Arc of the Comet

by Greg Fields

ISBN 978-1-63393-481-8

This is a work of fiction. The characters may be both actual and fictitious. With the exception of verified historical events and persons, all incidents, descriptions, dialogue, and opinions expressed are the products of the author's imagination and are not to be construed as real.

Published by

210 60th Street
Virginia Beach, VA 23451
800-435-4811
www.koehlerbooks.com

ARC
OF THE
COMET

a novel

GREG FIELDS

VIRGINIA BEACH
CAPE CHARLES

AUTHOR'S NOTE

This is a work of fiction. But in truth there is no such thing as pure fiction. We absorb in some way everything we do, everyone we meet, every breath, every experience, every heartbreak, disappointment, exultation and joy. We absorb these things, and we process them, either consciously or subconsciously, and in the process we manufacture our own stories, each drawn from what we know, and who we know.

What follows is one of those stories, or, more precisely, an unfolding of the forces and strains that help define our shared human condition. The particular events, and the particular characters pursuing those events, are creations.

But they are creations built in pieces from the people encountered in a constantly evolving life, all of whom have their own stories, and all of whom have their own distinctive, remarkable character. What follows is fiction, created by the interpretation and elaboration of things known, things felt, things imagined, and the complexities of those who sparked these reflections.

DEDICATION

To Leonard G. Fields (1920-2009)
The brightest of comets

Come to us Father, in the watches of the night. Come to us as you always came, bringing to us the invincible sustenance of your strength, the limitless treasure of your bounty, the tremendous structure of your life that will shape all lost and broken things on earth again into a golden pattern of exultancy and joy.

—Thomas Wolfe

PROLOGUE

Liam Finnegan had never been a gentle man, but neither was he brutish.

Where his mates would squeeze every hour out of a day and leave a crushed, pulpy husk at the end of it, Finnegan measured his time. He moved more slowly, spoke more deliberately than his neighbors. To be sure, he thought no great thoughts, nor tried to. Finnegan merely felt no compulsion to plunge headlong into a way of living draped in monotony, consigned to failure and bereft of hope. Rather, he did what he had to do to keep his humble existence moving along, took his pleasures in small doses, and found nothing in his part of southern Ireland to excite him. He felt assured of his survival at the least and knew that no amount of work would make it any easier. His countrymen, lacking Finnegan's conclusions, took him to be a bit peculiar.

Liam Finnegan was a farmer, as were his father, his grandfather, and presumably every previous male progenitor since his ancestors crossed the Irish Sea from Britain. The Finnegans had survived Cromwell, had survived the Penal Laws, had survived the great famines. Their lands had been seized and rented back to them in the seventeenth century, and so it had remained for more than two hundred years. Fortunately, Finnegan women had never been overly prolific so the family holdings were seldom split between more than two sons each generation, one of whom usually ran off early to another part of the island, to Europe, or to Hell. Rebellions, famines and disease periodically pared down the Finnegan males as well, with tenancy reverting to the eldest son. As a result, Liam Finnegan, the older of the two issues of his father's loins, would always have enough work to pay the rent and to keep himself reasonably well fed.

And now, in April, Liam Finnegan sat on the headlands overlooking the Atlantic near the Finnegan lands in Dungarvan, County Waterford. The spring wind blew a heavy ocean mist into his face. Although springtime, Finnegan's Ireland shivered as cold and as barren as the earliest weeks of winter.

His father had taken him as a boy to visit an uncle in County Sligo, well to the north. They made the trip by cart, and it had taken them several days. Young Liam had seen ruins along the way—the Drombeg stone circle, and, later, the great monastery at Inishmurray. How strong the stones had been to a young boy, how thick against the wind that assailed them so fatalistically. It would take centuries to wear them away. Yet, he thought, in the end they would vanish, casualties of a relentless assault, and the resolute stones would come to dust and powder, blowing against the faces of future generations ignorant of the haunted silt that settled over them. At Inishmurray he walked through the old graveyard, imagining the rotted corpses that lay beneath the soil. And of the monks buried there he had thought, 'What, brothers, has your holiness won you?'

A young man now, in April, during unsettled times, going neither upward nor downward and not possessing the luxury of either alternative, Liam Finnegan felt his blood move within him. Instead of spending this Saturday evening at Mick Ryan's Pub as was the custom of the young Waterford farmers, Finnegan walked. He walked through the village, what there was of it, from north to south, passing Ryan's and hearing the familiar voices within. On other such nights he might have shared their company, and been glad of it. But on this particular evening what welled up within him, inarticulate but intrinsically lyrical, could not be resisted. He had felt it before, and always it had perplexed him. It plagued him as a virus for which the simple ways of his homeland knew no cure. They were an unsophisticated people, and he was part of them. He knew no more than anyone else. And so, for reasons he knew himself to be incapable of understanding, he bypassed Mick Ryan's and headed southward toward the coast. The sea in this part of Ireland he knew to be as restless as his own soul. Perhaps he could find an empathy on the headlands.

On a highland two miles outside the village Finnegan stopped walking, gazed below him to purple-blue water, and, satisfied that he had found the view he sought, sat down on the soggy ground. The sea washed in like old wool, its edges frayed. It drew him outward to the horizon where distinction between sky and water disappeared. The sun, hidden all day behind thick clouds, had fallen off to his right over the western ocean. A cold wind blew toward him, meeting the melancholy chill that rose from his breast so that, as with the sea and the distant horizon, distinctions blurred. Finnegan sat, oblivious of the murky ooze of the ground around him.

We are a dying land that will yet live for centuries. We are a people just slightly deformed—lame enough to be scorned and abused but still holding enough strength to survive on our own, and, on occasion, to fight back a bit against those who sneer at us. As a country we shall limp along, surviving, growing older, growing more lame.

(Sea beat upon shore. A gull cried. Wind and mist were cold, even for April, an April in Ireland.)

I am a young man. I am nineteen. I am a farmer, and shall be so until I die. In Ireland I shall sire sons who will grow as tall as I am. They will marry Waterford girls, and they will farm Finnegan lands when I grow too old to do so. And then I shall die. Perhaps I will not die in loneliness, but surrounded by a family I have brought into being, and the sons they have brought forth as well.

The sons and grandsons I have condemned to a slow demise.

And after my death I shall go down into the ground. Dirt will cover me in my box. And I shall join the holy monks at Inishmurray; we shall be together in our holiness.

(The April wind rose; the April mist thickened. It was growing dark, and darker by the minute . . .)

Ireland is a dying land, and though I am but nineteen I am dying with it, as are we all, as are my unborn sons. We all know it. The boys up the hill at Ryan's know it, and they cannot drink it away. Maire Coghlin knows it, knows that even behind her gentle beauty is a waft of the grave no lemon scent can conceal. Fr. McCurragh knows it, too, although he would never admit it, either to his flock or to himself.

Liam Finnegan knows it, he feels it to his core, and he resents it. I shall not be stillborn here, living what little there is of my life without so much as a fuss. I am not a greedy man, and by God I am no hero. But Ireland is a dying land, and my fate here is set. I am granted not so much as a whimper against it all.

(Waves crashed upon the shoreline. The April mist congealed into a light rain. . .)

Liam Finnegan sat on a highland, spat upon the ground, and felt no cold. He was not a greedy man, nor was he a hero. Liam Finnegan had read few books. He did not know Ralph Waldo Emerson; the names of Whitman and Thoreau would have drawn no response. He was no Romantic.

Finnegan felt the same disquiet hat spurred his countryman Columbanus to the European continent, that sent Sir John Cabot westward. And in the simple ways of his Irish youth, he could never have understood it except for these restless Saturdays spent gazing over an ocean he had not yet sailed, feeling man's most basic longing—the frantic urge to stay alive.

The light April rain continued its bored persistence. It had grown completely dark. Finnegan rose from the wet furrow, pulled his damp coat around him and wandered along the Colligan River back toward Dungarvan. Even in the dark he knew his way. He passed Ryan's again, but did not go in. There was no point. As he reached the northern end of the village and started across an open land to his farm, he began to shiver. With the cold, he told himself.

He had never been a gentleman, but neither was he brutish. Liam Finnegan saw a dying land, and knew, as all men know, that it was time to leave.

CHAPTER I

My mind was a mirror;
It saw what it saw, it knew what it knew;
In youth my mind was just a mirror
In a rapidly flying car,
Which catches and loses bits of the landscape.

—Edgar Lee Masters, "Ernest Hyde" in
Spoon River Anthology

In the deep Virginia night, the narrow two-lane highway overhung by the heavy branches of unidentifiable trees, Tom McIlweath struggled against the wheel of the car, against the cracked and rutted pavement, and against his own instinctive craving to pull to the side of the road and sleep. His eyelids drooped with ten times their weight, his eyeballs flickered and darted from side to side. The day had been interminably long, hopelessly dull, the electric charge of anticipation and the heady intoxicant of unfettered discovery having drained out of him long ago. Now the road belied no mystery. No breathless adventure awaited him along the way. The only excitement his tired mind could derive lay in the process of passage itself. He was blood jetting through a vein, colorless and silent except for his own movement, which gave it whatever dimension it would ever possess.

Virginia. The word itself harkened Romantic images of dogwoods bordering rich green fields, of the wet lowlands of the Tidewater, flush with birds and foxes. Virginia had been a lonely boat sniffing up the James. It had been slavery and the Civil War, redeemed now by its own bloodshed. Virginia had been Jefferson, Washington, the Lees and the endless line of Byrds.

But here tonight, Virginia proved itself to be only a road, like all the other roads. Like New Mexico and Texas and the steamy, sticky roads of Alabama. Hell, he had not even seen Virginia. When they crossed the state line from North Carolina, it had been dark. All Virginia meant now was more of the same, a bit shadowy and somewhat foreign, but just as tedious as any place else. Days of mindless monotony had numbed Tom McIlweath's erstwhile nimble imagination.

McIlweath wanted desperately to sleep, but there was nowhere practical. On nights past they had stopped at highway rest areas and spent a few fitful hours trying to construct some comfortable posture in their cramped car. Even that seemed like deliverance now to McIlweath's exhausted body. Only one more day of this. It did not matter where they stopped. They didn't need a motel. Yet in this remote, empty swath of wooded bleakness, off the interstate and on a county road, they were unlikely to encounter even a wide spot in the road. Miles would pass, and still nothing. Only the blunt sword of headlights cutting against the darkness and the pinpoint swirls of the night bugs ambushed by the light.

To keep himself from complete vacancy he tried to scan the scenery behind the darkness. It was no use. Nothing penetrated the dead hanging weight of the trees, blocking both light and shape. McIlweath jerked his head sharply in all directions to shake some life into it. He took several deep breaths and stretched his arms against the wheel. He arched his back and yawned viciously. The road droned on, the clanking whirr of the old car deepening the sedation. McIlweath did not let his head stop moving. So many trees around, and deer peeking from behind them. Drifting off meant serious injury, maybe even journey's end. Too early for that. Just drive, he told himself. Drive through old Virginia, and watch for signs of life.

Amid his gyrations McIlweath turned his head to the passenger seat and gazed down at its contents, contorted awkwardly in the too small space, but sleeping soundly nonetheless. Conor Finnegan, as vulnerable now as a newly hatched robin. It was Conor Finnegan who had led hem both this far, Conor Finnegan who had caused them to be here, wherever this "here" really was. And, McIlweath mused, it was the most peculiar set of accidents that had allowed him to do it.

Finnegan relied on the accidental, the serendipitous and the unplanned. Conor Finnegan's accidents almost always seemed to turn into blessings. He was easily the most blessed figure McIlweath had ever known, causing the other to admit to himself that he was—there was no other word for it—jealous. He would have welcomed some portion of Finnegan's magnificent good fortune for his own. This entire expedition, in which their fates were temporarily joined, was for McIlweath an effort to conjure some of that mysterious quality that had so teasingly eluded him. His confinement with Conor Finnegan these past several days might have allowed some of that peculiar luck to rub off. He hoped so.

The road swerved in gentle turns around land that seemed to rise higher. Perhaps they were re-entering the Blue Ridge. McIlweath noted that it had been nearly half an hour since they had passed another car. Finnegan had speculated that the back roads would be more scenic, so they had abandoned the interstate in South Carolina. No other travelers here; only sleeping natives. God, it was lonely. And warm. The late summer night had fallen thick and humid, the temperature dipping only slightly after sunset. McIlweath's shirt clung to the seat. He felt his legs clammy with dried perspiration. The heavy Southern air drew reluctantly down his throat.

McIlweath looked at Finnegan, asleep on his side, legs tucked up under the dash, hair askew and mouth ajar. A thin band of spittle rolled out of one corner. *Not very dignified,* thought McIlweath, *and so very unlike him. If he could see himself he'd be embarrassed.*

Two weeks on the road had robbed them of all mysteries. They had no secrets now, at least no superficial ones. Yet, McIlweath still regarded Finnegan somewhat mystically, an emissary from realms he himself could scarcely hope to know. Finnegan might appear human now, or even subhuman, in these exaggerated and contorted poses, but once his eyes opened and his mind started to work, once that distinctive spirit became animated, Conor Finnegan would again assume outsized proportions.

What a horrible burden that must be, thought McIlweath. If he truly strives beyond what the rest of us conceive, who can be there to save him?

Finnegan shifted in his seat with an unconscious grimace. This sleep in its twisted discomfort was no sleep at all. He would wake as tired as when he drifted off, and sore in the neck and back from the awkward angles, ready to find something amusing or puzzling or moving in the day ahead, in the scenes around him. Irrepressible, sometimes insufferable. By contrast, McIlweath often felt his spirits repressed after long nights and ragged mornings. This very night was doing that to him.

And so, on an empty road in an empty land, hours before daybreak, hours since the last web of light tangled across the warm earth, Tom

McIlweath did the only thing his circumstances allowed. He drove on, wrestling a Protean fatigue. Next to him slept the favored Conor Finnegan, "St. Conor" to some of their more cynical friends. How strange to see him there, and how ungraceful for both of them.

* * *

This trip had begun in its way several months earlier. Although January, great rings of perspiration spread outward from underneath Tom McIlweath's arms. He sat jammed together, shoulder to shoulder, with a group of students he only vaguely recognized. His mistake. He had come too late to get the seat he really wanted, down there and to the left, near the attractive girl he had met during his first weeks here, the girl who shared two of his classes, the girl who haunted many of his waking minutes and most of his sleeping ones. McIlweath had wanted to sit near her so that he could see her, and perhaps catch her eye. He had watched her from a distance for many months, always from a distance. During that time, he had spoken no more than ten sentences to her, yet she remained a Romantic pursuit, an idealized version of youthful curiosity.

A faint haze fueled by the artificial humidity of too many bodies in too little space hung near the ceiling, just low enough to blur the people in the opposite stands. McIlweath's eyes were not good under any conditions. Tonight the crowd and the heat and the haze made him work twice as hard to follow what was happening on the gymnasium floor below him.

There, a blue contingent of scantily-clad bodies threw a ball over and around a similar group in white. Every few seconds the process reversed itself. In point of fact, Tom McIlweath knew very little about basketball, and cared even less. He attended these games as something of a social ritual, although he seemed to fall outside the society that ritualized it all. Tom McIlweath seemed this year incapable of asserting his personality among these new people.

Girls in particular baffled him, and to overcome his lack of self-confidence he reverted to Romantic posturing. He read the Cavalier poets and found something stirring in their idealizations. He preferred to remain passively enraptured of false versions, which he knew to be false, of the interplay between the sexes.

Not that he had any notion of cultivating high or deep emotion. Quite the opposite, in fact. But he found himself at that awkward stage of life when the inner core boils outward, creating new sensations that dictate fresh perspectives on familiar scenes. He saw people around him experiencing what he missed, and so felt that noticeable void. His remote vantage point in turn accelerated his reactions. He idealized the female form, its grace, its gentility, its kindnesses. He found himself perched on the edge of gallantry, a modern-day Herrick or Lovelace studying for his apprenticeship and yearning for the day it would begin.

Although McIlweath had been going to basketball games all season, the general schema—the gymnasium, the huge crowds, the sights and sounds and smells—still seemed quite foreign. People here took it far more seriously than they had elsewhere. All this excitement, the bolting out of seats to cheer good plays, the hooting at the referees, the obvious intensity of the players, all of it puzzled him a bit. Yet, he continued to come. In its own strange way, these games had become a personal forum, a hidden stage upon which he might enact his Romantic longings and quietly emulate his odd new society.

His father had changed jobs the summer before. A teacher, John McIlweath had taken a new position with the suburban Los Angeles schools that offered him better pay, more time to himself and a change in scenery, qualities he had always prized. So he had moved his family southward from the San Francisco area in yet another uprooting of what had been planted only a few years before.

From his first steps, John McIlweath carried a burn of time and place deep within him. Before he married he made his way through Canada from his native British Columbia, working as a lumberman, a singer, a fisherman, before tying himself to a wife and a life of teaching. But his burn had not lessened, and he concluded that his new respectability resulted more from a temporary stab of conscience than a lasting commitment to the stable life. How long, he had asked himself, could he really continue to be so formless? Each man had to face the time when, if he were to accomplish anything worthwhile at all in his limited years, he had to settle on one thing and try to do it well.

It had been a hard conclusion, and one that nothing throughout his previous ways had ever suggested. From an early age he knew himself well enough to know that he lacked discipline and had developed in its stead a passion for independence. They were opposite sides of the same coin, a coin he regarded as exceedingly rare and infinitely precious. He dropped out of high school near Vancouver and, with his father's curses ringing in his ears, set off for the other coast, a six-month journey fueled by odd jobs, quick encounters, and more than a little liquor.

He worked several weeks on a fishing trawler in Nova Scotia until he tired of the not inconsiderable rigors of maritime life. The salt air made him think of British Columbia. He headed back west but was sidetracked in Montreal by a girl who taught him how to play guitar.

He stayed with her a year, supporting himself as a clerk in a shoe store and aspiring to put his new talents to use as a songwriter. In time the city became too tense, too dense, and too dirty. His music lost its enchantment. It became a chore like all his other chores, a painful struggle to find words and melodies that malevolently lay just outside his grasp. If he finally grabbed a piece of what might become a song, he found it trite, or overstated, or dull. His woman, too, lost something, he couldn't say what. She became shrewish, she clung to him suspiciously, criticized his speech, his dress, his casual habits and his casual friends. John McIlweath started to long for less congested space. One morning he packed his knapsack, left behind everything he didn't need, including his guitar, and with no farewell headed west again.

Three months later he found himself back in Vancouver with nothing to do and little will to do it. As a last resort he entered college with a forged high school record, the pattern of his life confirmed in these two restless, unanchored years of wandering.

Tom McIlweath accepted his father's pace. Movement and motion became the standard, and he considered himself fortunate to be so raised.

His father changed jobs with the lunar cycles. With the new jobs came new places, upheavals, which carried with them the challenge of reacclimation. But Tom McIlweath had never found it to be so difficult as his latest adjustment. He had been here six months, yet he had yet to develop any rhythm for himself. He remained on the outside, pressing his nose against an imaginary windowpane. Tom McIlweath saw himself isolated, with no friends and few acquaintances, unable to penetrate the patterns that had existed in this place for years.

Part of the reason for this detachment was watery. To his surprise and overwhelming disappointment, his new school had no swim team. Swimming was what McIlweath did best, his body a lean, sinewy complement to the water. He had emerged as one of the premier swimmers at his previous school and thereby something of a jock, noted and admired. McIlweath had presumed that joining the swim team at his new school would give him a ready identity with at least one group. Without a swim team, his new school presented nothing at which he could excel and so leverage his way into some level of notoriety. (Except academics, of course, but no one ever paid any attention to the smart kids.) So McIlweath swam instead with a team at a private swim club each morning before school, with no one he cared to watch.

Tom McIlweath was not one of those favored few whose presence mingled with self-confidence to transcend any social gathering. He was not unattractive, although he would have disagreed—he considered himself hopelessly plain. McIlweath was slender but muscular—*stringy*, as his father called him—with a lean physique that masked uncommon strength. He carried a full head of light brown hair, the ends blonded during the summer through sunlight and chlorine. His angular face highlighted a mouth that turned up sharply at each end and eyes that seemed in a perpetual squint, a function of his poor vision. For several years he had worn glasses. Now, in an effort to lose his scholarly air, he had traded heavy black frames for wire-rims. They perched upon his heavy nose, a well-shaped ridge that skewed the dimensions of the rest of his face.

And so, in this new place, McIlweath's self-perceptions quietly deepened. On the rare occasions when he spoke to anyone, he presumed a disinterested audience. He resigned himself to his studies, his private swimming, and his Romantic fantasies.

Basketball games at his new school, always significant, this year rose to new levels. The team had never before been so good. Students, parents and the community at large reacted with unprecedented, obnoxious enthusiasm. The stands filled completely for every game. Ranked first in Southern California, the team had yet to lose. Heady stuff to be sure, and their followers responded with appropriate cockiness while the players swaggered across campus.

McIlweath did not totally understand the game, but he had come to like the sounds that accompanied it—the rhythmic slap of the ball on the shiny hardwood, the squeak of sneakers, the throaty chatter between teammates, the grunts of a defender, the snap of the net as the ball passed through it, the crowd's respondent roar. There was a lyrical surety in all that, a predictability based upon prescribed actions within clearly defined boundaries—the thick black lines around the court that locked the players in and everyone else out.

Tonight, as usual, his school's team led comfortably. Down below, McIlweath watched a solidly built player he knew only as Dave pull down a rebound and whip a pass to Finnegan near the sidelines. Finnegan caught it already in motion. On the court Finnegan always seemed to be moving, directing the offense, calling the defense, barking hoarse orders to his teammates, who, like chessmen, yielded to his hand. McIlweath enjoyed watching Finnegan more so than any of the other players. Finnegan embodied a restless movement, a driven force well below the surface. He took command intensely yet gracefully, eyes ever active, scouring the game around him for the best move, thinking two or three steps ahead of everyone else. He moved with a fluidity that implied his personal harmony with the game, with the crowd, with life itself. The balls of his feet never seemed to touch the court, his arms and legs never tangled. McIlweath, knowing little about the sport, would have likened Finnegan to a dancer, but of course he never could have told him that.

Finnegan grabbed the outlet pass and raced down the sideline. Slightly past half-court he cut to the middle. Bodies raced to catch up. The lone retreating defender challenged Finnegan just inside the free-throw line when Finnegan left the ground, his body screening the ball, his left leg pointing him toward the basket. The defender joined him in the air to block the coming shot. But at the top of his jump Finnegan pulled the ball down from his right hand, transferred it and deftly flipped it over his shoulder with his left. The defender watched without recourse as Finnegan's trailing teammate grabbed the pass and laid the ball through the rim. The crowd cheered lustily.

"Basket by Koscielski. Assist to Finnegan."

McIlweath, who cheered him too, shook his head. *My God,* he thought, *it all comes so easy for him.*

By the middle of the fourth quarter the game was put away. The outcome, never really in doubt to begin with, had been solidified. Some of the crowd started to leave, obviously with other places to go. McIlweath, with scant reason even for being there, fought back his envy.

"Ron Barber entering the game, replacing Conor Finnegan." The announcer raised his voice in enunciating he last two words as if he were introducing a Broadway starlet. The crowd, what was left of it, applauded loudly. Many stood; others yelled his name.

Finnegan trotted back to the bench, caught the towel thrown his way, took a slap on the back from his coach and went the length of the bench shaking every hand he could find. His face, reddened by exertion, glowed from the light reflecting off the perspiration there. Sweat darkened the front of his jersey in an inverted triangle. Finnegan draped the towel around his neck and sat back to watch the final few minutes, clearly content with his night's work.

At the final buzzer the crowd rose. Most stood in place for the school's alma mater, a dreadful piece of music reminiscent of an Old English dirge. At its end McIlweath stayed standing to survey the crowd. Unlike those around him he was in no special hurry. The cool January night air rushed against his face as he finally neared the door. After a couple of thick hours in a steamy gymnasium, he breathed it in deeply and let it clear the hazy dust inside him. The perspiration on his neck and armpits turned cold. Once outside, the crowd scattered in small groups, a bead of mercury dropped on a table. McIlweath, the remaining droplet, walked slowly to his father's car parked in a corner of the emptying lot. As was the case on most of these nights, depression hung on him like a disease.

Back in the gymnasium locker room, the team pulled off their uniforms while listening to their coach's summary remarks. The room quickly filled with thick clouds of steam. In the showers the young men exchanged the good-natured jokes and jibes born of self-assurance impervious to assault. Winning brought people together. This team had no rivalries, no jealousies, no cliques. They relied upon each other implicitly, both on the court and off. The postgame shower where they stood naked in each other's proximity, stripped of numbers, roles and responsibilities, had become a rite to which they all looked forward immensely. This was sacred ground where they stood, shared by a select handful. Here, amid the steam, the soap and the hissing of the water, they reflected upon the game and each other, then rambled onto the common topics of omnipotent youth while their coach, a gentle, scholarly man, retreated to his office. The shower baptized them, reminding them that they had been chosen apart from all others, and sent them out to an appreciative world to claim what was rightfully theirs in their youngest, strongest years.

Conor Finnegan enjoyed the postgame rituals as much as any teammate, yet he was usually among the first to leave. Tonight was no different. While the loud voices rang behind him, he stepped out of the shower, the starchy towel rasped across his skin. He dried quickly to avoid a chill and pulled on his clothes. By the time the next person emerged from the shower, he was fully dressed.

"What's the rush, Conor? Elaine waiting for you?" Jim Koscielski was one of Finnegan's closest friends. Finnegan looked up with a quiet smile.

"I thought so. What are you two up to tonight? I mean besides the obvious."

"I don't know. Probably just getting something to eat."

"There's a party at Macaluso's, you know. You ought to stop by, say hello to your admiring fans."

"Is that where you're going, Kos?"

"Of course. You know, Conor, I fear you're not making sufficient use of all this. The ladies respond to basketball players, especially undefeated ones. You're limiting your opportunities."

"The pleasure of the flesh, and all that?" responded Finnegan, tying his shoes.

"Something along those lines. Not that Elaine isn't a nice catch."

"Thank you, I think."

"I mean it, Con. She's gorgeous. I've lusted after her myself. But a man shouldn't restrict himself to one flavor, no matter how delicious."

"Christ, Kos, I'm not going to marry her. She's good company, that's all."

"Objection sustained. But I do believe you're shutting yourself out on some of life's greatest pleasures. Why don't you two stop by? You'll have plenty of time for gazing into each other's eyes later."

"Maybe," said Finnegan, rising from the bench to pull a light jacket out of his locker.

"Where women are concerned, 'maybe' usually means 'no.' Your loss."

"Perhaps, Kos. Give my regards to the other animals."

Finnegan hustled down the hallway, his step light despite the usual fatigue that settled in after a game. That would vanish though, as soon as he set himself about the rest of the evening. His body could recover at night, after he went to bed and pulled the covers up against the darkness. Then he would sleep deeply well into the next morning. But at night, between the game and bed, he was alive, completely alive. The energy he poured onto the court stayed with him, ebbing only in a slow, syrupy ooze.

On this night, as on most nights, Finnegan found himself overwhelmed by the vast panoply his life presented. There were so many corners to it, even at his young age, so many tendrils. It spread before him with no apparent boundary, limited only by the constraints of time and the tethers of imagination. Invigorating, rhapsodic passions surged through him like boiling water.

Let choices come later, and restrictions, and responsibilities, and sorrow, and death itself. Tonight there was life, only life, magnificent, powerful, glorious and mystical life, the trill of an angel's harp. Let the body respond while the body still could, let the mind grow lyrical, let the soul go on forever. Let the brewing, brimming chalice be guzzled down in a desperate thirst, and let the sweet meat be torn from the bone in a frantic hunger. For there is no other way, no other way at all, and the succulent flesh must nourish us, or we die.

* * *

Conor James Finnegan. Six foot, one inch, in the heart and prime of his most graceful years. Friends and acquaintances considered him rather handsome with his light brown hair, deeply set brown eyes and a naturally rounded, open, amiable face. His countenance radiated dynamism, a good natured love of action, of being in motion. His body, well-proportioned for his height, effused strength. He had no waist. His broad shoulders tapered only slightly to a firm midsection that flared outward again along muscular legs. He might have been a boxer, or, under different circumstances, a street fighter. His body suggested power and contention even though perched atop it was a face that only intimated charity.

In a biographical essay for an English class Finnegan had written, "I don't consider myself favored in any important way. My background is humble. But I've expanded by diligence whatever has been given me by fortune."

By his final year of high school he had indeed achieved a great deal for one of tender years—a nearly perfect academic record, an equally impressive athletic history, and a large coterie of friends that responded to the various aspects of his entertaining personality. Conor Finnegan had every reason to cast off the insecurities that commonly plague late adolescence. He had vaulted past them with a Herculean leap that scarcely taxed his remarkable abilities.

From the start, Finnegan had been blessed with a vision of the idyllic. He had always known what he wanted for himself, and so his life had progressed through a series of goal-oriented stages. The process had begun early. As an only child he was spared the distractions of a sibling's demands for attention. All his resources could be self-directed. As a result, Finnegan's life revolved around his own attainments, his own successes.

Finnegan's athletic development had been carefully planned, a consequence of his desire for the recognition the best athletes receive even as children. Somewhat chubby as a child, he had one day caught sight of himself in the full-length mirror hanging in his parents' bedroom. The rotund view startled him. Deciding that he wanted no future as a weeble, he dropped several pounds over the next two months through exercise and good diet.

He saw, too, how his friends looked up to those few coordinated graceful ones whose physicality outpaced everyone else's awkwardness. The best athlete in his group, Craig Masters, was the biggest, strongest and fastest among them, the one against whom they measured their own performances. Masters strutted around the schoolyard almost regally, but Finnegan found him to be arrogant, insensitive and a bit of a bully. He became obsessed with beating him in something, anything, some sport where Masters had always been considered unbeatable. Finnegan wanted to beat him simply for the joy of seeing him lose, of seeing that brash ego momentarily toppled.

After school each day Finnegan worked on his body. He would shoot baskets in his driveway until dark, or throw a rubber baseball against the garage, or just run around with his dog, concentrating on keeping his feet in front of the small, quick spaniel so that he might develop similar quickness. Finnegan felt himself grow fast. He began to master the fundamental skills of the team sports, especially basketball, which seemed to come easiest. After a few schoolyard successes of his own that ran the risk of swelling his own ego, Finnegan decided to focus on basketball above all other sports. Even so, he knew he lagged behind Craig Masters, although he sensed himself closing the gap with each season.

One afternoon following a practice during their first year of high school, Finnegan challenged Masters to a game of one-on-one. He had not planned on doing so quite this soon, but something inside him had launched a quiet fury. During practice Masters had ridden one of their teammates, an undeveloped, awkward boy who had little taste for the game, so viciously that the boy had been close to tears. The coach had no backbone for bringing his star into line. Finnegan watched, burning, at the cruelty of it, but said nothing until practice ended, when he issued his challenge. Masters stood three inches taller and was twice a strong, with muscles in places usually held together by soft tissue. He took Finnegan's challenge with a smirk.

Finnegan said nothing, did not smile, took the ball, and put the game into motion. He played superbly, better than he had thought himself capable. By game's end the entire team had gathered around to watch what had become a close contest that no one expected. When Finnegan stole the ball off Masters's dribble and then spun past him for a driving layup, the taller boy began to react desperately to the prospect of losing. In his tension he bounced the ball off his knee; it caromed to Finnegan, whose eyes now burned bright with focus. He drove to a spot fifteen feet from the basket, gave a quick head fake, and, with Masters off his feet, threw in a soft jumper for the game's final basket. His stunned teammates cheered wildly.

His academics took care of themselves. He knew himself to be intrinsically very bright. His intuitive mind usually arrived at the core of a topic several steps before others got there. He loved to read, and in his spare time he practically devoured whatever he could find—classic literature, history, poetry, current events. His teachers found him to be well organized, although they would have liked him to work harder. Finnegan had learned to gauge what it took to receive the grade he needed in each course. He would do as much as was necessary but no more, leaving him enough time for other things. In his first year of high school he misjudged an algebra teacher and came up a grade short. Mortified, he resolved never to make a similar mistake. Finnegan completed high school without further blemish, although during his final year he realized that his earlier error cost him the chance to graduate as valedictorian.

As he grew older, his native restlessness emerged piece by piece. He became edgy and bored around the house, wanting, in the most naked sense, to see what was around him. At the mercy of others, he could only go where they went. That no longer satisfied him. After he reached the right age and showed the right competencies, from time to time his father allowed him the family car and he would drive to hills bordering the suburbs. There, with the sun dropping low and no one else around, he could see a distant outline of Los Angeles, twenty miles to the west, smell the wild grass and observe a blend of colors swarming amid the day's dangling end. He could drive himself away from the mundanity of interchangeable streets, houses and lives to someplace new, someplace undeveloped and so virgin, as virgin as his own spawning emotions. Alone then, truly alone, he reflected upon the dynamics of his unfolding life, the marvelous potential there and the profound changes that lay ahead which he knew to be outside his comprehension. What he felt in those moments carried him forward for days. These sporadic wanderings captured the freedom he was coming to crave.

Despite his overriding self-confidence in most of what he did, Finnegan had never been assertive with the girls who attracted him with greater frequency as he grew older. Buried in his subconscious was the image of the round, awkward child reflected back in his parents' mirror, and so he could not fully believe that any girl might be interested in what he had to offer. On those occasions when he spoke with an attractive girl, he lost his usual fluidity, becoming tentative, nervous and unsteady, the fragile stem of a dandelion in a high wind.

All that changed at the start of his final year when, feeling the pressure of friends who were far more active than he was, he stammered an invitation to Elaine Sturgis to attend the formal homecoming dance. She accepted, and the mystical fear of his young psyche began to fade away, replaced with a burgeoning confidence that he welcomed with relief.

Elaine—tall, thin, beautiful and wickedly intelligent—became another status symbol. She showed herself to be witty, well-rounded and a bit vulnerable. The daughter of an investment banker, she had grown up with certain advantages. Elaine played the piano, had been to Europe twice, dressed impeccably. Finnegan perceived himself to be in a faster lane than he had previously thought.

But to his surprise, Finnegan found that he enjoyed her company for its own sake. Elaine challenged him, made him look at life differently, more gently, and opened him to what might be. They continued to see each other after the autumn formal. Finnegan tried to dispel his naiveté through contrived sophistication. He attempted to impress her as much as she impressed him. He took her to dinner at very good restaurants, he took her to the theater, he took her to museums. Always he affected an air of false confidence, acting as if he knew what he was doing in these rare places. To Elaine's delight, he never totally succeeded. Always there was the uncertainty of which fork to use for the salad, or how much to tip the parking valet. Finnegan had indeed impressed her, but not in the way he had planned. Rather, he had impressed her merely by the effort, and because of his awkward efforts she developed a genuinely sympathetic warmth that ran as deep as weakly shaped emotions allowed.

After those early attempts, they spent most of their time together in simple ways: walking along the beach, driving to the mountains for picnics, studying together or just talking in each other's backyard. Elaine faithfully attended every basketball game, although she never liked the sport. Finnegan would find her in the stands, and he would play to her. He always knew where she was.

It all meant nothing, of course. They each knew that their time together was little more than lessons for later relationships. What had begun as a search for status had yielded a serendipitous friend, a new dimension to the time-honored social rituals. Finnegan was extremely pleased. Through Elaine's gentle effort and his own receptivity to what she offered, the final element of a beautifully conceived panorama fitted into place. Life in that most favored of years ran full and high.

* * *

For Tom McIlweath, with the winding down of his final year of high school, another relocation loomed. This one, though, he would control.

College had always been a foregone conclusion. From his first days in a classroom when he learned to read, write and finger-paint, he had been conditioned to expect that his education was pointing him to four years of higher study, at least a bachelor's degree and possibly something beyond. Now, with college looming as a practicality rather than an abstraction, McIlweath recognized the need for some decisions.

John McIlweath often reinforced in his son the notion that college provided opportunity. To his son, that opportunity transcended formal education, a degree of some value, and the birthing of a profession. If opportunity beckoned, then Tom McIlweath sought its full advantage, and that meant, in the simplest sense, a redefinition.

In fact, this past year's lingering sense of isolation had wounded him at his core. It was more than just the people who surrounded him, generally ignored him and denied him, as an awkward outsider, entrance into the well-established patterns of their lives. They seemed to McIlweath little more than reflections of the general tenor of the place, which he considered sterile, designed to sedate rather than stimulate.

Perhaps it was that rare time of life in a young man's evolution when discontent manifested itself bitterly, and disproportionately. Perhaps he would have reached the same conclusion had he stayed in one place most of his life, coming to interpret stability as stagnation. But regardless of its genesis, the conclusion stood firm, and Tom McIlweath knew that a change was needed. He did not know precisely where he belonged, but he knew—with a certainty born of a year's frustration, a year's cold regard of the unchallenged and unchallenging faces that swirled around him, a year's rapping at doors that would not open— that it was not here.

Truly his father's son, Tom sensed the nameless, inarticulate longing for something broader, something purer, something more deserving of his best efforts. Had he been born in the south of France or in the Peruvian Andes he would most likely have stoked the same fires, for such are a function of character more than circumstance. Yet circumstance fed the fires as the year ran on, and caused them to burn hot.

In November Tom McIlweath had received a letter from the swim coach at Rutgers encouraging him to apply for admission there. An alumnus of the college swam at McIlweath's club, and had a daughter on the Rutgers swim team. He took note of McIlweath's times and forwarded them to the college coach, who saw a spot for a butterfly specialist in his struggling program. The letter McIlweath received went on for several pages and traced the history of the program, described the facilities in exaggerated detail, and promised great academic rewards at one of the country's oldest and most recognized universities. McIlweath applied without accepting the coach's offer of a weekend campus tour. New Jersey, McIlweath reasoned, had to be different, and, if nothing else, could never be like these cold, closed suburbs. Several weeks later he received his acceptance letter, and three days after that came notification of a full tuition waiver with a handsome stipend for room and board.

In May Tom entered his father's study to tell him of his decision. Hearing it, his father leaned back in his chair and sighed.

"New Jersey, right? That's a hell of a long way away." John McIlweath paused. "I suppose that's part of the attraction." He folded his hands in front of his face, then leaned forward to prop his elbows on the arms of his chair. "You know, you won't know a soul."

"That's bound to be the case wherever I go, don't you think? That's been the case before. Every time."

"Have you considered that you'll be totally on your own there? Totally, with no one to bail you out and no place to go if you get bored or lonely or tired or just want a good meal? Few things are as frightening, and it can change your entire personality. You start to make compromises for the sake of the moment."

"Spoken from experience, I presume."

The elder McIlweath smiled. "Of course. But I think I might have been better prepared when I headed out. I was harder, Tom. I had sharper edges."

"I would have thought you'd have a bit more faith in your bloodlines. But maybe I need the chance to sharpen my own edges. And at the very least, I won't be under anyone's shadow there."

"Meaning?"

"Dad, with all due respect, you've set the terms for every move we ever made. All I could do was follow. This time I'll be making my own move."

"You must know that I moved us for our own good. Every time. I moved us to something better."

"Maybe. But it always seemed to me that you moved for the sake of moving. You moved because you got bored. In any case, you did what you thought was necessary, even if it wasn't. That's all I'm doing now."

John McIlweath turned his head away from his son. He stared at a bookshelf for several seconds, his gaze following the shapes of the letters on the book spines without noting the words they spelled. For whatever reason, his son wanted to go away, as far afield as he could. John did not fully understand it, and could not see all of what lay behind the young man's ambiguous reasoning. And, despite that reasoning, John McIlweath did not empathize. Hurt crouched behind the hedges of this surprise, obscuring any recognition of the same impulses he himself had felt so many years ago. But John McIlweath knew, in these few moments, that the leaving was inevitable. He could not stop it, nor did he particularly want to. It all seemed too soon, though. And a remote echo reverberated within him that would play itself over and over again inside his thoughts for the rest of his life.

His youth was gone, and with it his power, agility and innovation. He recognized the last two decades as a futile attempt to preserve what could not be preserved, and so should have been left to die with dignity. He had made his Mephistophelean bargain, but the rewards had never fully materialized. The basic joys had turned sour. They had been souring for years although he deluded himself into thinking them still sweet and fresh. His passionate efforts to compromise responsibility with self-indulgence had failed. They had been doomed to fail from the start, as any rational and mature man would have seen. Tom's impending departure punctuated his folly. He knew himself, then, through his son, and shuddered at the grim reflection.

"Well," said John, turning back to the incarnation of a long-dead soul, "We've still got some time to get ready for all this."

* * *

Conor Finnegan, by contrast, took a somewhat different approach to his decisions. He strutted through that final year as Alexander through Macedonia—young, respected and thoroughly in control. His successes seemed endless, his capabilities infinite. Gratified by the domination of circumstances he himself had crafted, yet hardly surprised, he kept himself alert for additional challenges.

From October to March basketball consumed him. The team had been at the top of the rankings for most of the season, ultimately to suffer its only loss in the semifinals of the state tournament. Finnegan had played a key role, providing stability and leadership each time he stepped between the lines. Twice he scored as many as thirty points, and in half a dozen games he recorded more than ten assists. Such work had not gone unnoticed: at season's end Finnegan was named All-California, Honorable Mention. In early spring, several colleges recruited him to play ball, in the process offering him as much financial assistance as he would ever need.

But Finnegan resisted their seductions. Having confirmed his abilities on the hardwood, he lost interest in both the sport and what it promised him as the season came crashing down. He knew beyond the slightest doubt that there was more to him than a jump shot or a quick pass. As a result he dismissed out of hand those colleges who wanted him only for his basketball skills. There was nothing more to prove.

By spring he had secured his academic position in the top five of his very large class. He had scored well on a national scholarship competition, and had attained the highest college entrance board scores the school had seen in a decade. Local service organizations awarded him their achievement grants, and featured him in their newsletters.

In fact, Finnegan took his intelligence for granted; he was proud of the fact that he did so. Academics were just another sport. Those colleges that did not need him to play basketball courted him for his scholarly abilities, or what they perceived those abilities to be. Beginning in October, he would come home each day to find another letter, more likely a group of letters, asking him to apply. This university offered diversity, that college provided intimacy, the other boasted an experimental curriculum. It all became a bit tiresome.

What mattered to Finnegan was not size or atmosphere or reputation. What mattered was challenge. The prospect of challenge invigorated him, and speared his imagination. He wanted to shape the soggy loam that was the nexus of his fine spirit into a sleek and glossy statue, the highest expression of personal dignity, the most refined manifestation of his remarkable potential. He weeded through countless offers with an eye toward that singular compulsion.

Finnegan began dismissing the smaller colleges. Instinctively he gravitated toward the larger, nationally recognized universities. There, with their conglomeration of intellects and personalities, an opportunity to prove himself amid the strongest competition would be available. As the year wore on and his self-confidence deepened, Finnegan eliminated everything local, even the best multidimensional universities. He toyed with the notion of going away and, as he played with it, the notion grew stronger. Its shadow lengthened across his imagination.

The drunken exhilaration of youth ensnared Finnegan more deeply by the day. He considered that his greatest challenge would lie in cutting the rope. He had done well amid the security of familiar scenes and familiar faces. He had shouldered a broad space for himself among his peers, all the while reinforced by the fundamental concept of home. Therein lay his security, and hence his confidence, dancing on a high-wire above a thick and pliable cushion.

If that indeed were the case, then he needed to take away the cushion. He concluded that the most stimulating places were elsewhere, in new territory, under new ground rules, surrounded by the best, most diverse minds and bodies of his time. And so, in an exuberant hubris fed by the remarkable course of his unsullied youth, Finnegan weeded out every college and university that did not fit into his now rigidly conceived pattern of what must come next. He weeded them all out, and when he was done, only one solitary stem remained, a cosmopolitan blend of intellectual heterogeneity, distance, reputation and affordability. He would go east, nearly as far as the continent permitted, to find his unopened oyster.

He would go to Rutgers.

* * *

Tom McIlweath knew they were approaching Portsmouth, a town of some size that would offer an opportunity to rest. A road sign dimly seen through the headlights told him that Portsmouth was only thirty-three miles away. Less than an hour. He thought he could make it, although the prospect of keeping himself awake that much longer promised a struggle.

But to McIlweath's delighted surprise that would not be necessary. As the road turned one of the wide bends, a sign appeared announcing a rest area in half a mile. Half a mile—less than a minute! McIlweath pushed his weary legs against the floorboard as far as they would go. He yawned again and blinked his eyes to sharpen their focus. His foot lightened on the accelerator.

There it was, nothing more than a parking lot, but that was all they needed. The area was empty. As McIlweath turned the car off the road the headlights scanned only vacant asphalt, two conical trash barrels, and, in the background, the omnipresent dark trees. Here was rest, such as it was.

As the car slowed, Finnegan shook back to life. He sat up unsteadily and looked around himself to discern time, place and mission.

"What time is it?" he croaked, his voice dry and bristly. "Where are we?"

"It's nearly three, Conor. We're in Virginia somewhere. I can't stay awake anymore."

"Virginia, huh? What are we close to?"

"Exhaustion. Shut up and go back to sleep."

"You want me to drive? I could drive for a while."

McIlweath groaned. "Jesus, no. You can drive tomorrow all you want."

He nosed the car to the curbing and turned off the tired motor, which shuddered to a stop and then gave a gaseous wheeze. As he killed the headlights McIlweath plunged the entire area—Virginia, the South, the world itself—into a hushed darkness. Only the chirping of the night bugs punctuated the smothering black, alive amidst death.

McIlweath could barely make out Finnegan's contours in the seat next to him. Finnegan rustled a bit, shifted so that he faced the door and sagged again into his seat.

"Jesus, Mac, it's dark as hell!"

"It'll be daybreak in a couple of hours. Make sure your door is locked."

McIlweath sighed, stretched again as far as he could, and let the barren Virginia night cave in around him to claim whatever parts of him it could find.

CHAPTER II

There are two gates of sleep. One is of horn, easy of passage for the shades of truth; the other, of gleaming white ivory, permits false dreams to ascend to the upper air.

—Virgil, *Aeneid*

Glynnis Mear was eighteen when her father died. She would spend the rest of her life trying to patch the hole of his leaving.

Dr. Robert Mear had been a surgeon, one of the very best in a highly competitive field. Twenty-two years at Massachusetts General, nearly three dozen scholarly articles and more lecture appearances than he could remember had earned a hoary reputation for him and a great deal of money for his family. That was the key, the bedrock of his satisfaction, for he was, above all else, a family man. Professional success had meaning primarily for its impact on his family's well-being. He had no sense of greed in the usual context, seeking only security and comfort without undue luxury. For these traits his colleagues regarded him as somewhat odd.

Until he was thirty, Robert Mear equated his very existence with medicine. Nine years earlier he had entered medical school timidly, fully gratified by his acceptance, which he thought proved his innate capabilities, yet fearful of the intellectual and physical demands that loomed ahead. But his studies had been his revelation. A staunch Catholic, he came to believe, passionately, that the highest expression of adherence to God's abiding laws lay in the healing arts. There lay *agape* love, and acceptance, and mercy. The more he studied, the more he saw medicine as an instrument of regeneration with which he could perform God's most sacred intentions. Buoyed by this conviction that his professional life could be an extension of his Creator's Divine Will, Robert Mear threw himself into his studies with all the enthusiastic single-mindedness of a convert. Unlike many converts, though, his exuberance never waned, nor did skepticism creep into his faith. He came to define himself, along with his entire view of a divine system, through his study of medicine. Imbued with saving grace, Robert Mear exuded a quiet, soft-spoken dignity. He took himself very seriously.

One afternoon he noticed a young nurse eating alone in the hospital cafeteria. He boldly took a place at her table, passed his meal with standard innocuous hospital conversation, and, taken with the black depth of her eyes (which, he thought, could well hide a multitude of sins), asked her to join him for dinner later that week.

So began his courtship of Florence Parlovecchio, whose middle name was Melpomene. Twenty-three years earlier she had been born in Boston's North End, and there she had remained all her life. Florence was not at all what Robert Mear had imagined he would be attracted to, but then, he had had very little time considering the opposite sex outside of their anatomical curiosities. While his colleagues would have never allowed themselves to become serious about a young nurse from an Italian family of modest means, Robert Mear had little concern for ethnic or class distinctions. Florence was a healer, and so passed his only real prejudice.

Florence was a simple girl, and the Parlovecchios were thrilled when she informed them that she was seeing a young surgeon. As a matter of course, they jumped to conclusions far in advance of the circumstances that might have warranted them.

She had become a nurse out of a fundamental desire to work some good with her life. Florence had been a bright girl but upon completing high school had found college out of the question. Mama and Papa Parlovecchio had created a brood of eight, of which she was the eldest. There would be no college. The nursing program at Mass General, evening division, rose as a suitable compromise between Florence's ambitions and her father's means. Nurses made good money and worked regularly, in her father's view. In the meantime she could secure a day job, study at night, and help the family as much as she could.

As a result of such planning, Florence still lived at home when she met Robert Mear. She did not consider herself unique; the ambitions of nearly all her neighborhood friends had been subjugated to financial necessity, and, in most instances, destroyed altogether. She typified the condition of Boston's North End Italians, or so she thought, and so she never grew bitter. She carried on with her spirits intact.

Robert Mear, for his part, had never experienced the attentions of a woman since early in his undergraduate days. Florence in her simplicity showed him a gentility he had not encountered, a way forward that was less compulsive, less kinetic. She refreshed him. Florence never hurried, and when she left the hospital physically she left it emotionally and intellectually as well. Her instincts told her that this was a man who viewed the world in a single dimension. Her calm reserve could soften his edges.

The young surgeon found in Florence's placidity a resilient fiber that surprised him. And when, and the end of an evening they would bring themselves back to his apartment so that they could lie together, she stroking his neck rhythmically with the barest of motions, Robert Mear's innate tension then subsided and the healer himself was healed.

They wed fourteen months after they met. The groom reached thirty-one, the bride twenty-four. The wedding was an ornate affair and well attended, for the Parlovecchios had spread numerously as well as widely. Branches extended in twists and turns throughout New England and into New York, New Jersey and Pennsylvania, and all converged to watch the union of young Florence with her doctor. The father of the bride marveled that his little girl had done so well.

Through marriage, Robert Mear procured for himself another outlet for his intense disposition. No longer could he afford the luxury of tunnel vision. He had been forced to display another facet of an evolving character—more comforting but no less demanding than his surgical career: Robert Mear, the domestic man. In this new role the young doctor was as attentive and considerate as his professional demands permitted. That Florence continued her own career helped her understanding of those demands. For the times apart there was disappointment, but never resentment. Their comfort with one another grew by the day to become immense, and immeasurable. They belonged together in this life.

In a relatively short time the Mears proved themselves as fertile as the wife's forbears: two years after marriage Florence gave birth to a daughter, whom they named Glynnis, a lyrical, floating name they both loved. Their procreative efforts did not cease there, nor did they want them to. Perhaps their constant mingling with illness, suffering and death led them to seek the creation of as much healthy life as their bodies could produce. Within five years three more children followed.

Glynnis Mear grew up amid children smaller than she, under the steady and loving guidance of parents increasingly devoted to what they had made. She came of age amid the squawking, the fighting, the support and the euphoria that a family of that size invariably produces. She came of age under the eyes of a mother who herself had grown up in a large clan and expected no less, and a father who, like Narcissus kneeling at the pond, had found a fascinating new reflection which transfixed him.

And so it continued until Glynnis's eighteenth year, when her father, plagued by a series of headaches increasingly stronger, turned his medical expertise upon himself. At first he dismissed his pain as the reaction of an aging body to the stress of his profession. He had, after all, known several surgeons who had had to retire early because the intensely delicate balance of human life beneath their fingertips had in time exacted a huge toll on their mortal souls. They developed twitches, tics, sallow complexions, and other signs of degenerative exhaustion. They often lapsed into long, unbroken depressions or withdrew behind hollow stares to wrestle with the horrific skeletons of failure. Many took to drink, and others found uses for pharmaceuticals beyond mere healing. They were athletes at the end of glorious careers who still tried to respond to the demands of their sport, even as their bodies broke apart.

But after several weeks of regular attacks Robert Mear feared that his case might be something beyond fatigue. He decided to investigate his condition in some detail as soon as he could muster the strength to do so. The attacks continued with heightened ferocity. One morning, his head afire, he submitted to a colleague's PET scan. The result jolted him to the core: a melanoma tucked into the corner of his brain under the hippocampus, necessarily malignant and completely unreachable.

Together, Robert and Florence Mear told the children several nights later, after more tests, consultations and analyses, after they had had time to consider the facts of mortality. There was no way of knowing how rapidly the malignancy would progress, they said. There were things that could be done—surgeries and chemotherapy—but they offered no hope for a cure, and would only compromise Robert's remaining time and make it less livable. Father might still be with us for months yet. Years, if our prayers are heard. And the children believed this through their tears. They had no choice but faith.

Ever the logical man, Robert set about preparing for his death with the same calculated precision with which he had approached his life. These children and their mother must be well provided. He liquidated his investments, annuitized them for his wife and established trust funds for each of his children. Within a week he had dictated a long, detailed will to his attorney, taking care that assets accrued through his medical career, including residuals and intellectual property claims, were equitably divided between each son and daughter so that each would have a sizeable college fund. Once in college, he reasoned, they should be able to do well enough for themselves.

Details in place, Robert Mear sought then to live his life as he had before this terrible news had been learned. He continued to work as he could, appreciating that his time was limited. There would be too few miracles allotted him, and none in his own behalf; he could not afford to turn his back on a single one. If his life was to manifest an affirmation of the dignity inherent in every body, in every soul, he had only a finite number of days to reavow that testament. Concurrently he sought to savor his time with his family without abandoning himself to moroseness. Christ, we all have to die. He had the advantage, he told himself, of preparation. There would be time enough for mourning later. Thank God, he would not have to see it.

The time he spent with his family grew richer—less frivolous but not morose. It was, he thought, simply a greater appreciation of each other and where they were, even among the children. The younger Mears put away the vicious edges that children sometimes possess. They became more considerate, almost to the point of tenderness, almost serene in their sadness. They collected themselves gently, bracing singularly and collectively against the great darkness whose smothering depth they could not imagine in any particular but which they knew to be just beyond the next horizon.

The Mears had always vacationed in the autumn, usually in October shortly after the last traces of New England summer disappeared. Robert Mear loved the sharp crispness of the season, the barren quality that followed so closely upon the boisterous summertime. For years he had taken his family to the Maine coast, to Ellsworth near Bar Harbor. There they would hike through Acadia, rent canoes and paddle inland, crawl along the shoreline rocks, boil lobsters. The crowds of summer dispersed, few people intruded upon their pace and time. Cottages were plentiful, and the rates cheap. The children relished the special week when their parents took them out of school years just begun to steal away from friends, neighborhood and homework. In time, each of the Mears came to savor the contrast between the pressing throb of Boston and the pensive, crisp solitude of their week in Maine. Robert insisted that this year the family would head northward in October.

Nothing in the routine of their vacation changed, save the solicitous behavior of the children. Two months had passed since the pronouncement of their father's illness. They had grown accustomed to their grief, had grown into it and absorbed it, but the initial effect it had had upon their deportment toward one another became indelible.

This year, the year of her father's approaching death, Glynnis Mear looked forward to this time away more than she had in years past. Despite being the eldest, she had never been particularly assertive. She had grown up a quiet girl, treasuring time to herself. She did not enjoy taking responsibility for her brothers and sister, even though she loved them dearly. Until she was sixteen she shared a room with her sister, three years younger. Martha, it seemed, was a constant presence, and knew Glynnis's every move and every thought. Adolescence was a difficult enough time; she should at least have the opportunity to go through it by herself. The annual week in Maine had always provided the space she craved. There was enough room up there for everyone.

Glynnis did not try to shrink from her father's condition. She did not pretend. More so than the others, she accepted the fact that he was terribly, terribly ill, that he would die soon, and that, once that happened, her world would never be as secure as it was now in spite of any trust funds or annuities. While sadness governed the mood of her siblings, Glynnis tried matter-of-factly to come to grips with the practicality of what lay ahead. Always a pensive girl, she withdrew more and more frequently in the days following her father's disclosure.

And in her introspection, all thoughts were derivatives of her father. To Glynnis, he was gracious, gentle, omnipotent, omniscient, and ever the quiet hero. If the eyes were truly the windows to the soul, then she knew her father's to be bright, warm and eminently placid. How long she had envied his serenity. Since she was a little girl she had taken heart in that quality alone. Nothing seemed to ruffle him—not crayons on the wall, not a scratching fight between brother and sister, not a cold dinner after a sixteen-hour stint at the hospital, not even the death of a patient. Faith, however that nebulous, amorphous quality defined itself in his magnificent soul, reaffirmed that he, Robert Mear, had a purpose and that everything that touched his complex existence had a purpose, too. Glynnis could not imagine a kinder man. He loved humanity with an unspoken, generalized appreciation for the diversities of the human character. She could not remember her father ever uttering a disparaging remark toward colleague, friend, relative or total stranger. How she had prayed as a child that she would inherit that wondrous serenity.

Yet she knew, too, that her father could be hard. Because he based his life in an inviolable faith in man's inherent dignity, he reacted quickly when that faith was breached by a careless word or action. He could reprimand sternly, his words probing to the heart of the alleged transgression, the reason behind it, and how that lone sin, whatever it might have been, soiled its perpetrator. Glynnis blushed at recollections of some of her father's more intense lashings. Afterward, though, her father's face would always soften, and he would ask her if she had learned anything, if she were sorry. Often, a few hours or even a few minutes after the severest reprimand, her father would grab her in a great hug and press his face against her neck. She would glow then in her readmittance to his glorious heart, certain even then that she had never really left it and recommitted to avoiding the things that would disappoint him.

Her father constituted the core of her life. He united all the disparate ends into a single body, infusing it with a worth underscored by his loving example of what the human spirit could attain. He loomed larger than life, a hero, a demigod, the finest, most complete expression of man's compassionate nature. Glynnis loved all her family, but she revered her father.

And so, one evening, the second of their stay at the usual cottage near Ellsworth on this last getaway, Glynnis came to absorb another quiet and unexpected lesson from the man at the center of her heart.

She had set off for a twilight walk. For as long as she could recall, this had been her habit here. She liked to walk along the craggy shoreline during the broad edge between daylight and nightfall, the day turning cold, the Maine ocean changing by shades to orange, to purple, and finally to nameless colors man's eye sees too rarely to catalogue. Birds flew by, mostly seagulls, bleating at the vanishing light. Glynnis would walk for a mile or two, seeing no one, absorbing the shapes and hues and sounds that she would never be able to perceive elsewhere, that would forever elude her as she grew older. She would keep her gaze focused outward on the water. This shoreline, she would think, where Cabot sailed. It looked no different then.

Her father and the two boys had gone canoeing that day and were just returning as Glynnis stepped out of the door of the cottage. The boys, thoroughly chilled, dashed for shelter as soon as the canoes had been toted back to the shed. Their father, by contrast, moved slowly about his task of securing the canoes on their perches in the small shanty. The cold had not penetrated.

"Hey, lady," he said as he fastened the final lash across one of the boats. "Going for a walk?"

Glynnis smiled at the sound of his voice, calm and casual. "As usual, Daddy. I'll be back in time for dinner."

"Do you want some company? I could protect you from the sand crabs. Vicious creatures, you know. Eat your toes right off."

"But you must be cold. You've been out all day."

"I don't mind. I get too little time with my darling daughter these days."

The air hung silent for a second or two. Glynnis loved her father's company, but she feared in these waning days that he would attempt to do too much for her. She felt herself vulnerable to a dying man's platitudes. She wanted no discussions about responsibility, about example, about being strong for the others, about whatever would rob her of the delicate poise she had crafted to confront this final cycle. Wasn't it enough that she, more than the others, recognized his impending death? She would be able to handle it so much better because she had dispelled all illusions. Must she, even in light of such pragmatism, be subjected to a misbegotten effort to put things in order? His words would become memories; they would, all of them, react and carry on as their spirits allowed them. She had confronted the horrible reality from her own position. Must she confront it from his also?

The evening blustered around them as they walked. Wind blew a mist into their faces, and grey clouds moved in along the northern shoreline ahead of them. Glynnis, accustomed to the late-day bite, was wearing two sweaters and a windbreaker. Still, she felt the chill eat through her. Her father wore only a single hooded sweatshirt. For several hundred yards neither spoke. The surging ocean pounded against the rocks with a roar that would have made any conversation difficult anyway.

They stopped beside a projection of rocks, and Glynnis pondered the silence, seeking carefully a topic that might prove safe. At length she timidly brought one out. "How was canoeing today, Daddy?"

"Good. It was good. We followed that stream that crosses under the highway north of the town. I guess we must have paddled back about five miles or so. Long enough to wear me out."

"The boys enjoyed it, no doubt?"

"No doubt. They're strong, that's for sure. Stronger than their old man. But that's not saying much these days, is it?" He smiled gently, but Glynnis did not respond. Perceiving a tactical error, he backtracked shyly. "They're big by anyone's standards. I can see them winning some football scholarships before they're through. And they'll only get bigger."

"I hope they realize that they can't play games all their lives."

"No. But they should take every opportunity to play them while they have the chance. I wish to Christ I had been more like them when I was their age."

"Let's go sit on the rocks, Daddy." The formation of rocks jutted into the sea a considerable distance. Glynnis had been on these rocks before. She did not wait for her father to reply. The rocks, she hoped, might provide a breakwater from the inner storm now raging upward that had the power to dwarf the evening sea. She had not been wise to let her father come along tonight.

Glynnis hopped quickly to the rocks and began scaling delicately over the slippery boulders. Her father, with no real alternative, followed her lead, but more slowly. The incessant ocean spray slickened the rocks so that neither trusted a sense of balance. They propped themselves up with their arms as they crawled their way to the outer half of the formation.

"We look like two giant spiders," he called out. "How much farther do you want to go?"

"Far enough to feel the spray from the waves," yelled Glynnis over her shoulder. "A few more rocks. You can go back if you want."

Glynnis stopped fifteen feet or so from the formation's edge. Robert Mear slipped up behind her and they sat on adjacent boulders. The late evening waves tumbled in with no great speed, but they burst apart in spuming fury as they hit the rocks at the end of their run. Water shot high into the air and mist sprayed over the rocks toward shore. The grey clouds from the north moved closer.

Robert Mear looked at his daughter in the mist. Droplets of water clung to her temples, adhering the roots of her thick hair to her skin. Her rich brown eyes squinted through the moist air at the ocean ahead of her. The edge of a continent, butted angrily by the void that wanted to go on forever.

He closed his eyes and softly prayed, "God, she's so beautiful, and so quiet, and so composed. Let her avoid the desolation of human error. Let there be some happiness still."

Glynnis sat transfixed for several minutes. Both of them shifted on the rocks to find some comfortable position, and when stone pressed on bone too long, shifted again. What type of communion she had entered with the wind, the mist, the salt and the rocks, Robert Mear could not say, yet it seemed to be profound. He let her sit for uncountable minutes before he spoke.

"What are you thinking, lady?"

Glynnis turned to him, looking him fully in the eye to strip away whatever pretension he may have been holding. She spoke gently. "I was hoping that you'd spare me a parting testament. That's what you have in mind, isn't it?"

Robert Mear threw back his head and laughed, breathing in the wet salt that passed for air. God, how much he loved her! How he would love to be able to stay. She was just now beginning to hack through the constrictions of childhood, and the result was bound to be thrilling. God, how he would love to see it all happen.

"I suppose so," he finally replied. "After a fashion, that is. You know, Glyn, we talk so little. I tend to think that that's a function of temperaments. I know too that I can't make up for all the things I haven't said in one evening. I couldn't begin to sort them out anyway, so it's pointless to try. That would just make things awkward for both of us.

"If you're looking for some statement, I have none," he continued. "Only this: that you're the sole author of your own future. Nothing I can tell you now, or ever, will do you any more good than that. The seeds of your character were sown long ago, and they're indestructible. You can't change that, no matter what threatens you or tempts you.

"So my 'testament', as you call it, is just that there is no testament. There's just you, as you were from the start and as you will always be. You're my testament. It's as simple as that."

No sound, then, except for the seabirds' complaints and the whoosh of spray over the rocks. No sound, until Glynnis slid over to her father's side and wrapped her arms around his neck. She held him; they held each other, relishing the physicality, the heft and press of unbounded love. Glynnis tucked her head into the crook of her father's neck.

"You know, lady," he began again, "When I was your age I knew exactly what I wanted to do with myself. I had wanted to be a doctor since I was about four. Even so, when I got to college I tried everything. Economics, history. Even art. I wasn't impatient. I figured if I would be practicing medicine for the rest of my life, then I owed it to myself to sniff around the other things a bit.

"My second year in college I was forced to take almost all biology and chemistry courses, nothing else. I was bored to tears. I remember one test in particular, in late October, around midterms, and everyone in my dormitory was up all night for a week studying. But I was taking it easy. I think I was even doing some light reading, Fitzgerald or Dreiser or something like that. So everyone was amazed when I got the highest mark on that test. By far."

"What does that have to do with anything, Daddy?"

"I'm not certain. It just occurred to me for some reason. It probably has something to do with self-confidence, or knowing who you are. Or faith, I don't know."

"Everything comes down to faith with you."

"Do you find that odd?"

"I find it reassuring. Faith is a rare commodity these days."

The mist thickened into a light rain. Ahead of them, out over the water and down the coastline, gulls invisibly screeched. Like banshees, thought the doctor, which he had heard before.

"I have faith in such a great many things. You have no idea how valuable that is, how much that sustains me. I want you to know that I have faith in all of you, in all my children. But I've got a bit more faith in you than in the others."

"You flatter me, Daddy. There's no need."

"It's not flattery. And it's certainly not idle. You've got more depth, Glyn. More than the others."

"I'm older. I should have more depth. They'll follow."

"To a point, I think, but not totally. You're like your mother in so many ways. Sometimes she sees things or feels things that catch me completely off guard. And she can put things into perspective so quickly. She can make sense out of chaos better than anyone I've ever known. I think you're the same way. You're not a simple person, Glyn. I hope you're wise enough to trust to patience. There are precious few revelations in this life. Everything worthwhile takes time."

"You're starting to pontificate," Glynnis chided. "You promised not to do that."

"Forgive me. One of the privileges of age is inconsistency. It's getting hostile out here. What do you say we head back?"

Glynnis nodded and stood. She pulled up the collar of her windbreaker. The evening chill set in deeply. It penetrated their clothing, settled into their bones, dove into their lungs. They noticed the dampness in each other's hair, the misty droplets hanging on their eyelashes. The wind picked up, waves grew more violent, spray rose higher. Nightfall in Maine.

Both father and daughter moved carefully back over the rocks from the promontory. In the cold their muscles reacted slowly. Upon reaching the sand, for the first time since she had entered the nebulous boundaries of young adulthood and for the last time in her life, Glynnis Mear took her father's hand. In that way they returned to the cottage, and to dinner.

* * *

Of the death of Robert Mear little need be noted. It was the standard demise associated with that particular illness. Shortly after returning from Maine the headaches grew sharper and more frequent, the painkillers increased in strength and dosage. In time he resorted to morphine and became addicted. He ate little, grew thin, grew thinner, became emaciated. During the final stages he remained on morphine virtually each waking hour, growing less aware of the world around him, less aware of his family, yet ironically more aware of his decaying self, each limb, each membrane, each atom. His mental processes dulled, his memory lagged, he failed to recognize old friends and his wife's relatives. He faded into a fog, an ever-blackening mist that suffocated his sight, his words, his very thoughts. At length even his self-awareness disappeared as the fog closed in. He entered the hospital where he had served so many years, knowing in his rare lucid moments that the final act had at last come to be played. One evening in February the suffocation became total, and Robert Mear passed from this earth in numbness, unaware that his wife sat next to him, stroking his forehead and weeping to herself in the timeless manner of new widows.

* * *

"Hello, Petey. How's the boy this morning?"

The old man walked out of his bedroom into the apartment's small central living area. He walked in slow, measured steps as if he were crossing a brook on wet stones. His thin frame was clad in faded red pajamas, covered by a blue plaid robe equally faded. Plain cloth slippers kept his feet warm. The chilly morning shot against his window, a roundhouse punch thrown by Lake Michigan not far away.

The old man's apartment was not large, but it gave him all the room he needed. The place cast an aura of age. The walls, an off-white, in the dim light of morning seemed prison grey. A red carpet with a black design, as faded as the old man's clothes and threadbare, covered the floor of the living room. The furniture was of a fashion long outdated, solid hardwood frames with unattractive floral designs. Against the window that looked down to the street sat a high-backed sofa, once dark red, with scrolled arms. In front of it stood a companion coffee table, scratched and begging for refinishing, with a small portable television. Across the room in the opposite corner was an easy chair, beige, with a slight tear in its cushion just large enough for its linty innards to seep out in a wispy bubble. Bookshelves filled with a few volumes and standard bric-a-brac filled the wall nearest the single bedroom.

"Hello, Petey boy," repeated the old man as he arrived at the object of his attention, a canary whose cage adjoined the couch. The curtains, off-white like the walls, were closed so that little of the morning filtered through. The canary's small brain recognized its benefactor and flapped its wings briskly.

"You got a song for me today, Petey?"

The walls were barren save for a crucifix near the entrance to the kitchen. The old man saw no need for adornment. There was but one picture in the room, sitting on the second shelf of the bookcase near the bedroom. The picture, framed, was of the old man and his wife. She smiled broadly while he, grinning rather impishly, wrapped his arm around her shoulders. The picture was many years old.

After greeting his companion, the old man moved to the kitchen to switch on the radio there. Within a few staticky seconds a news station crackled in. Always it was news; the old man had never cared much for the music this country produces. The kitchen had little more to offer than the living room: only a solitary table against the wall, with chairs at either end, broke the space. The old man went to the old stove, lifted the teakettle to make sure it was not empty, and put it down on one of the burners. He sat in one of the chairs to wait for the kettle to boil. When it did, its steam whistling shrilly, Petey started to twitter from the next room. It was shortly after eight o'clock.

The old man listened to half an hour of news while sipping his tea and eating two slices of buttered toast for his breakfast. After placing the cup next to the sink he returned to the living room.

"Well, Petey, it's supposed to get pretty cold today. What do you think about that, boy??"

He checked the bird's cage to see if there was enough seed and water. Satisfied, he made his way back to the bedroom to dress himself. The living room remained dark.

A desk, an old thing with three drawers on the right side only, occupied one corner of the bedroom. Along with the bed and the dresser it was the only furniture in the room. The same style of rug as in the living room covered the floor here as well. The curtains were closed, the room dim. The old man turned on no light. By habit he knew his way around the room, where to step and what to avoid. From the closet he pulled on his clothes for the day, the same as yesterday's.

Three books were stacked in a pile atop the old man's desk. One was the Bible, the other two literary books: James Joyce's *Dubliners*, and *Hard Times* by Studs Terkel. Some stationery lay on one corner aside a can of pens and pencils. In the top drawer the old man kept his correspondence. Despite his advanced years he still received letters and responded promptly to each piece of mail that came his way. He kept one letter in particular on top of the others, needing response:

Dear Dad,

I trust this finds you in good health. Your letter came last week and it was good to hear from you again, as it always is. I hope the cold isn't slowing you down too much, but then you've always been pretty sturdy. I remember well how cold it gets there. I remember once when the furnace broke and we couldn't get it fixed until the next day. Albert and I spent the whole day in bed under the covers. We didn't even get up to eat as I recall. I think we only went to the bathroom once, and I remember running back to the bed afterwards and diving in, it was so cold.

We are all doing well here. Mother wants me to take some time off so we can get away for a few days. Maybe to San Francisco or down to San Diego, but I don't know.

You asked about Conor. He sends his love. He's gotten big, Dad, since the last time you saw him. You would barely recognize him. He's beginning to remind me of you when I was just a boy. That's strange, isn't it? But he looks a lot like you. Strong body, big shoulders. When he gets angry his eyes look exactly like yours did before you grabbed the belt. I can't really describe it. They burn almost, like he was looking right through you, and his jaw sets firm. When he's angry he never raises his voice. Instead he speaks slow and low, like a priest winding up his sermon. Again, he reminds me of you when he's angry. Fortunately, that's very rare these days. He's doing well. I wish you could see him.

You know Conor is going away to college next year. I told you that in my last letter. Rutgers, in New Jersey. Only the Good Lord knows why he's going so damn far away, but I think he'll do okay. He's a good boy, Dad, and I think he's smart enough and clever enough to get by without us. You'd probably understand him a lot better than I do in this regard.

Anyway, Conor's leaving gives us an extra room. You know what I'm going to ask even before I write it, and yes, I know we've been over it before. Allow me to try again. You're welcome to come out here and stay with us. You can even bring that damn bird. With Mom gone you're lonely as hell, even if you don't admit it. We're good company here. The fact is, I expect we're going to be a little lonely ourselves next year. I know you don't want to leave Chicago. It's always tough to leave home, no matter how old you are. But what's left for you there but memories, I'd like to know? And not all of them are good ones. Sometimes we have to burn a few bridges if we're to go on at all. It's warm here, and we're your family. We're what you created. We care for you, Dad. We don't want to see you alone.

Dad, I know the four of us have spread out all over the country. I don't even have an address for Jamie anymore. I

*don't know where he is. Allow me to flatter myself—I think
of the four of us, I've tended to the family better than any
of the others. It's not a question of taking you in out of pity.
I want to do it because you're my father, I miss you, and I
want the best for you. From my point of view, I've never put
much stock in self-denial. Please come.*

*There it is. Again. The decision is yours, but I'm not
going to argue with you forever. We've done enough of that
over the years. In fact, I'll try not to say anything more
about it. Let me know what you want before we close the
subject for good.*

Love,
Eddie

The old man had not reread the letter for the past few days, but it
had been very much on his mind, not because it posed a difficult choice
but because he did not know how to respond in any way his son could
comprehend, for his son was still too young.

* * *

Man ages, and in so doing becomes haunted. His mind is a Gothic
mansion, acquiring ghosts, and as his days become more drawn the
ghosts become darker, their shapes more defined, their shadows more
distinct. In time the specters assume recognizable forms, both good
and evil, and so their presence, fearfully perceived by an aging psyche,
is confirmed in each dying day. They haunt houses and gardens, lurk
in corridors and corners; he sees them on the street; he rides in their
taxis, he buys their groceries; they come crawling to his doorway
through the snow, drinking from a brown paper bag; they cheer at the
ball parks, they swim in the lake, they bring his newspaper. They assert
continually their right to exist, and become capricious. The ghosts wear
plaid skirts and play hopscotch on the sidewalks; they wear blue jeans;
they play basketball in the park and run home not to miss dinner; they
come out of movie theaters, and he catches their eye momentarily in
passing; they ask him for change on the street and taunt him because
he has grown so inexplicably old; they wear their finest and step out for
the evening in tailored suits and high-bodiced dresses. They carry with
them the potential of what might have been, and the ashes of what was.

He hears them. They speak to him at all times, but especially at
night, these ghosts. He will lie in bed sometimes, late at night, and hear

them as they say a great many things and change their voices. What is it, then, to be old, and to hear the ghosts we all acquire?

The old man's ghosts say such things as these.

"Sail away, then, and leave them here to die. How I envy you to be out of these troubles, but my eyes see the sorrows that await you. Changing time and place merely changes the form of the pain, lad. I shall miss you when you go, but I can see it in your jaw and hear it in your tones that your mind is set. I shall pray for you. I shall pray that you not be trading one desolation for another . . ."

And

"My lovely man. My lovely dreamer, weavin' your dreams out of breadcrusts. We've nothing, lad, but your dreams. But know that I love your visions, as deeply as I love the man who conjures them. We'll need to be content ourselves stayin' here with each other for warmth, and you can weave your dreams for me alone. My lovely, lovely man . . ."

And

"Come now boys, the turkey'll be up in a few minutes. Your father is carvin' it now. Just once a year you lads could be civil and mind your manners at table. The animals who tended Our Lord's manger had more decency than the lot of you. Now come hug your mother before you sit . . ."

And

"Pa, the Cubbies are playin' the Cards today. Can we go? You got a couple of dollars for us, and we'll sit in the bleachers? Or maybe you could call in sick and we'll all go. Come on, Pa, it's a perfect day."

And

"Are you sorry, Molly, for all the sins you have committed against the Lord your God? Can you give me a sign? Squeeze my hand. Can you hear me, Molly? *Ego te absolve in nomine Patri, et Filii, et Spiritu Sancti.*"

And the ghost who spoke to him most frequently, the one he could not lose even to his own final days, who rallied him and even cheered him despite its distant shadowy form, repeating the words again and again that would no doubt be his last conscious thought on this planet, the last syllables his brain would formulate before passing into the waiting ether:

"Good night, my dear love," it whispered as it had so many years ago. "I'd not change a day of it. I love you dearly, my lovely man."

And then a silence that broke only through these lonely echoes.

Insofar as the old man's ghosts had life, they had it here. In his aged solitude they intensified, and he welcomed them. He had more time to study them, indeed, to feel them. They had grown into him; he had absorbed them. They were in his bloodstream, racing through his veins, motivating his thoughts and ultimately dictating the rhythm of his days. They entwined themselves with his most vital parts so that, if he ever ripped apart from them, he would die quickly and with great regret. They possessed life here, in this place, in this city, amid the walls, and nowhere else. He played by their rules now, and, in the cold bitterness of old age wasted alone, he did not seek their release.

No doubt his son had ghosts, too. He could not help but have them, although they must certainly still be too faint yet. Their forms still cloaked themselves in imperceptible mist, and their voices mumbled softly, and without clarity, easily unacknowledged, and thus ignored.

But the old man could not ignore his, nor wanted to. And so, in the dwindling ashes of his life, he could not go from this place. At last, after years of disquiet, after years of feverishly searching for the elusive grail, he concluded that the very act of searching for it had put it in his grasp. He would not now release it.

The old man did not go outside that day. There was no need. He had food enough; the mail and newspaper were delivered. No one came to see him. No one called. He had expected no one, and most likely would have been miffed if someone had surprised him with a visit. The only sounds that punctuated his day were the common noises: the traffic in the street below him, the singing of his bird, the radio and the television. He nibbled on crackers for his lunch, prepared a small dinner. During the afternoon he read a bit of Terkel, whom he enjoyed because the man lacked all pretensions. Terkel made him think of the times of innocence, when, as a younger man, he felt secure amid the nation's heartbreak. He had proven himself a capable, independent man then, and he had never forgotten the pride he took in forging a stable, simple life for Molly and his boys. While reading he dozed from time to time. After dinner he watched an hour of television without liking it much, then read some more. By nine he was ready for bed.

He placed an old pillowcase over the bird cage to keep out the light. "Good night, Petey boy. It seems we're sleeping away what little we've got left. But that's no more than most folks, I suppose." He chuckled to himself, and to the bird. "Our advantage is in knowing we're doing it and being happy with the process. There'll be sleep enough for both of us in due course. I'll see you tomorrow, Petey boy, God willing."

The old man crossed himself, turned out the light, and went to his bed.

CHAPTER III

*Homesickness is . . . absolutely nothing. Fifty percent of the
people in the world are homesick all the time. . . . You don't
really long for another country. You long for something in
yourself that you don't have, or haven't been able to find.*

—John Cheever, *The Bella Lingua*

Back in May, Conor Finnegan and Tom McIlweath had been careening down their separate paths, one more in control than the other. McIlweath's frustrations had subsided somewhat at the prospect of finally getting away. If this vacuous and alienated existence were, as it was proving to be, only temporary, then he could endure it a bit longer in order to reach the complete break that was on the close horizon. He immersed himself in his studies which under different circumstances he had found stimulating. Now they were merely time killers, necessary and of passing interest, but most satisfying for the way they bridged his days. He marked off time from assignment to assignment.

Having become so meticulous with his work, McIlweath was consequently dismayed one afternoon to discover that he had left a textbook he needed to review back at school. Borrowing his father's car, he scooted back to campus to fetch it from his locker. He parked the car in a nearly empty lot. The campus was likely deserted.

The late afternoon sun cast shadows across the blue buildings as he made his way across the wide quadrangle. In early May, even in

California, a brisk clarity can ride the air. McIlweath paused by one of the thick stone benches. The faint chill heightened his perception of the contrast between the present quiet and the drone that customarily filled this place during most of his time there. After a few seconds of quiet innocence he went ahead to retrieve the book. His reverie was broken by a voice behind him.

"What do you say, Mac?"

He turned to find Finnegan trotting up to him from the direction of the gymnasium. McIlweath suppressed his annoyance.

"Conor. What are you doing here?"

"I was shooting around in the gym. That's about the only real exercise I get now."

"You're not playing baseball?"

"Not this year. I wasn't going to get much playing time. Shortage of talent on my part."

"That's too bad."

"Not really. It feels good to have the afternoons to myself. Basketball season seems to run the whole damn year."

"Wasn't it all worth it, though? You guys did great. It must be a good way to go out."

"We lost in the playoffs, Mac. That's all I'm going to remember."

'Who are you trying to kid?' thought McIlweath. 'You'll probably remember every basket you made and every time the announcer called your name. You'll remember your free throw percentage until the day you die." But all he said was, "I guess I can understand that."

"Did you walk back to school? Can I offer a ride home? And why are you here anyway? This is too nice a day to be stuck on campus."

"No, I've got my dad's car, but thanks. I forgot my physics book. We've got that lab assignment for tomorrow, remember?"

"Damn. I'd forgotten all about it. I can knock it off tonight, I suppose. I'm glad I ran into you. You know, Mac, I've gotten incredibly lazy these last few weeks."

"Why's that?" McIlweath asked without any real interest.

"I don't know. A lot of things, I guess. We can see the end of the road now, so the work just doesn't seem important. Now that everything is set for next year it doesn't really matter what I do. I'm not going to graduate any higher or lower regardless of my marks this term. And I did well enough earlier in the term so that I can probably screw up totally until the end of the year and my grades won't change. We're just playing out the string, you and I. It all seems a bit pointless. We're passed this stage, so let's get on to the next one. Is your car in the south lot? So's mine."

They walked together in the direction of their cars. A light film of perspiration lined Finnegan's forehead and cheeks. McIlweath could smell him faintly.

"Mac, do you ever get scared about next year? Whether you'll do all right, and whether you're making the right move?"

Finnegan had asked the question more for McIlweath's benefit, to draw him out about the coming year. In truth he really wasn't too concerned. He was, as always, supremely confident. And he certainly didn't want anyone, Tom McIlweath included, getting the wrong impression. Most of Finnegan's friends in fact had hinted at some uncertainties. But he wasn't like that, and his decisions, once made, provided blueprints. Finnegan expected that the quiet, private and largely unknown Tom McIlweath would have his share of doubt. Accordingly, McIlweath's response came as somewhat of a surprise.

"Conor, I can't tell you how much I'm looking forward to it."

Finnegan arched an eyebrow. "Tell me why. It's bound to be a hell of a change."

"Precisely what I'm looking forward to. Face it, Conor, I really don't know many people here. I never did. This is just a way-station. Very pleasant, but I've never been a part of it. I've never been accepted, even by you, although in your kindness you'd deny it. I'm anxious to move on to something different, someplace else."

Finnegan ignored the complaint and responded to the act rather than the motive. In his fashion, he turned it upon himself. "So am I, Mac."

"Are you? You've got everything you could want here."

"Maybe. But there's so much more out there that I don't even know about yet." Finnegan paused, then began again. "You know, it sounds almost silly to say it this way, but in basketball, coach always said that even the weakest teams can win at home. The really outstanding teams are those that can win on the road. That's what I want to do."

Tom McIlweath did not know where Conor Finnegan would be taking himself, nor did he particularly care. Let Finnegan find his own new playground and leave him in anonymous peace. Even so, the question was natural.

"So where are you going next year, Conor? How far on the road will you be?"

"Pretty far, Mac. I'm going to Rutgers."

McIlweath stopped in his tracks while adrenalin shot fiery arrows through his limbs. Air flew from his lungs, and he felt his face palpably grow red. Dumbstruck, he could think of nothing to say.

Rutgers. Despite his best intention to sever this distasteful chapter and start fresh as the sole author of the next one, a piece of this place would follow him there.

With Conor Finnegan, *Conor Finnegan* of all people, accompanying him across country to college, there would be no escape, at least not a total one, from a self-image he had come to loathe. One figure, a popular and persuasive one, would be a standing reminder of that which he had sought to dispel. Whether by false luck, or chance, or fate, or the malevolent mischief of unseen gods, with one word, his aspirations had been challenged beyond reasonable response.

Noting that his companion was no longer walking alongside him, Finnegan stopped and turned over his shoulder to see McIlweath's perplexity displayed in a furrowed brow and hard stare. "What's the matter, Mac? Have you heard of the place? A lot of people don't even know where it is. It's in New Jersey."

"I know," he croaked through a constricted throat. "I know where it is. In fact I'm going there, too." They had stopped just outside the gate to the parking lot. The sun hung low enough to attenuate the shadows of the adjacent buildings and keep them in shade.

Finnegan's eyes grew wide. "Are you kidding me?" he practically shouted as his excitement leapt from his lungs. "I can't believe it. Nobody from here goes to Rutgers. Nobody's ever gone there from here, and now there's going to be two of us? That's amazing. You're kidding me, right?"

"I'm dead serious, Conor." McIlweath started to walk toward his father's car. "Let's go home."

"But wait, though. I can't believe this. How did you pick Rutgers? I mean, why there of all places? Come on, Mac, talk to me."

"It's a long story. I'll tell you sometime. Not now."

McIlweath had parked next to the gate, right beside the entrance to the lot. Thank God. He could make an escape without having to explore further this perverse turn of events. He was too stunned to think rationally, or to sort through the avalanche of reactions that caromed around his reeling mind. He opened the car door to slide inside even as Finnegan continued asking him to wait.

The car spun around, nosed through the gate, turned right and headed for home. McIlweath dismissed the notion of running Finnegan down, although at the moment it had its appeal. Instead, he sped away, leaving his friend leaning against his own car, shaking his head in bewilderment.

* * *

For the next several days, Tom McIlweath went out of his way to avoid Conor Finnegan. Because they did not travel in the same circles this was hardly difficult, but some extra precautions were necessary nonetheless. His desire to avoid Finnegan took on neurotic proportions. Instead of buying his lunch in the cafeteria or eating in the quad, McIlweath spent his lunchtimes in the school library, munching on a sandwich at a study table, thumbing through magazines, the only student there. The librarian, a matronly lady of indeterminate age, would sit across from him, quizzically skewing her face from time to time, but she never said a word.

Nor did McIlweath take his usual seat in the second row of the English and physics classes he shared with Finnegan. Through the short remainder of the year he took to sitting in the rear, close to the door, so that he could arrive and leave with the passing bells without having to cross paths with Finnegan, who was customarily one of the first in the rooms. Finnegan, for his part, did not notice his friend's shift in position.

McIlweath also took great care to leave campus each day as soon as he could. To be sure, few students lingered after the final bell, but there was always a handful who might sit in the quad after the last period to talk, to gossip, and to watch the campus empty. Finnegan was occasionally one of those, particularly now that his afternoons were free. McIlweath made certain he had all the books he needed to take home before going to his final class so that he could bypass the quad afterwards and head straight out.

In this way Tom McIlweath avoided any contact with Conor Finnegan for nearly a month. May passed to June, and graduation, an event to which McIlweath had looked forward as his final release, impended at last.

On the evening of the ceremony itself, McIlweath had no more places to hide, yet he expected that Finnegan would be far too busy with his closer friends to pay him any mind. For once, the young man felt protected by his anonymity. Besides, they would not be placed anywhere near each other in the procession. Finnegan, second in his class, would march in next to last. McIlweath had not attained the necessary honors to pull him out of the alphabetical lineup.

Fifteen minutes before the procession was to begin faculty marshals nervously attempted to put some order into things. While counting down alphabetical lists of names, they scoured faces and sniffed breaths for the faintest whiff of alcohol. At the same time they tried to herd students into line.

Into the midst of this neurotic chaos strode Finnegan, shaking hands and smiling like a politician. He was enjoying himself fully, paying what amounted to last respects to those with whom he had shared his time. As second in the class, he was to give one of the graduation addresses, but he showed no sign of nerves. He walked down the forming line, stopping to speak to those he knew, taking no more than a few seconds with each, resting his hand on their shoulders in a gesture of intimacy, then quickly moving on, the light blue graduation robe flapping behind him.

McIlweath saw him working his way through the alphabet and ultimately heading for the "*m*"s. Exposed, he instinctively looked about for some type of cover. In the open assembly area, locked into place by his name, he had nowhere to go. He hoped that, in the interval of several weeks, Finnegan might pass right by him, or stop only to wish him luck before moving on to more important people. Still, he did not wish to tempt fate. He shuffled to the side of Peter McGuiness, a tall, heavy, incredibly full specimen who was set to march ahead of him. Pete's girth could cast a shadow, quite a large one, and provide some hope for concealment.

No such luck. Finnegan had arrived, his eyes twinkling squarely on Tom McIlweath. He dismissed the obstruction immediately.

"Pete, how are you? Good luck, buddy."

"Right, Conor. Good luck to you, too."

"Let me get to this guy back here." Finnegan extended his hand around the great McGuiness. "McIlweath, where the hell have you been? I haven't talked to you in weeks."

"I've been around, Conor. Congratulations."

"Never a doubt, Mac. For either of us. Listen, I've got to talk to you before we head east. You'll be around this summer, won't you? Are you going to work?"

"Yeah, I'll be here. I'm lifeguarding at a swim club across town." He tried to deflect the conversation. "What about you?"

"Nothing special. I'm a referee in a kids summer basketball league. Lousy pay but easy work." Finnegan would not be deflected, though. He had an agenda, albeit a brief one. "But look, I'll give you a call sometime after graduation. We've got to talk about next year. I've got some ideas about the whole thing."

'No doubt you do,' thought McIlweath. 'But, please, is there no way you can spare me your sickening enthusiasm? I can't be bound to you.'

Finnegan concluded and moved down the line. "Congratulations again, friend. We've got great things ahead of us."

Tom McIlweath was not so sure, and with Conor Finnegan's words still warm in his ears, he felt the oppressive air of his anonymous youth little changed by graduation.

* * *

The metal grandstand bit into McIlweath's back as he stretched himself across three empty rows. Below him, two teams of sweating adolescents ran up and down the basketball court. Order was being kept by two striped shirts, one of which covered the frame of Finnegan. The gymnasium seemed particularly cavernous. Only a handful of people, virtually all of them parents, watched the game. Their periodic shouts or cheers echoed around the building.

It was late July. Two nights earlier, Finnegan had phoned McIlweath suggesting they get together. They had not spoken since graduation night, and McIlweath had hoped hat that would be the end of it. Realistically, he expected to encounter Finnegan next year. That would probably be unavoidable. But Rutgers was a big place, and McIlweath anticipated keeping a goodly distance. He would go to class, he would live in his dormitory, he would swim, all apart from Finnegan and what he represented. At best, they should be able to travel in separate circles.

McIlweath dwelt on the idea of a clean slate, with no definitions, expectations or judgments appended from his past. The more he dwelt upon it, the more it drew him in, until Rutgers became for him the River Lethe, where all memory would be indelibly erased.

Even after Finnegan had called, McIlweath was unsure of what he wanted. Despite his best intentions he had agreed to meet. Still, he remained determined to keep himself unfettered for the coming year.

As the game ended McIlweath stood, stretched, and made his way down the bleachers. He did not think that Finnegan had seen him come in. Finnegan, though, had mastered the art of searching the stands while running up and down a basketball court. He had always liked to be certain of his audience. Consequently, after receiving his night's pay at the scorer's table, Finnegan headed straight for McIlweath. They shook hands, Finnegan smiling warmly.

"Mac, how are you, buddy? How's the summer?"

"Not bad, Conor. Quiet. I've been swimming a lot."

"At the beach?"

"No, with my team. Chlorine and natural sunshine."

Finnegan led McIlweath to a small bag sitting on the edge of the bleachers. He reached inside it for a towel, pulled the referee's shirt over his head, and dried the perspiration on his torso as best he could. Afterward he pulled on a polo shirt.

"Listen, do you feel like something to eat, pizza or a sandwich? I haven't had dinner yet. I'll pay."

McIlweath consented. They agreed on the restaurant and headed there in separate cars. Although the place was a fairly popular gathering point for young people, McIlweath had been there no more than two or three times the entire year, and then by himself. They were seated by a server no older than they were. McIlweath noted that, even though Finnegan had toweled himself off after the game, he still carried the sharp, acrid pungency of dried sweat. On Finnegan such an odor was particularly noteworthy. He was one of the few young men of his age to wear cologne daily. Where that type of vanity would usually be mocked by his friends, Finnegan was able to pull it off with no comment by even the crudest among them. It all seemed somehow natural for him.

They ordered. Finnegan got right to the point. "Mac, how do you figure on getting to Rutgers at the end of the summer?"

"I thought I'd fly back, of course."

"You think you'll be able to take everything you want with you?"

"What do I want to bring? Just clothes. Maybe a few books. That'll all fit into a suitcase or two. Everything else I'll need I'll get there. What's your point?"

"Listen, Mac. I don't want to fly back there. There's no adventure in that." Finnegan's voice picked up its intensity. He sat on the edge of his chair, his elbows resting on the table. As he continued to speak, his hands opened and he made quick, chopping gestures for emphasis.

"I want to drive to New Jersey, cross-country. I want to take about two weeks and go everywhere I want between here and there. No schedule, no map. Just follow the roads. And I want you to go with me."

Genuinely surprised, McIlweath could only ask, "Why?" in a soft, almost hidden voice. He could not imagine what purpose Finnegan might have in asking him along.

Finnegan had not expected anything less than a blind, shared excitement. The question caught him off-guard, and he stammered what passed for a response. "Hell, Mac, you've got to . . . I mean, Jesus, it should be obvious. You've got to get back there, too. If I'm driving back you may as well come. I think we'd have a great time of it, and it would be a terrific way to start college, with that kind of trip behind us. Thrill of the open road, and all that. Read some Whitman."

Composure regained, Finnegan lowered his voice slightly, and leaned across the table.

"Besides, Mac, you *are* my friend, you know."

All pretense fell away in a single sentence that McIlweath would remember clearly years later. With the lightning-quick reaction of human thought, McIlweath saw it all through these simple words. It had not mattered to Finnegan, then, that he had kept his distance for the past several weeks. Perhaps he had not even noticed the estrangement at all, or, if he had, defined it as something without personal implications. Finnegan ran through his world with a Romantic idealization of man's youth, aware of his own lofty station, accepting it as humbly as he could as some fruit of an unnatural, random selection, but accepting it nonetheless. So favored, he could love who and what stood around him. Everything in his existence up to this point had contributed to, or at least had not interfered with, his own ascent, and he perceived his life as a series of blessings personally bestowed by a kind Providence. Whatever he encountered—from his old car that still ran well enough to suggest a cross-country trip, to his friends at school, to the clothes on his back—manifested that special favor, that metaphysical embrace.

If, then, the world breathed such grandeur for his benefit, he could love it without qualification. Tom McIlweath was a small part of it, but part of it he was, and so Conor Finnegan accepted him as fully and as innocently as the sky accepts a sunrise. Even when McIlweath tried to resign from it, or, total resignation being impossible, tried to withdraw to its most remote corners, Finnegan's world held him fast. McIlweath may have had very sound reasons for doing what he did, but in the glorious personal schema of Conor Finnegan, they could not be related to character, action or promise.

"Conor, I don't know if it's practical," McIlweath spoke finally after the tides of sudden thought curtailed. "Do you think that car of yours is going to be able to make it? And even if it could, this little expedition would be too expensive. We're poor, struggling students, remember?"

"If we do it right, it's not going to cost much more than an airline ticket. Maybe less."

"What do you mean by 'doing it right'?"

"We don't have to stay in motels. Christ, that would be boring. We can camp out, or stay with friends along the way." The excitement returned in Finnegan's voice as McIlweath considered that there was no chance he knew anyone in Kansas, Wyoming, Indiana or any other state between here and there. "We probably wouldn't have to eat much, either."

"Conor, we've got to eat. What are we going to do, forage dumpsters for half-eaten sandwiches?"

"Think of it, Mac. We could go anywhere we want."

They were interrupted by the server returning with their order. McIlweath had ordered only a soda. Despite Finnegan's speculation on food intake levels, he had ordered big—a large turkey sandwich and a couple of sides.

"Anywhere we want," continued Finnegan. "And at the end of it, we'll be at college. Classes start September 12th, so I was thinking of leaving around August 28th or 29th. That'll give us two full weeks."

McIlweath caught his use of the plural. Already Finnegan presumed that McIlweath was on board. "Let's not get ahead of ourselves," he thought.

But the prospect of such a trip, totally inconceivable until a few minutes earlier, took on an immediately attractive luster. By the end of the evening, Finnegan's grand enthusiasm for the plan claimed a fellow traveler. McIlweath told him that he would have to think about it. There were logistical problems, he said. He would have to quit his job earlier than he had planned, he would have to convince his parents, he would have to check his finances, and so on. But Finnegan knew underneath this subterfuge that McIlweath had been bitten, and that, when things settled, the two of them would make this trip together.

It was ambitious, thought Finnegan, this idea of two young men—boys really, in terms of experience and wisdom, boys who knew almost nothing about what was out there—traveling across country on their own. But how stagnant would man be without his ambitions? Besides, he could not predict when an opportunity like this might come along again.

As the time for going drew near, both Conor Finnegan and Tom McIlweath prepared for it in their distinctive ways. Both grew increasingly excited; both stared deeper and deeper into the face of what they were on the verge of entering. With their excitement there mingled apprehensions that each confronted alone.

Finnegan paid heed to his Romantic tendencies. He had always been a great believer in his own potential, the embodiment of the potential of all young people, had felt the strong surges of power flow through his veins and brace his spine, had felt frequently the joy and wonderment of discovery, of finding things within himself that he had not known were there, and which were always worth finding. But he had never ventured far afield to exercise that potential, to test his own capabilities. It had always been so safe. Although he had no shortage of confidence, he was untried, like a soldier on the eve of battle: sure of his own invincibility, certain of survival, but wary of the wounds he may have to suffer to procure it. Finnegan had shown his abilities only in small, secure, well-protected arenas. He was about to enter a new, more vulnerable dimension.

As a result he became mindful of the world he was about to leave. He took notice of its physical details and tried to memorize as many of them as he could. On certain evenings, when he had nothing else to do, he would sit on the patio and stare at his backyard, absorbing the shape of every tree, the line of every bush, the texture of the grass. He would consciously remember the moments that had taken place there—throwing a baseball with his father, running the length of the yard with his dog, the heavy sensation of mowing the lawn on a hot summer's day. Or he would walk down his street and around the block, looking seriously at the colors of each house, noting the different designs, the way the asphalt changed hues in certain places, and the roll of the sidewalk. He became sensitive to the sounds with which he had grown up—not the voices of his friends or family, but the normal mechanical sounds that helped punctuate his daily routine: the resonant ticking of the living room clock, the springs in his bed, the squeak of the garage door when it was raised, the metallic cracking of the patio awning as the sun heated it. Finnegan tried to absorb it all, to make a complete record of what had formed him, so that he could better carry it with him.

He noted, too, the feeling of the place. In the early evenings his bedroom would capture all the heat of a summer's day. The sun would be low enough to cast the light-colored wall in orange or yellow, and the room would turn perceptibly warmer than the rest of the house. There he would sit and read in that special light, or review his books, or look through old pictures, and feel that warmth that he knew was part atmospheric and part emotional, knowing that this could never be felt anywhere else.

In the mornings he would lie in bed and let his body sink into the contours of the mattress, noting as he did so a softness made for him alone. The blue bedspread would be kicked to the bed's edge, or onto the floor altogether, and he would be wrapped in a sheet and light blanket. Then only was his whole physical existence turned to comfort—rested, softly spread across his own embracing space, thoroughly at ease.

The days themselves held no pressures. Because he worked only two or three hours each night, he had a great deal of time to himself. He took care to see his friends, but his attitude with them betrayed no apprehensions. He tried to continue as he had before: amiable, self-confident, universally excited. If anything, he added new pretensions, rarely letting an opportunity slide to remind his friends that he would be going away. Around them, he felt again in himself the ambitious daring that had allowed him to take such a step.

Above all, Finnegan took note of his parents. And during this summer of preparation he marveled at them as he never had before. They would be losing him, at least as a child, yet their demeanor was unchanged. They had not become sentimental or overly solicitous. As they had always done, they gave Conor whatever space he needed or wanted while making certain that he knew he had their confidence.

Yet despite their appearances, Conor surmised, they must be terribly puzzled. The specter of mortality presents itself in whispers and hints. He became attentive to them, and sought for ways to soften the impending blow. He spoke often of coming home for the holidays, of the following summer, or writing them long, descriptive letters.

For Edward and Katherine Finnegan, the process of watching their only son prepare to leave was indeed a painful one, but not without its rewards. Edward Finnegan, as his father before him, prized independence. 'I will bind myself to another man for wages,' he reasoned; 'my spirit no one can have.' He had raised his son the same way.

Ed Finnegan had always been proud of young Conor. Ever since his son's first few steps, he believed the boy was rare. Conor possessed intelligence, he had strength. Ed sought to guide his son gently in such a way as to allow him to bring out his best qualities, to try new things so that he could discover more of himself, and come to know the world around him, always assured of a safe haven in his own home. When Conor was a baby, Ed Finnegan one night leaned over his crib and whispered to his sleeping son, "I promise you that you will have everything you need, and most of what you want." As Conor grew, Ed remained true to that pledge.

Ed Finnegan also had a firm conviction of what was right and what was wrong. He believed in the inherent dignity of the human character, that everyone he might encounter had value no matter who they were or how they presented themselves. If any act curtailed a man's freedom or insulted that dignity, then it was wrong. Such acts should be condemned when seen, and shunned when tempted. He had little concern about being in the minority on even the simplest issues of personal justice. A man had the capacity every day to do something that might be of benefit to someone else, he believed. He needn't try to change the world, but he did have an obligation to make his part of it as gentle as possible. If he could raise his son with some of these values, keeping him mindful of the world around him and his responsibility to it, then Ed Finnegan could allow his boy to set his own course without worry.

Consequently he had never tried to bully his son, or prod him, or live out his own frustrations through him. He had merely sought to guide him. And Conor had rarely been disappointing. That the young man could feel strong enough to embark on his own at so tender an age was proof enough to his father that he had raised him well. Whatever loneliness might ensue, then, was worth it: his son had proved to be his finest labor.

Katherine Finnegan had never perceived herself as an independent soul before she married Edward, but their years together had instilled something of an appreciation for her husband's proud character, even though she could not bring herself to emulate it. She, too, was well satisfied with her son. She saw in him that same spirit that distinguished her husband from other men, that same sense of justice, that same tenacity. But she felt as well that Conor was far more sensitive than her husband. He had fewer rough edges and tended to be more trusting of others' intentions. She took credit for imparting in him that sensitivity. Yes, her son was an independent sort, as was her husband, and he would do well for himself wherever he went, but a mother cannot watch her child become an adult without pangs of sadness. She would miss him fiercely.

For the three Finnegans there hung over that summer an ominous air of finality. A part of their lives, irrevocable, tottered toward conclusion. No one spoke about it, at least not directly. Still, it pervaded their every action, their every word. And as the summer drew to a close and Conor's boyhood flickered away, the atmosphere grew heavier despite their best intentions. The end of it all would be bittersweet: an exultation of what was to come, a rejoicing and release of the young man's spirit, but a permanent rending of the security of what used to be.

Man's life is full of passages. We come from the womb in a spasm of blood, a fit of crying. This, too, was a passage — another birth, another escape from another womb, another bloodletting for the sake of something that had to be.

Across town, Tom McIlweath spent the summer where he felt most comfortable—in and around a swimming pool. He worked out every morning with his club, trying to maintain his competitive edge and suitable conditioning in preparation for the coming year, and then spent eight hours lifeguarding. He was seldom bored.

He did not view his flight across country as an act of finality. Unlike Conor Finnegan, McIlweath did not spend his last few weeks at home remembering his past and romanticizing his present. He did not account as completely as did Finnegan what he would be leaving behind. His parents, of course, he would miss, but he considered their impending distance merely a redefinition of their relationship, which he deemed, for the most part, healthy. His father had set off at an even earlier age, and he had never stayed more than a few years in any one spot even after marriage, so Tom had a slightly different view of what might be regarded the normal course of things for himself. John McIlweath, once presented with his son's choice, and recognizing that because of Tom's swimming scholarship his expenses for four years of college would be far below what he had expected, viewed it with sympathy.

Tom McIlweath knew it was time to get away, had desperately

wanted to do so, and consequently looked at the world he was leaving with a cold eye. As summer wound down his anticipation was no less than Finnegan's, but it stood on different legs. He spent his summer working, swimming, and, until Finnegan called him that night in late July, he saw no one. Whatever Romantic tendencies he had during this restless summer were well suppressed.

At least until Finnegan proposed his cross-country drive. McIlweath had told him he would think about it, but there was really no need. A chord had been struck. Within two days, Tom had decided to go along, infused with a surprising new fondness for the purveyor of this notion. Now the method of escape promised to be as intriguing as the escape itself. He began to think Whitmanesque thoughts. A continent lay before him, and he would approach it, wide-eyed and care-free.

* * *

In late August on the morning of departure, Conor Finnegan took leave of his parents. He preferred to leave quickly, before the sun was up, before he was fully awake. He told himself that he would not be overly sentimental. The world, he thought, lay fresh then, in the pre-dawn.

His mother had made coffee and they sat, the three of them, as the kitchen table. Conor had packed the car the night before, taking care to leave enough space for McIlweath's things. There was nothing left to do but drive away.

"How far do you expect to get today?" asked Katherine Finnegan.

"I'm not sure. We're heading north. We can make San Francisco if we want." Conor spoke slowly, measuring every word, knowing that he would remember this early morning conversation in all its particulars. "Does the car look okay, Dad?"

"Yeah, you're in good shape. As good as that heap can be. Now, if you have any trouble, call me. No matter where you are."

Conor chuckled. "Dad, what are you going to do, fly out with your tool box? I'm afraid we're on our own this time. But you know I'll keep you posted as we go along."

"Well, I just want to know. Let us hear from you. Often. Call us whenever you can."

Edward Finnegan, too, would remember this conversation, as simple as it was. He sat at the table, outwardly composed. Inwardly, though, his emotions tumbled and churned. He could not sort them all out. He felt again his intense pride in his son. But as he sat there looking at him, the father felt that, from this point on, the boy would no longer be his.

The elder Finnegan had marked his life through his son the same way he had marked off young Conor's growth on the kitchen wall. When Conor was born, Ed Finnegan had lived thirty-four years. It is a late age for a man to become a father. His own boyhood had lacked a mother, who died too young, and, with a father consumed with feeding himself and his four sons, Ed Finnegan was too often left to his own devices. He had never been taught to plan a future. Even after several years of marriage he still lacked a long-term vision for himself and his wife. Not that he squandered money or behaved irresponsibly. Rather, Ed Finnegan simply made no plans. He had worked at a number of jobs—auto mechanic, light construction, assembler in a farm machinery factory—staying at each only until he became bored. He had tried the military, too, staying three years and rising to the rank of staff sergeant. He left the Army having given no thought to a military career. He was looking forward to sleeping late for a while.

When his son was born, less than a year after Katherine, fearful of a ticking biological clock, had virtually demanded a child, Ed Finnegan settled himself. The change took subtle forms. At the time he was working as a grocer in a small store owned by an old man from northern Italy. Within eighteen months he changed jobs again, but this time the choice was more reasoned. He saw no future with his Italian friend, so he left him to join a large, multistore supermarket chain with a pension plan and unionized job security. He had a family now; he had to work himself along. In an instinctive way (for Ed Finnegan did not think in philosophical terms), his son's birth had forced him to consider his own mortality. Such was the whisper that someday he would die. While he was here, he had an obligation to take care of his own. Ed Finnegan remained in the grocery business for the remainder of his working life.

From then on, the father reckoned his own life by his son's. Years later he would be able to identify the day, the time and his frame of mind when Conor reached milestones of growth: his first word, his first day of school, his first report card, and so on. Ed Finnegan's perception of himself in his own maturity became woven around his son as young Conor shed, one by one, the trappings of childhood.

This morning, too, was another of those sheddings, but Ed Finnegan knew it to be the final one in the framework that had defined his life for the past eighteen years. What would come after this could only be foreign to him, and so his own uncertainties ran far deeper than his son's.

"I suppose I better get going. I'm supposed to pick up Mac five minutes ago." All three had been reluctant to state the obvious, or to make the first move. They had remained at the table well past the coffee, well past the limits of ordinary conversation. With Conor's pronouncement they rose and went outside to his car parked in front of the house. The extra weight of the packing caused its rear to sink lower than normal.

"Nice night."

"You've got a good day to travel, it looks like."

The three reached the car at the end of the front sidewalk. Conor, who was a step ahead, stopped first and turned around. His heart beat rapidly, adrenalin pumping through him in tiny darts. At that instant he felt a silent, invisible hand squeeze his chest like a child squeezing a handful of clay, wrenching it with all its unseen might. He could not hesitate now. The realization he had hidden all summer could not catch him, not now. Please God, not now.

"Well . . ." he paused, could think of nothing to say. His mother grabbed him.

"God be with you, son." She felt warm as he held her against the morning chill.

"Mom, take care. I'll be back soon." She was not crying, but neither could she speak.

Conor released her, and she him. Both he and his father stood motionless. Their eyes met. Neither wanted to make a move, and the few seconds they stood so fixed seemed frozen, so that years later Conor could remember his father's face, set with a firm chin, brown eyes glistening with a rich pride, and think then that there could be no greater confirmation of a father's love.

Conor reached out his hand, his father grasped it strongly. Conor followed his father's grip into an embrace.

"Be good, Conor. God bless you." Ed Finnegan's handshake had been much firmer than his voice.

"I'll do the best I can, Dad. You take care of Mom. And thanks. Thanks so much."

Conor pulled himself away, turned sharply and half ran around the car to the driver's door. He got in and started it up, noting oddly that he could see his breath. He put the car into gear, and, as it began to move, looked up to capture, consciously, a parting impression.

His parent stood there on the curb. They did not touch. Both father and mother smiled rigidly, a final forced benediction. 'They're trying too hard,' thought Conor. His mother's robe was white, his father's plaid, and now one plaid arm and one white arm were raised in a wave, moving very slowly, scarcely moving at all. It was his movement, the movement of the car, that gave any sense of motion at all.

Conor waved back. He did not smile. He was grateful that there were no tears from any of them. At least not there, not then.

CHAPTER IV

It was at the highest point in the arc of a bridge that I became aware suddenly of the depth . . . of my feelings about modern life, and of the profoundness of my yearning for a more vivid, simple, and peaceable world.

—John Cheever, *The Angel of the Bridge*

The midday sun was hot, the landscape unbelievably dull. In every direction, a solid dirty-white monotony ran to the horizon. This was, after all, the desert, and what could they expect? This was reality: no Romantic *Grand Canyon Suite*-like setting here, only a hot, dry, earthy plain, less intimidating certainly than to those who first challenged it by foot, horse or wagon, but no less boring.

Finnegan and McIlweath had roared down the Sierras of Northern California in an exhilarating bolt. They had left San Francisco early that morning, before dawn. They had seen the city lights below them and the great bay beyond. It had been cool then in the darkness. There in the hills of the East Bay the air had been fresh and bracing. Finnegan had paused as they packed their camping gear and stood for a few minutes gazing at the lights and the water, conjuring images of porcelain and crystal. He had been able to make out the Golden Gate Bridge with little trouble, for the night was totally clear even into the Bay. No fog shrouded his view. The whole city, and everything within sight, appeared to be *papier-mâché*.

Several hours later the freshness had vanished. They cleared the Sierras and drove through the high desert plains of northern Nevada, east of Reno, until boredom and fatigue forced them to stop early at a shabby campground near Elko. After a fitful night's sleep, dreamless and uninspired, they hit the road the next morning, to find more of the same dull, dusty, flat tedium.

Despite only a light shirt and blue jeans, Finnegan perspired freely in the afternoon heat. Driving a car presented no physical challenge in the typical sense. He had to stay awake and keep the car where it should be, but that required no strength at all. Still, he felt drained. The sweat clung to his body, dampening his brow, cheeks and forearms without cooling him. It lined him with a clammy, sticky film. His shirt adhered to the seat so tightly that from time to time he would reach behind himself and pull it away with a muted swish of wet fabric. The air conditioning in the old car was dead on arrival when Finnegan bought it a year ago, so all windows were wide open. But the cross-breeze did little to cool him. The wind that blew in was dry, almost abrasive. McIlweath sat next to him in the same condition. Boxes, books and clothing that did not fit into the trunk packed the back seat. It was a small space they had, and this afternoon for the first time it closed in on them in a hot, cramped, sticky, boring contraction.

"Hey Mac, aren't there any towns out here?" asked Finnegan. "I feel like stopping for something to drink."

"No towns. No one lives in Nevada."

"I guess not. If there were anything coming up in the next fifty miles we'd be able to see it, it's so damn flat."

McIlweath opened a road atlas and perused it for a few seconds. "There's some town coming up in about seventy-five miles. At least there's a dot on the map. I don't see anything between here and there."

"Whose idea was this?"

They drove on without speaking. McIlweath had turned into good company for a trip like this. In fact, Finnegan had been pleasantly surprised by McIlweath's broad knowledge and relatively quick wit. He also seemed to know about a number of things which to Finnegan had always been remote.

Such as camping. When first conceiving of this trip, Finnegan had assumed that he could save money while savoring the great outdoors by camping along the way. The fact that he had neither camping equipment nor had spent so much as a single night without a firm roof over his head never entered his mind. Fortunately, McIlweath had a large enough reserve of both gear and experience. He had a tent that would do, a pair of sleeping bags and some cooking equipment. More importantly, he had served a term as a Boy Scout and knew what to do with it all. Finnegan hadn't a clue. That first night they pitched camp, illegally, in a wooded park outside the San Francisco suburbs, Finnegan had fumbled about with the tent pegs and support ropes while McIlweath drove out to get something to eat. By the time McIlweath returned, the tent was firmly rooted on the corners but sagging in the middle, and Finnegan was thoroughly confused. Within five minutes McIlweath had run a rope along its spine and tethered it to two trees. From then on, Finnegan would leave all practical camping matters to his friend.

The drive up the coast to San Francisco had energized them both. Finnegan and McIlweath talked the whole time, about friends left behind, about family, about women, about sports. They had spent two days in the bay area where McIlweath had not been an outsider, and had several friends with whom they spent good time. And now, on the drive out, for the first time Finnegan was bored. A perfect complement to the physical discomforts, he thought. He presumed, too, that, from his silence, his friend felt the same way.

Nevada had no speed laws, at least none that were ever enforced. Although Finnegan maintained his old car at seventy, faster vehicles whipped by them. At one point a late-model Jaguar appeared in the rearview mirror, grew larger almost immediately, changed lanes, buzzed by and disappeared in the distance, all in the span of two or three minutes.

'Easily a hundred and thirty,' thought Finnegan.

At once, a glint came into his eye, and he straightened himself in his seat. "Mac," he said, "do you think this old thing can break a hundred?" Finnegan looked over to the other seat with a sly grin.

"Are you serious? If this thing hits eighty it'll start to disintegrate. We'll have to stop to pick up loose parts."

"I bet it will. It's really not in bad shape for a car with this many miles on it."

"Conor, small sedans weren't built to go that fast."

"Then why is the speedometer graded up to a hundred and twenty?"

McIlweath leaned over to check it out. "It is, isn't it? I hadn't noticed that before."

"We haven't had the opportunity to consider it before. Mac, it's only right. We're within a couple of hundred miles of the Bonneville Salt Flats where they set all the land speed records. I think we owe it to ourselves to try to set a new record for a twelve-year-old Dodge."

Finnegan depressed the accelerator gradually. McIlweath leaned over again across the bucket seat to watch the needle. Slowly it crept upward . . . seventy-five . . . eighty . . . eighty-five . . . ninety. The car began to shake slightly. Finnegan leveled off for a moment to make certain all parts were still intact. Satisfied, he continued the climb.

Ninety-five…ninety-six…ninety-seven. The accelerator was fully depressed and the car's vibration had intensified. McIlweath, his arm around the back of the driver's seat, stared hard at the speedometer.

"Come on, Conor," he shouted above the rushing air. "We're almost there."

The quivering needle touched the hash mark of ninety-nine. Finnegan had the pedal to the floor and was leaning forward as if to nudge it faster. The needle advanced just enough to touch the thick mark that noted a hundred.

"Hey hey, baby, we did it!" screamed Finnegan.

But before the words cleared his throat, the car shook violently. Something under the hood exploded with a huge clanging bang that left their ears tingling.

Finnegan immediately took his foot off the accelerator. In the same instant he turned to McIlweath. They looked at each other, eyes wide, mouths open, not speaking but listening intensely for another noise that might cast them to the side of the road in the middle of the Nevada desert at midday. Something resembling panic rose up from their bellies.

The car decelerated rapidly. It had coasted down to fifty before Finnegan dared try the accelerator again. He put his foot back on the pedal and gingerly pressed down. The pedal was firm; the car started to go faster. A faint rattle from somewhere deep in the engine was its only new sound. Finnegan took it back up to sixty and held it there.

McIlweath spoke at last, his voice several octaves higher than before. "What do you think that was?"

"What do I know about cars, Mac? I can't say. Maybe we dropped a rod. If we did, we're damn lucky it's still running."

"Will it get us to New Jersey?"

"I've got a feeling this thing would get us to the moon if there was a road going there."

They drove on for several more minutes, listening to see if the car made any other sounds they should worry about. After a bit they both relaxed, out of immediate danger.

"How does it drive?"

"Seems okay. You notice it was fine at ninety-nine but the instant it touched a hundred it exploded. Maybe that should tell us something."

"Yeah. A man's reach can't exceed his grasp."

"Or no guts, no glory."

"Do we claim victory?"

"Of course. The needle touched a hundred, and we both can verify it. I daresay no other Dodge of this vintage has reached that threshold."

"You're one amazing driver, Conor."

"Luck of the Irish, my friend."

The lucky Irishman and his companion drove on and on that day, stopping only once for a late afternoon meal and twice for gas. Across the salty neck of Utah they went, then north into Idaho and Wyoming. The terrain changed dramatically, the bleak desert of Nevada growing at first slightly less dusty and a bit greener, a line of mountains on the horizon looming larger and more present, then rising almost straight up so that they hid the late afternoon sun. The land rose, with trees beginning to appear alongside a roadway that was increasingly curved and narrow. The mountains exuded a rhythm—rises, mountain valleys, small towns, then greater rises, mountains growing out of mountains. The air cooled and thinned. They felt it first when they got out of the car to stretch their leg and pump their gas. Their breathing quickened; their pulses quickened. They felt cool, and Finnegan at least could understand in part what it was that made men forsake other men and head far back into the mountains. They had left the interstate and traffic was slight. The towns, such as they were, drifted by more slowly—a few homes, a store, perhaps a gas station, sometimes a post office. Everything seemed made of wood. Few people were to be seen, fewer still to talk to. The sharp land complemented the sharp air—the space so vast, so remote, and man merely a guest to be tolerated rather than entertained.

The sun fell low, tucked behind the mountains. The sky deepened through blue shades unlike any the urbanite Finnegan had ever seen. As the sun declined, the outlined forms of the mountains ahead of them darkened. Behind the mountains where the highway pointed, tendrils of pastel orange shot upward. McIlweath leaned his arm out the window and glanced from side to side, breathing in the magnificent scenery, trying to absorb everything at once. Finnegan, with the obligation of driving, was fixed on the curving road ahead. It had been a long day, and he was tired. Yet the majesty of that setting, the great height, the thick woods and jutting rocks, the softly flashing colors, conjured serenity such as he had felt only at his most sublime moments.

Purified, and purged of contrivance and complication, Finnegan saw himself atop a magical country, opened at last before and beneath him. He imagined looking over his shoulder to the coast, sparkled by the lights of San Francisco and Los Angeles. He imagined the freeway as night fell, ribbons winding around the tall buildings. He imagined the northwest timberlands, and the coastal mountains like footstools, green and plush. He imagined looking across the plains at his feet stretching eastward, forming criss-cross patterns of farmland and grazing lands, silos sticking out of the ground like matchsticks. He saw in his mind at the heel of the great blue lakes the city of Chicago, where his grandfather tended his now-quiet life. He imagined the glorious cities of the east and wondered when he would see them, and if he would be able to tell them apart by their feel and their character, Boston from New York, Baltimore from Philadelphia. From these mountaintops there could be no place higher. From here he could imagine an endless view, and see how all these pieces he had yet to come to know might fit together.

Neither spoke as they drove into the darkening mountains. They remained as they were for a considerable time, quietly overwhelmed, subtly humbled, immensely content.

Finally McIlweath broke their meditations. "Conor, we'd better find a place to stay tonight."

"Yeah, there should be a lot of campgrounds around here. The Graaannd Tetons."

"This is the country for it. Camping, I mean."

"It's quiet up here," said Finnegan. "That's a hell of a change from what we left behind."

"These are the Rockies, Conor. I've been in this area before, with the Scouts. You're not going to find much commotion up here. Not by humans, anyway."

"I like the change. We're at the top of a continent."

"You've been reading too much poetry. Let's find a place to pitch camp. I'm beat."

By the time they found a commercial campground, night had nearly fallen. The tall trees engulfing the roadway cast strange shadows that waved slightly in a whispering breeze. Finnegan drove up to the office, which was only a small cabin near the ground's entrance. A wooden sign declared that a campsite would cost $5. Finnegan got out of the car and went up to the cabin door, knocked, tried to open it and found it was locked. Do campgrounds ever close?, he wondered. He returned to the car.

"Nobody there, Mac."

"What do you think we should do?"

"I think we should find a campsite. If a ranger comes along, we pay him then. If not, we get a freebie. In fact, let's plan on getting out of here early enough tomorrow morning to miss him."

"That's illegal, you know."

"And so my life of crime begins. Besides, we haven't exactly been respectful of camping laws to this point anyhow."

They drove up the winding road leading back to the campsites. Finnegan felt more comfortable after passing camps already pitched. There were other people in these parts after all.

By the time they found an empty site it was totally dark. They had only one standard flashlight to find their way about. McIlweath used it to search for soft ground in proximity to two trees to pitch their tent. He stumbled around for several minutes, periodically mouthing curses as he came across rocky or uneven ground. Finally he found a suitable spot and went to work putting up the tent. In the dark Finnegan could be of no help outside of holding the flashlight. As a result it took longer to pitch the tent than it had on previous nights. By the time the tent stood firm their fatigue was complete. The day had caught up with them.

"I'm exhausted, Mac. Let's turn in."

"Don't you want to build a fire? That's pretty fundamental."

"What for? All we're going to do is sleep. We can roast marshmallows tomorrow. Anyway, why draw attention to ourselves?"

McIlweath was too tired to pursue it, even though he had never camped without a fire. Tonight he was willing to let it go. Finnegan set the flashlight on a rock so that the beam shone into the tent. They both used the narrow light to undress.

Sleeping arrangements fell a bit short of regal. Their tent was only a two-man pup. After fitting their sleeping bags they slept as close as man and wife, each insulated in his own cocoon. In a way he would never admit, Finnegan took great comfort knowing another human body was so close in these remote places. He preferred a roof, but without one at hand, he realized that McIlweath had become a security blanket. Whatever Conor might have to face at night, at least he would not have face it alone.

Subconsciously, too, Conor Finnegan found security in Tom McIlweath. As always, Finnegan remained confident in himself, keenly aware of his capacity to meet people and face new situations with intelligence, wit and composure. But now the process of removal was at last underway. It was one thing to plan, to talk boldly, to scheme of personal integrity and independence; it was quite another to encounter it. He had become aware from the first day, as soon as the exhilaration had worn off, that he had chosen not so much freedom as responsibility. The realization deepened in Nevada when their impetuous attack against boredom had nearly stranded them both in the desert. He assumed responsibility now, perhaps prematurely, but indeed irrevocably. He sensed that, from these days forward, he would face the age-old challenge of trying to take logical steps in an illogical universe.

Tom McIlweath shared these first few steps with him. They assumed this fledgling responsibility, not together, but side by side. And Finnegan felt comforted by that. It was like having a twin, he imagined. Moreover, McIlweath had known him in the commanding glory of the year just passed. They were well on their way to becoming close friends, Finnegan thought, and even though the parameters of that friendship might, and should, go beyond the superficial, McIlweath knew the image. He was a rope around Finnegan's waist, tied to the rock of his past.

Each man crawled into his sleeping bag. Finnegan could feel McIlweath's heft in close adjacency. The night was given over to the wildlife.

"Goodnight, Mac. Let me know if you hear anything out there that might eat us."

"You'll be the first one I tell. See you in the morning."

As they had since their journey began, both Finnegan and McIlweath slept soundly. The tedium and confinement of the day's drive combined with the freshness of high altitude air to sink them even more deeply into a dead night.

Finnegan awoke first the next morning, or what he assumed to be morning, for it was still dark. He woke to a sound he had not heard before. In his semi-conscious state, newly aroused, he blinked at his strange surroundings to sort them out, to remember just where he was. The strange sound continued, and he could not be certain where it was coming from. It sounded far off, distant and remote, something outside and away, but still present. As his alertness grew, though, so did the sound. It became clearer, sharper, until he could have no doubt that something was lightly tapping the roof of the tent just hard enough to be noticeable.

Finnegan rolled to his side and propped himself on his elbow to get a better reading of what was happening. As he did so, he heard a splash, and felt it, too, on his elbow and at the foot of his sleeping bag.

Water. The sound was raindrops. The tent was flooded.

"Mac. Wake up." Finnegan reached over and shook McIlweath's shoulder. As he leaned across he surveyed the tent, what he could see of it in the dim light. There was no solid ground. Everywhere he looked he saw the broken ripples of water, underneath him and around him, to the walls of the tent.

"Mac, damn it, wake up."

"Huh . . . Whazzat?"

"It's raining, Mac. We're flooded."

"What?" McIlweath groggily rolled over to face his friend. As he did, he too rolled into water.

"Son of a bitch. We're flooded."

"What I said. My bag's soaked from head to toe."

McIlweath sat up and squinted the length of the tent. "Jesus Christ, mine too. The whole tent's under water."

"How did this happen?"

"How do you think, fool? It rained."

"Yeah, but I thought we were on a rise. The water should have drained away from us."

"No way to tell how high we were last night. For all we know, we might be at the bottom of a ravine."

"Let's get to the car and dry off."

They pulled on their wet clothes, which had lain all night beside the bags, and broke camp, regularly muttering their standard curses. From what they could see the entire area was muddy and puddled. As they carried their gear to the car they sloshed through muck, splattering their already soaked jeans.

"Where do we put this stuff so it'll dry?" asked Finnegan.

"It'll have to go in the back seat."

"You mean lay it over? There's no room."

"Unless we lay it over the boxes there."

"And get everything else wet? No way. Let's cram it back into the trunk for now and lay it out when we get the chance."

The sodden tent and bags were difficult to handle. It took a while to roll them up into a tight form that would fit into the small trunk. The space where they were usually stored was too small for them now that they were saturated. All the while they worked at the gear it continued to rain. When they finished they crawled back into the car.

"Mac, we look like we swam here."

"I'm cold. We've got to get into something dry."

They went back out to the trunk to retrieve their bags and, maneuvering in the cramped space, found a change of clothes. Finnegan grabbed a towel to dry himself. McIlweath's towels were out of reach. When Finnegan was done he passed the towel to his friend. Squirming and shifting in the tiny seats they managed to make a complete change. By the time they were dressed the window had fogged over, and the air was rank.

"What do we do now, buddy?" Finnegan asked.

"What time is it?"

Finnegan checked his watch, delighted to find it waterproof. "5:30. The sun should be coming up soon."

"We're not seeing the sun this morning, Conor. Let's rest here until it gets light enough to drive out of this slop. I don't feel like facing the road just yet."

"God, I'm tired. I feel like going back to sleep."

"It must have rained pretty hard all night. I'm surprised we didn't wake up."

"We did wake up, Mac. That's why we're sitting in this goddamned car."

"Welcome to the great outdoors, Conor."

With that, the two put their heads back and closed their eye. Finnegan dozed uncomfortably for less than an hour. McIlweath didn't sleep at all. He wiped the fog from the windows near him and watched the rain.

When Finnegan woke again his neck was sore and kinked. It was barely light. No doubt the camp ranger would be coming soon. "If we want to avoid paying for this glorious experience," he said, "we better hit the road." He started the car and pulled onto the muddy access road. "Damn it, I still feel cold and damp."

"Think of it," said McIlweath, "as another form of baptism. You'll feel better."

* * *

They continued north and drove through Yellowstone. In the park they saw wildlife that neither had seen before—a family of bears below them on a hillside, and, in a wide clearing next to the road, a moose. The bears, accustomed to such travelers, took no notice of them. The moose, though, paused in his meal of meadow grass, raised his broad head and looked at the car that had stopped to watch him. After a few seconds he returned to his grass.

Nothing else appealed to them in Wyoming. They left Yellowstone via the southernmost entrance late in the afternoon. They had not eaten since breakfast, which they had had at a diner standing absolutely by itself on the road north. It sat there, an anomaly in a wide land, with no other building in sight. Now, hungry again, they decided to stop for an early dinner and plan their next set of moves.

They found another diner several miles outside Yellowstone. As Finnegan pulled into the parking lot, he said, "Better bring the maps. We can figure out where we're heading while we eat. Not that it matters. The land here is so damn big we'll never find the end of it."

The diner itself was just a place, like a hundred other places along the highway, squat and small. Neon signs flashed the names of beers in the two main windows on either side of the entrance.

Finnegan and McIlweath had begun to show wear. Neither had shaved since leaving home. This made little difference for McIlweath, who had a sparse beard. Only an inconsistent stubble grew under his chin and up the underside of his jaw. He had neither mustache nor sideburns. Finnegan by contrast had a darker complexion. A noticeable growth wrapped completely around his face, although the scraggly furze he carried was not thick enough yet to be a full beard.

The rain had tangled and matted their hair, uncombed since the brushing out of the morning rainwater. Each head was taking a shape of its own, wild and bohemian. They both wore faded blue jeans and frayed tees. Finnegan's jeans had faded to an off-white, and McIlweath's shirt showed patches of dirt on the sleeves.

When they entered the diner, heads turned and conversations paused. They seated themselves only to wait a full ten minutes for a server to fetch them menus. They were too tired to complain, except to each other.

"Do you feel a little unwelcome here?" asked Finnegan in a low voice.

"In what way?"

"Well, for one thing we're the youngest ones in here by about twenty-five years. We're not exactly dressed in the cowboy style, and we look pretty hairy. Other than that, we fit right in."

"Don't worry about it," replied McIlweath. "As long as we can pay, that's all they care about."

"The management, sure. But I don't know about our fellow diners. They're looking at us like they want to tie us up and drag us behind their pickups."

"We probably smell like two dead rats, too," said McIlweath.

"Who'd notice? The folks in these parts are used to sniffing cow dung all day. We're not likely to offend these crusty nostrils."

"Come on, Conor. Be charitable."

"I'm tired. I don't feel like being charitable."

"Where are we going to be tired tomorrow?"

"I don't know, Mac. What do you think?"

"Well, if we get out of here alive, we could head north and go through Canada."

"I'm not wild about that. We'd be backtracking, for one thing. Besides, I thought we wanted to stay domestic."

"Are we off to discover America?"

"Someone has to. What do you think about the South? It's a different world down there, or so I hear. It might be worth a look."

"All the way south, like Houston, New Orleans, Alabama? Is that what you mean, or are you thinking Kentucky and Tennessee?"

"If you're going to do something, you may as well do it all the way, don't you think? Let's head for the Deep South."

"Do you speak Southern?"

"No, but we can pick up a dictionary along the way."

They had carried their maps into the diner with them. Now, as they ate, they spread out the United States along the edge of the table as they moved their plates toward the wall. Between bites they mapped out a route southwest, through Colorado, across a corner of New Mexico and then downward like a stake through the length of Texas to Houston. From there they would head along the gulf to New Orleans, Mobile and Pensacola. At that point, they agreed, they would take stock once again and determine which direction appealed to them from there.

"Do you want to go interstates the whole way?" asked Finnegan.

"What's the alternative?"

"To go off the beaten path a bit. State highways. County roads."

"I'm not sure I want to mingle with the natives."

"I'm not sure we'll be able to avoid it."

They had eaten quickly. It was still relatively early, not yet five o'clock. "You know, we're going to have to find a motel tonight," said Finnegan. "Our sleeping bags are still soaked."

"Tough break. That means we'll probably have to shower and shave and change clothes."

"Yeah, goodbye to the rustic look."

"And none too soon. I feel like the floor of a city bus."

Finnegan paid the bill and they returned to the car. Again, the regulars watched them as they left. "I felt like we were trespassing, Conor," McIlweath commented. "Jesus, we were like Jesse Jackson at a meeting of the Aryan Brotherhood."

"Yeah, but that may have been our fault."

"You're kidding, right?"

"No. We just can't expect the world to welcome us at every turn."

Ironic, thought McIlweath, that such a statement should come from the lips of Finnegan.

They spent the night in a motel just across the Colorado border. They had driven until the sun set and by the time they checked into their room both were exhausted. Just the sight of the beds made them feel luxuriant. As they walked into the air-conditioned room the cool air hit them fully, almost physically, like a slap in the face. The carpeting, standard motel issue, seemed exceedingly soft. They took turns showering and shaving, then immediately went to bed. Finnegan unpacked an alarm clock and set it for 4:30 AM.

The next day they drove and drove, endlessly, through the great mountains southward. As before, they started fresh, in the cool air of pre-dawn. But the day wore on and it grew hotter. The mountains diminished, grew less majestic, and eventually gave way to the flatlands of New Mexico, then the grassy, infinite plains of Texas. There were no cities once they passed through Denver until they got to Amarillo. They stopped for a mid-afternoon bite there and got lost. It took half an hour to find their way back to the appropriate interstate in the appropriate direction. The horizon hung thick with dark thunderclouds, but the rain remained in the distance. The air hung heavy and humid. It was deadly hot.

All day Finnegan and McIlweath had said very little. Tedium had crept over both of them, and neither felt the energy or the urge to say much. They communicated silently, like spouses after years of marriage. This, too, was a marriage of sorts, a forced unity. As linked as conjoined twins, they spun through this experience, in the same process, in the same transition. And although each tended to define it differently, in the last analysis it was the same, possessing the same elements. They were crossing a bridge. What they would be aware of the rest of their lives was that they were crossing it together, unlikely partners united by the accident of logistics.

Back on course, they passed through Amarillo, then headed across the plains toward Dallas and Fort Worth. It would be well past dark when they arrived. As late afternoon burned into early evening an odd tranquility settled over the two of them. Their bodies reconciled to their constrictions, and their minds, facing no great or immediate challenges, relaxed. They fell into harmony with the motion of the automobile, felt the air cool as the sun went down. The mood fell upon them both equally and simultaneously. During such a time this trip presented to strain at all. To the contrary, the young men intuitively concluded that life's purest and most natural state was on the road, with responsibilities only to themselves, where roamed the ultimate freedom. Fatigue left them, replaced by the exhilaration of youth, of power, of change, an infusion of divinity. The land stood before them, they moved to it, they embraced it, absorbed what parts of it they liked and let the unabsorbed retreat back into the loamy soil like rainwater.

In such a peculiar mood, the first such mood of their journey, both Finnegan and McIlweath could indeed believe that they were somehow favored above the common vein. Serenity obliterated all obstacles. What lay on the horizon behind the gathering thunderclouds could only be good and comforting and fine.

"So, Conor," McIlweath spoke as he looked out the window at flatlands washed in the filtered light of a clouded sunset, caught in the moment's quiet mood, "where does all this lead?"

"What do you mean?"

"All this. Escape, and freedom, and the open road. College. Growing up. Growing out. Where are we heading with all this?"

Finnegan paused, caught in his own evening-spawned reflections. "I'm not sure how to answer that. How deeply do you want to go?"

"Tell me what you want to do in this life. Where are you heading?"

"Ah, Jesus, Mac. How can anyone know at this stage?"

"You've got ambitions, Conor. That's no secret. Start with the specifics, and we'll see where they lead."

"Well, to be specific, and more than a little superficial, I'd like a career in the law, I think. I want to be a lawyer."

"Another lawyer. Just what we need. Okay, say you're a lawyer. Then what? Do you expect to get married, settle down into a fixed career?"

"Eventually, yeah. But I don't want to get too comfortable too soon."

"Comfortable?"

"The middle-class American scenario—a house in the suburbs, station wagon, country club, 2.4 kids all above average, Golden Retriever."

"I've got a hunch we're starting to go deeper now."

Finnegan smiled. "Yeah, I guess so. But it's not easy to put goals into a simple form. 'I want to be a lawyer.' How is that any different from what thousands of other people are saying to themselves this very moment? It's not, not in the least. But I really mean so much more than that. I don't want to lump myself with everyone else."

"How are you different, then? Other than not wanting to live in the suburbs."

"I'm almost afraid to tell you, but I've been thinking about this for a long time. I think by and large the way we live points us down paths that have little meaning. We live for ourselves, we grab for what we can, we screw over anyone who's in the way and call it happiness. And when you think about it, that's exactly what's been drummed into us since our first conscious moments. The American Dream is all based on material goods, personal gratification and excess, and we're each conditioned to play our part in keeping the dream alive. Nobody thinks too much about those on the outside of it. But they're there. We saw them in that diner outside Yellowstone. They're all around us, and we make them invisible—the poor, the addicts, the kids without fathers, the poor bastards so traumatized by fighting a war that they practically wet themselves when someone claps his hand. No one gives a damn about anyone outside his little circle of success and attainment and comfort."

He continued, "And I don't think there's any way to change that, at least not during our lifetime. We're too cynical, too complex, too interconnected. Not to mention too brainwashed into thinking that we've already built the greatest civilization the world has ever seen. So there's no incentive to alter it, to make it more inclusive.

"But if a man can't change the whole of society, I believe he can at least affect his part of it. I think he's obligated to leave a positive imprint on what's around him. On who's around him. If he can't change the world, he can change *his* world. Does any of this make sense?"

"I'm with you so far," said McIlweath.

"So if I get to be a lawyer, I don't want to practice law solely for my own good. I don't want to try to turn the world on its ear either. But I think I can be an attorney with enough of a social conscience to try to make things better in some way. I don't even know the particulars. Maybe inner city work, or maybe government. And I'm convinced that I can go through life with attitudes that will leave that positive imprint. On everybody—family, friends, clients, even total strangers."

"What kind of attitudes?"

"They're not easy to define. I suppose a sense of decency, a sense of fairness. Charity, in the most classic meaning. The belief that every one of us has something to offer, has some dignity."

"That sounds pretty religious, Conor."

"It's not. In fact, I see it as the opposite of my rather strange Catholic teachings. I think man comes first. We've got to provide for each other. We can't trust to God. The best we can do is invoke His name in our efforts, but that in itself is incredibly dangerous. And hypocritical."

"So basically," said McIlweath, "you want to be a lawyer, but you want to be a nice guy, too."

Finnegan laughed. "Way to cut through the pretensions. Yeah. A nice guy. To bring about some change where I can. To stand up against this maddening trend toward depersonalization. To be socially aware, and socially alive. All that. Affecting the quality of life for anyone who comes into my environment. Mac, I just don't think we can live our lives for ourselves alone. That becomes incredibly lonely, I think. It must. If you live like that, what's left behind you when you're gone? What legacy? Nothing. You've contributed nothing. A family, maybe, but chances are they'll have the same set of values, or lack of values. It'll all be self-perpetuating."

"But do you think it's easy to live that way?" asked McIlweath.

"I guess I don't have much faith in modern man. I think society breeds self-interest. It encourages it. Our whole commercial structure is based upon acquisition, more and better, on having more than the other guy. Our power structure is just a collection of special interests, fueled by money. Democracy is dead, if it ever really was alive. Another myth strangled by greed."

Finnegan rolled on, "Look at most of the advertisements you see these days. How many of them even describe the products they're trying to sell? They're selling quick gratification, status without complications, without challenge or effort. Our system places us in competition with one another, and we take it personally if we don't have what everyone else does, if our neighbor gets more than we do. We tell ourselves we're failures because our car is too old, or not fast enough, or we drink the wrong cola, or our television is too small, or we wear last year's fashions. And we accept those values like sheep, blind-eyed and unquestioning. Then, in our frustration, we circle the wagons, Mac, and take shots at whatever rides around us. I don't want to live like that."

"Do you think you'll have a choice?"

"I'll force a choice. I'm not afraid of being an outsider, if that's what it means."

"That sounds odd to me, Conor, coming from you. I mean, you've always been in the center of things."

Finnegan did not respond right away, and when he did his words were calmer, fully measured. "I know. It's been pretty easy up to now. And I guess I've never really stood up for anything. We're a cruel species, Mac, right from the start. The way people ignored you back home was unfair, and I knew it, but I never did much about it. I could have been a better friend when I thought that you might need one, but I was too wrapped up in myself. So I can imagine it might be a little difficult to picture me stepping out of 'the center of things', as you put it. I don't know myself. All this talk sounds impressive, but when it comes right down to it, who knows? I might wind up like everyone else, scrambling for a buck, underpaying my taxes and flirting with my administrative assistant."

"You never know, Conor. But if you mean what you say, you're in line for more than your fair share of disappointment."

"What about you, Mac? What do you see for yourself?"

"Too early to tell," and with that McIlweath dismissed the subject, at least his side of it. They settled back and drove on in silence.

By the time they reached Dallas they were ready to stop. Even in late summer, with its long days, it was dark well before they reached the northernmost suburbs. With McIlweath behind the wheel Finnegan looked hard at the lights—lights of the tall buildings, lights of the traffic on the arteries, lights of the airplanes above them. They had been so long in the prairie's flatness that the city seemed an anomaly, a giant bauble to be turned and inspected by its own light. Drowsy until they reached the city, Finnegan perked up as soon as the glow from the lights came into view.

South of Dallas, then, headed for Houston and the Gulf, they once again met the plains. They had not eaten since Amarillo. In the boredom of the dark drive they discovered their hunger. McIlweath pulled off the interstate into Waxahachie and they found an all-night diner. Both were disheveled and tatty, but this time no one noticed. They ate their usual meal of hamburgers, salads and soft drinks. Back on the road.

With food in their bellies they found they could drive no further. Finnegan, back behind the wheel, drove ten miles down the interstate, saw a rest area and pulled in. McIlweath had already fallen asleep in the passenger seat. Finnegan locked the door, rolled on his side facing McIlweath, and, cramped, sore, but contented, joined his friend in slumber. The night passed quickly, and in the morning boredom loomed again.

* * *

It rained in Pensacola. Actually, it had rained all that day as they drove eastward from New Orleans along the Gulf. It rained in Mobile as they crossed the bay. It rained hard, and the water level seemed high, even though neither Tom nor Conor had any way to judge. It just seemed high, and dangerous.

They had decided to find a motel in Pensacola. The past two days had been dull. New Orleans, which they had expected to be a highlight, a gem tucked into the southern crescent, provided no enchantment. They were both tired, dreadfully tired, and they got lost looking for the French Quarter. Finnegan drove, McIlweath tried to make sense of the city map. Traffic pushed them along too quickly to read the street signs or to plan an appropriate, rescuing turn. They were too stubborn to stop for directions. They drove around New Orleans for two hours and, in the end, lost interest in finding the French Quarter. Frustrated and short of temper, they opted to skip seeing anything at all of the city. Instead they would drive on. "To Pensacola," McIlweath said, "where we can find a decent place to sleep."

"Why Pensacola?" asked Finnegan.

"I like the name," snapped McIlweath, and stared out the bleary window.

They changed places in Alabama, and McIlweath was driving as they entered Pensacola late in the afternoon. This would be the earliest they would stop, but neither could stand any more that day.

As they passed an intersection McIlweath saw a blue and white city patrol car pull out from a side street behind them. Its light flashed a red rhythm.

"He can't be after us," said McIlweath aloud.

"Who?" asked Finnegan, straightening himself at once in his seat.

"The cop behind us." But even as he spoke the patrolman was motioning them to the roadside. McIlweath's heart leapt into his throat.

He had never before been stopped. He had never had to deal with the police in any way. And he had heard stories, perhaps true, of the Deep South and its lawmen.

The policeman pulled his car to the shoulder ahead of theirs. He had no partner.

"He's huge," said Finnegan quietly as the policeman approached the car. "He looks like a shaved gorilla." McIlweath almost quaked with nerves.

"License and registration, please."

McIlweath handed him his license while Finnegan pulled the registration from the utility compartment. McIlweath's hands shook visibly. 'Great', thought Finnegan. 'Let's give this guy a reason to think we're guilty of something.' For his part, he was far more curious than worried.

The officer looked over both documents and noticed the difference in names. "Who's Mr. Finnegan?" he asked.

"That's me," said Conor, leaning over. "This is my car."

The policeman returned to his car and spent some time on his radio. McIlweath continued to shake in silence.

When the officer came back, he asked, "Where you boys headin'?"

McIlweath responded quickly in a voice that had risen several octaves, "We're on our way to college, officer. In New Jersey. We're just passing through."

Finnegan joined in brashly, "Actually, we're looking for a motel here. Could you recommend one? We'd like to spend the night in your lovely beachfront city."

McIlweath shot Finnegan an open-mouthed glance, near panic in his eyes. What the hell was he doing?

"You know you just went through a red light, son?" said the officer.

"Where?" McIlweath swung his head back to the officer.

"About two blocks back."

Finnegan again spoke up. "No way, friend. We couldn't have."

"Two blocks back, son. I saw it."

"Impossible," barked Finnegan. "You came out of a side street well after any intersection with a stoplight. You didn't see anything. And anyhow, the only light we went through was clearly yellow."

"I say it was red, son."

"And I say you're trying to set us up. And don't call me 'son'."

McIlweath was terrified. 'Shut up, you ass,' he thought. 'What's the worst this guy could do? A fine, which we can afford. You weren't even driving. He can fry both our tails, but he'll make mine a little redder.'

"Boy, don't challenge my word. The light was red. And I'm the law here. You think anyone'll believe a coupla California boys?"

At the word 'boy,' Finnegan started to rise further in his seat, but he checked himself. He did not trust what he might say next. He stayed silent.

The officer continued, "But I'm not going to write you up. I'm going to be nice to you fellas today. I don't know how it is in California when it rains. I never been to California. But here in Florida the streets get real slick. You can slide right through these wet intersections real easy. You can slide right through without realizin' a red light. But I'm not going to give y'all a ticket. I'm going to give y'all a warning. Drive slow. On your way out of town. Now."

McIlweath responded in his quavery voice before Finnegan had the chance to open his mouth. "Yes, officer. We will. Thank you. We'll be extremely careful."

"That's good. Because if I see you in Pensacola again I might not be so kind as to ignore your infraction." He turned and walked back to his car, but he did not get in. He stood beside it to watch McIlweath and Finnegan drive away.

As McIlweath started the car, Finnegan said, "I guess we don't stay in Pensacola tonight, huh?"

McIlweath's hands still shook. As they drove by the patrol car Finnegan shot the officer a wave of his hand and a big smile. McIlweath gripped the wheel with both his hands and looked hard at the road straight ahead.

"God damn you, Conor, you could have screwed us both."

"He was a jerk, Mac. He was trying to scare us. You know as well as I do that he never even saw us go through any intersection except for the one he came out of. He saw the California plates and wanted to strong-arm us. I just didn't feel like being intimidated by some cracker cop."

"You could have just gone along with him," McIlweath's voice was returning to somewhat normal ranges. His hands, thought, were still shaking. "He could have made real trouble. We could have spent the night in jail. Maybe longer."

"Come on, Mac. He didn't have a leg to stand on."

"Unless he took us to some judge who doesn't like strangers any more than he does. They're probably all cousins down here."

"No problem. Besides, Mac, there's a principle involved. The right of free passage, or something like that."

They found a motel, but it was not in Pensacola. The next morning they slept late, not hitting the road until almost noon. Both felt fresh again. After days of rain, the sun radiated a clear blue sky. Their tempers, grown increasingly short, returned to normal. They headed north, through Georgia and the Carolinas, finally crossing into Virginia well after the sun had set.

* * *

Theirs was still the only car in the rest area when they awoke shortly after the Virginia dawn. Finnegan rose first and groggily stepped out of the car to stretch his legs. 'Let's finally put this trip away,' he told himself. 'It's time to get on with things.'

For exercise he sprinted the length of the paved area, perhaps a hundred and fifty yards. At the end he took a deep breath and sprinted back. His cramped and compressed legs reacted stiffly. He did not think he was running very fast at all. When he returned to the car McIlweath had begun to rouse himself.

"Good morning," said Finnegan as the other yawned widely. "And where the hell are we?"

"Damned if I know," replied McIlweath through his yawn. "Virginia somewhere. Southern Virginia."

"Where does this road go, do we know?"

"North. Past a bunch of toothless old rednecks who don't like young guys from the suburbs."

"And us two such lovable creatures. Come on, let's find some breakfast. I'll bet there'll be grits."

"Then let's get this trip over with," said McIlweath, retreating back into the driver's seat.

They had made better time than they had planned. Along the way there had been precious few diversions to renew their excitement. They would be able to make New Brunswick that day, arriving days early and well before the dormitories were scheduled to open. But they did not for a moment consider any alternative. They were too tired; it was time to alight.

* * *

On the outskirts of New Brunswick, near the New Jersey Turnpike, Finnegan and McIlweath once again checked into a motel. Money at this late stage posed no problems because they had spent little of it by traveling so simply. If they had to, they could spend the next week in motels until campus housing opened. But enraptured at the prospect of finally being a college man, even a premature one, Finnegan wanted to petition the housing office to let them stay in their rooms. But they had arrived too late that afternoon to do so that night. The offices would be closed, so again they would sleep in the sterility of a cheap motor inn. They would wait until the next day to take a look at the campus. The center of their next few years, and the focus of so much Romantic affectation, thought Finnegan, needed to be first viewed in the morning's freshness.

The next morning, early September, they drove across town to the campus. At the eastern end of New Brunswick the congested, narrow flow of traffic thinned and the tattered buildings of a thousand eastern downtowns gave way at once to something different. Crossing under the railroad tracks, there it was, rising at first on a small hill to their left, marked by a wrought-iron gate, then settling back to its long, flat, rectangular main campus. The streets, main roads of New Brunswick, ran around it without being part of it.

They drove down George Street, and on the right the river, the old Raritan—dirty, sudsy, murky, a repository of filthy runoff—flowed steady and silent. Around the bend of George Street, then, to the three river dormitories, identical brick and coldly austere, but to Finnegan and McIlweath powerful sentinels which stood watch in front over the creeping river and in back over the remainder of the campus.

At the base of the rectangular campus sat Buccleuch Park, a sprawling green expanse that was remarkably well kept. Turning left onto College Avenue they continued their introduction: the library, brick with white pillars, on their left; the gymnasium, appearing to both of them by its colonial architecture and traces of ivy as another classroom building; further down the road, fraternities on one side and the heart of the old campus, Queen's Mall, on the other. The buildings ringing the Mall were clearly older, their grey stones faded unevenly, the ivy thicker, the gables more pointed, their windows more deeply set. This campus was old, Finnegan thought; it had its ghosts.

Ghosts indeed. Finnegan imagined them, his reverie engaged. This campus has stood for more than two centuries. And each year its halls received a group fueled by the furies of youth, guided by aspirations, unleashed and wild and brave and thoroughly convinced of their own distinctive splendor. He imagined the young men of the post-Revolution, apprentice gentlemen, men of good breeding whose families could afford to send them off. They gave way in his mind to a rougher group, with nineteenth-century cockiness, more serious in their straight-backed suits, developing traditions and songs that stood to the present day. Finnegan saw the sport coats and baggy white trousers of the early part of the twentieth century. He saw the great Paul Robeson, a curious, proud and immensely strong black man, moving through this mall to his small white room. Finnegan saw too the years of the Great Depression, the war years, and afterward the mobs of new students who had survived the worst of all of it, deprivations and warfare, and in their survival grown older and sadder.

Finnegan sensed the ghosts in the walls, heard them tread the stones of the old walkways. Outwardly different, all of them, but come here for the same purposes. Motivations rarely change. And what had they found here? What had become of them?

What is a ghost if not the residue of a man's desires? Here, all around them, they felt the passage of two centuries of those desires, and the faces that held them. Finnegan was to consider later in depth what only flashed through his mind briefly as he beheld the core of the campus for the first time. And he would come back to the mall at odd hours, with no one around, on Sunday mornings or late at night when he could not sleep. Under moonlight, at dusk, on deadened and soggy afternoons he would walk the mall, sit on a bench, lean against a tree, and try to put himself into context. At those times he would feel completely the ghosts he only now glimpsed. He would seek their wordless empathy. And, in the end, he would find himself considering the limits of his youth, the finite nature of all desire.

Finnegan sensed the entire panoply of a young man's experiences. He could sense the heartbreak of unrequited or aborted love, the excitement of intellectual discovery and the curiosity behind it, the morose sorrow of the death of friendship, the prideful joy of accomplishment, the drunken frenzy of celebration, the anguish of rejection, the stark fear of indecision, the loneliness of distance and time. All, all had preceded him here. He could add nothing new to the wisdom of these walls save his own interpretation, however insignificant, of the age-old processes of the expanding man.

A wind blew up behind him, warm and dry on his neck. Crawl now into the crucible and await the flame that, for the silent, surrounding ghosts had long since died.

These thoughts passed through his mind instantly as a spasm. The seed of his future ruminations had been planted. He shook his head, and returned to present realities.

But McIlweath had put his own first impressions aside immediately. There would come a time he might ponder where he was and what it all meant, but not now. There was a task at hand—they had to find their beds. Besides, he reasoned, there really didn't seem to be anything terribly distinct about this place. This is a campus, an old one, and not particularly attractive. Old stone, new bricks, a goodly amount of flora. McIlweath's initial exhilaration, shared with his friend upon first seeing the campus, had faded to mild disappointment.

They had parked the car illegally in a restricted lot adjoining the mall. The housing office stood across the way, in Milledoler Hall, which McIlweath translated as 'the hall of a thousand sorrows.' The housing office was on the second floor, up a slate-grey staircase. Paint peeled off the walls.

The assistant appeared, the embodiment of matronly love. She wore a dark print dress with a light red floral pattern. Her grey hair was pulled back in a bun, sitting high atop a face marked by a smile, seemingly as permanent a part of her features as a nose or two ears. Here was a woman who had no struggle with the nature of her work. She was a comfort, someone whose very presence might reassure not only a young man away from home for the first time, but his parents as well. She would do the college far more good here than anywhere else.

"Can I help you boys?" Her voice complemented her appearance. She spoke in a lilt.

"We're incoming students," Finnegan replied, "and we were hoping we might get our dormitory assignments and move in early. I know we're ahead of schedule, but we've come across country and there's really no place else we can go other than a motel. We're from California." Finnegan considered this last his trump card. He would come to use it often.

"Oh my, that is a long way," she cooed. "What are your names? If your dormitories have been approved by maintenance and have been cleaned, we may be able to help you. Some of them have been finished already. Of course we would have to charge you for the extra days."

Finnegan told her their last names, and she flipped through a file of room assignments. "Conor Finnegan? You're in luck. You're in one of the river dormitories. They were the first to be made ready. Campbell Hall, Room 605. You'll even have sheets on your bed," she smiled.

"Luck of the Irish again," said Finnegan as she went back to her file. "Thomas McIlweath?"

"Yes, ma'am," he responded, stepping forward from behind Finnegan, whom he had willingly let do the talking.

"Campbell 609. It looks as if you two will be neighbors. There's some paperwork you'll need to complete. You can start on the registration forms, but there's also a legal waiver for the extra days. The new charges will be appended to your tuition bill. I'll get your keys."

The two looked at each other as the lady spoke. Finnegan nodded his head slowly toward McIlweath to acknowledge his surprise that, yes indeed, they would be neighbors. Neither of them had considered that. There were too many dormitories, too many floors. Rutgers prided itself on mixing its students. First year students were not segregated, nor were out-of-staters. For them to land two doors apart was the wildest luck.

And so, McIlweath's desire for an anonymity in which he could reconstruct himself with no remembrance of things past had been futile from the start. Had he known in springtime that he would not only be unable to lose Finnegan but would have him at the closest proximity around the clock, he might well have declined to come here at all. In fact, he was sure of it. He had other offers, all tempting in their own way. He didn't have to come here. But it was as if fate had welded the two of them together. The situation defied coincidence.

But it was not springtime, and Tom McIlweath had changed his attitude. Or rather, Conor Finnegan had changed it for him. Finnegan had approached their mutual destiny with an openness and excitement that broke down barriers. He had not considered that McIlweath hovered on the periphery of friendship; it had not mattered. He drew McIlweath along with an innocence that bordered on naiveté. Finnegan's world had precluded the possibility that one might prefer solitude or anonymity, that one might be so discontent with the course of his life that he might choose to go to abnormal lengths to redirect it. He could not imagine it, so it didn't exist. As a result, Conor Finnegan had approached Tom McIlweath with an open hand.

They had thrown themselves together in a confined space, a metallic wheeled womb. Finnegan through it all had been a partner, genuinely interested in McIlweath's thoughts and reactions. He had never been overbearing. He respected their conversations, probing the line of McIlweath's ideas, picking up pieces of his words and turning them in his hand, examining all sides. McIlweath had done likewise. He had responded in kind so that, although much of the trip had been couched in boredom as it invariably had to be, there had been an unfolding, a recognition of one another as characters of merit. And not once had Finnegan invoked the past. Not once had he played a superior hand or made McIlweath feel awkward or unaccepted. Not even the slightest nuance had conveyed anything less than a fraternal, uncomplicated affection. Through fatigue, through discomfort, through boredom, they had remained in tune.

McIlweath's surprise at their room assignments turned at once to satisfaction. He would be starting college with an advantage he could never have foreseen.

The assistant returned with their keys. "Of course you know that your meal plan won't begin until next week. You'll have to find some way to feed yourselves. If either of you has a car, you'll have to register with Public Safety and get a parking sticker. Do you have any questions?"

"No, thank you. You've been a great help," said Finnegan.

"Welcome to Rutgers."

CHAPTER V

One writes of scars healed, a loose parallel to the pathology of the skin, but no such thing in the life of an individual. There are open wounds, shrunk sometimes to the size of a pinprick, but wounds still. The marks of suffering are more comparable to the loss of a finger, or of the sight of an eye. We may not miss it, either, for one minute in a year, but if we should there is nothing to be done about it.

—F. Scott Fitzgerald, *Tender Is the Night*

Jordan Brophy leaned back in his chair and watched the leaves rustle outside his office window. Unlike most of his colleagues, he did not share his office. Age, at least in this instance, had its rewards, although he still flinched at hearing himself referred to as the "Dean of the Department." He did not feel old; he merely felt relaxed.

Comfort comes through familiarity, which itself breeds security. After thirty-one years in the same place, Jordan Brophy felt comfortable indeed. He had, almost from the earliest days of his learning, set himself upon a scholarly career. Even as a young boy he had been fascinated by the processes of education. Knowledge was the ultimate stimulant. He often found himself physically stimulated by intellectual discovery. The mind could step outside the body, cross unknown borders and keep going. He would not be limited by his thin, rather brittle physique, nor by his retiring personality. What his classmates saw as shortcomings he would turn into assets, for he would have fewer distractions. While others developed themselves physically and socially, Jordan Brophy would build his mind. Therein he would establish his own dignity, his own standards of self-worth. And, while he had few other excitements with which to compare it, his genuine thrill of learning made this alternative not an alternative at all, but a destiny.

As a young man, Jordan Brophy experienced no doubts about his future or how to go about attaining it. He would study. Endlessly, forsaking all else. He did not see this as a sacrifice. He was simply translating his love into duty.

Jordan Brophy attended Harvard on scholarship, studied English literature and graduated Phi Beta Kappa. He passed four years without developing a single lasting friendship. He would not have seen it so. Instead, he would argue that he formed the greatest most trustworthy friendships—he had gone boating with Melville, walked the streets of Cambridge with Matthew Arnold, sat under an elm tree with Eugene O'Neill, climbed into bed with Edna St. Vincent Millay. He carried these people with him constantly, reflected upon their thoughts, honored their judgments, viewed the world through their unique prisms. They did not counter him, nor did they argue; they built him, and, from their graves, defined his very nature.

From Harvard he moved to Yale, earned a master's, then a doctorate. His doctoral defense completed one early May afternoon, Jordan Brophy could no longer delay the obvious: it was time to get a job.

He had, of course, realized this long before. In fact, he had known from boyhood that he would teach, and so he faced this reality with only the slightest fear—that his teaching duties would limit his own personal pursuits. In actuality, Jordan Brophy was home free. Once employed he found it easy to curtail virtually all social obligations. His personal library grew and grew.

His graduate studies had specialized in early twentieth century literature, where he had cultivated an intimate relationship with Theodore Dreiser. His dissertation, examining the impact of Dreiser's late adolescent Chicago years on the writer's traditional themes of social power, turned the heads of other scholars throughout the East. His advisor at Yale recommended him to another of his former students, then English Department chairman at a private college near Philadelphia. It would be, explained the advisor, the perfect place to start a brilliant career. The young scholar could establish his teaching credentials before going on to a truly outstanding position at, say, one of the Ivies.

Thirty-one years later, Jordan Brophy had yet to move anywhere. Not that his ambition deserted him, for, in truth, his only real ambition had been fully met. Here he could teach, he could read, he could pursue his research. Whether he taught the industrious middle-class students of this college or the distinctively brilliant minds of the great North American universities made no difference. The comfort of this situation became apparent during his first year there. He had no need to look elsewhere. In his own unusual way, Jordan Brophy was a fulfilled man.

Over the course of those years, Dr. Brophy had formed his habits. As he sat in his office watching the leaves, he indulged in one of his most familiar. Brophy chose to teach his courses in the late afternoon. He had not taught before lunch in more than a decade. After his last class of the day he would retreat to his office, shut the door and brew some tea. He would sit then at his desk, sipping slowly with no distractions, and examine the view from his window. His office faced away from the college itself, with a view that spanned across the wooded, rolling hillsides that ran up to the campus edge. Each season lent its own texture, and, as he sat, Brophy would reflect upon the class just concluded and the day that held it. The solitude, the quiet, the tea, the view—the serenity—was Jordan Brophy's personal buffer between realities.

This day's last class had been a freshman literature survey. Most senior faculty steered clear of such basic assignments, preferring the upper-level courses that allowed them to display their specialties like peacocks spreading their fans. Here was as much intellectual stimulation an undergraduate college could offer. And while Brophy shared these sentiments, he had never surrendered his survey course. It was another habit, and teaching it offered no strain. At the same time he could evaluate the younger students and possibly identify a bright light here or there who might be persuaded to major in English. The department always needed more majors.

The classroom specified social roles without ambiguity. Brophy's place as instructor defined itself, so he did not have to contend with the egos, idiosyncrasies or nuances that most social occasions engendered. He did not have to worry whether or not he was well liked, or even tolerated. He was professor, they were students. Nothing else mattered. In the classroom Brophy could relax and present his material with an élan that spoke to his own devoted love of it. He had become one of the college's favorite instructors. Students regarded him as a touch odd, but he knew his stuff and taught it so that it could be understood.

Jordan Brophy sipped his tea and reflected on the class just concluded. A typical group, somewhat awed by their surroundings, as are most freshmen, but most were eager, and trying very hard to be impressive. It was late October. A few were beginning to develop something approximating literary appreciation. And a sense of critical thought, too, seemed to be coming around. Freshmen were so malleable.

The semester was half over, yet Dr. Brophy knew few names. Unless a student particularly impressed him, he or she remained anonymous. Even if a student should climb the stairs to Brophy's office to solicit help or advice, he or she rarely penetrated the professor's memory. Brophy was universally polite, sometimes warm, but never transgressed the line between teacher and friend. Students were fluid: they came and went in annual herds, never aging. Only Brophy grew older. Students were replaceable, coming in endless supply. Brophy might concern himself with them collectively; individually, they would only clutter his well-ordered mind.

Except one.

A young girl had walked into his survey class on the first day, had sat down in the front row and then fixed her attention on the professor. She possessed none of the outward uncertainty that usually denoted first-year students. She carried herself confidently, although her actions were never bold, nor called attention to her in any way. She did not come forward to answer questions, and infrequently took part in discussions, nor did she speak much to her classmates. On those rare occasions when she did open her mouth, she spoke without hurry or tension. Brophy noticed that she seemed to speak in complete sentences, her thoughts well formulated. Her soft voice resonated. She was pleasant to his ears.

It was the rarest occurrence for Jordan Brophy to think about a student of only average ability, one who did not make herself noticeable through intellectual strength or agility. The fact that this young lady's face stood in his mind now disturbed him, and disquieted his reflections. He struggled with himself to see why.

Through the years, he had had young women in his classes who were nothing short of gorgeous. This one would not qualify as such, but none of the others had engrained themselves in his mind as did this catlike girl, who, Brophy mused, moved through her world without being a part of it.

She possessed a rare beauty, soft and subtle, that could cause an immediate ache in one seeing her for the first time. Her hair, a gentle brown, hung long down her back. Her face radiated a visual sensation of softness, so that a heavy touch might pass right through her skin. Her eyes, deep and brown, contained mystery and magic. She kept her gaze upon Dr. Brophy as he lectured. Confident, unhurried, slightly detached. The corners of her mouth curled ever so slightly into a half-smile, half-smirk. Her high cheekbones accented those remarkable eyes, or so it seemed. One would be hard pressed to forget those eyes.

Jordan Brophy was not well versed in the opposite sex. He was, in fact, a virgin, a state about which he carried few regrets. The sexual urges he regarded as annoyances, something that cluttered the roadway to a higher plane, not unlike a runny nose, and were easily dispatched. Where he could not imagine Nathaniel Hawthorne dripping mucus across his upper lip, neither could he picture himself in the passionate embrace of a lustful female. The language of love and all its attendant rituals lay far beyond this wise man's comprehension.

But this girl disturbed him, and ruffled his thoughts. She transmitted in her cool bearing a definite sexuality, and it was not lost even on so naïve a soul as Jordan Brophy. The professor looked at her, she looked back, and his thoughts strayed, became vacant. More than once he had had to stop his lecture to regroup the ideas that had dispersed under her gaze. He would feel an alertness in his loins, a subtle quickening of his pulse. His extremities might lose their warmth, his voice grow lower and more hurried. Thinking of her later, after class, his reaction might be the same. She would walk out of his classroom, and Dr. Brophy would watch her go, measuring to himself each slow, distinctive step.

He could not fathom his reaction to this fine young woman. What he could not fathom, he could not control. A lack of control made him uneasy; it shattered his orderly patterns. No student had ever drawn his attention so, not in thirty-one years of impersonal discipline.

Jordan Brophy sat back in his chair, drew the final swallow of his tea, and watched the leaves. Where was she now? Was this haunting impression merely illusion?

The leaves by his window had lost their color. The sun had nearly set, and the walk back to his apartment would no doubt be a cold one. Jordan Brophy gathered four books he wanted to skim that night in preparation for a class on Dos Passos and placed them in his ancient briefcase. As he left his office, he shut off the light. His footsteps echoed without companion in the empty hallway.

* * *

Where lies the bridge between love and contempt, and when do we know that we have crossed it? What compels us to thrust away that which once we held to our bosom? When does the sacred become the profane, the shapely become the grotesque? And, when at last we see it so, what do we do? Where do we go? Where do we find once again that which we can hold dear?

Come now, nighttime, and shroud the day. Like Lazarus, we are too soon entombed. Like Lazarus, we slumber, and for a time seek not beauty, but peace. Like Lazarus, we wait again for a savior, for a new day, to stretch our limbs again, to breathe the air that we now find.

Where lies the bridge between love and contempt, and when do we know that we have crossed it? To what new land does it bring us?

My father was a gentle man who loved us well. In our time he nourished us, grew us true and hearty. We stayed with him to feed him in return. He grew lean, though, the bones on his sides protruding like nails. He groaned in pain while we watched, all of us. Nothing to be done. One night he was gone. The body became headless. Decay will set in, and we will rot. We will grow misshapen and warped. My father stayed with us. He is dead now. We are grotesque and brutal, not as we were when we were young.

Where lies the bridge between love and contempt, and when do we know that we have crossed it?

* * *

The blonde girl pushed her chair back from the hardwood desk that was tucked into the room's far corner. "Roommate, what say you to a coffee break?"

The roommate lay on her bed, a history textbook propped against her drawn-up knees. "Sounds agreeable. Student Center?"

"Unless you want the machine kind."

The roommate made a face. "I can't stand that swill. Let me put on a sweater."

"Yeah. You never know who you might meet."

"It's not that. It's cold out, is all."

The evening was still young. In point of fact, the two girls had not been back from dinner more than two hours. On a weekday night there was precious little to do on campus but study. Neither girl was a scholar, nor wanted to be. They grew bored quickly and often, usually together. When one thought of a suitable diversion, a pretext for delaying their studies or ending them altogether, and presented it to the other, declinations rarely followed.

The student center was one of the campus's older buildings, made of brick and adorned with white pillars in an attempt to cultivate elegance which, sadly, failed. The building could not bluff away the scars of forty years of heavy, abandoned student pillage. The snack bar sat in the basement at the foot of slick grey stairs.

"God damn, I'm tired," said the blonde, whose name was Lynda, as she stretched back in her chair. "I hope this wakes me up. "As if to prove her point, she yawned. As she came out of it, her eyes landed on the blue and gold banner bearing the mythical medieval creature resurrected as the school's mascot. The banner took up most of the wall adjacent their table.

"That thing's disgusting, don't you think? It belongs in a high school pep rally. Not very uplifting."

"Are you here to be uplifted?" asked the other, a slightly sarcastic lilt in her voice, for she knew why they both had come there.

"I'm here to get away. So are you. Don't kid yourself. But then, I don't think you're the self-deceptive type. You're clever, girl. You know that?"

"I try to be," she smiled. "But no one's hurt by it. I like to be in control."

"So do I," replied Lynda. "But I rarely am. I never have been, really. That's one reason why I like it here. So far, I'm pretty much in control. Of myself, I mean."

"It's still early, girlfriend. Do you think you can stay in control?"

"Hell, I don't know. But I've turned a corner, I think. I'm responsible for what I do here. No one else. That part of it won't change, no matter what. I won't let it. If nothing else, college is going to teach me how to take care of myself, and that's a lesson too damn long in coming. Yeah, I've turned a corner."

Her roommate listened to this and was not at all convinced that the girl believed it herself. "Lynda, can I ask you something? It's personal."

"Sure, kid. You'll learn all my secrets in due time anyway."

The other girl fingered the lip of her coffee cup thoughtfully, and when she spoke she measured her words with care. This was her friend, or perhaps someone who could be. "You don't seem very happy. You haven't, really, since I met you. It seems as if there's always something holding you back, bothering you and making you sad. And that's so strange to me because you can be such a warm person. You don't have to tell me anything, and I don't mean to pry where I don't belong. Maybe I'm just no good at reading people. But I want you to know that I can sense that something important to you is not right. Tell me if I'm wrong."

Lynda listened quietly. She was, in a real sense, amazed. Everyone had secrets. She had her share, and one of them had compelled her to leave her home to come to this place. She had an option immediately before her. She could deny the sadness her new friend had perceived, and build the walls a little higher, a little thicker, pretending as if what they could both see did not exist. Or she could, for the first time in her life, discuss what really mattered. Her roommate possessed a gentility that inspired trust, although she could also be almost inhumanly cold when her mood shifted. Lynda had seen some black humors, when she was so quiet and inward as to be almost haughty. Yet this girl was her roommate, her closest friend for the moment, both logistically and emotionally. They would spend at least this year together, and probably more. Something called her on.

"Let's go for a walk. I don't want to talk here. That is, if you want to hear a story."

"I'll listen. If you want to tell it."

"I don't mind. It's probably good that I do. You're right, you know. There is something. I'm trying to sort it out, to get over it and find some peace. You can tell me what I should do."

They left the student center and went along the pathway that led down to the slope upon which the college had been built, then around the campus perimeter. Few people would be out along this path on a chilly night.

"You're pretty amazing, roommate. I've always thought I could hold things inside. But that comes down to playing a role. Congratulations. You found me out, although I'm sure it was just a matter of time. Any role grows tiresome after a time."

"It wasn't difficult, Lynda. You might not be as complex as you imagine yourself."

"I've gone through something that almost ripped me in two. And one of the worst parts was that I couldn't tell anyone. I never have. You're the first. I don't know why I should be so trusting, you know. You're still more a stranger than a friend, although I sense you've got the makings of a great friend, maybe the best I'll ever have. I suppose you're still reasonably objective toward me. Are you willing to lose that?"

"I'm hardly objective. That leaves us at first glance. Tell me what's on your mind, Lynda. I have my hurts, too. Maybe we can hurt together a little bit."

"I'll pay you back some day. Okay?"

"I'll count on it."

"Have you ever been in love? I know that sounds unbelievably trite."

The other laughed inadvertently, a spasm that rose through her lungs and into her throat. But immediately she retracted and became serious. "I'm sorry. No, Lynda, I haven't. I haven't even come close, and I don't want to for a long while."

"That's good. Neither have I when it comes right down to it. But I thought that you might have a few battle scars. Something to judge the depth of my wounds. They're made of a different tissue, though. Thicker. It's all I think about sometimes, what happened. And it's so simple, really, and I'm not the first. Not a very mystical matter. I made a mistake."

"What kind of mistake?"

"I convinced myself that I had fallen in love. Hopelessly, irredeemably in love, with the perfect man. Two years ago. I was sixteen. Can you imagine that?" she chuckled bitterly. "I wanted to be sophisticated, so cosmopolitan. The world at my feet, advanced beyond my tender years. God, I was so confused. I was so taken by illusion. I had no definitions, so I let a man fill in the blanks. He told me what I was. He told me who I was in love with. I believed him."

"Who was this man?"

"Ah, girl, there's the rub, and therein lies the heart of my mistake. It would have been stupid enough to become involved with anyone, but I would have been much better off if I had chosen someone less complicated, less demanding and just as naïve as I was. I would have been better able to weather the whole stormy mess. In fact, there would have been no stormy mess at all. Then we might have both learned something from it and I wouldn't have been the sole casualty. But I chose no ordinary man, roommate. He was older, with a family. And he was my English teacher."

There followed a silence of several seconds, perhaps longer. They walked without speaking, with only the soft crunch of pathway gravel and dead leaves underfoot. The other remained quiet, waiting for her friend to continue.

"He was a handsome man. Tall, tanned. Dark wavy hair and darker eyes. He dressed in sport coats and designer shirts. He was thirty-four. I guess he was going through some premature midlife crisis. He didn't want to grow old, not doing the same mundane things, not wasting the wider opportunities he thought himself deserving, not wasting away with that woman who was his wife. I made him feel young, he told me. 'Lynda, with you I can defeat time, at least for a while.' God, can you believe that? That I fell for that? His wife didn't love him, but he couldn't leave her. Too messy. Too many responsibilities. But she was dragging him down with her traditional ideas, her sense of comfort. He told me that she was stagnant, that she would never take a risk or look for a new experience. He sure as hell wasn't like that. He took a huge risk with me. And I guess I was his new experience.

"Anyway, he kept coming on to me in class. Smiling at me, winking, asking me to come see him to discuss my papers, that sort of thing. I was attracted. I was flattered, too. I can't lie. He seemed so clever, and of course I had never cultivated anyone's attention before. I fell for his act completely. In class he was very animated, hopping around the room and making these outrageous gestures. One time he even perched on an open window ledge to illustrate something about a Philip Roth story. "Defender of the Faith", if you've ever read it. He made the story come alive. We thought he might actually jump, maybe because it was only a second-story window, and he made us recite some nonsense and swear we believed it before he would come down. We all talked about that class for weeks. It was exciting for us. He excited us. And me.

"But he could be so gentle, too. He recited poetry so softly. Some of it was his own. And he could sing. Sometimes he'd put his poetry to music and sing it. Everybody loved him."

"Some more than others, I take it."

"Yes. Some more than others. I would go to his classroom after school to talk about my work, like he asked. Almost every day. I'd stay, and we'd talk about . . . all types of things. Me, him, his family. What he wanted to do after teaching. How he wanted to become great. He really moved me. I felt close to him. I felt unique, like I was the only one to whom he could relate. I guess that's what he wanted. He may well have tried his act on others, but I was the one who bit.

"I thought about him more and more," she continued. "At home. At night, in bed. I convinced myself that I could save him. Please don't be judgmental, kid: I was young and stupid and terribly naïve. Besides, my home life was no picnic, as well you know. You've met my parents. I needed an escape."

That much was true, thought the other. She had met Lynda's parents that first weekend when they had dropped off their daughter. Both of them had struck her as totally humorless, especially the father. Lynda told her later that they were fundamentalists. They tolerated no deviation from the literal word. They were fiercely conservative. Lynda had nearly been sent to a Bible college. Only the intervention of Lynda's counselor had convinced them that their daughter could get a fine education and successfully elude Satan at the place she had chosen. Her roommate considered that Lynda had retained little of her upbringing.

"One day in the classroom he touched me. We had been talking about his wife, how cold she was. He told me that he got more out of our conversations than he had ever gotten from his wife. I challenged him, he said, and I made him feel good about himself. Not worn or frayed. Then he leaned over and put his hand on my wrist. Nothing else. I went home that night and couldn't sleep. My wrist still tingled. This was the first real warmth any man had ever shown me. I wanted more. It was all such a contrast to what I had become accustomed to, that pious, frigid boredom I thought was all a man could be capable of. And I trusted him. I trusted him to show me more, to follow up on what he had begun. I looked at it as another type of lesson, another lesson he could bring alive.

"The next day I went to his classroom again. He wasn't expecting me. He was alone, thankfully, because I don't know what I would have done if anyone else had been there. He was standing at his bookcase. I just went up to him and threw my arms around his neck. And he looked down at me, so afraid and formal. He didn't flinch or back away, though. And I didn't do anything else. I didn't know quite what to do, to be honest. I just wanted to hold him. But at last he smiled, and then he kissed me. Hard, on the lips. Up 'til then I think I had only been kissed twice, each time at the end of a well-chaperoned date, and we had to sneak it. But he kissed me, and I told myself he meant it.

"He closed and locked the door. We spent the rest of the afternoon necking on his desk. I don't think we spoke more than a dozen words between us. I didn't think we had to, and he obviously didn't want to. He would keep breaking away every few minutes to unlock the door and check the hallway, but no one was ever around that late. At the end of it he said that he had to be getting home. Goodbye, see you tomorrow. That was it."

"Where did you go from there?"

"It was pretty apparent that he had sparked something in me. I wanted more. I had such a warped view of things growing up. I had always been taught that sex was evil, necessary between married people but a straight ticket to hell if you weren't. And any woman who toyed with a married man was a harlot, pure and simple. There was no give in it. And now all those silly teachings in themselves seemed evil and warped because they restricted something wonderful, this wonderful situation, this wonderful man. I wanted Peter. I wanted to be everything to him. Anything that stood in the way of that couldn't be right. Those stupid doctrines couldn't apply anymore. I needed him, and he gave every indication that he needed me, too.

"I wanted to be sophisticated. I wanted to be old enough for him. I changed the way I carried myself, and tried to change the way I dressed. I spent less time with my friends, almost no time at all. I became less outgoing, less girlish. I wanted to think about Peter, how I could make myself adequate for him.

"After about a month of sneaking around after school, he told me that he wanted to sleep with me. I was a virgin, of course, and underage, but he said that didn't matter. You know, after we started getting physical we didn't talk as much as we used to. I should have been suspicious, but I didn't care. I just wanted to make him happy. I was looking for some fulfillment myself, too. I don't know. I was confused, but I knew that I felt good. I was looking for a quick and easy answer, and I thought Peter was it. I wanted to live my life for him, to go away with him. After that step, the rest of my life would be as it should. All conflicts resolved."

"Did you ever think of his family?"

"No more than he did. He told me he wanted to leave them. But he never once told me he wanted to take me with him. I just assumed that's what he meant."

"And of course he didn't."

"Of course. We took me to dinner one Saturday night, then we went to a motel. It was so laughable. I had to be home by eleven. I guess he did, too, although I can't imagine what excuse he gave to his wife. After that we got together as often as we could. He even screwed me once right in his classroom. The ultimate act of power, I suppose. Usually I'd tell my parents that I was going to the library and he'd pick me up down the street. We'd do it in his car out in the woods. I never saw the inside of his house."

"How did it end, Lynda?"

"Real simple. We went on like that for about six months, throughout the autumn and the winter. Then one night he told me we couldn't go on like that anymore. He had just fucked me in his car. There we were, sitting in the front seat, the windows all steamy. We couldn't see anything. Our clothes were all messed up. You know, except for the few times we went to a motel we never took our clothes off. We just unzipped and unhooked the relevant areas.

"Anyway, he just came out with it. 'I can't see you anymore, not like this.' Of course, this poor naïve child was stunned. I cried. I asked him why. He didn't really say. I know he never mentioned his family as a reason, or guilt, or responsibility. He said he'd always be my friend, and that he'd do anything he could for me, but that was as far as things could go. He was so smug, too. He knew I'd never use our affair against him, even though I could have gotten him fired and thrown in prison. That's probably the reason why he picked me. He knew I was too timid, too locked in, to do him any harm."

"So he just used you as a dalliance and then cut you loose."

"For a long time afterward I tried to attribute some noble motivation to what he did, and to how he ended it. His family, I thought. He didn't want to cheat anymore, he was afraid of hurting me. Whatever. Then it dawned on me finally that he didn't care about me in the least. I was a diversion. I made him feel sexy, feel young. I wouldn't expect that I was the first student he ever tagged. I would expect he's doing the same thing to someone else right now."

"What about you, Lynda? What did you do?"

"The admissions office here accepted me conditionally. My grades, all my work, went straight to hell that last term. My senior year wasn't any better. I couldn't concentrate. I couldn't hold myself together. I'd break into tears sometimes just thinking about Peter and what he did to me. I couldn't control it. I didn't spend any time at school. I didn't talk to anybody. I was so afraid I'd run into him in the hallways, or I might let myself slip around my former friends. I got to campus in the morning right before classes, and left at the final bell. And of course I didn't dare tell my parents.

"I thought about Peter and I came to hate him. I still do. Even the memories turned sour. All it was was raw sex, nothing else, nothing deeper. He used all his charms as bait. He turned it all on and off. He was never mean, but looking back I can tell he never really cared about me, certainly not above the waist.

"You know, he's almost ruined me. I haven't seen a man socially since him. I haven't felt comfortable around men. I keep thinking they all want only one thing, that no one cares. We're all biological, kid, women as well as men. Peter knew that before I did, and he snared me. Now I know it, too. I'm not getting snared again. Ever."

"And that's why you came here. You couldn't stay home any longer."

"Yeah. Everything changed complexion. I couldn't face my life there. I suppose I was ashamed, and so I ran. It's better here, I think. At least I've got a chance to reconstruct some things. I won't ever get over the bitterness that you so cleverly sensed, but I can begin to learn to live with it here. Human nature is black. It really is. I know that as sure as I know that the earth is round. And so we keep spinning along, trying to outmuscle everybody else, trying to take whatever we can get. No morality, so no regrets."

"I'm not going to disagree with you. Lynda, in one sense don't you think you might have been fortunate, though? I mean, to learn something so hard, and what did you lose, really? Your virginity. A piece of your youth. Your emotional involvement wasn't real, you admit that. Wouldn't it have been worse if you really loved him, if you had given up everything to him, and he in turn really loved you? Wouldn't the scars have run even deeper? Here you lost an illusion and it's made you harder. Peter may have done you a favor in that. But what if you had lost something even rarer than an illusion, something that you might never find again?"

"You may be right," she replied after a pause. "But I won't know that until I experience something more complete, and I'm not sure I ever will. To get there you have to make yourself vulnerable. I can't do that. I won't do that, at least not now, and probably not for a long, long time. The damage is done, girl. I'll leave Romantic love to all you wide-eyed innocents. I'll never experience that. Peter did me no favors. He just did me."

They walked on, silently, each falling back into her own interpretations to sort out the pieces Lynda had brought forward, to shake them, to examine their color and textures, then put them into some type of order that made at least a little sense. It was a private process for each of them.

Years from now the other would remember this confession in detail and feel similar wounds, derived less harshly but still echoing the same conclusions. Human nature was black, and cold, and barren. Anyone approaching it with a childlike simplicity would be eaten alive. She would come to learn this in greater depth, but in fact she would be discovering nothing new. She walked on, side by side with her mutilated friend, arms occasionally brushing. She felt nothing beyond the vacuous emptiness in the pit of her stomach and the tension in her elbows and knees. Her eyes held the ground in front of her feet. At last, the evening could take hold.

"Let's go back," she said. "It's getting cold."

"If we stay on this path it'll take us around to the front of the dorm."

"Let's hurry." She noticed for the first time that she could see her breath. She thought instantly of her father, the image passing before it could be captured or considered. Around the path's bend they came into view of the main classroom building. They quickened their pace wordlessly and headed up the gentle incline that led past the old building to the warmth of their room.

*　*　*

A week later, Lynda Hoelscher ventured out of her bitterness. Or rather, she acknowledged it fully and wielded it as a weapon against what had heretofore been unassailable. She shook her bitterness by its roots.

She attended a party at one of the college's fraternity houses. There she got incredibly drunk, drunker than she had ever been before. She had arrived shortly after dinner, the first girl to walk through the massive front doors. She headed straight for the bar in the basement, parked herself on a stool and made certain she never saw the bottom of her glass. As the evening progressed men came up to talk to her in a steady stream. It had all the earmarks of a ritual; she was the prey. Her senses dulled, then rose again, swimming and twirling. She grew evil.

One young man in particular caught her eye. He had spoken with her briefly, like all the others had been rebuffed, and now sat on a bench in the corner of the dank basement, temporarily by himself. Lynda refilled her glass, tottered off her stool, tripped across the room and dropped herself next to the pleasantly surprised young man. She had noticed him because as the evening wore on, he appeared to be among the youngest in the room. His eyes were wide with wonder.

She said nothing to him. She merely leaned onto his shoulder and stuck her tongue into his ear. She would not remove it. Instead she probed deeper, making little sucking noises. The young man, absolutely stunned, made no sense of it, but he had no desire to fight it. He leaned back, half closed his eyes, and let the show continue. He was amazingly aroused, and drew his arm around her shoulders to hold her in place.

After a time Lynda's tongue grew weary. "You got a room here?"

"In Courtney," he replied, indicating the freshman men's dormitory.

'Perfect,' thought Lynda. 'How wonderfully perfect.'

They walked the short distance up then hill to Courtney, Lynda unsteady, the arm of her new friend tightly around her waist, bracing her. His roommate had gone home for the weekend. The dormitory itself was quiet, too, its residents prowling through the Friday night. The young man led her through the door to his room, shut it slowly and locked it behind him.

Lynda turned to look at him in the better light. 'Lord,' she thought, 'he seems so innocent.' For indeed he was. His young face had no lines to it, retaining the soft roundness of adolescence. His cheeks and chin had no whiskers. His blue eyes stood out clearly. Although he had had a few beers his demeanor had not blurred, his body had not become droopy or liquefied. His long blond hair curled under his ears, but it only added to his childlike quality, as if he were a young boy whose mother had let his hair grow out to see how it fell and what color it would be. 'He looks so young.'

"Take your clothes off," she purred. "I want to see you naked."

The young man complied, his excitement mingling with his nerves, compelling artificially slow movements and a weak, scrawny smile that he hoped would convey confidence. He was, to be sure, puzzled as to why this was happening to him. He knew, though, that he should feel fortunate. This girl was gorgeous, a fantasy come to life. His friends, most of whom not sharing his virginal state, would be impressed. And he himself stood to learn something.

Lynda watched him undress, not bothering to take off her jacket. She grinned as she evaluated his body, which did not carry the softness of his face. It was hard and fairly muscular. 'Not unlike Peter's,' she thought.

He laid his jeans across the chair and turned back to her wearing only his shorts. He took a step toward her, but she backed away and held up her hand, smiling as she did so.

"All the way," she said.

"What about you, babe?"

"You first."

Again he complied, obediently peeling off his shorts and kicking them under the bed. He stood before her, tumescent, trembling slightly in spite of his best intentions.

"That's better, lover," Lynda cooed, her voice growing low and throaty. "That's much better."

She walked up to him, each stride catlike in its calm, unhurried deliberation. She wrapped her arms around his neck, pressed herself to his naked body, kissed him full on the lips, parted them and wetly entered her tongue into his astonished mouth. She waited for him to respond. His breathing deepened, his already firm erection grew firmer. He rubbed himself against her loins, sucked rapturously on her tongue. Soft groaning sounds slipped from his unplumbed depths.

Lynda Hoelscher, too, responded. She had her man. It was time now to use him.

With a breathless fury she drove her knee upward into his unprotected scrotum. Instantly he doubled over in shock and agony. Her arms around his neck kept him from falling, and she drove her knee into him a second time. The young man collapsed on the floor, writhing spasmodically as he clutched his exploding groin.

"So long, lover. Take care of yourself." Lynda bent over the young man's quivering body and planted a kiss on his cheek. He did not respond except to roll to his side. Lynda walked to the door, unfastened the lock and passed through. She closed it behind her on the first sounds of her young man retching violently, the vomit splattering off the carpet and onto the tiles floor beneath his bed.

* * *

Tom McIlweath drew himself through the pool in long, relaxed, powerful strokes. That was his style—to propel himself with seemingly little effort, taking advantage of his overly long arms and strong legs. His slender trunk offered small resistance to the water.

Workouts had become ritualistic for him. Where other swimmers looked to the daily training sessions with resignation, McIlweath saw them as a release, a buffer between the zones of his day. He had always kept himself in good shape, better, he discovered, than his new teammates, so the physical demands of the workouts, while considerable, posed no great problem. He could swim his laps well within the coach's times for him. He could push himself on the sprints then, having a store of energy unburned from the longer parts of the regimen. He would be fresh enough to refine his strokes. Tom

McIlweath's body could withstand the workouts without draining itself to the last spasm and twitch. His fear that he would be too scrawny, too slow, too weak to swim at the college level vanished within the first week of training.

His body secure in the demands placed upon it, McIlweath was free to approach his workouts intellectually and, on some days, even spiritually, a touch of Zen. It had to do with the water.

As a boy, McIlweath had been frightened of water. His father would not long put up with the boy's fears. He took his son to the beach at the height of summer and, suddenly made aware of the child's reluctance to enter the great ocean, pulled his eight-year-old body into a pair of swimming trunks, grabbed him by the arm and dragged the boy with him into the surf. Tom, whose only experience had been gazing with overwhelmed awe at the ocean from a safe distance, who had been too timid even to risk putting his head beneath the surface while taking a bath, kicked viciously to break away. All that water, his brain screamed—so angry at the edge, and then endless to the horizon. Within a few seconds, young Tom realized that if he were to struggle against the bounding force of either his father of the ocean, he would most likely drown or, worse, be dragged back to dry land in humiliation. His irrational fear of the water dissipated under his very rational fear of his father's wrath. He swam.

In fact, by the end of the day he was doing more than swimming. He was running into the surf, plunging headlong into the smaller waves, and, with a sense of timing that surprised even his father, ducking under the bigger ones to come up laughing on the other side. Young Tom concluded that in water only one rule applied: if you're underneath it, don't breathe. Once he discovered he could float, and better still, that he could propel himself a bit in whatever direction he chose, his initial relief at conquering this potentially disastrous situation turned to joy. To his astonished father, Tom made a remarkable turnaround. The remainder of that summer Tom begged his father to take him to the beach every day the elder McIlweath was free. Tom frolicked through the surf like a warm-weather sea otter. He was not interested in combing the sand for shells or studying the tide pools for surprises. He only wanted to swim.

The next year Tom's father joined a swim club and Tom began to swim competitively. After the ocean, a swimming pool seemed tiny. If Tom McIlweath could not control the vast seas, he could at least master the small waters in which he now swam. He threw himself into his swimming, and became better each year, his times in key events dropping steadily. The move to Southern California where his new school had no swim team almost broke his heart. He swam with a private team throughout his last years in high school to stay competitive, to stay sharp. The Rutgers swim coach, always in search of young talent, took note of his times in the California state meet for sixteen-to-eighteen year-olds after an alumnus had sent a letter suggesting that Tom McIlweath might be worth looking into. McIlweath, discontent and dispirited at the time, had sought an escape, as far away as possible. Swimming had given him that chance, pointing him in a direction he could never have foreseen.

Now, in this new pool, McIlweath found another type of release, more personal, more immediate. The water buoyed him, it carried him. The turbulent state of a swimmer in motion could hardly be peaceful in itself, yet the water calmed Tom McIlweath. So soft; so yielding. He plunged into it, it folded over him, womblike, until he parted it, broke the surface to draw air, then back again, head moving side to side, breathing in sips, rhythm, rhythm. In the water nothing mattered. No friendships mattered, no classes mattered, there was no heartbreak, for him no stress. Breathing in small sips, rhythm, rhythm. In the water it was warm. In the water he saw nothing but the green blur through his goggles, the grey brick of the wall, no depth beyond it, nothing above him. In the water he heard only the attacking splashes of his strokes, the sounds he created, and his own lungs, inhaling, exhaling, breathing in sips. Rhythm, rhythm. In the water he need have no thoughts, he need be concerned with no ideas, he need have no reactions; his mind might be like the very water in which he swam, quieted after the swimmers had left—unmoving, without the slightest ripple, where a few moments before all had been churning and twisting. He grasped the irony of it, that in the churning of the swim he found his tranquility. Once he ceased, he became ordinary again.

He swam in a trancelike state, numb to his physical exertion, the sensual stimuli around him muted and regular. His mind, too, emptied itself; he became lost in rhythm, lost in the water that lifted him. Split the water, and go with it. And if he could, split the walls at the lane's end and swim invisible, forever, through other people's common space.

McIlweath hit the wall as if to push right through it. "Time, 17:26. Good swim, Mac. Wait for your teammates. We're going to finish up with some sprints."

McIlweath leaned one arm over the lip of the pool and watched the other swimmers move up and back in the lanes around him. He breathed heavily tiny drops of water spewing from his lips with each deep exhalation. It would be several minutes before all his teammates completed the distance. He would be well rested for the sprints. He would be well rested for the evening.

* * *

Conor Finnegan meanwhile catered to his urge to play basketball. This was to be his first year, since he was eight, without organized ball. He found early on that he missed it. Three or four days a week he would walk across campus past the library to the old College Avenue gymnasium to spend a couple of hours after classes doing what he believed he could do very well.

Basketball was a self-assertion, an exercise through which Finnegan could thrust himself forward and apart from the thousand strange faces he encountered every day. On the court he might be more than the casual student. He might be a touch less anonymous, even if he were only known as a white kid with a good jump shot. It was, in the least, a degree of distinction he suddenly discovered he missed, a part of his identity to which he had become accustomed.

And so Finnegan inflated these pick-up games to take on more significance than they deserved. He believed that most of the outstanding basketball talent at a major college played on either the varsity or the freshman squads. Consequently those young men who spent their afternoons playing pick-up at the gym were bound to be a cut below. Finnegan believed that, had he wanted to spend the time and effort, he himself would have been able to play freshman ball. If he were lucky and stayed healthy, he might well have made the varsity as a walk-on. So he believed. The casual games he played at the gym, then, would necessarily be against slightly lesser talents. During the early part of the year, in late September and October, he found nothing to disabuse him of that notion. In most games he did indeed stand out as the best player on the court. Those in which he didn't were the products of his own poor effort, or soft concentration, he told himself, and not a shortage of talent.

On this particular afternoon Finnegan had had no trouble finding four teammates to play against the winners of the game currently underway on the center court. He had previously played with two of them: a heavily muscled, dark-complected guy about his height, and a tall, bony blond fellow. His other two teammates he did not recognize. They all introduced themselves at courtside as they waited for the current game to end. As it did they walked onto the court and headed for the far end to take their warm-up shots.

Finnegan loved the sensation of first setting foot on the hardwood. He tended to saunter a bit as he did so, thoroughly in control, returning to familiar lands. He loved the sound of the ball bouncing against the glossy wood. The cool, stale air flared his nostrils. He broke a slight sweat taking his warm-ups. Finnegan felt at once relaxed and powerful, a racehorse in the starting gate, his muscles tensed, his mind fully aware of what lay ahead, what he would be called upon to do.

The game started with Finnegan's team bringing the ball up court. The first basket came when Finnegan cut behind a screen set by his tall, bony teammate, took a pass and sank a twenty-foot jump shot with a flick of his wrist. He ran back down court lightly on the balls of his feet, in no particular hurry, pleased at his quick demonstration.

His man took the ball at the top of the key as Finnegan crouched defensively. The short black guy started a series of head and shoulder fakes, one after another, back and forth in opposite directions. Finnegan had seen it before. He would wait for the real move. Instinctively he backed up half a step. His opponent launched his move with a quick step to the right then a crossover step back to the left. Finnegan reacted, but too slowly. His man shot by him, and his teammates, each concerned with his own man, turned around too late to pick him up. He went down the lane untouched for a layup. Finnegan said immediately, "My fault" with a confidence that indicated that he did not expect it to happen again.

But it did. His opponent went around him twice more, once to score and once to pass off for an uncontested basket when Finnegan's teammate, the heavily muscled fellow whose name was Lou, dropped his man to help out. Finnegan tried to compensate for the other's quickness. He sagged three or four feet off him, laying back in the key to give him a split-second more to adjust to the other's moves. His man read it immediately, a tiny grin settling onto his face, and with the extra room sank three long jump shots before Finnegan could step out to challenge him.

Finnegan's teammates changed their expressions as the game progressed. They frowned, muttering profanities after each basket, and Finnegan knew the object of their frustration. It might take the losing team half an hour to gain the court again, depending on how many others were waiting to play. The five of them had waited themselves to get this game, and now it was slipping away.

Finnegan grew more intense. Unused to being beaten like this, he felt a desperation to do something in return, something to redeem himself, something to save the game. He got the ball to the left of the free-throw line, twenty feet from the basket. His opponent stood against him, virtually chest to chest, too close for Finnegan to let go his jump shot. Instead he took a short step to his left, then dribbled the ball behind his back and drove to the right. A good move, and he was sure he had beaten his man. Off the dribble he pushed his right leg upward to begin his shot, no more than five feet. As he brought the ball above his hip, his opponent, who had followed Finnegan's drive, reached across Finnegan's body, knocked the ball out of his surprised hands, then sprinted by him to recover the loose ball and lead the break in the opposite direction. Finnegan could not catch up.

The next time his man got the ball, Finnegan got on top of him as tightly as he could. He pushed himself next to the shorter man, so close that he could feel his opponent's breath on his neck. As his man made a move to his right Finnegan stayed with him, leaning hard on the other's shoulder. His opponent stopped at once, Finnegan lurching ahead of him, off-balance. Just as quickly, the shorter man spurted to the left. While Finnegan could defend the first move, he could not recover quickly enough to defend the second. His man scored again.

"Jesus Christ, what're you doing?" said Lou, his face a scowl.

"He's quick, damn it."

"Or you're too slow. You take my man, I'll handle yours. Jesus Christ . . ."

Against his will, Finnegan blushed. Regarded by the grunting Lou and undoubtedly by the rest of his teammates as a liability, Finnegan's desperation to prove himself deepened. The game was to fifteen baskets. With the score fourteen to eleven against him, Finnegan shook free with a sharp cut to his left. He got the ball two feet under the top of the key, his favorite shooting spot, where he was almost automatic. In the instantaneous movement of thought, Finnegan made certain he was properly ready to shoot: hands across the seams, feet together, shoulders square to the basket. Up he went, drawing the ball smoothly to the side of his right ear. He fell into an autonomous rhythm, the actions rehearsed tens of thousands of times, his muscles tapping their collective memory to work harmoniously. There is a sense of order in that. There is a sense of control, of agreement, almost euphoric when it works correctly.

Finnegan saw nothing but the orange hoop of the basket. His eyes burned a hole in the back of the rim. His muscles released in a pattern that had grown to instinct. The ball arced forth and Finnegan followed it with his eyes, the dirty brown sphere outlined against the dark forms of the gym's second level of bleacher, now heading gently downward, spinning slightly in its usual rotation. Finnegan took three quick steps backward as he landed to get set to play defense, so certain that the ball was going in because that was how it had all felt.

Except the ball let him down. It hit the back of the rim, bounced very softly to the front, then bounded away into the outstretched arms of an opposing player. Finnegan stood there, incredulous. The shot had been good, it had to be. Everything had been done properly.

The missed shot robbed Finnegan of his last reserve. He defended limply, a balloon with no air. His man went inside and Finnegan followed, leaning on him to keep him away from the basket. A shot was put up. Finnegan's man hooked his leg in front of Finnegan's and pivoted toward the basket. The ball bounced off the rim right to him, and he put it back up for the winning basket. Mercifully, it had come to an end.

Finnegan walked off the court, his eyes riveted on the floor in front of him. Three members of the winning team walked up to him in the established ritual of shaking hands, saying "Good game" as if they meant it. Finnegan shook hands in return, but made no other response. It had not been a good game, not at all.

Three young men had been waiting to play the winners. They came onto the court now. "We need two more guys. Give us a couple of minutes," one yelled over to the other team.

"Get two guys from the losers," someone yelled back.

The three turned to one another. "Who do you think we should get?"

Finnegan had overheard this, so he stopped at courtside. Perhaps another game, another team, might work for him. He would have a chance to get his rhythm back. It was obvious that he knew how to play, and play well. He had just had a bad game, that was all.

One of the three new players came to the side of the court where the leavers stood, four near the baseline and Finnegan at mid-court near the exit. He glanced at Finnegan, then turned to the group of four. He pointed to Lou and to the tall, bony blond. "You two guys want to go again?"

Finnegan picked up his sweatshirt, pulled it on and headed out the door. Usually he would run back to the dormitory, a short enough sprint to finish the workout. This afternoon he walked, very slowly, head down. Along the way he picked up a flat, smooth stone and tossed it at a tree on the library lawn. He missed. Finnegan chuckled to himself, certain that it all meant something but not having a clue as to what, and continued on.

* * *

Lynda Hoelscher had immediately gained a reputation among her college's male population as a black widow, beautiful yet deadly, and to be avoided at all costs. As her roommate, Glynnis Mear became guilty by association. Not that this bothered her. She would not have to deal with the advances of people whom she preferred not to know. Her short experience at college told her that most friendships made here would likely prove shallow, the products of their particular situations of loneliness, of being thrown together in one place, of responding for the moment to the strangeness around and between them. Besides, those who tended to regard her suspiciously were men, and there she could not for the life of her imagine a relationship beyond the superficial.

Glynnis Mear did not mind. She measured her friendships in quality rather than quantity. Without the distractions of people who mattered little, she could tend more freely to her own concerns. And, although her outward manner remained calm, although she invariably appeared poised and very much in control of herself, she did have her concerns which at times broke her down.

She found ways to step outside herself. When the reality of being Glynnis Mear proved oppressive, she would escape in an anonymous flight into the congealed mass around her. She loved the city. It invigorated her to pass through crowds of people who did not so much as know her name and who, if they did, would not care. It was like being invisible. And, if she was invisible, she could go wherever she wanted without fear.

In her depressions she would take a bus into Center City, near Philadelphia's city hall, grey and baroque with its asparagus tower. Usually she would come into the city near the end of the day. She enjoyed watching the day grow dark, watching the numbers dwindle. She would walk around downtown, glancing occasionally into shop windows but looking mostly at the people. If she had time, she would walk up the Benjamin Franklin Parkway, past the cathedral, past Logan Circle, past the science museum and into Fairmount Park. She loved the greenness there, the sharp juxtaposition with the asphalt, granite and steel a few blocks behind her. In time she began to establish her favorite pathways in and around the city's heart. She came to feel as comfortable in Philadelphia as she had in her native Boston.

Her few friends, of course, thought it peculiar at best that this attractive young woman should want to stalk around the city streets by herself. At worst they thought it suicidal. It would only be a matter of time, they told each other, before Glynnis was assaulted, or raped, or worse.

Glynnis, though, never felt endangered. She went into the city to forget herself, to drain her mind. In the simplicity of young logic, she concluded that it wouldn't be fair if something happened to add to her concerns. It didn't work like that. When she was a small girl, the parish priest had once looked her squarely in the eye, smiled a gentle smile, and pronounced that she had special angels hovering over her.

"How can you tell, Father? How do you know?" she had asked.

"I can just tell, Glynnis. Your angels will always be there to protect you. Always."

"Can I see them?"

"No," the priest replied. "But you'll know they're there. And if you're ever a bad girl and they decide to leave you, you'll know that, too. But that won't happen. I can see your heart as well, and there's no evil there. Your angels will never have reason to leave."

The priest had been right. Glynnis believed the angels were still with her. In her girlish fancy she imagined them to be tiny, no bigger than matchsticks, and dressed so lightly in silver that they were transparent on those rare occasions when they, teasingly, might allow themselves to be seen. Their eyes were blue. Glynnis's angels would protect her and bring her good things. She did not know why they should select her, but she was infinitely glad that they had.

Glynnis believed that, aside from the angels, no one she might encounter on those streets cared whether she was there or not. They would not go out of their way to harm her, so all she had to do was give any potentially uncertain character or situation a wide berth.

She had become fascinated with the city when she was fifteen. She had escaped after a particularly vicious argument with her mother to walk in downtown Boston for three hours. She had no place to go, and at the time she had had to get away. The vibrancy of the city drew her in, bleached her thoughts and tranquilized the sudden burst of anger she had kindled. Glynnis had found a catharsis; she returned time and again. Not once had she ever been even remotely accosted.

And so she walked, slowly, unhurriedly, her head up to watch whom and what she passed. The city fascinated her as a locus, as the site of an infinite outpouring of human passion. Each individual she passed had his story, his reason for being where he was. She often overheard their conversations as she walked by, and she tried to fill in the gaps. If an individual appeared distinct for any reason, by appearance or dress or action, she tried to imagine his life, what he did how he felt, why he looked as he did. No group was exempt. She gazed with equal curiosity at the businessmen hurrying to their trains at day's end, the students going into and coming out of the museums near the park, schoolchildren shuffling along the sidewalks in groups, the tourist families wandering confusedly, cameras in hand and children in tow. She even regarded the winos and the panhandlers, grizzled, smelly old men who appeared as if from ether and grew more numerous as the night drew on. Her curiosity was not the clinical kind of a sociologist, for she did not care about societal types or collective behaviors. Her curiosity was personal, based solely on her wonder at the gamut of human emotions and experiences.

If she could, Glynnis would have crawled into the skull of each person she passed. Humanity enchanted her; she craved understanding of it so that she might in her own way define both mankind in general and the peculiar creature that had become Glynnis Mear in particular. In the bottomless perspective of the eddies swirling about her, the cares and rejections that propelled her to take flight invariably became muted. The strange beasts that prowled within her bowed to the equally strange and wondrous beasts that created the tide sweeping her away.

In early November, Glynnis received a letter from her mother. She dreaded these letters. Almost always before reading them she grew physically upset, her stomach tightened, her nerve ends tingled. She picked up her mail at the campus post office in the basement of the student center. When she pulled the letter from her box and saw the postmark, her initial reaction was to shove it back in and slam shut the tiny metallic door. Perhaps it would fly back to where it came. But logic, of course, dictated otherwise. She turned the letter over to confirm the return address, to confirm the recognizable script, placed it in her jacket pocket and went upstairs for coffee. She was in no hurry to read it.

Later, she returned to her room. Lynda thankfully was out so she would have space, and no need to mask her reactions, whatever they might be. Sometimes, without knowing it, she would clench the hand not holding the letter into a tight fist and drum it against her thigh. The first time she did this Lynda had become a bit concerned—Glynnis never betrayed such tension—and had asked a string of annoying questions that Glynnis had had to sidestep, with moderate success. Lynda remained curious as to why letters from Glynnis's family should upset her so. The letters came frequently, for her mother loved to write them, feeling the paper beneath her fingers, once or twice a week. Glynnis received three or four for every one she answered.

She sat at her desk, tore at the end of the envelope, pulled out the letter, and read:

Dear Glynnis,

It's raining here as I write this, and I'm cold. I'm sitting here with a big mug of coffee, which I dearly need. Tonight it might freeze. I'm trying to keep the heat turned down so we can save our oil. It's too early to be worrying about winter but I'm afraid it's a fact we have to face.

Martha, Bobby and Peter continue as always. Martha was named cheerleader two weeks ago, but I think I told you that in my last letter. (Two letters ago, Glynnis thought.)

She doesn't get home now until nearly six. We always have supper late, sometimes in shifts. She looks very attractive in her outfit. She'll be having the boys beat a path to our door by the end of the year, I think.

Bobby and Peter are still playing football. Their seasons don't end until mid-November, and then maybe the playoffs after that. Bobby's team won again last week, so they're still in first place. Peter's team got beat, but Pete scored a touchdown. He was so proud. He ran about 40 yards to score it. To hear him tell it you'd think he just won the Rose Bowl all by himself—you know how excited he gets. They're both always asking about you—'Did we get a letter from Glynnis today? What do you think she's doing right now?' That sort of thing. (The first not-so-subtle attempt at guilt, thought Glynnis. Stay tuned, more to come.)

Of course, even with the three of them around, the house still seems awfully empty. I never considered myself a lonely woman. I have lots of friends. As many as I need. You remember how they filled the house after your father's funeral? Some of them I barely knew. They kept coming for days afterward, too, always bringing food, like I was incapable of lifting a pot or pan. They forget that we were so well provided for. I guess they just wanted to help. Most of them still come around, and I see many of them at the hospital. I go out sometimes with one or two of them, to a movie or dinner, just to do something. Still, it gets quiet here. I'm not accustomed to that yet. I miss your father.

And I miss you. (Here it comes, thought Glynnis. No more subtleties. She's ready for the frontal assault.) I know we've been over it before, but for the life of me I can't understand why you were so anxious to go away to school. What did you have to prove, Glynnis? We have always been such a close, close family. With your father gone, I could use you here. I want you here.

You went away assuring me, assuring us, that you would come home as often as you could. Here it is November and we have yet to see you. I know you're busy getting used to things there, but you could spare us at least a weekend, no? And now you're hesitating about Thanksgiving for God knows what reason. That I won't take quietly. I expect you the Wednesday before the holiday. No excuses. I'll make your plane reservation, Philly to Logan, 6:15, USAir #628. I'll be at the airport to pick you up. Like I said, no excuses.

You don't even call much anymore. It's been nearly a month. My God, Glynnis, I don't know what to think. It's as if you had only been a visitor with us these past eighteen years. What have we done, my lovely daughter? Please tell me. Or if you can't, then come home, where you'll always have a place, and hearts enough to love you forever. Come back to life for us again. We've already lost your father. We couldn't bear another passing.

With love,
Mother of the Mears

Glynnis sat in her chair for several minutes more, not reading but retracing with her eyes the forms of blue ink on the paper. It had become so difficult, and it drained her. Her mother now moved bluntly where before she had lightly danced. Glynnis concluded that she could postpone the inevitable no longer. She could no longer hide at a distance. She would be on USAir flight 628.

Prior to her father's death, Glynnis had been uncertain how she would react. She alone among the children had accepted the fact that he would indeed pass, that the illness that daily sapped his energy and lifted his sensibilities into a pain-dulled, cloudlike ether would not go away. As the oldest child, she had always been the one most prepared, most ready, to face adversity. She had had to be, and she took quiet pride in her composure and resiliency, whether shooing a bat out of her brothers' room or repairing her sister's torn best dress. While Glynnis had been a soft-spoken girl, it would have been a mistake to confuse silence with weakness.

She knew her father would die, knew it months ahead of the fact and, because she acknowledged the reality, thought she had properly braced for it. In the closing stages of his disease she consciously tried to construct their lives without his presence. She tried to determine her world without him there. The result did not necessarily frighten her, although it made her sad beyond measure. The family would lose his stability, his constancy and his gentility, she concluded, but there would have to be ways to compensate. He had provided well for them financially. They were all good kids with well-developed attitudes of responsibility. His death would bind them even more closely; they would stand beside their mother, each supporting the others. We would miss him, she thought—his wit, his firmness, the way he made us laugh, his wisdom, his grand, glorious, unbounded love for all of us.

We would miss him, but we would survive. We can do nothing else.

The fault with Glynnis's conclusions lay with their basic construction: they were purely logical, projections of their current status with one of the pieces clinically removed and the others continuing down their previous paths. But when one of the pieces, in fact the central piece, is removed, the other pieces stagger and fall out of line. They would struggle mightily to find their places again, but they never would. In falling out of line, the pieces themselves had changed.

Glynnis herself changed most of all, in ways she could not possibly have foreseen. With Robert Mear's death the others caved in, giving way to a grief they had suppressed for months. Glynnis's mother initially tried to bear up stoically, but her muffled sorrow could not long be restrained. By the end of the second day after her husband's death, she, too, had fallen into a weeping desolation. Glynnis alone functioned efficiently, tending to her family, preparing the meals, even doing the laundry. She had known what was coming. Her grief had spread itself widely over several months, and she had swallowed it in sips.

She grew tired of the wailing and the mourning. Whether the result of some subliminal guilt of her own or the product of a mind grown weary, she began to question silently the direction of that mourning. Was it grief for the departed father and husband they were expressing, or grief for themselves? They did not see in Glynnis's eye the spirit, the resolve, the brooding anxiety of the man just passed. They did not absorb his anguish, the bitter flame of a life wrenched from its socket, a life that had paced, that had surmounted, that had embraced all it could in the time it had, a life from which had sprung issue, a life that had experienced the tears, agonies, exultations and vivid wonder granted us by a chuckling God. They did not see it enough at all.

Change comes. Profound, life-shaking change comes in time. There can be no escape, for we are consigned to it from our first suckle. It is what we do when we encounter the great currents and spasms of our lives that helps define us. Change comes, whether it scars us, and, if it does, whether the skin grows back thick and hard, or febrile, easily broken at the next bump.

Glynnis Mear saw her family respond to her father's death by changing in ways that she had not anticipated. In the dark corners of her considerations, places where she looked only reluctantly, she saw their fears, which she had dismissed, and saw their grieving loneliness, which she had compartmentalized. Grieve now for the man, if grief be in order. We are *not* lost, we are *not* forsaken. But we *are* changed, and changed forever: we are new pieces that cannot fit into old forms.

CHAPTER VI

—Euripides, *Alcestis*

Neither Conor Finnegan nor Tom McIlweath had ever been to New York City so on the short drive up the New Jersey Turnpike they were all eyes. Their heads flipped back and forth trying to take in everything on all sides. Six young men packed into Reg Coleman's old Chevrolet, Finnegan and McIlweath jammed knee to knee in the back seat. They were the only two of the group who took any notice at all of the bleak, grimy, smoky, belching landscape of the turnpike route in North Jersey. To the other four, this stretch of road was an annoyance to be leapfrogged before landing in the city.

The first spires of the mythic apple came into view over a junkyard ridge. The towers of the Verrazano Bridge, bluish-green in the fading sun; the needle-point of the Empire State Building; the Deco spire of the Chrysler Building, dimming sunlight reflecting off its glossy facades; the other tall buildings rising like grass.

"What bridge is that?" asked McIlweath.

"Verrazano, son. The third greatest bridge in the world," replied Lanny O'Hanlon, Conor Finnegan's roommate.

"What are the top two, Dice?" asked Finnegan.

"Brooklyn Bridge, number two. And the Charles River Bridge to Somerville, number one." Lanny O'Hanlon had grown up in the Boston suburbs.

"Explain that last one, Mick." Dan Rosselli leaned over from the front seat with his left arm. In the luck of the roommate lottery, Rosselli had been paired with Reg Coleman, the two of them placed next to Tom McIlweath and his mate, Rick Murdoch. Finnegan and O'Hanlon roomed down the hall. Due to logistics and common temperaments, the six of them had grown close during the year's first weeks. On this evening, the three dorm rooms had emptied in search of adventure and alcohol in New York City.

"A personal preference," responded O'Hanlon. "I wouldn't expect you to understand, big guy, unless I clarify. Jeannie Anthony. The Charles River Bridge spans more than a river. On the far side rests physical ecstasy whose name is Jeannie. For that reason alone, this one bridge will be forever special. Across that bridge I became a man, and I can say that about no other bridge in the world. You'll find your own bridge someday."

Rosselli turned back to the front seat, shaking his head.

In a few more minutes the entire city came into view. An upward surge of . . . something, perhaps passion, welled through Finnegan's breast. The sun had not quite set, and its final rays passed through a crystal blue autumn sky to paint Manhattan orange. Fitting, thought Finnegan, that my first view of this incredible city should be like this.

What lay in its bowels, on its streets, in its buildings for one like me? An infinity of possibilities, built on an infinity of faces. Millions of people, working there, eating, walking, cursing, fighting, screwing, each passing through his own universe come together here. The lights shooting down the streets, changing in their colors, highlighting the faces here in differing moods. No space, no air; throbbing, alive in its own plasma, breathing its iron, its glass, its stone. Sounds piercing off its sides, causing echoes, reverberations, until one could not tell where real sound dies and echo begins, a cacophony rolling back onto itself.

Infinite variations, infinite themes. Food, drink, women, dance, music, art. What lies within the city's sprawling, weblike system of streets? No, that is not the question. Rather, what does *not* lie there? If a man has a sense of himself, if he knows what he wants and why he came, how can he fail to achieve it in this glorious place?

This journey had arisen from basic goals: the group wanted a good meal, and they wanted to get drunk. The city, with its endless restaurants and taverns, could irresistibly satisfy them.

To add a degree of dignity, Lanny O'Hanlon had insisted they all wear sport coats and ties. He explained to them that this was indeed necessary. "No matter how shitfaced we get, we'll look at least somewhat respectable, not like drunken misfits. Trust me on this one. The city is loaded with cops looking for an easy arrest."

To the casual observer they appeared in fact as proper young men who might be on their way to the theater. Tweeds predominated. O'Hanlon wore his prep school tie, Rosselli a plaid touring cap. The air created, not accidentally, was that of a polished group of young men exploring their options. The gentry had their fox hunts; young men had their night in the city.

They crept through the dark, slow-moving tube of the Lincoln Tunnel and spun into the Port Authority Terminal, a ghastly, cavernous tomb that allowed neither light nor air. Before leaving campus they had settled upon a restaurant, cheap but pseudo-elegant, offering all the beer one could drink with the purchase of a top-end dinner. They would park the car and walk the fifteen blocks or so.

The city at twilight is a marvelous place—fluid, twinkling and cool in the fading October day, the kaleidoscopic swirl of colors and patterns of the streets at once sunning and invigorating every sense. Conor Finnegan stepped from the immense parking facility into the pulsing streets and, in a heartbeat, felt the deepest, most profound hunger of his life.

If the drive into the city and his first glimpse of its jabbing granite towers had aroused Finnegan's desires, his first few seconds on its streets awakened them fully so that they screamed in every corner of his mind. In this sprawl lay greatness and immortality, potency and power. But within it first lay a groundswell, a teeming, blank-visaged throng that set its own ceaseless throb. Crowds swept by him, some rubbing past him so firmly as to knock him down. Now and again he would overhear snippets of the conversations of the gray people rushing by him. Their words spun past him like dragonflies, as subtly heartbroken as their blanched faces.

"It's the art of the deal, Jocko. No prisoners."

or

"Knicks plus seven. I'll take it. A dime, that's all."

or

"Can't touch that bitch. Can't get near her."

or

"That's all I coulda done, ya see? To shut her up. Youda dun the same, wuncha?"

. . . and the ever-present figures darting out from storefronts or on corners handing out tickets for discounts at electronics stores or massage parlors. And the cases of ties, watches and cheap jewelry hawked in mid-block, almost every block, by sharp-tongued hustlers. And the worn men, with unshaven grey whiskers and tatty clothes, that appear like ghosts or zombies, shuffling ahead of you, conglomerations of bad smells and unrelenting despair.

And the homeless, the addicts, the winos, sticking out their hands, "Yo, Jack, whachew got? You got a dollar for sompin' to eat? I swear to Christ I ain't gonna spend it on booze or drugs. Swear to Christ. I useta be an altar boy. Gimme a hand, hey?"

Finnegan heard it all in bits and pieces, passed through it without stopping, his feet moving automatically, his head turning from side to side, his eyes wide to miss nothing. He saw their faces, saw their eyes, and wordlessly recalled fish he had seen in the supermarket. He saw their complexions and noted their walks, each signifying station and purpose, and wondered in God's name how anyone could carve a place in this congestion. From time to time he would see a figure standing out from this miasmatic swarm: a young man whose face shone with animation, whose walk was light, whose mouth might form an unconscious smile, or a young woman who captured all the glamour, the poise, the latent sexuality that femininity could possibly convey. But he did not dwell on these scattered exceptions. He merely noted that they did indeed exist, and felt reassured by this, less alone, and passed on as the crowd demanded.

And in his first few steps he perceived an undercurrent of brutality, of violent force, of abomination that, unleashed, could strip human existence to its barest rudiments. The souls of fifteen million people were bound in this city, and so many of them blank, interchangeable, the city itself a process of working, pushing, acquiring, distributing, acquiring again, thrusting against the anonymous, overpowering and impersonal forces that defined it all to begin. The city could not be a place to live in the traditional sense; it could only be an arena, a testing ground for valor, creativity, and resource. The cost of failure might be tremendous, might indeed be the ultimate cost, for if the city were only an arena, and all the faces anonymous, then how might a man convince himself that he is not a brute and, in so being, the subject of brute forces? What compels him to civility?

A single touch, perhaps, or a warm bed where he knows he belongs. A voice that belies his own anonymity. A welcoming glance, and one who knows his name. Of little more than this do we build ourselves against the merciless tides.

Finnegan watched it all, and the hunger rose within him, his heart surged with an exultancy that he had not realized. For he had never witnessed this savage fury except in his imagination, and yet he might be a part of it. Finnegan had a mind, and he had a soul. He had not been beaten down by the vicious demands of responsibility, of propriety, of thwarted ambition. He stood out with his quick and agile mind, his strong body. Finnegan walked into the teeming sea of humanity around him and saw at once that he was different from this mass. He thought at once of the bodies of his ancestors lying in the ground in dust and decay, fetid husks of now-nameless souls passed into an unknown ether. He looked at the anonymous faces here whose collective fates would differ little from those of a forgotten past. And he rejoiced inwardly because he was different from all this. He possessed more than a soul, he possessed a spirit. And, above all else, he possessed the one component that, once lost, would seal his doom with all the others. He possessed his youth.

Finnegan's hunger for all things good and rich and meaningful swept through him as if he had swallowed a burning coal. For if this city stood at the center of man's highest achievements and greatest longings, what could he not attain, what could he not hold as his own, should he desire it? The nature of Conor Finnegan, he knew, ran stronger, sharper, quicker, brighter than any he had seen around him here. If these shapeless forms rushing past him might, in their own fashion, partake of the contentment of accomplishment, if they could make their way in this most turbulent of places, then what flaming glories, what profound mysteries, might he not in his day achieve?

The six young men walked down Lexington through the upper forties. They were headed for 55th Street. Lanny O'Hanlon, smooth and very self-assured, took the lead. He walked with a quick, businesslike pace, paying little heed to the streets around him. O'Hanlon possessed a callous urbanity that his friends so far lacked. Perhaps it stemmed from a youth spent outside Boston, another vibrant, congested Eastern city, or perhaps it was from his frequent forays into the city when he was in prep school in central Massachusetts. Perhaps it was all a façade. Keeping O'Hanlon's pace, the group arrived at the restaurant in seemingly a few short minutes, although the walk had taken more than half an hour. The evening had been brisk enough so that the walk had not tired them. Only Dan Rosselli, slightly overweight, was breathing the least bit hard.

The maitre d' approached them. The restaurant itself was darkly lit, all wood and mock leather." We'd like a table in a far corner," said O'Hanlon. "We may tend to be a bit boisterous tonight."

"Certainly, sir. Wait right here and I'll see what's available." Their host spoke with a slight undefined accent. He had obviously seen groups like this before and knew what to expect.

"Phony accent," said O'Hanlon as he turned back to his charges. "Probably lives in the Bronx and takes the Yellow 7 line. A man of the city, that one."

The maitre d' rematerialized quickly. His black suit blended into the restaurant's motif. Even his complexion seemed dark—Hispanic, or perhaps Middle Eastern. He smiled a patterned smile, smooth and well-practiced.

"Right this way, gentlemen," and they were seated in the most remote corner of the building, three strides from the kitchen door. They sat three on either side of a booth with high wooden backs that shielded them totally from other diners.

"Nice place, Mick," said Rosselli. "You've been here before?"

"I know it by reputation. Guys at Fairfield used to come in here on weekends and get completely hammered. Without question this is the cheapest drunk in the city, if you're so inclined."

"How's the food?"

"No one could ever remember. Play it safe and order a steak."

"You know any other places we might go after dinner?" asked Reg Coleman.

"Let's take it one step at a time, boys. We may be in no condition to show ourselves in public. Besides, why are you asking me? You guys grew up in Jersey, God help you. Except for the two wandering Golden Boys here. They wouldn't know New York City from fuckin' Malibu. But the rest of you should have spent more time in this jungle than I ever did."

"Never got in here much," said Rosselli. "Anyway, Mick, you're twenty years older than the rest of us. You could run through a waterfall without getting wet. We'll defer to your judgment."

"I judge we stay here and drink our asses off. We'll worry about what comes next later."

Drink they did. They ordered dinner, each requesting a steak of some sort. With a basket of bread came their first pitcher of beer. They drank it quickly and ignored the bread. When the waiter returned with their salads he brought the second pitcher. The race was on.

Finnegan became conscious of the rich, pungent smell of the place. Although one thick blanketing aroma hung over them all, Finnegan could pick out individual odors, and they pleased him. He could smell, of course, the deep juices of the meat before him, and the bitter tangy air of the beer. He caught scent of his own cologne. Vaguely he could smell the cologne of his roommate who sat next to him. The six of them, jammed into that close space, created the healthy, acrid odor of perspiration. The leather itself on which they sat emitted the rugged gruffness of old rooms. It was a man's world in which they sat and dined and drank tonight; there could be no mistaking it. Every smell that penetrated Finnegan's nostrils confirmed the uniquely masculine nature of this night. In it he felt quietly strong, a champion at rest taking his pleasure, surrounded by his new friends whose growing bonds of loyalty were becoming apparent. It was, above all else, a sense of belonging.

As the empty pitchers of beer accumulated, the conversation became more animated. "The problem with Rutgers," Lanny O'Hanlon was holding forth, "Jesus, did I say 'problem'? Let me modify that. *One* of the problems with Rutgers is that nobody gives a damn what you do there. You've got administrators who don't give a rap what you're up to as long as you don't break anything and your bills are paid, counselors who don't even know your name, who counsel by reading a list of courses and say 'You decide', and worst of all you've got professors who stand up in front of a class of 500 kids and say 'I'm gonna come in here three times a week and teach, and I don't give a damn if you learn anything or not.' To them we're all the same. They lump us all together, everybody. Can you imagine what we're going to be like after four years of this? We won't even know who the hell we are. We might not even know our own names."

"Ah, Christ, Lanny, you're exaggerating," countered Rick Murdoch, unusually assertive. "You were a hot-shot in prep school and you expect college to be the same. You expect the world to eat out of Lanny O'Hanlon's fine young hand. It doesn't work that way. We're in a class of 1,600, all types and varieties, but all of them damn good or they wouldn't be here. You've got to earn your distinction all over again."

"That's not what I'm talking about," responded O'Hanlon. "I'm not talking about being a frickin' all-star. I'm talking about having any identity whatsoever. We're in a class of 1,600 all right, but I don't think it's too many for a supposedly major college to handle on a more personal level."

"What do you want, Mick? A housemother to tuck you in at night?"

"No, you moron, and there's no point in exaggerating. But you know how they had my schedule screwed up so badly at the beginning of the year? They had me enrolled in eight courses, for Christ's sake, including Discrete Mathematical Structures. There's a guy who's a junior now named Larry Hanlon and they gave me four of his courses, just for laughs. I can imagine how confused that poor guy must have been when they had him signed up for Freshman Composition and

French 101. Anyway, it took me three weeks to get that cleared up. The idiots in the Registrar's Office couldn't get it straight. They kept telling me that I had no business taking freshman-level courses and I could only drop them with the professor's permission, and I needed their signatures in triplicate. Three weeks it took for them to convince themselves that I am only a humble freshman. And then this past week I get a note in my mailbox telling me I got a B-plus on my Engineering Physics hourly exam. They're getting confused again, and I know it's going to continue until Larry Hanlon graduates or Lanny O'Hanlon throws himself in front of a bus."

"Don't you see, roomie, that's just the challenge," said Finnegan excitedly. He put his hand on his roommate's shoulder. O'Hanlon looked down at it in surprise, regarding it as if it were a dead fish. "All along there's going to be snares and pitfalls and foul-ups and confusions. That's the nature of this place. Hell, that's the nature of every place. But you'll find a way to get by it all. We've been thrown together with hundreds of other people who are just as talented as we are, and it's clear that we're not going to be getting much help. It's up to us to do everything we have to do to make it work. We've got to make our own friends, take our own tests, fight our own battles with the registrar, everything. That's a pretty radical change, but we'll come out okay. It's not just Rutgers, roomie. It's like that everywhere, and we're always going to have to face it."

"Tell me something, you two guys," responded O'Hanlon, pointing at Finnegan and McIlweath. "You came clear across country to go through this nonsense. Do you honestly think you made the right decision?"

"Absolutely" and "No doubt" were their replies.

"Why?"

"Just what Conor said, Lanny. We're on our own here. We've got a chance to redefine ourselves, and that appeals to me a great deal. No preconceptions. We do it all for ourselves, and make ourselves what we want to be."

"Couldn't you have done that a little closer to home?" asked Reg Coleman. "I mean, *New Jersey,* for Christ's sake."

"Yeah, we could have," answered Finnegan. "But I think we wanted to commit to something without being able to back out. No safety net, so let's see what you really can do. I can't speak for Mac, but I think that was one of my main reasons. To see if I could do well outside my comfort zone."

"Yeah," said McIlweath. "Once I committed myself to going away I wanted to go as far away as possible. It added a dimension to what I was trying to do. It made it irreversible, at least over the short term, and all the more important that I do well."

"Besides," added Finnegan, "I wanted to see what East Coast girls were like."

They continued to drink, vast amounts. The six of them finished their dinners quickly, each much hungrier than he had at first perceived. The drinking and the camaraderie sharpened their appetites. They ate the bread, asked for another basket, then another. And always the pitchers of beer kept coming. Finnegan, for all he had done with his young life, had never been drunk before, and he found that he liked the taste of beer. The simple act of drinking bonded him to his companions, made him a part of a heady brotherhood, and he saw his new friends as the brightest, bravest, finest men he could possibly know. Only Tom McIlweath, sensing the weakening limbs and slowing reactions of the other five, held back. Someone would have to drive back to campus that night. Someone would have to remain sober.

Their conversations wove and spun random patterns, increasingly wider, dipping one way, darting another, never holding course long enough to have much meaning. Their voices grew louder, their gestures more animated.

For Finnegan, the room started to shorten. All images beyond the booth in which he sat became blurred, then got lost altogether. He no longer noticed the servers hustling in and out of the kitchen or the diners at the tables standing free in the room's middle. He no longer noticed them because they ceased to exist, their forms obliterated as his vision lost periphery. His world continued to contract; soon the outlines and features of his friends blurred, too. The sharp lines of their warm, active faces became fuzzy. The room itself, now that its walls had closed to just outside their booth, began to spin, very slowly at first, but as the evening drew on more and more rapidly.

"Lissen," slurred Dan Rosselli. "We're all Rutgers men, an' we godda sing a song. We godda sing the alma mater, right? 'On the Banks,' right? We godda sing the damn thing."

"Yeah," said Finnegan. "Danny's right, we got to sing. Even you, roomie, even though you hate the goddamn place. Sing or I'll kick your Boston ass."

"If you animals want to disgrace yourselves, who am I not to join in? Besides, it's one of the best drinking songs I've ever heard."

And they sang, softly at first, reverently, in slightly more than a whisper.

> *My father sent me to old Rutgers*
> *And resolved that I should be a man,*
> *And so I settled down*

In the noisy college town
On the banks of the Old Raritan.

They grew louder throughout the verse. By the start of the final lines, their voices were full throated, slurring no more. They sang a statement of youth's power, their pride in being strong and whole, and, for a few moments, free and released. The crescendo rose.

So sing aloud to Alma Mater
And keep the scarlet in the van.
For with her motto high
Rutgers' name shall never die
On the banks of the Old Raritan.

On the banks of the Old Raritan, my boys,
Where old Rutgers evermore shall stand,
For has she not stood
Since the time of the flood
On the banks of the Old Raritan.

As they repeated the last chorus the crescendo had swept them away. They sang now, not of their own accord, but of a joined spirit that stood them together, and, in so doing, stood them apart. They sang with the voices of love, of glory and, ultimately, of destiny. They sang not for themselves, but for each other and for the school that had stitched them together, wary and alone, to draw from one another. They *had* identities, Lanny O'Hanlon to the contrary, each growing more precise by the minute yet none different in substance than that which had led every young man to stand erect ever since he discovered he could stand at all. They sang with the growing confidence that they had each, at last, stepped outside the thin shell of childhood and were now running down the singular pathway that, in the end, would take each of them to their disparate fates.

When they finished, the group in the booth behind them cheered.

During the final verse the maitre d' had approached the table, the same plastic smile set on his face. He stood at the corner of the booth while the group sang. His smile did not change even as the song rose in spirit and volume. He continued to stand there, smiling, as the singers ended their song and joyously reached across the table to shake each other's hands, proudly, warmly, laughing buoyantly. They had ignored him. No one noticed him there, but he did not seem to mind. He had seen all this many times before.

"Gentlemen," at last he said in his sharp little accent. The six looked at him, wide-eyed and a bit surprised. "You must keep your voices down. Sing, yes, but quietly, please. We have other guests."

"Oh, yeah, sure. We're sorry," replied Finnegan, genuinely contrite. "We musta got carried away. No hard feelings, okay?" He rose and shook the maitre d's hand.

"None, sir. Continue to enjoy your evening."

"The guys in the other booth liked it," O'Hanlon called after him as he walked away.

"Mus' be a Princeton grad," mumbled Murdoch. "Shows what an Ivy League degree'll do for ya. He could be a waiter in any restaurant in the city. Degree like that opens doors."

Finnegan felt warm, at first in his extremities then creeping centrally along his arms and legs to some undefined destination in his interior. His limbs became elastic. As a result, his beer mug had become quite heavy. He lifted it carefully with both hands, not so much to avoid spilling as to avoid dropping it altogether. For a long while he said nothing. The room itself, close now around them, began to rotate. In a few minutes it was spinning faster, its colors, dim to begin with, blended increasingly together. The faces of his friends, too, grew fuzzier and fuzzier. Across from him McIlweath's head moved onto Reg Coleman's body, then hopped to Rick Murdoch's, whose own head hovered in midair across the table. McIlweath, before Finnegan's very eyes, grew another nose.

From time to time, each of the six had to make his way to the restroom. As the evening passed the trips grew more frequent. For Finnegan they also grew more difficult. By his fourth or fifth trip he had memorized the route, fortunately, for he could no longer see well enough through the dim light to breach new territory. On his seventh trip he knocked against a table on his left, jostling the diners there and spilling a bit of their beer. He did not think to apologize. His mind, able now to absorb only one task at a time, was programmed to move his body to a place for urination. If he had stopped to apologize, he might well have relieved himself right there in a water glass. To compensate for his error, on the next trip Finnegan stayed to the extreme right. He lurched too far and his shoulder slammed into a wall. The wall provided stability. He kept his right side pressed against it all the way to the rest room.

The evening continued, and, despite their stupor, the six kept calling for more beer. The servers took only slight notice, for this was not uncommon. The place's management was currently reevaluating its all-you-can-drink policy. Although it had attracted some reputable customers, the youth of America was making it more costly than they had anticipated. The servers, though, could only continue to do their jobs.

Finnegan knew that conversation at the table was continuous, and he knew that he was taking part in it. But he could not remember what they were talking about from one moment to the next. Once a topic passed on, it was gone forever, vanished into an obliterated past. Nor could he distinguish his own comments from those of his friends. There were voices, six of them, all whirling together. His own sounded foreign to him, coming from outside his head. He knew that they all were talking as rapidly as their benumbed lips permitted. Finnegan offered opinions and anecdotes, that much he knew, riding the full crest of conversation merely for the present joy of being part of it. Yet he did not know what he was saying. His mind was in no condition to formulate precise or logical thoughts. As did all the others, he spurted out reactions, interrupted boisterously, responded immediately when the soft, bulbous fetus of an idea, hatched from their collective efforts at profundity, made its way into his liquefied consciousness.

All real sense of time had, of course, been distorted. They might have been at the table an hour, or three, or six. No one bothered to look. Again, it did not matter. And still they drank, yielding to the occasion, enormous amounts passing down their gullets. The beer started to taste tinny. The carbonation mixed resentfully, belligerently now with their stomach acids and echoed back to their mouths. Somewhere in the evening the beer had lost its smooth good humor. It had even lost its measure as a means to an end, for that end had long ago been passed. It was now just a process, a habit before them in glass and gold. They drank mindlessly, and as automatically they urinated it away.

Finnegan all of a sudden felt exhausted. He could no longer keep his head erect. For a while he tried, but it dipped and bobbed from side to side, adding to the dim, blurring whirl of the room. He told himself to rest, just for a bit. Finnegan leaned his head into Lanny O'Hanlon's shoulder and closed his eyes.

He woke when O'Hanlon stood to go to the rest room and Finnegan crumbled to the bench where his roommate had been seated. Pulling himself up, Finnegan assured his concerned friends that he had not been hurt. They believed him.

When O'Hanlon returned, they agreed at last that it was time to head back through the streets, to the car, and back to campus. They called for the bill. Being the only one of reasonably sound mind, Tom McIlweath calculated it into six parts and exacted from each of them the right amount, or so they trusted. Later he would tell them that they had consumer thirty-seven pitchers of beer.

Finnegan rose with the greatest effort. His muscles, reluctant before, had become rebellious. The same command for movement had to be issued three or four times, very deliberately, before his body would respond. He found it impossible to focus on anything. Since opening his eyes after his brief nap he could find nothing solid. Nothing stood still. He felt as if he were looking into a kaleidoscope, or, worse, that he himself were trapped inside the tube, turning and tumbling with the colors around him.

As he moved to the doorway, his stomach forced the crisis. Finnegan was too weak to fight it. By the maitre d's stand next to the entryway, he doubled over and vomited. Some of the debris splashed up on Dan Rosselli's trousers. Rosselli, oblivious, kept on walking. Late diners stopped in mid-bite. Those with food already in their mouths screwed up their courage and swallowed hard.

Finnegan did not pause for a second. He kept going, as quickly as his insensible legs would move him, out the door and into the light of the street. Behind him he would hear Reg Coleman, who, by virtue of a late restroom trip, was the last to leave, speaking with the maitre d', whose voice, as ever, remained unruffled.

"Hey, waiter," said Coleman quite loudly, "Lookathis. Somebody puked in your lobby, for Chris' sake. Iss a goddamn stinky mess."

"I know, sir. We will clean it up, But it *was* one of your friends."

"Naw, my friends wuddin' do this. Naw." Coleman left the restaurant shaking his head and continuing to protest, mostly to himself, that his friends were too good a group to vomit in a restaurant entryway.

But when he emerged he was greeted by the sight of Finnegan, one hand in his pocket and one hand bracing himself against the side of the building, head lowered prayerlike, regurgitating the last contents of his stomach onto the sidewalk. Coleman began jumping up and down, pointing and yelling.

"Yeah, yeah," he screamed. "God damn, Conor. It *was* you. Conor, way to go, pal."

"Leave'm alone," snapped O'Hanlon. "This is good for him. He needed this."

For Finnegan's part, retaining some shred of dignity became essential. He had to counter the impact of what he had just done. Consequently, as he completed his vomiting on the sidewalk, he had tucked one hand into his pocket in a gesture designed to affect a casual air while he scrupulously tried to stand as erect as possible with his other hand propping him up against the wall. He vomited into one spot between the tips of his loafers.

The walk through the streets of New York back to the Port Authority Terminal helped clear all their heads. Although the hour was late, the streets were by no means dead. Within two blocks of the restaurant, two prostitutes spoke to them from the doorway of a tavern. They wafted out, white and glittery, make-up and black stockings providing their masks.

"Hey fellas, you lookin' for some fun? We're real fun. We're fun enough for all of you."

Finnegan, McIlweath and Rosselli slowed down to look at this. O'Hanlon, still leading the way, charged ahead with Murdoch and Coleman at his shoulders.

"Not tonight, ladies," replied O'Hanlon without breaking stride. "Maybe some other night when we're sober."

"Your three friends seem interested." One woman walked out of the shadows to slip her arm around Rosselli's and Finnegan's shoulders. Finnegan looked at her closely, unable to move.

She was not unattractive by any means. Finnegan looked into her face, seemingly level with his, although she must have been several inches shorter. She had a small face, tapering down to a point of a chin. Her eyes were clouded by blue shadow and heavy mascara, but Finnegan could see that they were green, a haunting, remote color. Her thin lips broke into a mischievous smile over teeth that were still white. The girl's hair was a strawberry blond, parted in the middle and hanging freely to slightly below her shoulders. She had curled it subtly so that gentle waves ran its length. To Finnegan she did not seem cheap. She did not fit the image. She looked fresh, not worn or jaded, and she smelled wonderful. She smelled like orchids. Finnegan felt himself becoming aroused.

"What do you say, lover?" she cooed. "The three of us could have a real good time." Finnegan smiled at her shyly, and she leaned over to kiss his cheek.

O'Hanlon, noting that he had lost half his squad, stopped at once and looked back. He turned and walked briskly to Finnegan and Rosselli, then grabbed their elbows.

"Come on, you idiots. Don't waste your time." He tugged them away forcefully. "Sorry, sweetheart. We come as a group or we don't come at all."

"Your loss, fellas. See you soon."

"We weren't going to do anything, Mick," said Rosselli as he was led away. "We just wanted to see what they were like. Seemed like a nice enough girl."

"Jesus Christ on a pogo stick, Dan, she wasn't interested in making friends. She's a working girl. Jesus, you probably caught some kind of disease just talking to her. What am I going to do with you guys?"

"Just love us, Lanny."

On they marched. The lateness of the hour made restrooms impossible to find. Even though the walk back took no more than forty-five minutes, relief became necessary twice, with some urgency. On the first occasion they ducked down a subway station. Finding no restrooms, they started to go back up the steps when Rosselli spotted a bank of old-style wooden phone booths. He went into one, picked up the receiver and cradled it to his ear. In a few seconds a stream trickled out from under the door. The other five got the idea and made similar calls.

The second occasion struck without a subway station nearby. Rosselli again provided the answer. "Boys, gather round me," he said as he walked up to the corner of the MetLife Building. They did so, shoulder to shoulder. Rosselli, protected against whatever scrutiny there might be at that hour, relieved himself against that great black tombstone. When he was done, the others took their turns. Even years later, Finnegan could not look at the MetLife Building without wondering if there might be an indelible stain on its 45th Street corner.

He remembered nothing of the drive back to campus save that McIlweath, thankfully, was behind the wheel. Finnegan put his head against Dan Rosselli's arm, outstretched along the back of the seat, and slept. As he did, the city disappeared behind him. For now, Conor Finnegan's hunger had been sated. Or rather, it had been numbed into a quiet state of suspended energy.

* * *

Two weeks later it rained. It had rained occasionally in the intervening days, too, but the rain then had not pierced the skin and crawled into the marrow, spreading there as a sickening damp chill peculiar to November. The wind rose from the east, sweeping across the Atlantic headlands into the towns, villages and suburbs of central New Jersey, blowing the rain horizontally in gusts like so many tiny needles. The welcoming greens of summer and early autumn faded in the growing blear of shorter days until there was no green at all, only browns and grays, covered in the rain by a nighttime blackness so thick as to be suffocating—the bottomless black of a nature gone comatose, consigned to a long and bitter sleep. The only light was what man provided: streaky windows, the coming-coming-gone blare of headlights on roadways, the loneliness of streetlamps. When it rained as hard as this, the only sound the conscious mind absorbed was the staccato pattern, a crescendo as the showers intensified, of rain on pavement, on rooftops, on flesh. Everything else muffled and dimmed until it ceased to exist altogether. On a night such as this, the rain is all.

Finnegan had neither raincoat nor umbrella. He walked along George Street toward his dormitory, soaked to the skin. Upon leaving Van Ness Hall, he had started to sprint through the rain in hope of getting to his room before he got too wet. Within his first few strides, though, he knew it to be futile: the rain was too hard, the dormitory too far away. He would get wet, perhaps wetter than he had ever been before in his life. He slowed at once to a walk.

Cars along George Street sped by at their usual pace. It had rained sporadically during the day, but as daylight ended the clouds had split apart. During early evening it rained continually, and very hard. The gutters had filled. Standing water spread from curbside into the street. As cars drove by they sent up arcing walls of water toward the sidewalk, splashing those who walked too close to the curb. Finnegan was splashed once, and cursed aloud in response. But there was no point to it. He moved to the extreme inside of the sidewalk, but the great fins of water churned by the traffic still reached him. He gave up trying; on this night, he would remain wet. Let both nature and man soak him down.

Finnegan had had a late class, the last class period of the day, beginning at 5:00 and ending at 6:15. Class at that hour became more than just a learning experience: it took on dimensions of punishment. By the time he got out of class his friends would be at dinner. Some would, in fact, already have finished their meal and be returning to the dorm. On these nights he went to the massive dining hall, invariably seeing no one he knew, and ate alone. It was late autumn now, and well dark when he emerged from the old classroom building. Queen's Mall would be deserted except for the scattered other students heading back to their own rooms. Few people willingly took courses in this time slot. Not even the graduate students were around. The emptiness of Queen's Mall in early evening contrasted with its boisterous quality during the day and intensified Finnegan's loneliness. On rainy nights such as this, the atmosphere smothered him. The timelessness of the old buildings no longer seemed stately. Instead they were barren, devoid of any human presence, mausoleums preserving stale, fetid air.

Into the dark, wet, cold, impersonal night Finnegan stepped out from the high-ceilinged echoes of Van Ness. This late class was his economics course. Finnegan did not like economics. The countless graphs and curves confused him. He considered them divorced from real human reactions and so could put together causes and effects only with the greatest difficulty. He would spend hours trying to relate the Law of Diminishing Returns with shifting interest rates. Finnegan did not react well to things outside his immediate grasp. He resented them deeply, taking their evasiveness as a personal insult. In his room at night he would rail against economics, complaining to O'Hanlon that too much was expected of him, that the textbook was not clear, that the instructor, with his thick German accent, was purposefully vague. He would approach assignments with a physical dread, his stomach tightening, his palms clammy, his head throbbing as he pondered what it was he had to do. He would wrestle with his assignments as Jacob wrestled with his angel. Desperately, wringingly, he would try to squeeze every drop of comprehension from his text before finally, weakened and sweaty, he would put it aside in wavering belief that he had learned all he had to know. Finnegan hated economics, but he had heretofore done fairly well at it, thanks to this tenacity. It had always been a matter of pride.

Lately, though, the concepts had grown even more elusive, the problems more esoteric. The early semester war of understanding had taken its toll. Over the past two weeks, Finnegan had put his books aside without even the unconvincing rationalizations he had previously employed. Rather, he quit because he had had enough. He would leave it up to his rudimentary understanding and native quickness to do well.

As a result, on this coldest and wettest of nights, Finnegan trod back to his dormitory with his economics midterm, graded only slightly better than a complete failure, in his notebook. He had had no idea when he took the damnable test that he would do so poorly. He had not been prepared for the stark letter that leapt to his eyes in exclusion of everything else on the front page. When the graded test was returned, handed to him by a disinterested teaching assistant, he blushed deeply.

Finnegan walked up the sidewalk that rose the slope to his building. Lights burned in a few of the windows, but Finnegan noticed at once that only two or three were lit on the second floor, and none in familiar rooms. No one was in the lobby, no one in the elevator, and, as the doors opened on his floor, no one in the lounge or down either hallway. Finnegan, still dripping, went to his room, unlocked the deadbolt and flicked on the light.

Finnegan's room overlooked the Raritan River, a grayish brown ribbon of sludge that moved slowly from left to right. Across the river spread Johnson Park, a sprawling expanse of green. In front of it, riverside, ran River Road. Slightly to the right, through a break in the trees, a horse track was usually visible, its white railings set off from the surrounding green. The track was a small one with no bleachers. On Saturdays and Sundays owners would take their horses to the park to work them leisurely around the track. Beyond the park, the tops of the large, stately homes of that section of Piscataway stood above the trees.

In the far distance smokestacks, usually belching off-white, created an odd contrast with the well-ordered foreground. On clear nights the spire of the Empire State Building, surrounded by New York's lesser towers, would shine like a beacon, an urban lighthouse, signifying the boundless power, energy and glamor of the city. Finnegan found the view from his window calming. He could look out on a part of the world he did not yet know, one well divorced from the pace and drive of his studies, his friends, his life in general.

This night, though, the view was not a view, but a smear. All he could make out was the river. Beyond it hung a liquid blackness punctuated only occasionally by a light from one of the cars making its way on River Road, passing in and out behind windswept trees, now visible, now gone, sparse, erratic and dull. Nonetheless Finnegan leaned forward on the ledge, looking out. He stayed that way for a long while. He did not let himself be disturbed by the elevator, the voices, the slamming doors of people returning from dinner. Finnegan held his pose, staring into a black, wet nothing.

Finnegan let himself feel nothing, no wetness, no cold, save the creeping desolation of hopes grown timid. 'Perhaps I've been fooling myself,' he thought.

Transfixed, he stared into the womblike void. Staring ahead he was, yet staring behind him, too, his eyes trying to penetrate a depth that had no depth, searching for a core that did not exist except in his fertile imagination. His thoughts repeated themselves without expansion, the same words racing around his mind until they became a litany. The blackness, the echoing words—they numbed him. There, in the dim light, looking outward, looking inward, Finnegan stood suspended, stunned by a reality that, for the first time in his life, had no soft edges.

Lanny O'Hanlon broke Conor's trance when he opened the door quickly, as he always did. There was nothing subtle or halfway about Finnegan's roommate.

"What do you say, roomie? What're you looking at?"

"It's raining," answered Finnegan slowly, "and it's black out there."

"No shit. You eat yet?"

"No. I'm not real hungry. Maybe the sandwich man'll come by later."

"I don't know, Slick. He went through last night. He usually doesn't hit two nights in a row."

"No big deal. I'll get some candy from the machines or something. The food in this place will kill you anyway." Finnegan had at last turned away from the window. He frowned unconsciously as if disturbed by O'Hanlon's intrusion.

"How'd your class go? Economics, right? The one you hate."

"Shitty, friend. Purely shitty. A 'D' on the midterm."

O'Hanlon had taken off his raincoat, hung it on the back of the door and sat at his desk. He leaned back now, right foot propped on the desk's edge. "Jesus, Conor. That's not like you. I must be corrupting you, I'm afraid. McIlweath says I am. Leading you down the path of sin and perdition, as any good friend would."

"It's not you doing it, Dice. It's me. I've never gotten so low a grade before. On anything, let alone a midterm."

"You'll live. At least you didn't fail. Nobody up here is what you'd call a genius, pal. We're not supposed to be. Not yet. Some of us never want to be. Too much pressure, no room to screw up. I'll pass on the privilege. Trust me, you'll have more fun being ordinary."

"I don't want to be ordinary, Lanny. That's not why I came here."

"Christ, roomie, loosen up. Be thankful you're doing as well as you are. Look at Reg Coleman. At last count he was failing four out of five. Only French is keeping him from a perfect record, and he had three years of that in high school. Reg doesn't let it bother him."

"How can you tell? Maybe it's eating him up inside, you don't know. Reg isn't the world's most talkative guy. "

"No, Reg doesn't give a damn. And neither should you. Reg's like the rest of us. He knows he'll come out all right in the end."

"I'm not so sure, Lanny. I mean about me. It's such a goddamned struggle sometimes. I didn't expect it, that's all. I'm not convinced I'm as ready for it as I thought I was."

"Get used to it, friend, because it's not going to get any easier. How could it? We've had the world by the balls ever since we were weaned. The only way to keep it easy is if we don't expect too much. That's the only way. Otherwise we're going to find ourselves on the short end at one point or another. It's inevitable. Don't let one lousy grade get you down, for Christ's sake. Everybody slips up. You're not perfect, roommate, I hate to tell you. Today it might be your economics midterm, five years from now you might get fired, ten years from now you might get divorced. That doesn't make you a failure."

"Yeah, but goddamn it, Lanny, that's not what bothers me. I didn't do well on the midterm, sure, but why didn't I? I worked as hard as I could have for this. That kind of leads to doubts, you know? That maybe I'm not smart enough, or quick enough . . . or just good enough."

"Jesus God Almighty, Conor, don't give me that shit. You're as smart as anyone around here. Besides, what the hell difference does that make? What do you want out of this place? Ask yourself that. It seems to me that the only goal should be coming out of here better than when you came in. I'll tell you one thing right now—you're better off for getting that low grade. If you thought you'd sail through a school like this without a hitch, then you're much better off. You're no superman, pal. This could be the best thing in the world for you. It might give you a kick in the ass, or it might even lower your expectations, and that couldn't hurt. I'm sorry, Conor, but I've got no sympathy for this particular line of self-pity. I'd much rather reserve it for the sad fact that you've had almost no contact with anything feminine since you've been here. The rest of it just doesn't matter as much as you think it does."

Finnegan moved from the window ledge and sat down at his desk as O'Hanlon spoke. He responded, again speaking slowly. "I don't know, Lanny. It seems to matter. To me, that is. I want it to matter."

"Then you're only punishing yourself, Conor. No need to do that, but it's up to you. You going to study here tonight?"

"Yeah," Finnegan sighed. "I don't want to go out again into that slop." Finnegan knew full well that if he stayed in the room he would study very little. Their room was one of the floor's most popular, and people would be stopping in all evening. The thought didn't particularly bother him.

"Roomie," said Finnegan after a few minutes of thumbing through *On the Road*, assigned for completion the following week. "On second thought, I don't feel like doing anything tonight. What do you say we go see who's around?"

* * *

The rain fell throughout the night. After a while the wind died down so that the drops no longer whipped diagonally to sting whatever they met. The rain, like the wind, grew calmer. It fell straight down through the blackness without urgency. Hard, steady, unrushed, it would fall forever, or so it seemed. The wet, cold night would go on forever, as black and dark as death.

November in New Jersey, and the best of the year had been wrung out. What remained was only the musty, clammy underside prior to year's end, prior to the inevitable demise.

Down the hall that same night, Tom McIlweath wrestled with a calculus assignment. McIlweath of late had become self-disciplined to the point of regimentation. His days carried a regularity which strengthened him. He could compartmentalize his thoughts and program his reactions for the standard blocks of time allotted to each. Swimming had had no small role in this, for it ate up three hours daily. McIlweath realized that, if he wanted to swim, he would have to eliminate the fat from his day. And so Tom McIlweath prohibited himself from wasting time. His days swung past in tidy blocks: classes, meals, study, swim, study, sleep. On weekends he studied less and allowed himself some play. Weekdays, though, were confined to the tasks at hand.

He had expected that such an approach would be burdensome. When he arrived at college his ambitions were rather simple: to do well academically, to swim competitively, to make new friends, to carve a new self-image. Concentrating on these basic ends would cleanse him. Like all gestures of this sort, it would probably be somewhat harsh, or so he thought. The end result, a new Tom McIlweath, wiser, more assertive, truer and less encumbered, would be worth the effort.

But McIlweath made the mistake of focusing solely on the mechanics of the process while ignoring the substance. He soon found that the various pieces of his life fit together wonderfully to create not a brutal regimen of self-denial but an exciting panorama of intellectual, physical and emotional gratification. McIlweath grew more content by the day as he immersed himself into this new life.

His studies stimulated him constantly. The intricacies of calculus fascinated him, as did the give-and-take of economics. English literature and political science lifted veils from the full range of human experience. And Latin . . . ah, sweet Latin, aroused a monumental timelessness and a supposition he wished to explore, that man may have progressed materially over two thousand years but his best, purest, and truest means of expression were well behind him. McIlweath's studies became deeply personal. He delved into areas of humanity he had never recognized before. The resultant invigoration was as profound as anything he had ever experienced.

Swimming provided a pause from this. In the pool he existed purely as a physical being, and so revived his mind by letting it dangle. He felt his body grow leaner and stronger. He swam well, better than he had anticipated and better than most of his teammates.

McIlweath found, too, that he made friends easily. His naturally quiet manner did not drive people away or give them an excuse to ignore him. In the dormitory he had been tossed in with hundreds of young men of diverse character and personality. On his floor alone there were fifty-five other residents, and he had come to know them all. Everyone approached each other predisposed to friendship. It was easier that way, since they were all in this together, sharing space and sharing experience. Part of it, too, was based on the assumption that everyone, simply by being here, had something to offer. Tom McIlweath relished it all. It did not matter that he still saw himself as quiet and skinny, with thick glasses. He was well accepted here. People took the time to know him, and he reveled in the community of it all.

And so, that Tom McIlweath should be at his desk late on a rainy November night, grappling with differential equations, should have surprised no one who knew him. It was merely a part of the routine, one which imbued his life with a cherished richness. There was nothing else he could do, nor would he have chosen to do otherwise.

McIlweath's roommate had not yet returned from the library when Reg Coleman knocked on the door and sheepishly opened it before McIlweath could answer. Coleman saw that Rick Murdoch was still out. His timing had been good. Unlike Dan Rosselli, Coleman's own roommate, McIlweath possessed a sincerity of purpose that Coleman found attractive and comforting. McIlweath blended friendship with detachment. If Coleman felt restless and wanted to talk, he could do so, then retreat to his room afterward. The opportunity for a cooling-off period, that was it. That, plus McIlweath's quiet empathy, tacit though obvious.

"Hey, Mac. What're you up to?"

"Calculus, Reg. But I can tell it's time for a break." McIlweath rose from his chair and plugged in the small hotpot that sat on a shelf above his bed. "Some tea? I don't have any coffee."

"Yeah. I probably won't sleep too much tonight anyhow. What kind do you have?"

"Nothing caffeinated, so no worries there. I picked up some herbal tea at the health food store downtown," said McIlweath, tossing him the box. "It's not bad stuff." Coleman caught the box, looked it over once and placed it on top of McIlweath's dresser. He sat down on Murdoch's bed, steel-framed and low to the ground like all the others, leaned back against the wall and let his feet dangle from the narrow width.

"Where's Rick?"

"Library. He'll be there until it closes, then he'll come back and sleep through his morning class. Happens every week." McIlweath switched on the radio near his bed, went back to his desk and turned his chair around to face Coleman. He propped one leg over an arm of the chair.

"How's he doing?" asked Coleman. "Academically, I mean."

"Not bad, not good. He's passing everything, or so he says."

"That's more than you can say for me."

"Hang in there. It'll come sooner or later."

"Right. You know, Mac, I've never gotten the good marks. I mean really good marks. I think the only reason I got in here was because my father graduated from the place. Played football, joined a frat. A real big man. They probably felt the least they could do was accept his all-too-mediocre son." McIlweath noticed Coleman's eyes as the other spoke—darker, slightly sunken and flat—and felt uneasy.

"Relax, Reg. You'll be okay in time."

Coleman snorted. "Yeah. Sure I will. Can you imagine how dear old Dad would react if his oldest son flunked out of the school he had whipped through? You know, he sends this place five thousand dollars every year. He's one of the school's biggest annual donors. He's got one room, his den, loaded with old pictures and pennants, football trophies, yearbooks. He's got a rocking chair in there with the college seal on it. Cost him a fortune, and it's really a piece of rickety crap, but he didn't bat an eye when he ordered it. He loves this place, more than me, and ever since I was a little kid he's been telling me how I was going to go here and how great I was going to be. Yeah, I'd say there's a little pressure associated with all that."

The water in the hotpot boiled. McIlweath unplugged it and pulled two mugs from behind the books on his shelf. He dropped a teabag into each. Steam rose as he poured the water. "Sounds as if he's reliving his youth through you. Not a good formula."

"No doubt. He's come up this year for every football game. He wants me to get him season tickets for basketball, too. He wants to sit in the student section."

"Does he know you're having some troubles?"

" 'Some troubles'," Coleman snorted again. "Mac, for God's sake, I'm failing four courses. That's more than a few troubles, wouldn't you say? That's a total academic breakdown. How can I tell him that? He'd go crazy on me. He'd probably throw me through a window."

McIlweath pulled the teabags out of the mugs and tamped them on a spoon to drain, letting the last drop of each fall into its mug. When he was done he pitched the bags into a wastebasket and handed Coleman his tea. McIlweath sat down again at his desk.

"Reg, regardless of his motivation it's unfair to put those expectations on you. And really, it's unfair of you to accept them. Your problems might be a little self-imposed. You've got to do what you can and what you want to do. It's just my opinion, but maybe you'd do well to take your father less seriously than he takes himself. Let me ask you something: Do you really want to be here?"

"Yeah, I guess so. It's something I have to do. If I ever want to get a job or earn any real money, I've got to go to college, right? That's what they tell me."

"But you could go someplace else."

"Dad wouldn't pay for it. For him it was Rutgers or out onto the streets."

"Ever think about taking some time off and working? You could earn some money and pay your own way."

"I've thought about it. But how long would it take to get what I needed? And once I get out of school I won't ever want to go back."

"I don't know what to tell you, Reg. You're going to have to draw your own conclusions."

Coleman said nothing, and looked out the dark window. He had not intended to speak of his father, but the topic most likely could not have been avoided in this context. His father hovered over him like smoke. It was his father that was the deep-seated, ineradicable root of his discontent. While his immediate problems revolved around his inadequate response to a new and demanding set of circumstances, he knew too that there were other matters to consider, related but vastly more complex. These he tried to suppress, slamming his interior doors tightly shut as soon as they made the faintest appearance. He carried with him a perception of ugliness he dared not try to articulate. His limited command of the latticework of these complexities haunted his introspection, but he knew that all of this related to his father and the tremendous void his father had created within him, created through emotional distance, through a detached brutality, through incessant demands of activity and thought, through an enforced regularity, through construction of an idealized model he could never hope to match. It was his father at the root of this. His father, and no one else.

"My own conclusions. You're right, of course. You have a talent for being right, Mac, and that's why I'm willing to listen. But did you ever feel totally worthless? Worse than worthless. Did you ever feel as if there was something so wrong with you that you were really pretty hideous, even though no one could see the deformity except you? That all the parts didn't fit together right."

Coleman's face flushed, his brow furrowed, his mouth quivered. He was on the verge of digging deeper into himself than he had ever done in the presence of another, and there was pain in this, something painful beyond comprehension. McIlweath, unnerved, remained outwardly calm. He sipped his tea and looked hard at Reg Coleman's anguished face. If there was something profound here, so be it. He would not try to squelch it.

"I never felt that way, Reg," he answered slowly. "I'm not perfect, but I think I can define my shortcomings. Is that what you're getting at?"

"I can define things too, Mac. And I can tell the difference between a definition and a condemnation, even if I can't do a damn thing about changing the one for the other. That's what I'm talking about."

"You want to tell me your conclusions, Reg?"

"I don't know why I'm talking to you like this at all. I can't tell you any conclusions." Reg Coleman fought his desperation to make himself vulnerable. He perceived in Tom McIlweath a warmth, an honesty, a simplicity, a humanity that inspired trust, that might permit vulnerability even though he did not know him well or long. McIlweath was not as harsh as the others on the floor. Not so cavalier as O'Hanlon, nor as smug as Finnegan, nor as callous as Rosselli, nor as self-absorbed as any of a hundred others. It was not by accident that Reg Coleman sat in this room tonight.

Yet now that he was here, he could not go on. Instinctively, protectively, he fought a mammoth battle to regain the control he had so quickly let slip. He was a thief who no longer felt compelled to steal, who does not need the goods he takes but who continues to do so in the hope of being caught. Tom McIlweath, he hoped, might apprehend him, and, in so doing, might compel the help he so frantically and quietly sought.

But it would not come that way, not tonight and not here. He would steal again. Reg Coleman's control returned, his nerve evaporated. Better to face things alone.

"I can't be doing this," he said slowly.

"Reg, if you want to talk, I'll listen. It'll stay in this room."

Coleman shook his head. "No. Thanks, Mac, but there's no need. It's just that every now and then I feel things ganging up on me, you know?"

"I know. That's why I'm glad I swim. It helps to drown yourself for a couple of hours every day."

"Too bad I don't swim. Dad wouldn't like it anyway. For him there's no sport but football. Anything else is for fairies." Coleman rose off the bed. "Listen, Mac, thanks for your time. I hope I didn't disturb too much of your evening." He put his half-empty mug on the shelf.

"Any time, Reg. But you know you don't have to go. Everybody's got problems."

"None worth wasting your time over. Maybe the rain just brought out my grim side. See you later."

Reg Coleman left the room quickly, as if some evil presence had suddenly appeared to him over McIlweath's shoulder. He did not look back at his friend, still sitting at his desk, still calm, still a bit bewildered. The urgency in Coleman's speech had disappeared although it remained in his movements. He left the room hurriedly, shut the door behind him with a solid thump and went next door to his own room. McIlweath did not hear him through the walls. Whatever

road Coleman had been about to follow, whatever he had been close
to ready to explore, remained within him, walled away again behind
bricks thicker than before.

> *I am no prophet—and here's no great matter;*
> *I have seen the moment of my greatness flicker,*
> *And I have seen the eternal Footman hold my coat*
> *and snicker,*
> *And in short I was afraid.*

CHAPTER VII

*When from a long distant past nothing subsists, after the
people are dead, after the things are broken and scattered,
still, alone, more fragile, but with more vitality, more
unsubstantial, more persistent, more faithful, the smell and
taste of things remain poised for a long time, like souls,
ready to remind us, waiting and hoping for their moment,
and the ruins of all the rest.*

—Marcel Proust, *Remembrace of Things Past*

Perhaps it had been true, in one form or another, that every journey,
every exploration, conjures both wonderment and longing. It is
so easy to stay put, to cultivate the deepest comforts through
familiarity. A desire for security, to feel secure, pulses most basically
through man's veins. It is an urging as old as time and shared by every
living creature who must have his home, his lair, his nest, his den.

And when man in his moments of sharpest consideration realizes
that an adherence to the familiar boundaries of his homeland is
acceptance of the boundaries of his soul, he knows he must find what
to him is unknown. It is an ancient force, primitive, uncontrollable
and irresistible. It is what drove the Phoenicians westward and the
Venetians eastward. It is what sent man to the moon.

Imagine LaSalle first viewing the great falls of the Niagara, the
morning crisp and dewy, quiet save for the thunder of the mysterious
waters. Or Hudson sailing the silent river to view the deep, cliffy

greenery on both sides, steam rising from the flat surface. Or Caesar parting the forests of Gaul and Germania, thick and plush. What oddities the people there must have held for him, there in their rough beards and Teutonic hides. What is it that drove Peary to the crackling void of the frozen North Pole, or Jacques Cartier up the great Canadian river? Whose map did Francisco de Orellana follow up the Amazon, and what guided Pedro Menendez and Jean Nicollet? It has never ceased; it will never cease, and let man be praised for it. We are a restless species.

Yet when at last we give in to our curious urges and at last step outside the familiar into something new, do we not become nostalgic for what we were once so anxious to leave? There, on the banks of the Niagara, after viewing the majesty of the falls, could not LaSalle have thought of the calmer Seine? Wordsworth wrote,

> *I traveled among unknown men,*
> *In lands beyond the sea;*
> *Nor, England! Did I know till then*
> *What love I bore to thee.*

And Cartier, weary of the rigors of his new lands, wrote in his journal, "I am rather inclined to believe that this is the land God gave to Cain." It is the course of man to hunger for wider vistas, then, getting there, to look fondly behind him.

By late November, Conor Finnegan, too, had grown weary of his new lands. For the first time in all his existence, he did not merit special notice. He did not stand out there as the unique, gifted, distinctly talented individual he knew himself to be. The college routine, so stimulating in September, had faded into a predictability that wore him down. When the weather turned in October and the gray, rainy, murky days that dominate late autumn settled in, melancholy came with it. Finnegan's self-pitying despondency that soggy night in early November never completely left him, although he was able to control his frustrations outwardly and store them in the back of his mind, trotting them out again when appropriate, usually on weekend evenings when he found nothing to do and no one around.

He would rally himself by cultivating a nostalgic view of that he had left to come east. In California he had been appreciated for the versatile, accomplished creature he truly was—California, where he had grown up, its sandy beaches hugging a warm sunset, its mountains backdropping the endlessly exciting city where lived a thousand friends and a million pleasures—California, where it did not snow, ever, and where it did not rain this coldly penetrating rain so common to a Jersey autumn— California, where his parents thought of him proudly, kept his trophies dusted and waited for his letters with traditional parental anxiety. In California he would not be obscure or anonymous or, worst of all, indistinct; he would be respected, his friendship would be coveted. Not so here. At least, not yet.

Throughout the term Finnegan found himself wishing he could share his discoveries with his parents. At first this was because he wanted them to have a taste of the excitement his life had assumed. He remembered sitting in the football stadium on a beautifully clear early autumn Saturday, the green ridges tucked around the sunken field, the sharp scarlet of the Rutgers uniforms below running against the pristine white of the visitors. Around him the students cheered a traditional cheer, contrived the century before and handed down through generations of new students. He saw the color guard in Revolutionary War regalia. He saw it all, heard it all, felt the sun warm his shoulders through the cool afternoon, and wished with all his heart that his father might be there to watch it with him. His father, who loved sports, would revel in the tradition, in the color, in the tight press of vibrant young students acting out their meaningless drama.

Other times, too, he found his thoughts working this way. He wanted his mother to meet his new friends, for he knew she would be entertained by their loose wit. He wanted his father to see the campus with its stone and ivy so that he could be as impressed as Conor was when he first saw it himself. He wanted both of them to come to class with him, to see him at dinner with his friends, to go up the turnpike to New York City. He wanted to show them that he was alive, that he could take care of himself in the deep, unexplored lands. In short, he wanted his two lives to merge, the love and security of his home wedded to the stimulation of a new kind of living.

Later, though, as the term wore on and Finnegan wore down, he found himself wishing he could share these times not from excitement but from a need for justification. If the immediate course of his life left a bruise—from a class, a basketball game, a vacant social life— his parents could be counted upon to put matters into a more fitting perspective. And so by late autumn, he wanted his father to see him beaten on the basketball court and note the subtle, silent humiliation. He wanted his mother to watch him study hard for grades that were less than perfect. Frustration is more acute when faced alone.

As winter vacation loomed and his courses wound down, his excitement returned, focused in large measure on the fact that he would soon be going home. A few weeks in the sun, sleeping late, eating well and visiting with longstanding friends would revive him. His melancholy faded as December dawned. Despite his frustrations (which were, he was forced to admit to himself, relatively inconsequential), he appeared to have survived his first term. From here on, it was bound to be easier. Yes, to be home again for a little while would certainly stand him back up. He would refresh himself, the returning hero, and come back east in January to try it again, wiser and a bit more confident because he had at last been slightly humbled.

Finnegan's anticipation grew. On December 16, the day after the first accumulation of snowfall whitened the ground, he booked his flight home. A week later he was sitting in a 747 at Newark Airport, waiting to fly home as a prodigal son, bruised and shaken, but unbloodied.

* * *

The train ride from Philadelphia north passes first through some of the most grotesque, fetid scenery man has created for himself: Central Philadelphia to North Philadelphia, a squalor of neglect, where once the train stations were civic jewels in the cities' hearts. They stood now rundown, decrepit, passed over by newer and quicker technology moving travelers ever more in a hurry. It is true of Philadelphia, and Trenton, and New Brunswick, and Newark, and all the small or medium cities between Philadelphia and New York (excepting Princeton, of course, where all rules of suburban development have been suspended indefinitely), cities that once boasted of the Pennsylvania Line stopping there and built stations suitable for the honor. The grimy cities, the flat, murky lands, slums, oil refineries, smokestack industries, the bouncing side-to-side jostling of a ride on the old tracks, the acrid smell of grease and fuel—that is the way north now.

Then through the tunnels into New York City and Penn Station, where the crush of people and metal culminates in an intensity that makes breathing itself difficult. Newsstands and cheap snackeries line the platforms near the tracks, and the lights dim, and the smells draw closer, always, it seems, punctuated by the odor of perspiration. This station, too, is old and neglected, but it is too large, too populated to be truly rundown. It is not at all like the lonely ghosts standing in the smaller cities, abandoned by disinterest. The plaster here is cracked as well, the colors on the walls, drab to begin, has faded. But there are people in Penn Station—oceans of them, scattering askew like spokes on a whirling wheel—and so the station here in New York is not dead. Far from it. To remain calm and poised while people press and swirl and push about—that is the challenge here. It comes with practice. Breathe deeply, breathe the pungent, nauseating, oily odors, until the train at last pulls away. The pounding hum of the station, its separate noises indistinguishable from one another, lessens in the background, overrun by the rush of metal wheels on metal tracks, picking up speed.

"Tickets, please. Show me your tickets."

The voice is as metallic as the sound of the rushing train, the click-click of the ticket puncher, the shuffle of heavy shoes on the hard floor. Through the tunnels again, into a womblike blackness where the reflection of the train's interior on the window is sharp and well defined, then out and outward, away from New York City.

Into New England then, and at last a change of mood. The land seems greener, calmer. It all seems cleaner in the tight, trim Connecticut suburbs. The stations in the small towns are not as large, not as desolate, although they still lie in the poorer sections. The rush of the train settles into a purring whirr, the rhythms of movement gentler. Mixed with the oil and grease is the faintest hint of salt air only a few miles away. Few factories here; just a wider, greener, more pristine space, old and rocky but quieter, calmer. The train itself runs through as an aberration, a dartlike intruder upsetting momentarily a long-cultivated tranquility. But not an intruder, really, for no one pays it any mind. It is not important enough for anyone to object to it.

And so it passes through Connecticut—New Haven, New London, Groton, small towns all in the scale of things—then into the wink of an eye that is Rhode Island, encountering Providence, its first real city on this leg of the trip. For a few moments it is a throwback to the southern part of the ride, for Providence may as well be Trenton. But there are hills here, a few on the northern outskirts of the city. The land starts to break. Providence fades. So does the day. The whirr of the train resumes, the rhythm settles back in. The train enters its last homeward sprint, and finally it is good. The day has been long.

Through the last few villages and towns, northeastward to Boston, the train makes its closing run. The land sinks slightly, becomes lower, becomes flatter. The villages pass into cities and become denser, become suburbs, become Boston. Into the train yards, the trip is now ended, the changes along the way now boring. All that matters is standing up, stretching a set of compacted muscles and ultimately throwing oneself into the swarm to find, somewhere, sanctuary.

The sounds return, the press of flesh, the station dotted with the same newsstands and snackeries. The greasy smell still hangs low in the air. It could be anywhere along the journey. Only by fortune is this the last of it.

And, at the end, one asks himself, What have I seen? What did I just pass? Am I anywhere else than where I began, than when I first settled into my seat? A city with a different name, but the mask of humanity is the same. My life is the same. All the same, everywhere.

* * *

Glynnis Mear propped her elbow on the lining of the window and rested her head on her hand. She stared out at the passing scenery but took no notice. She had traveled this same route by plane a month earlier, equally as reluctant as she was now. The view was not likely to be different from what she had seen from the air; being closer made no difference. She stared at it merely to occupy her eyes while cleansing her mind. She aspired to numbness.

New York City was two hours behind her. She was somewhere in Connecticut although she didn't know where, precisely. Nor did she care. She considered only that she had another three hours on this train before she arrived. The train bored her, but she wished she could make the trip last longer, make it five hours more, or seven, or a whole day. Or several days. Then they could just turn the train around and head back south. It would all be over, and she could return to where she was becoming increasingly comfortable.

As Glynnis blindly stared through the window, a young man sat down beside her. He was in his early twenties, no older than twenty-two or twenty-three. His hair fell well below his ears but did not quite touch his shoulders. Above a flannel shirt his face carried an expression of self-confidence bordering on arrogance. His smile was a smirk. The young man was not unattractive, and he knew it. As he fell into the seat, Glynnis Mear did not turn around, nor give even the slightest indication that she had noticed him at all.

"Hey," he said, but Glynnis did not respond, nor even turn her head. She remained staring out the window.

He leaned in closer to her. "You look like you could use some company. So could I." Again Glynnis did not respond, did not move. "I'm just trying to be friendly."

Glynnis spoke at last. "Fuck off," she said. Still she did not look away from the window.

The young man recoiled, burned with a verbal poker. He rose from his seat and shook his head, hesitating just a second as a similar answer leapt to the tip of his tongue. He swallowed it, though, and walked down the aisle to the front of the car, opened the door there and went into the car ahead. Glynnis at last turned away from the window to watch him go.

He would not have been so friendly if I were eighty-two, or if I weighed 200 pounds, or, more to the point, if I were male. Hardly. There's no need for subtlety.

For what is the order of things? A man may set his life on whichever course strikes his imagination, and his woman goes along, a can on a string tied to a bicycle fender. The energy is man's, man the creator, and he must be strong enough to pull a woman. Or so it can be. Then a man builds his life in his own pattern and time, and his lover comes along. She draws from him, derives who she is from him until she cannot make out what is his, what is hers and what is theirs. What dreams she holds for herself merge away. In trying to make him strong, she can make herself weak. If his is the energy, her role must be to feed it. That's the rule. And even is she surrounds herself with children, if she secures every luxury imaginable and attains as much comfort as any person can stand, she owns none of it. Man the creator. She is merely along for the ride. If it is a pleasant one, she can feel blessed; if not, then her sacrifice is a complete waste. That is too often the order of things, and has been for generation after generation. That, so much of the world would tell me, is my condemnation.

Then, after tying her dreams to his and doing all she can to make him strong and good, in drinking in the reflected comfort of a well-constructed life, what if he dies? What then, Mother? What if he dies?

Then there is a void at the top, and we have become profoundly weak. We are misshapen. God help us, we are weak. We are weak, and we flounder about in a frantic, vain search for what has left us. It cannot be, it can never be, as it was. Father, wherever you are, come back to us in some way. Let us eradicate the mistakes we have made and let us make ourselves strong again, for we wallow now in our weakness.

What then, Mother? What if he dies? What is left of you? Of us?

Glynnis's head began to ache; the train's clanking rhythm did nothing to soothe it. She dozed off, but only for a few moments at a time, gravitating in that nebulous fantasy-waking world halfway between sleep and consciousness.

Once as she dozed, she shut her eyes but still managed to make out the scenery outside the train. They were in Rhode Island, or perhaps even near home in Massachusetts, and they were passing through some woods. The trees, many of them, seemed to have faces. Not distinctly defined at first, the faces were just suggestions of eyes, ears, noses, mouths and hair brought about by the sweep of trunk, line and branch. As she peered harder into the darkness, staring intently as the trees coursed by, the fuzzy outlines clarified. If she looked hard enough she could determine who they were, for it seemed now that they were all recognizable. And as they continued to resolve, there lining the tracks were the faces of nearly everyone she had ever known, all looking back at her as intently as she looked at them, each one firmly planted in the ground yet staying in front of her long enough to be counted before passing on. Everyone was in those woods—all her friends, some whom she hadn't seen since childhood: Jordan Brophy and the rest of her professors; Lynda, a wispy branch falling across her sad visage; and then her family, starting with her cousins, aunts and uncles, then her brothers and sister. Finally her mother, but she did not sweep by with the rest. Her tree hovered slightly off the ground a few feet outside the train window. She stayed there, not moving, simply looking back at Glynnis who was now fighting a creeping horror. Her mother, watching her with a peculiar sorrow, was alone among the trees now faceless.

After a few seconds her mother, too, whisked out of view. No new faces appeared. They were just trees now, like any others, interchangeable and inanimate, purely incapable of judgment.

The train rocked onward and Glynnis continued to drift, peering bleary-eyed through the window hoping to see more trees, hoping, hoping, always hoping . . . Broken dolls, broken windows lined with steam from wintry days, and children's stories . . . the Pied Piper tooting 'Follow me', and then down a long, long, sandy slope to the seashore . . . he takes off his green tunic, throws his pipe aside and then, shirtless, runs down the sand, stumbling, not falling, awkward as a crab, and reaching the water dives headlong, arcing his back and shooting out his arms like tendrils to see what he could reach, and then the splash as his body breaks the water, and then . . . silence. As deadly and dank a silence as man can bear, the silence of loneliness in nature, just the sea, endless to the horizon, a rusty blue, inky, deep, no swimmer, no body, just the sea, and all that silence.

Glynnis woke with a start, jerking her head up from the window. She blinked her eyes rapidly and shook her wrists before leaning back against the seat to compose herself, to realize where she really was. She breathed deeply. The train, and Boston. Ah, yes. She turned back to the window and looked outward: only trees, and nothing else. Another hour and a half to go. She checked to make certain her bag was still in the rack above her. She reached up to lift it slightly, feeling its weight. The heft reassured her. Something heavy, something substantial. Glynnis sat back down and leaned her head back against the seat once more. She closed her eyes and slept, dreamlessly, the rest of the way to Boston.

Later that same night, after her mother's welcoming hugs, after a cup of steamy coffee, after a conversation with her brothers and sister that was a bit too proper to be truly comfortable, after a phone call from her mother's sister, matronly Aunt Rita, who always called to be certain that a wandering child had arrived safely, after a few stolen words with Martha, who excitedly showed her sister a picture of her new boyfriend and tried to summarize his matchless qualities in a few breathless minutes on the second-floor landing, after her mother's ceaseless questions about her classes, her friends, her clothes, the city of Philadelphia and the joys of freedom in a faraway place, after this and so much else that wore her down and frayed her already weather-beaten edges, Glynnis went up to bed. Just as she had when she was still living at home, she would share a room with young Martha. When Glynnis moved away, her mother changed nothing.

Glynnis, pleading fatigue, preceded Martha to bed, although her sister came up shortly afterward. Glynnis anticipated that Martha would want to stay up with her and, in the old familiar habits of girlhood, turn out the light so that under the cover of a cloaking darkness they could trade secrets, gossip, dreams and tales. Glynnis had genuinely loved these late-night sessions. She usually looked forward to curling up in bed and talking well into the night until would both grow so tired that one or the other would drift off despite her mightiest struggle, sometimes in mid-sentence. Glynnis did wish to preserve this custom. But not tonight. She could conjure no warmth tonight, no willingness to open herself up to display her soft, moist, perennially jeopardized interior. She only felt weary, as if speech itself would drain the last of her sagging energies and her equally sagging spirit. When Martha came into the bedroom several minutes later, Glynnis feigned sleep.

Martha undressed in the dark and climbed into bed. "Glynnis," she whispered, but her sister did not respond. "Glynnis, are you awake? Come on, you must be." Glynnis kept her eyes closed and continued to breathe in a deep, somnolent rhythm. "Glynnis," she whispered more loudly in one last effort. Her sister did not move. It became apparent that there would be no shared secrets tonight. "Oh, damn." Martha threw herself back on her bed. "Well, good night anyway, you big jerk." Within a few minutes Martha's breathing, too, took on the measured resonance of sleep.

But Glynnis did not sleep. She could have if she had wanted, for she was quite tired, but really she had her entire vacation to sleep. Tonight a strangeness pierced her heart, a nuance of mood brought on by the peculiarities of time and distance. She wanted to feel it a bit longer. She wanted to know more what it was.

Sometimes a child who has cut her finger will remove the bandage to dig her fingernail into the tender flesh around the wound, then into the wound itself. She does so knowing full well that it will hurt, but she will still want to explore the sensation that pulses through her damaged finger, up her arm and into her brain. She wants to investigate the rift, the fire in her finger. She wants to see what it is.

Glynnis Mear lay in her bed, the covers to her shoulders, stared at the ceiling above her, and remembered how Christmas used to be.

There was, first of all, her father. He assumed a different air during the Christmas season. He shed the serious determination with which he customarily went about even the simplest task and became more spontaneous, more solicitous, more reactive. When Glynnis asked him once whether this was truly so and why it was, he answered that all year he fought with disease and death. During Christmas he would allow himself, force himself really, to deal with life. The holidays for him had to be different; he had to make them so, or else they were no good. He wanted to celebrate his own life, his own family and the goodness he perceived around him. Glynnis understood completely. While she loved and admired her father year-round, she absolutely adored him during Christmas.

The simplest acts of the season took on a significance that she now remembered fondly. She remembered her father bringing home the Christmas tree each year. He never permitted any of the family to accompany him. Always he sensed their excitement and wanted to build it to a peak by the time he made his appearance, pulling the tree behind him and littering needles everywhere on the way to the family room. And then the pent-up excitement would burst around him. The children would rush to help him with the tree, each stumbling over the others and jockeying to get closest to the bounty. Once the tree was inside they would wrangle over where in the family room to place it. That decided, their mother would pull boxes of ornaments and tinsel out of the closet, place it all on the coffee table, then go into the kitchen to make hot chocolate and tea. The children would grab for their favorite ornaments and try to get the skinny hooks to wrap around the too-thick branches with their pointy needles. Their mother would join them again as their father finished wrapping the strings of lights around the tree. Always their father would insist that their mother put the angel on top, and so she would after setting her tray of mugs on the now-cleared coffee table. Glynnis knew that they must have had a Christmas tree before her brothers and sister were born, although she could not recall whether it ever meant anything then.

She remembered, too, some nights when she was much younger. Bobby, Peter and Martha were just babies, or perhaps toddlers. Her father would take her onto his knee in the big leather chair near the fireplace in his den, that most mysterious of rooms. She felt the cold, smooth leather against her side. There he would read the Christmas books. She particularly liked Dylan Thomas's "A Child's Christmas in Wales" because it made her sense the cold and smell the wonderful, warm kitchen smells that the young boy savored so much.

She remembered going to Mass on Christmas Day, and the pungent odor of incense, the priest's melodic incantations, the booming Christmas carols sung lustily by the people around her. She thought back to one Christmas where, during *Hark, the Herald Angels Sing*, she began to cry, right there at Mass. It all felt so powerful and so whole.

They would take drives then, at Christmas time, to see the lights. Their father would pile them into the car after their mother had bundled them up, then out into the Boston suburbs to look at the displays and the lights on the houses there. Then they would head back into the city itself. The old churches all had displays, and some of the tall buildings had special lights that formed giant red stars or white angels. Sometimes on the drive back the younger children would fall asleep, but when they got back home there would be hot chocolate to revive them, and fruitcake, and Christmas candy.

As the days of December wore on, presents would appear under the tree. Each new present would draw an immediate inspection to see, first, whom it was for, and, second, what it might be. Judgments were rendered by weight, shape and feel. Usually the children were totally wrong, but they relished the challenge.

Her mother, too, changed for the season. She became less harried, even though the holidays always brought much more for her to do. As if responding to her husband, she took on a more peaceful demeanor, calmer, more loving to him and to them all. She reveled in the season, and it showed in everything she did. Glynnis remembered her mother returning from shopping on cold December days wearing a knit scarf, her cheeks red as she entered the hallway. The crowds never bothered her, and she would come home smiling, going about the house humming to herself and keeping that incongruous smile on her happy face.

Sometimes during the season her mother would tuck Glynnis into her bed at night, then sit there talking with her for what seemed like hours. There they would share their deepest secrets, as Glynnis would later do with Martha. But this was her first time for any of that, and first times are indelible. Her mother listened to her then. No story was silly, no dream too wild. Sometimes, too, her mother would sing to her in her clear, vibrant soprano. Her mother had a lovely voice that she used too rarely. She would sing quietly to Glynnis at the edge of her daughter's bed: Christmas carols, hymns, lullabies, popular songs, whatever came to her mind. She would never start to sing until after they had talked a while. Glynnis would listen to the crystalline voice, close her eyes and abandon herself to the most profound cognitions of warmth, of security, of love itself in the purest of forms, there smothering her into a holy bliss.

And then Christmas morning itself. Glynnis remembered waking early, always, and waiting to hear stirrings from the other bedroom. Sometimes her small brothers woke before she did and peeked into the girls' room to see if they were awake yet. They would all mobilize there in the upstairs hallway, waiting for one another. Then, as quietly as they could, they would slip downstairs to lift and feel the mysterious packages once again. It was so hard to wait for their parents to rise, but they would not open their presents until all were together. Somehow it felt wrong, despite all the excitement and wonder, to want to open something without the entire family around. But such fragile convictions did not stop them from dividing up the presents and inspecting all sides of them. After a while their parents would hear them and come down.

Real joy would explode then, without fetters or restraint, the six of them in their bathrobes ripping through paper, holding up their newest treasures and the children squeaking with delight. In their excitement over the great packages the little ones never remembered to check the den where their stockings had been hung. Always their father had to remind them to take a look in the other room, take a look at the stockings, and they would jump up from where they sat to run into the den. There they would find the stockings jammed, with toy soldiers, or little dolls, or oranges, or candy, or books, or all these things. As they dumped out the contents of their stockings they would often get their gifts mixed, but it never mattered. Nothing mattered on these most magical of mornings.

Glynnis, lying in the darkness, looked back and remembered the deepest, most essential feelings of her childhood, all revolving around this special time, reflected in an amorphous blending of traditional images. Snowmen on the lawn, and snowball fights, and snow angels; the shopping plazas and department stores with everything looking so big; Christmas music; the special food, like roast duck and Christmas cookies and mincemeat pie. All that defined the innocent, excited wonder of childhood for Glynnis Mear was captured in this season. As she grew older she found herself marking her passage each Christmas, when the essence of life itself was made clear to her once again. She would reach back, and, as her father did, put aside all else to revel in the most basic of emotions, to strip away human complexities so that the purest of joys might come forward, to believe ultimately that she was part of something so great, so vast, so protective, that it would never, ever pass away.

In time she wearied of looking at the ceiling. Her thoughts, her memories bumped into each other as they skirted about her mind. They beat against her, as rain against a proverbial windowpane, and in so doing benumbed her. Sadness then, an old grief digging back into her. She had spent the night inspecting it from a distance, observing the images that, when juxtaposed with her present, defined as profound a pain as she could fathom. Her mind had worn too thin to fight it off, to keep the distance that kept her strong.

Glynnis Mear rolled over and pulled the covers tighter around her. She looked out her window at the shadowed forms of the backyard trees. There, in an icy December, for the first time in months, she began to weep.

* * *

The winter vacation rolled on soberly, removed from all past values and so forfeiting the expectation of joy. Glynnis Mear took little pleasure in the respite from an increasingly comforting routine of classes, study and embryonic friendships. In her estrangement she had consoled herself with the constructs of a new, entirely personal order. It was, for her, an assurance that she did indeed retain her own unique non-Mearsian identity. All that was suspended now. Through distance, she girded herself against the futilities of once again coming under the familial yoke. The calm, softly smiling, quietly energetic Glynnis Mear of her youth had gradually become listless, a scarecrow with all the straw shaken out.

She passed her days at home with scarcely a rustle. She slept late into the morning, for she did love to sleep and that was one pleasure usually denied her at school. After rising she would read through the afternoon, or go into downtown Boston with Martha, or alone, to shop, to walk around without aim, to look at the people in their wintertime guises. On occasion she got together with her closest friends, one at a time, to brief each other on the past months. Even then she did not retain her excitement beyond the first few minutes of reunion. They were old faces, and too familiar, reflective of less complex days. Whatever she might do during the day, she made certain she was home for dinner. Glynnis saw no need to cause petty disturbances by skipping family amenities, and her mother was a very good cook.

After dinner she would watch television with her brothers and sister, or, more frequently, retire to the study, a room at the rear of the house where her father's books were kept in wooden shelves, where also stood a history of family portraits on two desks at opposite corners, where sat two heavy leather chairs in which her father and mother might sit for hours, talking in retreat or merely feeling each other's presence, where a classic bay window looked into the small patch of their back yard. Glynnis loved the study which, since her father's death, had been largely ignored by the others. Here in the evenings she would read again, or sometimes just sit in one of the leather chairs and look out the bay window into the clammy white of a Boston Christmastime. She relished her solitude. Within two days of returning home she had timed her family's routine so that she would emerge from the study only as her siblings were going to bed. Then she would spend ten or fifteen minutes with each of them, paying them singular visits like some vague avatar, assuring them and herself that all feeling had not been completely lost.

One evening in early January, after Christmas itself had faded and the New Year's celebration, spent by Glynnis as any other night, had been quelled, Glynnis's mother joined her in the study. Her mother's entrance surprised her. Florence Mear, above everyone in the family, understood the sanctity of solitude and could be counted upon to honor it. As her mother entered, Glynnis was sitting in the chair nearer the bay window, reading Emily Brontë.

Her mother opened the door with a shy smile and walked to the other chair. She did not sit down immediately. Glynnis noticed that she was carrying a collection of Shakespeare.

"Evening, baby. If you don't mind, I thought I'd join you tonight. I'd like to do some reading, too," she gestured with her book, "and the atmosphere in here is so lovely. I've totally taken it for granted."

Glynnis returned a quiet smile. "What are you reading?"

"Shakespeare. Another attempt to get through those things I should have read decades ago. *The Merry Wives of Windsor*. Go ahead and keep reading. I'll be quiet." She settled into the chair opposite Glynnis.

They read there together in silence for several minutes, but Glynnis's concentration went wandering, disrupted by her mother's soft presence. She knew it to be intentional. Her mother had not come in here to read. Glynnis saw herself as the prey of a crafty leopard lying in wait in a tree branch over a pathway she had to take. She knew it was only a matter of timing now. There was little she could do about it.

Her mother also grew restless, and after a while she broke the silence. "I'm sorry, Glyn, but I'd like something to drink. Can I get you anything? I think I'd like a brandy."

Glynnis dropped her book to her lap. "I think a brandy sounds wonderful. In one of those big snifters."

"Of course." Florence Mear left the room and came back a few minutes later with two snifters of Armagnac. She had changed her clothes and now wore a thick floor-length housecoat.

"I feel so luxurious in this," she said, reentering the study. "This is so warm."

"The brandy should be warm, too," said Glynnis. "It gets so cold in here." She took the brandy and immediately drew a sip. The liquid plunged through her at once, sending a warmth her entire length as the vapors pricked her sinuses. She knew there would be no more reading—the leopard stirred and stretched.

"I felt a bit odd offering you brandy," said her mother. "I've never seen you drink before. I just assume you've gotten to know a few spirits at college. That's fine. You're not too young." She paused. "In fact, you look to me to be a full lady, and an elegant one at that." Florence Mear smiled her shyest smile.

"I don't drink much at all, Mother. I've never been drunk. When a group of us go out for dinner, I might have wine. I don't like beer or hard liquor, at least not yet. I don't think I'm quite prepared to have my senses confused. I do like brandy, though, on cold nights."

"I do too, my love. And I think I developed a taste for it when I was about your age. I was living at home and going to school downtown. My father used to keep it around for nights like this. He gave me some one night when I had been out late. I was frozen and it warmed me right up. Of course, after he warmed my insides with the brandy he warmed my ears with what he had to say. I had been out far too late with a young man, and he had been worried, so perhaps it was a combined effect. But you know, I don't think Italians are bothered so much by alcohol. I remember drinking wine with dinner as early as ten or eleven. I grew up with it in milder forms. Never whiskey, always wine."

"I don't remember much about Grandpa. How old was I when he died?"

"Just a little kid, Glyn. You must have been five or six. He was always so proud that I had married a doctor. Your father was like some kind of trophy to him. But he came to love him for his own sake, too. Everyone loved your father."

"You never speak much about Grandpa. You never really told us much about him."

Florence Mear took a sip of her brandy, leaned back in her chair and looked at the ceiling, her eyes alive. "He was such a good man, Glyn. He worked so hard. You know, most of the Italians in the North End worked menial jobs. On the docks, or janitors, or construction. Papa worked in a market, though. He didn't own it, but he always acted as if he did. God, he took such pride in everything—himself, his home, especially his family. It was just natural for him to take pride in his job as well. That may be one of the most valuable things he ever passed on to me. We never had much, but we were required to take such good care of it. We made do, and we were very happy because he kept us that way. It was all a matter of pride.

"I wish he could see me now," she continued. "See all of us, I mean. He would be so gratified to know that I'm comfortable and have such a lovely family. That was always the most important thing to him, having a close family. 'That's the limit of what you'll need,' he'd tell me. He knew I'd do well materially when I married your father. But he didn't live long enough to see all my family. He'd have been very pleased."

"He died of a heart attack, didn't he, Mother?"

"Yes. Very quickly. He came home from work one day and went to bed early. He said he didn't feel too well. He woke up in the night with chest pains, but he didn't want to wake my mother, which I suppose was typical of him. He took a few deep breaths and tried to go back to sleep. When he got up for work the next morning he told my mother about it. Then he went into the bathroom and collapsed. By the time the ambulance arrived, he was dead. Very quick. I'm sure he didn't suffer much, and I'm glad my mother was with him. I wish I could have been. Just to thank him and to tell him I loved him, that he had been the best of fathers. To say all those trite things one thinks of at the time. He knew how I felt, of course, so there was no need for words. We say them more for ourselves, anyway."

Glynnis stared hard at her mother, stared into the leopard's eyes. "How did you react when he died, Mother? What did you do? You've never really told me."

"What could I do? I had my own family and they needed me. I grieved a bit, as we all did, then I got on with my life. You and Martha were the only children then, but you took my mind off things. I think above all else the two of you were the confirmation of life I needed just then. You were both so animated and innocent. You were a joy, and that was necessary for me more so than anything else.

"We go on with what's at hand, Glyn," she went on. "We have to. Or else we lose the good within ourselves, and then we profane the passing. It's so tempting to take our grief to distant levels, but that helps nothing. It's indulgence. If just kills off those parts that we still hold on to. You can grieve for a loss without turning your back on what you still have, on what still defines you."

"Do you think that's what I've done?"

"I do. My darling daughter, I don't know how you rationalize it to yourself, or how you regard this process of grieving. I'm sure that however you do, it makes perfect sense to your way of thinking. But in the end you'll regret it. Whatever you think, we remain a family, and we're good for you. We love you, and I invite you formally to partake of that love fully, even in your grief. Let us heal your wounds, however you perceive them, and come back to us from wherever it is you have gone."

"You misread me, Mother. My grief for my father, your late husband, is long extinguished. I grieve for something else."

"Tell me."

Glynnis summoned her courage, sipped her brandy and chose her words as carefully as her mind could sort them. "We're a family, yes, but we're a family without a head. We're misshapen, grotesque, a parody of what we used to be. We became functions in an equation when all the values were suddenly skewed.

"I miss him, Mother. I miss him every day. But it's like taking a picture from the desk here, dusting it off and putting it into a closet. He should be a living presence, but he isn't.

"And I come back here, now that I've moved away," Glynnis continued, "and things are so different. I imagine there's no avoiding it. You can't stop people from growing older, from recovering from the pain. Martha and Bobby and Peter are different, and you're so different, and Daddy's not here, and everybody is proud of how they haven't let it affect them. But that's so false. It *does* affect us, it will always affect us, and I resent the façades.

"When Daddy died, something irrevocable passed away. Nobody sees that. We're not what we were, and what we are now is . . . Christ, I don't know. Some odd unit of individuals, too prideful, too independent of their own pasts. There's such a void here, and no one seems to see it but me."

Florence Mear sat in her chair, hanging on every word which dug through her flesh and pricked her softest tissues. A piece of her wrenched itself away, like a second labor. What her daughter was saying, she supposed, was a type of grief, but it had mutated.

How else could Glynnis have misread the tremendous hurt that she, his wife of two decades, had suffered, how Robert Mear's death had killed the Romantic in her, how her own sense of conjugal love had been lowered into the ground with him? The man had crept into her veins and become inseparable from her own fiber. If the family, collectively and singly, viewed their lives now in practical terms, how could they be blamed? It was as her own father had said, you had to go on living, you had to nurture what you could still hold. And in so doing, perhaps the resounding pain could be ameliorated slightly by the struggles of coping without him. Why must a single death multiply and claim other victims?

Florence Mear knew that it was all a form of grieving, which comes in infinite variations, an acknowledgement of incomprehensible loss. It could not be obliterated all at once. It would have to break down gradually under its own weight, which, she reasoned, must be terrible.

"Will you then, carry these thoughts forever?" she asked gently. "We grieve for the same reason, all of us. We feel a loss. A forfeiture. We grieve for the man who had to make this sacrifice. Yes, there is a void here. A great big wide one which will never fill, and no one feels it as much as I do. But if you fall down and cut your knee, how long do you keep picking at the wound? Do you never let a scar form to protect the hurt?"

Glynnis twisted in her chair to avoid her mother's eyes. She did not respond for several minutes. The clock on her father's desk ticked loudly in the silence, a haunting phantom of the lost presence. Glynnis took a long, slow sip of brandy, saw that only a few drops remained in the snifter, then finished it off. "Is there any more?"

"Yes. I'll get it for you," her mother replied softly. She took the snifter and left the room. Glynnis scanned the portraits on the desk. Warm flesh and blood, each one a mirror. Pieces of a single glass, broken. The sons interchangeable, no doubt like the daughters. Different stages of the same process, and a bitter, bitter disquietude. Martha, Martha, sweet Persephone. I call you back.

Her mother returned and handed her the snifter, filled to its previous level. She had added some to her own as well. When Glynnis at last resumed, her voice had lost its certitude.

"I suppose Daddy's death was a watershed for me. Before, we were so well taken care of. We took everything for granted, including each other. I mean, none of us ever had any conception that anything could change, did we? We were still children, each one of us, including you, Mother. And we were so secure. You look at all these portraits of the stereotypical American family. That's what we were, a Norman Rockwell painting, quaint and cute."

She paused to sip her brandy again, and took a deep breath. Her voice grew tremulous, low and throaty. "Then Daddy died. He tried to warn us, you know. He tried to make us ready for the change, to caution us that our whole world was about to be redefined, and we'd better be prepared. That was so typical of him, and he was probably grateful he knew beforehand that he was dying so he could take care of matters before he went. We should have been ready. But even after that, after all his gentle warnings, he died so quickly. It wasn't like a death after all, really. It was like he was going away on some kind of last-minute trip. To an AMA convention. And I keep expecting him to come back.

"He died, and nothing seemed secure anymore. If Daddy could die, then nothing else was truly safe. He made us a family. Without him, we're not children anymore."

"So you don't feel as comfortable here," responded her mother, "under these new and sad conditions. And you think nobody else perceived the same transformation, that nobody else felt older when he died. We grieve both for your father, and for what we have lost. And many days I feel as if I'm ninety years old.

"I'll never get over it, my baby. Every night when I crawl into a cold bed I feel it all over again, and it never gets any easier. I loved your father in a way that you'll experience some day only if you're extraordinarily fortunate. And it will consume you if it happens, and you'll abandon yourself without wanting to and without being the slightest bit able to stop it. I gave myself to him, Glynnis, and I held nothing back. I haven't had a happy day since he died. I've resigned myself to the fact that I never will, not in the sense I've known before.

"But I do have the rest of you," she continued, "And I'm not going to cut my own life off out of heartbreak. I will not deny myself what's left. You lost your childhood. I lost all the sweet excitement of adulthood. There's no difference. But there comes a time when you don't dig at the wound anymore. It never stops hurting, ever, but you just stop looking for it. There's too much left for you to do with and for everybody who remains. You can never put your loss out of your mind, but you just have to stop reliving it. And you can't think any less of those who have already done what you must. Please, Glyn."

Glynnis watched the image of her mother blur and swim. The brandy had made her limbs weary, too heavy to animate, so she sank deeper into the warm leather. Her nose filled and she sniffled to hold it back. Blackness leaked inward through the bay window, covering the bookshelves, draping the desk and creeping behind her swimming mother. She felt a rift insider her, a fissure, splitting her from her neck to her knees.

"Mother, you make so much more sense than I do." She sniffled again. "And I suppose someday I'll be able to say how sorry I am and become the prodigal daughter." Her mother had lost all her edges, a wet, watery mess engulfing her chair. "But I can't tonight. I just can't." She sniffed once more before taking a deep breath to compose herself. "I must look pretty awful."

"Yes, my love, but you are still my darling daughter, and I still love you with all the heart that's permitted me. If you need more time, then take it. Take all the time you want, and know that we shall be here when you're done with this horrible process. We will always be here. Take your comfort where you can, even if it's away from us."

Glynnis Mear had not lost all control. She would not allow that to happen. She blinked hard until the blackness around her mother receded and the form again resumed a definable perimeter.

There was no resolution. There could be none within the young girl's confusion, for the rages of loss, of time, of denial are as ancient as humankind itself. Every life brings with it a thousand thousand forms of death, spread among those who touch its web. Only at the final death does the web collapse, sucking those closest into a swirling, vicious vortex. Each will land somewhere on the far side, but one cannot know precisely.

Glynnis rose from her chair, and, for the first time in immediate memory, embraced her mother of her own will. She kissed her goodnight before climbing the stairs to her room, her heart no less heavy, her mind no less troubled. But for this evening at least, she would sleep a dreamless sleep.

Three days later she took the train back to Philadelphia. Lynda Hoelscher had arrived earlier that afternoon and was waiting for her when Glynnis got to her dormitory room. As she entered, she saw Lynda, put down her bag and walked over to her friend. There, silently, she hugged her fast, holding on to the strong warmth of Lynda's shoulders with all her might.

* * *

Tom McIlweath, too, had gone home for the holidays, flying across country back to California although swim practice demanded that he stay in New Jersey two days longer than Conor Finnegan. To his parents he was unchanged, and Tom went through his three weeks at home as if they were any other three weeks of his earlier life. He worked out daily with his old swim club; he slept late when he could; he ate well. His parents, particularly his father, asked him ceaseless questions about college life, all of which he answered precisely, showing glimpses of the burgeoning confidence for which he had left home in the first place. Tom remained quiet and saw only two or three of his old acquaintances—he could not really call them friends—over the course of his rest, and those only by chance on those days when he was shopping or running errands. He did not seek them out, and he felt no great exhilaration at seeing them again. Save his parents, he had missed no one.

In short, Tom McIlweath saw himself as a lithe, graceful snake in the process of shedding a worn skin. When he flew back to New Jersey in January, he counted this vacation as the best of his young life, and these holidays the most rewarding he had ever experienced.

Conor Finnegan by contrast had plunged headlong back into his old lifestyle with a fervor that bordered on the religious. He would be home for three weeks—twenty-two short days to accomplish what he wanted, to see the people he needed to see.

He accepted humbly the adulations of his parents, which began of course as soon as he stepped off the plane and continued until he left. His mother became particularly solicitous and took great pains to prepare his favorite meals, to leave him undisturbed as he slept late each morning, to wash and iron his clothes. After nearly a four-month recess, Katherine Finnegan felt like a mother again. She allowed herself to behave like one to excess.

His father, too, reacted warmly. Conor and his father would sit up late at night after his father came home from working an odd shift. Together they would eat something, Katherine having gone to bed early. Then, with the television providing a mindless background, they would talk, openly and without pretension. Here Conor would try to fulfill the frequent longings he had had at school to share his new circumstances with his father, who, he was certain, would find them as stimulating as had Conor himself.

Ed Finnegan enjoyed his son's stories and looked forward to them as he locked the store at night. As does every father, Ed Finnegan had always lived a bit vicariously through his son. If his own existence might now be locked into place, he could, for these few weeks, find a profoundly practical release through young Conor. With every phrase, Conor's voice betrayed a barely suppressed excitement with life itself, enhanced through his inestimable joy of discovery. Conor tried to paint for his father a complete portrait of what those discoveries were—not only a tradition-filled campus with a hodgepodge of personalities and experiences, but also the new angles, depths and dimensions he had found within himself. For Edward Finnegan, it was as if his son was learning to walk again, and each evening he would look forward to watching him take a few more steps. Ed Finnegan did not know if he would ever see the Rutgers campus, but, through his son, he had a broad picture of it and its people. More importantly, he could also see the impact this mysterious place had had upon his only son, who returned home in his father's eyes stronger, slightly more polished, equally as confident as he had always been, and undoubtedly wiser.

Conor took great satisfaction in the provisions his parents made for him. To be sure, he acknowledged a warm emotional surge in seeing them again. They were a receptive audience for what he wanted to share. While he was home, the doubts, the insecurities that had begun to rise up, Gorgonlike, to freeze him into stone during the latter part of the first term seemed so far away as to be unreal. He was slightly embarrassed that his boundless self-confidence had ever been challenged. Now that he was back again in the most familiar, most comfortable surroundings, he felt invincible once more.

Conor managed as well to see a great many old friends. He went to two parties while he was home, each packed with people he knew and who knew him. To them he recounted the exhilaration of being away, the magic of the mythical and distant East. They in turn seemed anxious to hear, for Conor in going so far afield had defied custom. He had always been popular—so strong, so versatile and quick. Had he changed? Would he? Finnegan held forth with warmth and wit, glad to be with his old friends. They knew him in ways no one at college ever could. It is the old friendships that are best.

One afternoon Finnegan got together with several of his former teammates to play basketball at the high school gymnasium. One of them had called the coach, who had invited them to watch the current team practice. Afterward they would have run of the floor.

Finnegan sat in the bleachers with his friends and watched the team go through its paces. The gym itself brought back a rush of familiarity. He loved the shiny hardwood, so bright that it gave back clear reflections. He loved the pungent wood-and-sweat smell, the echo of the ball through a near-empty cavernous building, While his friends bantered among themselves and made comparisons with the current team, always to their own enhancement, Finnegan sat quietly, looking carefully at all aspects, all corners of the gym.

He looked at center-court with its black circle ringing a script 'S', the initial of the team name, and recalled his coiled nervousness each time he walked onto the court for the opening tip. He looked at the bench area and recalled the flippant offhand remarks between teammates near the end of a game already won. He looked across at the empty bleachers and recalled the cheering which he had never noticed until he came out of a game. He looked, too, at the thick rope attached to a disk a few feet below the high ceiling and recalled his fear at having to climb it as a freshman in physical education class, one more fear eventually overcome through a strong will.

In due course the team's practice ended, the sweaty bodies walking off the court, breathing hard, glassy-eyed and anxious to shower, leave and get on with their own vacations. The coach waved the others onto the floor. After a few minutes of shooting around to loosen up, they chose sides. The coach, a tall, scholarly gentleman who taught English (unlike most of the other coaches, who comprised the departments of physical education and vocational arts) called to them from the end of the court.

"I'll be back in a few minutes, gentlemen. I have to go instruct my team, which needs it badly. If you need me or if anyone gets hurt, I'll be in the usual place."

"You gonna come back and watch your old boys, Coach?" asked one of the old boys.

"Of course. I want to see if you people remember anything," and with a smile he ducked into the hallway leading to the lockers.

With the coach's departure the game began. Finnegan, to his delight, had been teamed with his old friend, Jim Koscielski. Finnegan had learned that day that Kos was the leading freshman scorer at the University of Oregon. They had always worked well together, both on and off the court. Finnegan relished the chance to relive some of their old magic, to communicate wordlessly amid a swirl of running bodies and know in advance how it would all work out.

And so it was. As the game progressed Finnegan found himself running up and down the court with no strain, not winded, pushing the ball quickly before him when he had it, cutting to open areas when he didn't, playing tough, tight defense. This is still a boy's game, he thought. His shots dropped, one after another, through a very kind hoop. He passed the ball with flicks of the wrist, firmly, to open teammates. He drove the lane, whisking by his defender, either to score or to flip the ball to a free man underneath. Basketball was joyous again, a fleet exercise that confirmed his youth, an exercise at which, on this day, he excelled.

Resurgent, he took his dares, lunging for balls at which he had only remote chances but coming up with them anyway, taking twisting, spinning, mid-air shots, throwing passes between several defenders to an open man. He took his dares, and did not fail. Still his breath came easily; he did not feel the knifelike pain that often dug under his ribs when he had pushed himself too hard.

What finer confirmation of youth than this? What nobler way to spend an afternoon, or a lifetime, sporting at a game in which one's true vitality might be found? Finnegan felt an exhilarative joy pulse through every vein—a joy of sprinting, crouching, leaping, stretching, even falling. His body had come alive once more, and with it his mind, his heart, his very spirit.

The game was to fifty baskets. With his team leading comfortably and one basket away from victory, Finnegan watched his man dribble up court. He crouched defensively, knees bent, feet shuffling, palms upward, looking for one last opportunity to impress himself. His man took his eye off Finnegan momentarily to look underneath the basket. When he did so, Conor shot out his right hand, a serpent's tongue. Before his man could cover up, Finnegan flicked the ball away, then stepped around him quickly, picked up the loose ball and was off in the opposite direction. No one would catch him, and his layup sealed the game.

Conor Finnegan looked to the bleachers, as was his habit. He had not seen the coach come back in and sit down, so he did not know how long he had been there or how much he had seen. But in looking over he had caught the man's eye, and the coach, in acknowledgement of the final basket at least, gave a slight thin-lipped smile and nodded his head. After that, Finnegan met his friends.

They walked to the bleachers to grab towels, dry off and rest before pulling on their sweatshirts to go home. The coach walked over to them. "You fellas still look respectable. Conor, you scored more today than you did all last year."

Finnegan laughed, "A man's got to take his shots, coach. I've got a lot of points in this arm that have yet to come out."

His friends jeered and hooted.

After a few minutes the coach returned to his office and the players filtered out of the gym. Where most of his friends had cars, Finnegan had walked. Now he felt so good that he thought he would run home. It was only a couple of miles. He paid his respects to his *compadres* with typical boyish jests.

"Listen, we'll get together this summer. I'll be back home."

"Yeah, good luck, Conor. Give us a call when you get back."

"Show those eastern guys how to do it."

"And those eastern girls, too."

Finnegan did not start at once for home. He stood in front of the gym and let his gaze sweep the campus once, slowly. He was no longer a part of this place, despite illusions. Whatever he conjured this afternoon had been transitory. Odd it was, to be here and not belong, to be flesh transmuted. His limbs were a bit numb, and the dried perspiration on his forehead grew cold. No longer a part of this place. How odd. How very odd. And how strangely sad.

Before leaving, Finnegan thought to have a word with his coach as well. He went into the locker room, down the short corridor and turned right. The dank, sweaty, slatey smell hung in every corner and every hallway. He found the coach at his desk going over a practice schedule. The older man looked up as Conor swung around the open doorway to the office.

"Coach, I just wanted to wish you well before I head back." Finnegan extended his hand. "Good luck." The coach rose and shook it firmly.

"To you, too, Conor. You've got a heck of an opportunity. You're at a fine school. I know you'll do great things with it."

"I've got a good background, sir. Good coaching. I've been well prepared."

"You know, Conor, I always considered you to be one of the smartest players I ever coached. You were the best shooter on the squad, but you never cared if you scored. You were always ready to pass the ball off and make sure that everyone else looked good. A lot of players end up doing that, but I never had to force you. I never had to correct you for not running the offense or for taking a shot when you should have passed. It seemed to me that that quality would serve you well the rest of your life, in whatever you do. "

Conor smiled. "I'm still doing my best, Coach. There's no other way."

"Give me a call when you get home again. I'll fill you in on how this year's group turns out. I think they'll be quite good, actually, if we can find a point guard to run things."

"I'll do that, Coach. Thanks for everything."

Finnegan went back down the short corridor and, as he came out of the locker room into the campus quad, he took three or four deep breaths to rid himself of the stale odor. The late afternoon sun hung low and the air was crisp, the campus now totally vacant. Finnegan heard the floppy, rubbery footsteps of his sneakers echo to the empty buildings. He turned in the direction of home and started to run, slowly at first until he caught a rhythm, then faster. The campus disappeared behind him. He was alone, running down the deserted sidewalks.

On the mantel the old clock ticked and clucked, its innards rusty but regular, a pattern of movement worn into it that no shock could alter. Books flanked it on either side. Above the entire mantel hung a wide mirror, mysteriously foggy around its perimeter. The fireplace had been blocked off for years. Its dirty gray border, once considered somewhat ornate, was now cracked on both sides. Along one crack the gap in the slate was so wide that a man could insert his index finger. If he were to do so, he would most likely encounter small insects crawling back and forth there. From the base of the old fireplace ran a threadbare carpet with a floral design that was once off-white. Now it had become so soiled that it blended into the bleached-out red that formed its backdrop. A few feet in front of the fireplace sat an old wooden coffee table, one leg broken and perched on bits of newspaper to level the table. The top of the table was ringed with stains of cups and glasses, its varnish long eaten away. Magazines, some months old, littered its surface between the stain-rings. Before it sat an old, deep easy chair, its once-green leather faded now to a mucusy hue. Each arm had a narrow split running its width where a man could rest his elbows.

In the chair, reclining as far back as it would let him go, an aged, brittle man sat humbly in flannel shirt and baggy workpants. His eyes stared across the small living room at the mantel. In an adjacent corner on a kitchen table, there was an ancient RCA radio. From it came a series of Christmas carols which the old man recognized, his mind tracing over nearly forgotten lyrics. Usually he watched the television on the other side of the room, but this was Christmas Eve and he felt it more appropriate tonight to listen at least a little to the holy carols. Near the television, perched in his cage, a canary chirped mindlessly along.

The old man took his eyes from the mantel, which had been only a vacant target for him anyway, and looked around the room. He sighed deeply, his thin, worn lungs bringing in then throwing out bundles of air. His eyes lit upon the kitchen table next to the radio where he had displayed, to no one of course, for he had no visitors, the Christmas cards he received this year. There were three: one from his son, one from his grandson, and one from his landlady.

Behind him, a window looked out from his second floor rooms. Earlier this week it had snowed, and the snow had not yet cleared. The traffic had ground it down to a gritty sludge lining both sides of the street. There was no traffic below, either on the sidewalk or the street itself. On a Christmas Eve, that was perhaps most appropriate.

The old man's mind punched through the radio's Christmas music. They became a draping for his wanderings. He returned his eyes to the mantel and tuned out whatever it was they saw.

It was not always like this on Christmases. He saw himself as a young boy, helping his soon-to-pass mother prepare a pudding. He was tending the fire in the stove while his mother stirred the thick contents of a heavy black kettle. He remembered the wrinkles in her face as she smiled down at him. He would receive no present this year, nor for several years. The richly sumptuous Christmas dinner, the best meal of the year, was gift enough for all of them. The small boy did not mind, for he had no concept of anything else. Once done with the stirring and the feeding of the fire, he pulled up a stool in a corner of the kitchen to watch his mother at work. She sang Christmas carols, ancient ones the lyrics of which he could no longer recall, some in Gaelic, and, as she sang to him, he sat smiling back at her, wishing he knew enough to sing along with her.

His mother, and father too, dead these many, many years, lying now behind the parish church, thousands of miles away.

Molly, ah, my sweet and beautiful Molly. She would fairly glow at Christmastime, a childlike excitement in her leaping eyes. Once he got on his feet here, he was able to afford some things—a tree and some simple gifts—and he remembered now clearly the thrill with which he offered them. She would decorate the tree simply, yet with the greatest care, hanging delicate gingerbread figures which she had baked and placing them near the striped candy canes. Later, after their first son was born, they would bring his crib into the living room so he could be a part of their gentle ritual.

Molly would bake then, endlessly it seemed—cookies and cakes and candies—and what they could not eat themselves she would take around the neighborhood. She would invite people to stop by. She invited their friends, who arrived in laughing, bundled couples, and she invited people they knew only remotely but wanted to know better, and they would come, too, for no one could resist Molly's invitations. Here, in this living room, they would serve the traditional drinks and the products of Molly's baking. They would sing then, too, producing a sound the old man remembered as surprisingly harmonic and truly inspirational.

Later, on Christmas Eve, he and Molly would exchange presents, usually simple items, but he occasionally could surprise her with something so obviously beyond their means that she would be stunned. He bought her one year a dainty necklace, with a real pearl tucked into a nest of gold filigree. Molly cried when she opened it, knowing the sacrifices it must have wrought in their fragile lifestyle. She wore it only at the most special of times. When she died, her grieving husband asked that she be buried with the necklace in place, and so he took comfort knowing it was with her even now.

Once their first son was born, Christmas focused itself on his boyish excitements, which in turn excited his parents to new levels. The baby added a rich dimension to the holiday, but the old man thought back to his Christmases with Molly alone and knew that, as much as he loved all his sons, those early years were the most precious.

And so the old man heard the voice inside him say, Molly, Molly, my one true and final love. You were light enough to clear any gloom, and at no time did your loving heart shine brighter than during these most holy days. I have known no happiness since your passing, my dearest love, none at all, and I look for none. My soul is with you now, as ever it has been. I wait only for my body to follow.

The old man sat in his bleakness, a tear running down each cheek. He did not feel them. His remembrances of holidays past ran no further than his last with his wife. What followed was hard, just him and the boys. Then his boys went off and never came back. The father was left to share his holidays with his friends, who became less frequent as age and death claimed them, too. His sons would call, send gifts, suggest trips to visit, but none of that could work. The old man presumed he would pass from this mortal realm alone without ever wrapping his once-strong arms in loving embrace around another human being.

He had chosen his course, from restlessness, from pride, from desperation, from deep unknown wells of commitment. Whatever

Finnegans were left in Ireland he could not know, for he had lost his family the day he stole passage.

The old man sat in his easy chair and continued to review past holidays throughout the evening. And, although he was saddened, he could not be disappointed. He had shaped himself alone, and now, even in age and solitude, he could recognize that few men ever accomplish what he had done so thoroughly so many years ago.

Let sleep come when it will, the long, cold, dreamless sleep of all mortals, for it would truly be a reward. Yet Liam Finnegan was not a bitter man. He wore the cloak of sorrowful age as fully as any other guise of his long life, and he knew that these bleak, haunted rooms were the logical conclusion of what he had set about as a brash, discontented young man decades ago.

> *The world owes all its onward impulses to men ill at ease. The happy man inevitably confines himself within ancient limits.*

> —Hawthorne

CHAPTER VIII

In tragic life, God wot,
No villain need be! Passions spin the plot:
We are betrayed by what is false within.

—George Meredith, *Modern Love*

Reg Coleman did not look well. Perhaps it was the ceaselessly bleak, slushy days of mid-January. Perhaps it was the resumption of classes with all their attendant demands after the lazy, well-fed holidays. Or perhaps Reg Coleman looked so ill because he had contracted some subtle disease that chews away one's health almost imperceptibly from within. Perhaps it was any of these reasons, or perhaps it was none of them.

He reappeared on campus in January as a gaunt, muted specter, speaking infrequently, and then never venturing into conversation but only reacting when spoken to. His once-full frame had thinned: his friends saw bones on him—elbows, long and stringy forearms, and in the shower ribs and sharply pointed hips. His cheeks had fallen away to pockets. His roommate, Dan Rosselli, would watch him sleep, lying on his side, and imagine small pools of water collecting in sockets above his jaw line. His eyes had gone blank. Where before his friends had seen the flitting, dartlike depths of Coleman's moods reflected there, they now saw cold, dead slate. It was like gazing into wet clay.

He no longer took care of himself. Reg Coleman went about campus in rumpled and wrinkled clothes that now appeared sizes too large.

He combed his hair not at all and shaved infrequently. Rick Murdoch found him in the communal showers one morning leaning against the tile, the stream of water shooting into the side of his face then running down the length of his body. Reg did not move even when Murdoch entered the adjacent stall. He made no effort to wash himself, nor took the slightest notice of his friend. He just stood there, head and shoulders braced against the cold tile wall. Rick Murdoch thought it strange, took his shower, but told no one about it until much later.

Reg Coleman followed a routine, exerting himself only so far as was required by his responsibilities and going no further. Classes, meals and study; no deviations. Study, it should be noted, was by no means thorough. He would sit at his desk, in his room or at the library, and stare at a book, rarely turning any pages. In this way he might pass an entire evening, reading, if so it could be called, twenty-five or thirty pages in all, then going to bed at 10:00 or 10:30, ridiculously early in the eyes of his dormitory mates. He did not socialize. He went to no parties nor did he join his friends in the floor's lobby when groups of them would sit around to pass the time. His friends noticed his absence. Reg had enjoyed their company before the holidays, or so it had seemed, and he had taken a drink or two with them as often as he could. His friends noticed his absence, but they did not discuss it beyond "Where's Reg?", "In his room", and then an obligatory grunt of acknowledgement. To do otherwise, to dwell on it at all, would have been rude.

And so Coleman passed his days through January and into February. The weather did not brighten, nor did Coleman. He did not speak, he did not respond: he remained wooden, a lifeless puppet controlled by strings of destiny visible to no one.

One night in late January, Tom McIlweath put down his Latin book and walked next door. Dan Rosselli was out, crashing a fraternity party in search of women, so McIlweath knew Coleman would be alone. Of all Coleman's friends, Tom McIlweath was most empathetic toward a soul he saw as isolated. McIlweath had observed it, had looked into those sullen eyes, and he had felt a pang. It shot through his ribs, up his sternum and caught in his throat. He had begun to fear for his friend.

McIlweath rapped lightly on the door, did not wait for a reply, and entered. "Hey, Reg. I thought you might want to take a break," he said in a voice he recognized as too bright for its audience.

Coleman looked up slowly through eyes rimmed in red. An open book lay next to him on the bed where he reclined. He spoke slowly in a low voice. "I don't think so, Tom. No. No, I don't think so. I'd like to finish this," and gestured with his book, *The Collected Short Works of Edgar Allan Poe.*

"That's pretty grim stuff."

"Yeah. I like it. I'm reading 'The Premature Burial.' Great piece of work. I've started to develop an appreciation for Poe. I think I might have liked him if we'd ever had the chance to meet . A drugged-out, alcoholic pervert."

"Sounds like a lot of guys walking around campus."

Coleman did not smile. He continued to look quizzically at McIlweath, who had not moved from just inside the doorway. He stood where he had entered, hands in his pockets.

"You picked the wrong guy to take a break with," said Coleman. "I'm not in the mood for company." He turned back to his book.

McIlweath took a step further into the room. "Listen," he said, "Murdoch has a bottle of wine in his closet. What do you say we find a couple of glasses and relax. I don't want to study anymore tonight."

"Isn't that breaking training?" replied Coleman, almost in a sneer.

"Coach'll never know. Come on, it'll be good for us."

Coleman hesitated, but then said, "Get some for yourself, Tom. I don't want to drink."

"I don't want to drink alone, Reg."

"Then go find someone else," he snapped. "Go find Finnegan or O'Hanlon. Go find some of the animals around here who don't give a damn about anything. There's plenty of them to choose from. They'll be happy to drink themselves blind with you."

"I don't want to get blind. I want to relax. And so should you, Reg. Jesus."

"I'm as relaxed as I care to be. What difference does it make anyhow? And who the hell are you to tell me to relax? Look at yourself," Coleman's voice rose, "with your Dean's List and your swimming and your God damn friendships. You're on full scholarship, aren't you? It must be so easy for you that you can spend your time in charity work like this. Go ahead and relax, Mac, but leave me the fuck alone."

"What's the problem, Reg?" McIlweath bit back. "Your father again, is that it? Whatever it is, it's not me, so don't make me your whipping boy. And if it is your father, then screw him. You've got nobody to answer to but yourself."

"Maybe my father isn't the problem, pal. Maybe the problem is me. Maybe there is no problem. Maybe, just maybe, you can't see everything, Mac. You can't know everything, despite what you think. God damn your ass, go find someone else to help. Go bestow your blessings on some other poor bastard."

"Jesus, Reg, calm down. What's bothering you is your business. But I'll tell you again, I'm not the problem, so ease up."

"Get out of here, Mac. You don't know shit. I don't want to talk to you. About anything. Just leave me alone."

McIlweath turned to walk out. "Nice talking to you, Reg." He closed the door behind him and returned to his own room. A few minutes later as he sat at his desk trying to read Catullus and wondering what had happened to his erstwhile friend, he heard through the cinderblock a muffled pounding.

"I saw him, you know. When I was home. He called me and asked me to meet him." Glynnis Mear's eyes had not yet adjusted totally to the dim wood interior of the bar. She lifted her glass of wine blindly and took a sip.

"He looked exactly the same. Nothing changed, not even his attitude. You'd think he'd have mellowed after what we had gone through, but he came on like the same old arrogant bastard he'd always been. He made it seem as if he was doing me some great favor by seeing me. He kept talking about the risk he was taking, meeting me in a public place, and how his wife would never understand if some acquaintance mentioned we were together."

Lynda Hoelscher finished her beer. It had not been her first. She motioned to the server, and another was on its way. Lynda liked this bar. She appreciated its atmosphere. Very thick, very solid, low and dark. She came here often. Although it was a Thursday night, young people filled every corner of the open room and swallowed up the bar itself. She and Glynnis had been fortunate to get a table.

"Why did he want to see you, Lyn? What did he want?"

"What do you think? Like I said, he hadn't changed. There's an art, Glynnis, in making the seediest impulses seem honorable. It's a type of camouflage that men master more easily than women. To my credit, I had no delusions when he called me, although I admit I was surprised. He knew the damage he'd done."

"Yet you saw him anyway."

A wry smile curled the edges of Lynda's mouth. "Yes, my naïve friend. I saw him anyway. Unlike Peter, I saw no need to camouflage my own base impulses. It had been a long time."

She took a long draught of her beer. Glynnis could finally make out her eyes. They glimmered in the dim light, the fine layer of moisture covering the iris catching whatever color danced around the crowded room. Glynnis identified blues and greens in the reflection.

"He called me," Lynda continued, "And said he wanted to meet me somewhere, just to see how I was doing. He sounded almost apologetic. 'I know I'm intruding,' he said, 'but I want to make certain you're all right. I still care about you, no matter what you think of me,' and blah, blah, blah. A very effective act, I must say, although I didn't buy it for a moment. He suggested I meet him at a bar we both knew across town, a bit like this one. You know, even after everything I went through, there's still some magnetism between us. Nothing lofty, just basic animal magnetism. That's what started things in the first place."

Lynda paused again to take another swallow. Across the table, Glynnis sat transfixed. She had come to care deeply for her friend. After the holidays, she had perceived a subtle alteration in Lynda's character. Lynda had put the last vestiges of vulnerability aside. She had become even more aggressive, even more self-possessed. She had always had a hardness about her, but now the shell had thickened. She drank more, nearly every night, and had become more profane. Her studies, never a high priority, had lapsed even further. Glynnis believed the story she was now telling lay at the root of this sad change. It was more than self-abuse; it was a dissipation, slow, gradual yet apparent to anyone who cared enough to look.

"Once I got there," Lynda resumed, "we spent about thirty seconds talking about me and how I was doing, then he started in on how risky it was for him to be there, and what if someone saw us, and couldn't we go someplace private, just to talk, you understand. He really was concerned about me, right? I didn't even have a chance to finish my drink. I know what you're thinking, too, Glyn, and maybe I was a fool to go with him. I knew what he wanted, but in some perverse way I wanted it, too. Like I said, animal magnetism."

"I can't say anything against what you did," responded Glynnis. "There's no way I'd ever judge you unless I had been in your position. Go on. Where did he take you?"

"Can you believe it? He took me to the same old motel. All the way there he kept assuring me it was just to talk, just so he could get to know me again, to see how I was doing, to convince himself that I was strong. 'It's over, Lynda. I'd never do anything to hurt you, but this is the only place I know where we can be totally alone.' I don't think I said more than a dozen words on the drive out there. I let him go on with his line. Maybe he really convinced himself that his intentions were honorable, the poor idiot.

"We got to our room," she continued, "and as soon as we got inside he took off his coat and tie. He knew what he wanted to do. He was trying to set it up. Peter sat down on the bed, and I think he took his shoes off, too. I don't know how it all happened. I can't remember what he said or how long it took him to get me undressed and into bed with him. You know what's funny? I'm not even certain who made the first move. I can't remember. All I know is that I insisted he take me right back to the bar afterward. I wanted to get home early so my parents wouldn't be suspicious of anything. That was the only thing that was important to me then," she laughed softly. "Nothing else. He was just a piece of meat, after all. But God, he was still good. He was better than ever."

"Was that the only time you saw him, Lyn?"

"No. We got together five or six more nights. Same motel, same result. And each time I made him take me right home so I'd get in at an early hour. I didn't care about him. I just cared about what he did to me, and that was fantastic. I'd been missing that. I'm empty again," she said, gesturing with her glass. "You want another, what, Chardonnay?"

"I don't think so."

Lynda caught the server's attention once more and pointed to her glass. A few seconds later she had another beer in front of her.

"How do you feel about that?" asked Glynnis. "That must have been awfully difficult, wasn't it? I mean, seeing him just for sex. That must have brought back some hard memories."

"Why should it? We were meeting on my terms. No emotional complications this time. We serviced each other, that was all. We couldn't have done that before, at least I couldn't. Now I can. I took advantage of him, only he didn't know it. He thought he was performing some great humanitarian overture, helping me prop myself back up. The ass. The arrogant ass. As if I'd be lost without his attentions. Without knowing that he was still thinking about me and that I could still perform like a woman." She paused to take a long drink. "He did nothing for me, except give me a few thrills."

"I think it was important for you to know that, Lynda."

"Maybe. I think maybe I've known that for a long while. It was important for me to take my pleasure at his expense, no strings attached. If he doesn't see that, if he thinks there's still some affection there, so much the better. He made a fool of himself. I'm glad I got the chance to be a part of it. And I could ruin his life now if I ever chose to. There's immense power in that, and more than a little satisfaction."

"You're turning into a black widow," Glynnis said through a cautious smile. Lynda's tale had made her uneasy. It was all too cold-blooded, but this wasn't the time to challenge her motives. She had been hurt beyond all measure. Lynda looked to Glynnis tonight for an ear, not a conscience.

"A black widow," Lynda repeated, her own face showing a clever smile. "Kill your mate when you're done with him. I like that. I think I'll find a black sweater with an orange pattern in front. I'll wear it every time I go out. It's only fair to give a subtle warning, no?"

Two young men, college students obviously, had made their way unnoticed to the girls' table, sliding over in ministeps, allowing the crowded bar to push them in the right direction. They stood now only two or three feet away from the edge of the table. To all observers, including the girls, they carried on their own conversation. In reality, though, they were timing an approach, sufficiently casual. When the conversation at the table paused, one of them at last turned toward the girls, leaned over and said, "Good evening, ladies. My friend and I were hoping we could buy you a drink. Your favorite beverage, no limitations."

They were not unattractive by any means. Both dressed similarly, in tight sweaters that showed one with a small but firm build and the other, at least three inches taller than his companion, with a powerful, strong torso. Both wore slacks, not jeans, and both were very well groomed—short hair, styled, shaven, washed and scented. Lynda perceived the scent of cologne, although she could not tell exactly who wore it. Probably both.

They might be brothers, thought Lynda. She measured them in a glance. No doubt that they were students, upperclassmen, possibly even graduate students, and likely from the University of Pennsylvania. Penn bred this type. She had been on campus, and knew that they were coming out of the walls there, advertisements from *Gentlemen's Quarterly* come to life.

"Yeah," she replied. "You can buy us a drink. You sure you can afford it?"

The taller one responded as he turned sideways to flag down a server. "I spare no expense in the interests of friendship. What would you two like?"

Glynnis slid off her chair and grabbed her coat from the back of it. She wanted none of this; she had no stomach for it. She had seen all this too often in the short time here, variations of a single theme, a ritual never holy, never fresh. "I don't mean to be rude. I was about to leave anyhow."

"You can stay for one, can't you?" said the shorter of the two. "We don't even know your name yet."

"Come on, Glyn," said Lynda. "There's no need to go now. Things are just starting to get interesting."

"'Fraid I have to. Take care of yourself, Lynda. See you back at the dorm."

"You're no fun anymore, Glynnis," responded Lynda with a mock pout, although her voice betrayed no resentment. Now she might have her pick. Or maybe even take both. "See you back there eventually."

The shorter one persisted, taking a small step toward Glynnis as she pulled on her coat. "Can I walk you back to campus? It's dark and cold out there. No telling what you'll run into."

Glynnis smiled. Neither of these two young men struck her as unpleasant. Yet she remained totally disinterested in getting to know either of them. "No. Stay here with your friend, and make a new one. I really can take care of myself."

"It's no trouble. Really."

Glynnis held firm. "No. Stay here where it's warm." As she pushed her way through what had become a dense mob, she heard Lynda in the background. "Sit down, gentlemen. It looks like just the three of us for now. The Black Widow would like a Heineken."

Glynnis Mear returned through the four blocks between the bar and the campus without apprehension. This was a fairly reasonable part of town, the college part, where the only action centered around the student bars. Even on the darkest nights, nothing ever happened near campus. Glynnis instead felt apprehension for Lynda, not because of the two young men they had attracted—they were essentially harmless—but because of the vortex that had apparently claimed her.

Lynda Hoelscher was no longer a little girl, if she had ever been. How ironic, thought Glynnis, that one raised under such rigid strictures should become so scheming, so . . . dispassionate. Glynnis knew that Lynda had been forced out of her shell too soon and too violently, was in fact the victim of someone else's dispassionate scheming. Womankind, the quality of being feminine, had been such a mystery to her. This man, Peter, had manipulated her innocence, invoking new layers to the already confused process. He had exploded for her the traditional myths of security, of emotional protection. He had triggered a release of her emotional and physical natures before they had had time to gel. He had engendered reactions she could never have understood, was totally unprepared to understand, because the context of her youth prohibited such understanding, thinking it sinful because it was all too human. And so, driven by that humanity and the monumental grief of the collapse of every surety she had embraced, Lynda ran away to recover, to formulate a new system of securities, of beliefs. To create a new context.

Had she, in truth, formed anything? Or did Lynda Hoelscher function now nihilistically, a dispirited wraith, exacting a retribution from those who had invalidated her faith?

She had seen him again, willfully. Was it purely vengeance, as she had said, a conviction that she now had the strength to draw from him instead, to satisfy herself at his expense? Or perhaps Lynda, the constructions of her life shattered, sought penance by submerging again in the currents and eddies that had swept away the innocence of those constructions. Now there was nothing for her to believe in, nothing worthy of belief, and so self-gratification becomes the only possible reward. No cost exacted can be too high because nothing is left from which to pay.

Glynnis Mear arrived back at the dormitory, went to her room, undressed and crawled into bed. It was still relatively early, only 11:00, and she did not feel tired, but she had no desire to deal with anyone else this night, and she had no mind to study. Going to bed, pulling the thick blankets up around her neck, would be a suitable insulation. Sometime after midnight, she drifted to sleep.

The next morning she awoke early for an 8:30 class. Lynda had not yet been in. Glynnis rose, showered, dressed. She did not see Lynda until mid-afternoon when she returned to her room between classes.

The two young men were indeed students at Penn, seniors. They shared an apartment near campus. Shortly after Glynnis had left, Lynda asked them to take her there. She had sex with each of them, singly and together, throughout the night, allowing them to do everything their collective imaginations could conjure. Around noon she had taken a cab back to her own campus. She was tired now, and a bit sore. She wanted to sleep.

Glynnis closed the door behind her and went to the library. She remembered the young boy into whose groin Lynda had driven the battering ram of her knee early in the autumn. Somewhere, Glynnis thought, the violence, the vengeance, had been turned inward. Glynnis knew, too, that in the face of such nihilistic fury her friendship could offer little.

And, for reasons she could not begin to fathom, she thought at once of her mother.

* * *

Tom McIlweath pulled a mental plug and let all the thoughts run out. Then, intellectually formless, he sought to work himself into a trance. He knew that the mechanics of the body perform best in rhythm. No distractions exist to pull the rhythm away. The human body, devoid of interference from outside, works its own magic, and efficiently.

McIlweath saw nothing around him save the softly undulating green just below and before him. He did not see Finnegan and his other friends who were in the area. He did not hear their voices, nor the calls of his teammates. McIlweath shook his arms violently up and down, spasmodically snapping off his gyrations at the elbows and wrists. The air wafted against his body, chilling his skin although he did not perceive it. He did not acknowledge what he felt.

"Swimmers, take your marks."

McIlweath stepped up onto the blocks. The green before him had no texture. His motion in ascending the blocks was wooden; his muscles, loosed only with the greatest care, tightened down through the length of his body.

"Set."

The command was not a word, but an expulsion of air bitten off at the end. McIlweath heard it and reacted without thinking. Instinct dominated. He arched his back, leaning forward and pointing both arms to the green womb below him. Tense now, all tightness; wound like a spring for the timelessly eternal split-seconds in this pose, the mind a void, hearing no more, seeing no more, just tension, wrath and fury, legs taut, arms taut, back taut, and leaning ever so slightly, breathlessly, for the edge; don't think, don't listen, don't see, don't breathe, don't . . . Bang!

The gun released him. McIlweath stretched his every fiber into the water, his legs shooting him forward. He thrust out his arms and straightened his back. His gentle face contorted into a hideous, straining grimace. That image of Tom McIlweath's face, an anomaly to his quiet, brilliant nature, now twisted and medusan, would stay with his friends who caught a glimpse of it, Finnegan especially would remember it, in retrospect comforting himself that the beast lurked within McIlweath, too. In this blinking moment, he let it surface.

For half a breath Tom McIlweath was a semi-naked Superman, skimming the air above the water. In the next instant he headed downward and broke the plane. He faded beneath the water's surface, his back still straight, his arms and legs still pointed, but all outlines dissolved under the water that closed over him. He pulled his arms sharply back to his sides in an effort to draw himself as far along as possible under the water where resistance was minimal. He locked his ankles and knees together, then released his long, sinewy arms. It was time to stroke, feverishly, frantically, rhythmically.

If one sits above the water and looks downward at the stroke, the butterfly makes no sense. The swimmer does not swim. He fights the water in a struggle, if not for survival, then at least for dignity. He kicks both feet in one motion, a breaching whale slapping at the water with his flukes. His arms reach before him, then pinwheel around unnaturally. His back thrusts up and down as in an act of copulation. The water fights back to block his passage. He must wrestle it, Jacob and his angel, and it will not release him. Or perhaps it is like a street fight: he must take the water forcefully, brutally, in anger, in a flash of fury, and have his way with it, control it without loving it. He must pound it to submission.

For Tom McIlweath and for the five other young men against whom he swam, the butterfly stroke was little different than it appeared. It was a brutal race, based on an unnatural movement. More than once in practice McIlweath's rhythm had been broken: he would open his mouth at the wrong time, ducking his head as the stroke demanded when he pulled his arms back, and gulp a mouthful of chlorinated water. The water would not be a quiet mistress; it would not submit calmly. Even now in competition, his body working in a carefully contrived mechanical pace, he felt no peace, certainly not in the traditional sense. The race was a sublime struggle that he met most efficiently only when his mind held nothing of the pain, the breathlessness, the groping desperation of it all. During a race, the rhythm, the trancelike, mindless rhythm, was paramount, a holy flame to be tended and preserved.

The race covered 200 meters, or four lengths of the pool. McIlweath had no strategy. In many races of different strokes or distances, he could plan his attack: go out fast and strong, coast in the middle, keep pace slightly behind the leader, then pass him in a finishing kick—whatever it might take. Here, in the 200 butterfly, McIlweath just swam, as hard and as fast for as long as his rhythm would allow.

At the 100-meter turn McIlweath was even with the leader. He did not know it because he did not choose to look around him. He continued to swim hard, and his opponent weakened. McIlweath stretched past him, taking sole possession of the lead shortly after the halfway turn. The remainder of the race he increased his advantage, each windmill stroke pulling him farther ahead. Flip around at 150, then head for home. McIlweath hit the wall a full two seconds before his closest competitor. He clung to the tiling, breathing deeply, his lungs clawing for what they had forfeited the last two minutes. McIlweath realized he had won only after the coach approached him from poolside with his time. He did nothing to acknowledge his victory, no gesture, no smile. McIlweath had not lost a 200 butterfly all year. This was to have been his toughest race. The top swimmer on the other team had similar times, and had placed last year at the Easterns, but it had only been half a contest once the starting gun unchained them both.

After a few seconds, McIlweath climbed out of the pool, took a slap on the back from his coach and walked to his celebrating teammates. The trance had finally broken, but the young man still did not hear the cheering of his teammates or of the small crowd cluttering the bleachers. He took a towel and dried off. Exhaustion claimed him for the moment. All he wanted to do was sit. Tom McIlweath, victorious but hardly smug.

He had swum twice earlier that day, the more conventional 500 and 1000 freestyle events. He had won them both. The season had half ended and Tom McIlweath had yet to lose a race of any distance and of any stroke. The team itself struggled, winning a few, losing more, but the young freshman swam well. People had begun to take notice. McIlweath for his part wished that the team were doing better, that they could win more as a group. His performance so far pleased him, but it was not his nature to gloat. He knew, though, how rare his personal satisfaction was, and how hard he had worked to attain it.

He would not be smug. McIlweath feared that, if overconfidence caused him to relax his regimen, all his accomplishments would be lost. He worked harder than ever in practice to keep himself sharp, and he knew that he was in the best shape of his career. 'Glory at best is a fleeting thing,' he told himself, 'and meaningless, nothing more than an acceptance of other people's standards. I'd rather please myself.'

Among the small crowd watching the meet were Conor Finnegan, Lanny O'Hanlon and Dan Rosselli. O'Hanlon, feeling the hard wooden bleachers digging into his thin rump, decided to leave after McIlweath's last race. Rosselli and Finnegan stayed for the entire meet, Rosselli because he had swum competitively in high school and, friendship with the star aside, he enjoyed the milieu.

Finnegan remained because he felt a quiet pride in Tom McIlweath, something almost proprietary. Finnegan had found McIlweath back in California, or so he thought, had pulled him out of his shell, had dragged him across country and watched him set up here. Now Finnegan could share a stake in his friend and vicariously exult with him in victory. McIlweath's success meant more to Finnegan than it did to the swimmer himself.

"Did Tom always swim like that?" asked Rosselli after O'Hanlon had left.

"No one really knew. Our school didn't have a swim team. Mac always kept to himself and no one ever figured him for a star. Ironic that no one knew who the best athlete in our school really was. He had to come clear across country to prove himself."

"Well, he's damn good," said Rosselli, and then after a few seconds pause, "Maybe I should have done that."

"You swam in high school, Dan. Why didn't you go out for the team here?"

"No desire, Conor. I wanted to put swimming behind me and concentrate on other things."

"Like having a good time."

"Right. Like this. A lot of fun, don't you think?"

Finnegan smiled. "Absolutely. What could be more fun than watching a swim meet on a Saturday afternoon in a dank old pool?

That's what college is all about. Who needs wild parties and loose women?"

"We do, old chum. We just can't find them."

"Alas."

The meet ended shortly before 5:00. Rosselli and Finnegan rose to leave. "Danny boy, you feel like getting something to eat?"

"What do you have in mind? The Commons?"

"Tony's," replied Finnegan, naming a popular cheap Italian restaurant near campus. "I'll even pay as long as you limit yourself to one main course."

"Let's go, Chief."

Finnegan and Rosselli walked the two blocks to Tony's. The midwinter sky hung a low canopy. It would snow that night. When they stepped outside the gym it was already dark. A light breeze came across the river.

"You hear from Stephanie yet?" asked Finnegan as they walked along.

"No. Not since Christmas. She's probably busy with school and all. She works, you know. Waitress in a coffee shop."

"Yeah. She probably hasn't had a chance to write/"

"We had a great time over Christmas. I'd like to get her to come up here for a weekend. She'd love it. She'd like all you guys."

"No doubt she'd be a better roommate than Reg."

"Jesus, Frankenstein's monster would be a better roommate than Reg. All he does is sleep. He never talks anymore. He doesn't even study. The guy's a zombie, Conor. I don't know what's happened to him. He didn't use to be that way."

They reached the restaurant, a two-story bleached-brick building identifiable by a single blinking sign on its corner. The interior was cramped, the bar and dining area jammed into the same small room, the bar occupying the right half and a few tables scattered across the left. There was a rear room, too, but that was very compact and reserved for those few diners who liked the food but preferred not to mix with the raucous college crowd that dominated the main area. The restaurant had no décor: the floor was covered with tiles, many cracked or split; the tables were rickety wood, covered with oily cheesecloth in typical red-and-white checked patterns. On the walls hung several old pictures of the Rutgers campus from decades ago. Here and there, initials or a Greek fraternity marking had been dug into the soft wood walls. A thin layer of haze hovered over the bar and spread to the dining area.

Tony's filled a need. Its atmosphere spoke to the bawdy yet innocent stage of a young man's life, a stage of tentative emergence into responsibility and dimension. One could feel safe there, and because the clientele was overwhelmingly Rutgers students, part of something larger. Here one could go to relax, to take a meal far better than standard college fare, to drink some wine and share some ideas. And even if the latter did not happen, one felt as if it did simply because of the communality of the place. It was, above all else, a college restaurant. Finnegan loved it, and went there as often as he could afford.

They had arrived early enough to get a table. Shortly the place would be jammed with a noisy throng of drinkers and diners. They seated themselves near the door and took two menus, huge plastic things that were awkward to open because of their size. They didn't need them. Each ordered a veal parmesan dinner, spaghetti on the side, with a liter of Chianti to split.

"About Reg," continued Finnegan. "He's really gone downhill. I'm a little worried about him. Has he ever said anything to you about what's eating him?"

"Like I said, he's a zombie. He doesn't talk to anyone. I know he doesn't like his father much. That could be it."

"Why does he have a problem with his father, do you know?"

"He thinks his father forced him to come here and has all these expectations for him. His father apparently was a real star here thirty years ago. Big football player, good student. Went on to business school. I guess he expects Reg to be the same way."

"That's a tough order. Reg doesn't strike me as exceptionally blessed in the brains department. He seems like the type who has to work hard for whatever he gets. If he's not motivated, he'll get blown away."

"He used to work pretty hard. Now he doesn't do anything. I know he's on probation. Flunked four out of five first term. He's not going to do any better this semester unless he pulls himself together."

Finnegan shook his head. "A sad case, *paisan*. We should feel fortunate to be where we are."

"You know, Conor, the odd thing is that it hasn't been that hard. Not like I anticipated. We've got to work a little more, sure, but it's really not that tough. I haven't run into anything I couldn't handle with a little effort. Maybe I'm smarter than I thought I was."

"Maybe, Dan. Maybe you're a latent genius."

The wine arrived. They filled their glasses and drank. Rosselli took a slice of the pre-dinner bread.

"I didn't want to swim this year because I was afraid it would hurt my grades. I think I regret that now. Especially after watching Mac."

"How good were you, Dan?"

"I was good, Conor. Good enough to make this team. I swam breaststroke and the short sprints. I made states two years in a row."

"Maybe you can swim next year."

"Maybe I should. I miss it, and I never thought I would. Probably like you miss basketball."

"I do miss it," said Finnegan. "But I try to make up for it. I play a lot on my own."

"Not the same, Conor. No one's cheering for you there. I swim at the pool every time it's open, but I swim lousy. I can't get excited. No one's calling my name. No one's cheering me on. It's not the same if no one's paying attention."

Both Dan Rosselli and Conor Finnegan did indeed need the cheering. Their friendship had grown quickly from their first meeting because they provided a perfect complement to one another.

Dan Rosselli had grown up in a small town on the south Jersey coast. Rutgers had always been his destiny. His family was of relatively modest means and he possessed talents enough to warrant a fine college. Rutgers was affordable for in-state residents and close to home. Rosselli enjoyed the security of knowing his environment; he had no urge to go far afield. He frequently went home for the weekend, chugging down the highway in an ancient dirty-white Ford he nicknamed 'The Ivory Crusader,' toting a bag of soiled clothes in need of washing and enough books to impress his parents.

Rosselli, like Finnegan, was an only child and that one fact had formed the basis of his personality. Dan Rosselli enjoyed the spotlight. His parents provided him with as many material comforts as they could afford. They took their greatest pleasures in sharing good clothing, fine and plentiful food, and annual vacations with young Dan. In return, Dan cultivated their affections and interpreted their pride. He worked hard to feed that pride, to do well in whatever he might attempt, both for his own betterment and for his parents' approval. In high school he had done well enough scholastically, but discovered that, unless he were at the very top of his class, the rewards were intangible. He received no trophies for making the honor roll.

By contrast, he observed early in life that athletic excellence was applauded more loudly than the less visible forms. He enjoyed sports, but as a boy excelled at none. Football intimidated him, basketball sped past him, and baseball mystified him. He wanted very badly to find a sport, any sport. In high school he stepped onto the tennis court and dove into the pool, and in so doing realized his breakthrough. While most boys his age pursued the major team sports, Dan Rosselli lit upon two lesser sports with commensurately less competition. He played tennis for four years, advancing once to the state tournament where he was quickly dispatched. That got him a trophy. He swam, too, and did even better at that. By his senior year he was team captain, earning honorable mention all-state in the breaststroke. That got him several trophies. He gave each one to his parents and watched their admiration grow.

One day, when he was a tender fifteen, he took a walk on the boardwalk near his home. It was late autumn, and cold, so the beach was vacant. He heard from offshore a cry for help. Peering through the gray, windblown mist he saw, ninety or a hundred feet from shore, a flailing figure and, behind that, a capsized dinghy. Rosselli hesitated, weighing risks and rewards. A few seconds later he leaped fully clothed into the surf, swam out to the panic-stricken fisherman and began pulling him in. The fisherman was icy; even though he had been in the water only a few minutes he had entered the early stages of hypothermia.

Only in retrospect did Rosselli realize the full risk he had taken and vowed to himself to be more careful should something like that ever arise again. The local newspaper, though, found itself a hero. Dan Rosselli basked in the glow for months afterward.

Rosselli was tall, owner of a large frame that easily grew larger if he were not observant. He possessed, too, an outgoing, garrulous personality that fit his size. One looked at Rosselli and could not imagine anything devious, calculated or improper working through his quick mind. He exuded an innocent warmth—large brown eyes and a perpetual smile on a rounded face, topped with light brown curly hair, something *in toto* of a teddy bear. Rosselli told many jokes and laughed frequently. He enjoyed being with people and could not understand how anyone could favor the solitude of constant introspection. He did not brood, or ponder, or withdraw. He considered himself a moral man, and accepted that as an ongoing reality. He investigated matters no further.

He had been conditioned from birth to his enjoyments. He relished material comforts, and good companionship, and, perhaps above all else, approval. His life had begun with modest amounts of each. He learned his pleasures and over time developed ways to expand them. Dan Rosselli's personality grew from these desires. He was, in the end, a materialist unencumbered by the higher questions. The warmth of his personality was not in actuality a façade, for he did truly enjoy the people and the life around him, yet it was a device that facilitated the gain of his most sublime pleasures.

College, too, was a device. A degree meant a career. Whatever he might learn in the course of attaining the necessary grades would be incidental. It was all a means to an end, and the end was comfort.

Rosselli hoped for medical school. Doctors made more money than anyone, he reasoned, and people tended to respect them highly. It might even be a way to keep the applause ringing in his ears.

The friendship between Conor Finnegan and Dan Rosselli was complementary because, quite simply, they provided each other an audience. Rosselli, for many reasons, saw Finnegan as a special individual, distinct from the thousands of other students at the college. Finnegan perceived this and came to relish it. They enjoyed each other's company, the lightness of it, the unburdened levity, the stories, the sharing of common situations. Finnegan grasped again, in Rosselli, the self-justification he craved, while Rosselli, in an effort to add to his own image, wore Finnegan like a badge.

The two drank much wine that night. They put Reg Coleman far out of their minds, and Tom McIlweath, too, and virtually everyone else. They spoke of themselves, relating incidents from their pasts and presents. Finnegan grew philosophical, Rosselli giddy. Around 8:30, friends they knew from the dormitory came in and joined them at their table. The conversation broadened and became earthy. Near midnight Finnegan and Rosselli rose to return to their rooms. Each was very drunk but alive with the wordless exultation of youth, of companionship, of joy, of power. They staggered out the door, Finnegan measuring his steps to make certain he didn't jostle any tables.

They had eaten well, they had drunk extremely well. They had shared the peculiar company reserved for a carefree and innocently arrogant youth. Finnegan and Rosselli wrapped their arms around each other's shoulders and bumped their way home. Because they felt like it, as they passed the student center they sang the alma mater.

Conor Finnegan had always been a believer in Providence. Or rather, he believed that, for whatever reason, Providence was a believer in him and so sat perched comfortably upon his shoulder.

His whole life had reinforced the notion that the Fates regarded him as their special child. It had always been that way. Even now, in undertaking the most substantive challenge of his tender life, he could consider himself fortunate. He had weathered the bumps and absorbed the doubts. In retrospect, it had all been good for him. Those midyear uncertainties had served him well. The basic confidence of Conor Finnegan, that unshakable faith in himself, remained intact.

And so Finnegan was not given to worrying about his future. He possessed some real physical and intellectual talents. These, carefully refined, would be enough to cashier whatever opportunities Providence put in his path. Finnegan trusted the creativity of his own character. Let Providence take its course.

He projected for himself a career in the law, which, he felt, had a certain glamor to it, an intellectual vitality. Moreover, as he conceived it, such a career might allow him to accomplish some genuine good. Finnegan wanted to help people. About that he was sincere, for he possessed a latent, rigid sense of ethics. Where he perceived injustice (and it was all around him—racially, economically, socially), he felt an inward ache. Man's inherent brutality gnawed at him. His circumstances now permitted him to do nothing—he had no clout—but that was bound to change in due course. He knew intrinsically that the pleasures, the carefree amusement, the intellectual dabbling of his current lifestyle was nothing more than a prelude to something grander. He would enjoy what he had now—it would build him up—and then he would use it all, whatever he had, whatever he could, when he was able at last to wield his strengths in pursuit of what he knew, *he knew*, to be just.

Finnegan knew all this in a general sense. He trusted the details to take care of themselves.

One late evening in early March, Lanny O'Hanlon received a telephone call on the floor's phone at the end of the hall. He was gone half an hour. When he returned, Finnegan had already crawled into bed.

"Some woman, Lanny?"

"My father. Roommate, what are your plans for the summer?"

"Hadn't really thought much about them. I suppose I'll go home and find a job. Or maybe not. Why?"

"My father called to tell me his friend, the senator, is looking for a legislative intern. Someone to do research, a little writing. Shake a few hands and look presentable."

"In D.C.?"

"No. In Boston. The district office."

"So what are you getting at?"

"Dad says that internship will be reserved for me. The senator owes him a few, I think."

It was true. Kevin O'Hanlon was a U.S. District Justice in Boston. He knew the state's junior senator quite well. Their careers had more or less intertwined.

"Anyway," continued O'Hanlon, "There are ninety-nine other U.S. senators, and they all need interns. Dad asked if I knew anyone who'd be interested. I told him that nearly everyone I knew would be interested, but there was only one I'd recommend."

"Me?"

"You. I presume you'd want to work for one of the California senators. Dad said he'd tell our boy to put in a word for you with your boys. They'll be expecting a letter from you within the week. Take your pick. You can work for the old one or the young one.”

Finnegan sat up immediately. O'Hanlon had once again taken him completely by surprise, and an electric sensation rippled through his limbs. “What are you saying, Lanny? All I have to do is write my senators, ask them for an internship and tell them who I am?”

“Dad said it'll be all arranged. Write them tomorrow and wait to see who'll make the better offer.”

“Jesus, I can't believe that.”

“Listen, pal, these guys get hundreds of letters from people asking for jobs. Maybe thousands. They don't know who to pick. Everybody looks the same and they all look damn good. My dad's doing them a favor. He's giving them some guidance. As long as you write a somewhat coherent letter and don't drool or pick your nose during the interviews, you're in.”

“Holy Jesus, Lanny, I don't believe it! This is great!” Finnegan exhaled the words in an excited prattle. O'Hanlon, as ever, remained cool.

“The best part, friend, is that both senators have Los Angeles offices. You can still go home and chase beach bunnies.”

Finnegan and O'Hanlon talked well into the early morning, Finnegan in the rich, endless web of wondrous exuberance, O'Hanlon in his calm New England nasality. Finnegan at last dropped off to sleep around 3:00.

The next morning he rushed through classes and sprinted back to his room before lunch. He agonized over the precise language of his letters, taking special care with the one to the stylish junior senator who had caught Finnegan's eye upon his election and whose politics seemed more compatible with his own. After two full hours, a missed meal and an odd March sweat, Finnegan had his final product.

He sent an identical letter to each senator, then impatiently waited for response. As the week ended, his excitement waned. 'These things probably happen all the time,' he thought. 'They'll toss my letter in with the rest.'

He was wrong. Within two weeks he received a note from both senators requesting that he come to Washington for a brief interview. Would he call the senator's office for an appointment? One wrote, “I have heard your praises sung by my colleague from Massachusetts and I am confident that we can find a suitable place for you.” Finnegan dashed for the phone as soon as his pulse calmed enough for him to speak normally. He succeeded in securing two appointments within hours of each other. Both administrative assistants knew his name and were expecting his call.

Finnegan rose at 4:30 one morning in mid-March, showered, put on his best and only suit and crawled behind the wheel of his old car. His appointments were at 11:30 and 1:30. He calculated the drive to be at least three hours, down the Turnpike, across the eyelash of Delaware and through Maryland's thick neck. He wanted to leave himself plenty of time. Finnegan's most immediate concern was the car: it carried a ton of miles, and had not been running well this winter. But there was nothing he could do about that now. If it broke down, so be it. He would trust to Fate.

Shortly after entering the Turnpike, along the flat, spongy lands of Central Jersey, the sun broke to his left. Finnegan loved the morning, the stark, gestating purity of it. His radio pulled in a station from Richmond. Once again, he felt the entire continent at his feet—a clear, virginal continent fresh for the plucking. The morning would be sharp. No clouds blocked the sunlight, and the sky rose to a deep, deep blue with a gentle orange rim on the horizon. A classic, crystal morning. In his exuberance, in his optimism, Finnegan knew that the broad omnipotence of youth rose within him in parallel to the morning sun.

To himself he defined politics as the brokerage of position among those invested with the power to devise and implement public policy. And while the ethics of any particular action might be called into question, he had no doubt that the system remained unassailable as a whole. Power, he knew, carried its own arrogance, but it also carried immense potential to shape complex systems to the benefit of those on their margins. The system bestows certain individuals with the privilege of action, and he saw himself on the verge of some very small portion of that privilege. He felt exalted, he felt honored, but, in the final analysis, it was no less than what he ultimately expected for himself. He might be onto something here. Providence, his friend and lover, may have murmured her most profound whisper. He would have to wait and see.

Around 10:00 Finnegan reached the outskirts of Washington. The city rose up out of its suburbs almost at once: white, vertical, pointed. Finnegan tried to catch glimpses of the landmarks as best he could while negotiating thick traffic in unfamiliar streets. He had spotted the capitol dome and homed in on it as his target. Perhaps after his interviews he would have time to explore the city a bit. It looked green and white, a lot of open space and a lot of marble, unlike the conglomerated chaos of New York. The houses, though, were so narrow, and so close together.

Capitol Hill was a mass of confusion. Finnegan could find no place to park. At a quarter after eleven, after several passes through the capitol area, Finnegan at last parked at Union Station. He would have to walk a bit, and quickly, but it would give him a chance to stretch, to relax himself and to get a feel for the wonderful pace of these streets, these buildings and the people inside them. He felt himself close to the core.

Much to his disappointment, he did not meet with the senior senator. He met instead with the man's chief legislative assistant, a short, snarly man about fifty or fifty-five with deep lines around his mouth and forehead. His full head of hair had grayed only at the temples. The aide removed his suit coat when Finnegan entered his office, and his belly hung over his straining belt. Nothing about the man put Finnegan at ease. His entire demeanor gave the impression of a busy man putting up with an unnecessary and annoying interruption. Finnegan, feeling like an inconsequential worm, tensed immediately in response and came across as the young man he was. He stammered and stuttered through the brief, unsmiling interview. When he left, the aide merely said that they would be in touch, but it might be a few weeks.

Finnegan walked back down the Hill to a coffee shop he had passed on his hike from Union Station. He tried to recompose himself over lunch. He would have to be stronger, that much was clear. He would not be put on the defensive. The aide had no use for him, but that shouldn't have upset him. If the senator had not wanted him there, he wouldn't have been there at all trying to impress this unimpressionable man. The fact that this interview was even taking place should have been enough to bolster his confidence enough to make his words and thoughts flow smoothly. Finnegan would be ready for the next interview. That would not happen again.

He finished his lunch while reading that morning's *Washington Post*. 'Good paper', he thought. 'Good city.'

Finnegan walked back up the Hill to the Dirksen Building, down the street from his earlier appointment in the older Russell Building. He opened the door to the appropriate office at 1:28 by his watch.

"May I help you?" The receptionist was absolutely gorgeous, a blue-eyed blond with a rich, tan complexion. Finnegan drew himself up.

"I have a 1:30 with the senator. Conor Finnegan."

She picked up the phone and punched one of several buttons. "Joyce, Mr. Finnegan is here to see the senator . . . Thanks." She hung up and smiled. "His assistant will be right with you. Won't you have a seat?"

Finnegan sat, and for the next few minutes kept stealing glances at the receptionist. After a bit the senator's personal assistant walked briskly into the anteroom. She, too, caught the young man's eye—a soft redhead, green eyes, slender figure, maybe thirty, maybe a touch less. 'Jesus,' he thought. 'Are they all this gorgeous?'

"Mr. Finnegan, right this way."

He obediently followed through the door into a labyrinth of desks, bookshelves, file cabinets, cords, wires and bodies. The staff's work area seemed incredibly small. Beehives would not be more congested.

They entered a second foyer, one with secretarial desks adjacent to three doors on the two side walls and directly in front of them. The redhead opened the door ahead and poked the upper half of her sublime body through the space. "Senator, Mr. Finnegan to see you." She turned back to Conor, smiled and gestured.

"Thank you," Finnegan whispered as he walked past her, catching a deep, rich scent of orchids.

The senator stood to greet him, then walked out from behind the desk extending his hand and smiling warmly. "Conor Finnegan. So good to meet you. Please, sit on the couch. Would you like some coffee?"

"That would be fine."

"Two coffees, Joyce. Cream and sugar?" Finnegan nodded. "With cream and sugar," the senator called after the retreating goddess.

The senator was tall and tanned, still showing the marks of an athletic past. He was by no means old. In fact, he was the second youngest man in the Senate, having won his seat two years previously at the age of thirty-nine. He had captivated Californians with his crisp, dynamic oratory, his youthful demeanor and his glamorous lifestyle. His best friends were among the wealthiest people of a generation, he owned homes in West Los Angeles and on the Carolina coast, his schooling had been superb. The senator had grown up in the East. He had attended an exclusive prep school, then Harvard, then Yale Law. Along the way he had married an aspiring actress who had little talent but looked the part of young glamor. That beauty translated well to the political realm in which she thrived as the candidate's dutiful wife. She met the cameras handsomely, muttered memorized responses to predictable questions, and scrupulously avoided anything smacking of original thought. Her husband's budding legal career landed him in the House of Representatives by the time he turned thirty-three. After three terms he ran for the Senate. The California electorate had been thoroughly charmed by the whole attractive package, and he won easily. Politics had little to do with it.

Once in the Senate, the man spoke a progressive line when called upon, but generally kept a low profile. He wished to offend no one. The prospect of alienating one senator, or even one voter, practically terrified him. He knew that the quickest way to make an enemy in a pragmatic world was to appear doctrinaire. As a result, he gave lip service to progressive positions, but made it clear to his fellow senators that he was not a fanatic about it. Deals could be made. Meanwhile, he continued to seduce his home state by going to all the right places with all the right people, remaining tan and fit, and taking major stands on minor issues.

"Senator," said Finnegan, "It's a pleasure to meet you. I've admired your work for quite some time."

"Thank you. I wish more people shared your enthusiasm. I wouldn't have to worry so much about reelection." The senator smiled. He was indeed an attractive man, dark brown hair clipped short and hanging across his forehead, a thin face showing nothing rounded, all cheekbones, mouth and chin.

Joyce returned with the coffee. She gave a mug to the senator, then handed a smaller cup to the visitor, turned quickly, and left. The door shut behind her.

"So, tell me about yourself. You come highly recommended by my friend from Massachusetts. I'd like to hear more. How'd you come to Rutgers?"

"I suppose I was looking for a new challenge. New worlds to conquer. I wanted the best education I could afford, and I wanted to try the East for a while. Rutgers fit the bill."

"It's warmer out west."

"Especially now. But it's more challenging for me here. I prefer that."

"What do you aspire to, Conor? What do you want to do with your life?"

"Some good," replied Finnegan, and immediately blanched at his flippant, naïve response.

"I beg your pardon?"

"I want to do some good." He had to follow that up, but he would try now to steer it back to less juvenile terms. "I think that means a career in the law, possibly in government. But I want to think that I'll spend my professional life in some manner of service. I don't think I'd be satisfied with anything else."

"Indeed. You consider yourself an ethical man, then."

"Absolutely." Finnegan paused, hoping the conversation would turn away from this uncomfortable, potentially volatile track. But the senator said nothing. He had to go on, to clarify notions of ethics, morality and personal worth in a formal conversation with a United States senator. He wanted to find a way off this path, but it seemed the die was cast.

"I believe," he continued at last, "that every man has an inherent human dignity. Whatever destroys or compromises that dignity, whether an individual or an institution, is wrong and should be corrected, and if correction is not possible, then opposed intelligently, compassionately, but definitively. That's the basis of whatever ethics I have."

"I see. Let me ask you then, what do you think of our foreign involvements. The wars we fight."

This was a minefield, and Finnegan knew it. Perhaps the senator wanted to test his politics. More likely he wished to test his flexibility, his pragmatism. Finnegan decided at once to play the senator's position.

"I think on some issues we have to temper our moral stand with a faith in our system, and the leadership of that system. After all, that's why leaders lead. I believe you said earlier this year that if we could remove our presence from the Middle East without sacrificing the social and economic gains we've put into place there, then you would support it, but that you weren't certain it could be done immediately. You said that, in the end, the Middle East was responsible for solving its own conflicts, that Jewish and Palestinians, Iraqis, Iranians, and Afghans all had a greater stake in regional security than we did. But we need as a country to coerce their understanding of that responsibility. I think there are certain agreements that have to be honored before we leave altogether. It's a question of identifying our allies and supporting them as painlessly as possible while building their capacity to support themselves. There's a great deal of violence, a great deal of pain, and people don't like it. I don't like it either, but I don't fully understand all the eddies and currents swirling the waters there. I'm not sure anyone does. But until our part becomes clear and our interests are made sustainable, we have a stake there that we have to honor."

The senator seemed satisfied. No dogmatic rebel here. "Tell me, Conor, do you play any sports?"

For the remainder of their conversation, another twenty minutes or so, they talked of basketball, tennis and golf. Nothing even remotely political entered into it. Finnegan, realizing that his only political statement had been graphically compromised to the point of falsehood, felt relieved that matters had taken this more comfortable turn. At length, the senator moved to close the interview.

"Conor," he said, rising, "I've got a committee meeting in about half an hour. Something about fishing rights in the Gulf of Mexico. Boring stuff that I know nothing about, but I do have to be there. Thank you for coming down. I've enjoyed it."

Finnegan rose, too. "It's been a pleasure, Senator. Thank you for taking the time."

"I think I'd be very pleased to have you intern with us."

"Senator, I'd be honored."

"I'm sure you'd do a good job for us. The problem is where to put you. As you can see, there's not much room here, especially for temporary staff. We're quite crowded."

"I can see that, Senator. But all things considered, I'd really prefer to work for you in Los Angeles, if that's possible. That's home."

"I was just about to suggest that. The Los Angeles office has more space. Of course, that's where several million constituents are and it's very important that we know what they're thinking. I assure you you'd still have extensive legislative experience even on the other coast. There are a number of projects you could tackle out there, and I think you'd enjoy it."

"There's no question I would."

"Then it's done. My Los Angeles representative is Greeley Welsh. He's a young fellow about thirty-five. I'll give him a call this week and tell him to get in touch with you at Rutgers. He'll give you all the details."

Finnegan remained externally composed, serious, businesslike. "Thank you, Senator. I'll look forward to hearing from him. You can be sure of my best effort."

The senator shook Finnegan's hand. "Good to have you aboard. You can start in late May?"

"Yes, sir."

"Excellent. I'll tell Greeley." They walked to the door. "Have a safe drive back, and thanks again for coming. I'll see you this summer, I'm sure."

"Thank you, Senator. All the best to you. Good luck."

Finnegan walked back through the offices unescorted. No one noticed him except the receptionist, who gave him a smiling, "Goodbye, Mr. Finnegan." He was caught by surprise so thoroughly that he could not respond. He merely smiled in return and walked out the door.

Conor Finnegan fairly ran back down Capitol Hill to the Union Station parking lot. He did not want to drive around Washington as he had planned; he did not care if he saw the city now. There would apparently be other opportunities for that. Right now all he wanted to do was get back to school so that he could share this most amazing news.

Few things in life are as compelling, or as fleeting, as a young man's exultations.

* * *

Reg Coleman knew what it was he had become, and in this, as in most matters, he blamed his father. He hated his father. He hated himself. Reg Coleman looked in a mirror and saw a malformed ogre staring back at him.

The young man would have no more of it. Everyone has his limit, the point where he will no longer permit himself to be shaped without consent by environment, by natural forces, by temperament. Coleman had long since passed his limit, but he had not known it until well after the fact. By the time he finally lifted his tired head and looked around, seeing himself as if for the first time, the latest dimensions of his character had solidified. He had not known it; he had merely been trying to meet expectations.

It had begun early, very early in his young life. First evidences came subtly. He had not liked sports as a boy. They seemed so meaningless. Win or lose, what did it matter, what did it change? What was accomplished at play today would be forgotten tomorrow. Besides, there was something brutal about all that running and pushing and grunting. He would rather draw a picture or build a model airplane. That, at least, would be lasting.

But there was his father, never missing an opportunity to drag his son into the back yard to throw or kick some odd-shaped ball, maybe to toss it through a hoop. And all the while his father kept exhorting him, telling him how good he was bound to be, just like the old man, and scolding him hard when his concentrations wandered far enough to make him appear as the awkward boy he really was. Young Reg grew to hate these afternoon workouts. But there was no escaping them.

In school Reg would sit glassy-eyed and pursue the daydreams denied his afternoons. There he would think of all those things he would rather do at day's end: fly a kite, or chase the ice cream truck, or perhaps just lie on the ground and watch the bugs go by. He wished he knew how to play an instrument. He wished he could play the trumpet. He would join a marching band, then, and lead the way, blowing as loudly as he could.

Reg's teachers, of course, took a dim view of his mental excursions. By the time he reached the fifth grade, he had lost interest in most of his schoolwork. He had never been particularly good with books, and, as concepts became more complex, he simply dismissed from his mind everything that loomed as too great a challenge to remember. His grades suffered. Reg was a pleasant young man. All his teachers said so. But a pleasant nature doesn't pass algebra tests.

He felt trapped by it all. How could he do well if he would rather be someplace else, doing things he was rarely allowed the time to do because other things were expected of him? And always there was his father, asking for more than he could give, pushing him harder and never, ever being satisfied. Where could he go to escape this?

His father suffered no deviation from a narrow path he himself defined. He demanded in no uncertain terms that Reg be obedient, polite, hardworking and successful. He expected Reg to get high marks in the classroom, and it did not go well for the young man when he faltered. Reg remembered classic arguments, violent confrontations when his father would angrily toss him around the room while screaming his disappointments. But it was on the playing fields that the elder Coleman expected the most from his son. He would not be denied the proud pleasures that came with an All-American athlete in the family.

By the time he reached high school, Reg had been bound to a habit of life he despised. The duty of obedience, of striving to meet his father's demands, had grown into his very marrow. It could not be escaped now; it was part of him and all he knew. His father's approval, paradoxically, had come to mean little to him on those rare occasions when it was actually bestowed. Reg accepted it resentfully and considered that the approval of some other force, far more distant, would be worth immeasurably more. He was a knight in search of the Holy Grail, consumed by an instilled passion for something he could never realistically hope to find.

What did come to matter to him, very deeply, was the approval of his most special friend, his biology teacher. Clinton Davies had not taught long in the system. He was no more than twenty-six or twenty-seven, and still quite green. But from the start of Reg's sophomore year, Davies had taken an interest in the young man. The teacher saw an underachieving student and sensed that something serious, perhaps profound, lay behind it. Day by day, Davies attempted to draw the young man out. Reg would be asked into the teacher's office time and time again, just to talk, and never about biology. 'What do you like to do? What do you want to do? Want to be? Why?'

Davies was compassionate, empathetic. Reg told him of his father, the pressures, the cage walls closing in hot and hard, burrowing into his sides until he couldn't breathe. He told no one else. Even talking to this special man struck him as disobedient. It made him feel guilty to let his problems out like this, even though Davies could be thoroughly trusted, trusted more so than anyone Reg had ever known.

His last two years at high school revolved around his relationship with the young biology teacher. Davies offered Reg a singular release from his father's incessant demands. And beyond that, Clinton Davies suggested to Reg a new and entirely foreign portrait of an older man, a striking contrast to a rock-ribbed, uncompassionate, unloving father. That portrait stayed in Reg's mind, a wondrous piece of art to be scrutinized breathlessly in every light. Reg wanted more of it. He wanted to prove that this unique concept of the compassionate male was no fluke. He cherished Davies's friendship throughout high school. When he graduated, Reg Coleman wept at the prospect of not having access to his friend on a daily basis.

Clinton Davies had sparked in Reg a flickering sense of self-worth. He could be more than the vessel of his frustrated father's vicarious dreams. He could have dreams of his own, and be valuable in his own right. A man's world could indeed approve of poor, underperforming Reg Coleman. He relished the warmth of that realization, and he sought desperately to keep the revelation alive. He sought the nod of a head, the open smile, the glint of an eye that confirmed acceptance. Clinton Davies had pointed Reg to a door he had never seen. Reg stuck his head through, saw a vista so strange as to be compelling, and ran through the door in a frantic effort to become part of it all.

In time, a short time really, the vista became an obsession. He sought the haven of friends who would accept him without judgment, the strong handshakes, the deeply resonant voices. He became more animated among those with whom he felt comfortable. Yet as satisfying as his new realization might be, he sensed something slightly wrong with it. Things did not seem to be quite in order. In the harbor of his friendships he could withstand his father's bluster. Nothing mattered beyond these relationships which proffered a confirmation he had lacked for so long. Perhaps that was it—the imbalance of it all. Fears started to creep into the back corridors of Reg's fragile psyche. He noticed them from time to time, but reactively and without thought he chased them away.

Meanwhile, his father upped his demands. Reg played football in high school, but not well. He had been cut from the basketball team. His grades, never great, had sunk to mediocrity. He had little in the way of an acceptable social life. Reg Coleman would have one last chance to redeem himself in his father's eyes: he would go to Rutgers, his father's school, and he would do well there. By sheer force of his father's will, he would be a late bloomer.

Thus, when Reg set foot on campus during the autumn of that first year, he was an extremely confused young man. In reality he had no base, and little surety. He played to his father's demands at the same time he rejected them, and in the buried reaches of his subconscious he had serious questions about his very nature. He knew most certainly that he was unhappy. It took only a close and critical examination of the reasons to bring Reg Coleman to where he sat one evening in late March, alone and drunk at his desk.

College had provided no therapy. He saw at once that he would not do well academically. He was not equipped for it, and no amount of hard work could bring him up to standard. So he simply stopped trying. His father, in seeing his son's midterm grades, railed violently. For the first time, he had struck his son hard, throwing a fist into his face at

Thanksgiving when Reg broke a commandment by telling his father that he didn't care if he flunked every course he ever took.

"You worthless son of a bitch. You can give me a good effort if nothing else. You don't know what kind of an opportunity you've got there, one I set you up for, and now you're pissing it away. God damn you. God damn you. You make me ashamed to call you my son. You're worth nothing."

Reg stood up from the couch where he had fallen after taking his father's punch. He drew himself up to his full height, wiping the corner of his throbbing mouth. "I can't be your son," he said quietly. "I don't care about your silly dreams. Dream them for yourself and let me be. You've never been my father."

There would be no reconciliation. Both men stood speechless, cowed by violence and shame. Ralph Coleman looked at his son, dropped his head and shook it quickly, clearing thought and memory. The swelling bruise on Reg's lip startled the older man. His rage subsided immediately. Reg had had no rage, only resolve. He would take no more. There was no reconciliation, but for the remainder of the day at least there was peace.

And then Christmas vacation, one lonely night with nothing to do. His father, silent and morose, sat brooding in his study. His mother sat there with him, reading a dime-store novel and trying, in her sheltered simplicity, to pretend that her family stood intact, together and loving. Reg was bored, and when he was bored he sought the ocean, the ancient Atlantic half an hour's drive away. That bottomless, breathless expanse was anything but monotonous. He would watch it, sensing the life underneath and above it, seeing it change shape, color and texture—even at night. No one else, he thought, could see what he could see. No one else ever cared to look.

Reg drove to the shore, parked the car and walked along the rotting old boardwalk with its closed, deserted shops and arcades. A melancholy place this, an old dowager attempting to play the coquette once again through cracked, pasty makeup, but failing sadly, and in so failing exuding an aura of death. It was near midnight. Reg's lone footsteps caused the salt-soaked wood beneath him to creak. He walked slowly, looking out to sea, searching for the definition of forms he knew to be out there. To the north, up the coast, he saw the massive light in the skies that was New York City. The waves, washing in from Europe as he imagined them, whispered a steady backdrop.

Reg walked for a mile or so, stopping occasionally to hang over the railing and stare outward. For the love of God, and for the love of Man.

On his way back down the boardwalk, after he had had enough of this melancholia and was heading back to his car, he ducked into a restroom. He had not seen another soul all night, so he stopped dead in his tracks when he saw the two men inside, one leaning back against the sink, his pants to his ankles, the other kneeling in front of him. Reg did not move; he could not move. He could only stare, transfixed, hypnotized. The standing man kept his hands on the back of the kneeler's head. He looked Reg Coleman in the eye, smiled and winked.

"What do you say, stud? Look like fun?"

Reg Coleman's pulse quickened, his knees and elbows weakened. He swallowed hard, but he had no impulse to flee. Urges hidden away yet all too familiar, all too definable, held him there. Dante in the lower ring of a personal Inferno, but Dante not repulsed, feeling the Inferno burn alive within him.

"Come on, stud. You're looking pretty sharp. Come on. You know you want to. I can read those pretty eyes of yours."

It would all be anonymous; no one need ever know. A test, maybe, to see if there was anything worth salvaging. A chance to sample the pleasures, at last to be a part of them and then, when completed, to walk away a changed man. The pleasures drawing him onward, drawing him outward. Reg Coleman, his mouth dry, did not flee. He took a step forward, into the bowels of the restroom, into the bowels of the scene before him, into the bowels, the deep, stinking, rancid bowels, of what he ultimately knew himself to be.

* * *

When Reg Coleman returned to campus at the end of the winter break, his outward nature had been stripped clear of any frivolity. He wanted none of it. Instead he immersed himself in consideration of his own fate, his own future, whether he had any and, if so, what form it might take. Reg had always been made to accept the traditional values. These had failed him. He had twisted them, made a mockery of them, forged them into the keenest blade upon which his very soul had become impaled. The incident on the boardwalk had provided the last piece of evidence, the final confirmation, of a metamorphosis at which the young man could only wonder. And now that it was finally complete, what happens next? The confirmation stunned him, and kept him stunned.

Reg Coleman had skipped dinner this evening in March. He had, in fact, skipped his two afternoon classes. Instead he had locked himself in his room and taken from his closet a fifth of the cheapest whiskey, pulled his chair around to give him a view of the river, and drank straight from the bottle.

It had been nearly three months since the incident. It seemed sharper to him than ever. And, in the last analysis, he had to admit to himself that he was what he was. There could be no changing it now. Too late for that.

Reg drank through the afternoon and into the evening. His Falstaffian roommate would not disturb him: Rosselli would be at the chemistry lab all night. Nor would anyone else intrude. Over the past few weeks he had managed to alienate virtually all of his erstwhile friends through a complete lack of animation. It was time for some conclusions. Reg counted the hard realities of his life. It all depressed him, weighed almost physically on his slight frame so that he sagged in his chair. He drank some more.

He had been depressed for months, for years, really, and nothing had come close to bringing him out of it. To the contrary, with every step along his pathway he sank deeper. No part of him, nothing, nothing, was as he wanted it to be, and there was scant possibility for correction. Every task he had undertaken had ended in failure; he went through life without love, without assurance, without accomplishment. He had no family. His friendships were superficial, nor would he allow them to be anything but. There was no Clinton Davies here. And now, at last, he had abandoned the final shred of his pretension. The traditional normality he had been taught to worship turned out in the end to be a false god.

Reg Coleman sat at his desk, drunk, disoriented, immersed in self-loathing and devoid of any hope of ever pulling himself out of the muck. Without hope, what remains? He saw himself as a pitiable, grotesque creature, and so it would continue for as long as he lived.

The young man stood and stretched. He glanced at the clock near his bed: 10:07. Rosselli would be coming back soon. Reg was extremely drunk. He had to steady himself on the bookshelf over his desk. A resolution had presented itself to his soggy mind, drastic perhaps, but logical enough. He would have to bring himself to act on it. The fifth of whiskey had only an inch or so left in the bottom, yet despite the huge amount of liquor he had consumed, his senses felt acute. That was fitting, and the young man congratulated himself.

'Yes,' he thought. 'An idea. How simple, how very simple. Pity I had not thought of it before. I would have saved so much time.' He moved to the door, bounced against his dresser, caught himself and straightened up. As he opened the door the light of the hallway scalded his eyes. He stumbled across the hall to the restroom to look at himself in the wide mirror there. Reg leaned hard against the sink and brought his face close to the glass. The reflection swirled before him. He noted that his eyes were redder than he had ever noticed them before, and he was very pale. But no matter now. It was not the time to be bothered by any of that.

Reg Coleman stepped outside the restroom and walked into the lobby. Unusual for a weeknight that no one would be seated there in the gaudy plastic-covered couches and chairs. Reg could hear voices up and down each hallway, loud, profane shouts of young men bored with study and wanting to break out for a while. Nearly every night around this time they spilled into the lounge, to sit and talk, to wrestle, to throw a football around the room. Oddly, though, not tonight, not yet, and Reg felt relieved.

He walked through the glass doors that opened from the lounge onto the balcony. The sharp night air struck him flush, a slap in the face. Often he came out here to watch the river, to feel the same night air. He still did not feel steady—his drunkenness caused him to wobble as he walked—but his will stood firm. His pulse was normal, his palms dry. Behind him he noticed two people come out of the hallway opposite his own. He could not be certain if they noticed him there on the cold balcony.

'Yes', he thought again. 'A resolution. And how very simple.'

He hooked his left leg over the railing. Reg looked six floors below him to the dormitory's parking lot, then raised his head to look across the river. In the distance he could make out the familiar lights of New York, the spear of the Empire State Building and the surrounding glare. He took a deep breath, felt the cold, brittle air pierce his lungs with a sharp stab, then exhaled slowly.

'It's very fine up here,' he thought.

Reg Coleman sat for a few moments straddling the rail. Behind him he heard voices growing excited all of a sudden. One he recognized as Tom McIlweath's voice, calling his name.

No more delays. An answer now to all his loathing. Reg leaned to his left and released the rail with his right leg. For a split second he felt weightless, a free man at last unfettered from all judgment, from all condemnation. A giddy exuberance raced through him. As he tumbled he noticed the black sky with only a handful of white pinpricks scattered across it. In his joy he imagined himself to be one of them, a droplet of light released from smothering darkness. A freedom to this, so rare and all too short, until the solid, heartless asphalt rose to meet him.

* * *

In New Brunswick the last spasms of winter had wriggled and died by early April. The weather at once grew warmer; snow fell no more, and that which had covered the ground off and on since December melted away.

To Tom McIlweath and Conor Finnegan, spring came suddenly.

It crept up on them before they had a chance to notice, so wrapped they were in their own affairs. Neither had paid heed to the subtle changes around them. They took for granted that college life would continue *ad infinitum* as they had first encountered it: cramped, soggy, cold and demanding. They had quiescently accepted their routines as they were, so when spring at last sent forth its quick, tethery fingers, they were surprised and pleased. Their last few weeks on campus would be bathed in mellow satisfaction, a peaceful, all-enfolding serenity that springtime often commands.

The swim season had ended for Tom McIlweath, and it had been glorious. The team had not done well at all, but McIlweath had done his best, always, and had finished the year by placing fourth in the 200 butterfly at the NCAA Eastern Regionals. He now owned three college records and felt capable of several more. His teammates had voted him their most valuable swimmer. Even in his characteristic modesty he recognized that they were probably correct. As a freshman he had accomplished far more than he had ever envisioned. With time he would continue to improve and so, in the season's wake, he dared to dream dreams for himself, possibly even the Olympics. The spring for Tom McIlweath dawned gently sweet as he played with his own ambitions. He had come to college a disoriented young man; within these several months he had honed a self-definition—academically, athletically and socially—and so felt better about himself than ever before.

For Conor Finnegan, the year had been more of a struggle than he had anticipated. It had hit him squarely in the autumn, and staggered him. He had flown home for the holidays, reeling under the blows of unfolding uncertainties. But there he had regrouped. Confidence reinstilled through honest reflection and the familiarities of friends and family, he returned east in January to plunge ahead, this time more cautiously, more aware of his limitations. His appointment to the senator's staff provided a significant confirmation of his unique quality, something he sought almost desperately throughout the year. Now he had it again, a perfect complement to his growing academic reputation and his expanding circle of friends.

Those who knew the two young men generally respected them as distinctive individuals, unusual in dimension, despite their early identification as "The California Twins." In the eyes of their common friends, Finnegan and McIlweath both possessed a character that compelled appreciation. Of the two, McIlweath had the more even temper. He was the harder worker, the quietly intelligent one in whom most people on their floor had found it easy to confide. McIlweath was diligent, persistent, talented, and humbled. He inspired trust.

Finnegan was more outgoing, but his did not seem a false friendliness, for he, too, exuded a subtle compassion. Finnegan could be given to moods; at times he could be sullen and withdrawn. But these instances were rare. He customarily bounced through his days with a buoyancy born of his brimming self-confidence. He had also developed a reputation for brilliance, particularly during the second semester. Of all those on the floor, Finnegan seemed to have the quickest wit, the sharpest mind. He achieved excellent grades without much fuss. The fact that both he and McIlweath had left their homes to travel across country for the experience also caught their friends' fancy, few of whom had ever spent much time with anyone from the mythical west. They were a unique pair, these two. Their friendship came to be a valuable commodity.

For McIlweath and Finnegan, the year had proven to be uncommonly rich. It drew to a close now through a brilliant springtime. The days grew longer. Along the river, turtles came out to sun themselves on the rocks; they could be seen from the dorm windows. The trees around campus blossomed with delicate white and pink buds, and the air carried the pungent sweetness of vernal grass. Birds sang in the trees along the towpath under their rooms. They woke to that sound nearly every morning, the trilling coming through windows left open to bring in fresh night air. In all it was a spring they had never known in the suburban sterility of their paved youth.

As soon as the weather relented, Finnegan and McIlweath began to go for long runs whenever they could find the time together to do so. Each was in relatively good condition, and running would keep them so. Moreover, it cleansed their young minds. The areas around campus presented some outstanding backdrops for their runs. Finnegan particularly liked the towpath along the river, a narrow ribbon of land separating the Raritan from the Delaware Canal. The towpath went on for miles, stretching into the remote wooded lands bordering the town. Often Finnegan would run by himself along this way, seeing no one and hearing nothing but his own footfall. Once, after an especially long run in winter, he had stopped to watch the river. In the late afternoon chill he could see his breath, but more, he watched in wonder as steam rose from his panting body. He had never seen such a thing, and the scene remained in his memory—the stark trees, the brown river, and the steam.

Late one Sunday, before dinner, McIlweath sprang into Finnegan's room. "You feel like a run, Conor?"

Finnegan put down his book, a dull piece on Thomas Hobbes, stood and yawned. "Yeah, I should do something. I've been sitting around all day. Where should we go?"

"Let's head up to the stadium."

"What's that, about three miles?"

"Should be. Up and back, we can handle it."

"Let me get changed. How cold is it?"

"You'll need a sweatshirt."

Finnegan changed into his running gear and met McIlweath downstairs in the lobby. After some stretching they started out. Finnegan did not especially enjoy the demands running placed upon his body, although he liked where it took him. He savored the relative solitude and the serenity that solitude imparted, but he regarded the actual process, the placing of one foot in front of the other, as tedious. The ground pounded his feet and made his shins ache; he grew short of breath until he found his rhythm, the familiar knife finding his side too often; his arms grew weary and weak with their swinging. He could always keep up with McIlweath, who was physically better suited to running, but the effort exacted a toll. Only later, after returning to the dorm and taking a long hot shower, did he feel any renewal. When running alone, Finnegan most loved to stop and rest in the most remote place he could find. There, in a quiet that was unattainable on campus, he truly felt at peace, and dominant. It was for those scattered moments that he met the challenge of running at all.

Tom McIlweath fought no such battles. He could run all day, or so it seemed, and when he finally stopped he never appeared to be breathing very hard. McIlweath ran in long, regular strides, his heels never touching ground, his torso bent slightly forward, his breathing marked by an unbreakable rhythm that lent a pattern to his work. McIlweath ran the way he swam.

They ran down George Street to the old grating paved bridge and picked up their pace as they crossed it, the cars clattering close by them. On the other side they cut diagonally across Johnson Park, the grass at last soft beneath their strides after the hard New Brunswick asphalt. They kept their eyes fixed on the ground in front of them to avoid the marshy places. At the edge of the park ran two low fences, over which they hurdled side by side, onto River Road. After three-quarters of a mile they headed to their right up the long and rather steep drive that led past the old Rutgers Stadium. Beyond, the land opened up into broad green playing fields for baseball and lacrosse. The math and science buildings of the Busch campus, a mile hence, loomed over the entire scene.

Finnegan gestured ahead. "Let's go to the road," he panted, indicating an access road about 400 yards to their left.

"Okay," replied McIlweath evenly, his voice showing no strain.

Finnegan felt winded, his limbs leaden. He plodded ahead with a regular but thick step. McIlweath at his side kept gliding along.

Finnegan at once picked up the pace and, as he did so, took two long deep breath before creating for himself a tight rhythm of arms, legs and lungs. McIlweath was caught by surprise by Finnegan's burst. He scrambled to catch up, but Finnegan had shot ahead and kept pushing harder. He was sprinting now, legs kicking high, arms pumping near his neck, his eyes fixed rigidly on the thin gray asphalt finish line. He did not know how far his friend was behind him. He focused on the line in a manic desperation to reach it first.

McIlweath, though, had regrouped. He lengthened his stride in pursuit. He leaned forward, looking at the right shoulder that had exploded past him. Finnegan was about fifteen yards in front. He settled into his own sprint, counting on his longer strides to close the distance. The access road lay no more than 100 yards ahead of them now, the rolling ground before it falling and rising under their steps.

With fifty yards to go McIlweath had pulled to within a stride of Finnegan. He looked at his friend, struggling now, his rhythm breaking down, running on sheer courage. He could be caught. McIlweath knew it. He brought himself alongside Finnegan but did not pass him. Their right feet hit the access road in unison.

They both trotted a few strides before Finnegan stopped, leaned over and grabbed the ends of his shorts. His breath came in groping draughts. McIlweath slowed to a walk, his hands on his hips. He too was short of breath, but he could recover himself more gradually. He walked in a broad circle for several minutes until Finnegan at last came up to him. He smiled warmly, the perspiration dripping down his nose and off his chin.

"I thought I had you there at the end."

"Me, too. Let's start walking back toward the stadium. We can rest up and head back from there."

North of the stadium they paused. Finnegan filled his lungs, the sharp pain that had cut them apart earlier now subsiding.

"Hold on for a second, Mac. I want to take a look at this."

"At what?"

Finnegan pointed across the river. "At that. At the campus. At New Brunswick. At everything. There it is, Mac. All before us."

And so it was. They both looked then through a berry-blue sky. The sun pushed a last swath of orange to their right, and across the river, under a darkening cover, sat Rutgers and the town, all the life they had created for the past several months. They picked out the stately brick of the dormitories and the library, the clean spires of the old classroom buildings on Queen's Mall, the tops of the fraternity houses, all punctuated by a nascent vernal greenery. Then beyond, the smoky city—smokestacks here and there, the tall buildings of the commercial sector, the black brick of the decrepit unreconstructed houses near the river, the jabbing four-pronged tower of the city's largest and oldest church. It all sat before them, an Impressionist still life, uncaptured, fleeting and too soon gone.

Finnegan, watching, felt a surge of tremendous power enter him, an unrestricted exultation in where he was and who he was. His very existence, all he had known or could hope to know, culminated here, in this view, in the blood running through him now, in the sweat on his face. He had sought no more than this, for here, on this crisp Sunday evening, vibrant springtime consummated his youth. He knew his potential, he breathed it in, it cloyed to the linings of his throat and lungs, it braced the blood rushing around his brain, it seeped through every fluid and syrup within him. Every thought he conceived, every spasm of his grand Romantic heart revolved around the glorious brilliance of this quiet unspoken vista. He perceived it all together, here, on this hillside in the innocence of new spring.

Conor Finnegan looked at the angular features of his friend's face. They betrayed nothing of the reactions pulsing under Tom McIlweath's skin as he, too, stood there regarding the campus in the distance. Finnegan could not read him, could not read Tom's sentiment that it had all worked out very nicely. This was exactly what he had wanted.

They stood silently for a few moments, Finnegan unconsciously pawing the ground around him. At length his exultation calmed. He noted it, and marked the time of this new passage.

"Ready to head back?" he asked.

"Whenever you are. Let's take it slow."

And they did, into a fading day too soon lost and too easily forgotten.

* * *

Greeley Welsh leaned back in his leather chair, his right leg propped on the edge of his desk, a file folder in his tilted lap. He looked alternately out the window to Wilshire Boulevard below and across to Conor Finnegan sitting opposite him. The morning sun streamed through the window to cut his legs in half.

"What're you interested in, Conor?"

"What do you mean? Personally?"

"Professionally. What do you want to do for us?"

"I was hoping you'd tell me. You know what you need better than I do."

"Issue work, Conor. You've got your choice. I'd like you to pick an issue, maybe two, and dive into it. You'll be our point man out here on that issue, whatever it is. That means you'll have to know it inside and out, and be able to represent accurately the senator's position on it. We need someone to make studies, to write speeches, to recommend action, to get to know the right people. The senator's never been inclined to go into any depth regarding issues. He generally takes his positions by sticking his nose out of the tepee from time to time and sniffing which way the smoke is blowing. We try to give him depth. We try to get him to look at a question rationally rather than fashionably. Believe me, it's not easy. He's bright, but he doesn't have much time, as you can well imagine. We've got to feed him the relevant material to make him appear knowledgeable.

"Right now," continued Welsh, "We've got a guy here working on housing problems and another working on relations with the Hispanic communities. Everything else is wide open."

"What about the Middle East?" asked Finnegan. "Can I do something with that?"

Greeley Welsh sighed and pulled his leg down from the desk. He shook his head slowly. Finnegan noticed the sunlight catch the red hairs on his wrist.

"Jesus, I wish you could. I wish somebody could. Do you know what his position is?"

"I've read it."

"It's no position at all. 'Withdraw our military presence as soon as possible but only after we've secured our interests.' He's run up and down the state saying that, but what the Christ does it mean? What are our interests, other than easy access to the oil fields? And, presuming that we have broader motives, how do we secure those interests in that multiethnic zoo without a military presence? And what's the diplomatic plan? Makes no sense at all. If he doesn't change his song, we're going to get killed with that in the next election."

"Hasn't anybody tried to talk him out of that?"

"Christ, we've all tried, but on this issue, of all issues, he doesn't want any help. Gets angry if we persist. 'I have to go with my conscience,' he says. Well, that's bullshit. He's trying to be all things to all people, that's what he's doing. Wants to paint himself as a liberal but doesn't want to offend the war hawks because the hawks have all the money, and he likes money. He needs the right's resources to get re-elected, or so he thinks."

"So you've got one of the most volatile foreign policy situations for an entire generation and he's doing nothing with it," said Finnegan.

"Essentially. He's trying his damnedest to steer clear. Much to my amazement, he's been fairly successful, but that won't last. Sooner or later, someone's going to hang him on it. Politics by neutrality."

"Or by duplicity," rejoined Finnegan.

Greeley Welsh looked up at him and his face spread into a good-humored smile. "I think I'm going to enjoy having you around, Conor."

"You still haven't given me an area."

"Like I said, take your pick."

"What are my choices?"

"Anything you want. Taxation and tax laws. Entitlement reform. Environment. Urban problems. Drugs. The elderly. Whatever."

"Can I think about it and let you know tomorrow? Maybe I can spend today getting acquainted with his positions, pending legislation, and all that. Nuts and bolts stuff."

"That's a good idea. I can tell you that whatever you decide to do, you'll be spending a lot of time answering mail from constituents. We get a bunch of communication each week, and it all has to be answered. We divide it up, and everybody's got to do some, so it's good to know where he stands across the board."

"I thought most communication went to Washington."

"You'd be surprised how many people contact him here. They all expect a reply. Phone calls, too, which we log. People call every day with an idea or a bitch. Mostly a bitch. I've got a feeling we'll be referring most of those calls to you. I hope you've got a thick skin. Come on, I'll introduce you around and show you your office."

"I get my own office?"

"Share it. With Ruben Garcia, who's a Georgetown Law student. He lives in Santa Monica and he's here for the summer. Ruben's our man on Hispanic relations."

Greeley Welsh stood up and moved out from behind his desk. He was a tall man, perhaps 6'3", and seemingly too young for this type of position. But in reality Greeley Welsh had accomplished no small amount in his thirty-six years. He had graduated from a small Catholic college in New England, then spent two years in Kenya in the Peace Corps doing health outreach and vaccinations in the rural villages. From there he returned to New England with little money and a dread fear of malarial mosquitoes. He headed to California where it was warm, and landed a job as a city reporter with a San Diego newspaper. Five years later he had advanced to city editor, and it was in that capacity that he met the brash young congressman intent upon becoming a brash young senator. Three Novembers later, the senator-elect asked the city editor to drive up the freeway to Los Angeles to head his field office there. Greeley Welsh had tired of San Diego anyway; he had spent eight years there. There would be new women in Los Angeles, and better beaches.

Welsh walked his young intern through the office. Of the six people on staff, only one caught Finnegan's attention, and that was Jill, the appointments secretary. Jill had silvery-blond hair, lots of it, green eyes, a deep tan and dimples. Her body had been shaped by some sculptor out of Grecian marble. Jill smiled when Finnegan was introduced, and he knew at once that he would have a hard time acting relaxed around this young goddess.

At the end of the small suite Welsh opened a thick door to a rather large rectangular office with two desks. One had papers and books heaped in piles, the other had nothing on it but a phone, a blotter and a computer monitor. The white walls were covered with enlarged photos of the senator, old campaign posters, and a California map.

"Ruben's in Bakersfield through the end of the week. Some dispute with lettuce growers again. Until he gets back, this is all yours."

Welsh went to a bookcase in the corner and pulled out two thick volumes. "These are the senator's position papers on every issue that's ever come up over the past four years. Read through them and get an idea of who he is. Do some research online of the public records, too, and the news stories. There are lots of them. By the end of the day I want you to take any constituent calls we might get. I'll listen in to see how you do. You can say damn near anything you want as long as you're polite. Don't be afraid to argue, but do it respectfully.

"Tomorrow we'll decide what your area is and map out a game plan for the next three months. If you have any questions, just give a yell. Welcome aboard, pal."

They shook hands warmly and Greeley Welsh left Conor Finnegan to his thoughts. They were many. Finnegan walked over to the window whose view was virtually the same as that in the other office. On the opposite side of Wilshire was a veterans cemetery. Beyond that, Finnegan could discern the UCLA campus, and beyond that the chic shops and theaters of Westwood. The Santa Monica Mountains backdropped everything. Finnegan thought the view spectacular.

And in that instant, Finnegan heard the siren's call through the voluptuous, seductive pull of youthful power.

* * *

Across the city at an exclusive private swim club in one of the interchangeable eastern suburbs, Tom McIlweath sat in the guard's chair a few feet above ground level. The sun on his bare shoulders and chest warmed him. He was baking, and he knew it. Tonight he would feel the familiar sting of sunburn.

The sun reflected brightly off the pool below him. Even his dark glasses could soften only slightly the slash across his eyes. Eight or nine kids, all between seven and ten, splashed and kicked, a school of sleek sea otters at play. Around the pool's edge their socially conscious mothers spread oil on each other and sat in the hot plastic lounge chairs. When they stood up, McIlweath noticed the stripes from the chairs' bindings running across the backs of their legs.

He had worked out in the morning, the first time in several days. His arms and legs felt limply feeble, his back tight. He wished he could take a nap.

Tom McIlweath had flown home two days after Conor Finnegan. A late exam, Latin, had caused him to stay. He had hoped that he and Finnegan could have driven back across country, but Finnegan said no, the old car probably couldn't take it. Instead, he had placed it in the keeping of Dan Rosselli. McIlweath thought that if he earned enough money this summer, he would buy himself a car back at school. It would be nice to be mobile.

McIlweath sat in his chair, felt the warmth, and thought of Finnegan, whom he knew he had misjudged. He regarded Finnegan now as his closest friend, a link between his two worlds, east and west. Finnegan had not been a reminder of McIlweath's shallow younger existence; instead, he had enriched the human dimensions of his new one.

This summer they had both come home, and McIlweath knew that they might see each other only two or three times at most. But that didn't matter. They had come forth together from a womb, conjoined twins linked at the spirit, and if they spent the summer months in their own realms despite their proximity, then so be it. They would still be as close as friendship allowed in the autumn, in the east.

McIlweath reached into his bag tied to the base of his perch and pulled out a floppy white tennis hat. 'My crown.' He thought. 'He who wears the droopy white cotton rules supreme.'

After an hour or so he hopped down from the guard's chair. He walked to one end of the pool, took off his glasses, whistle and hat, and left them in a pile at the edge. Only two young boys frolicked in the shallow end, their mothers chatting under a sun umbrella a few feet away.

McIlweath dived into the pool, extending his body in a familiar arc. The water slapped him coldly. As he drew his arms alongside him underwater, he opened his eyes. The water covered the sun, making it a cycloptic liquid eye directly over and in front of him. McIlweath's head broke the plane of the water. He reached for his first stroke, and drew breath.

CHAPTER IX

Did ye not hear it?—No! 'twas but the wind
Or the car rattling o'er the stony street.
On with the dance! let joy be unconfined;
No sleep till morn, when Youth and Pleasure
        Meet
To chase the glowing hours with flying feet.

—George Gordon, Lord Byron, *Childe Harold's Pilgrimage*

In late autumn, after the leaves have finished changing and the first snowfall has come to cover their musty piles, a young man settles into a winter frame of mind. His collective memory silently takes sway, he becomes more primitive, more concerned with survival. And in a modern society if survival is not at issue, the elements of survival take on a deeper texture, and we relish them. Beds are warmer in winter; we sleep late, thick blankets pulled to our chins. We become wary of every sneeze and sniffle. Food tastes better. The grandest, most rapturous meals of the year we eat in winter. It is a way to confirm our place, this sumptuous feeding. We reassure ourselves that, through the cold, the ice and the snow, indeed we remain alive. We shall beat the devils of winter once again.

As he folded his notebook and walked out of class, Finnegan thought of food. It was mid-November, and as the cold air stung his face he could see his breath. In late afternoon the Mall was virtually empty. Finnegan hustled through it, past Scott Hall, and stepped onto

College Avenue. Music from one of the fraternity houses across the street blared through closed doors. Already it was dark. The headlights of passing cars cut broad lines through the asphalt. An acrid pain in his stomach drew up through his gullet, and Finnegan knew he wanted a big meal tonight. He would cook it. Rosselli would be there, and possibly O'Hanlon if he got back from Trenton in time. McIlweath would be at practice. Finnegan rarely cooked for McIlweath.

As he scurried down the cold avenue Finnegan smelled the pungency of burning leaves. The odor surrounded him in a wave, conjuring traditional autumnal images of football, apples and the coming of the great holidays. He noticed the earth beside the sidewalk was spongy. Several footprints sank deeply into the muck where people walking two or three abreast had over spilled the concrete.

At the stately white-pillared brick library, Finnegan turned left and headed southward down a residential street that adjoined Buccleuch Park. At the end of their second year he and his friends decided that they had outgrown dormitory life. They had split up each afternoon that spring, each scouring a different part of the city looking for a suitable place to live. After several weeks had passed unsuccessfully and a grim despondency had set in, Dan Rosselli met a fellow at the pool one night who said he had just pledged a fraternity and, if he could find someone to take over his lease on a two-bedroom apartment near the park, he would be moving into the chapter house the next autumn. After the four of them—Finnegan, McIlweath, Rosselli and O'Hanlon—had perused the place, they jumped at the chance to take it. At that stage they would have been willing to agree to anything with four semi-solid walls and a roof, but they had been universally surprised at the quality of this serendipitous flat. None of them had seen a place anywhere in the city so large and so comfortable.

The apartment occupied the upper half of an old house adjacent the park. The frame window looked out from the living room onto Buccleuch Park across the street. McIlweath in particular fell in love with the view. He would sit next to the window most nights with his books, quietly studying and intermittently pausing to look out to the street, the park and the sky.

The place itself had been well preserved. Obviously college students had only recently taken it over, for the damage was minimal. The door opened to a long hallway, the foot of which, adjacent to the entryway, was the extreme end of a blocky, square living room. Down the hallway, in order and opening to the left (for the right wall of the hallway was the edge of the building) were a large bedroom, shared by Finnegan and O'Hanlon, a smaller bedroom, the digs of McIlweath and Rosselli, and the kitchen, a greasy linoleum chamber with a rickety table at one end. Fittingly, at the head of the hallway stood the bathroom. The four learned quickly to stagger their wake-up schedules to get maximum use of the solitary bathroom.

To be sure, it was no palace, but in comparison with the grimy, dimly-lit hovels into which students regularly crammed themselves, the light-colored, orderly apartment seemed luxurious. O'Hanlon and Rosselli spent the summer ferreting unwanted furniture and dishware from relatives. By late August, when McIlweath and Finnegan arrived from the West Coast, it was furnished in a charmingly eclectic fashion: cinderblock bookshelves, threadbare rugs that did not match anything, and bunk beds for the smaller bedroom.

The house itself was a looming, wooden thing, painted a dull gray. Finnegan opened the outer door and then bounded up the stairs three at a time. The top door was locked. No one was home, but he knew that already.

Finnegan's hunger had become ravenous. Once inside the apartment, he tossed his books on his unmade bed as he bolted down the hallway to the kitchen.

'Spaghetti tonight. Big, thick, heavy spaghetti, with sauce a la Conor,' he thought. He pulled cans of tomato sauce, puree and paste from the cupboards. Only after he started to fry the ground beef did he realize that he had not yet taken off his coat. The scent of the sizzling meat and simmering sauce permeated the small kitchen and wafted down the hallway. While it cooked, Finnegan pulled an apple from the refrigerator and bit in. The animal joys of winter.

By the time the sauce was mixed it was nearly 6:00. Finnegan sat in the living room reading *The New York Times* while the dinner heated. He loved the *Times*. He loved the intelligent text and its cosmopolitan tone. He flattered himself in reading it and made a point each day to go through at least one article on a subject about which he knew absolutely nothing. In spite of his own sporadically slothful tendencies, he was faithful to that task. That was the whole point of a paper like this, he reasoned. He loved its weight, its very heft that intimidated so many others. He even loved the black inky smudge it left on his fingertips.

His reading was interrupted by the heavy thudding of feet on the stairway. Rosselli had come home. The roommate threw open the door and stomped each foot twice on the entry mat. He started to tug off his thick beige jacket.

"Son of a bitch, it's cold. If it's like this now, I hate to think what winter's going to be like." He sniffed the air. "Did some small animal die in the kitchen, or are you just cooking dinner?"

Finnegan put down his paper and headed for the source of the aroma. "Spaghetti sauce. My special blend."

"Are we having a vegetable?"

"Broccoli. I thought a *paisan* like yourself might appreciate an Eye-talian feed."

Finnegan set the table while the spaghetti boiled. It steamed the windows so that he could not see out. In the darkness there was nothing to see anyway.

"Hey Dan, you want some wine with this?"

"Do we have any?"

"Rotgut Chianti. Chief Sunset Vintners, I think, out of Hackensack."

"What year?"

"August."

"Let 'er rip."

Finnegan drained the spaghetti, heaped a large portion onto two plates and smothered each pile with his sauce. On a small plate he put the broccoli. He had made garlic bread, too, and he put that on the table. With the smell and the sight of it all, Finnegan almost caved in with hunger.

"Let's go, Danny boy."

Rosselli came out of his bedroom and sat down. Finnegan placed a steaming plate before him.

"I should really be taking you guys out to dinner tonight. I've got something to celebrate." Rosselli spoke between bites of his food. He had wasted no time digging in. Winter ran through his veins as well.

"What's that, big guy? Got a date with Easy Ellen Blackmore?"

"Better. Dr. Schwartz is recommending me for a chemistry honors project. He wants me to work under him next year."

"You're kidding."

"Why so disbelieving? I have my scholarly moments, too."

"Jesus, Dan, it's not that I don't think you deserve it. I'm just surprised. I didn't think you'd be interested in anything like that, but that's fantastic." Finnegan's genuine pleasure bubbled out. Perhaps he and McIlweath had had some influence on their friend. It was apparent to anyone who knew him that Dan Rosselli was far more motivated now than he had been when he first got to campus two years ago. Finnegan liked to take partial credit.

"We're going to do a project on x-ray crystallography. He says if we both bust ass we can finish by the time I graduate next year. It might be publishable, he thinks, but we'll have to see."

"Med schools might find that impressive."

"They'll fall off their chairs. Schwartzy's a big name in the field."

"Christ, Dan, that's super. When do you start?"

"As soon as he arranges it with the department. I'll get four credits a term for this, and it'll be a well-earned 'A'."

"It's not a Henry Rutgers project, is it? Not technically."

"No. This is a special independent study honors project within the Chemistry Department. They run it by themselves. It's all research for about a year, and then I'll have to write it up as a thesis. Have you and Tom heard about your Henry Rutgers applications yet?"

"No. We're up before the selection committee in January. I still have to finish my proposal abstract."

"How many credits is that?"

"Twelve for the year. If this works out, I'll only have to take two courses each term and I'll still be carrying a full load. I can schedule them for the afternoon and never get up early again until the day I walk up to grab my diploma."

"You know, if you two guys get your Henry Rutgers, all four of us will be on some type of independent study."

"Well, you can't call Lanny's set-up 'independent study.' There's nothing even remotely scholarly about it. He doesn't have to write anything, he doesn't have to meet with an advisor. All he has to do is drive down to Trenton three times a week and drink the Governor's bath water."

"Great work if you can get it."

"Yeah, Lanny's always been an operator. He'll wind up with more money and power than the rest of us combined."

"More women, too."

Finnegan chuckled. O'Hanlon had a new woman every weekend.

"Grab me some cheese, would you?" said Rosselli. "Mac still in the pool?"

"Undoubtedly. He won't be home until 7:00 at least."

They finished their meal quickly despite the conversation, for both were rapid eaters. Rosselli cleared the plates and washed them hurriedly, a chore he detested. After he washed the dishes his roommates usually noticed specks of dried food on the plates or greasy fingerprints on the glasses. Rosselli did a lousy job, but no one ever cared enough to do them over.

Finnegan went back to the living room and settled into the apartment's only easy chair. Unlike the couch, whose springs often proved adversarial, the chair sucked in its guest. Finnegan let himself be absorbed. On his way into the room he had flipped on the old television, and after a few seconds it warmed enough to give a picture. The black void lightened, images came clear. Some nights he and Rosselli would watch the six o'clock news, but tonight Finnegan did not feel overly serious. He had turned the channel instead to a syndicated rerun of an old comedy series he had watched as a boy. It still could make him laugh if he were in the right mood, and tonight he was, all parts coming together.

Conor Finnegan on this evening felt relaxed, confident, and, for a young man of twenty, quite secure. This shaky old place was home, and these roommates the brothers he never had.

Dan Rosselli soon joined him. He had changed into his standard evening garb, a tattered set of green surgical scrubs he had appropriated from a local hospital while interviewing for a summer internship. They hung loose on his large frame, like pajamas.

"Donning your 'After Six' wear, I see."

"The finest in evening attire. What's on?"

Finnegan told him, Rosselli agreeably flopped on the couch, and they passed the next half hour in mindless, communal silence.

Lanny O'Hanlon scaled the stairs shortly before seven. "Jesus Christ," he said as he opened the door, "I had to park my car three blocks over. There's no freaking room on this street anymore."

"What do you expect, Mick?" replied Rosselli. "The automotive population went up considerably when we moved in. How do you think the natives feel?"

"They'll be glad to see us go. How're you guys doing?"

"Danny discovered today that he's a scholar," said Finnegan, and Rosselli repeated his good news while O'Hanlon leafed through the *Times*.

"You sure you're not just going to do research on new recipes for Italian food, there, Chubby?"

Rosselli responded with an affectionate profanity.

"So what's new in Trenton?" asked Finnegan. "You been named Secretary of the Treasury yet?"

O'Hanlon snorted. "Not for a while. I spent the whole afternoon reviewing bills on God damn pothole repair appropriations. New Jersey's got more freaking potholes than people."

"The state's going to fix them? That'll be a nice switch."

"Don't kid yourself, pal. They do it every year, in spring after the snow melts. It's just that the roads are made so shitty they fall apart as fast as they get fixed. What do we have to eat?"

O'Hanlon threw his suit coat into the bedroom, aiming for a chair but missing and pitching it instead onto his desk. He pulled off his tie as he walked to the kitchen.

"Conor took a stab at homemade spaghetti sauce," Rosselli called after him.

"And you ate it?"

"Both of us."

"Jesus, you'll both probably be camped on the toilet all night. Conor, do me a favor and sleep with your ass facing the hallway tonight." O'Hanlon went to the refrigerator and took out the spaghetti. He sniffed at it, accepted what he smelled and threw it into a pan to reheat. Once it started to steam he slopped it onto a plate, grabbed a bottle of beer and headed back to the living room. Finnegan began to say something about his choice of dinner, but O'Hanlon cut him short. "I'll take my chances. Where's Aqualad? Still in the pool?"

"Apparently."

"He's usually home by now conjugating his verbs."

"How can anybody like what he does?" asked Rosselli. "I mean, *Latin* for God's sake."

"Spoken like a true scientist," said Finnegan. After an hour or so of television and banter, O'Hanlon went into the bedroom, and Finnegan and Rosselli began their work.

McIlweath was indeed late this evening. Where customarily he would be home shortly after 7:00, tired and reserved, dragging his books to the living room to sit near the window, he did not appear this evening until nearly 9.

"Where've you been?" asked Finnegan as McIlweath took off his coat. "The library?"

"Yeah. I had to pick up some books. How're you guys doing?"

Rosselli again recounted his news. Finnegan, who had been reading St. Augustine, saw the makings of a diversion, even though he had been reading for no more than half an hour. As Rosselli finished, O'Hanlon came out of the bedroom where he had been perusing a magazine.

"I'm heading out for a beer. Anyone want to come?"

"Not me, Lanny. I just got home. There's work to be done."

"How about you, Buddha?"

"Not tonight," replied Rosselli. "I'll save my celebration for the weekend."

"Rooms?"

Finnegan hesitated. He really was too relaxed, too much at ease, to concentrate on his work. His conscience rumbled. "Where you going?"

"Olde Queen's."

"Go on ahead. Maybe I'll catch up with you later."

"Okay. Don't wait up, boys," and O'Hanlon was gone, his footsteps fading down to the bottom of the stairs.

Finnegan went back to St. Augustine. Rosselli sprawled on the couch, a chemistry text and a notebook open in front of him, teetering on the sofa's edge. Finnegan read for another hour, his attention fluttering as his mind ran free in a forest of amusements, first peering down one path, then running in another direction, then investigating a third only to return to the center again. He absorbed very little of St. Augustine.

All the while he kept expecting McIlweath to come down the hallway to assume his normal position by the window. Perhaps the absence of his friend at his customary station diverted his concentration. There had evolved among the four of them a rhythm that transcended speech or action. They had grown together symbiotically. When one deviated from the rhythm, even in the subtlest of ways, the others could perceive it even though nothing had been articulated. It was more than McIlweath's position at the window; Finnegan felt rumblings of some sort.

He put down his book and headed down the hallway. McIlweath lay on the bottom bunk in the small bedroom, music playing softly. A Latin book, *The Complete Works of Catullus*, sat unopened alongside him. McIlweath's hands were folded behind his head and he stared upward at the bottom of the top bunk.

"How're you doing, Mac? " asked Finnegan as he entered the room. "I haven't talked to you all day."

"Tired of St. Augustine?"

"I was tired of St. Augustine the day he was assigned." Finnegan pulled the chair away from McIlweath's desk and sat on it backwards to face his friend. "You know, I'm sure it's an important piece of work, but it bores the hell out of me."

"That's part of what he intended, wasn't it? Whatever it takes to keep a young man from the fallen path."

"You feelin' antisocial tonight, Mac? You usually don't stay in here."

McIlweath continued to look up at the bed above him. "Not antisocial, Conor. Just quiet. We all have our moods."

"There's nothing wrong, is there?"

McIlweath chuckled. "No. God, no, there's nothing wrong. You just get thoughtful sometimes, you know? When you're not supposed to. I just didn't feel like doing anything so I thought I'd lie here a while and listen to some music. Maybe I should have gone with Lanny."

"Yeah. Well, drinking with Lanny beats St. Augustine."

"Or Catullus."

Finnegan rose to go, but as he stood McIlweath rolled over to his side, propped on an elbow to face him.

"Hey, Conor." Finnegan stopped, and turned back to look at him. "I've met a girl."

"You have?" Finnegan sat back down at once. This would be worth hearing.

"Actually, I've known her all year. I just got the chance to talk with her tonight."

"Tell me. Who is she, and where'd you meet her?"

"Listen, Conor, before I go on, I want to ask you to keep this quiet."

"Keep it quiet? Christ, Mac, it's no disgrace, being with a girl. That's part of what we're all after, remember? What are you afraid of? Is she a beast?"

"No, of course not. But you know how Lanny and Dan are. If they think I've got something going, I'm never going to hear the end of it. They're going to have their own expectations, too, about what I should be doing and all that. They're pretty base sometimes."

"Sometimes?" Finnegan shook his head and gave a quiet laugh. "The 'Use-Once-and-Throw-Away Boys.' Anyhow, what makes you think I'm any different?"

"Because you're the closest friend I have."

"Tell me about her."

"Her name's Anne Newbury. She swims on the girls' team. I've noticed her since the first workouts, but I've never spoken to her. I mean, not one word."

"Until tonight."

"Right. After I showered and got dressed I went back to the pool for my goggles. I left them on one of the benches. When I came out of the locker room she was there, too. She was about to turn off the lights.

"We just started talking then," he continued. "We said it was strange how two people could swim together for weeks and not even know one another beyond a name."

"What did you talk about?"

"Who we were, where we came from. You know, our families, that sort of thing. What I was doing at Rutgers, how long we'd been swimming. Small talk."

"Small talk. What about her, then? Her name's Anne. What else?"

"She's a junior, too. Her father's a full professor in physics. Her mom's a gourmet cook. She lives at home with them in Piscataway."

"The central question: what does she look like? Tell me she's gorgeous."

"I think she's very attractive."

"You say that almost defensively."

"Well, she doesn't have what you would call classic good looks. She wears glasses. I never knew that until tonight. Her hair's light brown, down to her shoulder about. Blue eyes, broad forehead. Slight body."

"And you've admired her from afar for weeks. Sounds typical of your Romantic infatuations, Mac."

"Yeah, I know. But she's always attracted me. I don't even know why. It seems as if there's something vulnerable in her. She's been protected all her life, and it shows. I can't explain it any better than that. She's traditional, and that appeals to me. And she's obviously very bright."

"How can you tell all this after so short a time and so few words?"

"Just instinct. She's very quiet. All the other girls joke around a lot, but Anne's different. She never joins in, almost like she doesn't know how, or doesn't trust herself enough to be witty or clever. I guess that all adds up to a hunch, but I don't think she's real comfortable with people who aren't close to her. She seems timid."

"That's perceptive."

"I told you I'd been watching her for a long time."

"So what comes next? Did you ask her out?"

"No. We just talked. For about an hour."

"Are you kidding me? You sat alone by an empty, musty pool for an hour, wet towels in the corner, the romantic whiff of chlorine in the air. Didn't you at least ask if she wanted to get something to eat? You could have run over to the commons together."

"No. I couldn't bring myself to do it. I was thinking about it, though."

"Mac, you've got to do better than that. Jesus, if you're attracted to her, and she's crazy enough to sit on a wooden bench by a smelly pool and talk to you rather than go home to eat her dinner, you've got to ask her out. All the signs are there."

"I can't, Conor. At least I couldn't tonight. What if she turns me down? I've never been very good with women."

"How in Christ's name are you ever going to find out unless you take the initiative? If you never ask, then it doesn't matter if she would turn you down. You're in the same place, and that place is by yourself. And if she's as naïve as you think, she's never going to come to you. In any event, if she turns you down then you won't waste any more time worrying about it and you can move on to your next quixotic fantasy."

McIlweath said nothing, so Finnegan continued, gently. "I think I can understand you, Mac. You were the same way in high school with what's-her-name."

"Kim."

"Yeah, Kim. You admired her ever since I knew you, but you never did anything about it. You didn't want to risk it. As long as you kept your distance, you kept the remote hope that something might come about of its own accord, but if you made your move and she turned you down, then that was the end of hope, end of fantasies, end of Romantic idealizations.

"But you can't do that anymore, Mac," he continued. "I haven't had an evening out with a woman in months. There aren't enough women at Rutgers to afford the luxury of fantasizing them out of your life. If you've got one in tow, act on her. Take a chance. Believe me, the real thing beats fantasy every time. And if this girl's intelligent enough to give up her dinner to spend time talking with you in a fairly disgusting setting, then I don't think you've got a whole lot to worry about. Just do it."

"I don't know, Conor. I'm just not good with women. I'm not confident or comfortable. "

"You can't hold back, pal, and you know it as well as I do. Sooner or later you've got to put yourself on the front lines. Maybe with Anne, maybe with someone else, but you're going to have to make a move sometime."

McIlweath rolled back and put his hands behind his head again. "Maybe I will, Conor. I know you're right."

"Give yourself a chance, Mac."

"Listen, don't tell Lanny or Dan about any of this, okay? I don't feel much like being teased."

"No problem. But if this pans out you're going to have to introduce us all to her in due time. No secrets then." Finnegan rose and walked to the door. "Keep me posted. The prospect of watching Tom McIlweath stalk a female promises to be fascinating."

Finnegan headed back to his room, and to bed. For a brief moment, inexplicably, an image of McIlweath and himself running down the towpath flashed through his mind, an image from a while ago, when McIlweath passed him and, in doing so, inadvertently elbowed him in the upper arm.

* * *

For weeks Tom McIlweath maintained his boyishly distant pose. He hovered on the far periphery of Anne Newbury's life, content to look for a safe entry to the core. Young Tom went out of his way to give himself the opportunity for fortuitous chance encounters that no one could have expected. He lingered in the locker room after workouts, hoping to repeat the circumstances of their initial conversation. He looked up her address and drove through her neighborhood thinking he might see her walking somewhere and offer her a ride. During free moments he walked aimlessly around Queen's Mall hoping that he might find her coming out of one of the old buildings.

All his efforts, though, came to nothing. His relationship with Anne reverted back to a non-relationship. Never did his locker room timing pay off, never did he see her walking through town, never did she emerge from class at the right moment. The only times he saw her were, as before, in the pool during workouts. She occasionally smiled at him from pool's edge, and he smiled back, but they did not speak. Through the chlorinated water their images were fuzzy and ill-defined.

Conor Finnegan told no one of McIlweath's infatuation. To be sure, he considered McIlweath's approach to the entire situation laughable, but he dared not betray his friend's confidence. He knew that Rosselli and O'Hanlon would ride McIlweath cruelly if they knew how any specifics.

That sentiment, though, did not prevent him from leaning on McIlweath at every turn. Each night Finnegan would corner McIlweath in secret, in one of their bedrooms or the kitchen, and ask how the day went.

"Did you see her?"

"Only at workout."

"Well, did you speak to her?"

"No. I didn't get the chance. I handed her a towel when she got out of the pool, though."

"Didn't you at least say 'good workout' or something?"

"No, Conor. It wasn't the place. Too many people around."

"To say 'good workout'?! And what do you mean it wasn't the place? It's a pool, for Christ's sake, and she just worked out. Mac, I'm begging you, just make conversation. Anything small and dull will do. You're good at that."

Finnegan did not understand, but he was willing to go along with it as sympathetically as he could. Tom McIlweath, he concluded, had a problem. He, Conor Finnegan, might be able to help him with it if they both were lucky. To do so, he would have to be patient and persistent.

Because McIlweath had taken him into this deepest of confidences, Finnegan felt an almost proprietary responsibility toward the situation's outcome. He went so far as to try to devise a way in which he could make the approach on Tom's behalf, but he knew that nothing he could do along those lines would make any sense. He'd no doubt brand himself a fool in the process. One way or another, though, Finnegan would see this relationship come off.

McIlweath fell back on his dreams and fantasies. He concluded sadly that he lacked the simple fortitude necessary to bridge the gap between Romantic daydreams and a more exciting reality. To take a chance with Anne and to lose it . . . Anne was too special. She was an ideal, Dante's Beatrice. He could not bear a rejection here. Better to be timidly lonely than to suffer a thoroughly crushed ego. McIlweath kept his distance in a melancholy, bittersweet silence.

Until Fate, which McIlweath had pursued so meticulously, turned around and ambushed him.

McIlweath took a Latin course across town at Douglass College. On most days he drove the few miles through New Brunswick's sooty streets, but he had been asked this day by his coach to stop by the pool to review his events for the coming season and so had no time to hustle back to the apartment for his car. He would have to take a campus bus to get to class on time.

The bus stopped outside the gymnasium on College Avenue. McIlweath expected it to be crowded, but for some reason it was not. Only a handful of students occupied the plastic seats. As McIlweath stepped up to the aisle, his heart shot forth a burst of adrenalin: one of those seats was occupied by Anne Newbury, her head buried in some type of textbook. There could be no escape from this, nothing short of turning around in full view and stumbling back down the steps to the street.

With mock assurance, McIlweath walked the aisle to her seat. "Hello, Anne." She looked up, startled. Her blue eyes widened and shone alertly through her glasses. The pose froze itself into McIlweath's memory. "Mind if I keep you company?"

"Tom, no. Not at all. I'm surprised to see you. I've never seen you on this bus."

"I rarely ride it. Coach had his annual preseason meeting with me, so I'm running late."

"You have a Latin class?"

Tom was pleased. She remembered at least what he was studying. Or perhaps she just noticed the nature of the books he carried. No matter, it still counted. "Yes. It's an upper-level course I can't get here. The Romantic Poets. Propertius, Tibullus, Ovid, and the rest of the boys. Dull stuff, and some of it is pretty juvenile, like a boy going through puberty." Tom inwardly flinched at his careless mention of 'puberty.' He wasn't back at the apartment anymore. He was with Anne, and he couldn't risk treading through offensive references.

He continued, "I had forgotten you took a course across town, too."

"I'm not sure I ever told you," Anne replied. "It's a mathematics course. Probability and Statistics. I wanted to get it out of the way and it's not offered here this term."

"So you can calculate the odds on things?"

"Some things. The easy things. Like how often you can expect to draw a certain poker hand. That's an example they always use to get us started. But I don't know anything about cards. Their examples always confuse me," she smiled.

"I'm not much on odds. What's going to happen is going to happen. There's no predicting it. We're human, and that means we're fallible, flexible and unpredictable."

"That's rather fatalistic, Tom."

"Well, I think it's important to devise statistical formulas and probability tables, but they can't apply to the human condition."

"Obviously," said Anne, "You're not majoring in the sciences. But doesn't studying the humanities get frustrating because of that very unpredictability? Man's history is so misdirectional, like a moth caught under a lampshade. Just when you get him figured out or come up with a theory why something happened the way it did, something else comes along to controvert it. There are no formulas, and no surety, in the humanities. It's all so confounding."

"But that's the beauty of it, Anne. Flesh and blood, with all its mistakes. Confused intentions, pomposity, arrogance, greed, altruism. Man's highest accomplishments and his greatest blunders. That's classics, and history, and sociology, and economics, and literature. And it all applies to each of us as we are."

"Maybe that's what confuses me. You strive to find the best of what mankind has created and his highest thoughts. But then you look around and see the brutality of where we are. Killing each other, bombing, raping, cheating and swindling . . ."

"Vietnam, Charles Manson, Rwanda, the Holocaust . . ."

"Right. Do we ever really learn anything from all this studying?"

"What alternative do we have other than to try to find the greatest avenues for our potential? It's the best chance we've got to overcome our primitive nature."

"I don't know, Tom. It's all so confusing. The sciences are much more logical."

"I've had this discussion before with one of my roommates. Science versus the humanities, and all that."

"It's whatever our temperaments allow."

"Are our temperaments that different?"

Anne looked at McIlweath with a smile, then coyly turned her head. "That no doubt remains to be seen."

The bus turned a corner so that the momentum pressed McIlweath's body against Anne's. Tom noted her scent, the light, pungent sweetness of his hair. Her body felt softer against his side than he had expected it to be. He had anticipated the firm musculature of a swimmer.

Tom McIlweath for weeks had sought a sign. In Anne Newbury's surprising tactility, in her teasing response to his leading question, he had found it. With his mind rebounding from their conversation, his senses drugged by her presence, his instincts triggered by the pleasures of these past few minutes, he placed himself at last before her. He did not know what he had said, nor did he perceive himself in the action of saying it, until the words had passed from him.

"Anne, do you think you might like to have dinner with me Saturday night?"

* * *

The first time Conor Finnegan set eyes on Anne Newbury, something indefinable snapped within him creating a tiny fissure, a hairline rift along a previously solid wall. Had he been asked why this was so and what he felt, he could not have explained it, certainly not in any rational way. He felt as if he were in bed, in the dark, and heard voices outside his window, not threatening necessarily, but merely unknown and unexpected. Anne Newbury carried something with her he had not seen before, an invisible specter lurking over her shoulder, voices in the dark. Finnegan could not articulate it, but he most definitely perceived it.

Perhaps it was just that Anne Newbury at first glance was not the girl Tom McIlweath had described. She was not overwhelmingly attractive. That was Finnegan's first disappointment, although, to her credit, neither was she completely without her charms. Most noticeable were Anne's sharp blue eyes, hidden behind the blur of thick glasses. She wore her hair to her shoulders. McIlweath had described it as light brown and thick, but in reality it seemed stringy. Anne's body was slight. She had hips and breasts, but they were not immediately discernible to the naked eye. There were bulges where bulges were due, but in neither location was there a great abundance. Finnegan thought her small breasts to be jagged, and running his hands over them would be like grasping a pair of pointed rocks.

McIlweath had brought Anne by after dinner. He wanted her to grant his new home the benediction of her sweet breath and soft footfall. It would be, if nothing else, a confirmation of this latest reality.

Only Finnegan was at the apartment that Saturday night, though. Rosselli and O'Hanlon had gone to a fraternity party in a quest for alcohol and women, guaranteed of finding at least the former. They would not be stumbling up the stairs until much later. Finnegan had not wanted to go along. He had no need tonight of the noise, the press of bodies, the false banter. He had the opportunity for a quietly introspective evening, a rare enough occurrence, and so he would take advantage of it. Besides, unlike his other two roommates, Finnegan was excited by his friend's prospects. He alone knew what had gone into bringing it all about, the risks involved. He had helped nurse McIlweath through his uncertainties. In a small sense, it had been like sharing the birth of a child. Conor Finnegan, midwife, felt quite proud.

But all that pride tarnished when Anne Newbury walked through the door. Finnegan had been listening to music in the living room. He sat back in the easy chair with his eyes closed, mouthing the Dylan lyrics. When the door opened he sat up at once. Anne walked through first, and Finnegan perceived instantly that strange quality that dissembled his nerves.

Anne stood there with a shy, manufactured smile. Her whole expression struck Finnegan as contrived.

"Anne, I'd like you to meet Conor Finnegan. Conor, this is Anne Newbury."

Finnegan stood up. "It's a pleasure, Anne." He smiled, self-consciously sticking his hands into the rear pockets of his jeans.

"Hi" was all he got in return.

"Would you like to sit down?" asked McIlweath, gesturing to the couch.

"I hope Tom hasn't been telling you too many stories about what slobs his roommates are, Anne. We're actually a pretty friendly bunch of guys, and reasonably clean."

"Tom says you're all good friends. That's enviable. This is a nice apartment, Tom. I like the view." Anne sat down in the chair nearest the window, leaving McIlweath to sit by himself on the couch. Finnegan resumed his seat in the easy chair across the room. 'Awkward,' thought Finnegan.

"Where'd you two go for dinner?"

"Tony's," answered McIlweath.

"Not much on atmosphere, is it?"

"We didn't mind," replied McIlweath, a thinly rapturous smile affixed to his narrow lips.

"What do you do?" asked Anne. "Besides study."

The question seemed to Finnegan to come out of the blue, a blunt projectile hurtled forth from the clouds. He had to regroup himself. "What do you mean?" he finally stammered. "I do the usual things. I eat, I drink, I sleep. I kid Tom a lot. I drive an old Ford. Am I doing okay?"

"But what do you do?" she persisted. "You don't swim. Do you play any sports?"

"Conor used to be a great basketball player in high school."

"But you don't play here."

"Well, no. Not on any team. I play in the gym on my own quite a bit."

"Oh. Are you on the debating team, or do you play in the band or anything like that?"

"No, Anne. I guess I'm rather dull." What the hell was this all about?

"Conor worked the past two summers for a United States senator," said McIlweath. "He's our political expert."

"Oh, I don't pay any attention to politics," said Anne.

"Well, after working for the senator I'm not certain that I want to, either."

"Isn't politics rather disgusting?" she asked. "People contentious, mouthing at one another, calling each other names. People making deals behind everyone's backs, and taking bribes." She made a face.

"I haven't taken many bribes in my day, and I can't remember calling anyone a foul name. Not for a while, at least."

"Would you like some coffee, Anne?" asked McIlweath. "Come on. I'll show you the apartment." They left the room and headed for the kitchen. Finnegan felt a rush of relief.

'Whatever strengths she might have,' he said to himself, 'tact certainly isn't one of them.'

The two remained in the kitchen for several minutes. Finnegan heard their voices and knew they were carrying on a conversation, although he could not discern any words. He did not want to. Every now and then one of them would laugh in a childish spurt. Another couple and Finnegan would have been tempted to join them, but here he had no desire to do so.

Tom and Anne at length returned to the living room. They sat side by side on the couch this time after walking into the room, completely oblivious to anyone else. Finnegan chose not to initiate conversation. 'The ball's in your court, folks,' he thought. 'Let's see what you do with it. Let's see if there's anything you *do* like.'

But they said nothing to Finnegan. They talked to each other alone. They talked of people on the swim team, of workout lengths, of stroke technique, of the delicacy of balancing a heavy work load with the demands of the pool. To them, Conor Finnegan had disappeared.

After an interminable half hour or so, Tom McIlweath wrapped it up. "I should get you home, Anne."

"What time is it?"

"Nearly midnight. Can I get you anything? Something to eat or drink before we go?"

"No. I'm fine, Tom. Let's get going."

McIlweath fetched their coats. For the few seconds he was out of the room Anne stood awkwardly near the door. She said nothing to

Finnegan, nor did she look in his direction. When McIlweath returned, she hurried into her wrap.

"I'll see you later, Conor," said McIlweath.

Anne had already taken a step down the wooden stairway. "It was nice to meet you," she called over her shoulder. An afterthought.

"Yeah. Take it easy, you two," and they were gone.

Finnegan went back to his music, tuning in something moody and low. 'Jesus,' he thought to himself as the first song rose through the low notes, 'What the hell was that? But it's Mac's concern. He knows that he's doing. Or at least he should by now. If he doesn't, it's nobody's fault but his own.'

The concept of 'fault', though, was as far removed from Tom McIlweath's mind that evening as Halley's Comet. His night with Anne had been a glorious time, one of the singular chapters in his young life. He viewed her through the gloss of moonlight; everything she had said had somehow been lyrical, touching or witty, every move she had made had been as graceful as the birth of Venus. She had accepted him, spoke low to him. She had even held his hand briefly. It was just the two of them. Tom McIlweath felt as if his entire existence these past several years had pointed him to this one evening. Perhaps it had. Sentiment plays itself off circumstance to create Fate. Tom McIlweath soared rapturously in Romantic intoxication. He was, on this particular evening, Lord Byron on the shore, or Shelley walking his moors.

McIlweath drove Anne back to her home, the large suburban house where she had grown up and still lived. He walked her to the door. A single light shone through the living room window. Although Anne's parents were reportedly in bed, McIlweath felt inhibited.

"Thank you, Tom. I had a wonderful time."

"So did I, Anne. I hope I can see you again."

"Of course you can, silly. We see each other in the pool every day."

"That's not what I meant."

"I know. I'm teasing. I'd like to spend more time with you, too."

"Maybe next weekend?"

"Of course. Whenever."

They stood facing each other. They did not touch. McIlweath's hands hung self-consciously at his sides.

"I've got to go in. Thank you again. Good night."

She had unlocked the door and spun inside with one quick motion while McIlweath stood there awkwardly. The door closed before he could take a step toward her. He paused a second, then walked back down the driveway. He had not been quick enough to kiss her good night.

But nothing could taint that evening. He would let no disappointments rise within his timid psyche; he would not judge himself. It had all been what he had hoped.

McIlweath climbed behind the wheel of his old car, started it, revved it and turned on the radio, which played a song he recognized. As he drove back down the dark, sleeping street he started to sing along with it, loudly and with feeling. Electricity rippled through him. He knew it would take some time before he could calm himself enough to go to sleep.

* * *

A day or so later, Conor Finnegan and Lanny O'Hanlon had a conversation as they lay in their beds in the dark.

"What was she like?"

"Fair."

"Only fair?"

"No more than that. I don't know, Lanny. There's something about her that was really off-putting. I can't describe it. I think I've blocked the whole ugly experience from my mind. A coldness, I guess. She's pretty aloof."

"How do you mean?"

"It's hard to tell, rooms. I only talked with her for a few minutes, but she seemed as if the ground never touched her feet. She has a hard time relating to anything outside her own little world, that much was obvious. She doesn't *like* anything. At least that's what I sensed."

"The perfect woman for him. Do you think the rest of us will ever get the chance to meet her?"

"I don't see how you can avoid it. Christ, the way things are going, we're all likely to be ushers at the wedding."

"Do you think he's getting into her pants?"

\"Rooms, I don't think he even knows where her pants are. Mac's not the most worldly guy you're ever going to meet."

"No joke. See you in the morning."

Tom McIlweath's life, comfortably pleasant to begin, took on a vibrancy he had never before experienced. He viewed all issues now through one prism, and that prism was Anne Newbury. She lent an excitement to even his simplest tasks, for he reasoned that these must first be completed before he could see her again. She deepened his colors and drew new lines on his portrait.

He saw her daily. After workouts they would wait for each other and eat dinner together in the Commons. There they would review their days. Anne became for McIlweath a confidante, a barometer of all things personal and academic. Aside from his friendship with Finnegan, he had never before known such trust. Anne, for her part, was less introspective in their conversations. She preferred to speak furtively about friends or common acquaintances. Anne was a bit of a gossip, and a catty one at that, but McIlweath did not mind. He was flattered that she chose to share these things with him alone, even if they did seem somewhat trivial.

McIlweath wove his entire existence around her nexus. He drove her across town to her classes at Douglass. He called her each night even after spending the early evening with her. If he were going to the grocery or to the drugstore, he would call her to see if she needed anything. Some nights, if they knew their studies would not be too demanding, they would go to the library, spread their books on a corner table and alternately study and chat. Each weekend they spent as much time together as they could. When McIlweath could afford it, they would go to a movie or a play or a concert somewhere on campus. If not, they would sit in her living room and watch television, often with her parents. McIlweath began to go to church with Anne and her family, an oddity for which he drew much teasing from his friends, including and especially Finnegan, who knew that McIlweath had never been terribly religious.

In short, Tom McIlweath was smitten, thoroughly and totally. He had found something he had only rarely imagined himself attaining. Anne Newbury embodied the idealized traits of femininity to which he had long been attracted. She was intelligent, self-confident, poised, athletic, and, in her own way, very pretty. Moreover, *she* had accepted *him*. Anne accepted his insights, she used his strengths when she needed them, she was amused by his wit. She became a vortex into which swirled and spun Tom McIlweath's sense of self and with it, all hopes, all aspirations, all realities.

His growing involvement seemed to be a major event in the young man's life. As such, it compelled Finnegan, who paid close attention to the process, to take a hard look at his own status.

What he saw did not displease him. In fact, he was generally content with where he was and where he perceived himself to be going. The struggles of his first year had evaporated. He had carved a place for himself at one of the finest universities in the land. He had made Dean's List each semester he had been eligible. The past three terms he had received only one grade below the top mark, and that in a political science course in which he had had a philosophical difference with the instructor that, Finnegan was convinced, had led to an artificially low mark. He had settled into a major in history, where he truly excelled, for his great memory enabled him to catalogue details while weaving them into comprehensive theories. Finnegan had grown close to one professor whom he had taken for three consecutive terms. Dr. Miller, a small, tattered man who had been at the college thirty years, was now sponsoring him as a Henry Rutgers Scholar. It was considered at the time a great honor, and Finnegan knew in fact that he would be selected. Academically, then, he was accomplishing all he had set out to do. If he continued down this course, Phi Beta Kappa would await him, the crowning glory of a marvelous career.

His years at college had developed in Finnegan a genuine enthusiasm for learning. Although a history major, Finnegan did not lock himself into just one discipline. The great ideas of man attracted him almost lustfully. The perplexities of the human condition expressed themselves in many forms, and Finnegan wished to investigate as many as he could. Each exploration taught him something new, so he delved not only into world history but into English literature, religion, economics, political science, mathematics. He studied German, fascinated by its phonetics and logical constructions, and inspired by its literature, until he was nearly fluent. In all the questions were the same: How do we work? What does it mean to be truly human? How do we all fit together? And what do we want? What, as human beings, do we truly want?

Where did he project that knowledge to take him? Conor Finnegan rarely dwelt on the specifics of any future direction. His work with the senator these past two summers had quickened his pulse. He had fallen instantly in love with practical politics, and love soon grew into passion. His issue focus had been the concerns of the elderly, and within that context he had written speeches, advanced the senator's public appearances, represented the senator before various groups. Finnegan told himself that it was important work. In truth it appealed to two central aspects of his character: the desire to do some good, and the desire to be recognized for what he did. Finnegan did find gratification in his work. He had spent a good deal of time uncovering the depth of his issue, and his research had been reflected in at least three pieces of legislation introduced by the senator, one of which became part of a broader omnibus bill that eventually passed and was signed into law. The senator had read on the floor of the Senate a few speeches Finnegan had written, including one particularly literate attack on the current administration's Middle East policies.

There was a glamor to it all that had turned Finnegan's head. He had appeared on television, he had spoken to large public gatherings, he had lunched and dined with major local, state and national political figures. He had even met several well-known entertainers when the senator appeared on a charity telethon. The glamor settled into Finnegan's blood. In his position with the senator he believed himself to be working fully to his own excellent capabilities and, in so doing, cultivating the attention of a grateful constituency.

All this led him to conclude that his first choice would be a career in politics. He thought that he would go to law school, one of the fine Eastern ones like Harvard, Yale or possibly Virginia. From there he would go to Washington and work in government. The legislative branch appealed to him, but he could see himself in a top spot at an agency within the executive branch. Later, who could tell? Perhaps he might make his own run at elective office. Finnegan relied upon his boundless self-confidence, as he had always done. The right things would happen. He merely had to set a general course and ride the currents of circumstance. He had no doubt that it would all flow to his advantage.

In the meantime, Finnegan was truly enjoying his time at college. His love of learning did not preclude him from enjoying as full and as active a social life as he could cultivate. He continued to stay fit, playing basketball as often as he could, playing handball or the newly discovered, thoroughly eastern game of squash, or running. He had many friends. His living situation surpassed any of his previous expectations. He had a comfortable apartment with his three closest friends, brothers really.

Tom McIlweath's relationship with Anne Newbury disturbed him slightly, though, for it pointed out the one gap in it all. Finnegan knew several women, most of whom he had met in class, and he had spent some time with many of them—occasional dinners, a football game, perhaps a play. But he had never been close to any type of involvement. He had, quite simply, never wanted to entertain anything which might limit him. Yet there was something in Tom McIlweath's total immersion in Anne Newbury that captured Finnegan's curiosity. Since he had connected with Anne, McIlweath seemed fresher, more personable, sharper, and, in general, a better, happier person. That was, by all knowledgeable accounts, the way it should be, yet Finnegan had never before observed the process. While he might have some misgivings about Anne Newbury as an individual, he could not help but admire what she had done for his friend.

At present there was no prospect of anything like that happening for Conor Finnegan. He was not particularly certain that he wanted it to happen, even though his curiosity had been piqued. He resolved that there was nothing he could do about it in any case. Finnegan was attracted to women; he enjoyed their company, he enjoyed their touch. But for now, he would not go out of his way to find the kind of relationship his friend had found. He would wait, and watch what happened, for he reasoned that there must be some downside to this puzzling process. "To every action there must be an equal and opposite reaction," so said Newton. So be it.

Human emotions are not governed by physical laws, but he would wait and see. In the meantime, Finnegan felt slightly deprived that it was Tom McIlweath, his shy, sometimes awkward friend, who had entered into the experiment, and not he.

* * *

"Anne, have you ever thought about moving into the dorm, or getting an apartment, maybe?"

"Why on earth would I want to do that?"

"I would think you'd just naturally want to. You'd be more independent. You could do what you want."

"I'm independent now. I can do what I want. My parents don't bother me."

"That's probably because you don't bother them."

"I try not to. I do what they ask."

"But that's my point, Anne. I would think a bright girl like you wouldn't want to be answerable to anyone."

"That's ridiculous. I don't mind running errands for my mom or dad, or keeping my music low, or being in at a reasonable hour, especially if they're taking care of everything I might have to think about. I don't have to worry about what I'm going to eat, or fixing anything that breaks. I don't have to worry about paying bills. We get along fine. Why should I want to change that?"

"You'll have to leave someday, Anne."

"I suppose so, but I'm not looking forward to it. I'll never understand why you did what you did, no matter how you try to explain it. It's almost as if you resent me living at home and being happy about it. I'm sorry if I have none of your angst."

"I don't resent it, Anne. Your parents are fine people. But sooner or later we all have to make our own way. I think you learn more when you're away from home. There's none of that security you mentioned. You have to create your own. That's a massive task, but it has its rewards. No, I don't resent you living at home. I'm just curious as to why."

"I guess I'm just a simple girl, Tom."

The simple girl had made plans to watch an old movie on television one Saturday night. She had heard it was good, noticed its schedule, and thought a night in sounded fine. McIlweath, not wishing to concede a weekend evening to a few reels of celluloid, suggested they watch together at his apartment. She agreed.

What McIlweath had not known was that Conor Finnegan and Dan Rosselli, with nothing planned for the evening and no prospects in sight, intended to watch the same movie. When Finnegan told McIlweath that morning that he and Rosselli would be home that night, McIlweath at first was dismayed, but then he considered that this might be an excellent opportunity for his two friends to come to know Anne a little better. In fact, it might be great fun having everyone together.

The movie, a classic World War II film, was to start at 9:00. Anne arrived at 8:45, McIlweath scurrying down the stairs in a rush of arms and legs to meet her.

Finnegan and Rosselli had already settled into their seats, one in each chair at opposite corners of the room and thereby leaving the couch free. At McIlweath's urging they had dressed civilly. Usually on Saturday nights, if they were not going anywhere or seeing anyone, they would be dressed almost slovenly, Finnegan in gym shorts and Rosselli in his pajama-like hospital greens. McIlweath feared that that might be offensive, and so he had lobbied for street clothing.

Tom and Anne sat on the couch after perfunctory greetings. Until the movie started they spoke only to each other. McIlweath, ever solicitous, asked Anne if she wanted anything to eat, to drink, to sit on, to warm her, or to cool her down. No, she said, she was fine just the way she was.

The movie began violently, war footage backing the opening credits. The grainy grays and blacks dived at various lengths across the small screen. In the darkened living room the picture cast light patterns on the walls and ceiling.

A few minutes into the film, a new character (they were all new at this early point) walked onto the screen. He was portrayed by a veteran character actor often seen in war pictures like this. "Who is he?" asked Anne.

"I can't think of his name," replied McIlweath, slightly above a whisper. "I've seen him a thousand times."

"No, I mean in the movie. Who is he?"

"Some colonel, I think."

The colonel spoke his piece to his commanding officer, something about American vulnerability should the Germans anticipate the planned airborne assault near a particularly obscure village, inland from the Channel.

"Where's that?"

"In the Netherlands, Anne."

"Why would the Germans want to attack it?"

"They don't. The Americans are looking to attack it from the air. The Germans already hold it."

"Oh."

Rosselli and Finnegan shifted in their chairs. Finnegan took his eyes from the screen briefly to look at Rosselli, who, feeling his friend's glance, shook his head slowly. Finnegan went back to the movie.

At a commercial break McIlweath leaned over and whispered something in Anne's ear. She whispered back, giggling. Finnegan tried to discern their conversation without being obvious about it. He picked up a few words, and what he heard was hardly mysterious or secretive. They seemed to be mentioning how someone on the swim team resembled the German colonel. Why whisper? Finnegan, for all appearances intently watching an advertisement for a stomach antacid, tried to interpret something deeper, but he could not.

McIlweath stood up. "Anne and I would like some popcorn. Anybody else?"

"What's a war movie without something to munch?" replied Rosselli.

"Especially something that sounds like bones breaking. Make enough for four, Mac."

McIlweath disappeared down the hallway. Anne said nothing as she watched the movie, nor did she let her eyes stray from the screen. The smell of popcorn wafted down the hall from the kitchen with the bullet-like sounds of exploding kernels. The movie had resumed. War had resumed. Anne sat rigidly in place, her hands and eyes immobile. Finnegan and Rosselli, growing progressively more uncomfortable, could think of nothing to say, and so watched in silence.

McIlweath returned, thankfully for all concerned, with a salad bowl full of popcorn and several napkins. Anne reentered the realm of the senses, turning her head to him with a smile. "I missed you," she whispered as McIlweath sat back down beside her. Finnegan and Rosselli both heard it. They looked at each other as they leaned over to the coffee table to grab some popcorn. They had read each other's minds, and discomfort began to morph into amusement.

On the screen a group of paratroops huddled in the hold of an airplane. The plane bumped and swerved, knocking the unsteady men into one another.

"What's that noise?" asked Anne through the crunching.

"What noise? Where?"

"On the airplane. Why is it bumping around? There," she said as a muffled thump rocked the plane again. "What's that?"

"That's flak, Anne."

"Oh." She paused a few seconds. "What's flak?"

Only the tightest self-control kept Finnegan from bursting into a spasm of laughter. He shifted sharply in his chair, draping his left leg over the arm to turn his body away from the center of the room. He dared not make eye contact with Rosselli.

"Flak is what they call anti-aircraft fire, Anne. The Germans have spotted them from the ground and they're shooting up at them plane."

"Why? They don't stand much chance of hitting it, do they?"

"Better than you think. Just watch the movie for a while, Anne."

A few minutes later the paratroops made their drop. One landed hard and rolled over, grimacing and grabbing his leg.

"Was he shot?" asked Anne.

"No, I don't think so. He just landed wrong. He probably broke a leg."

"But he had a parachute."

Finnegan squirmed again. Dan Rosselli coughed, and Finnegan knew that Rosselli was fighting back his laughter as hard as he was himself, and that Dan was on the verge of losing. The cough covered an uncontrollable throat spasm.

"Why don't the others come?"

"They can't, Anne. They're occupied several miles away. They're all under fire."

"Wasn't that poor planning?"

"War tends to be unpredictable."

"What's that?" A German tank, then two, broke through the forest and turned toward the pinned paratroops.

"A tank, Anne."

"Oh. I thought so. Germans, right?"

At this Rosselli could take no more. He stood up quickly and half-sprinted out of the room, burbling under his breath about the bathroom. Finnegan smiled, recognizing Dan's desperation, then returned to the ridiculous farce taking place before him.

The Allied assault failed. Any attack on the village would have to come solely from ground forces without the aid of airborne troops. The American forces advancing to the village disengaged from the relentless Germans, retreating far enough to give them space to review a suitable new strategy, and leaving the stranded paratroops to their fate.

"They can't do that," said Anne. "The paratroopers are all going to end up in a prison camp, or dead. How can they leave them like that? That's not right."

"There's nothing else they can do, Anne. There's no way to break through the German position. Those paratroops are surrounded."

"Well, it doesn't seem right just to leave them out there. They'll be killed."

"It's wartime, Anne. They kill us, we kill them."

"But to leave them there like rabbits to be slaughtered. Not even to try to help them fight their way out. It doesn't seem right."

"All they'd do is get more people killed if they went in after them"

"It's not right," repeated Anne.

Finnegan and Rosselli again leaned forward for some popcorn. Finnegan took great care not to make eye contact. Since the movie had started neither had spoken. Finnegan for his part could think of nothing to say that would make any sense within the context of what was happening. 'I'm trapped in a Ionesco play,' he thought. 'Maybe it's like an onion and I'm just looking at the outermost layer, lying on the floor while they peel away at the rest.' But he really didn't believe that.

The show continued. Anne Newbury commented respectively on the characters' uniforms, the amusing sound of their names, their odd gyrations upon being shot, the homely girls who were supposed to be Dutch, and the fact that all the Europeans could speak fluent English.

"It's a device, Anne, so there are no subtitles. It's not real life."

"It just seems funny to me."

At 11:15 the movie ended, mercifully. Finnegan and Rosselli leaned back in their chairs. Unknowingly they had been perched forward during most of the show. When it was over they fell backwards, exhaling, two prize fighters retreating to their corners after a brutal ten rounds.

On the couch Tom and Anne sat whispering for several minutes. Finnegan this time made no effort to overhear. He could not believe that anything they were saying could possibly have any significance. He glanced across at Rosselli and could tell by the look in his friend's eye that amusement had turned to annoyance.

McIlweath, though, preferred not to notice anything but what sat next to him. He spoke low and earnestly. Anne smiled, and whispered back.

"Anne and I were thinking of going out for a bite to eat. Would either of you like to come along?"

"Not me, Dice. I'll see you tomorrow. That is, if you don't wake me up when you stumble in, you clumsy bastard." McIlweath flinched at the word. "Nice talking to you, Anne."

And with that Rosselli bounded down the hall, free at last. Finnegan followed soon after, first paying his respects to Anne and Tom. He heard them tromp down the stairway as he entered Rosselli's room. He found his friend naked to the waist and about to head for the bathroom.

"It's a good thing they're gone," said Finnegan. "If Mac thought Anne might see you like that, he'd be compelled to kill you on the spot. Protector of the young lady's purity, and all that."

"Can you believe it? Hold on, I'll be right back."

Finnegan sat down at McIlweath's desk and thumbed through a magazine until Rosselli returned. His friend climbed into his bunk, pulled the covers to his chest and rolled on his side to face Finnegan. "Can you believe it?" he repeated. "Conor, were we even there tonight?"

"Not so you'd know it."

"That really ticks me off. I mean, it's rude if nothing else. All they did was whisper to each other."

"Call it a blessing, pal. Otherwise she might have directed some of those questions to us. Jesus Christ, it was like watching with a little kid."

Rosselli rolled onto his back and laughed loudly. "God, I've never heard anything like it. 'Who's that? What's he doing? Why is he wearing those funny clothes?' It was unbelievable."

"Mac tells me she's intelligent," said Finnegan, breaking into a smile.

"Yeah, real bright. Christ, she doesn't even know where the fuckin' Netherlands is."

"But she's got a 3.8, big guy. She wants to go to med school. Just like you."

"Don't equate me with her, pal. She may have a 3.8 but she's thick as a brick."

"How does she make the grades then? There's got to be a spark of analytical intelligence buried in there somewhere."

"I've seen the type, Conor. Ever since I've been here. They live in the labs, all day, working on their projects or even devising new ones. Read their textbooks three and four times over, memorizing facts and formulas without ever considering where those facts come from, and what those formulas really mean. They're after the grades and they'll do anything to get them, but they never really learn anything. They never learn how to think or analyze or question."

"Seems to me," said Finnegan, "that Anne learned how to question very well."

Rosselli smiled, then continued. "They parrot back the things they've memorized without ingesting anything. A regurgitated education. They get the grades, but they're worthless outside of their textbooks. She's that type, Conor. She's shallow, and thick, and she's been protected all her life. Now Mac's going to play the gallant, chivalrous suitor. You can tell already, and it makes me sick to see it. I'm surprised he'd let himself fall into something like that."

"I don't know, Dan. Isn't that a bit harsh?"

"I'm telling you, Conor, I've seen her kind in action. They have yet to grow up. They're not adults yet, and they have absolutely no common sense. Their whole social development has been arrested somewhere around the age of thirteen. They still live the way they did then. They still have the same values, the same outlook. There's no need for them to change. Except that now, instead of getting the best grades in geography or biology, they're getting the best grades in organic chemistry and physiology. And they keep moving down the road, one step at a time, from high school to college to med school, because that's that they've been geared for. That's the proper way for them. The only way. The steps are hard but they know the technique. The problem is that they get there without picking anything up along the way. I shudder to think that Anne Newbury will someday be a doctor, deciding issues of life and death, but there seems to be no avoiding it. I just hope to Christ I'm never her patient."

"You really think she's like that?"

"Absolutely. What do you think?"

"I think she's pretty simple. And I also think that if Tom keeps seeing her, we're going to have a good time making fun of her behind his back."

"Such as?"

"Well, it's obvious Mac has to explain everything to her."

Rosselli went into a girlish falsetto. "Tell me about the colors, Tom."

Finnegan replied in a low, drippingly serious whisper, "What do you want to know, Anne?"

"Well, what's my favorite color, Tom?"

"Black, Anne."

"Oh. That's like the nighttime, right? When it's dark outside?"

"Yes, Anne. But I'll be there to protect you."

They both laughed. It was absurd, all of it. The evening, the girl, the boy, themselves, and their parody of it. Absurdity that made no sense. But they laughed, and abandoned their search for meaning. What meaning can be found between friends, at once slightly bitter, on a winter's Saturday night?

"Good night, Dan. I'll see you in the morning," and as Finnegan left the room he flipped off the light.

* * *

One late afternoon in the middle of the week, before dinner and after classes, Conor Finnegan went for a run. There was nothing strange in this. He liked to run three or four times a week if he could. He enjoyed keeping himself strong.

The day had been cold. In fact, it had been a cold week, a cold month. The temperature had not risen above freezing for several days. Finnegan pulled on his thick sweatshirt and zipped it up to his neck. He drew the string of his sweatpants taut. On his head he pulled a woolen hat, tugging it down over his ears. He bent over to tie his shoes. 'The right side of that one is wearing thin,' he thought. 'Pretty soon my toe will be breaking through.'

After stretching, Finnegan pulled on a pair of ragged cotton gloves, worn through on three of the fingertips, and bounded down the stairs. At the bottom he opened the outer door. Cold air stung him, and his first breath of it pierced his lungs. He stepped outside, shutting and securing the door behind him. There was no need to lock it. Pausing on the brick steps, Finnegan drew four deep breaths and looked at the approaching twilight.

The sky, cloudless, shot to the crystal blue horizon. It was the kind of color that shows only on a handful of days, and those the sharpest, freshest days of the year, broken-glass days. The sun had moved behind the house, but it still cast fading shades of orange, the deepest hues nearest the roofline, then draining in brightness as they rose, creating shades for which man had not yet conceived names. Up the street on either side the trees stood bare, their thick brown arms topped with scraggly broken fingers. Across the way, Buccleuch Park still held a greenness, but it had been muted by weeks of snow and autumn rain. In more than a few places patches of snow remained, flecked with tiny spots of black grime. The houses on the street stood dumb, tightly shut. From one or two of the chimneys there issued a wispy stream of white smoke. *Habemus Papem.*

It smelled like winter. Finnegan smelled the setting sun, and his nostrils flared as he drew it in. He caught the rich, loamy scent of the spongy ground. He inhaled chimney smoke, and the crystal blue of the sky, and the colored reflections of the parked cars. He smelled the steam of his own breath. The cold air ran down his throat and filled his lungs, mixing with and driving out the warm apartment air that was as sedentary as he had been all day. He drew deep breaths, and held them, smelling what he had inhaled.

'It is winter, and I am here, far beyond anything I have ever known. Tonight the sun will go down into the warm Pacific, and I have seen it. The cold will not come there, where I grew up, and the waves will run into the empty sand, miles away; years away. On the beach, near the hills, near the mountains that are hard and rocky. It is cold here. It is winter, as it has been for centuries, yet I have never known it. I am here now, and it is all so strange. So cold, and so very different.'

Finnegan hopped down the four brick steps. He walked across the street to the park, bent over one last time, grabbing the toes of his shoes, took a final relaxed breath, and broke into an easy jog. He stayed on the road that circumnavigated the park. Three-quarters of a mile to the other side, then another quarter down George Street until he reached the old steel bridge and the towpath.

As he ran, Finnegan looked around him. The park was empty. Ahead of him to the left were the tennis courts, netless. Ahead to the right stood the gaunt white gazebo, useless even in the best of weather, but a landmark nonetheless. It appeared as stark as the trees that framed it. Finnegan looked behind him. He could see the sun now, a magnificent orange sphere throwing off light in blankets rather than tendrils. The colors shot up and out in nameless orange-blue-purple-white hues. As the road split, Finnegan veered left to avoid a small ravine. The road sloped downward then, not gradually at all, but sharply, so sharply that he really didn't have to run at all. His weight, caught now by gravity, pulled him effortlessly down the slope.

At the bottom of the hill ran George Street. To the left, tucked into the elbow between the park and the road, rose an apartment complex of several stories. It was a landmark, too, visible even from his own apartment, although Finnegan usually chose to ignore it. Somehow it didn't seem right, this huge modern tower sitting adjacent to such rare parkland. In the warmer months he would see residents sitting on their patios as he ran by, but tonight there were no signs of life. It was too cold.

He reached the end of George Street and, glancing for traffic, trotted across the roadway to the old bridge. One or two cars headed down from the other direction, most likely students returning from the Busch campus across the river. Even so, traffic seemed unusually light. Finnegan stepped over a cable and glided down the stony rise that led from the towpath up to the bridge itself. The ground underfoot squished with each step.

Finnegan was not tired although he paused briefly to check the footing. The ground had been washed into softness by the season's moisture, and stones, tree roots, and small divots ran across the path. Once before, in late summer, he had stepped on a root here and twisted his ankle. He had not been able to run for two weeks afterward, nor could he play tennis or basketball. Now he was always careful, especially as the darkness loomed.

To his left the murky water of the Delaware and Raritan Canal sat motionless. To his right flowed the Raritan River, a silty brown, even in patches of a bright twilight. Here and there pockets of suds floated on the surface, residue from some unknown plant upriver. Finnegan turned behind him. In the far distance rose the buildings of New Brunswick and Highland Park, simple structures that appeared deceptively clean in the dying light, their usual grime masked by a brilliant sunset. In the near foreground stood the three river dormitories. Only the sides facing the river were visible and Finnegan tried to pick out the window to his old room on the sixth floor in the closest building. But it was like looking at a sheet of pockmarked red cardboard, and he couldn't make out where he had lived for two years. He noted the balcony there, six floors up, shook his head twice and turned back to the towpath. A narrow strip of land split the river from the canal, the stark, barren trees lining it standing sentry. Finnegan took another deep breath and quickened his pace.

Above him he heard the traffic from the road running along the river atop the high thirty-foot slope falling to the towpath. In quick glances he saw the backs of the houses on that road. Most of them were completely hidden once the trees sprouted leaves.

Ahead of him lay an empty stillness. Finnegan ran on, keeping his rhythm, counting his steps. He could feel his feet kicking up specks of mud. His sweatpants most likely would be filthy from the knees down. He felt the strong, crisp air filling his powerful lungs. If it were not a good day for him, his arms and legs would become leaden, and sharp pains would knife through his side. But there was none of that tonight. Finnegan's limbs felt hard, almost rocklike, yet very supple. His muscles rippled his skin. His relaxed breathing dictated the pace of his run.

Finnegan passed a familiar tree on his right, a particularly gnarled birch beyond which he could see clearly the college's math building on the Busch campus. He had calculated this to be about a mile and a half from the bridge. By now he was usually a bit winded, and beginning to plod. Here it would be a five-mile run total, two and a half out and two and a half back. Here is where he would normally turn around. But tonight he felt light. Finnegan was still running on his toes. He would push onward, just a little further.

The light grew dimmer. The sun had sunk all the way below the horizon far behind him. The sharp air stung his face. A thin line of mucus trickled out the edge of his right nostril and froze there. Yet his breathing continued evenly, and his step remained easy. Just a little further.

He pushed onward and felt no pain at all, and no fatigue. The noise of the traffic above him had ceased altogether so he deduced that he was beyond the point where the road veered away from the river, a good three miles from the bridge, and maybe three and a half. As he ran he discovered new landmarks and new views. He was well beyond the

Busch campus now. Across the river were houses—clean, mostly white, shuttered and prim. He noticed a church spire he had never seen before.

With the sun gone, the evening grew dark quickly. There was little light to delineate his steps. He slowed his pace, and gradually jogged to a stop. He still felt fresh, his limbs as powerful as they had ever been. Through the dim light Finnegan saw steam rise from his body. It wafted upward and blended into the river's silhouetting darkness. He recalled the first time he had noticed it. It had fascinated him then, it was so bestial.

Finnegan stood still and listened. He heard nothing save an occasional lapping of the river. No traffic, no birds, no other runners. He heard only the rising and falling of his own breathing and his step underfoot as he turned to face the river.

'Silence,' he thought. 'And as much solitude as I could ever want. For what reason have I come here? What has brought me here tonight, to this space? What steps marked my way here, and why did I take them? To stand at the edge of a lazy ancient river, where soldiers almost three centuries ago watered their horses and bathed themselves before going off to their mortality; to feel a cold on my skin; to join my life to others whose histories are not mine.

'Am I not the same as every man who ever walked this earth, and do we not seek the same things? It is not the arrival that provides the excitement; it is the process of getting there. For who knows his own potential, how far he can run? And who can tell what a singular step, once taken, irretrievably produces, and what further steps will become necessary, what others will become impossible? Is that not part of our potential—the capacity to take our strides in as many directions as imagination defines, and to make them deep, pounding ones that imprint the soil?

'What is it I seek, and what has brought me here? I seek the footprint. I can feel it coming: here tonight, a rolling underfoot, a groundswell, an intoxication borne on the crisp air. My form grows harder, my outlines focus themselves around an amoebic center, this gelatinizing of substance, this settling of character. I have waited for it, tried to find it, as all men before and as all men following me inevitably will. It is as natural, as necessary as drawing air, as filling our stomachs.

'I am not the first here, to stand at this river and search through the flotsam, to feel myself congeal, to the feel the promises turn toward me and breathe upon my warm skin. I am not the first to stand here, amid darkness and the water, womblike, to consider my impending birth. I am not the first, and I wish I could have known those who preceded me, and known their times. But it is all for me to be here now.

This is all for me, here at this water's edge.'

After several minutes, cold pierced Finnegan's reverie, returning him to the immediate. The perspiration on his brow and up and down his limbs had dried. There were only a few vestiges of light behind him. He had run too far and stayed too long. The run back must be at least six miles, and he would have to make it in almost total darkness. With some relief he recognized that the strength that had pushed him out so far had not been an illusion. He still felt as if he could run forever. But the quiet and the darkness made him nervous. He had never done this before.

He turned back up the towpath and tried to find a rhythmic stride. He ran even quicker than before so that he might cut his time on the way back. But the total darkness unnerved him. Only the softly sporadic reflections off the river—reflections from houselights, the city and the campus well ahead of him—provided any light at all. He could see the vague rippling of the river now to his left, and the shadows of the trees.

Within the first mile Finnegan stumbled several times. He realized that, if he wanted to increase his odds of returning safely, he would have to run slower and step lightly. His breathing deepened, and sweat reappeared on his forehead.

At length he saw the dim outline of the bridge far ahead. His tension ebbed almost at once. A familiar sight, and he knew he could make it now. The traffic would mark the road, and he could see his way through the park, guided by the beacons on the other side. He picked up his pace once again.

Down George Street he ran, as far to the side as geography allowed, but no cars came close. He turned in to the park. The hill, that downward slope so friendly on his way out, now loomed menacingly ahead. Finnegan realized that he had become very tired, had been so for the past mile or so. The darkness, the solitude and the uncertainty of his return had kept his slow pace regular, but now that the end was in sight his fatigue became very real, moving in from the periphery where his nerves had kept it at bay. He debated stopping altogether and walking up the steep slope.

'No, damn it. One last hill. One last push," and he set his jaw and broke into a sprint. Weight of gravity tied his legs to the ground, the slope pulling his stride so that each gain was small. Yet he drove onward, almost angrily. His muscles tightened with every thrust. The will was a foe, a real one, evil and arrogant. He had to beat it, that was all. He forced his muscles to respond . . . just a few more strides . . . three more . . . two more.

At the top of the hill, as the slope gave way to level ground, Finnegan opened his throat and yelled at the top of his tired lungs. He raised his arm like a sword. His legs and arms ached, his great heart pounded against his ribs, but it did not matter. He spotted the far end of the park with the house lights beyond. Three-quarters of a mile more, maybe less. A shower and dinner were at the other end.

Finnegan shot his right fist skyward once again, and sprinted the rest of the way.

* * *

That winter had been a restless one for Finnegan. He could not have explained it in any logical terms, but that did not disturb him. If there were an underlying disquietude, then so be it. If he felt it only vaguely, and could not define it, then he must give way to it, in any event. Something was coming. He sensed it, but had not the first clue what it might be.

And so, on those evenings when all concentration left him, when he could not remember what he was reading from one sentence to the next, when he looked out the front window to the parklands and beyond wondering what he might see there and how different it would all be, he yielded willingly. If his wanderlust masked any discontent, it would work itself out. It would have to.

In his restlessness, the young man would climb behind the wheel of his car with neither plan nor direction. He would take whichever road attracted his fancy, and he would drive, music playing softly, the windows rolled tight against the cold. In this way Finnegan saw the learned, quiet dignity of Princeton and the rolling verdure that surrounded it. He saw the ancient worn mountains to the northwest, the Poconos, and saw the deadened expressions of those who lived there in their rural, rustic, ragged sameness. He saw the smoky grassy industrial suburbs near the city, was repulsed by their grime yet attracted, too, to the broad human pathos, the basic animal struggles that hid behind the smokestacks. He saw the names on the stores and the restaurants— "Dominic's," "Santini's," "Wojo's"—and felt the Romantic pull of great distances and new challenges. He skirted into New York State and drove through the nameless burghs scattered along the hills of Orange County, and he marveled that he was an hour's drive from the great city, for these towns looked like Alabama or South Carolina or Wyoming. In winter's dusk he could not tell the difference.

He traveled southward, to Trenton's dreary stones and pipes, and crossed the Delaware River there, reading the large neon sign on another bridge bragging that "What Trenton Makes, the World Takes," but still wondering why Trenton existed. He saw the Delaware, crossed the bridge and drove along the Pennsylvania side north to Allentown, then returned on the interstate.

New England fascinated him, but that was too far for one of his evening's sojourns. He had read of it—rocky and round, with the cool ridges of the Berkshires, the driftwooded beaches of Connecticut and Rhode Island, the barren pine forests of Maine, and the oldest of all cities, Boston, standing at the water's edge like a baroness sitting in a bay window, accepting her callers. New England drew him, old, settled, sparse. The people there were different, as stony as their land, and he wanted to know them, to see them in their homes. He wanted to smell their wood smoke, watch their snow fall, and pick up the soil of their earth to weigh it in his hands. He had never been there; it drew him by ignoring him.

Finnegan took his drives, then, almost maniacally. He loved to see the sun set in a new place, for even the subtlest change in location brought about differences, nuances of lighting and background, that made them unique. He could not explain why this was important to him, this rambling, but he knew that at this point in his life it was important, and that he could not pass up the rare opportunity he enjoyed now. He drove without a goal, but carrying the goal within him—to paint greater and wider swaths across the land, to know it all by color and scent and feel, to be a part of none of it because he could then truly be a part of all of it.

And always when he returned from these trips, Finnegan's head felt clearer and his thoughts gelled more sharply. He could go on again as he was supposed to. But even so, he knew that nothing had been exorcised, that the restless hunger he carried at his core was only partially and temporarily satisfied, that it would reappear in a few days for the rite to be repeated. And he also knew that, if he were lucky and very careful, it would stay with him forever.

CHAPTER X

Far out beyond that timeless valley, a train, on the rails for the East, wailed back its ghostly cry: life, like a fume of painted smoke, a broken wrack of cloud, drifted away. Their world was a singing voice again: they were young, and they could never die. This would endure.

—Thomas Wolfe, *Look Homeward Angel*

In the mid-nineteenth century a young Frenchman, fairly wealthy by birth, grew bored with his study of the law. Too dry, he thought, and really, what is the point? If I do not practice law, there are hundreds of others who will step into my place and do as well as I. Perhaps, because they would be hungrier, they would do far better. Really, what is the point of it all?

The young man had always taken to drawing, attracted by the meticulous blend of line and color. The same precision of thought that would have made him an effective lawyer allowed him to capture an exact likeness. He drew portraits of friends and family, and they were quite good, so everyone said. Even so, he came to detest portraiture. If he did not know his subject intimately, his work came out lifeless. What was there to capture, then? He stuck to drawing his friends, drawing them well, but all the while felt his creativity wane.

The circumstances of his birth had allowed him to grow up in comfortable circles. As a child he had known the best sort of people. His father had been "well placed" and provided well for his family.

The boy grew up with more than a passing knowledge of the theater. He knew how to tell a good horse. He could appreciate beautiful women.

Such things continued to attract him throughout his youth. He had abandoned his destined career to pursue his art. Now, bored with the type of art he was pursuing and looking for a new dimension to his passion, he turned once again to the familiar habits. Yet behind the elegance of Parisian life then the young man perceived a hollow tone, a striking of a cymbal while holding fast to its rim. Behind the grace of the theater, the fine lines of the ballet, the majestic power of the race track, there lay a panoply of human emotions, of a desperation to achieve, not fine lines or grace or power, but simple human dignity, of a quietly frantic search to attain belonging, love and accomplishment, of lifeless resignation on the part of those who have failed and have chosen now to pursue no more ephemeral dreams. The young man had always sensed it. Now he saw that he could articulate it, this well-masked but ancient human condition, with his hands. He could draw it, or as much of it as his own limited experience permitted him to discern, and the realization excited him to his core, even while the pathos he observed made him melancholy. He came alive again; he had a new conviction. He would create, yes, but not the artificial husks of men and women. He would work with the subtle beauty of line and color, he would depict the casual scenes of elegance he had always known, but he would do so with a newly careful eye, and as honestly as he could. The blend of message and medium would have to be delicate, yet it was all he could bring himself to do. And he knew there was immense beauty in the blending.

Color, not line. That was where it could best be captured. The nuances of light, backdrop, shading hue causing dissolution of line altogether. A radical concept, but one emerging in the late part of that century in the European salons, and in his mind a concept perfect to the task, for was he not truly painting atmosphere rather than form? Pathos was a dusky shadow, a commingling of the dark with the bright, an abandonment of cold and hard outline. Pathos was a texture.

The young French artist came to meet with a measure of success. As he grew older, people came to know his name, for better or for worse. His paintings were displayed in all the right places, at the best exhibitions of his day. He had acquired a mastery of pastels, a difficult medium but one which permitted him best to blur line, color and shadow in stages of increasing subtlety. He enjoyed what he was doing. He even enjoyed the controversy, for at least it showed that people were paying attention. Times change, he thought. Let the old die with the old.

But in time, though, he too grew old. His eyesight slowly failed him, the price of years of close scrutiny of small details. He retired to the country as the new century dawned, and painted very little. What he did create did not please him much; his subtleties decreased and hard lines reappeared in the stead of his beloved gentle colorings. He turned to sculpture, but nothing really came of it. He died quietly as a world war poked holes in his land and butchered the unknown artists of a new generation. He did not have as much money as he might have liked, but no matter. He saw his death coming in inches, knew he could not forestall it long, and, not particularly minding at all, gave himself up to it in dignity, respect, and, ultimately, joy. It had been a life well spent. He passed from it as he had sought to create it.

In death his reputation surpassed what it had been in life. Demand for his drawings grew. High prices were bid and his works subsequently dispersed—to Italy and to Spain, to Russia, purchased by the great impresario Diaghilev, to England of course, and to the United States. Later generations of artists used his style as a jumping-off point to create the bizarre intellectual and psychological modes that marked the twenties, thirties and forties. Scholars accorded him high praise, studied him meticulously, every drawing, every stroke, every tint. He and his cohorts had been pioneers. They had broken the Golden Calf of Line and introduced an entirely new way for esthetic man to view, and hence capture, his world. Their courage had given them an immortality they had not deemed important at the time but which they no doubt would have welcomed.

Of the young Frenchman's drawings that had found their way to the United States, most had eventually been secured by the great art museums on the East Coast. A handful sat preserved in Philadelphia, more in Washington, more still in New York. On a Saturday morning in early April, Conor Finnegan, forced to face the reality of a term paper for his class in Nineteenth Century European Painting, headed down the road to Philadelphia, where he could study closely three examples of his topic, "The Equestrian Drawings of Edgar Degas."

Finnegan had not chosen this morning for his trip. Rather, the morning had chosen him. The day dawned brightly and Finnegan had risen early when the sun crossed into his room through a window usually shaded. The morning was crisp, barely topping forty degrees, but after the cold and slushy winter it dug into Finnegan's lungs, slapped his skin and pricked his heart. Life reaffirmed, a Pasch at hand, sweeping through this golden, glorious, spirited morning.

He did not know precisely why the morning captured him as it did. Perhaps because it seemed so fresh, so un-winterlike; perhaps because he had slept well after a productive week; perhaps merely because the syrups, fluids and elixirs that flow through us to comprise our moods sat in the right positions. It did not matter why. Finnegan felt young, and strong, and handsome, and intelligent, and infinitely blessed. The day, the whole world, was at his command, and he would do something grand with it.

Finnegan arrived in Philadelphia around 11:00. The tall buildings of downtown stood sharply against the blue. At the end of them Fairmount Park sloped down to the Schuylkill River, a green swath curving downward through shade trees. A handful of rowers sculled along the river. The morning sun reflected off the water in white pockmarks. Finnegan did not park in the Museum of Art's lot. He drove instead through Fairmount until he found a space there in the park, on the side of the road, and walked back through the greenery, the shadows and the spring.

At the top of the steps to the museum he paused to look behind him at the city spread below. He looked at the gray spire of city hall, William Penn eternally perched atop it. From his position on the steps he felt as if he looked Mr. Penn directly in the eye.

The museum was not crowded. After roaming through the maze of rooms and chambers at the Metropolitan in New York, Finnegan was a bit disappointed with this museum's layout. It was wide and open, and in being so did not seem large at all. Degas and the Impressionists hung on the second floor.

An art museum does not generally attract a variety of types. It is not a menagerie, nor a cross-section of something broad and far-ranging. The people who go to art museums tend to be quiet, studious, serious. They wear muted colors and walk in slow, deliberate steps. There are never many children, and, among the men, facial hair predominates. The women look disheveled, and frequently wear their hair in braids.

The people at Philadelphia's art museum this morning fit the mold. Finnegan, as he always did in crowds, scanned them as he passed. Students looking ragged, dilettantes and aesthetes—a predictably colorless and dull group if one were accustomed to them.

But as Finnegan walked down the hallway to the Impressionists, he saw someone who was not so dull. She was standing before a painting by Thomas Eakins, studying it with the wryest of grins, the corners of her mouth turned upward ever so slightly as to give merely a hint of amusement or interest. She had not dressed in the casual bohemian fashion that typified most of the people there. If anything, she had overdressed in a black top stretching under a dark plaid skirt. She wore stockings and simple black shoes.

Finnegan tried not to be obvious, but she drew him to her in a quiet trance. She stood before Eakins with her arms folded and her weight shifted to one leg. Finnegan walked slowly behind her and, in order to see more of her face, took a pose at the painting next to the Eakins. He did not recognize the artist, but then, that was not the point. He stole quick glances at the woman until she turned to move past him down the hall. As she did, Finnegan furtively slid his eyes downward from the painting to watch her walk past.

She had long brown hair, acres of it, flowing down her shoulders to the small of her back. It hung in gentle waves, curling slightly at the ends. Finnegan noticed, too, her eyes—large, brown, somewhat almond-shaped. They tapered at each end to high cheekbones that softly punctuated her face. Her body seemed delicate, although Finnegan noticed well the rise of her breasts beneath the tight black top. She walked in long, slow strides conveying composure, confidence, elegance itself. As she passed, Finnegan breathed her scent and recognized the deep, richly pungent aroma of lilacs.

He watched her move down the hall, trying to read her direction. After a few seconds he followed the same way, again furtively, hoping he was not obvious. She enchanted him. Finnegan felt confused, not knowing how he might go about speaking to her, or even if he wanted to. But she *was* distinct. He wanted to see more of her, to study her as he would a fine painting. Her color and line seemed to him to be superb.

Finnegan continued behind her through most of the second floor. He put Degas out of his mind; he could always return to him if she left. For the time being, he was most intent on observing this new work of art. She moved about in slow steps, pausing here and there to study a painting or a small sculpture. She carried a notebook, opening it occasionally to jot some reaction. Finnegan at first tried to do the same, if for no other reason than to maintain his guise of serious study, but his concentration soon wandered even from this simple ruse. Her mere presence made him feel awkward.

At one point, near a group of works by Georges Braque, the girl sat on a long rectangular stone bench. She placed her purse and notebook beside her, crossed her legs and tucked her chin between her left thumb and forefinger, clenched into a gentle fist. She looked straight ahead, casually glancing from time to time at the Braques.

When she rose after a few minutes, Finnegan, only a short distance away in the same chamber, saw her notebook on the stone bench. She had left it behind, and now she was walking down the steps to the first floor, possibly on her way out—of the museum, and of Finnegan's romantic musings. He hesitated, then gathered himself, walked quickly to the bench and picked up her notebook. For a blind second the thought of looking inside it crossed his mind. He held it in one hand and regarded it. The name of one of Philadelphia's better colleges was emblazoned on its front, but her name was not. No, he thought, he dared not open it. That would be an unfair advantage. He hustled down the steps to find her.

Sweet Lorelei, singing on the Rocks of Time.

She was near the foot of the steps, walking her long, slow strides toward the entrance doors. Finnegan caught up with her.

"Excuse me," and she turned. Finnegan extended the notebook in his hand. "You left this behind upstairs."

She smiled and took it from him. Her voice came out sweet and musical, with a hint of mischief, as she responded, "I was wondering how long it would take you. You've been following me for several galleries, haven't you?"

Finnegan felt himself blush. "Caught me." He smiled, then leapt forward, "You're not easy to ignore."

"Nor are you. You're very handsome."

"And you're quite amazing." Smiling now, "Not to mention straightforward."

"I see no need to be coy. You don't come here much, do you?"

"No. How can you tell?"

"I haven't seen you here before. I would have noticed. I can recognize most of the regulars. Art students, mostly. A pretty dull lot. You stood out. You're not an art student. What brings you here?"

"Degas. A term paper for a course I'm taking. I wanted to look at some of Degas's things."

"And you looked at me instead. I'm glad you did." She had a lovely smile, subtle, not broad. "Where are you from, stranger?"

"I go to Rutgers. It was such a gorgeous morning that I decided to come down here for a look at the museum. What about you? You go to school in the city."

"I do. I'm one of those dull art students. I come here a lot."

"Even on gorgeous Saturdays."

"Especially. What's your name, my new friend?"

"Conor. Conor Finnegan."

"Ah, an Irishman with two last names. I'm impressed. You look Irish, you know. Your face is friendly. You look as if you should be wearing a great wool sweater, sitting in some pub with your friends, laughing and drinking ale. What do you think?"

"I think you're incredibly perceptive. And I think I'd like to find a pub, or at least a café. It's nearly noon. Can I buy you lunch?"

"That would be lovely, Conor."

"You haven't told me your name."

"Glynnis Mear. My father was Irish, too, but my mother was Italian. I suppose I'm something of a hybrid, not as pure as you."

"Even so, that's a name that rings of heather on the moors. Where shall we go? You know the city much better than I do."

"There's a cheap restaurant down the Parkway. We can walk. On the way back I'll show you the Rodin Museum. That is, if you've seen enough Degas."

"I've seen all I need to see."

They left the museum and walked down the steps to the Benjamin Franklin Parkway. There was little traffic, although the park itself had begun to fill. Runners, mothers with children, people strolling through. Even with minimal traffic, the noxious odor of the city's exhaust hung in the air.

On the walk they probed and bantered. It was necessary groundwork, this production of raw data. From there they would go on to more interesting matters.

"What brought you to Rutgers? Are you from New Jersey?" They had reached the restaurant. It lay on a short side street that ran into the Parkway near the beginning of Fairmount. "Not at all. I was born and raised in California, near Los Angeles."

"And you came clear across country just to go to school. My Lord, you *are* an Irishman. Restless and Romantic, no doubt."

"No doubt. It was a challenge. I think I might have been a touch simplistic about it."

"How so?"

"I had done extremely well all my life, academically, athletically and personally. I wanted to see if I could do as well somewhere else, where I was less protected. To conquer new worlds, so to speak. But I don't think I can look at college, or adulthood, or life itself, as some type of contest. It's a process, that's all. Everybody has his own victories. Some are just more obvious than others."

"We all have our defeats, too."

"Exactly. The struggle isn't to see if we can do better than everyone else. The struggle is just to see if we can get things right for ourselves."

They were seated and given menus, which neither read. The restaurant was small and dark, not at all crowded. The walls were of thick oak, as were the tables. The servers wore bright red vests.

"I guess Irishmen like to throw philosophy about, too," continued Finnegan with a smile. "The world thinks the Irish are such wonderful storytellers. But we're all so full of crap that it comes naturally. The stories, the philosophy, and all the lies we ever tell."

Glynnis chuckled, a small gurgle riding her smile. Her brown eyes shone in the dim light.

"And you, Miss Mear. Where are you from?"

"Boston."

"You don't sound it. There's no New England accent there."

"Thank you. I take that as a compliment."

"Just an observation. Why did you come to Philadelphia when there are so many great schools in Boston?"

"I'm part Irish, too, remember?"

"Restless and Romantic."

"Partly. I wanted to get out on my own. I grew tired of my family."

"A big clan?"

"Big enough. Two brothers and a sister. But the tipping point came when it got smaller. My father died a year ago. I had to get away."

"I'm sorry."

"So am I. His death changed the whole complexion of things. He did everything for all of us, even my mother. He was so devoted. After he died, I just didn't want to face them, or face the new thing we had become. I thought it best I get away so I could start to appreciate them again."

"And have you?"

Glynnis shook her head. "No. Not really. My life is here now. I don't even go home during the summers. I stay on campus and work in the library." A red-breasted server returned with their food. They had each ordered a simple lunch. "Do you get back to California much?"

"Christmas. And the summers, too, but I really go back there to work. If I didn't have my job there I'm not sure I'd go back at all."

"What do you do?"

"I'm a legislative researcher for California's junior U.S. senator."

"Very impressive," said Glynnis with a slight bow of her head.

"Speechwriting and answering angry phone calls. But there's some element of glamor in it, I must confess. I have an office on the fourteenth floor of the Federal Building, and I know a United States senator. There's something to be said for that."

"That should help you down the road."

"If the boss cooperates. A recommendation from him might open doors, to law school or whatever else."

"Will you be going back this summer?"

"Next month, after finals. Sometime around May fifteenth."

"I really hate the summers here. It's so hot and sticky. No one's around, and there's not much to do."

"Then why do you stay here?"

"There's really no comfortable alternative, Conor. That may sound harsh, but there's nothing else I care to do. I couldn't stand the thought of being home for three months. But tell me about California."

Conor did. And he told her about his family, and about Rutgers, and about his apartment there, with his three friends. For most of the meal Finnegan wove the tales of his past and his present. Glynnis listened deeply, drinking in his stories and looking at her new friend with her constant wry smile. He amused her with his diversity. There was no need for her to say much, and she preferred that. At the end of lunch Finnegan paid the bill and, allowing the red-breasted server to share in his billowing mood, left a liberal tip. They walked back into the sunlight.

On the way back up the Parkway, Glynnis took Conor to the Rodin Museum as promised. Glynnis loved Rodin, the strength and taciturn power of his great sculptures. Conor feigned interest at first, but found that, under Glynnis's enthusiastic descriptions and genuine understanding of the artist, Rodin took on an authentic vibrancy he had not seen before. He hung on Glynnis's words and studied the sculptures now coming alive through his new curiosity. Glynnis's excitement was almost childlike and Conor felt flattered that she should show this to him. She, in turn, felt completely comfortable; it was right that she should share Rodin with him.

They walked through the park for much of the afternoon. At one point they sat on the banks of the Schuylkill to watch the rowers. "They're always there," said Glynnis. "At every time of day. I like them. They're so strong and yet they're so graceful. When they row there's an element of anguish in them that I find intriguing."

"An Irishman loves the sea," said Conor. Glynnis turned her head to him, away from the river, and smiled.

"Do you love the sea?"

"I do. I miss it here. I miss the Pacific. The Atlantic's different, not the same. The Pacific is beautiful, especially when the sun goes down."

"And I bet you'd like to sail after it sometimes."

"Just to see where I'd be."

"Restless and Romantic, my Irish friend."

"The stuff of poetry."

"So why the law? Why do you want to go to law school and not the Merchant Marine Academy? Follow your Romantic leanings."

"I am, in a way. I don't want to live my life solely for my own benefit. I'd like to think that my life might have value for other people, for those who might gain something they need from what I do. That's the ultimate virtue, I think. We have the capacity to do that. The law is a means. Government work, too, if I can stomach it. I think you can do great things through existing channels, if you're committed enough. And if the channels don't work, then you have the capacity, maybe even the obligation, to try to change them. The system works through the law. If you can master the law, then you can master the system. And if you master the system, or at least your own part of it, then you can bring it to work for the right things. You can address injustices, and create your own peace. Does that make sense?"

"You've thought this through. Are you sure you're not just rationalizing? It would be easy to lose those ideals once you start to draw a comfortable paycheck, which lawyers often do."

"I think my ideals will remain intact. I really can't justify sticking my head in the sand if I see something that bothers me and I can do something about it. I'm just not put together that way. But I'm probably putting myself in line for a lot of grief, though."

"Only if you're strong enough. It's the strong who get broken. The weak just flow along with the currents."

"Do you think I'm strong?"

"I think you've got heartbreak written all over you. Not past, but future. Yes, I think you're strong. You're bound to get hurt terribly somewhere along the way."

Finnegan turned back toward the river. "What makes you so certain?"

"You're young, and you're trusting, and you've got a conscience. Burdensome traits, those are. The primary ingredients for pain."

"I've been pretty successful at avoiding it so far."

"All the more reason. Your luck will run out."

Finnegan turned back to her. "That's fairly pessimistic."

"That's part of being Irish, too, O'Finnegan. I remember reading what someone said after President Kennedy was assassinated—'I don't think there's any point to being Irish if you don't believe that the world is going to break your heart eventually.' That seems right to me. We're an ill-fated people, a sad people, even on these shores. There's heartbreak in our blood. You show it clearly."

"I hope I can prove you wrong."

"You won't. But in the end it might be good for you."

"We'll have to see, won't we?"

"There's no choice. It's getting late, Conor. The sun's going down."

"It's quarter past five."

"I should be going back to campus."

"Do you have plans for tonight?"

"No. But I should get back."

"Can I give you a ride?"

"That would be fine, Conor. Thank you."

They walked to Finnegan's car a short distance down the park road. Finnegan was reluctant to see the day come to a close. He had not considered going back to New Brunswick, and now the thought weighed him down.

Finnegan turned the car onto Schuylkill Expressway following Glynnis's directions. She spoke little except to tell him how to get to the city's west end. She, too, seemed subdued. At length Finnegan drove through the campus gates. The sun now was very low, and the entire campus sat in shadow. She directed him down a side road to her dormitory.

"Glynnis, I'd love to be able to ask you to dinner but I can't afford it."

"A poor struggling student. I wouldn't go with you anyway. I want to eat on campus tonight. I want tonight to be as quiet as possible."

"Let me walk you to your door."

"Oh my, you are a gentleman. I suspected as much."

They walked from the drive up a stone path to the entryway. The dorm was silent. No one entered or left.

"Thank you for returning my notebook, Conor," she said softly. "And thank you for a lovely day."

"Can I call you? I'd love to see you again. You have all the makings of an obsession."

"You don't mind driving to Philadelphia?"

"On the contrary, any escape from New Brunswick is always welcome, especially for such a beautiful reason."

She wrote down a phone number on a page of her notebook, ripped it out and gave it to him.

"Thank you, Glynnis. For the whole day. And I will call you. Very soon, I expect."

"Please do."

Conor took both her hands in his. It was his first touch of her, and years later he would recall the warmth that brewed up behind it, the soft strength of her long fingers. He leaned forward, careful to be neither too bold nor too rough. The lilacs drew him in, a web that snared his very marrow. There was no escaping this. He had withheld himself all day, but now he would unfold the merest glimpse of his passion. Conor did not seek her lips. Instead he bent his mouth gently to the crook of Glynnis's neck, just below her ear. He kissed her there, at the nexus, barely pursing his lips. Conor drank her down, and with a second motion closed his eyes and nuzzled himself into her rich, warm flesh. If he could, he might have crawled through her skin into the exotic fibers that lay beneath. For an instant, Conor released himself totally, alone, fulfilled, immediately and ultimately redeemed.

In a brief second Conor withdrew from Glynnis's neck as gently as he had moved to it. She smiled up at him, neither shyly nor brazenly, but with a glow of comfort. "Have a safe drive back."

"I will. Take care of yourself, Glynnis."

"I always do. Call me."

"Soon. Good night."

Glynnis turned back to her dormitory with a quick spin. Conor walked down the pathway. At the foot, near the entrance to the parking lot, he looked around him. Finnegan had never been on this campus before. Of course there had never been a reason. Behind him, on the far side of the dormitory, a wide green mall sloped down to a group of stone buildings. The road emptying from the lot ran to Finnegan's left and disappeared in a grove of shade trees. The morning's freshness had not faded with the day. Finnegan paused briefly to look around at the scene, to etch it into his personal archives. He could not help it as he broke into a bouncing, loping run to his car.

* * *

Finnegan returned through the heart of the city, although he did not have to. His body did not sit quietly; he shifted, he tapped his foot, changed his position. Every end of him pulsed and raced. His muscles had turned to jumpy impulses, losing their definition. Each part of him swirled into an excited, dimensionless eddy.

After several minutes of city traffic Finnegan broke through to the north end where he picked up the expressway. He drove back through the speckled darkness, his self-assurance confirmed as more than mere folly, his spirit smiling at yet another stroke of his limitless good fortune.

Later that night Tom McIlweath returned home after an evening with Anne Newbury. It had been calming for him, as it always was. They seldom ventured out. McIlweath had eaten dinner with the Newburys. They had played some ping pong in the basement and watched television. Near midnight McIlweath had run out to a doughnut store for cinnamon crullers. Shortly thereafter he said good night, leaving his favored one without so much as a parting kiss. He felt no incongruity in his growing regard for Anne. She ran through his veins; he paid no mind to the context.

As McIlweath parked his old car, he noticed that a light in the living room was still lit. He glanced at his watch: 12:58. No surprise that someone might yet be awake. As he got out of the car he turned his head up and down the street. Finnegan's and Rosselli's cars were parked nearby.

McIlweath ascended the narrow steps to find Conor Finnegan sitting by the window, an art book in his lap.

"Evening, Conor."

"Welcome home, Romeo. An exciting time with Lady Anne?"

"Not exciting, but nice enough. I had dinner over there and we watched some television. I enjoyed the food. Are Lanny and Dan in?"

"Both asleep, if you can believe it. They went to a couple of frat parties but they were in by midnight. Not much meat on the hoof tonight, I guess."

"What a shame." McIlweath headed down the hallway to the bathroom. Finnegan waited for him to return, but upon emerging from the bathroom McIlweath went to the kitchen instead. Finnegan put down his unread book and walked after him. He found McIlweath sniffing through the refrigerator. "We're not out of milk, are we?"

"Afraid so. We've got plenty of beer, though."

"Of course." McIlweath pulled out a pitcher of orange juice, reached over to the cupboard to grab a glass and filled it nearly to the lip. He sat down at the kitchen table.

"So how was your day? Did you get to Philadelphia?"

"Yeah."

"How was the art museum?"

"Nice. Really nice." Finnegan paused. McIlweath looked up at him, for the other's voice held something hidden. When their eyes met, Finnegan broke into a smile. McIlweath smiled, too.

"Yeah? What happened? Was the art especially fine?"

Finnegan turned his head downward and released a burst of silent air. He looked back up at McIlweath. "I met a girl."

"At the museum? You sly dog."

"Yeah. We followed each other all through the Impressionists. She left her notebook by Georges Braque. I picked it up and brought it back to her on her way out. We spent the rest of the day together."

McIlweath's smile broadened. He wanted to hear the entire story. Such boldness, the meeting of a girl by chance and thrusting into her life, he could never have conceived for himself. "What's she like?"

"Mac, she's beautiful. That's why I noticed her at first, but it's more than just beauty, really. She carries herself with, I don't know, *grace*, for God's sake. She's quiet. She dresses well, at least today she did. She's poised. Confident. Independent. There's an elegance about her. I guess all that adds up to 'grace,' for want of a better word."

"What does she look like? You said she's beautiful. Give me details."

"Long brown hair, slight figure and brown eyes. God! Big, soft, brown eyes as deep as the Marianas Trench. She's got a special air about her, Mac. I can't describe it really, but it's attractive as hell. Oh yeah, she smells like lilacs."

"Sounds like you got pretty close to her."

"Not as close as I'd like to."

"What did you do all day long?"

"From the museum we walked up the parkway and got some lunch. She showed me the Rodin Museum there. We sat by the river, then I drove her back to her campus. She goes to college on the west side. Then I came home. I was home by eight and I haven't been able to calm myself since. I'm glad you're back."

"Hey, what are friends for? So keep talking. You haven't told me her name."

"Glynnis Mear. She's from Boston and she went away to school because she wanted to get away from her family for a while, or so she said. Her father died, and I guess that distorted her family situation for her. An art major with no career plans at this point."

"Perhaps nothing more than snagging an aspiring attorney."

"Not so fast, pal. I've only just met her. Besides, there's no room for that."

"Don't try to kid me, Conor. I know you better than anybody else, and I can sense the start of something. You've been snared."

"You're sure of that?"

"Absolutely. You're struck with this girl. You're excited by her, or else you'd be trying to sleep through Lanny's snoring. She's under your skin now, for whatever reason. I can tell. You can't go to sleep yet because you don't want the day to end. You had to describe her to someone. You've been home for five hours now and I'll bet she hasn't left your mind once."

"How do you know all this, Swami?"

"You're subtle, Conor, but you're obvious, too. For one thing, it's in your voice. You're talking quicker than you normally do. That's a sure sign. Plus you've got this moony look in your eyes like some fairy godmother just floated down and whacked you with her wand. You're intrigued by the possibilities. You don't know where this might go, but it's bound to be exciting whichever way. It shows, Conor. At least to me. When will you see her again?"

"I'm going to call her."

"Tomorrow?"

"Next week. But I think you're reading a lot more into this, Mac. We're not all dreamy Romantics like you."

"You're right, Conor. There aren't many Romantics roaming about. But you're one of them, friend. More so than me, even though you try to hide it."

"Then you of all people should have some empathy."

"Indeed I do. In fact, I welcome the company. I'm smitten, myself, as you might have noticed."

Finnegan smiled and clapped his friend on the shoulder as he walked past him. He returned to the living room to stand at the window. Behind him he could hear McIlweath walk softly into the bedroom he shared with the slumbering Dan Rosselli. Finnegan could make out the swishing sounds of McIlweath undressing.

What is the indefinable attraction that makes a man favor one woman above the next? What do we read in a first glance, in a few meaningless words? What sympathies cultivate our passion, and where do we know them? How do we know them? I have known a thousand women in a million poses, but why am I drawn to you, walking slowly through a somber museum in a springtime city? Do I perceive something there beneath you, perhaps nameless even to yourself, that shapes you as you are, that sets the parameters of your very being and, unwittingly, unknowingly, echoes my own? And if so, how do I know this? What do I sense? What greater threat is there to a logical man than to react solely on instinct? But what choice do I have, for logic demands that this is whimsy, nothing more, and perhaps a good deal less, perhaps nothing beyond the most basic and primitive urgings.

If that is so, let it remain hidden. Logic has its place. But not here. For now, I will abandon myself to whimsy, and place my trust in instinct.

But still I cannot define it. I cannot know why you draw me so, why, hours later, I see nothing but your gentle form. Where is the mingling of thought and fancy that brings about my attraction to you? Where does it lie, how did it arise, and, God help me, how do I control it?

How do I control it?. For you, of all women I have ever known, you frighten me. You can devour me. Something unspoken is there that tells me you can chew me into bits. Still, I have no choice. I will abandon myself to whimsy, and place my trust in instinct.

Finnegan turned away from the window and went to his bedroom. Lanny O'Hanlon, pragmatist, lay in the far bed, his back to the wall, breathing the stertorous rhythm of a peaceful sleep. O'Hanlon resided in lands forever closed to Finnegan. He envied him a bit.

Finnegan undressed and crawled into his own bed. He had spent himself, and sleep crashed over him in a wave. He had put his musings aside. Finnegan that night slept in the dreamless sleep of a sea captain whose course may not be clear, but whose ship had been solidly built.

* * *

A few days later, after returning from a morning class, Finnegan found a note on the kitchen table:

Conor me boy,

You received a phone call this morning, around 10:00, from a gentleman named Greeley Welsh. Claims he works for the senator and that he's currently in Washington. Friendly fellow, he was, although we did not have time to chat. He would like you to give him a call sometime today—202-356-2200. He'll be in until 4:00.

I have a late lab. Try to fix something at least remotely edible for dinner. I'm thawing out a pound of hamburger. Be creative.

Danny Boy

Greeley Welsh. What the hell was this about? Why would Greeley want to speak with him? Some problem with his summer position? But that's been confirmed for months, ever since last summer. Maybe he's just in Washington for a while and wants to waste some time on the phone.

Finnegan dialed the number, waded through the receptionist on the other end, and, after a short wait, heard Greeley's voice break through the line. "Conor, how are you? Thanks for calling back so soon."

"Greeley, Jesus, I didn't expect to be hearing from you. What are you doing in Washington? The senator forget his tennis racket on his last trip west, or what?"

"Some hearings he wants to put together on Latino problems. He needed my expert counsel. I think he's getting tired of abusing the same old faces. He wants new blood. A new cushion for his pins."

"Been giving you a hard time?"

"No harder than he gives everyone else. But he can be a real bastard sometimes. Thank God I'm only going to be here another couple of days."

"Are you calling for a sympathetic ear, or is there another reason?"

"You know I don't waste time on the phone, pal. I'm flying back to L.A. out of New York in two days, an evening flight. I thought we could get together for dinner in the city before I go. I'll buy."

"What's that, Thursday? No problem on my end. I think you still owe me a dinner or two from last summer."

"Several cocktails at least. All right, then. There's a restaurant I know on Lexington between 40th and 41st." He gave the name. "What do you say we meet there about 5:30? That'll beat any dinner crowd they might have. My flight's not until 10:00."

"Sounds great. You sure you'll last through Thursday?"

"I never realize how good I've got it in L.A. until I come back here. He only comes west six or seven times a year. I get too accustomed to running my own show. I don't know how to take orders anymore. And I've never been good at being deferential."

"An independent and free spirit like yourself made to heel? The thought brings shudders."

"Too true, my son. Got to go. See you Thursday night."

The prospect of dinner in New York with Greeley Welsh almost superseded Finnegan's thoughts of Glynnis Mear. He would wait until after this dinner to call her. For now, he continued to wonder if Greeley had some hidden agenda. Most likely. New York was too far out of the way for a casual dinner, and planes fly from Washington to L.A. all the time. But then, Finnegan reasoned, who am I? He knows lots of people. Maybe he's coming on other business and wanted to have dinner simply because his evening is free.

We grow accustomed to seeing the people we know in given contexts. We come to identify individuals in certain roles, in certain positions. When given contexts are breached, we feel an excitement, as if encountering a stranger for the first time. Children often thrill to see a teacher in a supermarket or a laundromat; husbands are often fascinated by their wives at their workplaces, and conversely; the public as a whole stumbles all over itself when it encounters a celebrity walking down the street. For this reason Finnegan grew increasingly enthralled by the prospect of seeing Greeley Welsh in New York. Newer, subtler facets of a personality he thought he knew would become evident, and he would see Greeley as something fresh, and out of place.

Finnegan drove into the city in late afternoon and parked his car at the Port Authority Terminal. He wore a jacket and tie under a thin overcoat that he needed against the chill: April evenings could still be cold. Finnegan had time enough to walk the several blocks across Manhattan to the restaurant.

He enjoyed this immensely. After his first encounter with the city more than two years ago, he had come to love New York. The massing, pulsing sidewalks that had once intimidated him now filled him with what he felt to be an unfolding understanding of the various forms of the human character. He did not shrink from the squalor of certain side streets; he felt no fears in the tawdry areas around Times Square.

"I feel safer in New York than anywhere else," he had once told a disbelieving friend back home. "It's as if the underside calls a truce on everyone else because they realize they can't get away with anything. Everyone expects the worst out of the city, so everyone's on guard. The junkies and the thugs and the hookers stay to themselves. They don't bother me, and I don't expect them to."

Finnegan continued to be fascinated by the ubiquitous juxtaposition of wealth and poverty. Lexington, Madison and the pompously named Avenue of the Americas housed some of the world's most powerful corporations, yet only a few blocks away infants died of curable diseases and young men beaten into ennui by despair stuck needles into their arms to draw out the sap. It was a condition as old as the city itself, one that had outlived the musings of perplexed minds from Walt Whitman to Jacob Riis to Thomas Wolfe. Finnegan could not hope to solve it, nor even to understand it. Nonetheless it stained his perception of the city indelibly, and left an awful, pasty flavor to his trips there.

Those who did have the wherewithal to live well there lived extremely well. Finnegan appreciated the fine tailoring of the men—not just their clothes, but their bodies, too: styled, clipped, tan, lean, each piece fitted perfectly. And the women, of course. Finnegan had never seen more beautiful women than those in New York. They inspired his fantasies, but then, in an innocent way, so did the men. Everyone on these streets looked driven; they all had someplace to go. Finnegan wondered at their secrets, at the unique stories behind each confident, compulsive face.

Finnegan entered the restaurant a few minutes after 5:00. His eyes struggled to adjust to the darkness. He noticed a theater motif. On the walls hung posters from old Broadway shows, classics as well as bombs, chosen to hang there not because of their success but because of their esthetics. A long brass railing marked off one set of tables on a raised platform to the side. The restaurant itself was long and narrow, a great rectangle, with the bar immediately by the entrance and the dining area beyond. Where no posters hung in their frames, there were mirrors. The lighting came from pockmarks in the ceiling, bright and, when reflected off the mirrors and glass below, very glittery. To the right of the dining area stood a piano, not an elegant grand, but a simple block piano as might be found in any number of living rooms. The servers, men and women both, all dressed in pin-striped shirts and black vests. They spoke animatedly with their customers, smiled, gestured and, when finally walking away, fairly bouncing on their toes. Aspiring actors and actresses, thought Finnegan to himself. He speculated that this place had been opened by one who, drawn to the glamor and the glitter of the theater, had failed in his attempt to crack it. In his disappointingly common need to procure a living, he had bought this restaurant with his last cash. Here he could take part vicariously in what he had left behind; he could keep it alive for himself. He would hire only young people like he had been, those with gleams in their eyes and dreams in their heads. If one of his people eventually made it, that would be him there on stage, too. The city is made of dreams, Finnegan thought. He took a seat at the bar.

Greeley Welsh entered right at 5:30 and spotted Finnegan at the bar immediately. Welsh rushed to him with a broad smile. "Conor, Jesus, you look great," he fairly shouted as they shook hands.

"So do you, Greeley. You're tanner than I am."

"A California advantage. Been here long?"

"Long enough for my first drink. What're you having?"

"Scotch on the rocks with a twist."

Finnegan ordered two of the same. The bartender had not bothered to check identification, although Finnegan still looked very young. At times Finnegan did not like his boyish face, particularly in situations such as this, but the bartender had not pressed him.

"Let's get a table," said Welsh. "It's been a long day. I rode up on the Acela. Just got in."

"No bags?"

"I sent them ahead to the airport."

They were seated at a table on the raised platform, the only ones in that area. The rest of the restaurant was largely vacant, although the bar had started to fill. They reviewed the menus, speaking all the while of the senator and Welsh's work in Washington.

"You don't get back here very much, Greeley. Are these hearings really that important?"

"Depends on who you talk to. A poll in the *San Francisco Chronicle* last month had the senator's performance rating lowest among Hispanics. Something like only 47% thought he was doing a good job. He got hold of that and panicked, hence the hearings. And he wants a big production, lots of heartrending testimony from mothers barely able to feed their babies. He figures that because I work most closely with our Hispanic brethren that I'd be best to coordinate this little circus."

"But what's the point? What's the focus?"

"To get re-elected, of course. As you know, we usually have hearings to discuss publicly a specific aspect of a general problem, or even a single piece of legislation. Note my use of the word 'specific.' Not this time. Our boy wants two days of hearings on 'The Hispanic Condition.'

Everything—housing, nutrition, education, you name it. And he wants to do it in Washington. He doesn't seem to realize that there aren't a whole lot of Hispanics there. We'll have to fly them all in, put them up in hotels, feed them, all of it. It'll cost a fortune."

"Greeley, you could spend a week on any of those topics. If you try to cover everything in two days you'll come off looking like a fool. The boss is going to appear shallow."

"Conor, he *is* shallow. You know that."

"Yeah, but the whole state'll see that this is just a meaningless gimmick."

"Exactly what they've come to expect from their junior senator. He wants to do it, though. There's no stopping him once he gets an idea. Fortunately that's pretty rare."

They talked through another drink while waiting for dinner. Finnegan was not an accomplished drinker, and he certainly had little experience with Scotch. He felt warmed through his toes. His mind caught and registered details of the room, the servers, the patrons. He noticed in particular a beautiful redhead sitting with a young man a few tables below the brass railing. She had green eyes. Finnegan kept stealing glances at her throughout his conversation with Welsh.

They each had ordered seafood, so Welsh asked for a bottle of white wine, a California chardonnay. Shortly after they began eating, one of the servers sat down at the piano and began playing while another broke into "What Do the Simple Folk Do?" from *Camelot*. He sang show tunes for the next several minutes.

"I didn't tell you this place had entertainment, too."

"Singing waiters?"

"Common in New York, from what I hear. Young kids looking for a break. It's sad, really, in a sense. There's so much talent in this city going to waste. Maybe not good enough to break into the big time, but good enough to be doing something besides waiting on tables for the likes of us."

They finished their dinners and poured the last of the wine. Finnegan knew that he was still in control of himself, although he started to have some difficulty focusing on items beyond the table. Not great difficulty, but enough to compel him to order espresso. Welsh followed suit.

"So we come to the heart of whatever matter lies at hand," said Finnegan with a smile. "Why am I sitting with you in a restaurant in New York City? What's up, Greeley?"

Greeley Welsh leaned back in his chair and hooked an arm over one end. "You're a patient man, Conor Finnegan. We now enter the business part of this great dinner."

"So it's not just a random trip up the coast to see the wonders of Gotham. I didn't think so, but I wasn't entirely certain it had anything to do with me."

"You, my young friend, are the sole purpose of my journey. In fact, I was due to fly home from D.C. this afternoon. I changed my flight when you told me you were available. Not that I mind," Welsh lifted his cup to his lips and sipped the thick, dark coffee. "This has been great fun. I love New York City, with all the smugness of a westerner who knows he'll never have to live in this chaotic cesspool. How, in God's name, do you do it?"

"For one thing, I'm not in New York City. For another, you get used to it. I'm young enough to adapt to anything, I think. I'd survive in a God damn igloo in the Arctic Circle if I had to. But don't get sidetracked. What's so urgent that it couldn't wait until next month?"

"I've been dispatched by the senator. You know, Conor, you've really caught his eye. He thinks you've done some very good things for him. The elderly, and that whole nursing home thing. He told me he thinks you're also the best writer he's ever had on staff. Better than me even, I suppose that means. But I'm not jealous, you son of a bitch." He paused again to sip his espresso.

"You know, that same poll in the San Francisco paper that led to all this Latino nonsense showed him extremely strong among the elderly. Something like 76 percent approval. That's the highest rating the geezers have ever given him. He attributes part of that to you. He's introduced six or seven pieces of legislation on seniors that have stemmed from your reports and recommendations, and one of them is part of the omnibus bill that's about to be passed. The old folks like that. They'll vote for him in a couple of years, those that are still around. That's the problem with the senior vote. It's not long term."

"So the senator likes my work. I'm flattered, but why are you telling me this?"

"Because, old boy, he likes your work well enough to want you around permanently. I've been dispatched to make you an offer. Legislative Assistant in the Washington office, $37,000 a year to start. You'd come on board next month."

Finnegan's lips pursed in genuine surprise, but he quickly gathered himself. He was glad now that he had had something to drink. He felt more relaxed than justified after hearing the impressive proposal just made to him. And he felt very confident. No need to rush.

"What about college, Greeley? I'm not quite done yet."

"The boss says you can finish up at night. We'll find a way to cover tuition. He suggested Georgetown or George Washington."

"Law school?"

"The same. He can get you in at George Washington. He's on their board."

"He'd lose his clout as an ex-senator. What if he loses?"

"Then you do something else for someone else. I'll tell you something, Conor. In this business, if you're good you'll always be employed. No one stays in office forever. The staffs of the losers are picked up here and there. Besides, you could always go to law school full time. That's what you plan to do anyway, isn't it? This way, at least you'd have a couple years full time on a Senate staff under your belt. That in itself might open some very nice doors. If anything, Conor, this position gives you more options than you have now."

"What if I want to compromise?"

"What do you mean?"

"I work in Washington this summer, then go back to Rutgers in September with the understanding that I'll come on staff permanently after I graduate next year. Do you think he'd go for that?"

"You don't want to leave college?"

"No way. Not with one year to go. I've built a pretty nice life for myself here, and I've already got commitments for next year. I don't want to abandon all that unless it's absolutely necessary."

"Is that your answer, then? You want to see if you can delay for a year?"

"Let me sleep on it, Greeley. But if I work in D.C. this summer, then it's not even a full year delay. I can even do some assignment work from Rutgers over those months when I'm back there."

"I don't know if he'll bite, Conor. He seems to want you on board as soon as possible."

"Greeley, if I'm this important to him now, what'll I be next year once I finish my degree and get some more experience? I'll still be with him for the election."

Greeley Welsh laughed. "You know, Conor, you're amazing. I would have thought you'd jump at this. I'm sure the boss thought likewise."

"I am jumping at it. I'm just doing it on my own terms. I'm not going to change my long-term plans, even for an opportunity like this. If that's unfair, then I plead guilty."

"So what's the next move?"

"I call the senator after the weekend and give him my answer, and my terms. What do you think?"

"I think you're wise beyond your years. And I think the senator will be surprised, which is not a bad thing. I also think he'll ultimately go for what you propose."

"I hope he does. But I'm not exactly sure yet what that will be."

"I've got to get going, Conor." He picked up the check and put it back on the table with a credit card beneath it. In a few minutes the server returned with his receipt. Finnegan glanced one last time at the redhead. "Where are you parked? Or did you take the train?"

"Port Authority."

"Want to share a cab?"

"That's not on the way, Greeley. You're heading in the opposite direction."

"No matter."

"No. You've gone enough out of your way today as it is. And I do appreciate it. This has been great."

"It has been. Always good to see you, Conor. Drop me a note after you talk with Fearless Leader. I'd love to see you back in L.A., but I've got a hunch that's not going to happen. The boss is pulling rank."

"We'll see."

Greeley Welsh hailed a cab, which pulled to a stop.

"Take care, Greeley. I'll be in touch. And thanks."

Welsh got into the cab and waved as it pulled away. Finnegan hailed his own taxi and rode it back to the Port Authority. The city lights flickered in horizontal and vertical pockets, but the romance of the city vanished at the terminal. Finnegan inhaled the greasy fumes of bus exhaust and stepped through the sooty doors into the sparse interior. He ignored the night people and the panhandlers.

To his car, to the street, through the tunnel, to the Turnpike, and then home. Finnegan made the trip within forty minutes, but his consciousness took no measure of time. There were other things to consider.

* * *

The next day, Friday, Conor Finnegan called Glynnis Mear. He had been struggling with the age-old strategizing that plagues young men. He had not wanted to call too early in the week—that would have made him appear too eager. But neither did he wish to wait too long—that might seem too cavalier. Greeley Welsh had distracted him, much to his relief, and he put away all speculation until after he had met with Welsh in New York. The next afternoon, he called Glynnis.

"Hello?"

"This is your young Romantic Irishman, Glynnis. The one who loves the sea."

Glynnis laughed softly. "Conor, how are you? I'm so glad you called. I was thinking you'd forgotten all about me."

"No chance, lass. I wanted to talk with you sooner, but it's turned out to be a busy week, and somewhat eventful."

"What have you been up to? Chasing windmills?"

"In a way. Too much to tell you over the phone. Can I see you tomorrow?"

"I've kept it free for you. All day, if you'd like to come down early."

"I can bring a lunch and we can go back to the park for a picnic. Then maybe I could take you to dinner, if that's okay."

"That sounds wonderful, Conor. I'll bring the wine."

"Glynnis, you *are* the wine. Shall I pick you up?"

"No, there's no need. Why don't we meet in back of the art museum around 11:00. I'll find my way down there."

"If you want, but I could really come get you."

"No, Conor. I'll take a bus. Maybe I'll walk partway. But please feel free to take me home."

"I'll insist upon that."

"I'll see you tomorrow then, Conor. Have a safe drive."

"Glynnis," Conor spoke quickly, almost barking her name to keep her from running off.

"Yes?"

"You know, I think I'm going to spend the summer in the East. In Washington."

"Really? How'd you manage that?" Her voice betrayed more curiosity than excitement. It was not the question for which Finnegan had hoped.

"I'll tell you tomorrow. It seems I've turned a senator's head. At any rate, I thought you'd be interested."

"Won't you miss your ocean?"

"There's one here. Even though the sun doesn't set in it."

"It'll have to do. You roving dreamers sometimes have to put up with considerable hardships."

"It comes with the territory. I'll see you tomorrow, Glynnis."

Finnegan hung up the phone and went to the store to buy food for their picnic. He checked the money in his wallet, seeing that he could afford a nice dinner tomorrow night. That evening he would do nothing more than listen to his music, perhaps read a bit, and let the fermentation of chance settle into his veins like a vapor.

* * *

Tom McIlweath had other plans for Friday night. He took Anne Newbury to a play staged by the college's theater group. It was an original drama written by a Rutgers graduate who had won a national writing award. McIlweath enjoyed the theater far more than did Anne, but she willingly went along when he suggested the play. To her it was a concession, one she felt compelled to make in light of the time and money McIlweath spent on her. She could placate him this way, and afterward feel that he owed her.

Drama, though, good or bad, held no fascination for her. It all seemed such a waste of effort. Fiction, she reflected, rarely reflected real life, at least not as she had noticed it. At best, then, the theater was a diversion, and at worst a distraction, one that could distort one's view of human nature if one took it too seriously. The theater inflated itself much more pompously than did the cinema, which, she believed, existed purely for entertainment with no thought of enlightenment.

After the play the two went back to Anne's home, as they customarily did at the end of an evening. Unlike most evenings, though, Anne's parents had already gone to bed. A single light burned in the entryway. The rest of the house was dark.

Anne unlocked the door, McIlweath behind her, then went into the darkened living room to flip on a light. McIlweath followed her in and sat on the couch. Anne sat next to him.

"I wonder why my parents went to bed so early? It's only a little after 11:00."

"Maybe it's been a long week for them. I know it's been for me," and McIlweath stretched his right arm around Anne's shoulders. Anne sat rigidly and did nothing to acknowledge his touch.

'She's so hard,' he thought. 'Her body is so lean. There's nothing but bone and sinew. Whatever tender areas there are beneath them are well protected.'

"What did you think of the play, Anne? Was it," McIlweath took the playbill out of his jacket pocket and read, "'a delicate examination of the vulnerabilities in traditional man-woman relationships?'"

"No, I thought it was silly. What was the play we saw in March? 'Charley's Aunt.' I thought that showed more insights than what we saw tonight."

"But 'Charley's Aunt' is a farce. It's comedy."

"This might as well have been, too. I don't understand how the main character—was his name Andrew?—was so enraptured with Marie. That didn't make any sense."

"That developed prior to the play's start. We need to accept that as a given. That sets the basis for a tension brought on by their opposite perspectives working against a visceral attraction."

"Their lifestyles were too different. He was a bohemian and she was a prim and proper society girl. And he tried to draw her into his own dirty world. What amazed me was that she would even consider going with him and his friends. I don't think anyone in their right mind would ever have anything to do with a man like that, and here the playwright had her almost giving up her whole world to follow a base and disgusting little artist. I can't see that attraction, even if we have to accept it."

"But that's the writer's point, Anne. Their attraction was nontraditional, and based on what proper society would call the wrong things. You can't deny that attraction existed even though you don't understand it. Even a relationship based on a rebellion like Marie's has some merit and deserves to be nurtured. It worked, at least for a while."

"Tom, that doesn't make sense. A girl raised in an elite society is only accustomed to that type of lifestyle. She's not going to reject it, even for a little while, unless she's sure she's getting into something better. She knows she's comfortable, and well provided for, and she knows that her life with that artist would be dirty and clumsy and foul. She barely knew the man, so their attraction was primarily physical. No woman in the world is going to abandon a comfortable lifestyle just for physical attraction. That only happens in fiction. It's nice to talk about Marie's rebellion and nontraditional relationships, and maybe a writer has to do that, but it doesn't reflect reality, Tom. So what's the point?"

"The Greeks saw the stage as a forum for ideas more so than a stage of actions. That's the beauty of good theater."

"Which this wasn't. I don't want to argue, Tom. Do you want anything to eat or drink?"

"No thanks. But we weren't arguing, were we? We were just discussing something we had seen together."

"What's the difference? You believe one thing, I believe something else. There's no point in talking about it."

"That's where conclusions come from, Anne. Thesis, Antithesis, Synthesis."

"It just makes for hard feeling."

"Not for me."

"Well, I don't like it."

McIlweath raised his right hand from Anne's shoulder to her neck, tucking it under her light brown hair. He massaged her nape. "Let me soften those hard feelings for you."

She closed her eyes and leaned back her head, pinning McIlweath's hand between her neck and the base of her skull. She murmured low and catlike, "I like that."

McIlweath took off his glasses with his left hand and placed them on an end table. He leaned over to kiss Anne's parted, purring lips. But as soon as his lips touched hers she resisted, turning her head. McIlweath drew back.

"Don't, Tom. Don't spoil it. Just keep rubbing my neck."

McIlweath muttered no protest. He merely did as he was told. After a few minutes, Anne lay down, her head on McIlweath's lap. He slipped off her glasses and rubbed her temples.

McIlweath looked from her face down the length of her reclining body. Anne's small breasts had not retreated into her chest. They rose firmly, pushing out the contours of her red blouse. He followed the line to the cave of her stomach, then further still to her hips, her thighs and her legs. She had kicked off her shoes, and McIlweath could see her toes curling and uncurling slowly as he rubbed her temples. He looked back to her face. Anne's eyes were fully closed, her lips parted languorously to show her white teeth. Her thin lips wore no lipstick and appeared rather dry. McIlweath gazed at Anne's ears and the place there where her hair fell and hung down into the narrow space between his legs. He reached down to twirl a lock around the fingers of his right hand. At the same time he moved his left hand to the small valley at the base of Anne's neck, just above her sternum, and rubbed gently. Neither spoke.

At length Anne revived as if pulling herself back from some forlorn precipice. She stretched her legs and arms, nearly knocking McIlweath's cheek with her fist as she did so. "I'm tired, Tom. This is so relaxing. Maybe you better head home."

McIlweath sighed. "If you really want me to, Anne."

"I think it's best. It's getting late and I'm really sleepy. Call me tomorrow," she said as she sat up at the far end of the couch, "and maybe we can work out together."

"I wouldn't mind working out a little bit right now," said McIlweath as he rose to his feet. His limbs were heavy but he did not want to go.

"What?"

"Nothing. I'll call you around noon, okay? Thanks for coming tonight."

"Thank you, Tom. I had a fine time, in spite of the play."

"But that's all we did."

"I had a fine time anyway." She walked him to the door. McIlweath turned to face her in the entryway. He placed a hand on either side of her taut, narrow waist. Anne placed one hand on McIlweath's shoulder in return. They kissed then, once, twice, three times. Anne's lips were not especially soft—perhaps, McIlweath thought, they are too narrow to be soft—but they were warm. McIlweath liked their salty taste.

He parted his lips slightly and ran his tongue along the perimeter of Anne's mouth. Anne did not open her lips. She absorbed the play, then drew back. She looked up at McIlweath and smiled.

"Good night, Tom. I'll see you tomorrow. And thanks again."

McIlweath was out the door before he knew it, before he could even reply. He shook his head slowly and walked back down the driveway to his car.

Tom McIlweath did not sleep well at all that night. For most of it he lay with his hands behind his head, gazing at the stark ceiling. In the bunk below Dan Rosselli gently but regularly snored, although that was not what kept McIlweath awake.

It was Anne Newbury that robbed him of his sleep, as she did from time to time. In his more cogent moments McIlweath concluded that his relationship with Anne was not what he would call normal, and probably not healthy. Yet, as a young boy might kick dirt over an anthill, leaving the ants invisible for the moment but still crawling frantically below the ground, McIlweath covered his conclusions with a genuine affection for the girl herself. He had indeed grown to like her very much. The vulnerability he had perceived from the first still remained, but McIlweath had also discovered facets of her character equally as endearing. She was not a complex woman by any means, a fact which would most likely have turned him in the other direction had he determined this before he could get to know her, but which now intrigued and attracted him greatly. It was Anne's heretofore sheltered existence which made her appear vulnerable, and it was her simplicity, her lack of sophistication, the absence really of a hard intellectual formation, that deepened that vulnerability, making McIlweath want to shield her from every conceivable blow.

Simplicity. Anne Newbury was still a schoolgirl. She swam, she studied, she slept. She had a few friends. Whatever Tom McIlweath put before her was bound to be new, whether book, play or the ideas within, whether an afternoon in New York or an evening at the movies. Her sense of wonder attracted him, her notion that she might be, as it were, coming out.

She viewed the world in black and white, that was obvious. White were those things which agreed with the values her limited past experience had imposed. Everything else was black. McIlweath ignored the moralism inherent in this and found it somewhat refreshing, particularly in contrast with the ethical compromises espoused by professors, the thinkers and writers they studied, and most of his fellow students. To Anne Newbury it was wrong to take drugs, to swear except in moments of the most extreme provocation, to act contrary to the wishes of one's parents, to stay out late, to speak poorly of one's country, to drink alcohol except for a rare wine and the occasional summertime beer, to steal. There could be no exceptions for any of this. There could be no exceptions because she had never considered any. If it wasn't to be done, then it simply and finally wasn't to be done by anyone, anywhere. She had confidence in her beliefs. They were, really, more than beliefs: they were certitudes. McIlweath found her confidence reassuring in an era where few lines were drawn, where pervasive doubt was not only acceptable but widely cultivated. If Anne could adapt herself to the growing complexities around her, she might truly find a lasting personal contentment. That adaptation was a tall order, McIlweath thought, but one of which she was most probably capable.

Anne's character, too, absorbed him, so fascinating in its traditional simplicity. She absorbed him thoroughly, mind and body. They spent part of each weekend with her parents. They rarely went to McIlweath's apartment or spent time with his friends. They took long walks through her neighborhood and watched television in her family's den. They did not venture too far afield from the secure surroundings of Things Newburyian. A trip into the city to go to an art museum was a singular grand adventure and required days of planning. More usually they would spend a Saturday in the pool, then eat dinner at Anne's house. There was, at the time, no need for anything more exotic. McIlweath could see that the elder Newburys were just like their daughter—self-confident, simple, with the highest standards for themselves and the environment they created around them.

In short, McIlweath enjoyed Anne's company immensely, almost as much for what she wasn't as for what she was. He catered to her expectations and she in turn comforted him with her attentions, with her willingness to accept him into her world and with her belief in his quality as a human being.

She did not, though, comfort him physically. The incident on the couch that evening had not been atypical. Anne resisted any physical contact beyond the basics of a goodnight kiss or two and some occasional handholding. McIlweath did not consider himself to be excessively passionate. He had never had much experience with women and he remained a virgin. Nevertheless he still had his urges, not necessarily for full intercourse (although the thought did not intimidate him), but at least for something more graphic than he had been allowed. He had been seeing Anne for several months now, yet his most recent embrace was no more passionate than his first. McIlweath thought it odd. Very odd, especially in light of the early nature of their relationship, which revolved around a swimming pool wherein they exercised in various degrees of undress. Anne, in fact, had seen nearly everything of McIlweath's body there was to see, save for his genitals, which even so had been covered so tightly by a wet swim suit that little was left to fantasy. McIlweath, too, had studied Anne's body. He had seen her nipples hard and cold under a wet suit, and he had followed the tight curve of her buttocks. They still saw each other this way, almost every day. But what this aroused in McIlweath was universally suppressed by Anne's apparent lack of arousal. After so many months and so much time together, McIlweath had yet to touch Anne's breasts.

Yet through all the tumbling eddies of his thoughts and reactions, McIlweath could not deny that he felt a growing closeness with Anne. He did not think it bordered on love, but that certainly might be a logical and eventual evolution. She had assumed a larger and larger part of his life. She was a core that continued to grow, pushing the parameters outward and crowding the remainder of his life's pulp. McIlweath had created his own vulnerability in subconscious parallel to what he perceived in Anne by opening up his deepest ideas, aspirations and fantasies to her inspection. She nurtured that vulnerability and protected it. She shared it with no one. She became for McIlweath a reflecting mirror, an anemometer, a knotted twain. McIlweath looked forward to shared experience and, as a part of that, a shared intimacy. He wanted to hold her, to express physically what he had already expressed intellectually and, in so doing, if his body found gratification, could that be wrong? Hasn't she too felt some of this? Why does she suppress it? In the end McIlweath reconciled as best he could to the peculiarities of their relationship, as he always did. He sighed, and rolled to his side.

The next day he called Anne shortly after noon. They met an hour later at the pool and went through a leisurely workout. Although the season had ended the month prior they both wanted to stay sharp. For Anne in particular the stakes were high. She had qualified for the summer nationals in July, and was working out formally with her local private swim club. A strong finish at the nationals could earn her a spot at the World University Games, or Universiades, to be held later in the year in Belgrade. Anne had never been abroad. The prospect of swimming on the national team intoxicated her: she desperately wanted to go.

They swam for more than an hour, finishing with a series of five 100-meter sprints. McIlweath beat her in each, but that was nothing. He was supposed to beat her. He could not deny to himself that he enjoyed the sensation of grabbing the wall seconds before Anne.

As he finished his last sprint he turned completely around and spread his arms along the lip of the pool, his back feeling the hard tile in its square ridges. In the next lane churning foam hit the wall, and

Anne poked her head up, breathing hard.

"Good swim, Anne."

She panted four or five times before she was able to respond. "I stunk."

"No you didn't. Come on, you did okay."

"I felt," she panted, "so slow. I'm not in very good shape."

"You shouldn't be. Not yet. You don't want to peak until July."

"Yeah, but I still don't like the way I feel."

McIlweath vaulted himself out of the pool. He walked the length and back, swinging his arms to throw away their tightness. Anne slowly swam two more laps, then joined him poolside. McIlweath wrapped himself in a towel, then placed one around Anne's shoulders. "I'm going to shower. I'll meet you back here in a few minutes. Take your time."

After a while McIlweath reemerged, dressed and warm, his hair wetly slicked back. He sat on a wooden bench and waited for Anne. It was a long while, nearly forty-five minutes, before she came back out of the women's locker room.

"Mom asked if you wanted to have dinner with us tonight, Tom. What do you think?"

"I think three nights this week is an imposition."

"I eat there every night," replied Anne with a smile.

"But I'm not their daughter. I was going to ask if you wanted to turn things around a little and eat at the apartment with us. On Sundays we usually fix something pretty decent. Conor even prepares a vegetable. It's the only day of the week he eats anything green, except for the stuff that spoils."

"I don't think so, Tom. I'll just go home."

"Come on, Anne. You haven't been to the apartment in a long time. You've never eaten dinner with us."

"No, Tom. Not tonight."

"But what's the problem?"

Anne looked away, frowning. She did not enjoy being pressed for any reason, and felt very, very uncomfortable.

"Why don't you ever spend any time with me at my place?"

"Tom, you'll get upset if I tell you."

"You know me better than that. I want to know. Maybe I can fix whatever it is you don't like."

"You can't. You know I can't."

"Like I said, I want to know."

"It's your friends, Tom," she said with a deep sigh. "I am just so uncomfortable around them. I don't think they care for me much, and

I'm not terribly fond of them."

"Anne, that's ridiculous. They've never said anything against you. They don't get to see you very often."

"That's just the way I feel. I'm sorry, Tom."

"How do you feel about them, Anne?"

She turned to look him directly in the eye. Her frown had hardened into a look of the firmest resolve. Her grim mouth set in a straight line, her eyes two flared spears of blue fire. She had her chance to score a crippling hit, and she took it.

"I don't like them, Tom. I guess the truth is that I don't know how they really feel about me, nor do I particularly care, but I can tell you that I don't like them. At all. I don't like being around them even for a bit."

"Anne, you know these are the closest friends I've ever had. Be careful what you say."

"You asked me. You had to know."

"Why do you dislike them?"

"A lot of reasons. They're crude and base. Both in the way they dress and in their language. I think they're lazy. They're dirty and sloppy—you know that your apartment is a total mess. And I'm not sure they're especially bright. They've never said one thing between the three of them that wasn't obvious, or profane, or silly. There you have it, Tom, and I'm sorry if it hurt you."

It hurt indeed. Tom McIlweath saw a very clear line being drawn. As with everything else, compromise would be out of the question. And he sensed that this line was emblematic of a wider division between Anne's rigid standard and the entirety of Tom McIlweath—not just friends, but thought and environment as well. Yes, to be sure, it hurt.

"You're wrong, Anne. You don't know them at all. These are three of the brightest, most well rounded people I've ever known. And as for them being lazy, that's laughable. Maybe they just make things look too easy."

"Tom, you know you're not going to change my mind."

"I've known Conor for years, Anne. In some ways he's closer to me than you are. I know he's none of the things you said he was. And Dan might be a little crude, but he's also intelligent and witty. He's got a lot of heart. So does Lanny."

"He's an operator, Tom. I don't trust him."

"You don't have to trust him. Just enjoy his good qualities. Enjoy all of them. It's not hard, Anne, if you don't pass judgment. They're human beings, and they're all different—from each other and from you. Maybe you just don't appreciate things in variety."

"That's a pretty rotten statement."

"Well, maybe you don't. Anne, you still live the way you did when you were twelve. Things are different now. People are different, and you've got to deal with them."

"Why? I can still pick who I want to associate with. And you have to respect my preferences."

"But look at this. You're drumming three people of diverse character and considerable talents right out of your life, three people who are important to me, because your first impressions don't measure up to what you expected or what you thought they should be. And these three people have unique personalities, and unique intelligences, and unique ambitions that they'd be perfectly willing to share with you. You'd be better for it, but you're unwilling to bend. You're unwilling to relax your judgments. You're nipping them off in the bud not because the stem is crooked or broken but because the color isn't your favorite. You don't want any variety in your life, Anne. You want everything to be the same flavor."

"And you don't discriminate about anything," she shot back. "Everyone and everything is fine with you. You have no standards. You're too willing to conform yourself to anyone who'll have you."

"Maybe that's what I've been doing with you, then."

"Maybe it is. But I'm a hell of a lot better for you than any of those guys you're living with. If you think my standards are too high, then maybe you don't care that you've met every one I've set for you. But you want to waste your time with people who'll just drag you down to what they are. And you want to drag me along with you. But I'm telling you, I won't go."

"Wait, Anne," McIlweath's voice lowered its intensity. He paused, confused. Anne had never displayed such conviction, and it frightened him a bit that she did so now. He imagined himself, briefly, in a passing second, alone. Alone. She had become part of his core, he knew that, and he felt that core move, ever so slightly. He did not like the feeling. It rent a part of him and weakened his suddenly wobbly loyalties.

"Anne," he continued softly. "I don't want to argue about this. You *are* good for me, I know that. If my friends upset you, then we don't have to spend any time with them. But I think you're being too harsh with them."

"Tom, I told you— "

"No, stop. It's your prerogative to be as harsh as you see fit. I just want you to understand that they're important to me, and I'd like you to respect that if you can. I'm glad to know how you feel, because you're important to me, too. I don't want all this to jeopardize what we have.

Okay?"

"Okay," she said, but she had not softened. Her face still set like a mask and her voice still carried its tone of indignation. She did not like being challenged, not at all.

"We don't have to deal with my friends if you don't want to. And maybe in due course I'll see things more closely to what you perceive."

"I think you should. Let's not talk about this again."

"As long as we understand each other."

"All right, then. Do you want to have dinner at my house?"

"I'd love to. Should I change?"

"No, you look fine. Let's go. We like to eat early on Sunday."

McIlweath reached for Anne's elbow as they started to walk, but she stepped ahead of him. "I'm sorry if I upset you," he said.

"You said some mean things. I don't know if I accept your apology."

"Please, Anne. I'm sorry. You know how much I respect your opinions. I was too quick to jump on them."

"Yes you were. You also called me inflexible and judgmental, as I recall."

"I'm sorry, Anne. You're neither, of course. You just have high standards. That's not a bad thing."

"I know it's not. It's the best we can do for ourselves. Let's forget this whole conversation, shall we?"

"Fine with me. I don't like to fight. Not with you."

"Because I'm always right," she said, a coy smile returning to her lips.

And vain Arachne spun her finest fibers.

CHAPTER XI

*The force that through the green fuse
drives the flower
Drives my green age; that blasts the roots
of trees
Is my destroyer.
And I am dumb to tell the crooked rose
My youth is bent by the same wintry fever.*

—Dylan Thomas, *The Force That Through the Green Fuse
Drives the Flower*

Conor Finnegan's world became a jungle of logistical details. Once he had confirmed his position with the Washington office he immersed himself in the needs and necessities that position entailed.

First of all, he would need a place to live. The staff in Washington proved little help—they knew of nothing that was both inexpensive and safe—but, they said, people come and go so frequently in the capital that things open up without much notice. Finnegan should just keep checking. And so he did, throughout the month of April, with no luck.

In the meantime he realized that he would have to make drastic improvements in his wardrobe. He had one suit and several sport coats, acceptable garb for casual Los Angeles but, he felt, inadequate for the world of Washington politics. That same month he sniffed for a Washington flat, he bought two summer suits and a pair of slacks that matched one of his sport coats. It would have to do.

Both apartment and wardrobe cost money, much more than Finnegan had set aside. So, at the end of his telephone conversation with his parents explaining his opportunity in Washington, he broached the subject of cash.

"So you'll be in the East all summer, then?"

"It looks that way, Dad."

"You sure you want to do this?"

"Yeah, this is good. Very good. Although I'll miss you two."

"Well, if you're sure. Where are you going to live?"

"I'm not certain yet. I'm still looking for a cheap apartment. Housing is so damn expensive down there. Which brings me to the point at hand."

"Which is?"

"I'll need to put down a security deposit and first month's rent wherever I go. And, to be honest, I don't have it. I'll pay you back by the end of the summer."

"Damn straight you will. How much do you need?"

"I've got to beef up my wardrobe, too, Dad. A couple of suits, maybe a few ties."

"Christ be with us, Conor. You haven't been named Secretary of State."

"Not yet, no."

It took some assurance of repayment before Ed Finnegan would give in, but the check was mailed within the week.

Finnegan did not mind setting up his summer world. It deepened for him his conception of independence, his appreciation of responsibility. He looked at his own evolution from callow adolescence to a composed young man who was truly reaching the current limits of his capabilities and, in so doing, outperforming even his most naïve imaginings. It filled him with a sense of power, for he had in fact succeeded on a new playing field, one far more diverse and intense than any he had ever traversed.

Finnegan also did not mind because Philadelphia lay squarely on the way to Washington, and on each trip down to the capital he saw Glynnis. Sometimes he could only stay for an hour or so before driving on to meet with the senator's aides to discuss his assignments or to peruse the Washington papers for a place to live. It did not matter. She transfused his blood and sharpened his thoughts, always. Even in their briefest meetings she took him to new inner places. He came away convinced more than ever of his own selection, his own distinction, and felt very proud.

Owing to Finnegan's enforced frugality, their times together were simple. Most often they would sit in the lounge of Glynnis's dormitory or walk around campus. If Conor had time they would get something to eat. In truth, Finnegan's trips to Washington proved a mixed blessing. Although he saw Glynnis more frequently than he might under normal circumstances, he had no time to make his visits as relaxed as he would have liked. There would be no other chance to spend a full day together until Finnegan got settled.

In early May, Finnegan received a call from Steve Krall, one of the senator's other legislative assistants. Steve's aunt, an analyst in the Defense Department, would be spending the summer on assignment to the U.S. NATO delegation in Brussels. Would Conor like to take her place? He would pay no rent, merely keep an eye on things and make certain her place stayed in good repair.

Finnegan repressed his excitement. "Yeah, Steve, I think it sounds great. Where is it?"

"Georgetown. Actually, Foggy Bottom, if you know where that is. She has a townhouse on New Hampshire Avenue, near the Watergate. It's quite a place, Conor."

"When can I look at it?"

"This weekend. In fact, if you want it you'll have to tie things up by Saturday. She leaves for Brussels Monday morning. She really wants you to take it, Conor. The lady's desperate at this stage. You'll be doing her a huge favor. Otherwise it'll sit empty and God knows what'll happen. Washington has some pretty sophisticated thieves. They know when people are out of town."

"I think I'll probably be more than happy to help her out, Steve."

Finnegan drove to Washington Saturday morning and closed the deal. It was as Steve described it; no rent, just routine maintenance and a warm body to see that the household stayed put. Only one string was attached, and that was Leona Krall's Siamese cat, Jade, a haughty beast who would eat only freshly boiled chicken livers. Conor must make certain to buy enough every week, and he must not let them boil too long. Jade liked them with a smooth consistency. Oh, and the litter box must be cleaned every other day.

But the townhouse itself was beautiful enough to compensate for any obligation. It was tucked into a row of similar houses, each long and narrow, their two stories built solidly of brick in an old Federal style. Upstairs were two bedrooms linked by a short hallway and a bathroom. Downstairs the front door opened to a square living room, the kitchen appended to its rear. In back was a tiny rectangular squat of land, all the backyard the crush of buildings permitted. Finnegan noted the rich hardwood floors. The rugs looked expensive. The furnishings, too, were hardly humble: couches and chairs covered with plush brocade. The bed in the guest room, Finnegan's room, sat in an old brass frame. King-sized, it was easily big enough for two.

Finnegan spent an hour with Leona Krall reviewing the care and keeping of both the house and the cat.

"She sleeps where she wants, Conor, but usually in the upstairs hall. She likes to curl up on top of the old desk in the hallway. Sometimes if it's not too hot she'll come into my room. Just let her go wherever she wants. She won't hurt anything, will you, baby?"

Jade walked across Leona Krall's feet and arched her back against her mistress's shins. She yawled the deep baritone of the Siamese, oblivious to the fact that her leisurely lifestyle was now under scrutiny. Leona, a tall, attractive, worldly woman of nearly fifty, poured the limits of her affection on Jade. Finnegan noticed the artwork in the living room—prints and drawings of cats, framed, some abstract, on the walls, feline sculptures of ebony or stone on the tables. Finnegan did not wish to pass judgment, but he thought the woman's devotion to this cat might be a bit eccentric, and certainly odd for one who travels in some of the government's highest circles.

After a while she changed the subject to matters more human. "Now, the bus to the Capitol, the 'E' bus I think, stops at the circle and goes right to the Senate Office Buildings. Or you can walk several blocks to the George Washington metro stop. It's up to you, but the bus is more direct. If you've got a car, don't drive it to work. Parking on the Hill is impossible. Parking around here is impossible, too, so take any spot you can find and leave it there. And don't park illegally, even for a minute. The police ticket everything. It's their humble contribution to keeping the city coffers filled. You can do your shopping at the Watergate. There's a supermarket there, and a drugstore and some other shops. Prices aren't cheap, so be prepared." and so on. Leona Krall, once started, did not slow down. By the end of her discourse Finnegan had been well briefed on life on New Hampshire Avenue.

She gave him a key. Finnegan would move in as soon as classes were done next week. "Relax and enjoy yourself. Enjoy the city. Use whatever you want and replace whatever you break. Have parties if you want, but don't tell me about them."

"Thank you, Ms. Krall. I'll try to take good care of things. Enjoy Brussels. You know, I think I'd gladly trade places with you if you wanted."

Leona Krall smiled. "I wouldn't let you. I've looked forward to this for a long time. Good luck, Conor."

But as Conor drove northward toward Philadelphia and Glynnis, he suspected that there was no need for luck. Once again, all the pieces had fallen snugly into place.

Conor and Glynnis had dinner together at a small Italian restaurant near downtown. They spoke of Washington and what lay ahead. Or rather, Conor spoke and Glynnis listened, for the young man's excitement this evening rose unbridled, all restraints thrown aside. His finding such an elegant address at virtually no cost capped his anticipation at what promised to be yet another grand adventure.

* * *

The day had been hot—the smothering, blanketing, breathlessly mucky heat of dead summer. Around 2:00 it had rained, a thunderstorm rolling out of the southeast across the bay and erupting at once. But the storm did not cool things at all. It merely thickened the blanket. People stayed inside, unwilling to leave the air-conditioned, breathable space of their homes or offices.

Conor Finnegan, too, did not want to leave. He lingered at his desk after most of his colleagues had headed for the door. He knew how hot it was, and he liked being cool. He would not be so cool that night, for Leona Krall's townhouse did not have central air conditioning. Instead, he would strip off his clothes and open all the upstairs windows, hoping for cross-ventilation. He would kick the covers on the floor, turn the small fan directly on his sweaty, contorted body. Sometime beyond midnight his drained form would slide over the elusive edge of slumber, and there he would alternately doze and wake, crossing back and forth over that edge, semi-conscious of the room around him, until the fine first light of morning called an end to his poor efforts. He would be fully awake before his 7:00 alarm sounded. Finnegan always felt tired these days.

The heat notwithstanding, Finnegan delayed going home. His desk imparted an identity he cherished. The desk itself was a clanky metal thing thrown into a corner of the suite amid six or seven others, each as chinked, as dented and as cold. But he had stamped this desk with his unique perspective. On two corners were piled several Congressional Reports, hearings transcripts and studies, all dealing with the plight of senior citizens. Between them sat a standard desk blotter on which were sketched his doodles, most of which were imaginary faces, all male. Finnegan did not know how to draw anything else. His technique was residue from a distant elementary school art lesson. Occasionally he would draw pointed ears and antennae on one of the faces to make it a space alien, but that marked the extent of his creativity.

On the upper corners of his desk sat his in- and out-trays, three-tiered, each full of paperwork, statistical tables or printouts of charts. Tucked behind his phone were that day's *Washington Post* and *New York Times*. A small framed picture of Glynnis stood ahead of the clutter on the desk's edge. This was *his* space, a space in the Dirksen Senate Office Building, reflective of his projects and his presence. Conor Finnegan was here. *Is* here.

Finnegan swiveled his chair to face the window, an unromantic view of the back of the Russell Building, blurred through the horizontal slats of blinds. He picked up the *Times*, heretofore unread, and flipped through the front section to the editorial page at the end. It did not matter that Finnegan rarely found time to read the papers. Everyone on staff carried them into the office in the morning, and Finnegan wanted to be no different. It was a matter of image, he thought. When he did read them, in unhurried moments such as this, he seldom found them enlightening. News and issues traveled by word of mouth on the Hill. Finnegan could learn more about things from an hour lunch with Steve Krall than from both papers combined.

"What about the Kurds, Steve? Refugees still pouring out of Iraq and Iran?"

"In droves. I've got a friend on the Judiciary Committee. Majority counsel. He tells me that no one's going to take the poor bastards. The last thing Turkey wants is a few more Kurds, but at least they're not shooting the convoys, unlike our good friends in Azerbaijan, Syria and Armenia. Nobody wants any part of them. The whole region's scared to death of food shortages, not to mention the strain on health systems. And of course these are Kurds we're talking about, the folks on the bottom rung of the regional ethnic totem pole."

"Any chance we could help them?"

"Doubtful. Even the liberals are skittish. Too many practical concerns to make it a sexy issue. I mean, where do we put them, how do we reach them, are camps even the answer? Then the nuts-and-bolts steps of feeding them, societal reintegration, educating the kids. And who the hell pays for that? Nobody wants to face the backlash of refugee support for a group that no one gives a damn about. My friend tells me that State's trying to find some third-party nations to step up, maybe get them relocated to a safer place that nobody can find, like Moldova."

"'Land of the free. Give me your tired, your poor, your huddled masses,' and all that. Another ideal bites the big one."

"It bit it a long time ago, Conor. Not an ideal, just a slogan. Every immigrant group had always had to fight its way in. Krauts like my people, Micks like yours. Our tribes were at least recognizable. Nobody likes the Kurds."

Finnegan read the *Times* quickly, then tossed it onto the corner pile of old newspapers to be recycled. His watch said 6:42. Only the senator's administrative assistant remained in the suite, sketching out a position paper in the office directly adjoining the boss's. Finnegan envied that location: the assistant's desk faced out of his office in such a way as to provide a constant view of Joyce, the senator's red-haired, green-eyed secretary-goddess. Of all the attractive women on staff (and there were easily eight or nine), Finnegan lusted after Joyce most frequently. But there was nothing to be done.

He grabbed his suit coat from a rack near the window, rolled down his sleeves and looked at the city. The sky was a sweaty gray, a function of the humidity. In the upper reaches hung occasional thick clouds, their bottoms barely visible through the murk. The sun, its size exaggerated, hovered westward, a giant cycloptic eye. The marble buildings themselves seemed to drip moisture and glow with the subtle radiation of heated stones. Finnegan pulled on his coat and walked silently out of the suite and down the hallway to the stairs. On his way out he smiled at the security guards, who did not, could not, know his name but who were universally friendly.

"G'night, sir. See you tomorrow."

"Yes, sir. Have a good evening, gentlemen. Try to stay cool."

"Oh no, sir. We don't even try no more. Body's got to sweat itself out in the summertime," and the great thick gold door closed behind him.

The air, heavy and as thick as the door he had just closed, cast its own presence. Finnegan walked down the street to the bus stop. Beads of sweat popped out on his forehead and at his temples. They slicked the hair above his ears.

'Ninety, at least,' he thought. 'Both temperature and humidity.'

At the bus stop, a group of four young black men wearing shorts and tank tops talked among themselves. They punctuated their words with supple movements of their bodies, fluid waves of spines, wrists and elbows. The young men were no more than eighteen or nineteen, a year or so younger than Finnegan. They noticed him as he approached.

"Uptown dude," said one, his voice neutral, neither friendly nor hostile. Finnegan chose not to ignore it.

"Yeah, but I'm as hot as you guys."

"Shit, man, you be headin' for some cool rooms. Some air conditioning. All we got's a porch."

"No air conditioning for me. Just open windows."

One of them snorted, "But everything in Georgetown's cool."

"What makes you think I live in Georgetown?"

"Jack, you got it written all over you. Some young government boy on the move."

"Don't call me 'boy,' said Finnegan with a half-smile. A couple of the others smiled too.

"Ya'll are okay, White Bread."

"I guess," said Finnegan, "I'm just a friendly sort."

The E bus rolled around Maryland Avenue and stopped in front of Finnegan. He climbed the steps, dropped his fare in the steel box and quickly surveyed the length of the bus for a suitable seat. He was relieved to see that it was not crowded at this hour, so there would be no need to plop down next to a stranger. Finnegan stepped toward the rear. As the bus began again to move, he was thrown forward and had to take three choppy steps to right himself. He took a seat three-quarters of the way back, immediately behind a man in a three-piece suit and horn-rimmed glasses. The man was working on a book of crossword puzzles, moving the corners of his mouth as he read the clues and frowning as he penciled in his answers.

Finnegan glanced briefly at the puzzle man, then let his gaze ride the passing streets. Air conditioning blew up his left arm as it leaned against the window. Outside no one felt chilled. Men came out of government buildings—the Justice Department and, after the bus turned a corner, the Treasury—with their coats draped over their shoulders and their ties loosened, wilted well before they had hit the street. Finnegan saw the usually bright, confident, buoyant, beautiful career women sagging in the heat. He remembered a piece of doggerel learned in high school:

Here's a handy little ditty
You surely ought to know:
Horses sweat and men perspire
But ladies only glow.

Not true. Today, tonight, horses, men and ladies all opened to the brutal heat. They all sweated, gushingly. It was summer in Washington.

Finnegan did not absorb the scenery of the streets. Rather, he sat back and let it wash his eyes. Glimpses held in his memory: the cover of a tennis magazine seen in a newsstand, the starchy red blouse of an older lady leaving a drugstore, the amazing breasts of a woman in a tee walking her dog on Pennsylvania Avenue, the oily scent of the bus itself. Conor Finnegan felt especially tired tonight, and he was surprised by his fatigue. It had not hit him suddenly, but had crept up his spine all day and settled behind his eyes. His legs and arms relaxed limply, his left arm sliding off the narrow window ledge to his lap where it lay like some foreign, dead animal. Finnegan's legs stretched under the puzzle man's seat. He felt drained of all substance.

The bus bumped along Pennsylvania, past the rear of the White House and then near George Washington University. Finnegan saw in the distance the Gothic spires of Georgetown University silently overlooking the Potomac, a sight which inexplicably triggered a spasm of melancholy. The ancient spires, Oxfordian, looming on a headland, while always, always the river runs.

'Bless me Father, for I have sinned. It has been three weeks since my last confession. I accuse myself of the following sins. I am lustful, Father. I have lusted after girls I see every day. Sometimes I don't even know them. It is a sin of the flesh, I know. Father, I am also proud. I place too much value on myself and what I do. I have boasted to friends of what I have done well, and have not trusted enough to let my accomplishments speak for themselves. I have not let them glorify Our Lord.

'I am profane, Father. I take the Lord's name in vain, many times. It's almost a habit. Around my friends, when it's just men, I feel guilty if I don't swear, as if I'm trying to be better than them. But in my heart I know it's just the reverse. I need to let my serenity guide me. I need to rely more on my faith. To have faith in my faith, if that makes sense. I need to have confidence in the type of person I am, in the type of person I aspire to be. Forgive me, Father, for these and all my sins, both known and unknown.'

Finnegan rose from his seat and moved to the front of the bus as he saw the traffic circle ahead. The driver pulled to a stop, and Finnegan hopped out with two other people. He hit the steamy air like a wall. He dragged the two blocks up New Hampshire. At the head of the street, where it joined the circle, he looked down to the serpentine Watergate at its foot several blocks away. Beyond it rose the cool green of Virginia. An airplane came out from behind the east end of the Watergate on a landing approach to National. Finnegan did not take note. He had stopped for a second to draw his breath, and to imagine Virginia's lovely wooded exurban hills. The hills, cool, and so far beyond it all.

As he opened the front door, Jade strutted out from the area behind the staircase. It was probably cooler back there. She stretched and mewed her resonant mew. She and Conor were not on good terms— mostly Jade kept her distance—but the presence of a human, even this one, no doubt comforted her, if arrogance did in fact require comfort.

Finnegan peered at her food dish as he went to the kitchen: that morning's chicken livers were only partially eaten. He could smell them. Finnegan took a bowl of leftover fruit salad from the refrigerator, devoured it in four or five spoonfuls, then made himself a ham sandwich. He stood in front of the open refrigerator and wafted the cool air down his shirt, grabbed a beer from the door rack, and went back to the table to finish what passed for his dinner.

Afterward Finnegan pulled himself upstairs, hung up his coat and slacks, then tugged off his shirt, wet and clammy from the day's heat.

He took a shower to cool off and came out wearing only a pair of gym shorts. He then went into his bedroom, flopped across the old bed, grabbed the phone, and dialed his justification for all this.

"Hello?"

"Hi, Glyn. How're you doing?"

"Well, good evening, Senator. Home from a hard day of legislating?"

"A hard day of paperwork. And a bit boring. No, let me amend that. It was terribly boring."

"Is it hot there? Of course it is. It's brutal here. I wanted to jump in the fountain at Logan Circle."

"There aren't any fountains down here. At least none that are swimmable. God, what I'd give to be able to go to the beach."

"Me, too. You know, my family used to vacation in Maine every year. Right on the coast. I'd love to be able to go there now. It was so beautiful there, Conor. So cool, with the ocean spray and the rocks."

"You're in the mood for a vacation, then?"

"God, yes. There's nothing here during the summer."

"Did you work today?"

"Of course. I'm a diligent girl, whatever else you may say about me. But I feel like such a damn prisoner. There's no place to go and no one to go there with. When are you going to come and rescue me?"

"I'm not."

Glynnis paused. "What are you saying?"

"I'm not going to come and rescue you. At least I'd prefer not to. That's really why I'm calling, aside from hearing the lilting rhapsody of your lovely voice. Would you be willing to take the train down here this Friday? We could spend the weekend together. I could show you the city, or as much of it as I've managed to learn. It might actually be fairly exciting."

"Is that an invitation, Sailor?"

"Absolutely. Glynnis, I'd love to spend the weekend with you here."

"This sounds rather sinful. I think I like it."

"Then you'll come down?"

"What would Fr. Francis say?"

"Who?"

"Our parish priest. He's been in our family for years, like an old heirloom. My mother always consults him on knotty spiritual problems, such as when to inform her daughters about menstruation. He knows about such things because he's only slightly younger than God Himself."

"Sounds like a versatile fellow. But perhaps some matters are best left hidden."

"I agree. I accept your sinful invitation, Mr. Finnegan."

"Great. There's a train that leaves Philadelphia at 5:30 and gets to D.C. around 7:40. Just in time for a late dinner and a drive around the city to see the lights. The monuments are glorious after dark."

"You make it sound quite dashing, Senator. But then again, that's how you Irish Romantics do it, isn't it? You can make a soft boiled egg sound like lobster and white wine."

"My intentions are quite honorable, Miss Mear."

"We'll see. Are you sure you can put up with me for more than a few hours at a time?"

"I'd be delighted to try."

"I'll see you Friday, Conor."

Sweet Lorelei, singing on the Rocks of Time.

* * *

Conor Finnegan had not yet felt a full part of Washington. While he had been swept up in the glamor of its currents of power and solemnized by its marble, he had never believed he truly belonged in the capital. To be sure, his stay had been short, and a bit incredible. He still had trouble getting from one end of the city to the other. A grid of bus and Metro routes and a city map were his best friends at the moment.

Yet when Glynnis Mear stepped off her train, Washington opened itself up like a blossoming lily and sucked them both inside. To Finnegan, the city instantly became a home, as secure and endemic as any place he had ever set foot. What came before, the people and the places, seemed as strange as a dream. His most reliable reality lay at hand as it always would have, had he the wisdom to recognize it.

They whirled through the city's darkening streets, starting around the Capitol then passing the congressional office buildings. From there to the Ellipse, stopping before the Washington Monument and walking around that giant protruding stalk, leaning over the Reflecting Pool to see if they could really make out their reflections. They drove the short mile to the Lincoln Memorial and climbed the fifty-nine steps to stand at the foot of a countenance eternally grave. They stood there and saw the city spread behind them, pocked with the spires and hubs of the Capitol, Mr. Washington's monument, the Library of Congress, the Smithsonian, and the museums. To their right sat the whitewashed bump of the Jefferson Memorial, and through the distance they could see the old Virginian standing in the shadows. The lights of the city blinked on, gold and white dots stunting against a black backdrop, and to the side, in the far distance, stood the proudly ancient cool hills of Virginia.

'It is all so familiar now, this city and these lights, which have shone like this for generations. The timeless river. And the green hills. Lee walked in those hills as a boy, and, farther out, in the Shenandoah, men died. They're dust now, lying silently below the ragged, hole-worn places, pieces of lead clattering through their bones. Mortality is absolute, and it is also relative. And now, this clear evening in this old city, it is as if I've been no place else.'

"This is beautiful, Conor."

"Isn't it? I love the lights. And I like to look at the hills, out there. I try to imagine what's in them. Especially at night."

"I like the lights, too. You can see the whole city from here."

"I wish I could show you the whole city. Everything. I wish I could show you everything I've learned about it. It's really very old, you know. I mean in a personal sense. People have been doing the same types of things here forever, in the same places. There are ghosts everywhere."

"That's history, my Irish bard."

"Yes, that's what we call history. But it all seems so fresh—power, government, issues. The entire country is captured right here in this city. This is America, these few square miles. All parts of it, and all it's ever been. All the wars, and depressions, and riots, and demonstrations, and sorrows. They've all come through here. This city is loaded with ghosts, and we can see them, every day. We feel them because we're no different than they were. We fight the same battles and tilt at the same windmills. We're linked to everything that's ever been, just by virtue of being here, of standing on these stones. Do you understand any of that?"

"No. But it sounds lovely. Just think how you'd feel if you were standing in Athens, on the Acropolis."

"I couldn't comprehend. I take my metaphysics in small doses only."

"It's not metaphysics, Conor, it's Romanticism. And I like it immensely."

"I wish I could show you everything, Glynnis. I wish we could explore everything together."

"Just show me a place to eat. I'm hungry."

They ate at a Salvadoran restaurant Conor had noticed on Connecticut Avenue near the zoo. Latin food reminded him of Southern California. The Boston girl had rarely had it. Glynnis, hungry enough to experiment on almost anything, found she liked its earthy textures and devoured her dinner completely, scraping the ceramic plate clean with her fork. After dinner they drove to the townhouse. Finnegan had to circle the block several times before finding a place to park.

And now, all pretexts aside, Conor found himself upon new ground. He knew it as soon as Glynnis crossed through the doorway. There were no formulas for this, no prescribed movements or words. Before, he could always be secure that the image he had cultivated in her would be preserved through distance, but tonight there would be no separation. What he would do with Glynnis's proximity he did not know. Nor was he precisely sure how he would like to proceed. This was untrodden ground, and Conor did not know what to expect either from Glynnis or from himself. All that became apparent as soon as Glynnis tucked her bag behind the stairway and sat down on the couch. There she was, and there she would remain. His throat tightened, his pulse quickened. He could feel his body wind itself up, in his chest, in his legs, in the gentle pounding at his temples. He had not been this way in a long while.

Jade walked halfway down the stairs to see who had come in. She stopped, frozen, when she saw Glynnis. Someone new. Glynnis noticed her peering in mid-step between the banister railings.

"Oh Conor, you didn't tell me about a cat. She's not yours, is she? No, she couldn't be. Come here, sweetheart. Come on, don't be afraid," Glynnis purred.

"She comes with the house. Kind of a watch-cat."

"What's her name?" Glynnis made gentle beckoning movements with her long fingers.

"Jade. We're not exactly the best of friends. She's a temperamental thing, but she'll keep out of the way."

But Jade, acting out an unspoken defiance of Finnegan's curt dismissal, responded quite well to Glynnis's coaxing. She walked slowly down the remainder of the stairs and haltingly, with great suspicious care, crept across the room to the couch. There she hopped up next to Glynnis, who picked up the beast and placed her on her lap. Glynnis scratched behind Jade's ears, and the cat seemed to melt in surrender to this gentle new creature. Finnegan was amazed.

"Jesus, Glyn, what's your secret? I bribe her with chicken livers and she won't even let me touch her."

"I guess I just have a way with small animals. I like cats. This one likes to be petted," and Jade purred, arching her back at Glynnis's touch.

"A witch with her familiar."

"Hmmm?"

"Witches consorted with demons who often took the form of cats. The familiar would follow the witch around and share her secrets. Some sorcerers could control even the wildest beasts."

Glynnis smiled slyly. "Do you think I'm a witch? " She stroked the cat's head.

"I think you're enchanting, whether it's black magic or human charm."

"I won't tell you which. Why do you think you followed me that morning at the art museum?"

"You attracted me. And you left your notebook."

"Maybe that's what I wanted you to think. Could it be that I drew you on? And now, perhaps I have your mind so fogged that I can do with you as I wish, and all the while you'll be convinced that you're acting of your own will. Like my friend Jade."

"I know what I'm doing, Glyn."

"You think you do. But that's a huge part of it. To make you believe you're in control when you're really not. You're docile that way. You won't fight me because you still believe you're your own master."

"If so, then I place myself in your trust and care."

"And I will use you and grind you up."

Finnegan laughed. "I don't think you have it in you. Plus, I'm not a soft touch."

"That wouldn't matter. I'm accustomed to having my own way. And you, my Irish dear, are a childlike Romantic with a tongue of silver. If I wanted, I'm certain I could render you helpless—a quivering emotional wreck. But don't fret. I'm far too attracted to you to do anything of the sort. At least now."

"But I shouldn't cross you."

"Absolutely not. I'm heartless when aroused."

"There's some wine in the kitchen. Shall I get it?"

"Of course. And Conor . . . don't take me too seriously."

Finnegan smiled, shook his head slightly, and went to pour the wine. When he returned, Glynnis had put Jade down. She stood near the entryway looking at one of Leona Krall's prints. Conor handed her a glass.

"Your lady likes cats, I see."

"She lives and breathes them. It broke her heart to have to leave this one behind. Would you like to see the rest of the place?"

"I'm sure I will in time. I'd rather just stay down here with you for now."

Finnegan put his wine glass down on an end table. He opened the windows for some air. "I opened the kitchen, too. I have to close the downstairs whenever I go out. Unfortunately it gets really stuffy in here, and sometimes unbearably hot."

"Is it hot upstairs?"

"Always. It's difficult to sleep."

Glynnis walked around the living room, ostensibly looking at the

Krall artworks but, Finnegan sensed, taking her measure of the place, learning the feel of it, the smell of it. She walked in slow, long steps, relaxed but not casual. Perhaps she, too, felt a touch of nerves.

Finnegan put on some music and turned off all the lights save one. The music, a Gordon Lightfoot collection, complemented the hushed atmosphere. Finnegan sat on the couch and, as Glynnis walked near him, he grabbed her hand. He pulled her down beside him.

"Conor, careful. I'll spill my wine."

"I don't care." He shifted quickly so that he faced her as best he could, slid one hand behind the soft waterfall of her hair to the nape of her neck, and kissed her deeply. They kissed that way for several minutes, unhurried, broken only to relive the sensation of first touch.

When at last they paused, Glynnis looked into Conor's eyes and smiled, but in such a way as Conor had never seen. She did not recall her wry smile of hidden knowledge, nor her subtle grin of amusement, nor her unbridled smile of genuine happiness. Conor saw in Glynnis's expression a depth until then unplumbed, an abandon to his strength, a trusting accession to a now-welcome vulnerability. Glynnis's features spoke with eloquence in a whisper that betrayed no mystery, no suspicion, and nothing coy. And in that flickering moment, bathed in the golden-orange light of a single lamp burning in the cooling blackness, they were as open to each other as they would ever be. Conor would remember Glynnis's face at that moment throughout his life.

"You've helped me through my nervousness," whispered Finnegan.

"What on earth is there to be nervous about?"

"There are things left unsaid, Glynnis, that we've both been avoiding."

"Say them then. Please."

"They're things I've never said. And I'm not sure enough of myself even now to say them well. The Irish are supposed to be wonderful with our words. My blood notwithstanding, I'm afraid I'm not so graceful. Not now. I'm afraid that you might find me too forward, or too brash, or too presumptive."

"Conor, you're the sweetest man I've ever known. Nothing about you could be base. I know what you're moving toward, but I want you to say it."

"Okay." Finnegan backed away slightly, freeing his left hand from the small of Glynnis's back and grasping her own to hold it on her lap. "Glynnis, where will you sleep tonight?"

"With you, of course."

"You're sure?"

"Conor, nothing in this world could please me more than making love to you tonight."

She leaned forward and kissed him lightly. Glynnis stood and with both her hands pulled Conor to his feet. "All right then. I'm ready to see the rest of the house now." She continued to hold his hand as they walked up the stairs.

Glynnis undressed slowly in the dark, as did Conor. She came to him then, her flesh quivering. Conor saw the outline of her body against the dim light of the window. He smelled the deep rich lilac scent that surrounded her. Conor held her close, burrowing against Glynnis's neck, drawing in her scent, simply holding her and feeling the wonder of her there before him, trembling and naked. He kissed her neck, then her cheek and eyelids. Glynnis clung to him tightly.

"Conor," she whispered, "I want you to know that I'm still a virgin."

Conor stepped back a bit and smiled down at her. She had spoken without her usual calm self-assurance. He was not surprised, neither by her admission nor by her tone. In a way that made him slightly ashamed, he relished her exposure, yet knew that he would be thoroughly solicitous of it.

"So am I, Glyn."

"Please don't lie to me."

"I'm not lying," said Conor, very softly. "There's never been any reason until you."

She kissed him hard on the mouth, channeling every frustration, every moment of alienation and loneliness, every empty, listless day through her frame into the gentle, strong figure of Conor Finnegan. She saw him then as the final regulator of her current existence, an aurora quietly exploding along a darkened horizon. She pulled him to the bed and there, for the first time in their lives, they shared their tragic vulnerability.

> *Lay your sleeping head, my love,*
> *Human on my faithless arm;*
> *Time and fever burns away*
> *Individual beauty from*
> *Thoughtful children, and the grave*
> *Proves the child ephemeral:*
> *But in my arms till break of day*
> *Let the living creature lie,*
> *Mortal, guilty, but to me*
> *The entirely beautiful.*

—W. H. Auden

The next morning Jade crept into the bedroom and sat in the corner by then door, patiently waiting for some motion. After a while her patience wore thin and she began to yowl her throaty complaint. It was time to be fed.

Glynnis woke first and rolled to her side, throwing an arm around Conor, sleeping on his back. He opened his eyes and saw Glynnis, her face framed by her tousled hair.

"Hi."

Glynnis placed her head on Conor's shoulder. "You know, I slept pretty well for a fallen woman."

"You're not fallen, Glynnis. You've just blossomed. And so have I. I haven't slept so soundly in months."

"Mr. Finnegan, you inspire me. I may yet become lusty."

"You're off to a wonderful start."

They lay together in their wedded position, not speaking. Conor reveled in Glynnis's naked touch, her flowery scent, the silken tangle of her long, thick hair. He let himself feel each part of his own body. He became conscious of the pressure of the bed against his back; he felt the sticky softness of the sheets where they had made love. From the open window the branches of a tree cast morning shadows on the far wall. A cat's paw wafted through the curtains; Conor felt it blow over him and cool his body. He felt most of all the warmth of Glynnis—her head on his collarbone, her willowy arm lying across his chest, the firmness of her breasts at his side, her leg sprawled across his abdomen and resting against his delicate manhood. Glynnis moved her toes along Conor's ankle.

Conor had experienced the whole of his passion. Now he broke it down into its parts, analyzed and catalogued them for future memory. He thought it important to do so. Each piece must fit together, and he must know each piece, each sensation, each breath, each touch, each kiss, each rising and falling. A mosaicist, regarding the tesserae, in wonder at what they have joined to create.

Jade destroyed it all by jumping onto the bed. Glynnis started, and sat up quickly, but seeing it was Jade she merely held out a hand. Jade came to it, mewing.

"She startled me."

"She wants to be fed. And what Jade wants, Jade gets, or so I've been commanded."

Conor gave Glynnis a final kiss, then rolled out of bed. He became aware at once of his nakedness, intimately proper in the bed but now stark and bold. He reached for his robe hanging on a hook on the back of the door.

"Stop, Conor. Let me look at you." He turned around shyly. Conor sensed the irony that he should now be regarded for his body by an attractive young woman, just as he so often regarded the women he would see on the street, on campus or at the office.

"You have a lovely body, Conor. Did anyone ever tell you that? You're so strong and solid." Glynnis paused, but Conor had no idea what to say. He stood awkwardly, one hand holding his robe, the other on his hip.

"I just wanted to tell you that."

"Thank you, lass. I know I've told you how beautiful you are, but now's not the time. Tonight. I'll share my body with you, and all the thoughts it inspires."

Conor pulled on his robe and went downstairs. All romance was put aside, for it was now time to boil the cat's chicken livers. The cat followed his every move expectantly. 'The servants,' she thought, 'are getting lazy.'

A few minutes later Glynnis came down the stairs in her own robe. She had brushed her hair and it fell now to her breasts. She smelled the boiling livers and made a face. "That's disgusting. You have to do this every day?"

"First thing. I'll make some eggs and sausage once the odor clears. I've plugged in the coffee already."

Glynnis sat down at the round kitchen table while Conor pulled the pan of livers off the stove. Coffee perked on the counter.

"So what shall we do today?"

"There's plenty left to see. I thought we might go over to Arlington, to the cemetary. If you can get over the fact that you're surrounded by moldering corpses, it's very pretty, and quite inspirational. Then maybe we could just walk through Georgetown and look in the shops at all the things we can't afford. Or maybe we can just drive west and see the hills."

"That sounds terrific." She hesitated. "Conor?"

"Yes?"

"I bled last night. The sheets are very bad."

He smiled. "A small price to pay, wasn't it? I'll buy new sheets."

"It may have soaked through to the mattress."

"I'll see if I can clean whatever's there. I've got an organic solution that works on anything protein-based." Conor mashed the livers into Jade's bowl and he put it by the door to the basement. The cat bound across the room and plunged her face into the dish.

"It just seems so dirty, Conor. I'm sorry."

"Glyn, don't worry about it." Conor paused, then added lightly. "Do I detect a note of Catholicism coming out?"

"Fr. Francis wouldn't approve."

"Fr. Francis need never know. It's none of his concern. What matters is whether you approve."

"You know I do, Conor."

"But in the morning, looking at the blood, it somehow seems a bit different that it did at the time, right?" Conor's sat at the table and took one of Glynnis's hands in his own. "Glynnis, what happened last night was the most beautiful expression I've ever made. It grew out of emotion, lass, not lust. And I don't think God could ever condemn what the heart feels so purely. If so, then I want no part of Him. Fr. Francis might not understand that, but I believe it wholly. I was raised the same way you were, Glynnis, but what we did last night was the finest, richest thing, and we'll both remember it until we die. Please don't trouble yourself. Religion is just a series of formulas. What matters is ethics. What matters is the heart."

Glynnis leaned across the table and kissed Conor deeply, then again. "Thank you, Father Confessor."

"Any time. I could go on, but I told you I can take metaphysics only in small doses."

"I'll prepare myself. Someday you can give me the Conorian view of life in detail, from top to bottom. But not today. Feed me, and let's get going."

* * *

Summer had not been kind to Anne Newbury. The season had provided little of the carefree release from concerns, duties and pressures she typically enjoyed during her youth. Although it was still June, Anne had concluded that the pattern of these erstwhile vacation months now allowed for nothing in the way of relaxation. There was too much to do, and too much on her mind.

It began with her swimming. The World University Games were scheduled for August in Belgrade. Anne estimated the times she would have to beat to earn a spot on the national squad, and, as soon as the competitive swimming season had ended in the spring, she mapped out a comprehensive training routine to bring her to Eastern Europe. But, as the ancients discovered, the weaknesses of the flesh can undermine the loftiest intentions. Anne had fallen behind her training schedule, skipping a day here, shortening a workout there. Her times were slower than what she had wanted them to be. She felt weak. Unless she could pick up her training pace considerably, her summer would be spent solely in the smothering boredom of New Jersey.

Perhaps it was her frustration with her swimming that forced her into frequent conflict with her parents. Anne had never been of an independent mind. She had never had the slightest desire to go her own way. It was enough for her to remain safely protected under her parents' scrutiny. She did not wish to be bothered with the mundane details of daily living: let her parents provide food and shelter. She in return had little difficulty honoring the scattered requests her parents put forth regarding her clothes, domestic contributions or social habits. They were generally of the same mind concerning these things anyway. Anne had embraced the ethical, religious and social systems of her mother and father. That was the natural course, in any event. Anne allowed herself little room for deviation, and so she had never permitted the opportunity for conflicting views to incubate. She had grown up comfortably nurtured in the beliefs of her parents, and that was her preference. The strife of an independent evolution held absolutely no appeal for her.

So it disturbed her that, this summer, she had somehow managed to become involved in almost daily disagreements with her mother or father. Anne supposed that most of it was her doing, but that realization had little effect on their frequent jousts and barbs. Subject matter was varied, and, in the end, irrelevant. Virtually anything—any action, any inaction, any response, any movement—could set her off. In past weeks Anne had wrestled with her mother, her father, or both over such matters as whether Anne might want to cook dinner on a given night, whether the latest addition to her summer wardrobe was truly worth what she spent on it, which television show to watch after dinner, and how often the family car should be washed. More substantive issues, such as which medical schools to consider, would wait for later in the summer after these preliminary skirmishes subsided.

And then there was Tom. Anne had never bothered to think through their relationship. That sort of thing would be a waste of time, for any introspective analysis was bound to be subjective, and therefore invalid. Rather, Anne felt that what she and Tom had together would proceed of its own accord. She did not believe in counterbalances, that the wishes of one would find an equilibrium with the wishes of the other, giving in some places, pushing back in others until a steady, acceptable level of behavior and sentiment would crystallize for both. Anne had her own standards, her own habits, her own preferences. If Tom could fit into those patterns, then he would be welcome. If not, then she would rather be without him. He would only disrupt those things what were genuinely important.

Now, though, Anne had become uncertain as to where and whether Tom McIlweath belonged in the general scheme of her existence. She had grown fond of him for many reasons. She appreciated his quick wit and the broad range of his intelligence. Moreover, he was accommodating. He rarely disagreed with her, he was constantly solicitous of her opinions, and he willing to subjugate his own desires to hers. The times they shared had been quiet ones. Tom had provided companionship, support, amusement, reflection and human warmth, qualities that Anne had always enjoyed from other sources but which now came together nicely in Tom McIlweath's sinewy frame. In short, Tom had all the requisite characteristics to have earned a berth in Anne's affections.

And yet she was not completely comfortable with him. She could not define her unease. Perhaps she saw it as a foreshadowing, or perhaps it grew from being unaccustomed in her role as Tom's focus. That's what she was, after all. That was apparent, especially to her. Or perhaps it was a realization that, as the princess who slept on the pea, something, somewhere, lay out of line.

In the final analysis he was a very different sort of person from those to whom she had been accustomed throughout her sedate, sheltered life. He had fled family and friends to set himself up in the most distant part of the country. Anne could not understand his flight. It didn't make sense to her, this self-exile, despite his impassioned efforts to explain it. He used such terms as 'lack of identity' and 'suppressed ego' and it all sounded so inflated, so self-pitying. There was something strange about it. She was not certain she could trust someone who had abandoned those points from which most reasonable people fix their perspectives.

If Tom felt no loyalty to his past, what could Anne expect of his attitude toward his future? Tom had not yet set a firm course. With his final year of college looming a few weeks ahead, he had made no plans. Perhaps he would teach somewhere, maybe in a prep school, or he might go to graduate school in the Classics. Law school wasn't totally out of the question, but even Tom acknowledged that it was getting a bit late in the game to be deciding on that. He had even mentioned the possibility of the Peace Corps. Tom's lack of a solid career goal unnerved her. She preferred not to think about it.

Nor did Anne like Tom's friends. They were a crude lot, unversed in the areas Anne deemed important. Tom spoke fondly of all three of his roommates, especially Conor Finnegan, but Anne thought them all too loud, too base, too interested in fleeting physical pleasures. Finnegan and Lanny O'Hanlon even worked in politics, which Anne knew to be the lowest of the professions, fit only for the dregs who could not find more respectable paths. They dressed too casually. She had seen Dan Rosselli sitting around their apartment nearly naked. They spoke too casually, too. She did not like their easy, off-handed manner of getting along with one another. She could not understand them, and because of that, she could not understand why Tom would ever willingly spend time in their company. That he did merely underscored Anne's uncertainty in Tom's commitment to the higher things, like a good book, a good swim, or an evening spent walking in the park.

And on top of Anne's other cautions, subtlest of all lay her instinctive perception that within Tom McIlweath ran a stream of discontent so strong that, should he release it, it would sweep her away entirely along with all traces of his present character. Tom's demeanor hid it well, but something—a word, a series of words, perhaps a facial expression he thought she would not notice—had burrowed into Anne's suspicious subconscious, and there it stayed. She could not shake it. There was in Tom a heavy reluctance about him, as if his current state—his friends, his pursuits, his very self—were in transit, or, more frightening, devoid of meaning altogether. She knew that Tom's scope was broad and that he wanted to give it wide range. So, in the end, he might well be torn between aspiration and duty, for Tom too had immersed himself in ethical responsibilities, not the least of which he held toward Anne. If so, what must he do with the heat of opposing compulsions in frictional movement? Where might it lead him, and what, ultimately, did he seek? That Tom's discontent was volatile Anne had no doubt, just as she had no doubt that Tom would be wasting his time in any pursuit of a broader fulfillment.

One did what one had to do, that was all. The rewards of doing things well were obvious. One might look to enjoy some comfort, some companionship, a family and a sense of accomplishment. Anything beyond that was quixotic, Anne felt certain of that. And so what she perceived in Tom—his Romantic hope that he might find something more plausibly in step with his unnamed and unnamable longings—unnerved her most of all.

Anne sorted through her reasons, and sensed a lack of control. 'This is not at all what I thought it would be.'

Her summer had become, in all, a compendium of frustrations, all too definable and so all the more present. She was unaccustomed to dealing with patterns and reactions not of her own choosing, of having to face her own inadequacies. It made her irritable.

Tom McIlweath saw Anne's frustrations as they manifested in distance and reserve. He sensed, too, that somehow he probably had a hand in Anne's moods, but he could not see precisely where. Anne had been very quiet with him of late—not that they had ever spoken in unusual depth, but now there rose great stone walls that muffled even the sounds they did utter, forcing them to speak quickly, in short bursts of words and thoughts small enough to fit through the fissures. Tom never pressed Anne. If her reserve was just a passing humor, he could wait. It was more than that, he would know in time. Meanwhile, he felt it best to present himself as one who respected whatever it was she was going through, one who would be at her disposal, reflective and nonjudgmental, if she would only say the word.

In such a frame of mind, McIlweath walked over to the college pool on a Saturday afternoon in late June. Anne would be finishing her workout and Tom had agreed to meet her there. Or more precisely, Anne had agreed to let Tom come to the pool at the end of her stint. McIlweath had it in mind to take her to dinner somewhere, someplace simple. It might relax her a bit. They could talk there if they wanted to, or if Anne felt the need.

McIlweath walked into the rear of the old brick gymnasium and headed down the narrow stairway to the men's locker room. No one was there. He sniffed the pungently familiar odor of chlorine as he went up the opposite stairs to the pool. Near the top he could hear through the door the regular rhythmic slapping of Anne's strokes against the water. He opened the door and stepped down to the cold tile. Anne's father sat behind the officials' table at the side of the pool. McIlweath came up beside him.

"Hello, Tom."

"Hello, Dr. Newbury. How's she doing?"

The older man shrugged and made a face. "Not bad, although she won't be happy with it. But that's nothing new, is it? She's going 9500 today."

"That's great, especially for this time of year."

"Yes, but she'll say her sprints were too slow, or that she had to work too hard to make her splits. Something. It's always something. How're you doing, Tom?"

"Good. I didn't have to work today, so I thought maybe I'd take Anne out to dinner."

"Your tan gets deeper every time I see you."

"I've been guarding five days a week, sometimes six. At least forty hours. But it's easy work, and the tan comes with it."

"Just sit in the tall chair and flirt with the girls, eh?"

"Not me. Besides, most of them are twelve or thirteen, or at the other end of the spectrum. Sixty-five or seventy."

"Sixty-five is still the middle bloom of life, my friend. Women may still be feminine, men virile. That's less than ten years away for me."

"You don't look it, you know. You're still in great shape."

"Clean living. And a feisty daughter, whom I'll now leave to your care. Have her home at a reasonable hour, won't you?"

"I always do."

"You're a good man, Tom McIlweath." Dr. Newbury rose from his seat. "But someday you'll be tempted not to. Someday the two of you will want to break away completely. It's bound to happen, I'm afraid."

"Anne's hardly the rebellious type. And I'm sure it won't happen tonight," said McIlweath with a small smile.

"No, she's not rebellious, Tom, but she can be awfully willful. She's used to her own way. You know that. The best thing you can do is to stand up to her from time to time. Make her bend a little, even if it's difficult. She'll drag you after her if she can, just like a horse pulling a fallen rider caught in the stirrups."

Tom shook his head. "I don't think that's the case with me, Dr. Newbury. We're good for each other, I think. And we're partners."

Dr. Newbury smiled benignly. He turned for the exit. "Enjoy yourself, Tom. And have her home early," he called over his shoulder.

McIlweath leaned against the table and watched Anne swim, her lean form cutting through the green water, bulletlike. The sinew that propelled her, glistening as she rose from the water in her strokes, head, shoulders, legs, forming the rounded curves that could appear so soft; but all of it solid, unyielding to the touch, sleek, a tarpaulin over the unbent and unbending mounds, a feminine form chiseled in salted driftwood, exhibiting the standard attributes of sexuality but masking a focused, compulsive power. Anne pulled herself, kicking, twisting, gulping for air in turbulent spasms. There was no grace in this, not to those who knew it. But it made her strong. Stronger. Anne reveled in her strength, in the firm contours of her body, in the tight, stringy brawn of her neck, her back and her arms, in the elasticity of her broad legs. She reveled in her speed. She was not like other women. She was not like the soft, self-indulgent princesses who sat back in expectation of the attentions and affections of equally soft, self-indulgent young men. She needed no finery. Her body was her finery, the only gown she would ever wear.

After several laps Anne hit the wall to McIlweath's left and pulled her torso over the edge of the pool. She rested her forehead on her arms, flat against the poolside, and, head downward, gulped heavily for air, inhaling the rank chlorine. She drew it deeply into her lungs. Rappacini's daughter, surrounded by her poisons.

McIlweath walked over to the side of the pool. "Hi." She grunted in response without looking up. "Your father left a while ago."

"I thought he'd leave sooner," she said breathlessly. "Let me wind down a bit," and she threw herself back into the pool to take long, slow backstrokes. Halfway down the length she turned around and stroked leisurely back to the wall. She repeated the process three more times while McIlweath stood waiting. Finally she hopped out of the pool at the corner and walked to a bench a few feet away. McIlweath followed and sat down next to her as she wrapped a towel around her shoulders.

"How'd you do?"

"Lousy. I went 9500."

"That's what your father said. How did it feel?"

"It hurts more than it should at this point. I'm not as fast as I should be either. I'm lousy."

"No, you're not, Anne. You're working hard. You'll peak at the right time and you'll make the Games. I've got confidence in you."

"Stop it, Tom. You don't know. Nobody does. And I'm not working nearly as hard as I should. I should be doing 9500 every day, and I'm not. Two days ago I only did 6000, and the day before that I did 5500. That's terrible. Everybody else I'll be swimming against is going harder, and longer, and faster."

"Anne, it's summer. Give yourself a break. All you have to do is peak in late July."

"And I never will the way I'm going."

"Do you feel like dinner? I thought I might take you to Tony's."

"What time is it?"

"Four-thirty. By the time you shower and change it'll be around 5:00. Maybe we could take a walk in the park first or if you're really hungry we could go right over."

"Let me get changed." Anne rose, toweling one of her arms. She headed for the women's locker room.

"Take your time."

She did. McIlweath walked around the pool. He read the listing of school records, noting the appearance of his own name three times. He perused the clippings on the bulletin board. Anne did not reappear for forty-five minutes. She wore a pair of corduroys incongruous for the summer, and a print blouse. Her hair was still wet. They walked out through the door of the main gym.

"What do you want to do, Anne?"

"I want to go home."

"I thought we were going to dinner."

"I never said that. You did. Just take me home."

"But why? We've got the whole night."

"Tom, I just don't feel like doing anything. I want to be alone tonight. I'm lousy company."

"Is it me?"

"What?"

"Do you want to be alone, or do you just not want to be with me?"

"Don't be silly."

"That's no answer."

"It's as much as you're going to get. I want to be by myself tonight, that's all."

"Have I done something to offend you? What the hell is going on?"

"It's nothing. It's everything. God damn it, I don't know. Leave me alone tonight, Tom. I don't want to deal with anything."

"Is there something you want to talk about?"

"No," Anne raised her voice in real exasperation. She fairly shouted her reply. "There's nothing I want to talk about. I've got nothing to say. I'm just tired, do you understand? Not everything in my life has to do with you. I'm tired, and slow, and pissed off. And there's no point in talking about anything. You don't understand any of what I'm going through, so what's the point? Okay?"

"Come on, Anne," said McIlweath softly as they reached the street. "I'll take you home. And I'll call you tomorrow, if that's all right."

"You do that."

* * *

That same Saturday, two hundred miles to the south, there was no such contention. Glynnis and Conor felt a syncopation, the product of their evening's passion fully realized. Their thoughts and urges transposed themselves. What one conceived in one's mind found expression on the other's tongue. They told each other things they already knew; their steps fell automatically together. Their separate moods paired off—frivolity with frivolity, sobriety with sobriety, all subterfuge behind an eager receptivity to the needs, whims or fancies of the other.

After breakfast they drove to Arlington and walked respectfully through the cemetery. The Boston in Glynnis revived silently at the Kennedys' gravesites. She stood without speaking amid the stone arenas of their words; it brought a melancholy familiarity, recalling the sharp nasal twangs and Irish Brahmin accents. She did not like graveyards where Bostonians lay buried. Finnegan, too, stood mute, sensing the cold wind that had blown into Glynnis's humor, not knowing precisely its origin but knowing intuitively that it must be potent. After several minutes, Finnegan knelt before the eternal flame at John Kennedy's grave, said a silent prayer for aspirations shattered, for a generation abandoned and hence lost, then blessed himself and moved to Robert's grave, where he repeated his gestures. Glynnis watched. When Finnegan rose she followed him up the gentle hill away from the graves, tightly holding his hand.

They drove westward from the city, through Fairfax, through Falls Church, through Vienna. Glynnis loved the greenery of the suburbs, and especially the sight of sunlight broken by the branches falling on the undergrowth. They went there just to see it, just to get another perspective on a mild summer afternoon. Virginia. The South. The old Confederacy. Glynnis had never been there. They saw a sign for the battlefield at Bull Run and it thrilled them both, history made apparent. They could sense the age in the hills rising before them, and it oddly comforted them.

They got back to Washington early enough to explore the shops along Wisconsin Avenue. Finnegan bought a copy of *John Brown's Body* at an old editions bookstore. He looked in each shop they entered to see what caught Glynnis's eye so that he could learn her tastes. He would have liked to buy a gift of some sort but nothing seemed appropriate. Most of the shops they saw were clothing stores, which offered nothing which Conor could comfortably purchase, or specialty shops—antiques, leather goods and the like—which offered nothing Conor could afford. He bought nothing, but resolved to be better prepared for Glynnis's next visit.

They walked up M Street, near the University, to look at the old, quaint federal houses. The cobbled brick of the streets made their steps delicate, and they took care not to stumble on the unfamiliar surface. Again a timeless quality to all of it—houses, streets, lamps, trees—that simplified them. Finnegan, from the first time he had set foot in the city, had admired Washington for its history, the broken evidence of lives past. One could not avoid it.

They returned to the townhouse shortly before 6:00. It had been a full day, and somewhat exhausting. The hair around Glynnis's temples moistened against her skin, the product of their long walking. Still, she smelled of the now familiar lilacs. Conor had noticed her richly exotic scent all day. He had wanted to preserve it somehow, keep it with him when she left. Glynnis's lovely purple aroma excited him. It had become her mark, channeled permanently into Conor's memory. He would not be able to think of Glynnis without smelling the lilacs of her hair, her breasts and her neck.

They did not go out to dinner that night. Instead Conor prepared their meal: salmon with ginger, zucchini, salad and black coffee, iced. Glynnis sat at the table while Conor went about his task.

"I didn't know you could cook," said Glynnis as Conor at last set a full plate before her.

"You haven't tasted it yet. I really can't."

"Don't be absurd. This looks delicious. I couldn't begin to put something like this together."

He poured them each a glass of Pinot Grigio. "It's a survival skill, pure and simple. One of the requirements of apartment living with three other guys. I became creative last autumn when I got tired of macaroni and cheese with hot dogs cut up in it. Now my roommate Dan and I do most of the cooking."

"How's Dan?"

"Better than me. But then, he's Italian. The cooking instinct is in his blood, mixed in with garlic and olive oil."

"You don't look as if you're suffering."

"Ah, a thinly veiled hint that I might lose some weight. In fact I'm not suffering at all. Expensive weekend dinners with my lovely girl keep me from looking too lean."

"You know, Conor, you might well be on the way to spoiling me."

"I'd certainly like to try."

"But what can I do for you? I'm not well versed in all this, although I've heard that the way to thoroughly please a man is to keep his stomach full and his testicles empty."

"Too basic. That implies gratification is solely rooted in the creature comforts. That doesn't work."

"Explain, please."

"We're social, Glyn. As soon as you introduce collective relationships, you start to complicate matters. Read Plato's *Republic*. Society necessitates specialization, and we derive satisfaction from performing what's required of our societal role. We derive special gratification from improving our societal role. We become competitive, then we look for competitive advantages. Our specialization increases; pressures intensify, and we become more deeply embedded into a social fabric. And that's just for openers. I won't even mention our need for individual expression and identity, which leads to art, which is a separate compulsion in itself. We spend all our time carving out a place in a complex society, then trying to make some sense of it. So we need more than food and sex. "

He paused to take a bite of his food. Glynnis watched him with a bemused smile. She enjoyed Conor's frequent discourses simply because she never took them as seriously as he did himself. They provided entertainment; enlightenment followed only by permission, or by accident.

"We started to outgrow the basic pleasures as soon as our hairy ancestors banded together for mutual protection. In between bopping each other on the head with rocks, they learned security, cooperation, creativity, all the ways a semi-rational creature relates to a group and how he defines himself within it. Eating, sleeping and screwing have always been important, but there's more to us than that. And we're stuck with it."

"But that's not so bad, do you think? We've become infinitely more sophisticated," said Glynnis.

"With a broader range of satisfactions, but with a broader range of reactions, too. I mean, what's war but collective self-interest—political, economic, even ethnic—wielded against another group's perceived interests? And on the individual level, we have thievery, rape, murder, extortion. It seems to me that every evil is the product of a frustrated or perverted quest for one of our sophisticated satisfactions. The more complex we become, the greater our potential for evil."

"So where does the good come from?"

"Personal fulfillment attained without disturbing the common good, and in fact adding to it. That's a satisfaction all its own. In fact, I'd hazard a guess that the less self-interested an individual is, the greater his capacity to perform what might generally be called 'good works.' I suppose that follows from the idea that our complexities are the root of most of society's wrongs."

"Maybe the ancient ascetics had the right idea."

"I doubt it. They divested themselves of all self-interest, which is itself a horrible vanity. Perhaps that's the most self-interested thing an individual can do. Ironic, isn't it? But they took themselves completely out of the social order, and I think that's unnatural for a social creature. A better example might be the Mendicants."

"Where do you fit in, Conor Finnegan? How self-interested are you?"

"Enough to know that I wouldn't want to be anywhere else tonight, or looking into anyone else's eyes."

"Talk Irish to me."

Conor reached out his right hand and grasped Glynnis's across the table.

> *"When you are old and grey and full of sleep,*
> *And nodding by the fire, take down this book,*
> *And slowly read, and dream of the soft look*
> *Your eyes had once, and of their shadows deep . . ."*

He relinquished her hand and came back to English. "Yeats. A gentle Irishman like myself."

"You charm me, young bard. How do you remember such things?"

"'Tis you, lass, who inspires me to poetry. You and a fearsome English Lit professor in love with early twentieth century verse."

"That smacks of self-interest."

"So be it. It's a clever man who can combine Romanticism and pragmatism in the same gesture."

Their lovemaking that night did not spring from premeditated urges expressed spontaneously, but from a desire to extract every subtlety, every nuance from their shared passion, now an open part of their deepening regard for one another. They sat on the couch, wrapped in each other's arms, aware now of the mysteries that lay ahead and willing to approach them leisurely, without anxiety, without uncertainty. They drew long kisses from one another's mouth. Conor traced the contours of Glynnis's lips with his tongue, and she reciprocated. He felt the slithery firmness of her body, he ran his hands through the length of her flowing hair. Glynnis in turn captured the sinewy power of Conor's arms on her sides and back. She spread her hands across his back, around his broad shoulders and down his lean, solid arms, stanchions that surrounded her there in her feasting.

Nearing midnight, Glynnis drew back and sat upright, her right hand cupping the curve of Conor's cheek. "It's time for bed, my young hero."

She stood, Conor below her now, flecks of gold reflecting in the bottomless brown of her eyes. Her heart beat quickly in expectation, and a sensation spurted through her in an instant that reminded her of the cold, sharp winter mornings in late December when she was a girl.

Conor rose and took Glynnis's hand without speaking. He led her up the stairs. At the top, Glynnis dropped his hand, kissed his cheek and spun into the bathroom. "Let me make myself ready for you, Conor. We have all night."

Finnegan walked into the bedroom and undressed to his shorts. He glanced at his form in the mirror: strong, a solid waist, powerful arms. He feared every flaw, every tuck of loose skin, every disproportionate bulge or swerve. He feared disappointing the mystery that had unfolded the night before. He went to the bed and pulled the covers down.

Glynnis emerged in green. She wore a long nightgown made of something sheer, cut low and held up by two thin straps. A narrow elastic band created a high waist, accentuating her breasts. The sweet, rich scent of lilacs swept into the room with her. Light from the window, filtered through shadowy trees, softened her features to a gentle blur. Conor at once drank in every delicate section of her, and nothing at all. She became an illusion, a reflection of the suppressed aspirations of his youth, an embodiment of all hope, of all passion, of faith itself. She stood there, her face serious yet relaxed, and for the briefest of instants Conor became helpless, his very spirit unable to flinch in the merest response. The alpha and the omega . . . the first and the last, and everything that lay between. Conor grabbed her in his arms and drew her tightly to him.

What, then, of this most profound and most permanent rite of passage? What ageless mysteries, and mysteries not at all, lay in the twisting, the gropings and the thrustings of Conor's and Glynnis's passion?

It is at the root of mankind in all its forms to feel complete in its power, to know that, as a human being, he may dictate the variances of his physical experiences, his intellectual processes, his emotional sculptings. Passion is born of all these, and the body as conduit, the mind as interpreter, the emotions as provocateur. And as the parts of one's soul work together in this ultimate act of humanity, one finds himself at once consumptively powerful, and shockingly vulnerable. For if our mind and body and emotions are working in concert, what is left to protect us? As we devour the feast in front of us, a feast which makes us resoundingly strong and firm and whole, what will we not do or say that otherwise, in our moments of greater restraint, would sit undisturbed, neatly catalogued in some forgotten corner of our psyches?

Conor Finnegan made love to Glynnis Mear, relentlessly, breathlessly, in rapt self-absorption and in a worrisome self-denial. He did not know what it was he was trying to crawl back into when he penetrated her; he did not know what personal depths he had opened and allowed to be probed. He knew only that his soul at last was acting in concert, all parts fulfilled together, and that Glynnis beneath him was the cause.

Their hips rose and fell slowly together, languidly, for there was no hurry. Conor's mouth and tongue played across ear, neck, shoulder and Glynnis's round breasts. He marveled at the warm moistness sucking in his base, alternately taking and giving back. Glynnis's legs closed across his back; she ran her heels up the back of him and locked her legs around his buttocks. He returned each of her soft groans.

There was nothing out of the ordinary in this, for Conor and Glynnis were merely repeating an act rehearsed for millennia. Yet in their strength, in the fulfillment of all their power innately human, there lay a vulnerability. What we will not do or say—

Perhaps it was this naked state of abandoned defense that led Conor Finnegan, as he neared the moment of orgasm, to nestle his face into Glynnis's neck and whisper deeply,

"I love you, lass."

And afterwards, after Conor had sent himself well inside her and lay now stroking Glynnis's hair, after the walls of Glynnis's vagina had spasmodically contracted in her own answering orgasm, after they had collapsed together to pull themselves gently apart, Glynnis Mear turned her head to one side to let a single tear run out of the corner of her eye and down her cheek to dissolve into the blue fabric pillow.

* * *

Summer drew on with the fleeting quickness of a symphony that captures the heart as well as the ear, and in so doing suspends time itself so that, at its coda, one had little sense of beginning, middle or end. There is simply the music at hand, rapt, engrossing and transcendent. One passes through it as through a vapor.

Finnegan did not count the passage of time. The excitements of his current state did not come in a linear progression, from day to day, but rather created an atmosphere perpetually charged with elegance, purpose and romance. His elation never diminished. Finnegan held this new type of excitement up to the light; he turned it over and looked at it from top and bottom, felt the weighty substance of it in the palm of his hand, bit it, and found it real.

His work gratified him immensely. Within a handful of days he had established a camaraderie with his colleagues, most of whom were young, recent college or law school graduates. He saw the value of their work in general, and his work in particular. He continued to assimilate facts and figures regarding the elderly into readable reports, some of which were translated into legislation. He wrote speeches that were read on the Senate floor. He met with lobbyists from senior citizens' organizations. The people he encountered met him with respect, despite his youth. And the senator in turn relied increasingly on Finnegan's insights into this issue. Conor became, through both the quality of his work and the charming seriousness of his demeanor, the senator's leading counsel on the problems of the elderly. The confident young man began to recognize the trappings of power without its responsibilities, and it pleased him very much.

Weekends, of course, were for Glynnis. She came down every Friday on the 7:40 train and left again each Sunday afternoon. They saw all parts of the city in due course, always returning in the evening to make love for most of the night. Any fleeting sentiments of guilt had been put well behind them. Both Conor and Glynnis looked forward to their nights together with a lusty honesty.

On some Saturdays, Conor would drive them to the Virginia hills. There they would have a picnic lunch and walk through the wooded paths, encountering other couples or single hikers. Finnegan liked to look for the most remote spot, and often he pulled Glynnis off the path to stumble and slash through shaggy, shaded undergrowth. Under the aegis of the silent trees, he would take off his shirt and hold Glynnis to him, not for any sexual purpose but to feel her cool fingertips on the warm flesh of his back. Glynnis would kiss his neck and the solid muscular bulges of his chest. They might stand that way for several minutes, each cognizant of the other's resting form, taking deliberate account of their passive embrace.

One day Conor drove them all the way from Washington to the Shenandoah Valley, a two-hour drive. He had never been there. They found a creek in the backwoods, well off the footpath. There, in this ancient, haunted valley, they spent the afternoon, Conor shirtless and dangling his bare feet in the cool creek. Glynnis fell asleep with her head in his lap. He leaned back and slept as well.

They awoke much later with the sun low behind the tops of the high trees, and as they drove back to Washington a thunderstorm blew up from the bay. It rained in great wind-whipped sheets, slamming against the windshield more thickly than the wipers could disperse it. Pockets of water crept out from the side of the road. Finnegan drove through them and kicked up wing-like splashes that caused his car to plane. He drove tight-lipped, not speaking, concentrating fully on the road ahead and keeping his car in control against the suddenly violent elements. Glynnis, sensing Conor's concern, did not disturb him. She turned up the radio to be heard against the storm and sang softly with the lyrics. She had complete trust in her situation. Conor, for his part, struggled to see the road, now just a faint band streaming into uncharted black.

Near Fairfax the storm abated. As Finnegan rolled down the window he felt a rush of cool air sweep across his face. He breathed it in slowly to let its fresh tendrils probe every channel of his lungs. Around one turn and beyond a slight rise, they saw the city spread out before them, its sleek white marble standing solidly between green trees. The Potomac formed a narrow blue moat.

As Conor looked at the city he clasped Glynnis's hand and held it tightly. For at that moment he recognized all the grandeur, all the strength, all the limitless potential of youth in its prime, a time grasped once, and only once, a time against which all other later experiences will be measured. So rarely, so very rarely, does potential meet reality, does the full range of positive actions complement the breadth of intelligence and feeling. So rarely do all the tesserae of one's existence—physical, emotional, intellectual and spiritual—fit into so stunning a mosaic. So rarely do we comprehend the ability to fight any foe, to run any race, to shake hands with any man and call him 'brother.'

And when these rare, these ephemeral moments come, always there is in the back of our minds the troll under the bridge, the grim unspoken realization that it cannot last, that as humans we are destined to be swept back into a heartless, brutal maelstrom of suffering, loneliness and loss, of fatigue, of dreams made dust, of illness and of death; that, as humans, all our joys are terminal, all our triumphs are only illusions, for we cannot help but be dragged back into the muck that spawned us, that, as surely as red blood flows through us and sunlight warms our skins, we are destined from birth to be cut apart, to go through life as half-beings, or less, with the finest parts of us bludgeoned, bloodied, made insensate. We are too complex. We have known it since the epics of Homer and the Code of Hammurabi; we have known it since Vercingetorix and St. Augustine. We have known it in Carthage, in Tyre, in the realms of Ozymandias. We have always known it, and we cannot ignore it despite our best efforts. It stalks us, slowly, with great patience, waiting for us to relax, to become smug, to let our complacency grow up like vines, then it pounces, fangs bared, merciless, ripping apart our sweetest flesh and flaying us with the stark bleak character of our own humanity. We cannot avoid it; we merely stay ahead of it for a time until we can hide no longer.

Conor Finnegan, looking down at a city made cool by the rain and washed clean by the storm that brought it, felt noble, and strong, and ultimately worthy—an unconquerable spirit. Through the sheer radiance of his character, Glynnis Mear felt it, too. But, unlike Conor, she did not believe it. She knew it to be transitory, but that did not stop her from enjoying now this most glorious of moments while the beast lay far behind them. In time it would strike, because it had to. There could be no avoiding it. But for now, let this moment remain pure and uncluttered. There would be time enough later for the grim confirmation of their humanity, in whatever form that confirmation might take.

* * *

In the middle of July, Conor Finnegan picked up the phone one night after work and called Tom McIlweath. He had not spoken with his friend all summer although they had exchanged brief notes a few weeks earlier. But nothing can be read from such notes, so Finnegan, realizing all of a sudden that he had not thought of McIlweath in a great while, decided to call.

Knowing that McIlweath might well be working late at the club, Finnegan did not call until nearly 11:00. He dialed, then listened to the muffled electronic rings on the other end. Perhaps if Tom had gotten together with Anne after closing the pool . . . .

"Hello?"

"Mac, it's Conor."

"Well, how the hell are you, Senator? It's good to hear from you."

"Yeah, I just thought I'd give you a call, see what's up. You work tonight?"

"Until 8:30. I just got home in fact. I stopped to get something to eat."

"Haven't you learned to cook yet?"

"Frozen dinners and boil-in-bags. The life of a bachelor."

"You keeping busy, pal? What're you up to?"

"Nothing much, Conor. Guarding most days, and I swim some, just to keep the muscles toned. I've been reading, too. I want to get a head start on my Henry Rutgers."

"So you're spending the summer with your head submerged in water and Latin books. Sounds great."

"How's the political system treating you?"

"Can't complain," said Finnegan nonchalantly. "I feel right at home here, doing what I'm doing."

"What's that? Still trying to wring votes out of gullible senior citizens?"

"More or less. The senator is attempting to develop a soft spot in his heart for our elderly progenitors. I'm in charge of making him appear lovable."

"Any success?"

"Of course not. He's as lovable as a chunk of marble. But I keep trying. I'm setting up some hearings for him in mid-August. I understand he's thinking of arriving dressed in chain mail and riding a white charger. After this I may well be headed for a career in show business. Maybe choreographing clown acts."

"You sound cynical."

"Not really. All this is pretty glamorous—Capitol Hill, a townhouse in Georgetown, the corridors of power and all that. I can see myself being seduced."

"I'm anxious to see this townhouse of yours. It sounds a touch elegant."

"The door's always open, friend. Why don't you and Anne come down some weekend? I've got plenty of space."

"Maybe, Conor, but not until after the nationals."

"When are they? Are you in them?"

"Late this month, and no, but Anne is. She's trying to peak for them."

"How's she doing?"

"Hard to say. She keeps to herself most days. She says she doesn't want any distractions. If she does well enough she'll earn a spot at the World University Games. She'd be off to Belgrade for two weeks."

"Wonderful. She should be just in time for the peasant festivals. But how do you feel about that? I mean, if she makes the team she'll get a certain amount of national attention, at least in swimming circles. Plus being away for two weeks, although I'd guess after a few days of Belgrade even you would start to look good."

"Conor, she's been away all summer. Her being out of the country won't make any difference. Maybe it'll get her over whatever it is that she's going through."

"Trouble in Paradise?"

"Temporary. I've found I don't like being a lower priority. It'll pass."

"Her mood or your resentment?"

"We'll have to see. You're still seeing Glynnis, of course."

"Yeah. She comes down every weekend. I'll tell you, Mac, despite the job and the glamor and the house in Georgetown, her visits are the finest part of my life. Everything else comes in a distant second."

"Conor, you sound like a man smitten. I'm surprised. Washington's loaded with young lovelies. I thought you'd be sampling a full range of them."

"Not this time, Mac. Those young lovelies aren't Glynnis. You know, you've never met her. To be honest, that's one reason why I'd like you and Anne to come down."

"Unlikely. You'll have to bring her to New Brunswick."

"I run the risk of subjecting her to Rosselli and O'Hanlon, then. She may not be ready for the Lust Brothers. By the way, have you heard from those two derelicts?"

"Lanny's in Trenton drinking the Governor's bathwater."

"Dan's still working at the hospital, I assume."

"Apparently."

"You sound a bit lifeless, Mac. We may have to have a heart-to-heart. Get your ass down to Washington, damn it. Dr. Finnegan has all the right prescriptions. He always has before."

"I don't know, Conor. You're right, though, I guess I am a little down."

"Anne's got you that upset?"

"Yeah, that's most of it. I'm just not sure what to make of her."

'Make of her a memory, friend,' thought Finnegan. 'Put her in your past and find someone with a soul. Don't let her eat you up like this. Don't let her rob you of what is essentially and ultimately yours. Because she will do just that if she has the opportunity. That, Mac, is her nature. She'll fill her own voids with the best parts of you.'

"Well, hang in there," he said. "You two obviously care about one another."

"That's all I can do, Conor. I've got to hang in there."

'No, you don't,' Finnegan thought again to himself. 'You can still redeem yourself. You can throw off that rock-hard shell that's wrapped around your form. You're the pulp inside a mold now, but you haven't set yet, praise be. Once you do, you'll hold that grotesque shape for life. You were not born for that, Tom McIlweath. Other men, perhaps, but not you. I know you too well.'

Finnegan perceived the leaden melancholy that hung over his friend. Even in a brief conversation over a great many miles, his well-tuned ear could discern it. He sensed that the seeds of something grim and oppressive and ultimately lasting might be primed to mature. Finnegan, who knew McIlweath better than anyone, or so he thought, feared some irreparable damage to his friend's delicately marvelous character. But there was nothing he could do.

At length, they brought their conversation to a close. Finnegan resolved to call again in a few days to see if he could read something a bit brighter. But Glynnis came down again that weekend and Finnegan abandoned all thoughts of Tom McIlweath for the time being. When they resurfaced again the following week they somehow did not seem as troublesome. Finnegan did not speak to his friend again until he returned to campus at the end of August.

For Tom McIlweath, the remainder of those summer months passed drippingly slowly, maple sap from a tapped tree. Each day hung on the spigot and dangled there, refusing to let go, refusing to fall so that another droplet, equally thick and viscous, might take its place. July seemed to last forever. August, with the impending prospect of classes resuming and a subsequent return to normality, loomed as a distant beacon.

During those sweltering weeks Tom McIlweath was no more than a foil for Anne Newbury's moods. She acted, and he could only react. The intensive training for the nationals and the implied lure of the World University Games made her sensitive, demanding, withdrawn, at time vitriolic. McIlweath could not perceive any other sources of frustration beyond her swimming. Of perhaps he could, but fearing they might center at least partly on him, chose to ignore them. 'It was the swimming that makes her this way,' he thought. 'Only that. And I can wait until all this passes.'

Why Anne should be so obsessive about these games puzzled him in the first place. She was, to be sure, a fine swimmer, one of the best in the state at her age and in her event. But competition for these games was bound to be fierce. Anne would have to improve her best times considerably to have a realistic chance. She would have to pull a monumental upset at the nationals. Of course, the rewards stood to be rich. If she should make the team, then she would be well-positioned for the Olympics two years away. In the end McIlweath concluded that this was another goal for Anne, self-set, and because she looked at the payoff as something desirable, she had to work for it, push herself toward it relentlessly. Point A to Point B in the straightest of lines.

McIlweath himself was also an accomplished swimmer, of course. He had captained the Rutgers team and his rankings for two events placed him among the top five in the East. McIlweath took it all very seriously. Competitive swimming made him hard. He recalled how, in his earlier years, it had defined him and helped him craft a respectable self-image.

He enjoyed it still. He enjoyed being very good. The realization that, of all those who swam his events, he, Tom McIlweath, was among the top handful sometimes made him giddy. He hated to lose, and did so rarely. He had his ambitions, too. The Olympics would be a glorious thing, if he could make it.

Yet, after all considerations, swimming was only a pastime. Tom would define himself now, determine his worth, through other means. He could do that only now after the dissolution of his earlier uncertainties. He might embrace his swimming enthusiastically for a few months, but in the summer he had to walk away from it. He needed time away from the workouts, away from the fatigue, away from the adrenalin-charged thunder of the race itself if he were to renew the excitement of it all come autumn. The thought of intensifying his workouts over the summer repulsed him.

And so, even as Tom McIlweath could understand the motivation behind Anne Newbury's summer regimen, he could never have accepted it for himself. Let Anne train, let her abandon her free time to a strict, painful, exhausting routine, let her dismiss all serenity and shatter all peace, let her fatigued mind draw sketchy conclusions about the other more human elements of her life, let her build herself up for a crushing disappointment which, if it comes, invalidates all her previous effort. Let her do all this in pursuit of a self-imposed goal—Tom would support her any and every way he could, even to the subjugation of his own personality.

There are, sadly, different methods of suffocation.

And so, one Sunday evening with nothing to do and Anne out of bounds, Tom McIlweath took a walk. He had been restless all day. He had not had to work, but he had not known what to do with his free time. The day was hazy and humid with a light breeze. For a while McIlweath sat in a corner of the living room where windows on two walls created a crosswind. He read there, working on some obscure works by Ovid in which might be hidden a reference to the romance he was translating. Yet reading Latin on a summer's morning seemed completely out of place. Latin was to be read in dusty, musty libraries in the autumn when the leaves fell. Latin itself was dusty and musty and gray, an old hoary dowager. To read it during the sultry, fertile days of summer seemed incongruous.

After a few pages McIlweath went to the store for bagels and the Sunday *Times*. He turned on some music and read the paper leisurely. By the time he finished it was early afternoon. To kill a few more minutes he tried the crossword puzzle in the magazine. It took nearly an hour and he could not complete it. For the most difficult clues he tried to piece together answers using his linguistic and etymological knowledge, but some clues ran past language to remote topics such as baseball—"N.L. Home Run King"—or geography—"River in Spain." After a while frustration becomes boring. McIlweath put down the magazine and went to the pool for a swim. In late afternoon he wrote a letter to his parents.

When he had eaten his dinner, he felt agitated, more so than any other time during the dead day. He went from room to room, looking for something that might hold his attention. He flipped through Dan Rosselli's car magazines, he reviewed several months of telephone bills in a file on Lanny O'Hanlon's desk. He stood in front of Conor Finnegan's bookshelf and regarded the titles, reflecting history, political science and literature. Perhaps there might be something there to read . . . but, no, he couldn't.

McIlweath walked to the front window and looked out. He could not relax. The muscles in his back and legs flickered and twitched, his arms swung impulsively back and forth. His body did not want to rest.

Nor did his thoughts. He found he could focus on nothing for more than a few seconds before it passed on. His mind had taken down its walls—thoughts, memories and impressions raced across it from side to side, unrestrained, staying only so long as it took for another to shoot in and bump its predecessor to an empty corner.

The evening was warm, and a breeze blew. The sun was outlined through high, slaty summer clouds. A Sunday evening can inspire peace and serenity, or the most honest introspection. Tom McIlweath knew there was to be no serenity, yet he was not at all certain than he wanted to embark on self-examination. And so he took his walk to allow one of the other to come forward against his reluctance.

Queen's Mall drew him as the logical end. There was something reassuring there in the cluster of brick and stone buildings on the edges of the rectangle, and the ivy that grew along those stolid buildings. He felt the mall to be the nexus of all the life, all the passion, all the vain and ignorant strivings he saw around him.

The mall itself was empty. Classroom and administration buildings were just shells, darkened and strangled mute by the ivy. The only sign of life was in the seminary across the street at the campus-end of the mall. Several people walked up the rise to the cylindrical chapel there. Obviously a mass was about to take place, but it did not appear to be well attended. Few people were about.

McIlweath did not sit on one of the cold stone benches that dotted the mall. Instead he walked to a great elm tree that stood nearly in the middle, and sat at its base, nestling his legs between two thick roots. He leaned back against the solid tree. Knots and clumps of bark poked into his skin so that he had to adjust his position several times before he was comfortable. The emptiness of the buildings around him deepened his solitude. They stood blankly, as gaunt and as lifeless as the statue of William of Orange, frozen forever with one green hand lifted near his chin, standing watch near the seminary-end of the mall.

The humidity had thickened into clouds which hung now in a low canopy. The day had cooled noticeably. It was growing dark; the clouds extinguished the light more quickly and more thoroughly than on most days. There were no shadows. Tonight, ghosts would walk the mall, would empty out of the old classrooms, would sit and sob on the old benches. McIlweath knew they would; he could feel them, and knew they would come.

McIlweath sat against his tree and watched the thick end of a wasted day dangle down to nothing. He became conscious of Time—not the simply charted markings of the days, but Time as a material substance. He must be more than merely a point on a line.

And here in this ancient mall, where so many lives such as his had been determined and defined, where every possible human emotion had been played out, where young men had sampled for the first time the sweet narcotic of human pleasures, the bitter draught of frustrated heartbreak, the stark brutality of man in his spiritual loneliness, where these same young men had honed themselves to go forth from here to meet their common mortal destinies, here in this place, Time the material substance drew all fates together.

Tom McIlweath might have languished where he was, but instead he had come east out of a determined resolution not to be shaped by circumstance, but to shape circumstance to his own preference.

Here, in the relative freedom of anonymity, in the relative absence of expectation, he had pursued the things that attracted him. He had studied the classics and become an honor student. He had continued to swim competitively. He had met and developed friendships on his own terms without succumbing to the pressures of their preconceived notions. He had accomplished what he set out to do: he had resisted the compelling forces of conformity and molded a character, previously suppressed beneath a soft, pliant exterior, which invigorated him by its singularity. Time the material substance.

Yet, even in his temporary fulfillment, McIlweath felt uncontrollably restless. He could not explain it, or perhaps he dared not. There should be more than this. More than the mind's pursuits, more than the product of the body, more even than his rather proud self-image. What lay at the core of his discontent?

This was, he knew, a launching point. It had to be. But in what direction, and how fast? Where does a restless man make his bed, and with whom does he share it? And when the day's satisfactions grow stale, when the end of his strivings proves bland and sickens his tongue, where shall he go?

Change is the nature of man, and change is what makes him strong. Time the material substance, to be kneaded and slapped, gouged and twisted . . . into what? And how fast? Build something, and build again. Never stop, never rest, just build, build and brood. Turn it over, look at it through the sharpest lens, hold it to the brightest light. There will always be rises and small holes and cracks where the weeds grow through. It is what we are. Change is the nature of man.

Tom McIlweath leaned against his tree and the night sank down from the low clouds. There were no sounds—no cars, no birds, no breeze rustling the trees. A still, slow, low, dead night. He thought:

'I have come here to remake myself. And I have done so, better and more completely than I had ever imagined. But what is this gnawing in my stomach and down my legs? What is this echo deep inside me that I hear only on nights such as this? This is not what I thought it would be. This is not it at all. And so where do I go now? And with whom? Now that I have determined myself as I want to be, what do I do if I find it still hollow? Where do I go?

'Must I be redeemed again, and if so, where lies redemption, and by whose hand? What is this deep rat-like gnawing, what is this echo? Why do restlessness and discontent rise within me like the surf, gentle and small at first but ever more powerful as it rides in?'

> *I am thy father's spirit,*
> *Doomed for a certain term to walk the night. . .*

> —Shakespeare, *Hamlet, Act I, Scene 1*

Ghosts stirred in the buildings and the trees, the ancient ghosts of two hundred years of young men consigned to burn in the devouring flames of youth itself. Through the mall they paced, lending their shadows to the grass and walls, brooding in sullen formlessness. They had come out at dusk to walk for a while, and there were thousands of them. They dwelt here now, at the root of their eternal discontent, at the place where all doors had been thrown open to them and, by entering one, all had been closed.

They came upon Tom McIlweath and formed a circle around his tree, although he could not see them. They stood there then in the gathering darkness and regarded him with the blank, expressionless, masklike faces of those from whom all life, all promise, all expectation had been drained.

Brother, you shall not die. You shall never die. But Brother, neither shall you live. Poor haunted soul of man.

Tom McIlweath rose from his spot, the back of his jeans damp from the soggy ground. He walked slowly out of the mall toward College Avenue. Lights from the fraternity houses across the street broke the darkness while adding to the gloom. Seeking either serenity or self-conclusion, he had found neither. Whatever it was that lay within him was still there, and his acknowledgement of it only made it stronger. There was nothing he could do.

* * *

Anne Newbury continued to train hard, aiming for the weekend in late July when the nationals would determine her selection. She seldom saw McIlweath, who grew reconciled to his subsidiary role. He looked forward to when it would all be over, and counted the days.

The nationals were to be held in Philadelphia, at the University of Pennsylvania, close enough for McIlweath to accompany Anne and her family on the drive down. Three days before the meet, though, Anne said, "I don't want you to come with me, Tom. I don't want you to watch me."

"But Anne, why not?"

"I don't need that pressure, too. I wouldn't feel comfortable with you watching me, and judging me."

"I won't drive down with you, then. I can drive down separately and see you after the meet. You won't even know I'm there."

"I'll know, Tom. Don't go."

And so he didn't. He did, though, exact a promise from Anne that she call him as soon as she could after her heats. The preliminaries were scheduled for Friday night, the finals for Saturday.

The Newburys drove to Philadelphia Thursday morning. McIlweath wished he had some token of luck to give Anne before she left, but he could think of nothing. He rarely put any stock in such trinkets, although now he wanted her to have some physical reminder of him. He had driven to the Newbury house to see them off. While Dr. Newbury loaded the car, Tom pulled Anne to the side.

"You'll do fine, Anne. You've worked too hard not to."

"I hope so, Tom. I hope I've worked hard enough. You've been good not to be too demanding. I want you to know I appreciate it."

"Will you make it up to me?" he asked with a smile.

"No," answered Anne, unsmiling. "I did this for me. You did what you did and I'm grateful, that's all."

Anne's father threw the last suitcase into the trunk. "Anytime you're ready we can get going," he called.

"In a minute, Daddy," she responded, then turned back to McIlweath. "I've got to go, Tom. Thank you for seeing me off."

"I wish I could see you swim."

"You know how I feel, Tom."

"I know. Call me, then."

"Tomorrow night, after my heat."

"And Saturday after the finals."

"If I make it."

"You'll make it, Anne. I have every confidence." He kissed her cheek. "Good luck."

"I'll see you Sunday," and she was gone.

McIlweath stayed in Friday night waiting for Anne's call. Her heat was slated for 7:45 or so. The other heats in her event were immediately before and after. He figured that Anne would know whether she qualified for the finals by 8:15 at the latest. He expected her call by 8:30. Lanny O'Hanlon had stayed in Trenton for dinner and drinks that night, so McIlweath was forced to wait alone. He preferred it that way. He turned on an old movie on the television, sat down in his chair by the window and watched the clock.

7:30 . . . She'd be in the locker room now, and her parents would be flipping through their programs and nervously watching for Anne to come out. 7:37 . . . Anne would probably be in the warm-up pool loosening her muscles and watering her skin. She might catch a glimpse of the finishing heat. That was good; she'd know what she had to beat. 7:42 . . . She'd be pacing in the bench area, or perhaps sitting down, staring at the tile, trying to compose herself. 7:44 . . . Called to the pool, her lane assignment confirmed, she would snap her arms to keep them loose and take deep breaths to fill her lungs. 7:45 . . . Up top now—'Take your marks'—then the slapping bolt of the gun, and arching herself into the water. Stroking, kicking, breathing, pulling. McIlweath tensed vicariously at the appointed moment; he clenched his fists. God, why couldn't he be there? The culmination of everything she had sacrificed, and he, too. Right now, sitting in this hot, steamy room, far removed from it all, made no sense. If he had had the power, McIlweath would have lent Anne every ounce of his own strength to see her through.

But she would not need it, he reasoned. Anne had never been denied her goals. She wanted this as much as anything she had ever sought, and she had the peculiar talent to drive herself absolutely as hard as she needed to achieve what she wanted. The very force of Anne's character would pull her through this race faster than she had ever gone before. McIlweath was sure of it. To imagine Anne failing at something she truly and deeply desired was to imagine a grotesquery, as if she had lost an eye or suddenly developed a humped back. Still, he wanted to be there, to see these lost weeks finally bear fruit worth tasting.

7:48 . . . The race would be over now, if indeed it had gone off on schedule. Anne's fate, whether she would make the finals, the results of her training, all of it now coming to decision. All he could do was wait to learn how it had been put together.

And McIlweath did wait, twisting in his chair, watching first the movie, then the park across the street, then the movie once again. He kept clenching and unclenching his fists. At 8:15 he walked to the kitchen and, resting his hands against the counter, looked out the back window for a few minutes. At 8:20 he walked back to the living room. The call, he reasoned, would be any second. His ears anticipated the ringing. He stared at the phone.

By 8:30 his agitation heightened to all new levels. He paced the length of the hallway, back and forth. At one point he even stood at the corner where the hallway met the living room and put his hand on the phone as if to draw energy from it, or perhaps to feel its presence, feel its reality.

He paced, then paced some more. "Come on, Anne." He said aloud more than once. Each time he passed the phone he grew more urgent. "Damn it, come on."

But no call came. By 9:00 he started to wonder about his imagined timetable. Perhaps she had not had the opportunity to get to a phone as quickly as he thought she would. Or perhaps her heat had been delayed. That sometimes happened. Perhaps she had not even swum yet, and here he was getting all upset. He would sit down and try to relax. There must be a good reason for her not calling.

He sat, but he did not relax. He tried watching television again, but that did not distract him, so he turned on his music. Nothing worked, and no word from Anne. By 10:00 he was pacing again.

McIlweath had not gotten the name of the inn where they were staying. He cursed himself for his carelessness. It *must* be over by now. The clock said 10:17. Heats in all events were scheduled only through 9:30.

What's done is done, but there was no way to find out exactly what that was. McIlweath felt abjectly frustrated. By midnight he had resigned himself to the fact that there would be no call tonight. Something must have happened, he reasoned, either exceptionally bad or exceptionally good. His confidence in the order of things shaken, he had no idea which was more likely. McIlweath's entire weight had sunk through him to his ankles. Few moods are emptier than misspent anxiety. He would have no answers tonight, and, if not tonight, then possibly not tomorrow either. He felt robbed, and twist of resentment spiced his considerations. Why hadn't she called?

McIlweath crawled into bed at 1:30. He did not pull up any covers because it was another hot night. At 1:45 he heard Lanny O'Hanlon come up the stairs. O'Hanlon walked down the hall to the bathroom, then a few seconds later back to the other bedroom. He heard him throw his coat and tie onto his roommate's vacant bed, then flop down onto his own.

Where was Conor Finnegan this evening, and what was he doing? Tom McIlweath felt like talking to someone.

The next morning, Saturday, as McIlweath sat at the kitchen table eating his breakfast, O'Hanlon, hair disheveled and wearing only shorts, stumbled into the room in search of food. "Morning, Mac."

"Rough night, Lanny? You look shot."

"A few lagers with the boys from the attorney general's office. Maybe more than a few. I need eggs," and he pulled a frying pan from a compartment beneath the stove.

"I heard you come in. You weren't very late."

"Not by normal standards." O'Hanlon took a carton of eggs from the refrigerator and broke four of them into the ungreased pan. "But we'd been drinking since about 6:00. We went out right after work. Christ, I can't even remember if I ate anything. I'm starved."

McIlweath finished his cereal and got up to put the bowl into the sink. He poured a tall glass of orange juice.

"You want some of these?" asked O'Hanlon.

"No, thanks. You look like you need them far more than I do."

O'Hanlon stood over the stove stirring his eggs with a fork. McIlweath went into his room and got dressed. When he returned O'Hanlon was sitting at the table devouring eggs and toast.

"How'd Aqualass do last night? You haven't told me yet."

"That's because I don't know."

"Didn't she call you?"

"No. No word. Something must have come up."

"Right." O'Hanlon looked up from his plate with wry eyes. "You expect she'll deign to call you today?"

"I don't expect anything. She'll do what she wants to do."

"Do I detect a note of bitterness, pal?"

"Not at all. She doesn't owe me anything."

O'Hanlon took another bite and shook his head slowly, his thin lips curling into the hint of an amused smile. "Mac, after all your attentions she owes you big. Out of common human decency, if nothing else. She's turning you into a God damn lap dog."

"You're wrong, Lanny, but I don't want to get into it. I do things for her, she does things for me. You don't see all of it."

"You're a big boy, Mac. You know what's best. Just don't let her rape you, though."

"Rape me? She's not that type of girl," replied McIlweath with a forced laugh.

"That's not what I'm talking about, friend. I don't mean physical, for God's sake. But the other kind . . . Jesus, they're all that type. We might have the power to violate them physically, but they do other things to us that are just as bad. Maybe worse. And when they're done with you, you'll never be the same. You've been violated, only maybe you don't know it, and she walks away with a part of you you'll never regain. Before you even feel it she's used you, and she's gratified herself in a way you'll probably never understand. You cater to her, you do everything she wants even before she asks for it, you throw yourself on the floor so her God damned feet don't have to touch the soiled earth beneath her. That's conquest, Mac, not love. I've yet to meet a woman who won't take advantage of that if it's offered, and you're offering it daily. It's an act of violence. And when she's had enough, after she's had her fill of what you have to offer, then she's gone, and you sit behind with a hole poked in you that'll never grow back."

"And you're just warning me?"

"I'm just warning you. I've seen it happen too often. I see it happening now."

"I know what I'm doing, Lanny, okay? I know Anne, and I don't need any warning. Especially one as cynical as that."

"Sorry, pal. No offense intended."

"Are you going to be around today?"

"I thought I'd drive down to the shore and see Rosselli. You want to come along?"

"No thanks. I think I'll stay close to home today. Do some reading, maybe."

O'Hanlon put his empty plate in the sink. He turned on the tap to shoot a spray of water over it, then turned out of the room and down the hall. "I'll give him your regards. But I think a day at the beach might do you some good."

"Right. I don't get enough sun and water as it is. I'll pass."

Lanny O'Hanlon left an hour later. Tom McIlweath had, in the meantime, run down to the corner store to get the *Times*. He was halfway through it when O'Hanlon opened the door to leave. "I may not be back tonight, Mac. Depends on what we do."

"Or how you do, girls on the beach being what they are. I won't count on you."

"See you later." The door shut, a graphic division between the cavalier and the contemplative. McIlweath settled back into his chair and finished the *Times* in hollow, echoing, measured and measurable silence.

He did nothing with his day. There was nothing he could do. Tom McIlweath found he could not function with the unknown. His dissatisfied curiosity dominated him completely. After so many weeks of preparation, after focusing on this event mentally and emotionally as much as Anne had done physically, McIlweath felt cheated by having to wait for his culmination several hours after Anne had met hers. If nothing else, it felt like a breach of loyalty. His emotions ranged from frustration to anger to pity to fear, but he was in no condition to reflect upon that odd composition. He could only wait.

Near 6:00 that evening it came. The phone rang at last, and McIlweath bolted across the living room before the echo of its first bell had subsided.

"Hello?"

"Hi, Tom. It's Anne." A sullen and distant voice mouthed plastic words. At once, the secret was out.

"Anne, where are you? What happened?"

"I'm home, Tom. We came home this morning."

"You didn't make it. I'm so sorry."

"No. I didn't come close." Anne's voice plodded through the line. It was an effort for her to speak at all, a labor she obviously would have preferred to skip.

McIlweath pressed forward gingerly. "Tell me what happened."

"I finished third in my heat. I was never in it, Tom. I was so tight and I couldn't breathe. I started out slow, then I panicked and lost my pace altogether. Maybe I overtrained, I don't know. Or maybe I just choked. I was more nervous before that race than I'd ever been." She told McIlweath her time, and he knew it to be a half second slower than her best.

"Maybe we just put too much into this, Anne. We never relaxed."

"There was no other way to do it."

"Do you want some company tonight? I could come over, we could talk. You might feel a bit better."

"Nothing could do that, Tom. I'm tired and I'm depressed and I let everybody down. I just want to go to bed."

"If that's what you want."

"It is. Call me tomorrow, in the afternoon. Maybe I'll tell you the whole story then. There were some good races. Mine just wasn't one of them."

"I'm sorry, Anne. You know I thought you'd make it."

"Then we were both fools. I'll talk to you tomorrow."

McIlweath went to the kitchen for something to eat. He knew, of course, why Anne had not called earlier. He could imagine her state after her heat. She finished third, so she would have had to wait a short while to see if her time might have been fast enough to qualify for the finals. If they ran four heats, they'd take the winners plus the next four fastest. But with the time she swam, she must have known there'd be no chance. She must have been absolutely miserable. He imagined that she might even have broken down and shed useless tears.

He felt disappointed, but less upset than he should have. His first reaction was relief in finally knowing Anne's fate. The jumbled mix of emotions he had felt before her call vanished at once, and he now regarded that blue funk distantly.

McIlweath fixed a sandwich and returned to the living room. He turned on the evening news. For the first time in two days, he felt the urge to do something. Anything, it didn't matter. He wanted to be with people, and get out of this apartment.

After finishing his sandwich he called an acquaintance he knew from the club. They arranged to go to a movie in Princeton. McIlweath drove, and they rode down with the windows open. The wind sweeping across McIlweath's face cooled him, and he breathed deeply, relieved to be able to breathe anything at all.

CHAPTER XII

*I am part of the sun as my eye is part of me. That I am part
of the earth my feet know perfectly, and my blood is part of
the sea. My soul knows that I am part of the human race,
my soul is an organic part of my nation. In my very self, I
am part of my family.*

—D.H. Lawrence, *Apocalypse*

Conor Finnegan drank down the last draughts of his days in Washington with the slow, savoring relish a gourmand reserves for his finest dishes. Classes resumed in early September, the final classes of his final college year. He would be leaving soon. Finnegan thought of the places that had defined this remarkable summer, the sites he had visited with Glynnis, the monuments and memorials, the restaurants, the parks where they had walked to escape Washington's smothering heat and find some green space.

The site of deepest meaning remained Conor's upstairs bedroom. That Conor and Glynnis returned to it every week, reenacting and expanding their initial act, using that same bed to explore new levels of a tender sensuality, deepened their sense of passage. In the evenings they would climb the stairs quietly, hand in hand, saying nothing. Afterward, in the panting decline of their passion, they would strip away all defenses, all pretenses, lying there together as exposed emotionally as they were physically. A reverence crept over them. Conor, a Catholic who had somehow escaped any strong notions of guilt, vaguely equated what he felt in these moments with a deep spirituality. The warming quietude, the sensation of peace, the conviction of universal acceptance reminded him of what he often felt at the end of Mass.

Even during the week, when Glynnis was miles away, Finnegan regarded his room not as his alone, but as Glynnis's too. He kept it neat and made the bed daily, things he had never done at college.

In late August, during the last week, came a series of days cool and dry. The breeze blew not from the south but from the northwest, launched from Canada, the humidity lifted, the sky rose to a rich opaline blue. Summer for a while had broken and crisp autumn appeared for the first time at a distance, far off still but present and beckoning. The autumn mood snapped Finnegan into a deeper contemplation. He acknowledged the graphic passage of time, for when the sultry swelter returned again to this city he would be well north of here, adopting another, more basic persona. Autumn in any form, with its penetrating winds, brightly dying leaves and smoky haze, moved him to introspection. Premature autumn in a place far away thrust him violently into self-account. He was not displeased.

One evening, a Thursday, Finnegan went for dinner at a restaurant with sidewalk tables, a place where he and Glynnis had sometimes gone for a simple meal. He was alone, but he had long since rid himself of the awkwardness dining alone in a public place could instill. He could afford to do it now and then. It was a platform from which he could look down and around, or, if the mood was right, he could be alone and think. Finnegan took a small table under the awning on the sidewalk. Although the evening carried a slight chill, it was still pleasant enough to be outside. A couple sat several tables removed from him near the white railing that surrounded the patio. They were the only ones there.

Finnegan ordered a scotch and, when the server returned with his drink, a modest dinner. He had come directly from his office, hopping off the bus a few stops early then walking northward the seven or eight blocks to the restaurant. He carried his *Post* under his arm. To all the world he looked the part of the young and rising government executive.

He mused as he sipped his scotch. Washington, with its stolid marble hallways of power, its illusion of influence, its cultural and social glitter, its southern gentility, its northern ruthlessness, its legends and its glories, had seduced Conor Finnegan thoroughly. He had expected this in part so he was not completely surprised. Perhaps he had even created a self-fulfilling prophecy. But no matter. What's done is done. This was where he wanted to be.

Finnegan reviewed the life he had led these past few months. He marveled, truly marveled, at his successes. He had maneuvered himself onto a Senate staff, a position of service reserved for only a handful, and he had worked in areas that fascinated his young mind, that placed him on the near periphery of issues impacting the tenor of national life. He had written speeches on the conflicts in the Middle East, drafted legislation on Medicare, given talks before community groups. Government, he had seen, could be more than ennui and red tape. It could work, albeit slowly and reluctantly, and it could work in the interests of good people. He, Conor Finnegan, might be able in his own way and to the limits of his diverse abilities help make it work. There was a role he could fill, and now, with some experience behind him, he might fill it a little better. The thought that he could come to this realization, and come to it at so young an age, made him giddy. This indeed was where he wanted to be. There was no place else.

When the senator had first interviewed him two and a half years ago, he had asked Finnegan what he wanted to do with his life. Finnegan recalled now that whole nervous scene and his pretentious answer, "Some good." He blushed at the recollection. What must the senator have thought then in hearing Finnegan's naiveté spread out before him in just two words? But he had hired him anyway, perhaps because he had had to. The senator might conceivably have thought that a few laps around the track would knock Finnegan's idealism into a more realistic context, and teach him that the goal of one's life should not be to do some good with it, but to survive it.

And Finnegan had taken some knocks, that he could not deny. He recalled the aspiring congressman two years ago in Los Angeles who had offered him a large donation to the senator's war chest if he were included in a round of hearings for which Finnegan was coordinating presenters. He recalled times this summer when, tired and frustrated, the senator would utter a racial or ethnic slur. And he regarded a colleague who had jumped staffs to a senator across the aisle, one whose politics were on the opposite end of the spectrum, for a marginally higher salary. But politics reflected humanity in all its forms, the most noble as well as the most ignoble, the selfless and the self-serving.

He knew that power was a seductive allure and that some men and women would do anything to maintain their grip on it, regardless of the cost in human terms. They sought power for its own sake, and saw no need to consider the ends for which it might be used. These people were truly dangerous, and they could be found in every government corridor, of that he was certain. Yet their prevalence, their willingness to trample any cause or any human need for the sake of a vote, compelled Finnegan to cling tightly to his own idealism. He thought of the old politicians in the late nineteenth century who sought to break the labor unions, and who catered to every exploitive whim of the business sector because that was where the money was, and he thought of the Jim Crow politicians of the twentieth century South who disowned an entire race. They had their analogies today, and the motivation remained the same: power. What's mine shall remain mine, and what's yours might end up being mine as well.

Yet despite this realization (or perhaps because of it) Finnegan believed that his own brief stint of government service had yielded some positive results. He had thrown himself headlong into the issues assigned him. He had read everything he could find on the topics that interested him; he spoke to anyone who might know something he didn't. The senator had wanted Conor to work with the elderly, to serve as the liaison with the great national organizations that represented that demographic. He had done so, but he had not stopped at the level of those slick, highly paid lobbyists who hung around the office corridors. Finnegan might have been sympathetic to their causes, but they were not the people who captured those sympathies or who designed those causes. Finnegan wanted to see and hear the problems of the aged firsthand. He toured nursing homes, mostly under the watch of defensive administrators, although often he would break away to find some lucid patients who wanted to talk with him. Then he would sit by their beds or their wheelchairs for long stretches of time listening to their reminiscences and hearing their complaints. Their eyes haunted him. Their eyes carried age, and wisdom, and sometimes almost unbearable pain and loneliness. He had been moved to tears by one old woman, bedridden, with whom he had sat and chatted for nearly an hour. When he rose to leave, her bony birdlike hand clasped Finnegan's forearm and tears filled her imploring eyes.

"You're the only visitor I've had in months. Christmas, no, not even then.; don't go. Or come back. Please tell me you'll come back," and her crackling, brittle voice faded into the conclusion that this human contact had been too brief, and would not come again. Finnegan sat in his car in the parking lot and bent his head to the steering wheel. His own tears answered those of the specter he had just left, for he knew that he could not return. This lovely lady, intelligent, warm, struggling to recapture a long dead vivacity, struggling to revert to a humanity she had long ago taken for granted, would most likely die in her hated, bitter loneliness, an orphan, homeless at her passing.

Still, Finnegan knew that the institutionalized elderly presented only one aspect of the process of aging. To find another point of view, he dropped in on community centers and social clubs. There, too, he would start conversations with strangers, most of whom warmed to him at once. Conor listened far more than he spoke. He let his new acquaintances ramble on if they wanted, speaking about their families, where they lived, what they had done before they retired. He saw more pictures of grandchildren than he cared to remember. He inferred from his contact with these people that they greatly feared a world passing them by. They feared being considered dead before their time. They feared not being taken seriously, or, worse, being patronized. They did not care about national or international events nearly as much as they cared about companionship. Most of all, they feared exile to a place where they could be "cared for," and in that care, smothered by neglect.

Finnegan came to regard his work with these people as an expression of his own human symbiosis. *We had drawn from them; now we need to give back.* He constantly suggested new approaches to legislation addressing housing inequities, adjusting Medicare rates, providing transportation discounts, encouraging volunteer projects. Every call the office received from an elderly voice automatically found its way to Finnegan, who dove into the problems with a determined commitment not to fail them. If the voice needed help with government red tape, Finnegan would cut it for him; it if wanted information on a particular bill, Finnegan would discuss it at length; if it merely wanted to get something off its chest, Finnegan would listen sympathetically. He became passionately committed to this group, *his* group, *his* constituents, and wanted to serve them in their peculiar condition as best he could.

As the summer wound to its close, then, Finnegan found himself inspired not only by the glamor of government work—the respect, the sensation of power—but also by the conviction that he could in fact serve the human condition. He could, indeed, do "some good." It was what he had expected thirty months ago when he first considered government work. Now the realization of those old expectations was sweet and rich and clear.

As Finnegan sat at his table, watching the traffic pass, watching the sun go low and sipping his scotch, he knew that his old plans would no longer work as he had constructed them. There would be no law school, at least, not at once. After he received his degree next June he would come back to Washington and pick up where he was leaving off. The senator had told him that the job would be there for him. There was no way he could turn it down. After seeing so completely how fulfilling, how purposeful, how gratifying this lifestyle could be, he would have been a fool to consider anything different.

And what of Glynnis? She had been present through this wonderful and quick evolution. She had shared the best parts of this life. Conor did not know what Glynnis's plans were, for this would be her final year of college, too. She didn't know herself. But Conor presumed that they could work something out and that, if they did it right, they could be together. He knew that this glorious life would lose much of its allure if Glynnis were not part of it.

Dinner came, and Finnegan started it with deliberate, measured motions. The scotch had slowed him down. At the same time he believed it sharpened his thoughts and quickened his perceptions. The street seemed clearer to him, the few pedestrians more animated.

Again, Glynnis. There was not a day when he did not think of her, and once more a wonderment crept over him that such a remote series of accidents had brought them together. He could define in logical terms her attraction for him—her intelligence, her self-reliance, her deprecating wit, her quiet poise and grace, her rare physical beauty— but there was no romance in that. He could have described a house cat the same way.

Instead he preferred to refer to snapshot images and the sentiments that came with them. He saw her in the Virginia hills with the scent of rain sneaking toward them. He saw her over dinner one night speaking of her family with a horrible tone of remorse. He remembered his first glimpse of her and how she stood out so remarkably at the art museum that morning last spring. He saw the affectionate, respectful smile in her eyes as he told her about his job, what he had done, whom he had met and how much it all meant to him. And he saw her beneath him or above him in their wide bed, naked and warm, the soft press of human flesh, and he noted the lost, faraway expression on her face as they made love, a rapture for them both, taking them back to some protected secret place long forgotten except by an aroused subconscious.

There were, of course, countless images that Finnegan carried. Glynnis was to him a mosaic, intricately crafted, the compendium of all human emotion and promise. She intoxicated him, and by her love, confirmed his worth. She had become as necessary for Conor as hope itself.

While Conor dwelt on both Glynnis and the meal before him, the couple who had also been on the outside patio paid their bill and left. Only a few people were on the street. This part of the city had relatively little social life to draw a night crowd. The restaurant stood near the end of the commercial section of the street, and the area in general was largely residential.

At one point, toward the end of his meal something caught his eye. He looked up to see an old man, shoddy from head to toe, standing on the sidewalk just beyond the white railing. He wore a threadbare faded sport coat that was once a gray pattern. Beneath it he had only a polo shirt, dirty-white, a hole on the left side slightly above the heart. His pants no longer fit. They hung on him like dusty wrapping paper. On his feet he wore large hard brown shoes.

The old man looked to be about sixty or so, maybe older. Maybe younger. He had not shaved for a while, and a grizzled, bristly gray-black growth spotted his cheeks and chin. His lips were thin, his cheeks hollow. He had shrunk within his clothes, wasting to a smaller and smaller form, and soon he would diminish altogether, disembodied for all time through sheer want.

The old man was watching him eat. Finnegan could not tell how long he had been there. He had seemed to materialize in a blink, an emanation from the concrete under his feet. The specter's eyes grabbed Finnegan's, and held them. Finnegan at once harkened back to the tearful lady in the nursing home. It stunned him; a nervous jolt shot out of his chest and down his legs.

Silent there on the sidewalk, the old man did not move. He simply stood and stared. Finnegan, totally disarmed, looked back. They stared at each other for no more than a handful of seconds, but for Finnegan all time had stopped.

Hear now this, O foolish people and without understanding;
Which have eyes and see not; which have ears and hear not.

— Jeremiah, 5:21

"You look at me, boy, as if I'm not like you."

Finnegan had no words to answer him. He continued to look hard at the old man. His eyes had been drawn to something immovable and timeless. The old man croaked his words in a crackly, tinny voice.

"I said, you look at me as if I'm not like you. A hungry traveler, no more, no less. I'd ask you for some of that food if I thought you'd give it. But that don't matter. To you or to me. I'll eat all right, but I'll eat a different food that suits me fine."

The phantom moved a few steps down the sidewalk. He continued to regard Finnegan, with whom he was almost now directly face to face.

"You're a good boy, probably, but that won't do you no good. You got to be bad to keep up. You got to be bad to keep from gettin' hungry," and he laughed. "Bad man to get good food. Don't make no sense. But I know where I'm sleepin' tonight, and the night after, and the night after that. I know where I'll be ten years from now, boy. Do you? I know where I'll be lyin'. Ain't no trick to stayin' alive, boy. Anybody can do that. The trick is knowin' when you had enough." He chuckled again and moved on a few more steps. No one else was around.

"You ain't no different, boy. A hungry traveler, just like me. Take a good look. Take a real good look. I'm your God damn daddy."

The old man turned fully away from Finnegan and headed down the street in a stumbling shuffle.

Finnegan's appetite died away. His legs and arms pulsed with the start the old man had given him. There had been no scent of alcohol on him, none of the dank, stale odor that permeated the street people. Where he had come from and where he would go were complete mysteries. The old man had been as out of place in the casual elegance of this section of the city as an Eskimo in the desert. Finnegan thought back to the early chapters of *Moby Dick*, Elijah collaring Ishmael and Queequeg. "Shipmates, have ye shipped in that ship? Anything down there about your souls?"

He pushed his plate away, grateful that he had finished most of his meal. When the server came he paid the check and walked down the street toward New Hampshire Avenue. Normally he would have taken a bus but the evening cool refreshed him. It was what he needed, and he wanted to walk.

By the time he got to the circle, his reflective mood had returned to its original terms, the ones he had set for it as he had sipped his scotch. The old man had disappeared. Finnegan did not think further of him this evening, and, when he recalled the incident in the days ahead, he found he was able to dismiss him as a half-crazy, disoriented derelict, an isolated peculiar event in a summer heretofore remarkable in its harmony.

* * *

The house stood dark and cool, silent except for the ticking of the great clock downstairs in the entryway. It could be heard even on the floor above, its softly thudding, regular tick muffled there in the darkness, the heartbeat first heard in the womb, before time itself.

The lightest of breezes moved the tall trees outside just enough to create a rhythmic swishing that would have muted any night noise rising from the street—a neighbor walking his dog, a car passing, a party down the way. The unheated, unhurried winds of New England had snuffed out the day's candle. The night came quickly, insulated and tranquilized, the security of the dormant years implicit in its whispers and its rhythms.

Glynnis Mear stretched out in her bed in the cool New England darkness. She had come home for the first and only time this summer, here, at its end, when delay was no longer possible. In the next bed Martha rolled restlessly to her side. She was unused to having her sister with her, and so could not sleep.

"Glynnis, are you awake?" she whispered.

"Yes. I can't sleep either."

"Talk to me, Glyn. Okay?"

"If you want."

"I never see you anymore, Glynnis. I never get to talk to you."

"What do you want to talk about? Any deep, dark secrets you care to share with your older and much wiser sister?"

"Remember how we used to talk ourselves to sleep? Every night. God, that was so great, to know you'd be here in the next bed. I always felt so safe when you were here."

"We get older, Martha. We grow up, and some of us have to go away."

"I know. I think I want to go, too. I want to go away to college, just like you did. I want to get out on my own. I can't wait, sometimes."

"You won't go away just like I did, Martha. You won't be turning your back on anything. You'll just be going, and that's so much better. But what's wrong? Why do you want to leave?"

"Glynnis, there's so much I haven't seen. I know how trite that sounds, but it's true. I've lived in Boston all my life, with the same people, the same friends, doing the same things. And then I see you go off on your own, for whatever reason. To this day, Glyn, I don't know what it was you were running from even though you were running so hard. After Daddy died you got so distant. Don't worry, you don't have to explain anything. I know you love us and all that, and what you feel is your business. That's not the point. It's just that you seem to be doing so well and to be so happy now. I admire that so much, Glyn. I suppose I've never been more aware of the fact that you're older than me until the last few months. You've grown up and you've grown away. You seem so assured now, so confident. I think that's wonderful.

"Remember when we were little kids," she continued, "and you tried to teach me to swim in the ocean? We were up in Maine and I was scared to death. But you dove right through the surf and splashed around offshore, even as cold as it was there. You yelled back, 'If I can do this, so can you. We're made of the same blood,' then you slogged in and grabbed me by the arm. I can still remember how cold your hand was when you grabbed me. Then you pulled me into the waves, and I was kicking you and slapping you and crying. But it was all right, you know? It was cold, and the waves knocked me around, but it was all right. And after that I used to look forward to going back to the ocean, and I'd strut right up to the surf and march right into it like it was mine alone. I'll never forget that, Glynnis. 'If I can do this, so can you. We're made of the same blood.'

"You've gained so much by what you did, Glyn. I can see it in every part of you. I'm envious, and I want to catch up."

"Maybe you're just seeing illusions, Martha. Maybe you see what isn't really there because you see me so seldom now."

"No, Glyn. You're my sister. I know every inch of you. You want to know something? When you told me you were going off to school, I thought, 'She'll never make it without someone to look after her. She'll be back to stay inside a year.' I just didn't think you were tough enough, or that you could stand up for yourself. I thought people would walk all over you. Or through you. I didn't think you'd know what to do or how to get along with the different types of people you were bound to meet. And I thought you'd miss us terribly since we were everything you'd ever known. You surprised me, though. The first time you came home you acted like a visitor, like you really felt you belonged somewhere else. It's as if you grew up all at once, and that flustered, naïve girl who grew up ahead of me was gone. I saw it so clearly, Glyn, and I was so impressed by my new sister that I began to want some part of that for myself. And I do want it, more than ever. I've got to go away, Glynnis. I've got to see if I can do what you did."

"If I can do it, Martha, so can you. We're made of the same blood."

Martha rolled to her back and laughed. "God, it feel so great to talk to you again. I miss you, Glynnis."

"I'm still your sister. You know where I am and how to get in touch. A phone call now and then might do us both some good."

"It's not the same as lying here together, though. Besides, you've got someone else to bare your soul to. And you've told me nothing about him."

"He's a friend, Martha."

"Don't whitewash me, big sister. He's more than a friend. I can tell by that stupid romantic twinkle in your eyes. Sometimes you act as if you're not even on the same planet as the rest of us. You spend a lot of time with him, don't you? And even now you're thinking of him almost constantly. Now, come clean. What does he look like? Do you have a picture?"

"I do, but you won't see it. He's tall, about six foot one. Strong build. He's not thin but he's not overweight. He has broad shoulders and a hard flat stomach. Brown hair long enough to touch the back of his collar. A cute little round nose, a strong chin, a full and fleshy face. He's not gorgeous, Martha, but he's far from unattractive. It's his eyes that drew me first. Soft, large, deep, brown, dancing eyes. Oh, Martha, his eyes fix on you and ask you in, and how can I say no? I think he's beautiful."

"Not handsome?"

"No. Beautiful. Attractive with a hint of delicacy. I'm sure he bruises easily and it shows in his face. He opens himself so very quickly, and he expects you to like him. At least he's hopeful you will. He's hopeful for mankind itself, and that makes him delicate. I think we're a species beyond hope."

"Conor's his name, right?"

"Conor Finnegan."

"Oh God, a pure Mick. Dad would be pleased."

"Conor and Daddy would have gotten along famously. Conor's Irish to the core. I tease him about being a Romantic Irish poet, but Martha, if he had lived in the Middle Ages he'd have been a troubadour, roaming from town to town singing sad songs. He talks so sweetly, and sometimes he quotes me poetry."

"He's in Washington working for a senator. That doesn't sound too poetic, Glyn."

"That's why I worry about him. He *is* Romantic. He loves humanity and he loves his God and he wants to be of service to both. He thinks he can do that—help the poor, feed the hungry, end wars. He can be so trusting at times. He's bound to get hurt, and hurt badly. Someday he'll have the realization that mankind can be brutal and selfish and ruthless and God knows what else. It'll be beaten right into him. He's still a little boy in some ways, Martha. An innocent, loving little boy."

"Glynnis, your little boy sounds marvelous."

"He's from California, you know."

"You're kidding? What's he doing here? I just assumed he was from somewhere east."

"He came east to go to college. That's the Romantic in him. A lust for different places. He's said he wants to see humanity in as many forms as possible. He wants to set his own spirit independently so that he alone will be responsible for his success or failure. He's explained that to me several times. I think he might actually believe it."

"I think I'd like him, Glynnis. We seem to have something in common. I suppose I can be as envious of him as I am of you."

Glynnis paused now. She would not disclose Conor, to Martha or anyone else, in greater detail than was necessary for the moment. Conor was hers, part of her new self, an element in what she perceived as her emergence.

"Girl talk now," whispered Martha. "Do you love him?"

But of some things Glynnis need not be protective. Of some things she could be proud. "Yes. Yes, I love him."

"Have you slept with him?"

"Martha! There are some things that are off limits even for my darling sister. I won't tell you that!"

"You don't have to, Glyn. I have my answer. I had my answer even before I asked."

"Let's go to sleep, kid sister. This is going down dangerous paths."

"Good night, Glynnis. And I am envious of you. More than I ever have been."

The New England breezes had not intensified. The trees still swished softly; the old house creaked from time to time in weary protest against even the gentlest buffets of time and age. Downstairs the great clock ticked its thudding tick with a regularity that might defy the end of time itself or lead the morose to think of death, to think of the steady, stealthy, onward creep of man's timeless and haunting agony.

Glynnis Mear rolled to her back and pulled the light blanket to her lovely chin. Summer was at its stub end; the air had grown chill disproportionately early.

> *For now I should have lain still and been quiet, I should*
> *have slept; then had I been at rest, With kings and counselors*
> *of the earth, which built desolate places for themselves.*

> Job 3:13-14

The next day Glynnis and her mother went shopping through the crowded, cluttered, amorphous stores of downtown Boston. The day rose uncommonly cool for late August. The crispness of the air, blown over the harbor and carrying a hint of salt, of the faraway places, of the grandeur, spice and adventure of seaborne distances, put the city in good humor. The throngs pushing through the stores, usually impatient and grabby, moved in harmonious tolerance of one another. There were no arguments, no clogs, no delays. It was a spirit that descended on those rare serendipitous days when people are surprised by the clean, sweet, infinite exhilaration of life itself.

Glynnis shared in it fully. Browsing through the downtown stores with her mother, looking for nothing at all and so wanting to look at everything, she perceived at last a serenity that had been too rare since the death of her father. She abandoned for moment the twisting, wrenching pangs of divided passions; she saw no distortions, no grotesqueries in the life risen around her. She regarded her mother at once with a depthless well of affection, the force of which overwhelmed her and thereby weakened her. She saw her mother walk through the housewares section of an elegant department store and evaluate a lamp with her typically simple gestures—a gentle lifting of her head to rate the solidity of the base, her long fingers barely touching the cool metal when turning the price tag over and back. She walked delicately around the table on which it stood, her steps so light that they seemed ethereal, only the balls of her small feet touching the carpeted ground, her expression slightly quizzical but confident that whatever decision she might make regarding this object would be the correct one.

For Glynnis, watching her mother a few steps away, these simple movements summarized the boundless, piercing, self-abandoned love with which the woman had tried so passionately to collect the family after Robert Mear had passed, with which she had dressed every wound, dried every tear, given every gift, fixed every meal, and said every nighttime prayer to her children growing up, that defined the grace and beauty and soul of Florence Mear. When her mother returned and they resumed their walk through the store, Glynnis held her hand.

They shopped in the bright morning, then had lunch in a downtown restaurant neither believed they could afford. Afterward mother and daughter simply walked for the sheer pleasure of sunlight and sky. They walked through the Common, past the golden domed State House and up Beacon Hill to Luxembourg Square. They looked at the stately houses, the old city's grande dames, and it made them both think of eras long dead. They returned the way they came, viewing the city from the other side. During their walk they spoke ceaselessly, commenting on what they saw—the forms of the houses, the connotations they evoked, friends and family. For the first time since her father's death, Glynnis spoke of him with her mother warmly and comfortably, no trace of remorse. They relived their fondest moments and discussed the man's proudly quiet character. When they at length reached the car for the short drive home, a shared serenity of this rarest of days settled around them like a protective shawl.

By the time they got home the Saturday mail had come. Florence Mear picked it up from the table at the side of the entryway and looked through it while Glynnis walked past her toward the kitchen.

"Not so fast, my darling daughter. You seem to have a letter here."

"I do?" She turned back in surprise. Her mother held it out and as Glynnis took it from her hand she saw the District of Columbia postmark and recognized Conor's return address. Why would he write her, and here of all places?

"It's from the young man of yours, isn't it?" Glynnis mother said, her face carrying the beginning of an amused smile. "You've still told me precious little about him, you know. A mother deserves at least a few details, don't you think?"

Glynnis smiled back. "Perhaps I have no details to tell."

"Nonsense. You're marked with the stamp of romance. I think I approve, but I'm not certain yet. You have to reassure me."

"Have you considered that you might be reading signs that aren't really there?"

"I have but that's not the case. You are my daughter after all. I believe I can read your secret codes better than most. Go read your letter. You can help me with dinner when you're done. And really, I do think I approve of this young man of yours. I believe he's very good for you."

Glynnis went up the stairs to her room and closed the door. She sat on the edge of her bed, puzzled and excited. She wanted to read Conor's letter casually, to dwell on each separate thought, to replay his most attractive words and phrases. She loved his mind, especially when it unraveled before her like a tapestry. His rhapsodic intellectual wanderings, the boyish energy in his words, his lilting command of a language made romantic by his mastery of it continually charmed her. Glynnis wanted to take her time with this, to bathe in the words.

She opened the envelope carefully, pulled out the sheets, and read what Conor had written her:

Glynnis,

I trust I've timed this letter to arrive while you are still at home. It comes, really, on the wings of a pure whim. I've been thinking of you all week as usual. Tonight I have no desire to do anything other than sit at the small desk in my/ our bedroom and revel in every memory, every sensation, every response you've created in me. Writing is both a safe way to lay myself open to you, and a risky one. Safe because I can construct my words at my own pace and evaluate each thought completely before I relay it, and risky because, once committed to paper, each word becomes indelible.

I thought, too, that I might write you in Boston simply to reach you in a part of your life to which you've allowed me limited entrance. I've told you that I would love to meet your family, Glyn, and to see where it was those remarkable sensitivities and passions were nurtured. I'd like to get to know each one of them, and read parts of you in what they say and do, how they think, and who they are. If, as I suspect, you are a composite of all the people and places that have come before, then I must know them thoroughly. And they must be rare, rare people. So this letter, representing my thoughts and structured through my words, penetrates where you have not permitted my body. Romantics, particularly naïve ones, tend to view such tings symbolically.

Lately when you're not around I've been taking account of the course of my life over the past several months. The joy of each of my days has created a new standard for me, and I fear that the days ahead will have trouble matching the magic of what's around me now. I take careful account, and contrast who I want to be with what I see.

I've looked closely at the people who share this space with me—those with whom I work, the blank, sullen faces on the bus in the morning, the bored mothers in the stores with their squalling children. It's sad, Glyn. Perhaps it says something about human destiny, but I hope not. If so, then everything we've created for ourselves must be transitory. That thought terrifies me.

I've concluded what I think I've already understood for a long time—that most people find their lives a cold, burdensome thing. They feel too little harmony with what they do, and they define themselves solely by habit. Work is a device, relationships are predetermined to fail, pleasures are nothing more than diversions between obligations. You can see it in them, Glynnis. You can see it in deadened footsteps and glossy eyes and flat, lifeless voices. They're beaten down, hopelessly and thoroughly depressed.

I cannot imagine myself going through life that way. I cannot imagine not viewing my work as purposeful, or seeing it only as a paycheck to support the material way I live. I cannot imagine not believing in what I do. I cannot imagine relationships grown automatic and therefore unexciting. I cannot imagine rising each day and thinking only of responsibilities I would rather not meet, people I would rather not see, and tasks I would rather not perform.

How does it happen, Glynnis, and why do they put up with it? Why do they allow it to happen? The seduction of convenience? We are, in the end, an incredibly materialistic society, and we're obsessed with our gadgets and our conveniences. We're conditioned from birth, I think, to adjudge ourselves along material lines. We are besieged by advertisements that are essentially mindless, we feel the pressure of our peers. We see so rarely that there are alternative ways of going through this ether. In growing up, do you remember once hearing about Gandhi, other than the name, or Dorothy Day? My heroes were sports stars or actors and actresses, people who made a lot of money and led glamorous lives. We're given such things as our standards, as our goals, and we're taught to grab more, and earn more, and have more, but so seldom are we challenged to be more. And I think in the end most people come to feel a vacuum in their lives—a vacuum of purpose, of genuine human compassion, of true personal value, all swept away by a consensus that says we do not define ourselves that way. We define ourselves by what we have. And cheat if you can, lie if you must.

We've been so fortunate, Glynnis. I find myself now continually in wonder, and continually challenged. I see challenges all around me—the challenge to fit myself into a complex society in such a way that I can feed myself and those I love while doing some good within it, the challenge to keep my passions alive and fresh, to see something worthwhile in every responsibility I accept, to find dignity in the human character however it's presented, to remain aware that life can be a process of endless discovery.

I'm proud of the way I developed. Without sounding vain, I think I've worked hard to keep myself fit in every way—physically, mentally, spiritually, emotionally. Thank my parents, if you ever meet them. They instilled everything in me which you might perceive as good. They're older now, of course, and a bit jaded themselves. But there are moments when the excitement of living, the pure joy of being alive, breaks through their routine, and they become children again. I can see it in them, those rare occasions when I see them at all, and it makes me so proud. There's depth of character in both of them well beyond their circumstances. They've managed to avoid most of the snares, most of the deadening blows. They've denied the common and damning conclusion that life is merely a series of tasks, and they passed their sense of wonder on to me. For that alone, I'll cherish them until I die.

The room where I sit tonight is filled with so many memories of you. I can see that you have become the most precious component of what I've tried to create for myself. You are the final determinant of all meaning. You have taught me the sweet peril of commitment, the tender joy of vulnerability. I am a baby at your breast, and you convince me of the infinite newness, the majestic potentiality, the sheer raw ecstasy of human experience. All I create, all I do, falls softly in your gentle lap.

I do not sleep well without you. In my sleep I grope for your missing body and stir when I do not find it. Odd that I should perceive your presence now as the norm when we have had so few nights together. Still, I have a hard time adjusting to your absence at night; I do not want to adjust. In my restlessness, then, I am keeping a part of you with me. I think constantly of the comfort of just sleeping with my arms around you. Nothing more physical than that is needed to reassure me, although I think often of making love to you, too. The sweetest times, Glynnis, with you beside me asleep, my arms across your shoulders, the side of my hand brushing your breast, our legs bent in tandem. Sometimes I would stroke your beautiful hair without waking you, and I would nestle my face as deeply into it as I dared, smelling your constant scent of lilacs. Mornings, too, when we would fix our breakfast, and you smiling for no reason so that I would be moved to grab you and swing you around the kitchen, and then into the day. You in the dim light at day's end, your eyes dreamy and your body alive, reaching for me, the soft pressure of your clothing against me, the taste of your tongue and your hands on me to return to where we had begun.

I shall leave this house this week, and we shall not see it again. That note of finality saddens me because, what we've created between us, we've created here. This place is our cradle; it breathes our lives at the very core.

I will leave you now, my lady, to your mysterious family and the Boston summer. I will leave you, with your long hair that smells of flowers, with your soft skin, and with your secretive eyes that see all sides of me. I will leave you in word, but never in thought. I am with you there, in prim and tidy Boston, although you cannot know it. I shall always be with you. I shall haunt you, in body and in thought, all the days of your life, and you will haunt me. Love itself is haunting, and we cannot do without it.

Conor

Glynnis reread Conor's letter several times before folding it carefully and tucking it into her traveling bag. She would reread it countless more times before the pages tattered at their edges and the young man's words became so familiar to her as to lose their power. She would keep the letter, his first letter, close to her, carrying it with her when she felt detached from Conor by circumstances of time and space. She would protect it as she would an heirloom, or a precious stone.

Nearly an hour passed before Glynnis returned downstairs to join her mother in the kitchen. Her mother was chopping carrots. "Welcome back to the nether regions. Your young man's letter was not bad news, I trust?"

"No. He just wanted to write. Feeling lonely, I suppose," and Glynnis said nothing more about it. The rest of the evening she remained fairly silent, speaking in sentences rather than paragraphs, as the awesome weight of passion pressed in on her from its singular direction. It gratified her and troubled her. She went to bed early to allow the naked musings of a sleeping mind sift through her reactions. There were no conclusions. There were only impressions, fleeting and ephemeral, like hope, like terror, like life itself.

* * *

When Conor Finnegan arrived at the apartment in the Friday twilight, only Tom McIlweath was in. He could tell by the parked cars that lined both sides of the street: Rosselli's and O'Hanlon's were not among them. Finnegan found a spot a few houses away. He trotted the short distance of uneven sidewalk, leaving his bags in the car. He would tote them in later. Now he only wanted to see his friends. His excitement had grown proportionately the closer he got, and during the latter stages of his drive he had scarcely been able to contain himself.

Finnegan bolted up the narrow wooden stairs two at a time. He flung open the unlocked door to find Tom McIlweath, who had heard his approach, waiting for him.

"Mac!"

"Conor!" and they shook hands warmly, Finnegan grasping McIlweath's hand in both of his, then slapping him gently on the shoulder.

"Where are Lanny and Dan? Wasn't Dan supposed to get in today?"

"They ran to the store for some beer and steaks. You haven't eaten yet, have you?"

"No, I drove straight through. Three and a half hours of Maryland, Delaware and Jersey swamplands. I'm starved."

"Good. We're going to fix a nice spread."

"Then wash it down?"

"While we compare summers. Mine was dull, and that's all I'm going to say about it. But yours I want to hear about. In detail, with special emphasis on female experiences."

"I'm sorry you and Anne couldn't make it down."

"Me too, but there was no time. I would have enjoyed it, I'm sure. I should have come down alone."

"You'll have your chance. Maybe you can help me move down after we graduate."

"Then you want to go back?"

"More than anything. Mac, I couldn't begin to describe it all—what I saw, what I did. What I felt. It was tremendous. The best experience of my life. I came of age, I think, all at once, like a supernova."

"Typical Conorian overstatement. I see you haven't lost your penchant for hyperbole. That's good, and I'm envious. But I had no such experience, Conor. I'm still underdeveloped. A bit tanner, but still underdeveloped. Perhaps I should get into politics, too."

"Go ahead. There's room for all of us—you, me, Lanny. And then we can retire together in thirty years and become political consultants. McIlweath, Finnegan and O'Hanlon, offices in Washington, New York, Los Angeles, London, Paris, and World."

"You've given me top billing and I've done nothing to earn it."

"All you need is a total lack of ego and the willingness to make an ass of yourself. Convictions, ideals and ethics are purely optional. In fact, they're something of a burden."

"Have you finally shed your ideals this summer? Has Conor Finnegan been beaten into submission of reality by ruthless political operatives? Has he in fact become Machiavellian? Tell me the truth."

"The truth?" Finnegan smiled broadly. "Not a chance. I have come of age, but I'm still as naively idealistic as I ever was. I'll have no part of Machiavelli. Give me Burke instead. Because I've seen the ways of the world doesn't mean I've adopted them."

"Shall I go saddle your horse, Don Quixote? What windmills shall we attack today?"

"None, Sancho. We're just going to relax for a while."

Heavy thumping on the stairs in two sets; four feet clomping upward and two voices making indistinguishable sounds. The door popped open again and Dan Rosselli stood at the head of the hallway, his face a great, toothsome grin. He was holding two cases of beer. Behind him, peeking around the edge of the doorway into the living room, poked the smiling head of Lanny O'Hanlon.

"Conor, you son of a bitch! Great to see you. Let me put this down."

"Then you can give me a great big sloppy kiss. Lanny, how the hell are you?"

"Super, roommate. Been keeping the nation's affairs in order, I see."

They shook hands. "It all starts at the state level, as you know. What's in the bag?"

"The selfless offering of some poor steer and a few ears of corn."

"Christ, you're not going to cook that, are you? You have yet to prepare anything that I'd even remotely want to pass through my lips."

"No way. You and Chubby are going to do the honors. The *paisan* volunteered your services." O'Hanlon thrust the grocery bag to Finnegan. "And get going, huh? I've been looking forward to this all day."

"Come on. We can talk in the kitchen."

Rosselli was emerging from the kitchen as the other three walked down the hall. He threw a beer to Finnegan. "You're thirsty after your drive. I can tell."

"Thanks, brother. I understand we're cooking tonight." All four entered the small kitchen. Finnegan put the bag on the counter while McIlweath and O'Hanlon took seats around the table.

"So how the hell are you?" asked Rosselli.

And Finnegan told them. He told them everything he could think of, beginning with his awe during his first days there, moving through the elegance of where he lived, to the excitement of his duties, to the character of those with whom he discharged them. They listened between interjections and crude observations. Finnegan told them everything, with the exception of Glynnis.

O'Hanlon, too, recounted his summer at the state capitol, and Rosselli told of his experiences in the hospital at the beach. Unlike Finnegan's, their tales were well embellished with females, numbers of them, virtually all admiring of the young men's attributes and hopeful of pleasing them. Finnegan listened to the descriptions of conquests and gratifications, certain that they were grounded in truth but equally certain that somewhere in these narratives that some truth had been jettisoned as excess baggage. It was so typical of the two of them. He was happy to be back.

Finnegan prepared the steaks, Rosselli boiled the corn. They sat at the table's four corners and ate hungrily, noisily and sloppily, bursting out words between bites, spraying tiny bits of food on the table. They drank, too, several beers each, and it all made their hearts full and warm. It was good to be together once more. It was good to be home.

After dinner they pitched their dishes into the sink and returned to the living room. There they sprawled over every free inch of chair or couch, taking the space now to relax thoroughly. Summer's disorientations lay behind them now. What was at hand was the comfortable regularity of a place the four of them had adopted as their own. This was home, and nowhere else. And in their coming together here, they had adopted one another as well. The four, separate in fate and distinct in character, had united through the accident of circumstance. After several months apart, the thread running through each of them had been pulled taut again, and they rejoined each other in the common life. To a man, they took immeasurable comfort in that.

The sun had gone down and the night blew in coolly on the rumor of distant sea air. The stories swapped grew more remote. 'In the end,' thought Finnegan, 'the stories we tell are unnecessary. We know each other's characters, we know each other's lives, what's important and how we think. The four of us, in our disparate locations and with our disparate adventures . . . they do not tell us anything that we do not already know."

"Hey fellas," said Rosselli, "let's take a walk. Through the park. It's a nice night, and the air'll do us some good."

"Yeah," joined O'Hanlon, "there won't be anybody over there now. Grab a beer and let's go."

The four of them, beers in hand, tromped heavily back down the steps in a line and out into the night's freshness. They walked four abreast across the street and into the wide, empty, flat park.

"This feels icy," said Finnegan. "It was never cool in D.C. Except last week."

"It probably felt hotter than it was," said O'Hanlon, "with that woman of yours wrapped around you every night."

Finnegan scoffed, "Hardly every night, Lanny. Besides, that's privileged information."

"Well, how often then? I think Brother Finnegan has been holding out on us. You haven't told us much of anything about this babe. We need details."

"Why? To feed your own perverse little fantasies? I'll play no part in that, and neither will my woman. Besides, from what you and Dan tell me, you have no need for any of my fantasies. You're doing fine with your own lusty realities."

"Always room for vicarious entertainment," said O'Hanlon. "Even McIlweath here speaks occasionally of the Ice Maiden. You're obliged to do your part. We haven't even met her yet."

"All things in time, fellas. And anyway, what makes you think she's the only woman I had anything to do with this summer? Washington's loaded with young lovelies."

"It's all over you, Mick," said Rosselli. "You're caught like a fly in hot tar. We could see that last spring, and judging by that stupid romantic glow of yours it looks all the worse for you now."

"Maybe you're seeing things that aren't really there."

"No way," replied O'Hanlon. "You're about as subtle with your emotions as a runaway bus. I can read you like a map, and all roads lead to one intersection. I fear you're in love, roomie. All the signs are there, from the tone of your voice to your newfound reluctance to mention the young lady's name. Obviously you're been up to some pretty heavy breathing."

"Well, draw your own conclusions. I'm not going to give you any information you can use to skewer me."

"Your option. Now, young Tom here is another matter. Not only have we met his lass and gotten to know her as far as time allowed, we can see his actions toward her on a daily basis. It makes me look forward to the coming year."

"Yes, and we know," said Rosselli, "that Tom's habitual reluctance to discuss fair Anne masks passions running dark and deep. 'Tis a fearsome thing, this silence. It hides our soul's most thunderous rumblings. A calm we perpetuate before the coming tempest."

"Christ, Dan, you're talking like Finnegan," said McIlweath. "What have you been reading this summer?"

"Sex manuals and pornographic novels."

"My sons, my sons," O'Hanlon said, "I do have my fears. Women at this stage of your lives will only mess you up. You're too fresh, both of you. You haven't set yet. You haven't gelled. Everything about you is still tentative. Don't try to anchor yourselves to things that are just as tentative. Then everything falls apart—you, her, and the bond that's linked your pathetic fates. Wait until you're certain of your own substance, about which you still don't have the first clue. Wait until you're not still pulpy at the core and can take some knocks without being punctured."

"Feeling priestly tonight, Fr. O'Hanlon?" asked Finnegan.

But O'Hanlon ignored him. Alcohol loosened his thoughts and put them into a clear order, and, feeling nothing less than brilliant, he went on. "Whatever conceivable reason you might have for entering anything deep, I contend it's invalid.

"You might say that this woman's the only one who can make you happy, or the only one you feel capable of loving. You might say she's the greatest thing you've ever met. And I'd say that you haven't seen enough to judge. There are a hundred million women in this country, and, if you're lucky, you'll have the chance to meet thousands of them. Why shut yourself off to that incredible variety? And of the thousands you might encounter, there'll be hundreds who are going to appeal to you in various ways. The 'one woman' theory is bullshit, particularly at this stage of your life.

"Or you might tell me that you just want companionship. But there are lots of different forms that companionship can take. You don't have to fall in love or make some absurd commitment to spend time with her. Most of the women I know wouldn't want that either.

"Or you might try to say that she makes you feel secure. Well, brothers, we've all got our insecurities. It's a drastic step to tie yourself down just to feel worthy. There's nothing wrong with rejection, anyway. It's a normal aspect of growing older. Wrapping yourself around one woman and saying you're hers and she's yours doesn't mean you're secure. It doesn't mean you're attractive or charming or witty or any of those things we're so afraid we're not. All it means is that you've given one person, out of the hundreds of people in your life, the ability to blow you apart.

"You could try to tell me that she brings out a side of you that you never knew existed. Well, if there are sides to your character that are ever going to do you any good, they're going to have to come out of their own accord. They're either a part of you or they're not. No woman can create something in you that you don't already have. Besides, there are flip sides to all those arguments. The disagreements, the pettiness, the jealousies, all that. A woman can be a terrible inconvenience.

"It's all too risky, gentlemen. Any commitment, any emotional involvement, no matter how small, is fraught with danger. You're bound for far more harm than any good this type of relationship could ever produce." O'Hanlon stopped to take a long swallow of his beer. "Any questions?" he asked with a smile.

"Thus endeth the lesson," chirped McIlweath. "Praise be to God."

"Yeah," said Finnegan. "When does the time come clear to make a commitment? And how the hell do we control it? Emotions tend to have a will of their own. I contend that emotional involvement is a basic part of one's coming of age. Sure, it's loaded with risks, but you can't dwell on them. You can't be timid. There are rewards, too, that I think counterbalance the risks. It's a step you'll eventually take, and there's absolutely no way of knowing when it's right and when it isn't. You go on instinct and you take your chances."

"But Conor," replied O'Hanlon, "you can minimize the risks by evaluating where the hell you are. You don't even know what you want for yourself at this stage. It's ridiculous to incorporate another body into the planning. Hell, it's not even planning. We're scrambling, not planning, and we're desperate to find something, anything, that might be right for us. Why complicate it? Minimize your God damn risks. If you're behind the wheel of your car, you know you can take it up to sixty-five or seventy. But you don't do it around a mountain curve, because that would be suicide. You have to travel that road, but slow down and enjoy the view. You wait until you're on flat land before you start to speed."

"Unless you're Dan Rosselli," answered Finnegan, all of a sudden too light-headed for any serious discussion. "Then you'll floor it from the top of the mountain to the bottom, burning rubber on every turn."

"Did I tell you I drove a Jaguar this summer?" said Rosselli, lighting now on a topic that thrilled his blood. "My uncle's friend is a dealer and he let me take one out for a drive one Saturday."

"How fast?"

"One forty, and I was nowhere near the red line. And that thing handled so smooth it was like I was only going fifty. I told myself then and there that I was going to own one someday."

"How could you justify spending that much money on something like that?" asked McIlweath.

"It's a toy, I admit. But I think I'll be able to afford it once I'm out of med school and have my practice. Besides, there's the status of it. How many people do you know who actually own one?"

"Fast cars and faster women, eh, Dr. Rosselli?"

Rosselli smiled broadly. "Exactly, my friend. I want the best of everything. The fastest car, the biggest house, the most beautiful woman, the swankest country club. The rest of you can go work out your moral dilemmas. I'll be comfortable where I land."

"A creature of the flesh, Dan," said McIlweath. "A sad spectacle. What makes you think all that will be enough?"

"What makes you think it won't? They're not the pathway to happiness, but they're a hell of a start. You can be a hell of a lot happier living in comfort than you can living from hand to mouth. I'll find a woman eventually, I'll start a family and I'll make money providing a service that people are willing to pay for. Whatever philosophizing I do, I'll do from the lap of a thick, leather recliner. You've got to take care of yourself first, and then if there's time left, see what else you can do." "Is that why you want to be a doctor?"

"Partly, yeah, although I'm fascinated by medicine for its own sake. The human body is still our greatest mystery. What causes cancer, or birth defects? What makes the nervous system do what it does?"

"Why do fools fall in love?" O'Hanlon cut in.

"These are the highest challenges man will ever face," continued Rosselli. "But at the same time, there aren't too many other professions that provide as much financial reward. I'll have the best of both worlds."

"You're drawn by money, then," said Finnegan, "and Lanny here is no doubt drawn by power, right?"

"I like feeling some sense of control, yeah," responded O'Hanlon. "There's a certain satisfaction in being at the center of things."

"You ever going to run for office?"

"Who knows? All I concede now is that I'm paying my dues with this menial position I have now in Trenton. There are better things on the way, but I don't know what they'll be. The people I'm meeting and the connections I'm making are going to be immensely useful, that's all I know. One thing, though—you run for office and you've taken the first step to being out of a job, even if you win. But if you know how to work the system behind the scenes, somebody'll always have a place for you."

"So Dan is motivated by money and Lanny is motivated by power and, according to my cynical friend here, I'm motivated by romance," said Finnegan. "That leaves you, Mac. What motivates you?"

McIlweath drew on his beer, then paused before answering. "I suppose you'd call it a sense of belonging. Knowing that where I am and what I'm doing is right for the time. Knowing that those people I'm closest to accept me without qualification or prejudgment. Knowing that I'm leading my life in harmony with what I know and believe, that I'm not doing anything for false reasons. Everything else will follow from that, whether it's money or power or romance. I want to fit in with what's around me, and be comfortable in my own character. I want to live a life without compromise or accommodation."

"Jesus, Mac, that's a huge challenge. Is it even attainable?" asked Finnegan.

"I don't know. I know I've only felt it in bits and pieces, and most of that has been within the past two years or so. I don't know if it's ever completely attainable. Part of us might always be discontent, or even remorseful. We might always have to prostitute some part of ourselves. Maybe I just want to minimize the compromises. And be accepted for whatever it is I've become."

"That's more ambitious than the rest of us," said Finnegan. "We always tend to view each other in shorthand. 'He's an accountant,' or 'She's an art teacher,' not 'That's John Jones, who's honorable, intelligent, slightly compulsive, wears the color red too much and sometimes makes me laugh.' We almost never see the whole person. We define each other through our compromises."

"Well, I can't set standards for the whole society, but I can set them for myself. I just want to be content with my own circumstances, and to feel accepted for what those circumstances dictate. I want to know that I'm the sole author of those circumstances, that these are the things I want and not the product of other people's expectations."

"In our own distinctive ways," said O'Hanlon, "I would guess that's what we're all after."

"But it's easy to take that for granted," replied McIlweath, "or to assume that that's the way it will be when it's really not. We bend ourselves to fit, wherever we are. We bend ourselves to fit into the molds formed for us. I'd like to fit without bending."

"It feels like rain," Rosselli broke in. They were at the far side of the park where the road curved behind the tennis courts. In the low night sky they could make out the bulky forms of thick rain clouds.

"You're right," said O'Hanlon. "It's going to pour. Let's head back."

"Let's just keep going," said McIlweath. "It's the same distance back no matter which way we go. Let's finish the loop."

They quickened their pace around the park, but within a few seconds they were caught. The rain came in slanting, windblown sheets, slapping their faces and stinging their eyes. Lightning flashed above and around them, illuminating the entire park by outline, and the houses beyond. Thunder crashed in their ears with the basso authority of heavenly fate pronounced by God Himself.

The four broke into a run, their clothes instantly soaked and clinging to their churning legs and arms. It was a run of desperation, and a run of joy. They ran with boundless energy and power, believing that they would never tire, that together they could run through the rain forever to the ends of existence itself and back again. Their limbs pulled them along fluidly, their lungs filled and emptied effortlessly, the water splashing around their feet and into their eyes, cooling them. It was a benediction, holy water sprinkled lavishly on their chosen heads. They had to run nearly a mile around the far side of the park to get home. In the buoyant confidence of youth unleashed, they dashed down the road, away from all fears, away from all uncertainties, assured in their hearts that they were running toward those things they desired—toward security, toward glory, toward fame, toward the crowning ecstasy of life itself.

They ran through the rain together, no one pulling away and no one falling back. They reached the park's entrance and bounded across the street, then down the short block to the apartment, opened the lower door and sloshed up the stairs to their entryway. The walls of the stairway were splashed thoroughly, and small pools formed on some of the steps. The four piled into the apartment.

"Jesus Christ," said Rosselli between breaths, "I'm drenched."

"Take off your shoes and stay on the carpet."

"God damn, I've never been so wet. Mac, you ought to feel right at home."

Finnegan, shoeless, went down the hall to the bathroom and returned with four towels. "Here, dry yourselves off. We better take off our clothes before we do anything else or we'll saturate the rugs."

They stripped, wrapped their dripping clothes in their towels and went to their respective bedrooms. O'Hanlon tossed his bundle in the corner then went down the hallway, still naked. "I could use a beer."

"I need another towel," said Finnegan, and followed him. O'Hanlon pulled out four beers from the refrigerator, gave one to Finnegan, then carried the other two into the adjoining bedroom.

McIlweath and Rosselli were finishing toweling off and getting dressed when O'Hanlon entered with the beers, Finnegan behind him.

"Christ, you guys," exclaimed Rosselli. "Put some clothes on. You're disgusting." Laughing now, O'Hanlon and Finnegan headed next door to their bedroom where they got dressed. The four reunited in the living room.

"A toast," said Finnegan as he entered, extending his bottle in front of him. "To this evening, to the rain, and to friendship." The three others stood up and the four of them met in the center of the room.

"We have one year left together. Let's not forget that. Let's draw as much from it as we can, from ourselves and from each other, and at the end of it, let's be able to look back on four years of brotherhood. And let's carry those feelings for this year to the grave."

They clinked bottles and drank.

"Well said, Conor," said Rosselli. "We have to be aware of that. We're living the dream, right now and right here. It's something we'll never be able to duplicate as long as we live."

"You're right, Dan," rejoined Finnegan. "The way we live now is really unnatural. We have only a finite amount of time left. Appreciate it, and be protective of it. We'll never have it this easy once we leave here."

They drank then, and drank for the rest of the night, into the small hours of the morning, with the storm pounding on the roof and against the windows. They grew quite drunk and told their stories with great embellishment. They slurred their words and laughed at each other's mistakes.

Around 3:00, Tom McIlweath, slouching back in his chair by the window, fell asleep, his glasses askew and his mouth gaping. No one wanted to disturb him, and a few minutes later Dan Rosselli spread out on the couch to sleep, too. Finnegan, the room whirling about him, slid off his chair onto the floor and lay spread-eagle with his face toward the couch. O'Hanlon, the survivor, tried to rise from his chair, but his limbs did not respond. His hands slid off the armrests as he attempted to push himself up. Resigned, he slumped back and closed his eyes. There was no point in fighting it.

The four of them slept that night, lights on and fully clothed, in their contorted positions. They awoke within a few minutes of each other the next morning, each stretching groggily and gingerly taking account of their heads, their stomachs, and their dry, starchy mouths. A rankly acrid smell the odor of stale beer spilled onto the rug, filled the room. When the phone rang at 11:00, they cursed it. Only McIlweath moved to answer it, the other three falling back into their chairs and holding their heads.

"Hello? Hi, Anne, how are you?"

Rosselli groaned audibly and shut his eyes.

"Not much. We just had dinner and sat around. Conor and Dan came back last night so we had a lot to catch up on . . . Well, yeah . . . Okay, give me about half an hour. I'll meet you there . . . No, I'm not. I feel fine . . . Really. I'll be there in half an hour. Goodbye, Anne." He hung up and plodded wordlessly down the hall to his room.

"The Fairy Princess," said O'Hanlon huskily. "She'll give him hell for being hung over, then she'll make him swim an hour. The poor bastard's going to suffer mightily today."

Finnegan rose with effort. "You derelicts want some coffee? I'm going to make a pot." Interpreting his friends' grunts for assents he headed for the kitchen. Conor Finnegan felt truly wonderful. It was grand, it was glorious, to be back.

* * *

The following weekend Conor brought Glynnis to campus. She did not take the train; Finnegan drove to Philadelphia to pick her up. It had been three weeks since he had seen her.

By the time they got back to new Brunswick it was nearly dark. No one was at the apartment, where they stopped briefly to drop off Glynnis's bag before taking a walk around campus. Finnegan had arranged for O'Hanlon to sleep on the living room couch which folded out into a bed. His own narrow bed would fit them both.

With his boyish sense of wonder revived, Finnegan showed Glynnis the campus, the touchpoints of his life here, then they walked the short blocks north to Tony's. The restaurant was crowded, so they waited for a table at the bar. Few women were there that night, and when Glynnis entered Conor thought he noticed heads turn and linger on her a bit longer than normal.

They got a small table for two against a far wall. His head seemed light; he felt giddy, not because of the single beer he had drunk at the bar, but because Glynnis was finally here. All surety was once more dismissed. This was new, and he would have to inch his way through it. He was uncertain whether he should be protective, or solicitous, or cavalier. He sat on every one of Glynnis's reactions, every word, every gesture. If he was off-balance, how then must she be feeling? He tried to read her. At the same time he tried to accustom himself to the simple fact that Glynnis had walked next to him and now sat before him in places that previously were solely his. She redefined this part of his life by her very presence.

They ate and drank again, catching up on the three weeks apart. Glynnis talked of her family and her trip home. She spoke of school, her small circle of friends, her dissolute roommate whose youth had been aborted. Conor listened and when he spoke, his disjointed thoughts hopped from topic to topic. He outlined his honors thesis, reviewed his professors, spoke grandly of his friends. He told her how the river looked as he ran along it on late winter afternoons. He mentioned the funny names of the places around them—Rancocas, Weequahic, Metuchen. Finnegan felt compelled to lay open what this place truly was as far as he could see it, to stretch it across the table for Glynnis's closest inspection. In the end, he tried to make her comfortable, that was all.

After dinner Conor and Glynnis walked back to the apartment. For the first time since their greeting kiss, he touched her, putting his arm around her narrow waist and pulling her form to his side. Glynnis in response lifted her hand to Conor's shoulder and nestled her head against him. They walked on silently, dwelling once again on the renewed sensation of each other's presence. Conor breathed deeply, drawing in the combined scent of Glynnis, and of the quiet city streets of the late summer's evening. He pressed her side and spread his fingers to capture as much of her as he could.

To Finnegan's surprise, all three of his roommates were in when the two of them arrived at the apartment. They were sitting in various positions in the living room as Conor opened the door. The thought of introducing Glynnis to his three friends had heretofore made him somewhat nervous. Although he had confidence they would all get along, the uncertainty of Glynnis's reaction to them, and they to her, had given him pause. He would have to see if his confidence was justified, and there was nothing to do but proceed.

"Evening, Conor," Rosselli spoke first.

"Good evening, gentlemen." It was Glynnis who greeted them, a glint of a smile in her expression. Conor had not anticipated that she would speak up so quickly, even in greeting. Her eyes scanned the three forms reclined before her, the first impressions that most often prove indelible. The three sitting figures stood up.

"A few introductions are in order. Glynnis, this is Dan Rosselli, Lanny O'Hanlon and Tom McIlweath. Roommates and brothers in sin. Gentlemen, Glynnis Mear. She's proof that I have a side I never show you guys."

"I'm so glad to finally meet you all. Conor speaks of you so often that I feel as if we're old friends. And Lanny, it's so sweet of you to give up your room for me. I'll try not to be a bother."

"It's no bother," replied O'Hanlon. "In fact, it's a pleasure. I wasn't aware an animal like Conor could attract someone as lovely as you."

Glynnis laughed. "Conor's not an animal. At least not most of the time. I've been anxious to see where you all live. This is really quite charming."

"I was just about to go to the kitchen to get us something to drink," said Rosselli. "What would you like? We've got beer, soda, and some harder stuff if you want."

Conor and Glynnis requested beers, McIlweath scurried out to help Rosselli carry them out, and the two of them sat down with O'Hanlon on the couch.

"Nothing happening tonight, rooms?"

"Not a thing, pal. No parties, no ladies, no plans. I thought I'd sit around with Dan and Mac. Between the three of us we can probably manage an incredibly boring evening. What are you two up to, besides the obvious?"

"No plans for us either. Maybe we can all sit around together."

Rosselli and McIlweath returned quickly with the beers. They each took one, and Rosselli proposed an unexpected toast. "To old friendships, and to new ones."

None of the five left the apartment that night. No one had anywhere to go. They sat there in the living room, music playing softly, and talked among themselves. Glynnis took an active part, asking questions and making her own observations on whatever arose. She did not seem awkward or ill at ease. She operated with the assumption that, because these were Conor's closest friends, they should be her friends, too. The Transitive Property of Friendship.

And Conor's friends reacted to her openness in kind. They spoke without inhibitions or restraint, occasionally lapsing into subjects that were essentially tasteless, such as O'Hanlon's sexual habits or the adventures of Rosselli's incontinent uncle. No one stood guard. Conversation flowed back and forth freely, naturally and happily, and it seemed as if Glynnis might have been around for years. Finnegan's tightened veins relaxed in gratification. By the end of the evening when he crawled into bed and burrowed himself into Glynnis's soft body, he was thoroughly content.

The remainder of the weekend they spent simply. Saturday they walked in the park and had a picnic lunch. They walked down to the river. That night Finnegan fixed dinner, then they went to a movie. On Sunday morning they went to Mass at the little chapel next to Old Queen's. Glynnis had noticed some ducks in the park on the other side of the river, so after brunch they packed some popcorn and bread crusts and walked across the old steel bridge to feed them. The sturdy white ducks boldly nipped at the popcorn in their hands, squawking among themselves and pushing one another out of the way. Conor occasionally pitched a handful of seed into the pond to see the ducks dive over and into each other in pursuit of the popcorn before it sank. In the sleepy late afternoon the two walked back to campus and stopped in the student center's snack bar for ice cream. No one else was in the small bistro. They ate quietly and returned to the apartment, finding no one there as well. All of a sudden, the afternoon had emptied. They napped for an hour or so, then Conor drove Glynnis back to Philadelphia.

On the drive back to New Brunswick, Finnegan felt overwhelmingly tired. Leaving Glynnis behind after having her so near for two days instilled a graphic loss, a disruption of the contrived normality he was only too willing to accept. It would be days before he would see her again. She had been so warm, so animated, so central, and he knew she had responded well to being with him on his own turf. Washington belonged to neither of them—they had been visitors. But New Brunswick was Conor's alone, the crucible wherein the fatty textures of smug complacency had been burned away by the challenges of space, time and uncertainty. Finnegan, in his self-perceived conquest of this new place, had come to possess it. Now Glynnis took her part in it as well. She had felt comfortable with Conor's friends, and she had been relaxed all weekend. In her self-assurance, Finnegan thought, lay her independence, and he found that he loved her all the more for it.

But now she was not there, and the drive back to New Brunswick was exceedingly dreary. Finnegan checked off the miles on his odometer, counting down until he got to Trenton, to Princeton, to Rutgers. He wished it all would pass quickly, but it took the same ninety minutes his Friday drive had taken. He arrived at the apartment a bit out of sorts, a mood intensified when he considered the work yet to be done. He had a short essay due for his art history course the next day. All week he had put it off, resolved to write it on Sunday night after Glynnis had left. Now that Sunday night had come, he had absolutely no desire to write.

Finnegan forced himself to the kitchen table and plodded through his material while sipping a cup of tea. A note said that Rosselli and O'Hanlon were at the library. McIlweath had vanished without a trace again, sucked into the Newburyian vortex. Conor Finnegan felt utterly alone, the simple joys of the weekend just passed dispersed, and very distant. Something inside him ached; he could not identify it. He knew it had to do with Glynnis, but its precise contours eluded him. Was it a discontent that they were now apart, the flip side of that sublime weekend? Was it just a predictable letdown? Was it some foreboding, a subconscious interpretation of something she said or did, some posture she assumed that his mind has silently ingested? He couldn't tell what it was, beyond the yawning emptiness that had dragged him down.

An hour passed before Tom McIlweath came in. He joined Finnegan at the kitchen table, he to translate his Latin, Finnegan struggling with medieval diptychs. Conor had barely finished when his remaining roommates bounced through the door. They were cheerfully loud, and they stormed into the kitchen to pull Finnegan and McIlweath away from the table there. Rosselli grabbed Finnegan about the waist and hoisted him down the hall into the living room, challenging him to a wrestling match. When Rosselli put him down, Finnegan spun quickly around to put his friend into a headlock. From that point they were engaged, the smaller, more agile Finnegan and the bulky Rosselli trying to throw each other to the floor while taking care to avoid breaking any furniture. McIlweath and O'Hanlon, too scrawny to be anything but pacifists, yelled from the hallway.

The wrestlers groped at each other for several minutes before Finnegan made a dazzlingly quick move to Rosselli's side, hooked his leg around his friend's and buckled Rosselli's knee. Down went the big man. Finnegan slipped an arm around Rosselli's neck and kept his leg locked between the big man's legs to render them useless. With his free hand, Finnegan pinned Rosselli's right arm to his side. The other, for all his strength, was helpless. After acknowledging such, he was released.

"Don't mess with a Mick, Danny boy," panted Finnegan. Perspiration clung to his shirt collar and dampened his temples.

"A lucky throw. Best two out of three?"

"No. The guys downstairs wouldn't like it. We must sound like two dancing hippos. Thanks for disrupting my studies."

"What are roommates for? Besides, you study too much. You and Mac. You needed a break. You're next, McIlweath," and Rosselli turned to the erstwhile observer, chased him down the hall and grabbed him in a bear hug. He carried him back to the living room where Rosselli sought to salvage at least one victory.

Finnegan watched Rosselli throw McIlweath from one end of the room to the other before pinning him. He knew he would do no more that evening. His glum mood had dissipated completely as he regarded the scene in front of him, the apartment where it played out, and those with whom he shared it.

When they went to their beds later that night, Finnegan and O'Hanlon chatted a bit with the lights off as they drifted to sleep.

"I liked her, rooms. She seems like a down-to-earth girl. Not to mention gorgeous."

"Thanks, Lanny. I like her too."

"She's nothing like the Ice Maiden. She's got a head on her shoulders, and a sense of humor. You getting any physical gratification from her?"

"Privileged information, friend. Let's just say she holds my interest."

"Good for you. Really, that's good. And I wish you luck. But remember what I told you before. Just be careful and pay attention to where you are. That means reading the signs. And she'll definitely give you signs."

"Don't fret, roommate. I'm cagey enough not to get burned. And you know I'm certain of where I'm heading."

"You can't be certain of a damn thing, that's my whole point. There are no certainties at this stage. Only educated guesses. Stay tentative, Conor."

"Good night, Lanny."

"Good night, Conor. But don't say I didn't warn you."

* * *

There are times in our lives—remote, Romantic, long-dead times—when our existence falls into a pace so comfortably natural that our daily patterns are devoid of all struggle. We do not notice it at the onset, and sometimes, if we are very unlucky, we do not notice it until it is gone, disrupted by the call back to the bleak, exhausting nature of coping with a less-than-ideal humanity.

In the end, we cannot escape the conclusion that life breaks our hearts and our spirits, that it grinds us into bony gristle incapable of fitting into close space without thrusting a jagged edge into the soft rims around us, that humanity labors under the cruelest, most heartless death sentence imaginable. We cannot avoid the impression that existence offers little in the way of lasting fulfillment but at the simplest level, and that we are constantly teased by the specters of glory, ease and wealth beckoning to us just beyond our outstretched fingertips. We cannot lose sight of the perpetual and recurring disillusion, the chronic loneliness, the empty sense of abandonment, the crushing depersonalized inhumanity of a society carried by artificial values and desensitized souls. We cannot avoid any of it; we cannot escape it. The best we can do, if we are most fortunate, is to forget it for a time and set about the enjoyment of the haunting glimmers of harmony that fate occasionally conjures and that we, in our misguided hubris, interpret falsely as permanent, the logical state of things that come to us as a fitting reward for our planning, our hard work, and our basic decency.

Conor Finnegan, Tom McIlweath and their friends embarked upon their final year of college well in step with their surroundings. It was a rare time. They plunged through the autumn months and into the winter confidently assured that life's bounty had been reserved for them above all others, that their existence here and evermore would be a series of challenges met, conquests justly won and glories accrued. All aspects of their lives harmonized during these euphoric months. There were no conflicts, either within themselves or among each other. They pushed blindly on, silently assuming that the rarefied atmosphere of youth fulfilled would surround them the rest of their lives.

Finnegan and McIlweath worked on their honors projects with genuine intellectual curiosity. They researched and translated, wrote and edited with a fervor approaching the religious. Both enjoyed infinitely the realization that they were educated men, that the breadth of knowledge earnestly stalked was growing each day and that, in the process of understanding what was put before them, they were learning that rarest of talents: the ability to think critically. They had become intoxicated.

Rosselli and O'Hanlon pursued their independent study projects with a plodding acceptance that hid any intellectual excitement they may have truly felt. They had devised their projects not from a love of knowledge, but for personal gain. But their motivations really did not matter. They were locked into the responsibilities those projects created; it was up to them to identify their own satisfactions. Both young men regarded themselves as among the elite of the elite. At the same time, they reassured themselves that their inherent pragmatism set them apart from the boringly vacuous intellectuals that usually chased these types of projects.

Socially, too, these few months epitomized all that had come before. Conor saw Glynnis every weekend, sometimes in Philadelphia, sometimes bringing her to New Brunswick. They remained enamored of the simple pleasures—long walks, afternoons in the student center, the occasional play or movie. Sometimes, when no one else was around, they would just sit in a chair in the living room, Glynnis on

Conor's lap, and hold each other. There was nothing sexual in this. It was an acknowledgement of each other's presence, this gentle grasping of the firmness of both their bodies and their minds. Often they would walk to the pond in the park across the river to feed the ducks. As the weather turned colder, they became more conscientious about this. They had begun to feel paternalistic toward the forgettable waterfowl, who seemed too docile to make it through the coming cold.

While Conor Finnegan cultivated his rich affection for Glynnis Mear in simple human ways, Tom McIlweath clung tenaciously to Anne Newbury. She too clung to him, although that was not nearly so obvious. McIlweath remained overly solicitous of Anne's wishes and needs. He saw her daily, and after he returned to the apartment at day's end he would phone her before he went to bed. He would call her prior to running to the market to see if she might need anything. He drove her to her classes across town. He bought her small, meaningless presents. They spent most of their time at her home and rarely ventured out. Only seldom did he bring her to the apartment. Oddly, though, he drew tremendous pleasure from this limited routine. McIlweath protected Anne as he would a valuable gem or a family secret. He convinced himself that he must be constantly attentive of her or else she would fade away from him. For her part, Anne was quite receptive to McIlweath's indulgences.

Concurrently, Lanny O'Hanlon and Dan Rosselli had no use for female involvement except of the most physical kind. They did not miss the Romantic allure of fidelity, nor did they believe their emotional natures to be underdeveloped. Let Finnegan and McIlweath take their chances. Their rewards might be temporarily greater, but so was their cost. Instead of romance, O'Hanlon and Rosselli sought the sensual pleasures. That, of course, was much simpler. They knew women on campus who felt likewise, and, if none of those were available, they knew where others might be found. From week to week they sought their quarry and indulged in mutual pleasures that were often very sweet. Neither had any qualms about it. There would be plenty of time later to inundate themselves with responsibilities and obligations. For the time being, this was the way for them to go, and they were both inordinately happy.

For Tom McIlweath there was his swimming. When autumn dawned he began his workouts again in earnest. His body sharpened— muscles seemed stringier, bones seemed lighter. McIlweath swam hard to build himself back up, and by the time the season opened in late November he was in superb condition. He swam many different events, three races each meet. He did not come close to losing any of them. Against his traditional instincts, McIlweath allowed himself to feel proud of his records. Athletic recognition was no longer necessary for him, but it provided an extra dimension, a measurable excellence, to his increasingly well-honed character. Tom McIlweath was proud of his swimming, to be sure, but he was prouder of who he was becoming.

For all four young men, this was a year of smoke dreams borne of a Romantic finality. Each had grown supremely confident of his own worth, the people around him and his destined place in a complex world. The four of them had fallen into step with their expectations. They perceived their unique fortune silently, and the shared realization drew them closer together. Their lives orbited around each other like a distant solar system set off by itself. They reacted to each other's moods—if one were depressed, they all ached. Similarly, the elation of one could pull all of them along, and some nights were spent in mindlessly random laughter triggered by nothing at all and sustained for the sheer joy of it. And through their symbiotic humors each recognized the thick cable that held them together and would never break—even if assaulted by the gods themselves—a cable woven of friendship and youth, of the limitless excitement of limitless potential, of dreams crafted in each other's presence, of communal pleasures and communal frustrations, of wit, of power, of time itself.

They analyzed their special relationship and considered each other as close as brothers. In the drunken euphoria of youth that has known no destruction, of youth that perceives the world as its own, to be shaped and sculpted in accordance with its own grand design, they believed to the very fiber of their souls that their kinship would never end.

CHAPTER XIII

It was ours, this sun, we saw nothing behind
the gold embroidery
then the messengers came, dirty and breathless,
stuttering unintelligible words . . .
You told them to rest first and then to speak,
the light had blinded you.
You'd forgotten that no one rests.

—George Seferis, *Our Sun*

A driving bass rhythm pounded off the thin wooden walls and reverberated through whatever lay in its path, objects animate and inanimate alike. Behind it rode the sound of harsh metal and over it a throaty voice screamed a tale of dissipation in barely distinguishable lyrics. The thumping rhythm mingled with the diverse jumble of humanity jammed into the too-small room and down the hallway. Footsteps bounded up and down the hollowed stairs, doors opened and shut. An identifiable voice occasionally rose above all others, either in greeting of someone new, or when some discussion became excessively animated. Otherwise everything blended into a cramped, sweaty closeness that spoke of a contorted, impressionistic miasma.

April had broken through the monotony of late winter. Spring had been delayed by unknown factors. March remained cold and damp, causing a certain irritability among those who had expected winter to have dispersed by then. To change their frayed moods, the young men of Rutgers had planned a party. As if in benediction of what they were about, the day had dawned warm, and as it wore on it grew warmer. The four had spent most of it outside, playing tennis and running, the season's first excursions into the physicality they relished. Their pores opened again and they drew their breaths deeply. At once the dusty, dormant mantle that had subdued their spirits the preceding months had been ripped apart and joyously trampled. They were, once again, children at play.

The day's heat rose to the second floor and made the apartment too warm even before any guests arrived. Once they started to troop in, the place became stifling. The bathtub had been packed in ice and filled with beer. That alone was cool; everything else swam with heat.

By mid-evening, groupings had become apparent. Despite the flow of people back and forth between conversations, certain patterns crystallized. Diverse types had been invited, although not in the traditional sense of the word. Word had been spread that there was a party on Huntington Street, see if you could come and bring whomever you wanted. As a rule, there were always unexpected people who happened by, but no one cared. The greater variety made it livelier. That was something to be prized.

But patterns did develop. That, too, was predictable. In one corner of the living room members of the swim team sat slouched in a semi-circle, drinking heavily. There were five or six men and only two women, all of whom swam together daily. Lapsing frequently into inside jokes and making reference to their peculiar passion, they tended to be too specialized for outsiders. The swimmers felt comfortable together and did not look for new people.

Opposite them in the corner furthest from the front window, a group of Dan Rosselli's friends held an animated conversation about sports cars and commented furtively on the women who were there. Most of them, like Dan, had applied to medical schools and would be waiting for replies. Undertones of uncertainty manifested through their braggadocio and intermixed with their banter. They had grown friendly through a shared competition, and now they regarded themselves as survivors worthy of each other's company.

Around the kitchen table sat four young women, friends of friends, and standing next to them, entertaining them with his Boston accent, was Lanny O'Hanlon. He alone moved easily into conversation with attractive women. O'Hanlon was never intimidated. He knew how to accentuate his distinctive character once he drew their attention with his smooth wit. Everyone who knew him and saw the scene assumed that O'Hanlon's partner for the night sat somewhere within the apartment, even though she herself might not yet be fully aware of what was in store.

In the hallway, two on each side, stood a group of Conor Finnegan's friends, relatively unkempt and radical in both social and political thought. There were two men and two women, all with hair of approximately equal length and texture. The men wore stubby beards, and one of the women had a chipped front tooth. Finnegan had gotten to know two of them in a literature course. He was intrigued by their nihilism, and spoke to them outside of class whenever he was in the mood for a friendly argument. Here, though, they did not argue. No one sought to interrupt them or to join their conversation. They were oddities here, if such there could be at a party like this, and viewed with mild discomfort by those who did not know them.

Scattered throughout the apartment, in every room and at the distant end of the hallway, stood other pockets of friends, many met during the first two years when they had all lived together in the dormitory. They were part of a shared and very special past; they had helped nurture each other through their weanings. As such, their friendships were regarded dearly, not as much for who they were but for what they had seen, and what they had shared. They all had been different individuals when they first met more than three years ago. Now, as they neared the completion of the process they had set about, as they realized that a final and permanent displacement loomed just ahead, they felt more strongly than ever their particular bond. Some of these friends were closer than others, and some were better regarded, but each stood out by the connections their identity evoked.

Conor Finnegan and Glynnis Mear walked between groups, entering conversations and then leaving them quickly. Finnegan was a politician working the crowd, making certain he spoke with everyone at least once, and greeting all who walked through the door whether he knew them or not. Glynnis, who knew no one except Conor's roommates, stayed with him at first, although as the evening wore on she regularly left him to follow her own course. In time she entered her own conversations, speaking to those people who interested or attracted her without regard for Conor, who, she knew, would handle himself quite well whether or not she was with him. The wine she was drinking helped feed her quiet confidence.

Tom McIlweath and Anne Newbury worked no crowds, nor did they seek interruption. For them the people wafting through the apartment existed only as disturbances that were best minimized. They sat on the couch, turned enough to face each other, and spoke quietly between themselves. There they stayed throughout most of the evening. On only one or two occasions did anyone dare to violate their space. The intruders acted unwittingly, not cognizant of Anne and Tom's special dynamic. They were quickly and readily rebuffed, drawing back from their forays into the conversation as a child pulls back from a too-hot burner on the stove. Finnegan saw the two of them establish their turf early in the evening, and he paid little notice to them from then on. Each time he looked their way they were in the same position. He could not be certain what they might be discussing, but he guessed that somewhere along the way they took a dim view of what they were seeing around them. Why had they come, and why did they stay? Finnegan reasoned that it must be nothing more than a sense of duty.

Finnegan came into the living room in the middle of the evening after grabbing another beer from the bathtub. The night was going splendidly. The crowd was a good mix and he had been enjoying himself thoroughly with the diverse range of people here. He had also been drinking at a quick pace. The alcohol relaxed his limbs and he believed it sharpened his perceptions. He usually felt that way when he drank. His reactions seemed more calculated, his immediate recollections clearer. Before drunkenness set in, Finnegan always saw that was happening around him in distinctly memorable outline.

He walked into the living room with his beer and noticed one of his old dormitory friends sitting in a chair next to the couch. Whomever he had been talking with had apparently just left him. Finnegan sat himself down on the ottoman in front of the chair and slapped his friend's knee affectionately. "What do you say, Ted? I don't think we see each other more than once or twice a semester anymore."

"Now that you've moved into the suburbs. I miss it. We used to get into some great arguments."

"You were always my conscience, Ted."

"It comes with being a philosophy major. We have a habit of falling back onto the ideal. Hegel, Spinoza and the boys. It presents us with some excellent opportunities to be self-righteously obnoxious and arrogant. I think, if the truth be known, I've always preferred your kind of realism."

"You were a good influence on me," said Finnegan, "especially since I roomed with the greatest pragmatist of them all. O'Hanlon would be telling me that all success is based on someone else's failure and you'd be talking about the Moment of Negation or Critical Imperatives. I didn't know what to think."

Finnegan's friend sat back slightly and smiled a feral smile. Ted Rosenbloom had lived down the hall from Finnegan and O'Hanlon for two years in the dormitory. Finnegan indeed had always regarded Rosenbloom's reactions highly. He had been continually impressed with the sheer power of Rosenbloom's intellect, the breadth of his reading and his command of ideas or concepts Finnegan found obtuse. Philosophy had seemed a natural course of study for him, with its elaborate constructs and idealistic overlays.

Yet for all the strength of his intellect, Ted Rosenbloom had always come across as disinterested. He sometimes set himself apart for days at a time, and in more than one instance Finnegan had detected an air of condescension. Rosenbloom would smile slyly and look at Finnegan, or whoever might have engaged him, with a penetrating fix that masked a hidden conclusion. His replies could be sharp. When Finnegan and the others moved out of the dormitory, Rosenbloom had made no effort to continue the trappings of their friendship. He had been content to maintain the routine of his own existence as it was, relying only upon whatever chance encounters might occur with the relocated to keep their relationship intact. Finnegan, suspicious of Rosenbloom's hidden arrogance, had also not gone out of his way to keep in touch.

Rosenbloom had gained weight. When he sat back, a slight paunch appeared roundly above his belt. His face seemed fuller, too, and Finnegan could see a plump curve to his reclining arms. Rosenbloom wore a beard—he had had one as long as Finnegan had known him—and it remained scraggly with gaps throughout that allowed tiny patches of skin to show. Rosenbloom's hair was parted in the middle and rolled down the sides of his head to the tops of his shoulders. He was not an attractive man, but then, his entire demeanor eschewed the physical.

"Drink a toast with me, Conor," he said, extending his bottle of beer. "For luck. I've got an interview with Columbia Law this week."

Finnegan clinked bottles. "Here's to good luck, then. I didn't know you were looking to law school. When did you decide that?"

"Last summer. A bolt of reality shot down on me and I realized that eventually I would have to do something to earn my daily bread, besides being philosopher-king. The law holds a certain interest."

"Why?"

"Why do you ask? I thought you were interested in law school yourself. At least, you were the last time I talked to you."

"Those plans got waylaid by a better deal. You're right, though. My question is rhetorical. I've always seen some value in a legal career, but I'm a little surprised that you would. I'm curious as to your thinking."

"Like I said, it interests me. A philosophical conception put into very flawed practical use. That's a rare thing. I'd like to understand how something devised so nobly, then perverted by centuries of manipulation, works up close in a pluralistic society. Let me retract that," he added quickly. "I know how it works. It doesn't, certainly not as it's conceived. It's the translation of ideas into action that intrigues me, and how those ideas are compromised so that they can be acted upon at all. I want to see how we got to the point where winning trumps justice."

"That's pretty pragmatic, Ted. You're coming around."

"More pragmatic than you can imagine. Don't overlook the fact that a lawyer can be paid awfully well. Particularly a good one, with a rich combination of ruthlessness and arrogance, and I plan to be good. I plan to be good enough to make myself extremely comfortable."

"Any thought to playing a role in changing the way things work? In reversing a part of those centuries of manipulation, as you put it, and making the law come closer to its ideal?"

Rosenbloom drank his beer. "Don't be silly," he said. "What chance is there of that?"

"No chance if no one tries. But you're willing to play along with it all, something you see already as seriously flawed, if it provides you with some material comforts. Which, by the way, never seemed to hold your interest before."

"You make it sound so base," replied Rosenbloom. "But I am an American, after all, and I'd be following in one of our greatest and least publicized traditions. The system is less than perfect, Conor, that's obvious. Hell, it's more than seriously flawed—it's totally fucked up. No one knows how to apply the law anymore. You've got rapists and murderers walking the streets with suspended sentences while reporters who've spent their whole lives defending the system are locked away because they protect their sources. Where's the logic in that? Is the law deterrent or retributive? I don't have any answers, Conor. I'm not sure anyone does. So how do we go about changing things? You mentioned making the law responsive to a pluralistic society. How do you do that, for Christ's sake? A pluralistic society invites contradictions. Hell, it demands them. I'm not going to change anything. No one is, because the system is based on counterbalancing tensions that won't allow any movement forward."

"So you'll just go along with things the way they are and collect the rewards."

"Absolutely. The rewards are very seductive. When it comes right down to it, why would those people who might have some vague power to alter the way things work ever consider doing so? The system works perfectly well for those who know how to ride it."

"Ted, you're starting to depress me. You've gone way beyond pragmatism. You're well on the way to cynicism."

"Maybe so. In fact, that may be one of the highest compliments you've ever paid me. Put faith in nothing. Listen, after three and a half years of being a poor and humble student, I have no desire to keep making sacrifices for the sake of some unrealistic ideals. What's the point of that? I'm no martyr, Conor. It's not my place to divert the course of human history, even if I could. My interpretation of the absolute is just as subjective as anyone else's."

"You didn't use to think that way, Ted. You were always subject to the 'tyranny of the ideal,' as you put it."

"I take it you disagree with my cavalier attitude. You have designs to leave your personal mark on our small planet?"

Finnegan chuckled silently, then drank from his beer. "You know, Bobby Kennedy made a speech in South Africa once when he said that each time a man stands up for an ideal or strikes out against injustice, he sends forth a tiny ripple of hope, and that those ripples can build a current that will strike down the mightiest walls of oppression. I take a fair amount of comfort in that. We each have the power to affect what's around us. The stronger we are and the harder we work, the wider our ripples might be."

"And how do you propose to do that?" rejoined Rosenbloom. "Don't you think that if you find a satisfying job and work at it, you'll be playing your part as fully as can be expected? Society as a whole is going to move in its own direction no matter what you do. The most logical reaction is to find something that makes you comfortable, however you define it, and accept your role as a tiny, replaceable sprocket in a gigantic machine."

"But some roles carry greater influence, Ted. You can be a bigger sprocket. Influence a broader segment of that mechanism, and make a wider ripple."

"What are your plans, Conor? How are you going to put these grand ideals into motion?"

"Government," said Finnegan. "I've got a spot on a senate staff. I'm moving down to Washington after graduation and get back to it then."

Rosenbloom laughed. "And that's how you're going to change the world? Well, I wish you luck with that," and he raised his bottle. "It's not social work, *per se*, but I suppose it'll do. But tell me, Conor, how are you going to change a system while you yourself are part of it, and not a very big part at that? Especially a system that resists all reforms and lies at the heart of whatever injustices you perceive?"

"Who said I want to change the system? I want to have a positive impact. That doesn't imply revolution, for God's sake."

"Ah, but it does imply service in some form. Service to humanity, am I right?"

"To a degree. I don't want to sound naïve about it, though."

"You already have, Finnegan." Rosenbloom's voice took on an ugly, pointed tone, and Finnegan was startled. He realized at once that Rosenbloom had been leading him into some semantic trap which he was now about to spring.

"So, what it all comes down to for you is working for some nebulous, vague concept of 'The Good.' A positive impact with yourself as arbiter of what's positive and what's not. Aside from the arrogance in that attitude, there's a great deal of naiveté. You seem to imply that humanity is salvageable and that the magnanimity of your career will somehow contribute to that salvation."

"And you seem to imply that humanity is lost," shot back Finnegan. "Whether it is or not, we've got to make some attempt at the improvement of the species sometime. Maybe it's all futile, but that can't preclude the effort."

"'Improvement of the species.' God, Finnegan, you should have been a priest. It's not too late, you know. Although you'd have to give up that gorgeous piece of femininity that's been hanging on your arm all night, and I don't suppose that would be an easy thing to do. But if you're truly interested in reaching your potential for human service you might consider it. I'd hate to think you've been seduced by some creature comforts like the rest of us mortals."

For an instant Finnegan considered standing up and walking away entirely, leaving Rosenbloom to wallow in his inexplicable bitterness alone. But no, he was engaged now, and he felt challenged to defend his motivations. He fought to calm a rising anger.

"What's your point, Ted?" he asked, biting off the words.

"The species isn't worth saving, Finnegan. You're deluding yourself into seeing some good in it at all. And if humanity is, as I propose, inherently brutal, self-interested and corrupt, then all your best efforts to make a 'positive impact' will be transitory at best and pathetically naïve at worst. You'll be wasting your time. You'll be living your life for all the wrong reasons. At the root of our existence is survival. Nothing more. And those Romantic notions of yours make you look like a God damn fool, like some schoolboy who hasn't grown up yet. You want to live some fairy tale—Sir Conor of Finnegan riding around and whacking dragons. What makes you think anyone gives a damn what you accomplish or who you 'serve'? You can't make a 'positive impact' unless other people allow you to, and they're so busy with their own concerns that that won't happen. You'll stand out so God damn much that you'll invite suspicion, because saints these days are so hard to find. We're a society with blinders, and we place our egos and our comforts above everything else. Ego and gratification. It's taken me a while to figure that out, but it's true. And if you think you can alter that even the slightest bit, then you're a complete fool."

"So then, in your view we're a contemptible species unworthy of any improvement in how we live, how we think, or what we believe? What the hell's been the point of 10,000 years of civilization, then? Why do we agonize over our imperfections? Why have men and women died in pursuit of justice? Why Socrates and Aquinas, why Gandhi, Mohammed and Jesus Himself? Were they fools, too? You can't condemn man's finer instincts because in the end, they are all we have. And if we have yet to perfect ourselves, to sweep out and tame our most brutal instincts, then the effort becomes all the more critical. That's our last best hope for continued existence as a species, flawed as it might be."

"I'm intrigued," replied Rosenbloom, "by your comparison of yourself to Mohammed and Jesus. Maybe you're more delusional than I thought. But for every Socrates, there's been a Richard Speck, and for every Gandhi there's been a William Calley. I daresay the ratio is well beyond one to one. I daresay it's out of sight. You mention these great men, but they're exceptions. They stand out precisely because they've placed their emphases outside themselves. And what happened to them? It didn't end well for any of those you mentioned. That you bring them up at all merely proves my point. Mankind as a whole is beyond salvation. These men dedicated their lives to your 'positive impact', to softening man's inherent savagery, to ushering in a more humane approach. And they were viciously attacked and most of them were killed by a society that didn't want to become more humane.

"The collective will of man," continued Rosenbloom, "overpowers any effort to change it. We're born in blood, Finnegan. That's a fact of nature. What other species kills its own kind just for sport? What other species tortures its own kind, or practices slavery? What other species could conjure up something like the Holocaust, which is much closer to me than to you? What more graphic example of man's savagery do you need than the systematic extermination of millions due solely to the accident of their birth?

"We do it nationally, and we do it individually. We do it whenever we fail to suppress our most basic instincts. It's easy to be brutal in the name of one's country. Hell, that makes for heroes. We give awards to those who kill the most, and kill most efficiently. But we don't need the excuse of nationalism to kill. We don't need political reasons. Remember reading about Charles Whitman, the guy who climbed the tower at the University of Texas and had a grand old time shooting passersby? We called him crazy, but what does that mean? It means we lose our control and allow instinct to take over.

"We've even refined our capacities to the point where we can brutalize one another anonymously. The corporate structure allows us to do that. While we sit here drinking beer, farm workers in California are being harassed and beaten by growers who object to their 'outrageous' request for a living wage. 'Can't do that, you know. Might cut into the profit margin, so you poor slobs have to continue to live below the poverty line so that I can afford my winter home in Barbados.' And the labor strikes of the nineteenth century when strikers were clubbed down, with full governmental approval, because they had the audacity to request enough salary to feed themselves. And our wonderful tobacco companies that produce goods that they know will kill you. All of this for the sake of profit.

"Where the hell does it all end, Conor, and what in God's name do you have the power to do about it? How broad is your arrogance that you think you can make a dent in the brutal way we live? Even the purest of intentions are meaningless, and even the best works are only temporary. Mankind will never be able to escape its own condemnation."

Rosenbloom paused and took a long draught of his beer. When he was done he slapped the bottle down on his knee and smirked cynically. For some reason Finnegan focused on Rosenbloom's scraggly beard. The ends looked like jagged spikes of tiny wire.

"It goes well beyond the collective level," resumed Rosenbloom, more quietly than before, his voice more even. "Each individual carries the potential for destruction and he'll never rid himself of it. Let me ask you, what did it feel like when I started in on you? Be honest with yourself. My guess is that you wanted to throw me against a wall. At the very least, you probably wanted to come back at me verbally, as harshly as you could, maybe humiliate me in front of our common friends. Maybe you wanted to break a beer bottle over my head. I wouldn't blame you for any of it. And you, Conor Finnegan, are an educated individual striving for refinement and motivated by simplistic, sanitized notions of man's higher nature. You're near the top of the species. Consider what the average undereducated, unimaginative American might have done."

"But that's just it, Ted. I controlled it," replied Finnegan. "That's the battle. I can't deny man's brutality, but the cases you mentioned are aberrations. You can make any argument you want using extremes. But it's the mass of society that constitutes the norm. The struggle is to control man's brutality, day by day."

"So it's the mass of society that constitutes the norm? " said Rosenbloom. "Then God help us all. Then we're not only condemned to eternal brutality, we're condemned to mediocrity as well."

"What would you have us do then, God damn it? You're leaving yourself no options."

"No, Conor. The alternative is just to be aware of what's out there, and that you can do nothing—absolutely nothing—about any of it. So you consign yourself to a personally gratifying lifestyle and you realize that the only true satisfaction for anyone who views society as it is must be based in isolation, not involvement. Involvement, your 'positive impact', is necessarily futile. All we can do is gird ourselves against the prevailing influences and find meaning through our own comforts."

"And to hell with the rest of society."

"Yes. To hell with it, and with all mankind itself. We're a lost species, Finnegan. And we'll continue to eat ourselves away, bit by bit, until we ultimately destroy ourselves and our planet and everything that's had the misfortune to creep or crawl into our space. In blackness and blood we were born, and to blackness shall we return."

Finnegan shook his head slowly. There was no point in continuing this. Where had Rosenbloom's Protean cynicism come from, and when did it begin?

"You're wrong, Ted. Tragically wrong, and I'm sorry for you. If that's really what you believe, then you're gearing yourself for a stark and sterile life. I hope something comes along to change your outlook."

"Finnegan, you self-righteous condescending bastard, everything that's ever come along has only deepened my 'tragic' convictions. Now, play the good host and bring me another beer."

"Get it yourself, asshole," replied Finnegan. He rose and turned away, a wellspring of bruised anger percolating up from his base. He did not want to see Ted Rosenbloom for the rest of the evening. Drunk, he could not be responsible for what he might do.

Finnegan went to the bathroom, found it empty, and pulled another beer from the iced bathtub. He drank it quickly as he rejoined Glynnis standing by the entry to his bedroom and speaking with two girls he did not recognize. Finnegan drew into their conversation and composed himself through the mundane small talk that carried back and forth.

He returned for another beer, then another, then several more. The night swirled on and the apartment grew less crowded as people left for other parties, to clear their heads in the night air, or to pair up with newfound partners. Those who remained continued to drink until the beer lost all taste and became nothing more than a pointed texture on their tongues and throats.

Someone turned up the music in the living room. Finnegan, who had been down the hall for a long time (how long he was not able to judge) talking alternately with Glynnis, with O'Hanlon, with the girls drawn to O'Hanlon, and with the various present acquaintances, walked unsteadily into the now loud room. He was surprised to find it emptier than it had been all night. Ted Rosenbloom had disappeared, his chair now occupied by a grinning Dan Rosselli. Tom and Anne still sat on the couch, not speaking but looking with glassy, tired eyes to the center of the room where two couples danced to the music's virile rhythm. Finnegan saw a glum resignation in Tom McIlweath's eyes. Perhaps he just wanted to go to sleep, he thought.

He returned down the hallway for another beer and for Glynnis. She was speaking with two swimmers in the kitchen. Finnegan knew one of them well, at least by his rakish reputation. He might have tried to interrupt their conversation under any circumstances but now the driving music from the living room compelled him to dance. He grabbed Glynnis gently by the wrist.

"C'mon, lady, let's dance," and he guided her back into the hall.

"Conor, I was talking," she scolded, but she came along willingly. Finnegan held onto her wrist. God, it was great to touch her, to feel her there with him. He bumped into one wall, then back into the other as he hurried down the narrow corridor.

There in the living room he spun her around and faced her. Finnegan knew little about dancing, although he thought he was quite good at it. He danced best when he was drunk. The music shot forth in blunt-edged darts that pummeled his inner ear and vibrated the stem of his brain. Still grasping his bottle in one hand, he let himself be carried by the hard rhythm. His limbs reacted of their own accord as he moved in jutting motions to the music.

Glynnis moved more softly. She swayed and stepped lightly, a gentle counterpoint to the harsher music. Finnegan could not focus on her very well. All her features melted together in an indistinguishable blur. Once or twice her image duplicated itself so that two Glynnisses moved before him. Finnegan thought she was smiling her gently wry smile, but he could not be certain.

He did not care as the music pulsed whether Glynnis was enjoying herself. At that moment it didn't matter. As he danced, Finnegan felt displayed, exhibited in a new form to both his friends and his lover. He felt graceful and fluid and strong, serendipitously in union with an unknown, all-encompassing force. He danced, and expected—no, demanded—that Glynnis dance with him in this new form. She must be here, and he must know that she was there.

Finnegan did not know how long they danced there. He recollected staggering back down the hall once, twice (or was it three times?) for more beer, and to relieve himself. Each time he returned the music thumped loudly, he found Glynnis and they moved around the living room in motion to the music. He thought other couples were dancing, too. He thought O'Hanlon and Rosselli were out there with him, each with some new young girl, and the thought caused an unbounded love to sweep through him. Brothers together, even here.

The clock on the bookshelf showed a late hour. Perhaps it was 1:00, or perhaps it was 2:00, Finnegan could not discern. Still they danced, tirelessly, and still they drank, now only a handful left from the original crowd, no more than a dozen.

Willie Mark, a tall, angular swimmer made solely of bone, stepped into the room. A girl Finnegan did not know but supposed to be another swimmer stepped in behind him. "Hey folks," said Willie unsteadily, raising his voice above the music. "We need some air, don't you think? Whaddaya say we go down to the street."

"Ain't nothin' on the street," answered Dan Rosselli. "Nothin' down there at all 'cept a park and a dirty old river."

"Yeah, the river!" yelled Willie Mark, now excited. "We don't just need air, we need a swim. Let's go for a swim, right now. In the Raritan. You ever done that before? Anybody been in that river? Come on, let's go. A swim'll do us good."

One or two skeptical voices rose in protest but Willie Mark talked them down. "What's wrong with you guys? It's warm enough, for Christ's sake. The water'll be good for us. Wake us up and give us some exercise. Whaddaya say?"

Finnegan liked the idea.

"Yeah, Willie's right. Let's go for a swim. Come on, we need a swim," and Rosselli, O'Hanlon and three or four others added their concurrence. The idea all of a sudden seemed adventurous, and a bit charming. After a few minutes everyone but Tom McIlweath and Anne Newbury had been talked into it, but they came along as the group cascaded down the wooden stairs to the street. At the foot of the stairs, though, they broke away.

"I'm taking Anne home," said McIlweath to no one in particular. "I'll see you guys later. Good luck."

"Mac, you can't leave us now," cried Finnegan. "We gotta go for a swim. Come on, that's what you do."

"No, Anne's got to get home. Besides, I'm not drunk enough to go along and I'm not crazy enough to do this while I'm sober. See you guys later." Anne had already climbed into McIlweath's car parked three houses down. She had not said a word in parting.

"Oh, let him go," said Willie Mark. "He's got other commitments. Whose cars are we gonna take? Who's sober enough to drive?"

"None of us or we wouldn't be doing this," said O'Hanlon. "But I'll drive. I can fit five and so can Rosselli. Let's go."

Finnegan was not certain precisely whose car he piled into. He sat cramped in the back seat, his legs jammed together between two girls whom he only remotely knew. Glynnis sat in front, or so he thought. His neck could not support his head for long, so it bounced from side to side on the short drive. The girls, one named Barbara and the other Jill, kept up a conversation with him about some indistinct topic, but he paid no mind. He responded where his thickened mind deemed appropriate, and the three of them laughed through most of the trip. The girls were as drunk as Finnegan was. As they crossed the narrow steel bridge, Finnegan felt the one on his left, Barbara (or was it Jill?) slide her right hand between his compressed legs. She slid it quickly up to his groin and whispered something in his ear which the whirr of the tires over the metal grating drowned out. Finnegan wished he had heard. He leaned to his left and kissed her hard on the mouth. He liked the sensation, the pure, sensual wickedness of it, and wanted more. With a quick left turn, though, they were in the park near the river.

Theirs was the second car to arrive, and as they spilled out Finnegan saw that it was O'Hanlon who had been the driver. The ten of them moved toward the river. One or two excitedly ran ahead. Although the night was the warmest since the days of late summer, the light breeze blew a chill across them. Finnegan stumbled forward, found Glynnis and draped an arm around her neck. He found O'Hanlon too and threw his free arm around his roommate's shoulders. O'Hanlon in turn was folded around Barbara/Jill, who had now turned her attentions to someone less committed. The four of them teetered onward, bumping into each other and holding each other up.

The ones who had run ahead had already arrived at the river's edge and had removed their shirts. Finnegan, O'Hanlon and the girls were the last to get there. O'Hanlon disengaged himself and kicked off his shoes. Finnegan did the same, the muck of the shore clinging to the bottom of his feet. He was filled with a sensual excitement, an awareness of immersion not only into a body of water but into a state of sin, a twisted ritual of reverse baptism. The women there aroused him, but no more so than the men, indulgent partners in the unfolding, delightful, sultry scene. The cool breeze hit his chest as he took off his shirt. He smelled the renascent aroma of new grass, he heard the light slapping of the river against its banks.

Before him the group was growing increasingly naked. The first two young men, swimmers, had stripped to their shorts. They looked at each other, then back at the group. With broad grins they peeled off the final pieces of clothing, pirouetted to a round of applause, then dove into the black river. The cold of the water caused them both to shout out, but then they splashed briskly, kicking up water at one another, until their limbs refilled with warmth.

Finnegan looked at Glynnis, who stood next to him in bra and panties. She smiled at him impishly. Even in the darkness, Finnegan thought he could see her deep eyes twinkle. Her eyes continued to glint, never leaving Finnegan's face, as she reached behind her to unhook her bra. She tossed it beside her, then latched her thumbs inside her panties and pulled them down. Glynnis kicked them aside, still smiling, still maintaining even in drunkenness (Was she really drunk? Conor could not tell.) her remarkable self-control. Unhurried, unrushed, always poised.

"Come on, lover. It's time for a swim," she purred.

She unbuttoned Conor's jeans herself, slid down the zipper, and Conor obediently stepped out of them. His underwear immediately followed. Finnegan paid little mind to his own nakedness; he felt no shame, nor did he shift to hide himself. He was, instead, more intent on Glynnis. Her long hair fell around her thin shoulders and toppled onto her breasts, stopping at her nipples, stopping at her heart.

Unreality, all of this, for we are not here. Rosselli and O'Hanlon are not here; I am not here on the banks of this ancient river. Nor is Glynnis standing before me in her lovely form, Aphrodite upon the shore.

Finnegan looked down, now oddly detached and objective, on this strange revelry from an unknown height. It was as far away from the essential soul, the jellies and syrups that constituted Conor Finnegan, as a Bosch painting. He inspected each face, he noted each form and sought to memorize the stark details of this darkened scene. Glynnis a part of it, exposed from all illusion, dipped now and forevermore into our shared, fated humanity.

Glynnis, do not pursue my folly, do not follow my own besoiled destiny. I am not worthy to receive you, but only say the word and I shall be healed. You alone can reach me through the smothering mire and redeem the twisted hypocrisy of my jerry-rigged soul. Go back from me now, that you may return to pull me free.

Glynnis grabbed Conor about the waist and led him into the river. The cold water shot up Conor's legs and into his heart. Glynnis let out a yip, then gathered herself and plunged headlong into the murky water. Conor took several deep breaths trying to gather his strength. The breeze wrapped around his chest, head and neck. He stepped through the water until it rose to just below his loins. Around him his friends splashed and swam. The river was shallow; the only way to immerse himself was to dive in fully. He did so, up to his neck, and after a few seconds some feeling returned to his stunned limbs.

Glynnis swam over him and under him and on each side. She frolicked like a white, sleek dolphin, dancing through the water ahead of Conor's unsteady form. Others had moved down the river to spread themselves out. He saw O'Hanlon with Barbara/Jill a few yards away running his hands over his companion's slickly solid breasts, the young woman laughing huskily. Five men and five women, all now paired. Glynnis, too, was laughing, and under the water her own clever hands darted over Conor's most sensitive areas.

But Finnegan did not reciprocate. His excitement dispersed into confusion, into disorientation, into the shock of certainties disrupted. He sobered quickly, and wished he had not come.

He sloshed through the water back to shore. He expected Glynnis to follow him out, but she did not. Instead she turned into the river and pushed herself down near the others. Conor looked back from the shore as he pulled himself fully into the dry air. He watched Glynnis flip to her back, then over again, and he heard her call something to Rosselli and his mate for the evening, but he could not decipher what she had said. Rosselli called something back and they both laughed. Finnegan felt tremendously alone.

He plodded up to where his clothes had been strewn. The night air hitting the water on his body caused him to shiver, but there was nothing with which he could dry himself. He picked up his shirt, shook off the dirt and swabbed his body with it as best he could, then he climbed back into his clothes, his chest draped with the damp shirt. He felt no warmer.

Below him the river ran, and in it, downriver and away, his friends splashed in subtle foreplay. Glynnis, he could see, swam among the playful couples, talking to one, then another.

'I wish she were here,' thought Finnegan, 'with me, keeping me warm. I wish we had not come, and I wish I had not drunk so much. But April dawns warmly and bodes a spirited springtime. Glynnis in the water, and an Irishman who loves the sea. We lay equal claim.'

Finnegan leaned back into the dirt and sparse grass. He closed his eyes to ease the curious confusion out of him. Glynnis would be back soon, and it would indeed be a spirited springtime. All he could do now in the cold, lonely darkness was wait.

* * *

Behind the river in another direction Tom McIlweath sullenly drove his car through the empty neighborhood streets leading to Anne

Newbury's home. The evening had not gone well at all. He and Anne had quibbled all night, disagreeing on nearly everything that came their way. They had both been indefinably out of sorts. The very presence of each other had proven an irritant. Yet even as they could not identify the source of their sour moods, neither could they suppress the bitter humor that crept over them. There was no logical reason that they should be so brittle, so easily annoyed with one another, but while logic suggested a kind demeanor, the vague mists of emotion demanded something else.

So it was that neither Tom nor Anne had particularly wanted to be at the party. Each would have preferred to be alone. As one of the hosts, though, McIlweath was obligated to be there, and, as McIlweath's close friend, Anne felt obligated to keep him company. That was a natural aspect of the habits into which they had fallen. The two of them stayed anchored to the couch all evening, exchanging only desultory greetings with those who came and went. All the while, the haunting annoyances that had dictated their misanthropy ate away at the back of their minds, silently acidic in the insistence of acknowledgement.

The scene around them had grown cruder as the crowd thinned. Those who remained grew drunker, louder, and more boisterous. Their language took on a rough air of lustiness that made McIlweath flinch. Anne made it clear that she did not like the music that pounded through the room where they sat, she did not like the wild dancing going on in front of her, she did not like the great amounts of beer that had been consumed, and she did not really care for the people who were consuming it. She had been forced to share this evening, to endure it. In a general sense, McIlweath agreed with her, but he deferred her repeated requests to leave.

"Just a little longer, Anne. We can't leave now."

"But Tom, why not? I hate this. No one even knows we're here."

"It wouldn't look good. We can't leave this early."

And although McIlweath himself wanted to get out of the cramped, hot, primitive scene and fill his lungs with the rich air of the spring night, even though he would have preferred to rid himself of Anne's presence and end their bout of carping, he forced himself to stay. He knew that Anne was equally miserable, and probably more so. He took enough consolation in that to make himself last out the evening.

When Willie Mark drunkenly lurched into the center of the room and suggested a swim in the Raritan, McIlweath knew that the party was finally breaking up, or at least relocating. He and Anne had not yet talked themselves out. In fact, the strain of their conversation throughout the evening had weakened the defenses of their overly logical minds. The root of their unspoken annoyance had started to creep out. They both saw it coming and neither made an effort to avoid it. Willie Mark had interrupted its progression, but he had not destroyed it.

At the foot of the stairs, when the survivors had all tromped down to the street, Anne had turned wordlessly toward McIlweath's car. McIlweath took the time to tell Finnegan that he and Anne would not be going along. Conor, to McIlweath's dismay, seemed too drunk. He hoped that no one would get hurt.

He drove Anne home then, jabbing and poking at the topic that, once engaged, became so difficult to drop. It rose forward in a tidal wave of suppressed uncertainty and frustration, hovering above and behind them like a black vapor. It rang to the nexus of Tom McIlweath's self-perception and questioned the validity of all his strivings because, at its simplest, it dealt with the young man's destiny, challenging the assumptions McIlweath had set for himself. Anne Newbury had been the catalyst, and when she came to know fully her role, she played it to the hilt. She became almost predatory in her vigilance.

This late and tiring night, as McIlweath slowly drove Anne home, the conversation rose and fell, choppy, a small boat on violent waters.

"I don't understand it, Tom," Anne spoke with an obvious annoyance, or perhaps it was disdain. "I don't understand you, I suppose. Sometimes you seem to be so amorphous. You have no form of your own. You just conform to whatever shape is convenient to where you are at the time. That's no way to live."

"That's not true, Anne. Or maybe it is true and you're misrepresenting it by putting it so negatively. I don't know. I think I've got a pretty good handle on myself."

Anne snorted derisively. "That's foolish. Look at yourself objectively now. It's April, you have less than two months left, and you have no idea what you'll be doing next year. Or where."

"Ah, that's the heart of the matter, isn't it? 'Or where.' You expect me to go trotting after you to Boston like some obedient puppy, but because I've made no definite plans to do so you call me 'amorphous.' Anne, what assurances can you give me? Why should I bend my thinking to suit yours?"

"Because my plans are less flexible."

"And that's of your own making," McIlweath shot back. "I've never found rigidity to be very workable."

"Tom, I've gotten into Harvard Med. Do you know what that means? And do you realize how many excellent graduate schools there are in Boston? You could go to any one of them."

"But why should I? So we can go on for another year or two like this? Arguing with each other and taking each other for granted? Where the hell's the warmth, Anne? There's not much left anymore, at least not lately. I wonder if the stakes are high enough for me to follow you."

Anne sat in icelike silence. She looked straight ahead through the windshield. McIlweath, now engaged, would not back down.

"For more than a year I've catered to your whims, Anne. I've not been too forward, I don't think, and I've rarely imposed my own preferences when you've been at odds with them. You've dictated our social life almost totally. I've gotten to know your family intimately while I've ignored my own friends. Damn it, Anne, I've been absorbed by you. I've been sucked into your world without so much as a loose button left behind. I've been convenient for you."

"I'm sorry to have been such a burden on your free spirit."

"Don't misread me, Anne. I've done what I've done of my own choice, and it hasn't been without its rewards. You're a marvelous companion and I care about you deeply. You're brilliant and naïve and challenging and charming. I'm scared to death of losing you. But have you ever really made me feel secure? Have you ever really confessed your own feelings for me? You've never seemed the slightest bit grateful for my accommodations. You seem to expect them. And there are times when you seem so remote, like last summer when you were in training. Days can go by without so much as you calling me. Am I important to you, Anne, or am I merely a diversion who occasionally does you some service? Sometimes I have my doubts, and you play upon them. You use them very well."

"That's a hideous thing to say. I've never led you on, Tom. You act of your own accord. The decisions you make are yours, you've just said that. But you're no good at making them. You'd rather sit back and let things run over you and pull you along. Don't blame your weaknesses on me. I have a direction, Tom, and it's very important to me. It's the most important thing. I've always been that way, and you know it. I'm stronger than you. I suppose it's only natural that I lead and you follow. But don't accuse me of playing on your insecurities. You've let your insecurities dictate your whole life. That's why you came east in the first place."

They turned down Anne's street. McIlweath wanted to run this conversation to its full end, but he knew that Anne, now near home and a close to the night, would not allow it. Perhaps it was for the best. Neither of them was in the proper frame of mind.

"Thank God I'm home," sighed Anne as McIlweath turned into the driveway. "This has been a horrible night. I'm willing to forget it ever happened." Suspicions confirmed.

"Anne, please don't mistake my accommodation for weakness. You should know better after all this time. But what I've said is true. I am scared to death of losing you." He grabbed her hand. "And if I've made no specific plans for next year, that doesn't mean that I don't want to be with you. You mean the world to me. But don't pressure me, please. I go about these things differently than you. You might not understand it, but I'll make my decision when the decision becomes apparent, not before. I won't force myself into something that doesn't fit."

Anne smiled slightly for the first time that night. "Tom, I'm sorry. I just hate uncertainty. I hate not knowing what's going to happen. And I do care about you. We're good for each other, and I don't want to lose you, either. If I seem hard sometimes, it's just for your own benefit. I know you'll make the right decision. I hope I'm a part of it."

McIlweath leaned over to kiss her lightly on the cheek. It was late; he could hope for no more. "Get some sleep, Anne. We can talk about this again tomorrow if you want."

"We'll just get upset again. Let's let it lie for a few days. I don't understand you. You need a rudder to help you steer a straight course."

"A straight course sometimes means missing the best scenery."

"Think kindly of me, Tom."

"Good night, Anne." They kissed again, very lightly. "Let me see you to the door."

"No. Let's just let this night die. It *has* been horrible, you know."

McIlweath laughed quietly. "God, it was. I've never seen anything so sloppy. I wish we'd never decided to throw a party at all."

Anne laughed, too. "Your friends trying to dance was hilarious. They were so drunk they looked as if they were made of clay. They kept bumping into one another."

"I liked Willie trying to drink a beer and missing his mouth. He poured half a bottle down his shirt."

"You're going to have a terrible mess to clean up."

"I'll leave it to the others. This was mostly their idea. I just hope the industrial sludge in the river doesn't dissolve them altogether and they come back somewhat whole."

"I've got to go. Call me tomorrow." And with one last light kiss, a peck really, Anne had bolted out of the car and run up her sidewalk. Tom McIlweath watched her to make certain that she had her key, then he backed the car out into the street. He felt infinitely better than he had just a few moments ago. He had cleared a major hurdle. There would be others, but not for several days, and he would be able to relax.

On the drive back, McIlweath's tired mind turned over his options. There was, of course, graduate school, and he had applied to several. His study of classics had been immensely satisfying. Antiquity lured him. Graduate school would allow him to continue his studies in a different place and with different mentors and possibly with a different emphasis. An advanced degree would be essential if he eventually decided to teach.

To his surprise, he had received a totally unsolicited job offer two weeks earlier. The father of one of his teammates was headmaster at a small private prep school in the northwestern part of the state. McIlweath had met him on numerous occasions and they had talked casually. The prep school needed a Classics instructor and, coincidentally, a swim coach. The headmaster had called McIlweath to ask him to send along his resume and transcript. He wanted to offer the young man the job—it would be perfect for him, just starting out—and he needed the materials for the files before a formal offer could be made. McIlweath had sent them along, and four days later the headmaster wrote back with the complete breakdown of his salary and benefits. McIlweath was intrigued. Jobs were hard to come by. A prep school would be incredibly demanding, and he would have to learn by doing, but it could prove to be a handy steppingstone to something more permanent. He had not yet responded to the headmaster, nor would he until he absolutely had to.

And so, as April dawned and a severance with the sureties of his current way of living loomed only a few weeks away, Tom McIlweath sifted as methodically as he could through his options. He was forced to admit to himself that he really had no long range plans. The scholarly life appealed to him in great measure, but that could easily turn sour, just as teaching could turn sour, or business or law.

So there was no need to plan for it. McIlweath would permit himself the luxury of remaining flexible for just a little while longer, and he would fight any urge to conform himself again to what other people wanted or expected. Any decision about the coming year, and about the course of his life in general, would creep up on him like a hawk circling a field mouse. It was better that way.

* * *

Glynnis Mear sat in a local pub drinking a bitter imported ale. The taste was thick and acrid; it heldw to her tongue in a cloying film. A thin layer of foam coated the inside of her mug. She swirled the remaining ale around the mug to rinse the coating down, then put it heavily on the oak table. She looked across at Lynda Hoelscher, a swath of blond against a darkly wooden backdrop.

"I'd like to meet him, Glyn. Why don't you ever bring him around? Let him spend the weekend down here for once. I want to check him out. For your own good," Lynda smirked. "Unless you've become as world-wise as my fallen self, in which case we have a great deal to talk about. I'd hate to think that young Glynnis has grown up right in front of me and I missed it."

Glynnis smiled at Lynda's kidding. "What's college if not a place to grow up? But I've had to go far afield to find my romance. It would have been so much more convenient if Conor had gone here, if he had been one of those handsome young men standing at the bar there, or if he had gone someplace like Penn. He'd fit in well at Penn, I think." She paused to sip her ale. It crawled down her throat like a furry animal. "He has quite an air about him that the boys at Penn might appreciate. He'd probably outclass most of them. He might even be resented a bit because he can do so many things so easily. He can be as mature and as serious as anyone I've ever known. He can be almost elegant in the way he talks. But then he can turn around and be so earthy. He's really very spontaneous, Lynda, and he's so likeable. And I don't mean that as subjectively as it sounds. People who don't know him almost always take to him right away. He'll meet people with that innocent, genuine smile, and his eyes will be so trusting and warm, and he'll be so natural. People are drawn to him, Lynda. And once he meets them he hangs onto them. He values them, I think. He values their character, and what they show him. It's remarkable. He's like a big kid, and he can be so playful, but then something sets him off and he can go on a half-hour discourse about human suffering, and man's worth, and injustice, and dignity. Things like that. But in the end he'll usually come back to that innocent, playful kid again."

"He sounds exhausting," said Lynda. "And complex."

"I'm not sure he's as complex as you might think. In fact, you could really see him as rather simple. I mean, he relies on such an optimistic frame of reference. Nothing sad or tragic has ever happened to him, so he bounds along with this constant expectation that everything moves to his own personal rhythm. It's really an uncluttered perspective, and not very well developed. But so far he's had nothing to challenge it, so it's worked for him. He's lived an incredibly smooth existence."

"No heartbreaks yet, huh? Nothing to show him our slimy undercharacter, or to hint that humanity is basically shit. He hasn't turned over the rock to see the squirmy things underneath."

"It'll come, Lynda. It has to, and it won't be easy for him. I told him the very first day I met him, and I've told him since, but he doesn't believe me. It'll come, all that heartbreak, and it won't be pretty to see what happens to him. It's bound to be so much harder for someone so innocent and idealistic. He'll be shattered."

"And then," said Lynda, "he'll have to regroup like the rest of us mortals. This might sound tough, but it'll be good for him. It'll make him harder. And if he can come through it with a few bedraggled strands of that idealism intact, he'll be okay. He'll be better than most. And if he doesn't, then it won't matter because he'll be just like everyone else—bitter, cynical and altogether too human."

Lynda motioned to the server for two more ales, then turned back to Glynnis. "So to the really essential issue, my friend: how is he in bed?"

"Lynda . . . God," and Glynnis laughed.

"Level with me. We're not talking about any deep, mystical secrets, sweetheart. This is biology. Does he make you come or not? That's all that's important, I'm thoroughly convinced. If he doesn't, throw him aside for one who does. Nothing else amounts to anything. So level with your soul mate, won't you?"

"Let's just say the nights aren't dull," said Glynnis, still smiling.

"Good. Stay with him. For now. And let me meet him. I'm dying of curiosity to see this young man. I picture him in a great woolen sweater with a growth of beard and wind-tossed hair, sailing into the North Sea."

"Not quite, Lynda. He has no beard. But I'm not certain I'll be seeing him much longer anyway."

"A change of heart! What are the mysterious humors that bring about such an odd statement?" Lynda purred. She was surprised, although love and abandonment, after all, were commonplace.

"I don't know, Lynda. I really don't. I love what Conor offers, but I'm afraid of it, too. I don't want to get too serious." Disparate images flashed through her mind, and she paused to sort them. She sipped her ale. "I think of my mother," she resumed, more slowly, more deliberately, "and I see that she threw away whatever substance she may have had when she married my father. She's a brilliant woman, Lynda. She's witty, she reads everything she can get her hands on, and she's probably the most insightful person I've ever known. She can spot the slightest alteration in someone's behavior, or sense a word or an expression to see what it really means. She knows when you're out of sorts, or worried, or unusually happy. It's like she can read your mind. Read your heart. But it's just that she's so brilliant, that's all it is.

"Anyway," she continued, "what did she do when she met my father? She put her intelligence into mothballs for twenty years, she corked her curiosity and put away any sense of ambition. She continued to work, but not for herself. Her job was just to bring in some extra money to buy new shoes for the kids, or so she said, and that always struck me as incredibly sad. I mean, my father was a doctor, for God's sake, and he made a small fortune. But the only value she could fix to her work was in what it might provide for her family. She rarely went out with her friends, she was home every night. She said she couldn't afford the luxury of a social life because my father worked such irregular hours. She said that *we* were her social life. What a sacrifice she made, Lynda, and what I've never understood is why she did it. *Because she didn't have to.* None of it.

"And then, with the kids well on the way to being grown, my poor father dies. What was she left with, Lynda, when that happened? All of a sudden, the secure family life she had given up so much for, that she had paid for with the cessation of Florence Parlavecchio's continued existence, was lopped off at the top. We had no financial worries, Dad had seen to that. But our family had no nucleus anymore. Just memories. My mother did the only thing she knew how to do—she kept at it. But the rules had changed and all of a sudden it seemed so damn empty to me. The standards had been overturned, and we seemed so different. I think my mother saw it, too. She saw the end of our youth and she saw this idyllic family structure that she had worked so hard to preserve blown apart. But what could she do? What was she equipped to do? I think back on my father's death and I marvel that it didn't crush her altogether, especially after she saw that she really didn't have to pull things together the way she did, that our course as a family and as individuals had long ago been set.

"I loved my father, Lynda, and I loved what he provided. And, so you don't get the wrong idea, I love my mother as well. But her sacrifice scares me. I don't want to do what she did. I don't even think I'm capable of it, and I'm frightened that someone will come along to make it look so tempting that I'll take it upon myself anyway in spite of my better judgment. I don't want to be defined by a relationship and subjugate everything I could do, all my instincts and creativity, for its sake alone. Those are my greatest fears, Lynda, and I see them made handsome in Conor Finnegan."

"And yet," said Lynda softly, "you love him, don't you?"

"It presents quite a dilemma, don't you think? On one hand I've been looking to recreate the security of my youth, yet on the other hand I don't want to make the sacrifices required to make that happen."

"I think," said Lynda, "that you worry too much. My advice is to enjoy this young man, and when you no longer enjoy him, find someone else. Someday, if you're convinced there are no longer any alternatives, then join yourself to whomever makes you the most comfortable. And if you never feel ready to do that, then screw it. There are other ways to live your life. In the meantime, there's something to be said for the animal pleasures."

Glynnis smiled across at Lynda. The animal pleasures did indeed attract her. Lynda had, since the haunting self-imposed penance of her first year at school, been an active practitioner.

That night Glynnis and Lynda were joined at their table by two young men whom Lynda had met on campus several weeks earlier. Lynda had seen them walk into the bar and had called them over. One had already slept with Lynda, and the other, hearing his friend's stories, had his own designs. His friend had encouraged him. He had told him that it was well worth whatever effort it might take, and that that effort was likely to be minimal. Neither of them knew Glynnis, but just as Glynnis was avoided in her first year on campus as a friend of her neurotically brutal roommate, now she was regarded by the two as most likely possessing the same appetites as her companion.

They sat at the table for nearly two hours, drinking and, when a band started to play at the far end of the narrow room, dancing on the cramped floor. They had implicitly paired, the one who had already had his session with Lynda deferring to his friend and directing his conversation to Glynnis. Lynda, who had grown noticeably drunker, put her hands around the new young man's neck as they danced. She gyrated her hips seductively to the music.

Glynnis was not nearly as responsive, but neither did she put her own partner at a distance. She did not know that he had slept with her roommate, nor would she have cared. With each passing week there were fewer and fewer men around campus who had not sampled Lynda Hoelscher's carnal smorgasbord. He was pleasant, and passingly handsome.

At the end of the evening, toward midnight, Lynda's companion suggested they leave. He would drive them back to campus, he said, and drop them off at their dormitory. Perhaps they could do this again. At the girls' dormitory, he leaned over to whisper something in Lynda's ear, she laughed and nodded, then turned to the two in the back seat.

"You can get out here," she said. "Doug has graciously asked me if I would like to see his room. Some things," she giggled, "that I must review."

Glynnis patted Lynda's shoulder as she got out. The other young man slid out behind her, and together they walked up the slope to the dormitory. The young man fairly strutted. They stopped at the door, he took her hand and kissed her. "Can I come up?"

Glynnis hesitated. The thought of lying in this man's arms did not displease her, but neither did it have any great appeal. He was, after all, not Conor. Yet perhaps it might be good for her. Perhaps it would be cathartic, ripping out a gnarled branch to let a new one grow in. She pondered. An image of the Raritan, dotted with naked bodies of lovely youth, jumped through her mind.

"No. I don't think so. Not tonight."

"Are you sure?" He kissed her forehead. "I'd like to spend more time with you. I think you're something special."

"No. I'm sorry, Jeff, but I don't think we should."

Jeff sagged in disbelief. He was not certain whether he should walk away nonchalantly or show some anger to let her know how much he disliked being teased. "Well," he said, his course not so much decided as speaking for itself, "if that's what you want. Can I see you again, at least?"

"Let's not plan on it just yet. Maybe something will come up, though."

He left wondering where he could kill an hour or two while his roommate copulated with Lynda Hoelscher. Glynnis walked up to her room and quietly undressed. She was glad that she had turned Jeff down. But she could not deny that it felt extremely good to be asked.

CHAPTER XIV

*Orpheus—they've gone on now, the good as well as the bad
. . . They've done their little song and dance in your life . . .
They are that way in you now, forever.*

—Jean Anouilh, *Eurydice*

For Glynnis Mear, the cloying waters of the Raritan had been a Rubicon of sorts. As they splashed in her face and coursed over her slender form, the waters had awakened her from a drowsy malaise that had dominated her for longer than she had realized. She had been reinvigorated by the stark chill, and as she waded in to her knees, her thighs and beyond, she wanted more. She wanted the chill to shake her alive, to revitalize the placid blood at her heart that she recognized as stagnant. If it had been possible, she would have dived beneath the black waters altogether and never resurfaced.

The naked bodies of these men and women whom she only remotely knew stimulated her, too, and, slightly drunk but well enough in control to know precisely what she was about, she shed her clothes willingly to join them. Glynnis had never considered herself an exhibitionist: the only man who had ever seen the entirety of her splendid body was Conor. She felt no reluctance, though, perhaps because the shared stupor of those she was with provided a type of insulation. They would remember few details, she reasoned, and her body was likely to be indistinct from the others as leaves on a thick branch. She loved the raw sensation of the cold air and the colder water. She felt infinitely safe.

Glynnis had not ignored the frolicking nakedness around her. She regarded each body in turn, particularly, of course, the men's. She looked at their wobbling penises, incongruous under the circumstances, remarkably asexual, and their white buttocks. With the exception of Dan Rosselli, each of the men was lean, their stomachs hard, their legs and shoulders defined by bone and sinew showing no puffiness or droop. The water made their skins glisten. Glynnis wanted to run her hands over them, to feel them as she might feel the hewn marble of a fine statue.

When Conor had turned inexplicably back to shore, Glynnis had continued down the river, spellbound. It did not matter that Conor was not there. He would have been an encumbrance, limiting her sensual indulgences with the regularity of his presence, the predictability of his responses. She was glad she was alone. She paddled past Dan Rosselli and his mate, a girl she did not know. Rosselli had her in his grasp below the water and she was laughing a throaty laugh. Glynnis called to them, "You two behave yourselves," and Rosselli rolled his girl over and called back, "Always. I'm a very good boy. There's plenty of my goodness for everyone," and Glynnis laughingly responded, "Later, lover" before swimming on.

She felt as if she had pulled the curtain on an ancient bacchanalia where sensuality and sexuality, too long repressed, surrounded her and sucked her in. This was a celebration of the body in all its wondrous functions; she existed solely to be satisfied. The norms had been reversed, the forbidden glorified and the mundane forbidden. Conor, back on shore and bound to be sullen, could never understand. He locked himself inside his damned ideals. He would push his limits outward periodically an inch or two at a time but all the while remaining well within the prescriptions his tyrannical abstractions demanded. The next day he, no doubt, would reflect upon what happened tonight and conclude that they had all stepped too boldly over the line.

But who drew that line in the first place? On this glorious night Glynnis wanted no part of arbitrary constraints drafted by years of staid usage. Limit implied denial, and denial implied sacrifice, and sacrifice without reward was meaningless. Conor seemed drawn to sacrifice for its own sake—denial of the flesh beyond the normative indulgences, denial of the emotions beyond what was clearly definable, denial of the mind beyond what was unfathomable. Through it he supposed he would become more keenly honed, more devoted to what was already well prescribed, high and good. But to Glynnis this made little sense. Abandonment now seemed the proper pathway, shared pleasure with the consensus to eliminate any and all norms, any and all judgments.

There would be far more to be gained through experience than through denial. She could see it clearly.

My rigid lover, bend. My Romantic idealist who views each day as a churning sea to be crossed in the small and fragile boat of your intentions, yield to me and dismiss your dreamy notions, if only for a night. Place yourself in my trust here in this world as it is, with its vanities and its tears. Do not deny what you are. You are human, and you ache, you tire, you lust just as the rest of us do. There are times when we are meat, not gods, and you, too, for I have felt your body on mine at night and heard your breath in my ear. I have felt the rising and falling of your Irish passion, frustrated by the ropes tied around it and, when released at last, spent joyously on my own small frame, poured endlessly into me. Do not deny what you are, my lover. You are a man of infinite longing perplexed by finite ability. You are a man of the highest ideals sullied by the soil of your own humanity. And, my lover, do not be too rigid in either your actions or your perceptions. For be assured, that, from this moment on, I shall not be. Perhaps you do not know me well at all. Perhaps I am only one of your Romantic Irish ideals, a sleek and graceful porpoise swimming just beyond your reach as you navigate the small and fragile boat of your intentions.

When they returned to the apartment that night, each carrying with them the lingering tarry scent of the dirty river, they did not make love, although Glynnis, aroused by the sensual carnival she had just left, practically begged Conor to please her. She tried all the seductive glances and grasps she knew, but Conor pleaded fatigue, a rising headache and the river smell that filled the room.

"It would be like making love to a dead fish, Glynnis."

"I think I'm a bit more enjoyable than a dead fish," she purred, sliding her hand inside his shorts. "I think I might be offended by that analogy," then sucked his ear.

"Tomorrow, Glynnis, after we get a chance to shower and rejoin the ranks of humanity, okay? But not tonight, please. I'd only disappoint you."

'You disappoint me now,' she thought, 'as thoroughly as ever you could. And when, when, have you ever rejoined the ranks of humanity? You know nothing of being human. You may as well hope to sprout feathers and become an ostrich.'

"All right, then, we'll sleep. But you owe me, Conor, and I mean to collect."

And you owe yourself, too, if you'd ever see clear to realize it, not as a weakness but as an inescapable part of your very being.

* * *

Over the year, Lynda Hoelscher cultivated her own set of private jealousies regarding Glynnis Mear. Had she known what her subconscious was up to, she would most certainly have resisted it, outwardly at least. That, alas, was impossible, as impossible as it would have been to reverse the churning eddies of her confused and confusing past. The sad experiences of a youth thoroughly disabused of its naïve notions drew her perceptions of Glynnis toward an inescapable conclusion.

Both the concept of emotional involvement and the conviction that mankind was ultimately beneficent, or at the very least neutral, lay dead for Lynda Hoelscher, the Rosencrantz and Guildenstern of her psyche. They had not so much been lost at sea as they had been torpedoed by the unrelenting circumstances of her adolescence. Consequently Lynda saw all human activity, from helping an old lady cross the street to finding a cure for cancer, as motivated by self-interest. Man's emotional reactions could never be entangled with anything other than the ego. All else was false posturing, ignorance, or, in the extreme, vile deceit.

That Glynnis had so obviously controverted this rule of nature through her involvement with Conor Finnegan sat in the bowels of Lynda Hoelscher's subconscious like some indigestible piece of foul meat. It absorbed the smaller items around it and grew and bulged until it became a subliminally painful obstruction. Glynnis, with her faithful devotion; Glynnis, with the freshly revitalized glow she carried upon her return from weekends with her lover; Glynnis, with her phone calls and letters; Glynnis, with her naïve and sickeningly underdeveloped notions—it all lodged there, uncomfortable and misshapen, distending the limits of her very real affections. It was all too sweet, too pure, too clichéd to be real.

Lynda observed it all and, step by step, grew increasingly resentful of what appeared to be Glynnis's uncommonly good fortune. Her relationship with Conor smacked of artificiality. It would blow up in her face someday. It had to. In the meantime, its purity offended Lynda's hardened psyche. She would have been much happier and graphically more satisfied if something would come along to despoil that sweet Romantic purity.

So were the conclusions of her buried subconscious one Friday afternoon in late April when Glynnis asked her to call Conor to let him know that she would be finishing an art project for the remainder of the day and that he should not pick her up until three hours after the previously established time.

* * *

Conor Finnegan arrived at Glynnis's dormitory after the usual ninety minutes of expressway and city street. He had long ago ceased to find the drive fascinating. The scenery and names that had been so laden with the intriguing history of the area, that odd sense of time, had become mundane, mere mileposts on a dutiful journey whose true reward lay not in transit but at the end where his lover waited for him.

Finnegan hopped up the stairs to Glynnis's room after signing in at the desk. The building itself had always struck him as feminine, with its bleached white pillars in front and its stately brick. The interior was awash in light colors to create a brightness of environment that was no doubt meant to instill a brightness in spirit, however contrived and transitory. The broad waiting room contained solidly stuffed furniture that would not have lasted three weeks in Finnegan's old dormitory before its soft innards were distributed from wall to wall. The white curtains, ever clean, let in huge swaths of sunlight late in the day as the angle of the sun's descent set it flush against the west window, a giant, fiery voyeur whose pleasure was obvious. The stairway that Finnegan scaled in hops of two or three steps at a time was carpeted, and the carpeting remarkably showed little wear. Do they float up these stairs? he wondered. The building's refined, immaculate condition never failed to make him aware of his actions, every step, every gesture, as if the intrusion of his sizeable man's body into so delicate a world was a violation of the laws of nature. Too, he was afraid that a careless move or quick turn might pockmark a clean white wall or send a table lamp hurtling to a shattered oblivion.

Finnegan reached Glynnis's room and knocked gently with the back of his hand. A muffled feminine voice bade him enter; he turned the knob and stepped in.

When he saw that the woman inside was not Glynnis, he stopped in his tracks and bit off the flippant greeting he was about to deliver. A tall blonde with rich green eyes sat on one of the beds, her back against the wall and her long legs stretched out toward the center of the room. She had been reading. Her hair hung over her shoulders and fell across her forehead in loose bangs. Finnegan stood thoroughly surprised, thoroughly transfixed by the green pockets that were her eyes and which knifed into him like razors.

"Do I have the wrong room?" he asked as he regrouped. His voice came out higher than he wanted. That was a trait he abhorred, this piping of his voice an octave or two up the scale when he was nervous. And this girl definitely made him nervous.

"You must be the mysterious Conor Finnegan," said the young woman as she got up from the bed. Conor noted her thin, firm body. Her breasts were larger than Glynnis's, and her stomach appeared flat and hard. She wore a gauzy white blouse that set off the rich tan tint of her skin. Her jeans clung tightly to her slender hips. Conor tried not to look too hard, but she exuded a sensuality that he found compelling.

"I'm Lynda Hoelscher. Glynnis must have mentioned me to you."

"Oh, Jesus, yes," said Finnegan, although in truth Glynnis had said very little about her roommate. "I'm sorry we haven't had the chance to meet before this. It seems as if we should have, but I've always come down at the wrong time."

"Glynnis will be a bit late. She's finishing a project for one of her art classes that had to be in today, or so she said. I've been dispatched to keep you company until she gets back. Have a seat."

"Lynda, you don't have to do that. If you've got something else to do, please go ahead. I can amuse myself for a while."

"But it would be so much more fun to amuse each other, no? And there's nothing else I have to do. You're my number one priority."

"Well, then I'll content myself with being flattered. You know, it does seem strange that we've never met. I feel like I've been missing a big part of Glynnis's life."

"Me too. She can be distant sometimes. She'll tell you what she thinks is relevant and leave everything else aside. Not that she resents your knowing, but that she doesn't think it's important."

"That's true. I still haven't met her family."

"Her mother's a great lady. Quiet and confident and strong. But isn't meeting the family a terminal step? Doesn't that signify something, or am I mistaken?" she asked with a teasing smile.

Finnegan smiled back. "Nothing is terminal at this point. I'm just curious. You can tell a great deal about someone by their roots. What are yours, Lynda? Where are you from?"

"There's nothing Romantic or exotic about me, I'm afraid. Upstate New York. Loved and abandoned at an early age, a victim of a carnal bandit. Disillusioned and cynical, I headed south to this place where I've set about reconstructing things."

"It sounds as if there's a story there, and if what you say is true, then I'm sorry for it. But," he smiled again, sensing that he was being played, "you're being too glib to be serious, aren't you?"

"As you like," she smiled. "Glynnis, on the other hand, has told me volumes about you. She's told me where you live, and who your friends are, and how you work for a senator. She told me what you look like and how you talk. Especially how you talk. You have a charming tongue, I hear. I'm interested to see all it can do."

"It sounds as if Glynnis likes to exaggerate to her friends."

"We'll see. She was accurate about the physical description. I think I could have picked you out of a horde of thousands. You're very striking."

"Thank you, I think. Although 'striking' can have a few different connotations."

"Oh, it's positive in your case. I judge you to be a rare human being, Conor Finnegan. I'd like to get to know you better. Would you like something to drink while we share stories? There's a refrigerator down the hall that we all share. Beer, wine, and even some vodka, I think."

"No, I don't think so."

"Come on. I'm going to have a glass of wine. It's no fun to drink alone."

"All right, then. A glass of wine would be great."

"Good," and Lynda bounced off the bed and down the hall. He watched her tight, slender figure hop out of the room. Her breasts pushed the front of her thin blouse forward in firm cones that tapered to rounded points, and Conor stole sly glances at them as Lynda left the room. In her absence Finnegan remained where he was, seated at Glynnis's desk with his body twisted to face Lynda's bed. He felt incredibly self-conscious, and awkward at being here. He was alone on strange turf now. The safest thing would be to hold his pose and fix his gaze on the abstract, garishly ugly poster that hung on the wall above Lynda's bed.

She returned in a few minutes with two glasses in one hand and a huge bottle of chardonnay in the other. "I might want more than one," she said. "So might you."

The wine bypassed all of Conor's digestive organs and made straight for his blood. It relaxed him almost instantly, in part because he now had a prop around which he could wrap his hands and which, in turn, defined the current situation. Two new friends getting acquainted over a drink, no longer a young man who happened unexpectedly upon a beautiful young woman alone in her room. Finnegan's awkwardness, which Lynda did not perceive but which perched in the visitor's throat waiting to leap forth and direct any word that crept upward toward his mouth, diminished by degrees until it vanished altogether.

They talked for nearly an hour, Conor still in Glynnis's chair, Lynda reclining on her bed. They spoke of Conor's background, his work in Washington, what lay ahead, what he wanted to accomplish. Lynda was not willing to talk about herself, despite Conor's prompting. He tried to lead the conversation back toward her, but she kept averting it.

"I prefer to remain mysterious to my young men. Besides, you know all that's worth knowing. I'm here, I don't particularly like it, but there's nothing else I can do at the moment. I'm Glynnis's roommate and I love her dearly. I'm probably not a 'good' person in the traditional sense of the word, but then I really don't care for tradition in any form. I'm cold-hearted, oversexed and not to be trusted except by the two or three people in this world to whom I'm close, Glynnis being one. She could trust me with her life, and I'm very protective of her. She needs me, although she doesn't admit that to herself. There. Now let's get on with you."

"You make it too simple. And too gloomy. No one can summarize herself like that, in shorthand."

"I just did, Conor, and that's all I'm going to give you. Verbally, I mean. Now, tell me about this Italian friend of yours, the big one. He sounds adorable."

And the conversation continued away from Lynda, who skillfully choreographed it to the end. Lynda stayed reclined, her ankles crossed, her head propped back against the wall. Her eyes remained fixed on Conor, green stones beneath her blonde bangs. They burrowed into him and settled somewhere near his ribs, burning a path fiery and straight. She was in control, there could be no doubt. Conor Finnegan was merely a passenger booked for the ride, or perhaps a mouse running between a cat's paws.

Conor finished his second glass of wine. "More?" asked Lynda, and he smiled impishly in return. "I think I might. This is having a nice effect." Conor stood and took a step toward the bed to hand Lynda his glass. He stood there next to her as she poured. She finished, filling the glass nearly to the rim, tucked the bottle between the wall and her pillow, then held the glass up to Conor.

"You don't have to sit in that hard old chair." Her voice came out in a throaty purr. "Sit here beside me. We'll both feel better." Her eyes riveted on Conor's. The two glints of sharp jade held him fast. Finnegan stood spellbound, unable to move, unable to respond.

"Take your wine and sit next to me, Conor." She smoothed the bedspread with her hand. Slowly, languidly, ever in control.

"No, I don't think I should," replied Conor at last, helplessly, barely above a whisper.

"To the contrary," cooed Lynda, "it would be very good for you. But if you don't want to, then maybe I should try to convince you." She stood and reclaimed Finnegan's wine glass. She put it with her own on the desk. Finnegan took a small step backwards.

"What's the matter, lover? You don't find me attractive? Most men do." She slithered up to him and slid her hand around his neck as she spoke. Her breasts rubbed the front of Conor's shirt and she moved languorously from side to side to make him aware of them. Her lips brushed across Conor's, her breath warm against his mouth. Still her green eyes did not stray from his. Conor's lips trembled involuntarily; he felt his lower regions begin to stir.

Lynda pressed her lips hard into Conor's, parting them with her tongue. She drew him onward, confident now of her succulent power, confident now of her control, of her domination. Conor struggled against his better instincts, indefinable at this point except as reflexes, unarticulated and programmed rather than logical. He was incapable of sustained thought. In a victory of conscience, he broke away and retreated to Glynnis's bed.

"She won't be back for another hour at least. I lied. We've got all the time we want, lover." Lynda reached up and undid the buttons of her blouse.

"No . . . Not now," stammered Finnegan, confused and lost.

"It doesn't matter what's right," purred Lynda, now shrugging her blouse off her shoulders and slowly unzipping her jeans. "Not in the least. You want to, I can tell that, and so do I. Desperately. I want to do everything with you. Glynnis will never, never know."

Her bra fell next. Lynda cupped her breasts in both hands and rubbed them. Conor stared at them, fully rounded, much larger than Glynnis's, beautifully shaped. Lynda crossed the room to where he stood. She released her breasts and hooked her right hand on Conor's belt while her left reached around to his back to pull herself against him.

"I'm yours, lover. Don't disappoint me." She dropped her hand and rubbed the front of his jeans. Conor's eyes closed; he ran his hands through Lynda's thick blond hair. He found the soft solidity of her breasts, and his breathing quickened.

* * *

"Conor, you've barely said a word all night. What's wrong with you?"

"Nothing, Glyn. I'm sorry. I thought I'd let you do most of the talking tonight."

The dull familiar scenery of central New Jersey plodded by them. Conor felt as if they were not moving at all. He wanted this drive to be over. His head throbbed, a blunt edge pounding into his temples with each heartbeat. He wanted the long drive to be done, and this night to be done, and the entire weekend to be done. He wished that Glynnis would have found some excuse not to have come up this week. And if it were possible to transport oneself in time through the sheer power of thought, Finnegan would have done so. He would have pushed himself into Monday evening, where he could be alone with his reactions. Instead, he found himself behind the wheel of a car he did not wish to be driving and sitting beside his lover whom he did not wish to see. Not now. But no escape was possible.

"You must be tired, poor thing." She reached across and rubbed the back of Finnegan's neck. He flinched. Her touch felt like sandpaper. "Rough week?"

"Rougher than you could know. I just want to be home and in bed. My head is splitting apart."

"Poor thing," she repeated. "I'll make you feel better. I'm tired, too. Maybe we can do good things to each other."

"Glynnis, we do those things when we're not tired and when we're feeling fine. Tonight I think I'd rather just sleep."

"Conor, don't be mad at me because you had to wait. I had to get that project done, there were no two ways about it. You understand, don't you?"

"Yeah," he said after a deep sigh. "Yeah, I understand. And I'm not angry, Glyn. Just tired."

"Lynda kept you company, though. She's not bad company, is she? I'm glad you two finally got the chance to meet."

He said nothing.

"Well, I hope you were more at ease with her than you've been with me tonight. You don't seem quite right. Did she do anything to set you off?"

"I liked her well enough." Conor stopped, then started again. "Or maybe I didn't. I don't know. Maybe she's too wrapped up in herself to be what you'd call pleasant. Maybe she just tried a little too hard to be liked. I don't know, Glyn. I honestly don't know what I think of her. That'll take time to digest."

"You didn't have that much time with her, Conor, certainly not enough to form a lasting impression. Be gentle in your thoughts, won't you please? She's had a rough go of it. Rougher than anyone could rightly expect her to handle without some ugliness coming through. I know her much better than you ever will, and I know she can be crude and self-serving and dishonest and cruel. But I know, too, that those are her last defenses. I love that girl, Conor. She can also be quite kind and compassionate. Beneath her brittle surface there's a desperate longing to be appreciated. To be liked. She's given up her vulnerability, but there's still an innocence that she rarely shows, and never intentionally. I don't expect you saw any of that."

"In the short time I was with her I saw nothing that could even remotely be mistaken for innocence. Kindness and compassion reared their heads only for a brief peek."

"That's too bad. But at least she was company for you, even if a little jagged. Right?"

"Yes, Glyn. She was company."

They finished the drive in silence, arriving at last around 9:30, much later than normal. Conor wanted to go straight to bed. The thought of the soft sheets beneath him in the cool, chirping darkness covered his pounding head like a balm. Let Glynnis fend for herself tonight. Let her prepare her own food if she wants it, let her swap stories with his friends. He must sleep, and soon.

But at the top of the stairs there was noise—music and the clatter of many voices. Conor Finnegan opened the door to find a small party, no more than a dozen or so of their closest friends. He regarded the scene with a scowl firmly set on his dark face.

Dan Rosselli bolted from the center of the room, grinning wildly. "Conor! Glynnis! Where the hell have you two been? We've been waiting for you, and you need to be here."

"What's up Dan? I didn't know we were entertaining tonight."

"Had to. Great news, brother!"

Finnegan guessed it at once, and his frown reversed itself into a broadly growing smile.

"Which school?"

"Georgetown."

"Georgetown! Holy Christ, Danny boy, that's fantastic. That's . . ." and, unable to think of the right things to say, Conor Finnegan grabbed Dan Rosselli and hugged him with all his strength.

"Dan, I'm so God damned happy for you."

"Thanks, Conor. Now go grab a beer while I hug your woman." Which he did. Glynnis kissed him on both cheeks.

"We can talk about living arrangements later," Finnegan yelled down the hallway. "Right, roommate?"

"Is that an offer?"

"If you can come up with half the rent."

"Where?"

Finnegan returned with his beer. Glynnis had ducked into Conor's bedroom to put away her bag. "Wherever we can find something where we outnumber the rats. My sources are looking."

"Christ, Conor, that would be great, staying together like that."

"Yeah, wouldn't it? You'll love Washington. And in three more years I ought to be used to your cooking. Plan on it, Doctor."

Finnegan hugged Rosselli again. Hopes are only hopes until pushed across the border of reality. And now all uncertainty, all concern, all the frantic desperation of not knowing whether one's set course is proper, and, even if proper, attainable, could be jettisoned like the dead weight it was. Let arrogance and conceit, greed and egoism, creep in later after the thrill of accomplishment dwindles. For that would happen to a man of Dan Rosselli's incontrovertible nature. Tonight, though, he was just a little boy, joyously open, unshakably pure.

Conor's humor turned over. For an evening he could revive himself and toast his friend. He could ignore his headache, he could forget his self-pity. He could put aside all unhealthy notions, the burgeoning self-doubt, the crumbling sureties of passion. They would all be back with him tomorrow, or perhaps the day following. Jacob's Angel would be there to be wrestled so that salvation might at last be attained.

* * *

Graduation, then, rose before them all as an act of irretrievable passage. It was left now only to Lanny O'Hanlon and Tom McIlweath to determine where they would land on the other shore.

O'Hanlon had his options. Just as Conor Finnegan, O'Hanlon had settled on a career in government, or, rather, politics. No altruistic pursuit of the common good entered his decision. Indeed, his resolution had been no decision at all but the natural evolutionary outgrowth of a path set for him since childhood by breeding, temperament and circumstances. Lanny O'Hanlon enjoyed power, the sensation engendered by the realization that what he did compelled the work of others. He enjoyed walking into a room and being recognized. In the last analysis, he concluded that if his personal characteristics might not in themselves generate respect, if men did not look up to him for his intellectual or physical or moral attributes, then he could create the same effects by virtue of political position, the job superseding the man who performed it.

Lanny O'Hanlon had to decide whether to stay in New Jersey where he had been offered a permanent position on the Secretary of State's staff, a logical development of two years of interning with growing responsibility, or return to Boston where his father had (by dint of Lanny's solid reputation, embellished a bit by fatherly aggrandizement) secured for his son a position as legislative assistant to the Speaker of the Massachusetts State Assembly. Both possibilities excited him, and both made sense. They were both clear entries to a sturdy career that could be fed by good work and better contacts.

At length, in late May, two weeks before he was to leave college forever, he decided to till the soil in Trenton using his own tools rather than return to work Boston's using his father's. Lanny suspected that his father still viewed him as too callow to set his own course. That had, after all, been the elder O'Hanlon's motivation for arranging matters back home in the commonwealth. Trenton, on the other hand, had been created by Lanny alone. He decided to play the hand he had drawn for himself from an unstacked deck. His father understood perfectly and had no hard feelings, nor did the Speaker. He would always be there if Lanny found he ever needed his help.

Tom McIlweath had expected his decision to crystallize before him, a well-formed sediment of scholarly opportunities, financial realities and his increasingly confused, contorted feelings toward Anne Newbury. Long before Dan Rosselli had received his happy letter from Georgetown's medical school, Anne had been accepted three times over in three scattered parts of the east coast, with Harvard at the top of the pyramid. There had been no party for Anne, just lukewarm congratulations from Tom's friends and a celebratory dinner for two at an expensive restaurant. She would be in Cambridge for the foreseeable future, then. She had assumed Tom would readily follow, so when he balked at Boston University's acceptance to its graduate program in Classics, when he let it be known that he was not firmly in tow, Anne had become aggravated. She coaxed and demanded that he come to a decision about his own future. She termed him weak for not doing so at once, and his hesitation caused her to grow sullen.

But Tom McIlweath did not wish to be directed by a relationship that offered as much insecurity and bafflement as it did emotional satisfaction. He resolved to view Anne as but one factor in a decision to be reached under composite influences. McIlweath had loosely concluded that he would continue to pursue the scholarly life, at least for now. At Rutgers, his research and translation work reassured him of both the broad nature of man's intellect and his own capacity to understand it. That sense of accomplishment, the rarefied exhilaration of intellectual creativity, was not a small thing. It invigorated him daily. It allowed him to transcend whatever oppressive details of his humble lifestyle might at any given time be tarnishing his spirit. It allowed him temporarily to dismiss that haunting subliminal suspicion that, despite his efforts at devising an existence that defined his innermost character, all was not right. Nothing else he considered came close to exciting him as did the prospect of continuing his study of the classics on a higher level. This would do for now. It approximated what he wanted for himself better than anything else he knew at the moment.

McIlweath had applied to a number of graduate schools, taking care, in spite of his rebellious sentiments, that he had selected institutions that were not only good but were in cities that had medical schools to which Anne Newbury was applying as well. He told himself that this was just a precaution should he determine that his relationship with Anne was worth continuing. It would be a terrible development if, at the end of the year, things had progressed and their feelings had deepened only to have to navigate a geographic gulf between them. He would not have to attend near Anne, but he believed he should probably have that option.

Tom McIlweath was the last of the four to determine where he was heading. While his friends remained silent on the issue—Mac could decide for himself, they reasoned; besides, we have our own problems to solve—Anne constantly reminded him that he was still directionless, perilously so, and if he weren't a fool he would head for Boston come autumn. McIlweath for his part carefully weighed the Classics programs at the schools which had accepted him and compared their financial offers, trying to find a decisive difference in what was essentially identical.

'Perhaps,' he reasoned as he sat one night on the front steps of the apartment, 'perhaps I shouldn't be so quick to abandon something which I had sought for so long.' Images of Anne, her deep acceptance of him and the genuine emotional response she evoked despite all disagreements, despite all divergences of style and substance, flooded him.

'Perhaps I take her for granted. I don't want to be lonely again. No matter how I phrase it to myself or try to rationalize it, that's all it is, isn't it? I don't want to be lonely again. We need each other. It would be a sin, a tragic sin, to abandon one another. After what we've known of each other I could not stand it. I'd go blind, lifeless and numb, a creature of habit, a creature of response, but one incapable of projection.

'I see her there, with the depthless echoes of her blue eyes and the soft curl of her hair, the silky delicacy of her skin. I see her cold and alone, too, there in Boston, and it breaks my heart. I see her sadness, and I cannot stand it. She is a little girl still, afraid of the night. I cannot leave her there, and myself removed some place else, away from all warmth, all acceptance. I cannot . . .'

This last was true. Tom McIlweath could not leave Anne Newbury, not then, with any greater ease than a fetus can step outside its mother's womb and walk away. He had known it for weeks, for months, for years, and he had attempted to deny it through a coldly logical assessment of his opportunities. He had attempted to deny the undeniable. In the end, it was all a charade. His 'opportunities,' indeed. What opportunity did he truly have, apart from Anne? He knew it, had always known it, and no protest to the contrary could ever have dislodged the conclusion reached, without his consent that day, long before when he had sat next to her on a crosstown bus.

Tom McIlweath went back upstairs and in the quiet thickness of a gathering dark night penned his acceptance of an offer of admission to Boston University, a few miles away from where Anne would spend her next several years.

* * *

It all ended much more quickly than it had begun. The day dawned heavy with an impending rain that held off until after dark. No sun shone through the thick clouds that pressed down like a layer of turf on the occasion. The McIlweaths and the Finnegans had come east, the O'Hanlons had come south and the Rossellis had come north from the shore. They gathered to compare their sons and to recognize the processes of mortality that had acted upon them. They saw in each other indelible traces of themselves.

The Finnegans and the McIlweaths toured campus escorted by their son. Edward Finnegan, more than the others, was impressed. The great stone buildings, the wide trees, the crawling ivy formed an image of solidity, of permanence, of good people in worthwhile pursuits, and his son had been a part of it, a small niche in wood gnarly grown. He felt inestimable pride that young Conor, who bore a name reflective of a nomadic Irish heritage, should have come here on his own and, through the strength of his hard character, conquered it within his four years. He had indeed conquered it; he had made it all serve him, he had drawn from its energy, and his father saw that now. Edward Finnegan knew his son in these strange surroundings to be more alive, more confident, more assured, in sum stronger than he had ever been before. He knew, too, that through it all, Conor belonged here.

Katherine Finnegan was not nearly so appreciative. The campus dwarfed her, and she saw at once that it was peopled with men and women far different than her own traditional background had allowed her to be. Bold and confident intelligence, and the trappings of intelligence, had always intimidated her. She knew her son to be extremely capable, and that was obvious now. But he would have honed himself to this sharper edge no matter what he had done or where he had gone to college. Why had he to come here, to this strange place where the natives spoke with a peculiar accent, and rob her of eight years—four of his and four of hers? Now he would settle in the East and her only son, her only child, would be a world apart by emigration from the ways and elements which had nourished him so long ago. Nothing now could be regained; no recompense offered itself. Katherine feared her age and she feared loneliness. She was convinced that they both loomed immediately ahead. She wanted all this which was at hand to be done, so that she could leave this strange place, this place that had claimed her child, and return to the few sureties left her.

The ceremonies on that leaden gray day were long, made longer by the fact that both McIlweath and Finnegan had been elected to Phi Beta Kappa, and so had their honor bestowed at a breakfast several hours before commencement itself. The two young men had received notice of their election three weeks prior on the same day. Finnegan had stood motionless at his campus mailbox, reading and rereading the brief letter from the dean. As well as he had done during his time there, he had rarely considered this possibility. The reality of the honor made his lungs ache. He ran back to the apartment, an odd sight in slacks, a sweater and loafers, carrying several thick books, sprinting across campus, in front of the library and down the quiet residential street adjacent. His excitement and disbelief burst into a naked animalism, a primitive rush of mindless energy that compelled him to run and not stop until he was exhausted. He darted up the brick steps to the front door, then up the wooden staircase to find McIlweath standing in the center of the living room, flapping his arms wildly as Finnegan bolted through the door.

"Conor, I got Phi Beta Kappa!"

"Christ, Mac, you too?"

"You got it?"

"Hell, yeah," he screamed, and then they rushed together to pump each other's hands and pound one another on the back. Later that night they sat in the kitchen, too engaged by their own success to do any work and drinking an obligatory glass of wine in quiet celebration. In the course of their conversation, Conor said, "I never dreamed I'd do here what I've done. Mac, when we came here I was so brash, but I really didn't know anything. I had no expectations beyond some nebulous concept of 'succeeding.' Somehow. I was sure that whatever constituted success, I would find it. But in reality, Tom, it's so much sweeter than what some arrogant kid could ever make it out to be."

"Think back to what we've been through, Conor. We can both feel proud."

"But not complacent, Tom. Never complacent. As a reminder of that, I offer a toast, to our late friend Reg Coleman."

"Reg was hardly complacent, Conor."

"No, but those of us who knew him were. Especially me. We all thought that we held a certain amount of control over who we were and what we did. Reg showed us what happens when we lose that control, when we cave in to what others expect of us. We were all too self-absorbed to see it. We never believed that that type of ugliness could ever visit us here. We were complacent."

"Reg defined himself almost completely through what other people saw in him," said McIlweath, "and not what he saw in himself. His own ambitions never surfaced. That wasn't a living human being we knew, Conor; it was someone's concept of what should occupy that space. Reg had no idea of himself, so neither could we."

"I think about him often, Mac. I really do, especially at times like this, when it's all going so well. He was the other half, the lost half of each one of us."

"To Reg Coleman," said McIlweath, and raised his glass again. "May he find in his passing the peace he never knew when he was among us."

"And to us, my friend," rejoined McIlweath. "God damn it, to us."

After breakfast, the Finnegans and the McIlweaths returned to the apartment. The elders jammed into the living room while the four young men donned their robes. They stepped over and around the boxes and suitcases strewn across each bedroom. Their possessions were all arranged for quick departure. At the end of the day, nothing of value would be left behind. None of them had the urge to sit with the corpse of a body too soon dead.

The ceremony itself was a long, tedious affair on Queen's Mall. Graduates and parents kept scanning the sky for the impending storm but the day's speakers neither shortened nor sped up their addresses. Stertorous and dull, all of it. The graduates returned to their seats, each one of them, diploma in hand after having their names called to walk singly across a makeshift stage, a final instant of recognition before being swallowed by the anonymous swarm. Finnegan did not thrill to the tangibility of his diploma, as some did. It did not matter. What he had accomplished here could not be so easily symbolized or imprinted on any manner of document, so the document itself had little meaning, nor did the ceremony. It was all just ritual.

The rain held off. Afterward they all reassembled at the apartment and loaded their belongings into the appropriate vehicles. They would scatter from there—Rosselli back to the shore for one final carefree summer, O'Hanlon down to his newly rented flat outside Trenton, McIlweath back to California for two months before heading to Boston. He would leave his car and large possessions in Anne's care, who had promised to find a suitable place for him to live in Boston, something inexpensive but safe and close to campus. She had spent the day with her parents, had gone through the ceremony alone, and Tom had not seen her except to wave across the rows of seated graduates. Finnegan, too, set to leave. He would stay with his parents for several days, traveling down to Washington where they would help him settle into his new apartment before they started the interminably lonely drive back across country.

They would go now, the four of them, benumbed to their inner sense of deep, deep loss by the demanding new mantles they each had claimed. They would go now, sealing an unspoken brotherhood but never again able to share in it as they had at its inception, and so a hollow, empty, aching sentiment. They would go now, striding with innocence into a society devoid of innocence, confident of acceptance in a society oddly indifferent. They would go now, quietly assured of eventually achieving wealth, power, justice and peace by virtue of their great, good characters, assured of the favor of a benevolent Providence whose blessings had always been as abundant as they were apparent.

What chapters end, what begin, there on a precipice, a razor's edge between certainty and doubt, between love and abandonment, when past existence so clearly meets what lies ahead and swirls it around a single point? A black hole sucked them in there and left behind no sound, no smell, not the faintest trace of any of them. It drew them into darkness and the great mysteries, pulling them through a point no wider than a microbe or the sharpened prick of a needle. But therein lay the fiber of their youth, the heated energy of all hope and promise, compressed by the infinite, relentless power of time. They saw themselves there, victims as well as actors, inescapably linked to whatever seeds had been sown within them, timid in the face of their ultimate fruition.

Solitude impended, as did frustration and loss. They sensed it all without articulation, as a forest deer sniffs the air for a distant fire burning in her direction. They knew it by reputation even as they believed that it could not really touch them after all, this distant fire which so far had spared them, and so by nature in the days ahead they would continue unscathed. It is the arrogance of youth, tempered by a quietly lurking fear that all houses must one day fall, that all men and women, sadly, are mortal, subject to heartbreak, to anonymity, to death in life, to pacing dark and empty hallways in search of what has come to be lost. It is the fear that, despite all assurances to the contrary, man must suffer and bleed and claw at his face in the agony of despair, that he must cry in the night alone, that he must plead with himself to muster strength and pride in the maw of dejection, that he must convince himself anew of his own worth, that his life has value and purpose, that it makes more sense to plod hopelessly after a lost dream, or one unknown altogether, than to throw himself headlong off the highest cliff onto the jagged rocks below. It is the fear that he will soon be haunted by the brevity of his existence against the grand infinity of his desires. It is the fear that, in the end, life will prove to be grimly frustrating, sad and lonely, a crushing burden to a spirit once glorious and unfettered, a hateful and oppressive process that twists the soul into a grotesque, befouled, corpselike entity, the antithesis of joy, of peace, of life itself as he had always known it.

It was fitting, then, that after the final ceremony, after all cars were loaded and after all doors were locked behind them, the four young men left together for the last time. They excused themselves from their parents, who shifted to the far side of the street so that they might be out of the way. There they waited in a group of eight, exchanging their own formalized farewells with those whom they had only recently met but with whom the implicit common ground was obvious.

Across the street, the four graduates stood together in front of the closed door and dark apartment. No one quite knew what to say or how to begin the inevitable. The day's true ceremony hovered just before them.

"So," Finnegan began at last. "Listen, I don't want this to be awkward, but I also want you to know how hard it is to leave here. You guys have been more than family, and I'm grateful for the time we've had together. I'm grateful to all of you."

"It's been great, hasn't it?" said McIlweath. "Like nothing I could have expected, and like nothing we'll ever experience again."

"Well, listen," said O'Hanlon, subdued and strangely serious, "take care of yourselves. You won't have your wise New England roommate to bail you out with money, women and wisdom. In fact, I might even be tempted to worry about you guys. Babes in the woods."

"Conor, you and I will at least have each other," said Rosselli. "And Tom'll be with Anne, and Lanny has his ego. No one'll be alone. We'll be fine."

"I have no doubt," said Finnegan. They looked at each other, one at a time. First Finnegan, then the others, broke at last into a smile, and they shared their broad, boyish, unaffected grins.

Someone, maybe O'Hanlon, said, "Take care, gentlemen, and stay in touch." They shook hands warmly, then in common realization that such was not enough, they hugged one another tight and hard in clutching unembarrassed embraces, feeling the solidity of bodies on the verge of stepping into new forms. They separated, exchanged pats on the back and final handshakes, and then with the eulogistic finality of car doors thumping shut, drove off into their singular existences.

* * *

The several-day drive westward that night took the McIlweaths through the rich green mountains of northwestern New Jersey and eastern Pennsylvania, the Kittatinny range and the Poconos. Tom McIlweath sat cramped in the back seat. The sky which had hung dark all day at last opened up in a driving black rainstorm that pelted thick, bulletlike drops against the windshield. The swish-click of the wipers created a numbing monotony as the scenery washed away. Night came on within minutes and McIlweath found himself growing greatly depressed. Perhaps it was natural denouement of a day laden with such intense reactions. He closed his eyes and slept a jerky, uncomfortable slumber.

As the rain came, Conor sat on a bed in a motel room not far from campus. He sat alone. His parents had gone for something to eat and Conor, pleading a lack of appetite, stayed behind. He sat in darkness, with no lights, no radio, no television to break the gloom. He preferred it that way. When the rain began he took no notice. The heavy drops slammed against the room's large window, hidden by drapes that shut out most of the dying day's sparse light. Conor sat on the bed, head in his hands. He stared at the carpeted floor and breathed in a slow, ponderous rhythm whose contrived beat was marked in his imagination by the splash of the rain onto the unseen window.

CHAPTER XV

*Thus have the gods spun the thread for wretched mortals:
that they live in grief while they themselves are without
cares; for two jars stand on the floor of Zeus of the gifts
which he gives, one of evils and another of blessings.*

—Homer, *Iliad*

"Generally, sir, we take our patients on referral from the VA. There's no one here from off the street, as we say. I'm afraid there'd be nothing gained by your looking around."

"But my grandfather is in the VA hospital in Richmond now. They're going to move him in a month or so, as soon as they find someplace suitable. They mentioned your facility. I wanted to see for myself where he's going to be."

Conor Finnegan sat across the desk from the administrator, a slight, hawkish man whose entire face seemed hidden behind a massive pair of thick glasses perched atop the razor of his nose. His lips were so thin as to be transparent. Large ears stuck out beneath graying black hair slicked back and greased down. 'There is no blood in this man.' thought Finnegan. The administrator leaned forward in his chair and nervously fingered his nameplate: Brandon Carrecker.

"What do you do for a living, Mr. Finnegan? I ask only because I am interested in your family's ability to cover the expenses that will come should your grandfather join us here. I assume he has adequate medical coverages but there are always costs that no plan will cover."

"I'm an instructor at Georgetown University, Mr. Carrecker. And, yes, my grandfather has more than adequate coverage. Money will be no issue. He has a considerable sum he's saved for retirement, more than half a million." Finnegan mentioned the figure deliberately, and slowly. "It's sad that he won't be using it for what he intended, poor man."

"Yes. But we never know quite when the ravages of age will strike us, do we? Stay here, Mr. Finnegan. I must check with our director of nursing services to see if a tour would be appropriate right now."

Carrecker drew himself out of his chair and left the office. His suit hung on him, too large for his bladelike frame. As Carrecker walked past in a jerky gait, the image of a ferret passed through Finnegan's mind.

In the administrator's absence Finnegan studied his office. It struck him as unusually spartan. Carrecker's desk held only a handful of scattered papers, a telephone and a lone in/out tray. In the corner stood a metal filing cabinet and on the fading yellow walls there hung two framed diplomas. Beyond that there was nothing. The small room was a narrow cell in a great honeycomb. Finnegan could find no evidence of human warmth here at all.

He sat alone for nearly fifteen minutes before Carrecker slithered back into his office. "Forgive the delay, Mr. Finnegan, but as I'm sure you can imagine, we are quite busy. An unplanned tour takes away from everyone's time. However, we shall be glad to give you a quick peek at our facilities if you'll follow me. I will conduct you myself."

Finnegan rose and followed Carrecker out of the office. Some pungent indefinable smell flared his nostrils as soon as he set foot in the inner hallway. He had not noticed it upon entering, and he did not like it. This was not the harsh antiseptic odor of a hospital or of most other nursing homes. This was starkly bitter, a mixture, Finnegan guessed, of ammonia, urine and vomit. He fought to avoid showing his disgust.

"Thank you, Mr. Carrecker. I'm very grateful for your help."

"Please bear in mind, Mr. Finnegan, that you will be seeing the facility as it truly is. We have not hidden anything or spirited away our most unruly residents. We have not had the chance to do so in your case, to be quite blunt."

"You do so otherwise?"

"Everyone does. Everyone wants to put forward their best face, so for the families of prospective residents they take great care to see that everything is in order. Why agitate someone over an unattractive reality, however inevitable and natural it may be? It's part of the game and, as I say, we're very typical in that regard. Everyone does it. But I can assure you that your grandfather will get the optimum care here, certainly as good as he would receive anywhere else in Northern Virginia. You have my word on that."

They walked down a long corridor that was as starkly faded as Carrecker's office. Four or five other administrative offices opened onto this corridor, but there were no signs of activity. At the end they turned right through an open entryway into a large rectangular area. Several threadbare chairs were scattered around the room, and in a far corner one was overturned, its legs thrusting into the air hopelessly. Against one wall a television set alternately held then lost its picture. Actors and actresses of some daytime drama faded in, then were swept away in a maze of horizontal static. On the wall above the set were numerous pockmarks about the size of a man's fist or a hard shoe. The floor was a dull linoleum some shade of gray. There were no rugs to interrupt its flat monotony. The wall opposite the television console had two square windows, without curtains or shades, that looked out onto a central courtyard.

What Finnegan saw as he turned in to this room made him stop short, and Carrecker took two quick steps ahead before he realized that his visitor was not beside him. "Come along. We won't be disturbing anyone."

'Indeed not,' thought Finnegan, 'for the people in this room are purely incapable of being disturbed.' Before him were arrayed a macabre collection of scarecrows and skeletons, or wraiths and ghosts, of the incoherent, the incontinent, the dispossessed, of every form of death in life his young mind could conceive. It was not a collection of humanity as he had ever known it, and it was this horrific sight, combined with the harsh smell that he had noticed in the hallway, that made him stop in his tracks. At Carrecker's insistence, Finnegan stepped into the room.

As they walked through it, Carrecker made some type of explanation which Finnegan absorbed in only bits and pieces. "Common sense . . . come together during the day . . . some come and go as they please . . . meet with and talk to one another . . . the importance of contact . . ."

Finnegan did not, could not, listen. His impressions and consequent memory would be refracted not through the ear but through the eye. In one chair to his left sat a bony, unshaven form in pajamas, his mouth agape and a thin flow of saliva dripping from it to his chin. His glassy eyes paid no heed to the two walking figures that passed him. They seemed instead to be fixed on some point on the far wall, or possibly beyond. Across from this lost soul another man rocked back and forth in his chair, his toothless mouth opening and closing. Some substance had dried into a brittle cake on the front of his pajama top. He raised a hand as the two men walked near him, not a wave but a salute. Next to him an old man sat strapped in his chair by broad leather thongs. He laughed hysterically, mindlessly, a high pitched squeal of a laugh, the sound made by blowing across a blade of grass. Below his chair a fetid puddle of excrement grew by drips from the cuff of his pajama leg.

In the far corner, near the two windows, an emaciated figure leaned against the point where the walls met, his face burrowing into the concave molding. There was no meat on him at all. Near him, an old man bent over, his head hanging between his knees. He spat something onto the floor and let its remnants drool out of his mouth. Another patient sat with his back against a wall and uttered profanities to everyone, and to no one. Not a soul paid attention to him, so apparently he was considered part of the landscape. Other figures huddled in their chairs or walked aimlessly, silently about the room.

One of the strolling figures walked up to Finnegan and Carrecker. He was a shadowed form, his face carved in angles and lines with the scruff of his unshaven chin and cheeks matching the short growth on his head. He moved painfully in a slow shuffle. Finnegan was surprised to see that he was barefoot. The old man approached them from the side and, reaching out a bony claw of a hand, grabbed Finnegan by the wrist. Finnegan looked into the vacant eyes that had filled with tears.

"Jimmy," the old man croaked. "Jimmy, take me home. I want to go home now, Jimmy," and his voice broke over crusty cheeks.

"Now, Mr. Crenshaw," soothed Carrecker, "you can't go home now. You know that. But maybe in a little while you could, when you're feeling better. Why don't you go sit with Mr. Ellison. He looks as if he could use some company." Carrecker steered the old man to another shapeless figure strapped into his chair. Mr. Crenshaw reluctantly shuffled away, muttering, "Jimmy . . . Jimmy," as he went.

"A sad case, Mr. Finnegan, but no sadder, really, than many of our residents. As you can see, a fair number of them are mentally incapacitated. It's a shame, but there's little we can do for them."

"Do you even try?" muttered Finnegan under his breath.

"Pardon?"

"Nothing. Please go on."

"We have to keep several of them constantly sedated. We're heading now for the residential area. The residents you'll see here are those who are physically handicapped. I want to show you what a typical room looks like. The type of room your grandfather would have, you see, provided he has no special needs."

They walked down a corridor of closed doors. From behind two or three of them Finnegan heard groans, or maybe loud sighs. Sounds of dissolution. Carrecker rapped briskly on one of the doors and opened it before he could get a response. Therein lay a grizzled form with one leg. He lay uncovered on his bed, an intravenous system attached to a spindly arm. He said nothing as the younger men entered the room.

"Good afternoon, Mr. Herbert. We won't disturb you long. I just want to show this young man what type of accommodation we offer."

The room was a long rectangle made of plaster which cracked and peeled in several small spots. A single window no more than two feet square opposed the door. The bed sat against one wall and a small desk with a chair was situated in the corner beneath the window. A dresser abutted the desk. Finnegan did not notice whether there was a closet. The room was painted a drab olive green, as lifeless as the rest of the building and the people in it. Small, cramped, sterile, dead.

"What do you think, Mr. Finnegan?"

"I think it reminds me of my old college dormitory room, except without the charm."

"It's all the space a retired gentleman needs. We're fortunate to be able to offer a high degree of privacy. Most of our rooms are single. Many places can't offer that."

They went forth to inspect the dining area and the recreation room. Both places were empty. Finnegan noted that the dining area had not been thoroughly cleaned. A good deal of food was strewn across the floor, and some was smeared onto the walls. He could not be sure, but he thought he saw a tiny insect dart along a far wall. Perhaps it was that he expected to see it.

The recreation room contained a ping-pong table, a rack of magazines and four or five card tables with decks of cards and poker chips. The room was nearly as large as the common room, or so it seemed in its empty state. 'Which of these skeletons is strong enough even to hold a ping-pong paddle?' Finnegan thought, 'let alone swing it? This is ludicrous.'

"We provide a full range of recreational outings," said Carrecker, "To the zoo, a park, maybe even a high school football game. I'm surprised this room is not in use at the moment. Usually many of our residents pass some time playing cards."

"Maybe they just have other things to do today," replied Finnegan.

Carrecker let the sarcasm slide by. "Perhaps they do. I won't show you our physical therapy room. That's in use. But let me tell you that we do have a registered therapist, a P.T., on staff and that our therapy room is equipped with a whirlpool bath, a complete set of hand and leg weights, walkers, guide bars, and an adjustable treadmill. We run a complete therapy program for those who need it."

"I see. Tell me, how many people do you have on staff here? I've noticed very few. There was an orderly in the common room and a nurse's aide in the residential wing, but I think that's all I've seen."

"We have a staff of 26. That includes health care personnel, maintenance and kitchen. I assure you, we're adequately staffed. We exceed state regulations in that regard."

They retraced their steps through the grim scenes in the grim rooms. Carrecker kept up a chatter of statistics and testimonials. "Finest care available . . . VA referrals . . . waiting list . . . complete program of rehabilitative care." Finnegan paid no attention. His eyes darted quickly in all directions looking for further affronts, looking for scenes to memorize.

They reached Carrecker's office. "Do you have any questions, Mr. Finnegan?"

"How many of your residents ever leave this facility?"

"All of them leave, but very few walk out, I'm afraid. As you know, retirement facilities provide a level of care that cannot be attained in one's home, and most of our residents have serious physical or mental conditions that cannot be reversed sufficiently for them to be on their own. That's why most of them are here in the first place. It's a sad fact, but there it is. You're dealing with old men whose recuperative powers are either severely limited or nonexistent. But we do try to provide as comfortable a setting for them as we can."

"Do you allow unlimited visitation?"

"Oh, good heavens, no. We couldn't possibly do that. It would interfere with our social and therapeutic programs and be far too disruptive for the residents. Relatives and friends may visit Wednesday evenings, on weekends and by appointment."

"But isn't visitation itself therapeutic? Your residents should have the opportunity to keep close family ties without feeling as if they've been shuffled off to some remote outpost to meet their maker."

"Frankly, Mr. Finnegan, visitation is more a nuisance to the staff than it's worth. Most of our residents are beyond response to their family members. They just want to go about their existence. On visiting days, many sit and wait for visits that never come, and they go to bed at night more dispirited and depressed than when the day began."

"Mr. Crenshaw seemed to be waiting pretty hard for Jimmy. Seemed like he wanted a change of scenery, too."

"Most of our residents, to be blunt, are here to get it over with."

"That seems a cold attitude for a nursing home administrator, if I may be equally blunt."

"It's reality, Mr. Finnegan, and it stems from twenty-two years in the business. This is not an easy task, sir. One's ideals occasionally become trampled by the sadness of the conditions with which one has to deal."

"Thank you for the tour, Mr. Carrecker," said Finnegan abruptly. "You've been most helpful, and I know you've scrambled your day to accommodate me."

"Do you think your grandfather would be happy here? Tell me about him."

"He's a simple old man, Mr. Carrecker, with all his wits intact. I'm sure the VA will give you a complete summary of his condition, should they refer him to you. I'll request that they do."

Finnegan walked out of the building quickly, fleeing the pungent, vile odor that had followed him throughout the tour. Carrecker no doubt had grown accustomed to many things. It was exactly as Finnegan had heard. He filled his lungs with the clean warm air and climbed into his car. He drove back to the Hill with the tense excitement of a new battle about to be joined.

* * *

Glynnis Mear had taken a small apartment near campus and furnished it with what her mother had sent down, mostly old pieces that had been stored in their attic. Most of it was both sturdy and stylish, reflective of her mother's delicate senses. Over the years they had simply acquired too much of it, so some had to be put away. She hung her own paintings on the wall. The apartment, an upper flat on the fringes of Philadelphia's Main Line, quickly assumed her personal mark. It acquired a special comfort fueled in part by her own independence.

She had not wanted to commit herself to Washington. She had been reluctant to narrow further the already wafer-thin gap between her life and Conor's. Every rational impulse she had during her deliberations had pointed to heading south and taking a place in the city, if not moving in with Conor altogether. She had been sorely, sorely tempted. Yet each time she considered that course, something held her back, something irrational, illogical and deeply rooted in some remote abyss of her psyche. She could not bring herself to accept Conor's invitation, which, when he perceived her reluctance, became a plea. Nor, when pressed, could she explain herself. Conor surmounted his puzzlement with the conviction that Glynnis still felt strongly about him, still loved him in fact, but for reasons of her own would not move with him to Washington. The timing must be wrong, so he would have to be patient for now.

Upon graduation Glynnis took up residence in her new apartment. Her mother had come down with a rental truckload of furnishings then, the day following the ceremony, returned up the turnpike to Boston, slightly uneasy about her daughter's lack of definable direction. Glynnis had decided to pursue a master's degree in art. She did not, however, know quite what she wanted to do with it. Florence Mear concluded, in light of Glynnis's evasive, noncommittal actions, that her daughter was merely passing time.

Perhaps, in fact, she was, but if so, she was content with the forms her amusements quickly assumed. She had been awarded a graduate assistantship so her expenses for the coming year would be fully covered in exchange for teaching line and composition to a new generation of eccentric aspiring aesthetes. Consequently she saw no need to work during the summer months. She lived off her small savings and spent her days reading, drawing and taking long, aimless walks through the sultry city. Her restlessness, which had been absent for several months, returned and there were times she felt a desperate, almost frantic need to get out, to move her body in any direction, to see new faces and to smell new scents, to discover at any cost something different, some vista or sound or idea apart from anything else she had ever known. She had felt this way nearly all her life, but never so strongly since she had met Conor.

She took a cab sometimes to the middle of the city, and then, as the steamy days wound down, she would pick a street with an ancient, lyrical, inviting name and follow it. Broad, Walnut, Market, Arch and the numbered streets. She even headed down Spring Garden one night, supremely confident that even in that beaten, stark, hopeblown neighborhood she would not be menaced. At times she would spot a stranger sitting in a park and, because he looked pleasantly intelligent, start a conversation. To her dismay, most were reluctant to speak to her, but that did not stop her from trying to bring them out when the mood struck her. Most people, she was convinced, were inherently friendly.

Weekends she spent with Conor in Washington repeating the scenes of the previous summer. Conor lived alone for now with Dan Rosselli still working in the hospital near his home on the Jersey shore, but it would not have mattered had he been present. Of all Conor's friends, Rosselli made Glynnis feel most comfortable. He had not been pretentious; he carried absolutely no expectations of her. She did not dread the autumn when he would be moving in with her lover. His company, in fact, would be welcomed. It would provide a relaxing contrast to the intensity, the increasing seriousness and the growing demands of her relationship with Conor.

And so Glynnis Mear passed the summer idly, as indolently as at any time of her life. The world had been constructed to her specifications.

She had no complaints, then, as she waited for the coming of the autumn and the resumption of her casual studies.

* * *

Griffith Ross was a large, burly man who had always enjoyed the animal pleasures. He had been something of a rake in college twenty years earlier, and by the time he left the ivied halls of his alma mater he had cultivated a broad reputation as a ladies' man. Shortly after he received his degree and arranged to enter law school, one of the ladies upon whom his reputation had been crafted dropped by to say that the animal pleasures they had shared a few weeks previously had yielded a permanent reminder and that, consequently, some appropriate action must be taken. Ross knew his choices and opted for the decent route: by summer's end he was married, and a good thing, too. His new bride had sufficient family money to relieve the enormous debt he had counted on incurring to go through law school.

As a brightly ambitious law student, Ross concluded that, while criminal law carried a high degree of glamor and the greatest potential monetary rewards, it was also the riskiest of specializations. Too many criminal lawyers burned out, or became mediocre. Real estate law, Ross concluded, could be just as lucrative and was far less competitive. He would have room for both error and, when the mood struck him, indulgence. If he found the proper niche for himself, one in a prominent urban firm whose specialty might be closing transactions involving overpriced city land and the elaborate structures thereon, he might do quite nicely indeed. Before his graduation in the bottom third of his class, he made a favorable impression on a junior partner of a great Los Angeles firm who had come east to recruit among the ivies. The partner was looking for an ambitious young associate with an abiding interest in real estate law. Griffith Ross, his young wife and their three-year-old son headed west into the sunset.

In relatively little time Ross worked himself into a partnership. It was, in his mind, only a matter of intent. He found a partnership desirable because it would broaden his rewards, and so it did. As partner with the least seniority, he became the spearhead for the firm's community involvement. Within a few months he found himself on the boards of a local private college, two nonprofit health organizations and the Los Angeles County SPCA. He did not mind all this, even though he carried few convictions that did not change with his company. He realized that the firm would benefit from the community and that, as the newest partner and one who happened to be fairly personable, the task of community service fell to him. Ross carried out his volunteer duties with the minimum of effort and a complete lack of sensitivity.

During this time as divisional chairman of a United Way drive, Ross struck up a friendship with an equally ambitious young attorney who had just been elected to the House of Representatives. Ross, who paid little attention to politics, had not heard of him but he was impressed by the young man's outgoing personality and obvious aspirations. He sensed that there might well be bigger things ahead and that it could be worth his while to hang onto this new friendship.

His solicitous attention to his new acquaintance carved a sure and steady road to a shared personal confidence. When the young congressman made his bid for the senate, Ross helped engineer the campaign, a slick, well-packaged effort which blithely deflected any serious discussion of issues to emphasize the candidate's good looks and eloquent rhetoric. When the candidate returned to Washington as California's junior senator, he took Griffith Ross with him as his administrative assistant.

Ross's relationship with the senator was a healthy symbiosis. The senator provided a glamorous justification for Ross's special elitism, and a ready access to corridors of wealth and power. In return, Ross was the senator's eyes and ears. He had an instinctive understanding of how the senator's actions would play with his constituents. The senator had developed a blind faith in his assistant's instincts and so turned to Ross for guidance on virtually every issue that would require a public position. Ross had successfully steered the senator down a safe middle course regarding the most explosive topics of his day. He had constructed the senator's positions on foreign policy hotspots, ethnic conflicts in Africa and Europe, racial and economic inequalities in the United States, and every festering economic issue. He had demanded that his man avoid any mention of trigger terms. Each time the young senator took the floor to deliver an address to his bored, disinterested colleagues and their equally bored staff members, each time he drew up his long frame before an assembly of California voters, each time he faced a representative of the media, his words and ideas had been thoroughly edited, clipped, trimmed and washed by Ross, who kept his remarkable ear to the ground to hear the rumble of each senatorial footstep.

The senator, then, for Griffith Ross became a cause in his own right. Ross lived to preserve an image he had meticulously shaped. Nothing else mattered but the man. He lived in dread that the senator might someday be caught off guard and make some statement without Griffith's counsel that would undo that finely crafted image. Ross tried to imbue the staff with similar sentiments, to make them see that the continued political well-being of their man was not only a sufficient motivation for their work, it was the only one. Anything beyond that bordered on fanaticism.

Ross now leaned back in his swivel chair, legs crossed, and flipped absently through the twenty-four page memo that sat now on the great mound of his lap. He was not reading it, not at the moment. He had already done that. Now it was as if he were looking for an impression he could articulate, a word or a phrase that might leap up from the page and stir a thought. Across from him sat Conor Finnegan, the memo's author, who tried to feign a businesslike demeanor while struggling to control both his excitement, which flamed at the potential this meeting carried, and his nerves, which warned him that that potential might as easily be negative as positive.

Ross reviewed the memo without speaking for several tense minutes. The silence pressed the moment down hard upon Finnegan's delicate confidence; it seemed like an hour. All he could do was sit attentively, notepad in his lap, left arm propping his head pensively.

Griffith Ross at last broke the heavy silence. "So?"

"I beg your pardon?"

"So," repeated Ross, then continued with a paced deliberation, "What do you want me to do with this? Or, I should say, what do *you* want to do with this?"

"That's why I'm here, Griffith. You tell me."

"Some graphic things in this, if it's all true."

"It's all true. It's all verifiable. I saw those conditions myself, and from what I've heard, this place is hardly unique."

"Of course it's not unique. But what can we do, Conor? What do you suggest?" Ross spoke without any discernible emotion. His questions same out flat, almost disinterested, like asking his wife when he should mow the lawn.

"I'm not sure, Griffith. I thought you'd have some insights. Here's a facility that takes almost all its patients from Veterans Affairs, which is consequently deriving most of its revenue from federal sources, and it's not providing livable conditions. Hell, it's not even coming close. It seems to me that some action is in order."

Ross grunted and leaned back even further in his great leather chair. His face twisted into a deep frown. "Conor, do you know that there's already a series of laws on the books mandating sanitation and recreational standards for any eldercare facility that gets a dime of federal money, and that's damn near all of them. Everything's covered, from space requirements per patient to the caloric content of their daily diet. There's probably a clause in there about the amount of toilet paper they have to stock. We can't add anything to that. This strikes me as an enforcement issue rather than a legislative one."

"Well and good, Griffith . . . then those laws aren't being enforced. At least, not in this case. And people are suffering for it, and I've been able to verify it. If you want me to get some hard data to back this up, I'll do that, too, although God knows what that would be."

"Oh, I don't doubt the veracity of your report. I'm certain conditions are just as grim as you paint them. My question remains, what do we do? If legislative standards are in place, our work is done. We're not the executive branch, my friend. We only make the laws; we can't do a damn thing about enforcing them."

"But can't this report be the basis for some additional legislation to put some bite into the enforcement? Penalties can't be very severe if violations are so widespread. Or we might look at . . ."

"Enforcement is provided by the states," interrupted Ross. "All the federal agencies do is rubber-stamp state certifications. We can't go beyond that unless you want to create some huge, sprawling agency or add another layer to an already overblown bureaucracy. As much as I bleed for our elderly brethren, it's just not worth the effort."

"Couldn't violations be written into the federal code?"

"As it stands, failure to meet established health standards results in a cutoff of federal monies. What else can we do?"

"Prison terms."

"The courts will no doubt be extremely happy to add to their caseloads for this. Besides, gross violations or repeated offenses already carry the threat of license revocation. That's worse than jail for these guys. Any other suggestions?"

"Obviously I haven't thought through this all the way, but . . ."

"Obviously you haven't," snapped Ross, leaning forward now with his thick arms on top of his desk.

"What I'm saying," Finnegan continued doggedly, "is that this report points out some grave failings in the manner in which we administer long-term care through VA-supported facilities. At the moment I don't have any specific legislative solutions, but my report might well be a topic for discussion and a basis for further investigation. Ultimately some course of action might arise from that, but we'd have to see. That's the usual path for such things, isn't it? I'm not willing to dismiss this so quickly, Griffith. We're doing a huge disservice if we do. We'd be turning our backs on a serious social wrong that we might have the power to remediate, at least in part."

"How? What power? Waving our magic wands and conjuring up the Nursing Home Fairy? In case you haven't been paying attention, all legislation is compromise. We devise some type of bill to address the situation you describe, and then watch what happens. First of all, it disappears in committee for the remainder of this session. We're not dealing with a very sexy topic, you know. Then, if it ever gets on the committee's agenda, probably after we reintroduce it next year, it's likely to die there, or, in the extremely remote chance it comes to a vote, it'll be amended and diluted so much you won't recognize it. Once it gets past committee, then we all stand aside and let the lobbyists have at it. The whole process will end up taking years and accomplishing nothing. You're pushing an issue that everyone thinks is already thoroughly covered, that may not lie in the legislative province, and that has limited voter appeal. As I see it, Conor, what you're proposing is a serious waste of the senator's time."

"I don't see it that way, Griffith, and I think you're being overly harsh. There is . . . well, there must be something we can do."

"Conor," replied Ross, less stern, almost conciliatory, "if we pursue every worthy issue, we'll achieve nothing. Congress doesn't work that way. We have a limited amount of time to attend to all of the nation's domestic and international situations. It's too much for this body to handle, so we pick our spots. The worst thing the senator could do would be to go off after every noble cause. For one thing, he'll offend too many people, and for another, he'd lose all credibility with his colleagues. He'd become a cartoon.

"But," he continued, "I don't want you to be discouraged. You've shown some real initiative here. If you want, pass this report onto the VA and see if they want to take any action against this place. And, if you can think of some specific, like practical legislative steps we can take in light of what you've found, then outline them for me in some detail. Fair enough?"

"Fair enough, Griffith. I'll see if I can come up with anything."

"And Conor, I want you to know that you've uncovered nothing new. Violations of health standards by long-term eldercare facilities is old news. But if you can make something useful of it, you have my blessing."

"Something useful, then. That's the key?"

"That, my friend, is the way we live in this peculiar profession."

* * *

Tom McIlweath scaled the rickety stairs of his newly rented flat in a sour humor. He carried with him a box of his books, the last such box he would have to tote up these fragile old stairs in completing his move from New Jersey.

It was not the process of moving that had instilled his grim mood. He did not know what, precisely, had brought about his surly outlook. He had not bothered to analyze it. The drive to Boston from New Brunswick, boxes of his belongings crammed into every nook of his old car, had bored him thoroughly. He found nothing quaint or picturesque in his sojourn through the New England countryside. All he had noted was the hot, flat solidity of the turnpikes and the sooty grime of New York City and the industrial Connecticut suburbs, which he chose to notice instead of the office buildings and tidy residences that were equally visible. On the solitary drive he had not bothered to delve into his reactions to the new situation into which he was about to drag himself. His thoughts, mostly banal observations of the passing scenery or the music from the radio, repeated themselves monotonously. Wind—the stinging wind of passage—blew through the front seat and tossed over the flap of his winter coat sitting atop a pile of clothes next to him. The wind did not cool him. The late summer had been unusually hot and humid. The weather beat Tom McIlweath about his ears and brow; he perspired freely, but the wind dried it immediately, making him tacky and stale. He drove on numbly.

There had been no spirit of adventure, no sensation of discovery in this short trip. McIlweath had returned to California with his parents for several weeks. He had done nothing there, passing his time reading Latin and Greek, swimming occasionally and seeing the few people he considered worth seeing. He missed Anne. More so, he found he missed Conor Finnegan and the settled combination of security, intellectual challenge and excitement his life at college had been. He missed it terribly, and he had a hard time reconciling himself to the fact that, upon his return east, neither Finnegan nor any of his friends would be there for him. Only Anne. Before it had ever been finally dispersed, before its final echoes had ceased their reverberations, the camaraderie, the brotherhood that had set apart McIlweath's last four years from all other periods of his life had become his sweetest nostalgia. He did not really dread his impending new existence in Boston, or so he told himself. Even so, its prospect hung over his summer with a damp, leaden melancholy.

He had come to believe that his sole reason for setting his course northward was Anne. Certainly he looked forward to continuing his studies. He had never ceased to be fascinated by the literature of antiquity but, all things considered, he might as easily have done that at Rutgers, or back in California (so warm and bright), or in any of a dozen other places. It would be the same processes he had adopted years ago repeated on a higher level, that was all. There was something comforting in that; a tie, perhaps, to the surety of more stimulating times. Anne, too, provided security. It was her special certainty, the expanded dimension she brought to his self-definition that drew him on.

She waited now at the top of the stairs leading to the small flat Tom McIlweath had rented. She had spent the summer in Boston living off her father's largesse and acclimating herself to her new surroundings. Anne had, in fact, found this place for Tom. She herself had settled into university housing near campus, a clean and modern apartment complex whose rent was figured into her fees. With her own logistics in place, she had set about to mold Tom's, but she found that housing in the city, particularly in college areas, was exorbitant. After three weeks of daily phone calls to prospective landlords, she had discovered this one-bedroom flat on the upper floor of an old, old wooden house a mile from campus. It sat on a busy commercial street at the edge of a predominantly Italian neighborhood on Boston's west end. Anne took one look, found it charming, and arranged a lease for Tom to sign, which he obediently did upon his return. He had no choice.

Anne held the door open for McIlweath as he tromped up the stairs. He walked into the square living room and put the heavy box down in one corner. "That's the last of it."

"Tom, isn't this place wonderful? I'm so glad you finally have a decent place to live."

McIlweath looked around, hands on hips. 'No, Anne, it is not wonderful,' he thought. 'It is many things, but 'wonderful' is not among them. It is dark and old and dingy. It is furnished with faded and decrepit items—sofas that sag, chairs that show the outlines of their springs, bookcases with great, wide gouges, a bed that sinks in the center, a bathtub with cracks, a kitchen stove with burns, a refrigerator with a loose handle, ugly curtains that mask the light, threadbare rugs that have various indefinable stains, and pervading throughout, the musty, decaying odor of mildew. It is furnished with age, and pretensions long shattered, and the poignant throb of loneliness. It has chipped tiles in its bathroom and a fractured spirit in its soul. It is faded and decrepit, and it shall make me faded and decrepit, too. This is not a place to come to study, to ponder and to revel in the magnificent potential, the infinite energy, of one's youth. This is a place to barricade oneself against all life and light. This is a place to come to die. This is not a home. It's a mausoleum.' Tom McIlweath finished his review and turned to Anne. "It could use some work."

"Oh, of course it can, but what place doesn't need some touching up? It's comfortable, that's the main thing. And it's affordable. You should be grateful I was able to find it for you."

"I've already thanked you, Anne. Many times over, as I recall."

"Well, you don't seem so thankful. You seem annoyed. You have all day."

McIlweath moved to the window and sat down on a box of his belongings. He pulled back the curtain to look down onto the street below. He was across the street from a drugstore that had an old blue-and-orange sign. Its display window carried advertisements for mouthwashes and deodorants. He noticed its doorway had a retractable steel grid.

"Maybe I'm just tired, Anne. The drive up here was long and hot."

"You should at least be glad to see me." She walked over to him and put her hand on his shoulder. The gesture seemed to McIlweath artificial, the response to a cue, or the reversion to a proven method of erasing his petulance. The simplicity of it annoyed McIlweath all the more.

"What makes you think I'm not?" he snapped. "But do you expect me to simper and fawn all over you under these circumstances? I've had to move everything I own several hundred miles today. I'm in a new place in a new part of the world where I don't know anybody, not one soul besides you. Please forgive me for being worn out and edgy and probably, underneath it all, a little bit afraid. This isn't exactly what I bargained for."

"Don't you dare take your frustrations out on me," Anne replied hotly. She had removed her hand and walked back to the center of the room. "I went to a lot of trouble to set you up here. Besides, you've made your own decisions. You're here of your own free will."

McIlweath twisted his lips into a bitter smile. "Am I now? But you of course had offered your unerring guidance."

"You're damn right. Sometimes I think you're purely incapable of charting your own course. It took you months, *months*, to decide what you wanted to do with yourself. You should have settled on that years ago. Instead you drifted through college with no direction, no ambition and no goal. Yes, I helped steer you to where you are now and you should be damn grateful I cared enough to make the effort, because God knows it was anything but easy. If it weren't for me you'd still be drifting, 'trying to find your place,' or whatever you want to call it."

"It sounds as if I should be grateful to you for life itself. You've never had any sympathy for my perspective, have you? You've never understood that someone might not be completely driven to achieve some arbitrary goal, that someone can allow his conclusions to evolve rather than be carved in marble. You've never understood for one single minute what's most important to me."

"You're talking like a spoiled child."

McIlweath snorted a derisive laugh and shook his head.

"I mean it," continued Anne. "You assume that somehow the adult world is going to take care of you on its own initiative. You think some grand and glorious lifestyle is just going to present itself. That's nonsense, and you should know it by now."

"What would you know about the 'adult world'?" McIlweath mumbled.

"What was that?"

"Nothing worth repeating. I can't count the times we've had this same damn discussion. I'll never make you understand, so there's no point in trying. We'll only say things we don't mean."

"You always back down when you're cornered, Tom. That's disgraceful. You don't defend yourself because you can't. You don't have a leg to stand on, and down deep you know I'm right about it. You *know* it. It's not a matter of interpretation. It's a matter of responsibility, and your whole sense of it is ridiculous."

McIlweath flung a narrow volume of Plutarch across the room. It bounced off the thin cushion of the worn couch and fell to the floor.

"God damn you!" he shouted. "Who the hell are you to talk about responsibility? You're twenty-two years old and you've never left home. Even now you view this whole move like some kind of summer camp adventure, or an overnight senior trip. But Daddy's just a phone call away so you're really in no danger, are you? Just another change in your courses and everything's the same as it's always been, except maybe a little more expensive. But you needn't worry about that either as long as Daddy writes the checks. What in God's name do you even remotely know about responsibility? It's beyond your range of comprehension, like some Buddhist chant. You stand there so smug and pass judgment using those simplistic little words that you've never once called into question. But you refuse to believe that they don't apply to me or to how I think or to what I want to do. There's no give in you, Anne, and I'm getting so God damn tired of it."

McIlweath's outburst startled Anne to her core. He had never done this, had never been so violent, and by the end of his tirade beads of sweat had formed on his forehead. His eyes fairly burned behind his glasses, fueled by the red heat of frustration, anger and loss. She grew frightened not by his words, which she really did not comprehend, but by the savagery with which he shouted them. She stood across from him, her own eyes wide with surprised, fearful wonder, her limbs weak. She had absolutely no idea what to say. No one had ever spoken like this to her, and she did not want to provoke him further. What else might he be capable of saying?

McIlweath saw the shock in Anne's expression, and recoiled in confusion. He perceived the primitive emotions that had propelled him, caught them and consciously stifled them, for he, too, was frightened. Anne's helpless, childlike fear—fear of *him*—rocked him senseless and plunged past all rancor, all frustration, all resentment, shattering them so thoroughly that they left no vestige. McIlweath, spent and instantly remorseful, ran his hands through his hair in anguish, then stood before Anne speechless, unaware of what ultimately lay within him. His mouth opened and shut awkwardly in muffled, aborted apologies.

"Anne, I . . . I don't know what." He shook his head as he groped for an explanation, the beast now safely back within its cage. "I can't say what . . ." His whole body trembled, and he held out his hands hopelessly in her direction. Tears began to well at the corners of his eyes.

Anne, too, shook her head and moved to him there, standing befuddled in the middle of the room. She would have abundant opportunity later to press the advantage she gained from this little scene, especially if she reacted with a measure of compassion in the moment. She wrapped her arms around his quivering body and held him tightly. McIlweath's tears broke free; they ran down onto her hair. She felt the warm wetness there, so mortal, like blood.

"I'm sorry, Anne. Oh God, I'm sorry. Please forgive me." His pleading, penitent voice rose softly in pitch to become almost childlike. Anne was surprised that his words held together and did not crackle around his tears. "I'm so sorry," he kept repeating.

"It's okay, Tom," she whispered. "Don't think of it, ever again."

"I don't know what took hold of me. Please forgive me."

"Don't worry about it. It's the heat, that's all. And the strain of moving. You're tired, Tom. You need to rest a bit. You should forget the whole thing."

"I suppose you're right," said McIlweath, composing himself and drawing away from her embrace. "You're right about so many things. I imagine my greatest fear is that you're right about me, too. Maybe I do lack a sense of responsibility. I've made one bold act in my entire life. But how bold, really, was that? I always had safeguards. I knew I'd never be lonely as long as there were other people around, especially people with no preconceived notions of who I was. And I knew I could do the work. Distance wasn't a test of responsibility. It was only an insulation."

"You can't live off that one act forever," said Anne gently.

"I know. Perhaps that's what I've tried to do. I took it, and then I stood aside to marvel at the footprint instead of looking at the direction it pointed. I got angry with you because you saw what I feared might be true, and you had the courage to tell me."

"Not courage, Tom. Just compassion. I do care about you, you know. I want you to be the best person you can be. You have such wonderful potential if only you could put it into some context. It kills me to see you so aimless."

"Well, then I surrender to you. Point me in whichever direction you think best and fill me with your ambitions. It's apparent I lack any of my own."

"You think too much. And you worry too much. Sometimes our best course is so obvious that we're suspicious of it, then we try to look behind it, and we end up confusing ourselves with metaphysics and philosophy and all that 'meaning of life' nonsense. It needn't be so difficult. You've told me so many times that you're looking for some sense of belonging and a harmony between who you are and what you do. But I'm telling you that values define actions, and that actions define self-impression. You've found your harmony. You've always had it, but you don't seem to know that. Your harmony exists, Tom. It's here, with me, in this place, doing what you're doing."

A tiny smile curled McIlweath's lips as he looked down at Anne. "Do you ever have any doubts, Lady Anne?"

"Not a one, Tom. There's no time, and it's just a waste of energy."

"Perhaps you're right," he said weakly.

"Of course I'm right. And besides, you just surrendered yourself to me, and I accept your capitulation." She reached up to kiss him on the cheek. "Now, let's get something to eat and talk happier things. Boston is loaded with great restaurants. You can buy me dinner and we'll discuss the terms of your surrender."

"I trust you to be the sweetest and fairest of conquerors."

"You'll just have to see. Let's get going," and the two of them descended to the narrow, bent streets of Boston, alive with the vile, the profane, the holy, the indifferent. Anne took him by the hand and, draped regally in self-assurance, led her young man through the mobs to a safe port, where they dined and drank.

CHAPTER XVI

Once drinking deep of that divinest anguish,
How could I seek the empty world again?

—Emily Brontë, *Remembrance*

Early autumn night, black and cold. Rain aggressive on the window. The macabre whipping skeletons of the angry trees down the street. Open the door and walk into the light to see the glistening of the wet raincoat. Hang it by the doorway. It drips, rhythmically, a measure of time, a peculiar water clock.

The body sags as the coat; the mind sags, leaden and damp. They did not tell me how hard it could be. They did not tell me the cost. Inaction, frustration and disbelief. They did not tell me how truly hard it could be.

Somewhere, in a place I cannot reach, a place I cannot reach, a great bass drum is pounding against me, pulverizing whatever sensibilities I raise against it, thumping me into a depthless abyss, a numbness, a remote oblivion. The soft tissue grows insensate where it strikes, time and again. Water off a raincoat, blood from an open wound. And where the water-blood falls it forms no pool, but is absorbed into the soft, insensate tissue, which grows more insensate with each drop.

Conor Finnegan entered his empty apartment, relieved at last to be out of a driving October rain. Dan Rosselli was not in; he was never in. Dan took his studies seriously. He saw his validation in exercises that he could surmount through pure effort. His processes were given him in detail, and he could go about them secure that they were proper and that, at the end of his programmed work, he could step into a predictable situation which would most likely satisfy all expectations. Perhaps the scientists really do have it all over the humanists. How thoroughly comforting that must be, to know that by passing through Point A, Point B and Point C, one got to Point D. Rosselli had the good sense to realize that.

After hanging his raincoat in the doorway, Finnegan went to the kitchen. He had no appetite whatsoever, but he opened the refrigerator anyway to see if his stomach could be inspired by anything that might be in there. Out of habit, he made himself a sandwich from a cold steak he had prepared two nights before. Returning to the living room he turned on some music and set about the chore of eating his dinner. The bread crumbled around the corners of his mouth as he fought his way through the reluctant sandwich. The meat had become rubbery, and it had no taste. Finnegan bit off thick chunks and noshed down on them viciously. The flotsam sat at the back of his mouth like paste. He got three-quarters through it, then abandoned the effort. He rose from his easy chair and returned to the kitchen. After throwing the remnants of his sandwich into the garbage, he poured a generous glass of scotch.

Finnegan resumed his spot in the old chair and watched the windblown forms outside his window. The rain blew hard against the pane, blurring his view so that only the streetlights and headlights of passing cars gave any dimension to what he saw. He listened to the staccato assault of the rain against the glass to see if he could create a rhythm. He could not; all was chaos.

The music that played now was a dirgelike folk tune, some lyric of dissipation. Lost souls everywhere, he thought. I should consider myself fortunate.

He sipped at the scotch and let the strong smoky liquid burn its way down his throat and into his benumbed stomach. Let the numbness start from there and work its way outward. He mouthed the words to the song he heard, then softly started to sing along with it, closing his eyes to let the sentiment seep into him like an ointment. In this pose he passed the song, then another, then another. He rose to change the music, and he finished his drink. Tendrils of a loose warmth crept up his arms and down his legs. He breathed deeply in a sigh, but he felt far more relaxed, far more accepting than he had a few moments earlier. The scotch had begun its work, and defused him. He went to the kitchen for another, returned to his chair and let it engulf him—the chair, the liquor, the cold, brittle evening itself. It felt good not to have to fight something.

The great beast lumbers on and crushes what it does not devour. Its nature, then—neither benign nor malevolent, only consumptive.

I am haunted by the blank, lifeless stares, by the thin bones sharper than sticks, by meatless limbs and spiritless souls. I am haunted by the odor of them, the repugnant mingling of sterility and impending death. I am haunted by all lost days, by the dangling, useless ends of lives severed from all love, all hate, all thought. Existence without life, a pulse without a heart. They stare at me. They reach up to grab my sleeve and search for the briefest of instants and with the faintest of hopes for some touch, some glance, some word to invoke, once more, all they have abandoned, all that has abandoned them. Plaintive, beseeching eyes and the talons of their hands claw at flesh that, like theirs, is human, claw at a stuporous fantasy that they might evoke from another living being a human response. The talons claw at a prayer that existence might be more than merely physical yet, beyond all hope, beyond all fantasy, beyond all prayers, knowing that a hollow, echoing tomb yawns in their direction, and there shall be no reprieve, not by the young form before them, nor by any other living creature, nor by God Himself.

The great devouring beast lumbers on, and these poor, haunting phantoms who have been squeezed of all use are crushed, the grotesquely contorted rinds of once-sweet fruit. They have become inconvenient; they are devoid of purpose. We draw no gain from them unless we build elaborate institutions to tend them and charge them for life itself. Then, only then, do they have a purpose. The soft, pliant rinds might be squeezed one last time, and all remorse be forgotten.

Glynnis, where are you tonight? Does the wind blow your long hair about your neck and does the cold rain slap your delicate face? Do you walk through the lights and shiver? Or, my lady, do you sit warmly in your room that smells of lilacs, do you feel the plush, bottomless depths of your narrow bed? With whom do you speak tonight, and of what subjects? Are you proud with them, or profane, or do you lead them with a coy turn of your head and the charisma of your great brown eyes?

Why, lass, this distance? Glynnis, why are you not with me tonight, and every night? What made you stay away? Cold, ever cold, and so bitterly silent.

Sweet Lorelei, singing on the Rocks of Time.

* * *

When Dan Rosselli returned home around 10:30 he found Conor Finnegan still in the easy chair. An empty glass sat on the arm. Finnegan still had on the suit he had worn to work that morning, shirt opened and tie askew. His head lolled awkwardly to one side as if some giant hand had snapped his neck like a twig. Music continued to play, despite the lack of a sentient audience.

"Conor, wake up, you lazy Mick."

The sleeping form frowned, growled, and shifted positions. Rosselli walked up to the chair and kicked it. "Finnegan," he shouted, and Conor woke up with a start, sitting up wide-eyed and uncomprehending. He had trouble focusing on his friend. He shook his head quickly to regain a sense of place and time.

"Come on, Senator, go to bed. Have you wasted the entire evening like this?"

Finnegan swallowed to get the metallic taste out of his mouth. He squinted hard to clear his vision. "Like what?"

"Snoozing in your chair like some middle-aged slob. That's not the most inspiring sight to come home to after a long night in the library."

"Sorry, pal. Maybe tomorrow I'll greet you in something slinky."

Rosselli had made his way to the kitchen. "Didn't you cook anything tonight? Jesus, I'm starved."

"What time is it?"

"After 10:30," called Rosselli.

"Christ Almighty," Finnegan croaked.

"Didn't you cook anything tonight?" repeated Rosselli.

"I just had a sandwich. A bad sandwich."

"So there's nothing left over for old Danny boy. Shit."

"You'll have to reheat something. It's a hard life, Dan, and I've had enough of it for one day. See you tomorrow, "and Finnegan walked to his bedroom with Rosselli saying something to him from the kitchen. Finnegan could not make it out, nor did he really care to hear it, one of Rosselli's typical playful insults for which Finnegan this evening had no stomach. He undressed and crawled into a bed he deemed too wide. Sleep collapsed upon him like the wall of a decaying building, and the rain pelted against his window with the sound of crackling cellophane.

The rain did not abate the next day, or the day following. The mysteries of distance closed in on Conor Finnegan and made him uneasy. In the drab early autumn wetness, the city itself depressed him. Gone, drowned by the ceaseless downpours, was its cosmopolitan *joie de vivre*. People did not smile or talk lightly, the great marble buildings turned a dour gray, street gutters filled to the curbing and splashed up at those huddled figures hurrying by. The air smelled continually dank. Bus windows steamed up so that the rides to and from work were suffocating. Finnegan became as leaden as the weather.

He rarely saw Dan Rosselli. His other friends, those at the office, did not present any consistent companionship. Their friendships dissipated once the day ended. They interested Finnegan only in limited ways. No one tied into his own concerns, passion or background with any degree of efficiency. They were, essentially, strangers who had been thrown together circumstantially. They assembled in the morning and dispersed in the evening, Monday through Friday, and each preferred it that way. Only rarely did they share a night out, usually just cocktails. Finnegan, to his complete surprise and against all expectations, found himself frequently alone.

On a Thursday night, at the conclusion of another day of the great autumn rains, Finnegan slopped through the door to his apartment. The short walk from the bus stop had left him thoroughly drenched. To delay returning to the echoing shell of his residence he had eaten dinner alone at a modest restaurant near Capitol Hill. He ate his veal, drank two glasses of a strong red wine and read his newspapers.

Upon entering his apartment he took off every article of clothing that was cold or wet and left them in a soggy pile near the door. His suit would have to be cleaned. Mud had splashed up onto his trousers. Finnegan changed into a sweater and his corduroys, then picked up the phone and dialed. He had been anticipating this singular moment all day. A waste of energy, he knew, to put so much effort into fantasy, but given the sterility of these days, it was an effort that proved irresistible.

Five rings, six rings, seven, and no answer.

He turned on the television and watched nothing for an hour, focusing instead on the passage of time since his first call. In precisely sixty minutes he tried again. On the fifth ring, Finnegan heard the familiar click of a phone uncradled.

"Hello?"

"Glynnis?" Finnegan asked with some uncertainty, for the tone on the other end did not remind him of his lover, although the voice carried the soft inflection that was usually unmistakable.

"Conor, hello. How are you, love?"

"Lonely and wet. I tried to call a bit earlier but you weren't in."

"I've been spending a lot of time in the studio, but that's not why I'm late tonight."

"Been working on a special project?"

"No. It's just peaceful there at night, after all the other students have gone. No one else is around so I have it all to myself. I've been spending a good deal of time there lately. It helps to clear my mind."

"All alone with your thoughts. You must relish that." Finnegan could not suppress a tone of bitterness that rushed of its own accord into his throat. He hoped at once that Glynnis would not notice it.

"I do, from time to time. You do, too. Are you alone right now?"

"Of course. That's my constant state of late. How about you?"

"I told you that the studio wasn't the reason I was late tonight. No,

I'm not alone. Lynda's here."

The words sent an electric shock down Finnegan's frame. What was she doing there? She conjured his deepest fears, invoking them as a witch might call to the dark spirits.

Conor Finnegan had not seen Lynda Hoelscher since their one and only meeting in the spring. During the weeks following, he had scoured Glynnis's words and actions for any evidence that Lynda might have told her what had transpired during that surreal encounter. Finnegan had lived in mortal dread that Lynda might have baited Glynnis, that she might have resorted to embellishment where none was necessary, that she might seek to use a lie as a weapon, that she might try to sully what Glynnis alone possessed. After several weeks of normal behavior between the two of them, Finnegan shelved the incident and its attendant fears in a far corner of his memory. Even so, he remained aware of its tremendously destructive potential. Finnegan was glad that Lynda had gone back to New York immediately after graduation, there to settle into a new job and a place of her own several hundred miles away from Glynnis. Let the residue of that remote April evening stay there with her.

"Lynda's here." The words practically froze Finnegan to his chair. He took several seconds to respond, but before he could gather any intelligible words Glynnis spoke again.

"Did you hear me? Lynda's here."

"Why?"

"Her firm sent her to Philadelphia for a couple of days to work on an account. She's staying at the Hotel Fairmount, can you believe it? She got in today and she leaves tomorrow night. We had dinner, and she went back to do some work, but she's coming over in a bit. We'll probably be up all night reliving our sinful pasts."

"So she's not there now?"

"Oh no. She wanted to go back to the hotel to change and to write a quick outline for her meetings tomorrow. She'll be here soon. Shall I give her your regards?"

"Of course." His fears broke through their interment, ghoulish green specters that would dance gleefully around him all night. He would have to deal with them accordingly, and he knew that they would exact their price. A pound of flesh.

"Well," Finnegan went on, "the reason I'm calling, other than to hear your lovely young voice, is to alleviate my own state of loneliness. Can you come down this weekend, and which train will you be taking?"

Glynnis sighed audibly. "No, Conor, not this weekend. I can't come."

"Why not, Glyn?" Finnegan's words sank to a hurt whisper. His spirit, already tested by the reappearance of Lynda, plummeted through the floorboards, through the apartment below, through the ground and into the cold, silent, stifling earth. "Glyn, what's wrong?"

"Nothing's wrong. I just can't come. I'm sorry."

"Could you at least tell me why?"

"I'm not feeling quite right, Conor. I need a weekend to myself. All I want to do is curl up in bed with a good book and some brandy."

"Alone, I presume. You have a cold, then, or a touch of the flu?"

"Perhaps. Call it that. This week has depressed me thoroughly."

"It's done the same to me, Glyn. Don't you think we might bring each other back to the ranks of the living?"

"Not this week, my love. I just want to rest."

"You know, I'd be willing to drive up to Philadelphia and keep you company. I wouldn't mind trying to nurse you back to health."

"You can't, I'm afraid. Conor, it's not only physical. I feel run down mentally, too. I wouldn't be much good to you now. I wouldn't be good company and I'd be doing nothing for myself if I spent the weekend with you. You're sweet, Conor, and I love you dearly, but I think I should be alone."

"I'm not certain I understand, Glyn, but it appears I have no choice. I was counting on you, though, to bring me back around." Finnegan spoke slowly, sadly, tiredly. "You're all I think about, Glynnis, and nothing, absolutely nothing, lends any meaning to what I'm doing here except you. The rest is all ornamentation, all gadgetry. You alone are my substance. I do love you, girl. You hurt me by your distance, you know that."

"Oh, Conor, you make it so difficult. I hurt myself as well, you must believe that. But we've been over this so much."

"And I'm not going to resurrect it. I suppose I spoke unfairly, and I'm sorry. I'm saddened by being without you any longer than I have to be. As I said, Glynnis, I'm not certain I understand, but I'll honor your preferences. I don't mean to pressure you."

"But you do it so well, Conor. You're so subtle. You seem so much like a puppy that's been accidentally kicked and sits in a corner whimpering to itself. I know you don't want to pressure me, but the truth is, you do. This is not easy for me, Conor. I hope you believe that I'd much rather be in your bed than mine. Just not this weekend. There'll be plenty of time for us later."

"We get greedy for the present even at the expense of our future," said Finnegan. "We're all creatures of expediency."

"Exactly, my love. It's the rare individual with foresight, and rarer still the one who honors his foresight with discipline. Be patient."

"You sound unusually reflective for someone who's just put off her lover. That might cause me to worry. I think I'd be more assured if you just dismissed me out of hand without a preconceived justification."

"You get nervous when I think too much."

"Or too deeply."

"Fear not, love. I'm still yours. 'Til death, I hope."

"As you wish. Call me Sunday night, won't you, Glyn? That will at least give me something immediate to look forward to. And Sunday night alone is the most bitter. Sunday night always seems like the dead end of a broken arm, just dangling and useless."

"I'll call you Sunday, then. And Conor, it it's any consolation, I know I'll regret not being with you as much as you resent my not coming. I can't explain what gets inside me. But I do think I need the time away."

"You worry me, lass," Finnegan sighed. Security is at best a fragile thing, and at worst ephemeral. Finnegan knew he would get little rest over the next few days. He would not rest well again until he slept once more next to Glynnis.

"Please don't worry, Conor. I've never been more yours."

"Glynnis, remember when we first met you said that I was destined to have my heart broken? I never believed that, and I still don't. But you've made me vulnerable in ways I had never conceived."

"That's an awesome responsibility, my love. And whether you believe it or not, you're too innocent and good to escape this existence unscathed. You will be shattered, Conor Finnegan, but I pray that I'm not the one to do it."

"You're the only one who can."

"The subtle pressure again," replied Glynnis with a sly laugh. "I'll leave you now before you reduce me to tears. I'll talk to you Sunday, Conor. And I am sorry for your loneliness. My portion is just as great."

"Good night, sweet girl," and she was gone, leaving Conor Finnegan to face his specters, mocking him there in eerie, haunting gyrations as they grew in number.

* * *

"Pray, brethren, that our sacrifice may be acceptable to the Lord our God."

"May the Lord accept the sacrifice at your hands, For the praise and glory of His name, For our good and the good of all His Church."

He knelt, the soft board creaking beneath his weight. Two pews ahead a small girl turned around, kneeling in the wrong direction, her gentle head topped with a mane of white-blond hair and marked by two translucent blue eyes facing him directly. She looked at him, did not take her eyes from his face, fascinated by the young man's humble yet intense gestures.

'She stares at me,' he thought, 'and her world expands. She grows past it. She does not know that this is happening, what it is, or that it is inevitable. Her mouth chews around the back of the pew. Poor child.'

"On the night He was betrayed, He took bread . . ."

The church was half full, a smattering of people on both sides of the aisle but most, probably two-thirds, sitting on the right. An oddity, the young man thought. He noticed every week that people tended to sit in the right-hand pews. His own tendency was to sit in the area with fewer people to balance things out. Why are people so reluctant to sit apart? Why do they feel that they must always follow the lead of those who've preceded them and sit in areas already well-settled? He couldn't understand it. His young blonde observer still looked at him intently across the two-pew gulf. He shot her a smile. To his surprise she did not turn back toward her mother. Instead she continued to look at him, expressionless, her sharp blue eyes studying his face.

"Though Him, with Him, in Him. In the unity of the Holy Spirit, all glory and honor are Yours, Almighty Father, now and forever."

Above and behind the organ spat forth a series of echoing chords. They flooded down like ashes from a distant fire. He sang a throaty set of three 'Amens' as he always did, just loudly enough to hear himself apart from the muffled, horribly off-key voices of those near him. He enjoyed the sound of his voice. He thought it a rich, resonant one that could rise or fall with whatever tune it carried. Had he wanted, he might have been a singer, perhaps a distinctive voice in a great choir, or possibly a singer of the gentle folk songs he found so honest. Whatever there was to do, it was worth doing well.

He rose, the kneeler again creaking with his movement. His lips formed the words to the Lord's Prayer, but this was a mechanical exercise. Church, he had always believed, was a difficult setting for serious prayer. Too many distractions—the sounds of other humans, the breathing of the old structure itself, the statues and icons in every corner, even the way the light fell through stained glass upon the high triptych behind the altar. All this conspired to pull his mind away from God and keep it tethered to the mundane. He was certain it was no different for anyone else, no matter how they might pretend.

"Let us share that peace . . ."

He turned and stepped over to the old lady down the pew. She was a tattered, faded specimen, dressed in a dingy yellow topcoat, her furrowed head covered with a scarf in deference to traditions now irrelevant. He extended his hand. "Peace," he said. She turned toward him reluctantly, a tiny forced smile upon her lips. Her touch was brittle, like crumpled paper. She said nothing as she shook his hand quickly. The young man stepped back after his dismissal and she resumed her wooden pose fronting the altar, this unwelcome and awkward intrusion now complete.

Ahead of him, the young white-blonde girl turned around once more to look his way. He smiled again and this time, catching the spirit of the communion going on around her, she smiled back. He raised a hand in a small wave, his smile deepened and became sincere. The girl's mother turned then and he saw that his new friend had inherited her beauty from those who went before. Funny he should not have noticed her before, because she was truly eye-catching. Her hair, white-blonde like her daughter's, was pulled back to her neck where it formed a tight ball. Her face had been carved from white onyx. Her cheekbones set off a small mouth and framed eyes lightly shadowed in blue to reflect their natural color. He could see that underneath her coat she wore a delicate white blouse with a lace neckline that rose up to her long throat. She couldn't be more than twenty-five, he surmised. She looked at him and smiled formally, nodding her wonderful head in his direction while her thin lips formed the word 'peace.' She completed the gesture and turned forward again. The young man studied her from the rear, noting the slender form buried beneath the camelhair coat. Her tightly wound hair hid the nape of her neck. Fine white hairs spun away rebelliously from the ball although its shape was firmly tied down. He wished he could reach across to her and unleash her hair, detonate it, and let it explode over her shoulders and down her narrow back. He wished he could plunge both hands into it, lift the weight of it and feel its sensual, silky dimensions. Let her daughter watch if she wished.

He fell back to his knees. "Lord, I am not worthy to receive You, but only say the word and I shall be healed."

He rose and followed the woman and her daughter up the aisle. No one had been sitting in the intervening pews so he walked directly behind her. Her hands clasped in front of her, as were his. At the front of the aisle stood the priest with his altar boy but they were amorphous white and purple forms. He focused his gaze on the woman's back and the top of her lovely, proper head. Her daughter clung to one leg. Her mother was wearing a plaid skirt and, of all things, knee socks of a woolen blue. He found it unique, and therefore attractive. He had rarely seen such dress before.

Unclasp those fine hands, young woman, and let me replace your daughter at your leg. Let me peel down those warm blue socks and pull up your plaid. Together we can celebrate a sublime divinity that mortal man cannot see. We can offer our own Eucharist.

She received the wafer on her tongue and headed toward the side aisle to return to the pew with her daughter. He saw her out of the corner of his eye, a new, albeit obscured view, framed by an altar and a sacristy, that he wanted to be able to regard as inappropriate.

The priest stood before him, the transparent wafer held forward. Fr. Kovaleski was a tall, somewhat overweight man who took his vocation as seriously as any priest who had ever come before him. His black hair, touched with large shafts of gray, swept up the sides of his head and piled itself on top to make his head appear blocky. The priest's face, universally unsmiling, looked through its crags and crevices behind flimsy wire-rimmed glasses at the young man now before him.

"The body of Christ."

"Amen," he said, and extended his tongue. Fr. Kovaleski placed the wafer firmly upon it. For a fleeting instant, the young man thought of the base nature of this practiced gesture—reaching into the mouths of strangers to deposit something on their tongues, feeling their breath on the top of his hand, perhaps pressing down too hard with the wafer and picking up saliva from the slithery membrane. He walked back to his pew and knelt in silent prayer, the wafer having dissolved between his tongue and the roof of his mouth. He swallowed most of it, scraped the pasty remnants onto the back of his tongue, then swallowed again. To insulate himself against the common distractions, he raised his elbow to the back of the pew in front of him and covered his eyes with his hand. It was here, and only here, in the quiet moments after receiving what he presumed was the Body of the Risen Lord, while the faceless people around him shuffled back to their own areas, that real prayer occurred. All the rest of it was mere ceremony. He rubbed his hand over his eyes, wanting to articulate his thoughts but finding himself incapable of formulating a coherent supplication. Images of the past week mingled with his idealistic phrasing so that both elements became confused. He was confused over the nature of prayer anyway. Should it be an act of thanksgiving, an act of penance, an act of proposition, an act of dedication, a simple connection without definition to something broader? He knew, of course, that it could be different things at different times, but what should it be now when, in the serenity of the post-Eucharistic reflection, his thoughts should be clearest and his relation to whatever Supreme Being was most defined? There was always a danger of trying to do too much with this prayer, the only real one he would say all day, when his reactions to the pains and progress of his secular life were more confused than they had been in a great while.

The injection of uncertainty, the invalidation of basic assumptions, can be a terrible negation. It comes furtively, this doubt, a hidden disease that works its way secretly into even the strongest psyche and eats its way through the delicate tissue there until all values, all the accepted rules, are called into question. What was once secure becomes tumultuous, a maelstrom stirred by the threatening possibility that love, profession, God and life itself are not truly as they had seemed. In the face of such fears, what good might come of two minutes of prayer?

"Let us pray."

The young man rose once more and stood stiffly to listen to the priest intone something to which he paid scant attention. His mind still worked through the construction of his aborted prayer, a hopeless exercise. He felt ragged standing there, and wondered why he had bothered to come.

"Bow your heads and pray for God's blessing."

He stood unbowed. Fr. Kovaleski raised his right hand. The young man looked around at the parishioners. Most were buttoning their coats or reaching for handbags. The blessing had been a signal that the end was imminent. Getting out quickly seemed to take precedence over the good wishes of the Almighty Father.

The organ groaned a recessional that no one sang. Fr. Kovaleski led the retreat. The white-blonde girl and her mother had bundled up during the blessing and made their way into the aisle. The young man stood in his pew until they passed. The child looked up and this time, she smiled first. A blessing, he thought. A benediction. He returned it with his own smile and a small wave of his hand, then remained standing while several more people walked past. The girl and her mother disappeared out the back of the church followed by a train of unknowing worshippers. He genuflected toward the altar and stepped out into the aisle.

At the rear of the church in the vestibule Fr. Kovaleski greeted his people as they passed by him. The young man was among the last to leave. The priest extended his hand in an unsmiling gesture that was nevertheless friendly. That, as everyone had come to accept, was just the manner of a serious priest.

"Good morning, Father."

"Good morning, Conor. How are you?"

'What,' thought Conor, 'shall I say? Shall I say that I am troubled in ways that you could not conceive despite your years? Shall I say that I am plagued by demons, by horned and angular demons, that you could never recognize? Shall I say that I need an exorcism? Do you really want to know how I'm doing, Father?'

"Fine, Father," replied Conor. "And yourself?"

"Couldn't be better, young man. I could not be better."

'No doubt,' he thought. "See you next week, padre."

"Have a good week," replied the priest, and Conor Finnegan found himself out on the cold, windy sidewalk. He turned in the direction of his apartment and began to walk.

* * *

Lynda Hoelscher reclined along the thick rug and stretched her long, graceful legs to their limit as she propped herself on one elbow. She held a glass of red wine in one hand, weighing it there as if it were a glass filled with rubies. She raised it to her lips and drew down a good portion of it. After taking her drink, she shook her head quickly to clear away some loose strands of hair that had drifted across her forehead.

"You know," she smiled, "I'm really surprised to find you here."

"What do you mean? This is my place. Where else would I be?" Glynnis's eyes glinted mischievously. She reclined on the floor, too, across from Lynda with her back resting against her small couch. After dinner, a rich meal of pasta, veal, salad and coffee, they had eschewed conventional seating for the animal comfort of the floor. Great amounts of wine had been consumed with the meal, and afterward. Both young women had become slightly drunk in spite of all the food they had eaten. Both wanted to keep on drinking. This was a special time, and the rare contentment of ample food, good drink and close friendship had settled over both of them. They were two cats now, stretching and yawning by the fire.

"You know perfectly well what I mean. I had expected young Conor to sweep you away with him and the two of you never to be heard from again. That's how fairy tales usually end, isn't it? Everything seemed to be pointing to that."

"Everything was. I mean, that was the next logical step. I suppose that's one reason why I didn't go with him. I tend to be suspicious of things that are too tidy."

"Even so, Glyn, I'm surprised. Do you know what you've got with him? He's a rare man, my friend."

"So he is, and I do love him as much as I can. But that's not the point. It's just that I'm not certain that at this stage of my life I could handle what he's offering." Glynnis paused to drink her wine. "I know I've told you this before, but I can't get it out of my mind. I keep thinking of my mother and what she gave up to marry my father. God, Lynda, she became a cipher, just a function of my dad. She lived totally in my father's shadow and she made herself content with that. The first time I realized she had a personality beyond my family's image of her was after my father died, and then only because she had to assume one. I love my mother, Lynda, but she scares hell out of me. I just don't know if I'm capable of anything close to what she did. And even if I were capable, I wouldn't want to do it. I wouldn't want to end up the same way no matter what type of man I had."

"Does Conor expect you to abandon everything, though? It seems to me that he'd be solicitous of what you want to do with your life. The excitement might be in doing it all together."

"But why should he have to be solicitous, like I was some type of orphan under his care? I don't want to be patronized, and even the kindest master is still a master," and here she paused again to drink before she continued. "But, ah, Lynda, how to explain Conor Finnegan? My God, he is so innocent. He works with such a simple set of values and he can't fathom how anyone might question them or not want to assume them for their own. He's so sure of himself, and what he wants to do, and what he believes. It's unnerving sometimes to be around that much confidence. His whole life has just been a series of confirmations. He believes in his own inherent talents. Everything for Conor has been so orderly, all he's done is progress from one point to the next, and he expects that to continue all the way to the end. Why should he expect anything else?"

"And then you come along," said Lynda with a smile.

"Yes," said Glynnis, sighing, "but I've been just another affirmation, don't you see? I've fit perfectly into this glamorous little pattern he's constructed for himself. The man, the education, the job, the woman. The poor boy couldn't begin to understand anything falling outside those boundaries. But already I feel drawn into the same role my mother played for so long. She fit into a pattern, too. Willingly, although I'm not certain she knew the price of it. But there are things I want to do for myself, Lynda. I don't even know what they are yet, but I'm sure they'll make themselves known to me in due time. Or maybe I'm just rationalizing my fears. Don't you see, though, that if I followed Conor to Washington the mold might already be set? I'd be filling a role. For Conor it would be just another logical step in an infinitely logical progression, but for me it would be something else, something unsettling. I don't want to be locked into anyone's pattern."

"Don't you want that eventually, though? Sooner or later you'll have to decide what you want to do, and who to do it with."

"Sooner or later, yes, and I may well decide to go with Conor forever. I pray that I do. But not now. If I had gone to Washington, especially in light of his expectations of me, I'd never be certain that I hadn't rushed into it for all the wrong reasons. That would be tragic. I wouldn't even be sure that it was my decision."

"You could go down and then leave if it didn't work out. He's a big boy. He'll survive without you."

"No. That would be playing right into his expectations again. You know, Conor Finnegan can be incredibly seductive. And I mean emotionally and intellectually, not just physically. He's secure, and comforting, and safe, and he's created such an impressive life for himself already. What lies ahead is bound to be glorious for him, if he survives. It's only natural to want to be part of that. And so the deeper I become entrenched, the more readily I'd abandon myself altogether, and the more difficult it would be to disengage from it if I ever wanted to back out. No, before I make any gesture like that, before I commit to Conor, I have to be positively certain that there's no going back. There's no other way with him."

As Glynnis talked Lynda got up to bring the wine bottle from the kitchen. She refilled both glasses and sat back down on the floor, the wine bottle between them.

"You do love him, Glynnis. There's no doubt of that. I can see it very clearly."

"God, yes, or else I'd never be putting us both through this. I love him and I do want to be with him, perhaps for the rest of my life. But I'll do it on my terms. I have to. He's so uncomplicated, Lynda. He can't see that my reluctance is as much for his benefit as for my own. I couldn't bear to hurt him—he's so vulnerable, like a little wide-eyed fawn. But I'd do it to protect myself if I had to."

"Glynnis, does Conor ever mention me?"

Glynnis paused to consider, then answered slowly. "No, not really. I rarely mention you to him. Why do you ask?"

"I thought he might, that's all. He seems the compassionate sort, and my past is the kind of thing that might spark some interest. You know, he *is* a handsome lad, and so strong with those big shoulders. I'll bet he's terrific in bed. He's probably so grateful for the chance that he works hard to make it worthwhile."

"Lynda," giggled Glynnis, "you're treading on sacred ground."

"Glyn," Lynda replied, sitting up at once, "you should let me try him. After all, you have nothing to compare him to, do you? I could give him a workout and let you know if he's any good. You'd be getting the benefit of my experience with none of the risk. Really. You probably think he's amazing, but he might be just average, or even worse. I could tell, I've had all kinds. You know," she said in a low voice of mock confidence, "if he's really as good as he seems to be, you'd be a fool not to move in with him right away. If you don't, I might be tempted to take your place. A proficient lover is worth any price. They're as rare as nuns in a brothel."

"I never realized you were so generous, Lynda."

"I'm only thinking of you, Glyn. Well, maybe myself a little bit, too. I *am* in the market for a new adventure. If nothing else, this would at least be a unique situation."

"I'll pass for now. But thank you. I'm quite touched."

"Your loss, Glyn, but it's up to you. Would you mind a little independent research? I'll be going to Washington in about a month."

"Yes. Put it out of your mind. By the way, how's your love life doing, now that we've analyzed mine?"

"Fair. Actually it's about the same as it was here. I have my companions, and we do for each other."

"Nothing serious?"

"God, no. I've yet to encounter anyone who would ever tempt me into what might be called 'a serious relationship,' and thank God. Like you, I am reluctant to make any major sacrifices. I enjoy my lovers."

"Have you seen Peter since you left here?"

"Yes. Several times. Some weekends I visit my parents and end up giving him a call. We'll meet in the same restaurant and finish off our meal in the back of his car. Just like two God damn teenagers, and it's humiliating. You'd think I would have outgrown that. Once or twice we were honest enough with each other and just met at a motor inn. I much prefer that to any pretense that we care about one another. We've been through all that. Now we realize that we're just meat, and it's much better that way. We've done away with all complications."

"Forgive me for not congratulating you."

"I wouldn't expect you to understand. He still holds a fascination for me. I suppose he's a bridge between innocence and whatever it is I've become. That makes him special. He fills a role no one else ever can, that delicate transformation of purity to wickedness. Consequently I find sex with him to be better than with anyone else. It's like making love to two people."

"You say you've done away with complications. It sounds to me as if you're making matters very complex."

"We've eliminated all social complications. The internal complexities will always be there. Not unlike the internal complexities of your own regarding young Conor. That's usually the case with first loves and first lusts."

They finished the wine that evening and Lynda fell asleep on the floor. She did not go back to the hotel. Glynnis rose with wobbly legs and brought a blanket from the closet to cover her. She went to bed herself, the walls of her single bedroom blending into and out of each other.

Glynnis did not rise until late the next morning. Her gentle head felt thick, corseted by effects of too much wine. She sat up unsteadily with a groan. A metallic film coated the inside of her mouth, and her limbs ached.

Lynda had already showered, dressed and left. As Glynnis weaved into the living room, she saw the blanket folded on a corner of the couch with a note resting on top.

> *Glynnis —*
>
> *You're sleeping too soundly to disturb. We drank much more last night than either of us bargained. At least I did. My head is under assault from thousands of tiny hammers. I can imagine how you'll feel, so the best I can do is clear out silently and let you sleep.*
>
> *Thank you, Glynnis, for your wonderful hospitality and the great conversation that went with it. You've recharged my batteries. I don't suppose I've ever told you, but I miss you terribly. I took you for granted for four years, but all that time you were a kind of rudder for me. I could use you now again. Despite all my hardboiled surety, I'm not doing well at all. We'll save a complete analysis for later conversation.*
>
> *I do envy you, my good friend. I envy your decent character and the deep, great goodness of your soul. Armed with those advantages, you can't help but set a lovely course for the rest of your life. One word of advice, though, if I may intrude: hold on to your Irishman at all costs. You fret about sacrificing your identity to his 'patterns.' My guess is that it would be far worse to face the world on your own terms while knowing the horrible price by which those terms were won. A pyrrhic victory of the worst kind. Loneliness is awful, Glynnis, and it will destroy you much more quickly than would a few logistical sacrifices. Conor is a rare blend of admirable traits, but beyond that, he's a good man. You may never find one like him again anywhere.*
>
> *Stay in touch, and thanks again. For everything.*
>
> *Love,*
> *Lynda*

* * *

One aspect of Glynnis's new existence did not surface during Lynda's visit. It had not, indeed surfaced anywhere except to Glynnis herself. She hid it, not protectively as one might guard an object likely to inspire jealousy, but purely out of confusion. She did not know what to make of it or how to react. Until she could determine her own response, she deemed it best to keep this curious situation to herself.

The situation's name was Michael Halcón. Glynnis had been giving him a great deal of thought. He had appeared in September and from that point forward had assumed a close proximity to her own life. Three times a week, when Glynnis walked into the studio to begin, resume or complete a project. Michael rose forth with his gentle, appealing character, an inescapably unnerving component of an otherwise tameable existence.

Michael, Glynnis concluded the first day she saw him, was uncomfortably handsome. His quietly intense demeanor, a distinctive hybrid of simmering Latin passion tempered by an Eastern acceptance of the immutable forces that worked upon his world, intrigued Glynnis who saw in him at once a graphic, more placid contrast to Conor Finnegan's strident, active, sometimes painfully naïve idealism. Michael Halcón sought to change nothing. He placed himself in opposition to nothing and, if an individual or institution struck him as out of place, he merely ignored it, preferring instead to find his own peace rather than join battles in which he would be hopelessly outmanned. When Glynnis asked him once about his quiescence, he responded that, yes, he saw the world's brutality on both a grand scale and in his immediate surroundings, but that he would never be so arrogant as to propose a solution beyond simple kindness. He had no right to intervene, even if he could, for who was to say that his own subjective values were more just than those he would seek to replace? The only approach, then, was kindness, to the people and places at hand.

Michael Halcón preferred to search for more personal kinds of fulfillments. Ever since he was a boy he had been drawn to all forms of physical art. And sculpture in particular. He relished the feel of wet clay and the chip of chisel against stone. It was a way of shaping a completed, absolute view that was otherwise unattainable. He would be creator, judge and jury. What he shaped would be final, assailable only by his own standards, his own definitions of beginning and end, image, illusion and reality, concept and execution. Over the years he suffered with his shortcomings, that universal artistic torture of distortion between idea and formulation. Yet through a continuing pursuit of lessened imperfection (he dare not call it excellence) he had become highly regarded during his development. He cared little for any type of general recognition, and he yielded to the wishes of his instructors to display his work at public exhibitions only under the greatest pressure. Michael much preferred to work privately.

He found the academic environment ideal. Here he might pursue his own work in relative obscurity and according to his own pace while earning enough money to get by. His contact with the students he found largely tedious, although there were always exceptions. The vast majority struck him as mediocre, or worse. They lacked the discipline to edit the distractions from a piece so that they might concentrate on its soul. By and large they pursued art as a diversion. They did not share nor could they understand the passions it could evoke. Consequently Michael provided for most of his students only the rudiments of studio instruction. Their comparative indifference wearied him, and he thought it best to avoid overextension. He might teach them technique, but he could never teach them how to maintain their souls.

Glynnis had been fascinated by this gentle, remote man. She found herself drawn to him physically. He was lean, a sparse frame apparently undernourished from neglect rather than circumstance. Black hair curled around his ears and across his forehead to fall above eyes equally black that flared and flamed when, on rare occasions, he spoke of his art—the descriptive power of it, its glorious potential, and its uncommon wedding of mind, hand, soul and being. Glynnis saw in Michael's eyes an eruption of such unbridled force that it disturbed her. She perceived the bottomless well of his passion, and wondered how it might be if he ever chose to release it.

Michael's eyes were two black stallions thundering across the surf. His beard, too, was black, short-clipped in tight bristles that bracketed his mouth. Michael was woven of darkness and shadows. His skin was a rich brown, like coffee heavily creamed, and it blended well with his black features. Later Glynnis discovered that he was of Spanish extraction, that his father in fact had been born in Valladolid and had come to the United States with his family as a young boy to escape the violence and repressions of Franco. According to Michael, his resemblance to his father was eerie; they might have been twins.

Michael had, in turn, taken note of Glynnis Mear. She had taken his course only by chance. As a graduate student, she did not need to top off her schedule with an undergraduate offering, but she had wanted to explore sculpture beyond her cursory experience there, and Michael's course fit conveniently. Michael, during the first studio session, noted that Glynnis was a graduate student. He pulled her aside to inquire why she was there and was stimulated by her reply. Here was someone who conceivably might possess a grain of curiosity, a grain of passion. How welcome that would be. Welcome, too, was Glynnis's long brown hair and gentle body. She moved lithely around the studio and plied her clay with delicate fingers. Her face pursed in concentration did not hide its soft contours. And when she spoke Michael heard the crystal bells of New England on a winter night.

He was pleased when, one night early in the term, Glynnis showed up at his studio to put in extra work on one of her projects. He watched her furtively, pretending to be working on his own piece, and said nothing to her. When she cleaned up prior to leaving, he walked to her table and, purely without ceremony, asked if she would like to go with him for coffee. Glynnis, who knew that Michael had been watching her and sensed that he was delaying his own departure on her account, accepted his brusque invitation. They walked across campus to the student center and, over coffee and biscotti, talked for two hours, a perfunctory yet necessary conversation that set the basis for what might come later.

That was September. In the weeks to follow, Glynnis spent increasing amounts of time in Michael's studio. Occasionally they would repeat that initial evening and conclude their work over coffee. Glynnis did not tell Michael about Conor. There was no point, really; they remained on a superficial and innocent level. Twice Michael had asked Glynnis to have dinner with him on the weekend, and, bound to Washington, twice she had declined. She did not give Michael a reason, nor did he ask for one. For his part, Michael had little conception of romantic rituals. He preferred to be direct. He would keep asking, simply because he wanted to have dinner with her, and get to know her better. He could not deny to himself that he wanted to sleep with her as well, but that would come later, if it came at all. In the meantime, he would keep asking for her time. When she refused he was not discouraged, for his intentions, the final and ultimate arbiter of his actions, had not been altered. He would continue to pursue her, very gently, without pressure and without expectations, so long as they remained where they were.

Glynnis, of course, had been pursued by many men and had learned the art of the delicate rebuff. Michael, though, affected her differently than did the other young men. He was a vapor, invisible and odorless, that Glynnis inhaled without knowing. He had worked his way inside her; he played with her blood. Glynnis was attracted to him, intellectually to be sure, but more so physically. Conor, with his wild energy, his appreciation for all parts of her body, his untamed physicality, had always satisfied her most basic desires. Yet the contrast between Conor Finnegan and Michael Halcón was distinctive, and therefore intriguing.

Where Conor bubbled and burst with enthusiasm, Michael simmered. He held his reserve, and in so doing created a foggy, mysterious aura. His was a latent power. He stifled it; he would let it build. What walls might be ripped asunder when he finally let it go? Glynnis fantasized about Michael's restrained power; she fancied it filling her, rending her into tiny sections, flooding her being with the unplumbed depths of Iberian passion. Michael radiated a constant, overt sensuality which disarmed Glynnis thoroughly. Should she offer her bed, she knew he would accept. The possibility of something new, of momentarily throwing off all considerations of obligation and expectation, thrilled her. She wondered about the particulars of how Michael would be, but she assumed that he would be somehow marvelous.

As the weeks passed her curiosities predominated. She paid little attention to his quiet intellectualism. That, in fact, came to bore her, especially in contrast to Conor's boyish constructs which continued to charm her. The activism in Conor's intellect made it more complete. Not that she ever found Michael shallow. Rather, she tired of probing his constant reserve, the conclusions and convictions he only reluctantly shared. Conversations with Michael usually gravitated to the mundane simply because of the energy required to bring them further. Occasionally Glynnis discoursed on some point, some issue which excited her, in which case Michael remained passive and noncommittal. Glynnis enjoyed Michael's proximity for the unspoken act of rebellion it represented. She enjoyed the potential for a mysteriously wicked physical experience, although in spite of all fantasy she feared it coming about. Nonetheless, Michael Halcón—quiet, simmering, uncommonly and disturbingly sensual—flamed her blood.

In short, she had no idea what to do with him. She was certain, though, that until she resolved her intentions toward Conor Finnegan which, she presumed, would be accomplished when she finally developed the strength to honor her emotions and answer his call, she wanted to maintain her convenient relationship with Michael Halcón.

CHAPTER XVII

*The silence drew off, baring the pebbles and shells and all
the tatty wreckage of my life. Then, at the rim of vision, it
gathered itself, and in one sweeping tide, rushed me to sleep.*

—Sylvia Plath, *The Bell Jar*

Tom McIlweath absently fingered a paper clip while staring
out the narrow, grimy window of his new apartment. The
street below lay fetid and dark, intimating evil or, at best, cold
indifference. It had snowed that day. Slush lined the sidewalks; a horrid
black mire rose up against the curbing. The stores, shops and dusty cafes
stood hollow. Above them, in the cramped ancient flats not unlike his
own, lights shone sporadically to punctuate the vacuity. McIlweath saw
no one on the street. It was late and cold; all sensible life was home
now, in bed or reading, sipping hot chocolate. McIlweath sat at his
desk fingering the smoothly symmetrical, cool metal of his paper clip.
He started at the rounded end and ran its length, then spun it over to
repeat the process again and again. He looked at nothing. Insofar as the
conscious workings of his tired mind focused on anything at all, they lit
on his paper clip. Whatever might wait beyond that remained unnoticed,
merely part of the cold, heavy blackness that seeped in from all corners.

McIlweath had grown horribly bored, not with the transient
boredom of circumstance that besets all individuals of thought and
conscience, but with a boredom more profound, more pervasive than
anything he had previously experienced. It confused and disoriented

him. He did not know in any sense what to make of his disillusion. He had not had the time or opportunity to examine it, the demands of graduate study and Anne Newbury being what they were. For weeks (longer?) he had stumbled through his responsibilities, meeting them because he had to, because an innate sense of duty underscored by more than two decades of 'proper behavior,' of doing 'the right thing,' of doing what was expected from one in his position, had propelled him along this course. Yet he had fulfilled those responsibilities—he had gone to class, he had completed his translations, he had doggedly pursued his research, and, in the intervening moments, he had kept company with Anne—without excitement, without satisfaction, without the supreme sense of wonder that youth in a great city should assume.

The classics still intrigued him. He still reveled in his ability to read Latin and Greek, and, in so doing, to share in the ideas, the esthetics and the glories of antiquity. Had he been left alone to study those books he preferred and to push his research in directions entirely of his own choosing, his growing discontent might have lessened. No, the classics were still fine; it was their context which now seemed off. A miasma had settled upon his discipline, and it needed fresh air. This environment which he had pictured as intellectually pure and stimulating had, in fact, been stultifying. In this of all places, this oldest of cities, he had become bored. His work conjured images of dusty, frail, forgotten books hidden in the back rooms of decaying, mildewed libraries.

Environment had dictated all this. His studies had become a scapegoat for the general dissatisfaction whose long growing seeds had pushed through the surface of his loamy psyche. McIlweath had few friends here—he had no friends, really, in the true sense of the word. Among his fellow graduate students in the Classics Department, or those whom he might encounter in the library or student center, there was not one with whom he felt he could enter into a personal conversation. Nor was he the type of person to make friends easily outside the university community. His lifestyle was subdued and his natural reticence made it impossible for him to warm to another individual without a hook to draw him on. He had come to Boston assuming that those with whom he would share time and space would be similar to those he had lived with as an undergraduate. Instead, he found a group of students whom he saw to be aloof, elitist and so absorbed in their peculiar specialties that they could not readily step outside themselves, or let someone new enter. All of McIlweath's halting efforts to draw these people outside their stark, self-obsessed intellectualism and into areas of shared response were coldly met. They did not want friendship, he concluded, not on these terms, and his perception of their incredibly narrow personalities made him, too, shy away from any relationship outside classroom and library.

It alarmed him that he should now be surrounded by individuals intent upon keeping a discipline alive only for the sake of its perpetuation, rather than for the richness, the wisdom and the human understanding they could derive from it. To his fellow graduate students, the classics existed apart from all other human endeavor. McIlweath had always viewed it as intrinsically linked to what man had become, to the best of his thoughts, beliefs and emotions. But this sense now had little place in a discipline made competitive. His colleagues devised self-worth and evaluated others on the basis of grades won, of papers accepted for publication, of addresses delivered before professional societies. They resented accomplishments that outstripped their own, and those who authored them. McIlweath had overheard their resentments in cloistered conversations before departmental meetings, or in the few minutes prior to the beginning of a seminar, and they left him cold.

When he encountered his fellows separately in the student center and circumstance forced the awkward sharing of coffee or lunch, they would never speak of anything current—unemployment, the latest war, the latest murder, even a movie or a television show—and whenever McIlweath raised such a topic it either changed quickly or died from inattention. They would not speak of such things, he thought, because they could not. Their limited outlooks prohibited it. Instead they would raise a discussion of Moses Hadas's translation of Aristophanes or Gregorovius's interpretation of the Roman system of law enforcement. In time, McIlweath avoided altogether sitting down with other classics students. When he met them in the student center or on the T, he would exchange a brief greeting and go his way by himself. The result, particularly in contrast to the warmth he had shared the past few years, made his heart ache. He passed most days in abject loneliness.

It fell upon Tom's relationship with Anne Newbury to define the young man's existence in this strange and glorious city, but that too had grown bitter. It was Anne who had drawn McIlweath this way. Her presence here, her unswerving resolve that this would be the best course for him and her stubbornly self-righteous conviction that she could provide the proper guidance—all that had forced him here. In light of the power of Anne's personality juxtaposed with McIlweath's fragile emotional insecurities, there had been little leeway when it came time to decide what to do next.

But while Anne seemed satisfied with the scope of their relationship under these new circumstances, McIlweath felt increasingly frustrated, and thus increasingly lost. He saw her rarely: the demands of medical school were extreme. Occasionally they met during the day to share a quick lunch, and once or twice a week they could get together for an equally quick dinner before retiring to their separate ways to study away the evening. Anne had prohibited studying together—distractions might come too easily. On weekends they might spend an afternoon walking along the Charles or dining in a cheap restaurant. But even on those weekends their time was measured, the twin specters of their individual academic demands looming above and behind them. Anne for her part took her studies far more seriously than did Tom.

By the end of that gray, lonely autumn it had become apparent to McIlweath that he was expected to fill in the gaps in Anne's busy and well programmed days, and no more than that. He saw her only when she had the time, and then on her terms. He had become a companion of shallow substance and shallower expectations. When he called her, she put him off. When she called, he hopped to meet her. Now their time together lacked the unarticulated quality that, even at its most strained, their relationship had always had before.

Discussions of frustrations, annoyances, challenges, success, dreams and discouragements became less frequent and ever more brief. Anne's implications that she was too tired, too preoccupied, rang clearly. She preferred their time to be light and quiet, an interlude of mindless distraction from the pressing concerns at hand, concerns which McIlweath could neither alleviate nor understand, and so left unspoken. McIlweath perceived their worlds increasingly separating, joined only by proximity, and he was left stranded in a bland, lonely, uninteresting sphere that he had not chosen freely. They shared nothing but their time.

So then, he concluded, it had come to this. In spite of all his proud intentions to forge something for himself apart from any preconceptions, to produce a sophisticated thinking and feeling character that was above all else pure, unsullied by false motivations of conformity, prestige or convenience, he had ultimately bowed to his insecurities. His life had become no more than an outgrowth of someone else, one whose personality was stronger, more clearly defined, and unyielding. He had become a satellite, a shadow, an oblique reflection. Were his life to end this evening, he would have to consider it a failure, a waste of space and time.

Amid his growing depression, a thin vapor of resentment crept into his lungs. He breathed it imperceptibly, and it deepened his breathing and quickened his pulse. He must, he thought, resolve all this, resolve this failure while there was still time to extricate himself. For this was not right. This was not right at all.

Late that evening the phone rang. McIlweath, who had not moved from his desk all night, jerked back with a start. The ringing snapped him back from his dank musings. It was, of course, Anne.

"What've you been doing all night? Studying, I presume."

"Presume nothing. Actually I've taken the evening off. I've watched the street and looked at all the unhappy people going by. Have you been a good girl?" Conversation was an exertion. McIlweath went through the motions hoping that this call would end quickly, and the effort made him tired.

"I'm always a good girl, you know that," Anne said brightly. "I've been at anatomy laboratory poking around some grotesque body parts—I'll have to tell you about them. Be glad you're healthy."

McIlweath chuckled softly to himself as Anne continued, "After lab I stopped at the student center for a snack. I was hoping you might be there to surprise me, but there was nobody I knew, so I got a big dish of Swiss chocolate almond ice dream and ate it with a physiology textbook. Fascinating company, no?"

"You're getting to be on intimate terms with your little hard-bound friends."

"I'm getting to know them inside and out, front to back," giggled Anne. For some reason her girlish giggle annoyed McIlweath greatly. Fingernails on a blackboard.

"Anyway," she continued, "I can only take so much of this medical stuff. Do you want to offer me a diversion and go out to dinner Saturday night? Dutch treat, of course."

"Of course. Are you certain you can spare the time? And I'm not certain Dutch treat is quite fair. Your earning potential is about five times greater than mine. I think you should buy."

"Don't be silly. I'm in debt up to my eyelashes. We go Dutch. And it'll have to be late, say around 10:30. There are some things I need to get done that night. I have a huge physiology project that's due next week and I want to work all day on it. But by 10:30 or so I should be done, and my mind will be complete mush. Come by around then, okay? We can go to that cheap seafood place by the Charles that's open all night and eat crab legs until we can't move."

"Can't you make it any earlier? It's Saturday night. Can't you ease up a little bit?"

"I told you, I want to get this done. Once I start something I want to work all the way through it. Maybe if you're nice to me Saturday night we can spend some time together Sunday."

"I detect a touch of emotional blackmail. What if I don't treat you nice on Saturday night? What if I was a total brute?"

"Will you be throwing books again?" asked Anne, who knew how to press an advantage. From time to time she would wield that isolated and complex incident like a mace. McIlweath this time ducked the blow.

"I don't want to see any books on Saturday. I don't want to see them Sunday or Friday or Thursday, either. I'm tired of books. I'm tired of mildew and dust and boring, pointless books written in dead languages. If I could, I'd throw them all into the river."

"A bit disenchanted tonight, are we? I'll cure you Saturday. I promise."

'Ironic,' thought McIlweath, 'that the poisoner herself promises a cure.' He was silently glad that he would not see Anne for three more days. There was still much to work out.

"I'll give you every opportunity. But Anne, don't call me until then, all right? I plan on working each night. I've got to catch up on some things that are falling behind."

"The price you pay for squandering an evening or two, my friend. That's probably just as well. I'll be busy myself, as always. But I will look forward to Saturday night."

"So will I. See you then."

"Good night, Tom."

Back into silence; back into the interminable gloom.

* * *

The next day, one which assumed its usual pattern albeit viewed through a darker lens than usual, Tom McIlweath rose early and went to class, an excruciatingly dull seminar on Roman comedy. The professor had been at the university for nearly four decades, long enough for whatever enthusiasm he once had for his subject to be extinguished by repetition to the blank stares and stifled yawns of young people whose passions ran in different directions. He had become a brittle man—gray hair, gray face, faded coats and ties—yet it was clear that the university would allow him to remain on campus for as long as he wished, answerable to no one's evaluations, tucked away in its farthest and dustiest corner, free to follow any and all pursuits of his rapidly aging intellect. He had become as archaic as his subject.

McIlweath sat through the old professor's droning on Apuleus. He caught occasional bits of interpretation but knew that little of value would be said here. McIlweath froze a practiced look of interest on his face and daydreamed behind it.

For once he did not think of Anne Newbury. That would have been too much effort. He recollected instead his swimming victories as an undergraduate. He thought of the cool water flowing under his churning body and his arms pulling his form away from his competitors. He thought of the solidity of the wall when he touched, the draught of air he sucked into his lungs as his head shot up at the finish, and the blurred images of the other swimmers still struggling down the lanes beside him. He remembered the cheers of the crowd, the first sound to penetrate after the watery rasp of his desperate breathing and the lapping of the pool. The air so cold as he climbed out of the water, so harshly cold.

"And so, in *The Golden Ass*, we see one of the first uses of exaggeration in support of satire, here not of national or international political attitudes, but of the common human condition. It is a much subtler form and is given to very discreet nuances. Even today, after two thousand years of study, we still might argue about the devices Apuleus used, and what he intended in the particular."

McIlweath wished he were back in the pool, pulling ahead with the crowd cheering him on. How richly satisfying it had been to beat the elite swimmers from Princeton and Columbia and Penn. How surprised and dismayed the boys from the ivies had been to be out-matched by the scrawny, squinting kid from Rutgers. He had caught them unaware a good deal of the time. Even as a senior, well after his reputation had been established, he thought he saw some skepticism in his rivals, looks that said, 'How could this guy be so good? Are those times accurate? We'll see in the pool.' But time after time, he, slight, unassuming Tom McIlweath, had proven himself the faster swimmer.

'Name your stroke, boys. The butterfly at ten paces? The breast stroke perhaps, if you wish? No matter. I'll duel under any terms.'

Respect, he had been led to conclude, was even sweeter when it had to be wrenched from reluctant hearts.

The seminar, and McIlweath's concurrent daydreams, came to a halt at 11:30. He had not said a single word during the discussion of Apuleus's satiric techniques. He stacked his two books atop his notebook and left the room. Walking out of the old stone building he felt no compunction to study. The campus rose around him in its ennui like bars of a cage. Not knowing precisely how to fill the time before his next class but certain he had no stomach for anything academic, he headed for the student center. He was not hungry. His appetite had been almost nonexistent for several days, but at least he might grab the morning paper.

McIlweath settled at a table in the small basement cafeteria after going through the line to pick up half a grapefruit and some orange juice. He had also pulled that morning's *Boston Globe*. As he sat there reading and slurping what passed for an early lunch, an acquaintance from the English Department stopped by.

"Tom McIlweath, how're you doing?"

"Hello, Joel," said McIlweath looking up from his paper. He seemed to recall the other's name as Joel, and he hoped that he wasn't wrong about this, now that he had blurted it out. They had only met a few times on the bus from the west end to campus. Recognizing each other as graduate students, they had exchanged some superficial conversations. McIlweath had seen him around campus but this was the first time they had spoken while not in motion. "Care to join me?" McIlweath asked despite seeing that Joel carried a tray with an empty milk carton and two bare cardboard plates.

"I'm on my way out. How are things with the Classics boys?"

"Classically dull, but what can you expect? We're a dull group."

"Aren't we all? Listen, I'm having a little party this weekend—chasing away the winter doldrums and reacquainting myself with the pleasures of alcohol and loose women. You're more than welcome to come if you can stand the company of English and history geeks. Bring anybody you want and spread the word. I want a large, raucous and generally disorderly crowd."

"I don't know, Joel. I haven't been in much of a partying frame of mind lately."

"That's exactly the point. None of us are. Winter on this campus is oppressive like no place else. A good squawk will do you fine. Drive off a few devils. 134 Lexington, just inside the Boston city line. Big white house in a dumpy neighborhood. I share it with three other grad students. Park on the street or take a bus, but I hope to see your ass there Saturday. Like I said, bring whoever or whatever you want and spread the word."

"Don't count on it, Joel, but thanks anyway. I'll try to make it."

Joel smiled and raised his free hand in a gesture of resignation. "Suit yourself. Gotta run, Tom. Hope to see you Saturday night. If not, take it easy."

"You too. See you around."

McIlweath returned to his newspaper and read each section carefully, not to ingest any news but to pass the time. The grapefruit spat at his face when he cut it. It tasted of acid and started a small pin-sized fire in his stomach. At 1:00, having spoken to no one other than Joel, he rose with his tray. The room was nearly full, and as soon as he stood two young men took his table. McIlweath did not know if he had been holding them up, nor did he really care. He threw away the cellophane that had wrapped the grapefruit, the plastic spoon and the orange juice container, then placed the tray on the service sill. He walked back out into the daylight. For the next two hours he walked aimlessly around campus until it was at last time to go to his next class.

When one lapses into despair, when he comes to believe that the whispers and winds of his existence have led him haphazardly into a blind alley, when he finds himself hamstrung by Fortune with the strings contracting, he tends to extremism. He becomes likely to act as rebelliously as the limits of his temper permit. He seeks an act outside his usual character, outside the run of things, something new or unimagined, just to break things up, to break the ischemia of routine, to shine a new light, however tiny and temporary, into his blind alley.

Depression seeped into McIlweath like a gas, invading each pore and weighing down his lungs so that it hurt him to breathe. He did so reluctantly. The oppressive burden of his embryonic sentiment of failure never left him during those days. He could not know if this sentiment would be transitory, a perverse outgrowth of some foul mood or dark circumstance, or just a period of adjustment to the contrast with what had come before. He feared it was more than this, though, something more substantial than a temporary ill humor. He sensed its logical base and, as a logical man, he could not escape it. If, then, he could not escape it, he must ultimately change it. He must change the circumstances that were dragging him subtly away from his true character, the character he had aspired to create for himself against all circumstance.

After his brief conversation with Joel Whatever, McIlweath spoke to no one for two days. This was not his preference. He would have relished a long conversation into the night, probing and poking at his discontent with a close friend until his desolation could at least be partially expelled. McIlweath thought of Conor Finnegan, the accidental brotherhood they had formed through a proximity that McIlweath originally had dreaded. He wished Finnegan were near, that he were accessible for that conversation, for that cleansing. Washington was too long a drive for the weekend. They would have too little time together.

McIlweath spoke to no one because, quite simply, there was no one. The realization of his stark loneliness pushed him deeper into his depression. He had only Anne to whom he might unburden himself, and that, of course, would not do. That would only intensify the problem, ripping another tiny shred of the shrinking fabric of his individuality. And so He came to see his situation as cyclical—the source of his problem was his only available comfort, and, should he try to embrace that comfort, to call upon the source to provide him an outlet from his deadening days, his problem would grow.

On Friday, having heard no human voice directed his way for quite some time, Tom McIlweath paced his small apartment. As the circumstances of his existence had, he felt, abandoned him, he in turn abandoned them. He had not opened a book for three evenings, he had skipped his Friday classes to swim for two and a half hours at the university pool, he had not eaten a solid meal since the early part of the week, he had slept in sporadic naps and nods. In his apartment he watched television without knowing precisely what he watched, he stared at the traffic in the street below him, he looked through memorabilia—old campus newspapers and memos from the dean— from his undergraduate years. Twice he had begun a letter to his parents but, lacking words that did not sound morose, he had left off the effort. And at night he paced, music playing behind him, and did not sleep.

McIlweath glanced out his window at the street—quiet, even on a Friday, and virtually empty. The impression sickened him, his stomach and bowels turned inside him. At once he began to gasp through a tinny metallic taste in his mouth; he drew for air. 'I have to get out of here,' he thought desperately. 'I have to get out of this place. Now, without delay. Tonight.'

He pulled on a jacket and ran down the narrow stairs in near panic. The cold air from the dead street slapped him hard and subsequently calmed him with his first breath. The frantic pace of his gasping softened. He filled his lungs to capacity with the harsh, sweet, sooty air, then turned to walk to his car, parked three houses down.

He drove that night to downtown Boston, and found an open lot to park near the Common. He sought a radical act, although he did not perceive it as such; he did not know it. He needed to see people, real human beings in all their diversity and shared misery. Not homogenous, staid, bitterly cold people, or people bound to a single purpose, but people pushing and swearing and smiling, people reacting to human situations, people bridging themselves to other people and creating something peculiar and profane and hallowed, something that he desperately missed.

The young man had no goal in mind. Boston was enough. All he wanted was to walk its streets, see faces in motion, hear new and differently toned voices—the nasal twang of New England, the raspy snarls of the natives, Irish and Italians and Poles, redeeming their brawling individuality through a single night's escape. McIlweath sought to see them, to reassure himself that life need not be sterile and rote, that man's passions, even his basest, most hollow instincts, might still identify him. People, then—the primitive, gnarled, contentious, loud, brutal, swarming flood of mankind—that was what McIlweath sought. To observe it, to smell it, to hear it. Ultimately, to be reassured by it and, in so doing, to slacken the heavy chains around his throat. Around his heart.

He had parked his car southeast of the Common, locked it, and set out. He wanted to walk a bit. He felt no apprehension at being downtown alone, even though he wasn't familiar with the landscape. There were some clubs around here and, he thought, some theaters too. There would be people enough around.

McIlweath walked down streets whose names he did not know. They were not well marked. He passed restaurants, old ones with gouges in their doors and graffiti at the base of their walls but still issuing the rich, smoky aromas of meat being grilled. At the top of a rise nearest the Common, nicely dressed couples were plentiful—smart women on the arms of well-groomed men. No doubt they had come here directly from work, these professionals exuding confidence, control and place, exuding money and accomplishment.

Music spilled out from some of the places he passed. McIlweath knew nothing of jazz—he would have been purely incapable of discerning the good from the bad—but the sound of it stalked him like a prowling jaguar as he walked by the clubs. Squealing staccato horns, throaty saxophones, jabbing piano riffs conspired a restless harmony. McIlweath heard it inside him for days. Years later, in places far away on the darkest of nights, he would hear it again, because its mournful, wrenching wailing, the melodic sobbing of hopeless desolation, never really left him. The soft jazz emanating from one old club which had stood on the same spot for decades, pouring forth its haunting blues, echoed McIlweath's delicate mood. He stood outside its doors for uncounted minutes. People walked by, in and out of the club not noticing McIlweath, paying no heed but to each other.

And here he was then, a thin young white man, in sweater and corduroys and jacket, a misfit of sorts. This was no place for boys, and McIlweath's youth and naiveté shone forth like a beacon. The neighborhood of his wanderings began to change subtly, becoming as rough and forlorn as the music he heard. Even so, held by that music, attracted by the noise and movement of people in the street, breathing the crisp New England nighttime air, Tom McIlweath paid no mind. He was where he wanted to be.

He walked on, turning one block left and two right. His surroundings continued to grow meaner. Gone were the stylish restaurants and clubs that ringed the streets leading to the Common. Gone, too, were the mystically forlorn jazz houses. The streets grew emptier, and those that were still on them appeared rougher. Like a priest in a leper colony, he was intrigued yet removed from it all, knowing full well that he had been spared this as a permanency, but compelled to be here now.

What atmosphere there was had become glittery and false. Tawdry bookstores and dive bars spotted both sides of the street. The ubiquitous construction projects that never seem to come to completion chopped up the streets and threw barricades onto the sidewalks so that McIlweath had to step around broken concrete, hop off the curbs into mud puddles, and step carefully to avoid tripping on the uneven surfaces. There were no stylish couples here, no loners in search of an outlet for their blues. Some young men walked these streets, but they plodded their paths with neither bounce nor spirit.

With them were older men, beaten by the years, unshaven, gray of face, gray of mind, with hard and brutal eyes lurking below perpetual frowns. Their sneering animalism mocked the life that had mocked them. They had shaken off any and all notions of human compassion; existence was merely survival, and survival was made palatable by the simplest pleasures, a cheap beer or a cheap hooker. They did what they needed to get by, that was all. They expected nothing beyond that, would not know what to do with it should something better come along. All their lives they had been flamed in a singular primitive crucible of which this was the softest and coolest corner. McIlweath regarded these hard figures without looking at them. He respected their anonymity and would not have wanted to violate it. And beneath the veneer of the cheap bars and the dirty, broken streets he sensed an eerie, corrupt, voluptuous glow.

Tom McIlweath had had no conscious intention of walking these particular streets. Had he reasoned his course, or known the city better, he would have picked some other direction, perhaps Faneuil Hall or Beacon Hill, something less base and more removed from this subtly anarchic atmosphere. But now that he had happened upon it, this part of the city drew him in. He had sought human company, especially that company which stood in opposition to those who customarily filled his space. He had found what he had sought, and gone beyond it. He was Dante through the portals of the Inferno, lacking his Virgil but still able to observe the indulgences of man and the consequences of those indulgences. He sensed the nether side, that aspect of shared existence tinged with lust, with greed, with horror, with death itself. McIlweath walked on, transfixed by what he saw, but more so by what he sensed.

Stumbling forth from the shadows of an alleyway between two bars, appearing so quickly that McIlweath could not be certain precisely from where he had sprung, a disheveled figure lurched forward to block his path. Each part of him seemed shaky, as if he might tremble apart altogether and fall to the sidewalk in pieces. McIlweath's first glance at the intruder startled him. He felt a spear of adrenalin, a reflex of surprise tinged with fright, rocket through his chest and down his limbs.

The man was old, or so he looked. Most likely he had passed fifty, but quite possibly he could be younger than that, aged falsely through poverty or alcohol. He wore clothes that fit poorly—a tattered dark blue shirt, a black turtleneck underneath it, baggy pants stained here and there with some light-colored substance, like white or yellow paint, only thicker. His clothes hung from him. Most of his salt-and-pepper hair was covered by a ski cap with a deep rip on its front. His hair fell unevenly on the turtleneck and stuck out at odd angles on the sides beneath the cap. The old man had not shaved in several days, and a crusty gray-white stubble furzed his chin and cheeks. The old man's eyes were black, and hollow as if a flashlight shone into them might have revealed the back of his skull. It was not pain he hid there, but disassociation, an incredible distance between the poor possessor of those eyes and the rest of humanity. He had abandoned himself to the wolves, and so become one of them—bitterly resentful of any whose life contained those forgotten elements that, once without, he had come to scorn, and therefore poised to strike at the throat to rip away the soft, vulnerable flesh that tasted even sweeter in its despoilment.

The old man blocked McIlweath's random path, and, from the thin line of his mouth, growled some words the younger man did not at first hear. "What?" said McIlweath, his voice at once taking on the familiar high pitch of accelerated tension.

"I asked you if you could spare some change. Whaddaya say, buddy? I could use some help." His face remained set in a permanently etched snarling frown. "I swear I won't spend it for booze," but the stale acridity of his breath, his clothing, his demeanor, made the pledge ludicrous.

"Sorry, friend. Can't help you." It was true. McIlweath had no change in his pockets, and he was not about to part with a bill. Even in his malaise, he recognized the precarious financial position of a graduate student.

"Come on, buddy," said the old man harshly, taking a step to the side to block McIlweath again as he tried to walk around. Their chests bumped together and the old man, three or four inches shorter, drew himself up. The hot stench of his foul breath burned into McIlweath's face. He could feel it on his mouth, and the sensation sickened him. He detected a faint odor of urine from somewhere near.

"Come on, buddy. You got some cash, I know you do. You're gonna help me out now, God damn it."

"Listen, I'm telling you I got nothing. Find somebody else."

"No, you little shit, I found you." The old man grabbed McIlweath's left elbow suddenly with a calloused paw that felt more simian than human. He was strong, to be sure, despite his age.

McIlweath wrenched his arm, but the man held fast. The panhandler tightened his grip and wrenched back. A shooting pain charged up McIlweath's elbow to his shoulder. No one of the few figures on the street paid any mind to what was unfolding here, safe in their anonymity and choosing to be oblivious.

The old man pulled McIlweath against the wall of the alley, away from any sidewalk traffic that might appear. His breath filled McIlweath's ear. He had turned the younger man so that he now stood fast behind him while pressing McIlweath's side hard into the wall.

"Listen, you son of a bitch, come across with something or I'll break your arm. You fuckin' shitass kids." He drew back his head and spat, the warm gob of saliva hitting McIlweath's neck and then working its way down his back. "All your money, right now, boy. You ain't gonna get laid tonight, not with no money. What would you say if I dragged you down this alley and stuck it up your ass myself? Huh? Would you like that, boy? That'd be fun, wouldn't it? Now gimme your money, you son of a whore, nice and slow."

McIlweath moved slowly, his senses battered now, his world in spin. The man held his left arm tightly and relaxed his grip on the right only enough to allow McIlweath to turn enough so that he could reach into his back pocket. McIlweath's hand was trembling badly, and he had trouble clutching his wallet. Involuntary tears welled up in both eyes to blur his already clouded vision. The night scene had grown misty shapes in bright lights, some flashing, forms walking to and fro in another dimension, removed from the terror he now felt.

"The money, asshole. All you got. Give it to me easy."

McIlweath pulled his wallet slowly out of his back pocket. His fingers clasped hard around the solid leather, thick with pictures of family and friends, thick with identifications, thick with the proof of his survival. He felt its weight and clenched his fist around it as tightly as his rapidly ebbing strength allowed.

"Hurry up, you little shit."

McIlweath swung around in a flash, spinning in a whiplike motion to his left, his arm still pinned hard against him. Pain drove hard into his shoulder. The old man tried to pull back but he was not quick enough. The years, the alcohol, the dissipation had made him slow. McIlweath's free right hand, backed up by the thick wallet in its grasp, smashed into the hard bone of the old man's face. The impact made a muffled crunching sound. The attacker released his grip, and

McIlweath ran as hard as he could back to the street and down the block, dodging the still-oblivious figures ambling this way and that. As he broke away, he saw out of the corner of his eye the old man slump to the sidewalk. He had hit him as hard as he could.

He ran back up the streets he had come down, not stopping even after he cleared the tawdry, bawdy streets of Hades. He ran past the jazz clubs, and past the restaurants, not smelling the rich scents of food being prepared and cooked well. His running attracted the stares and startled the hearts of others, but that did not, could not, matter. He ran, and ran hard. The city had lurched forward as an evil thing breathing menace with the same intimate vulgarity as had his attacker. He must escape it at once, run past and away from its violating grasp and fetid whispers.

McIlweath ran to his car and unlocked it awkwardly, his hands still trembling, his lungs heaving and burning. He threw himself into the security of that old machine, then reached frantically into the back seat for his gym bag. He pulled out a towel and scrubbed the back of his neck. Most of the old man's spittle had dried. His shirt stuck to the skin along his back where it had run down. He reached back and scrubbed hard, scraping off the skin. The sensation of the wet, mucusy saliva would stay with him for days, and he would never be able to forget its feel completely. Years from now that spot of skin would tingle with the horrid memory, branded forever.

As McIlweath drove out of the city he calmed himself through many deep breaths. His powers of rationality returned. Even in the short time of the drive back, the marvelous salves of time and space had begun to work their wondrous cures.

He had, after all, felled the man with one blow. The man was old, and while he had no doubt done this before, he could not be counted upon to match strength with a much younger man. He relied upon intimidation, terror and surprise. McIlweath, once he had overcome his shock, had dismissed him easily. 'The poor bastard,' he thought. 'He must have taken more than his fair share of blows through the years. I'm not the first to deck him.'

McIlweath parked his car and went back up to his darkened apartment. His mood had oddly brightened. There was, it seems, life out there, even if a bit shady. He had seen it, and that, after all, was what he had sought. The city, for all its muck, presented a counterweight in the cosmic scheme of things to the stodgy, boring environment to which he had been consigned.

He took a hot shower to wash thoroughly the drippy run of saliva. Steam filled his lungs and he breathed it deeply, the warm vapor flowing down deep within him where it commingled with a burbling resurrected wellspring of . . . what, courage? He *will* do what was needed, to protect himself, to define himself, to make himself whole. He will not suffocate here nor anywhere else. These empty days are merely another rite of passage, nothing more than an incubation. It dawned at once, then, glorious, reassuring and indomitable, the joyous promise of the spirit's inevitable triumph over circumstance. All that he needed was a bit more time.

CHAPTER XVIII

There was a disturbance in my heart, a voice that spoke there and said, I want, I want, I want! It happened every afternoon, and when I tried to suppress it, it got even stronger . . . It never said a thing except, I want, I want, I want.

—Saul Bellow, *Henderson The Rain King*

Tom McIlweath awoke the next morning with more enthusiasm for the simple tasks of his life than he had had in weeks. The fragile reaffirmation of the previous night was still in place, a revival of sorts, and so perhaps destined to come sooner or later. McIlweath relished it.

What did his temporary failures and frustrations matter, as long as he remained mindful of who he was and the responsibility that came with it? If he wanted, he could climb into his old car this morning and head in any direction he chose, abandoning this sullen way of life to find something new, something more in step with the unarticulated pulse of his deepest character.

Perhaps Anne was correct about his lack of direction. But she did not understand what this really was. She was incapable of such understanding. McIlweath never lost sight of the fact that any commitment had some finality to it, and that had to be considered, which, McIlweath thought, few people ever did. Most were willing to rush headlong into what seemed to be the right path, and in so doing gave up a bit of themselves, and maybe more than a bit. For his part, he would not be coerced into fulfilling someone else's expectations. He had done that, and tasted ashes. In the end, he sought to create his own expectations and attune himself to them. He would do what contented him, in a place where he felt comfortable. And if that wasn't what was now at hand, then so be it, as long as he could keep moving toward it, whatever it was.

In this way McIlweath reconciled his loneliness and restored his delicate confidence. But as the day wore on, the ennui of the pattern of his current fallow existence set back in. He might be cognizant of his potential for self-determination, but the reality of his day-to-day lifestyle was still with him. It stifled him; it squeezed him dry. Morning crept into afternoon. He tried to read a critical study of Roman tragedy. His work had fallen drastically behind, but he could not concentrate for more than a few minutes at a time. His eyes bounced from the book to his drab apartment, crammed with other books equally dull, and he daydreamed endlessly.

He took himself back to his undergraduate days and thought of his three roommates, recreating incidents he remembered clearly—a party, a football game in the park, nights watching television together, even something as mundane as fixing a dinner on the weekends. He took himself back to the pool, to the cheers. He remembered the thrill of tremendous pride when he saw his name go up on the swimming record board. He took himself back to his first meeting with Dan Rosselli. It was a boisterous session—they had sat in the dormitory lounge until 2:00 in the morning swapping stories in the infusion of excitement born of a new friendship in a new place. He took himself back to his drive across country with Conor Finnegan, the first rite of passage, and the peculiar mix of apprehension, wonder and burgeoning self-confidence as the country and their innocent youth passed before them en route to a new, marvelously unknown corner of their lives. This was his earliest recollection; he did not care to examine anything before that.

McIlweath accomplished little that day. He grew restless with his inability to study. His lack of focus caused him to read no more than two or three pages at a time before putting down his book. He walked around the tiny apartment, then walked around it again. At one point he dropped to the floor and did thirty pushups, then flipped over to do fifty sit-ups. He wanted to be in motion and still, he spoke to no one. His despair returned, more gently than before but present nonetheless. It glossed his renewed convictions, it glossed his resolve. His day clouded over, the mist in front of it growing thicker as the afternoon waned.

Once again, an impetus to action called him forward. He needed to do something, to see something, to be with someone. Last night's frenzy put the city out of reach, but still he needed a place apart, something different.

In late afternoon he remembered his conversation with Joel earlier in the week, and the loose invitation to a party. Maybe that was it. He knew he was due to meet Anne for dinner around 10:00, a date which promised nothing different than all the other times they got together. Perhaps, before he met up with her, he might stop in Joel's party for a bit. He'd enjoy the noise. He'd enjoy seeing if he could talk to someone new. There was, too, the consideration of his relative anonymity. Most of the people there he would not know. No expectations, and if he were extremely lucky, he might even have a good time. He saw few risks in taking Joel up on his invitation.

McIlweath let the afternoon die and ate a tasteless meal in front of the television. He watched the news and felt foreign. Nothing he saw had any bearing on him at all. He found himself to be envying Conor Finnegan once again. How exciting it must be to be in the midst of things, to sense that one's actions had some impact on other people's lives, to possess at least a dollop of influence. McIlweath discovered that his knowledge of current events, never comprehensive to begin with, had evaporated during his time in Boston. Names and places issuing from the television were mostly unfamiliar. Ironic, he thought, that he could name the rulers of Greek city-states twenty-five centuries ago but could not name the Greek president today.

At 7:00, hopelessly bored and more than three hours away from Anne Newbury, McIlweath pulled on a jacket and headed out the door. It was the first time he had stepped outside his apartment all day.

Joel's party was an unknown quantity with unknown possibilities, and McIlweath's timidity reasserted itself. He would, he told himself, just drive by and see if he might want to stop in. No commitment to go, just a little scoping out to see how it looked. Besides, the cold air would do him good. Before he left he combed his hair, splashed himself with cologne and put on a pair of his best slacks with a clean sweater. If nothing else, he was prepared to meet Anne.

McIlweath drove to the side of town where Joel lived. He found Lexington, then slowed his car to cruise past 134. It was an old house, probably built right after the second world war. At first glance it reminded McIlweath of the place in New Brunswick, wooden and warm, thoroughly comfortable. Forms moved behind the front window. Even though the curtains were open and the lights were bright, McIlweath could not tell how crowded the place really was. Old houses had a way of distorting space. Cars were parked thickly on both sides of the street.

He sped up gradually and drove around the block, still undecided.

He glanced at his watch—7:23. He might stop in, he reasoned, and stay a few minutes, just to say hello to Joel. It had been, after all, an unexpectedly friendly gesture to invite him. They barely knew each other. If he found someone to talk to, he could stay longer. He would still be able to meet Anne at 10:00. This would just kill a bit of the gap between now and then.

McIlweath returned to Lexington and found a spot to park near the end of the block. As he neared the house he saw that indeed there was a good crowd. Figures moved in both the upstairs and downstairs windows. On the sidewalk in front he heard music and voices, not loud or garish but assertive, pleasant, altogether friendly, the sweetly rich resonance of youth which he had not heard in months. The sound created a subtle stir within him. He walked up the wooden porch, fully curious now to see and to feel what was inside.

A sloppy handwritten note was stuck above the door handle: "Don't knock. We're too drunk to answer." McIlweath opened the door and stepped inside, and, upon entry, he returned once more to the realm of the living.

Joel spotted McIlweath as soon as he was inside the room. He had been standing in sight of the door speaking with a slightly built, darkhaired fellow. They both came up to greet the newcomer. "Tom McIlweath. Hey, I really didn't expect to see you." Joel shook McIlweath's hand warmly, and with force. "Glad you could come, thanks for coming. This is one of my roommates. Doug Fleming, History Department, this is Tom McIlweath, Classics."

The other extended his hand with an equally warm smile. "Pleased to meet you. We've got beer, wine and liquor in the kitchen, food in the living room and drugs wherever you can find them. Help yourself. Here, let me take your jacket."

"Thanks," said McIlweath, and his jacket was taken away by Joel's roommate, whom he did not see again for the rest of the evening.

"We've got an interesting mix of folks here tonight, Tom. You'll find them pretty entertaining, I think. How've you been?" Joel walked McIlweath to the kitchen to see that he got something to drink. McIlweath recognized several of the faces in the crowded living room although he knew none by name.

"Fair. I wanted to get out tonight and be with some new people. It gets lonely sometimes."

"You live alone, right?"

"Yeah."

"Big mistake, especially in graduate school. You find yourself sinking into your studies and not doing what you have to do to stay alive. You've got to waste some time doing mindless things, and you've got to have people around. At least that's the case with me." They had arrived at the small kitchen, equally as crowded as the living room. McIlweath pulled a beer from the refrigerator and popped it open.

"You're right. I lived with three guys as an undergraduate. I miss the hell out of them. But I didn't know anyone here, so I got a place by myself."

"You should have held out. There are plenty of guys around here looking for roommates. You run the risk of ending up with a slob or a geek, but at least it's company. Keeps the costs down, too. This city is wicked expensive. Come on, let me introduce you to some folks. You probably don't know anyone here."

Joel took McIlweath to two young men standing near the passage between the kitchen and the living room. Both were tall and thin, one with blond hair, the other with black hair complementing a well-trimmed beard. Both had the sunken, sallow faces of students— undernourished, removed from sunlight and divorced from all forms of exercise. They halted their conversation as Joel and McIlweath approached.

"Gentlemen, I want you to meet a delegate from the Classics Department. Tom McIlweath, this is Owen Lee, English, and Kieran Mulrooney, Political Science." They exchanged greetings and McIlweath tried to remember that it was Mulrooney with the beard.

"I'll leave you folks to your interdisciplinary discussions. I've got more guests to greet. If you need anything, flag me down. Tom, the bathroom is up the stairs when you need it," and with that Joel was gone.

"I've seen you on campus many times . . . Tom, is it?" said Owen, the blond. "You study in the library quite a bit. As do we all, I suppose, graduate school being what it is."

"Yes, I believe I've noticed you as well. How far along are you?"

"Doctorals this summer, writtens in June and orals to follow if I pass. I look to have the degree in four years. How about you?"

"I just got here. This is my first year, and to tell you the truth, it may well be my last. I'm not all that taken with the scholarly life these days."

"Oh." Owen audibly shrank, as if McIlweath had committed a *faux pas* too obvious to ignore and too gross to be commented upon, like hitting on the host's wife or walking about with a slip of toilet paper jutting out of his pants. Owen tried to pass over it with as much grace as he could muster. "Well, to each his own. Do you have any prospects?" He said this last word with something of a hiss.

"Not at the moment. I don't know what I'd do. Perhaps," said McIlweath, recoiling a bit, "I'd do well to stay here and finish my degree.

That would be the logical course, but I'm not certain I have the heart for it."

"For myself, I can't imagine a better way of life than what we have here. It's rather idyllic, you know. We can surround ourselves with great books and great ideas and people with common temperaments. Our needs are few. We content ourselves with the simplest of gratifications, those of the mind, something we can always indulge very simply but which only a few people are able to do. I believe we are the elite. We live by our minds, we follow our curiosities. Our only responsibility is to learn, and if that is our passion too, then how could we be happier?"

"You're making me feel guilty," McIlweath said with an awkward chuckle.

"Perhaps you should be. We really have been favored, you know. We are grandly fortunate to be here. I'd stay here for the rest of my life if I could. My dearest hope is that I get a solid teaching position in a similar environment after I complete the degree. But such things are quite rare."

"But don't you feel somewhat isolated here?" McIlweath suggested. "We really are apart from society in general. We build our own little universe here. Unless we make a special effort we hear little of what goes on in the world. I saw the news tonight for the first time in a month, and I found I miss it. Here, our whole world is introverted. It's as if we've been cut off from the remainder of mankind and told our sole purpose is to swell our knowledge, but that no matter how much we learn, there's only a tiny fraction of it we'll ever really share, simply because we *are* so cut off."

"And what's wrong with that? When you do have cause to observe 'the remainder of mankind,' as you put it, what do you see? Belligerence, bloodshed, intellectual mediocrity or worse, bigotry, greed, self-absorption. Whether it's an international conflict or someone stealing a loaf of bread from the convenience store down the street, it's all so apparent. We are a sad, sad species, I fear. We're self-devouring. Why on earth should you be remorseful at being cut off from it to a degree, particularly when you can indulge your own intellect in ways so comprehensive that you'll never get to the end of it? The only chance we have at elevating ourselves is through pursuit of the highest ideals and the best thought, like we do."

"I have a friend," replied McIlweath, "who's one of the few people I've ever known whom I would call truly brilliant. He has a clever, intuitive mind that can grasp an idea immediately, before you've even articulated it or understood it yourself. We went through college together. He never took his studies very seriously. Not that he didn't want to do well, but he always said that there was too much else he wanted to do to devote himself to the books. He studied only as much as he had to in order to get what he wanted, and he came away with as many academic honors anybody could attain, including Phi Beta Kappa. I did well myself, but I always got the impression that he was much happier than I ever was because he wasn't isolating himself. He never built walls around his intellect. He had a lot of friends, he was a good athlete, he had a beautiful woman, and he was able to indulge himself, too, in the ways you described."

"Where is he now?"

"Washington, working for a senator. He couldn't be more involved with this 'sad species,' to use your phrasing."

"Then he is bound to compromise that wonderfully intuitive mind to expediency. Perhaps he already has. In any event, the demands of his job and his lifestyle will catch up to him, and then his personality will begin to change. He'll be drawn into the mediocrity he's so far been able to rise above. Then what will all his practical knowledge avail him? Don't you see, he was able to do all those wonderful things you mentioned and he was able to develop that unique character simply because of the isolated environment you both enjoyed for four years. When he steps outside it, he loses its protection. He becomes increasingly ambitious, materialistic, and ultimately jaded. It's unavoidable, I'm sorry to say. It's the forfeiture of the intellect to a cold-blooded pragmatism that's necessarily imposed upon him. Excuse me, you two. I've drained my wine. I'm off to get another." Owen Lee turned abruptly, not waiting for response, and ducked into the bowels of the kitchen.

"Your friend has the smugness of his convictions," said McIlweath to the tall, dark-haired, bearded fellow who had stood silently throughout the entire exchange. "That's an admirable trait in small doses."

"Not at all. Owen's a bloody pain in the ass. He's a complacent bastard, but he can give a good laugh sometimes." The other spoke in the crisp, flat accent of Australia.

McIlweath cocked his head. "Where are you from, Kieran? I didn't notice your accent before."

"That's because I kept my stupid mouth shut. I know better than to tilt with that pedantic bastard. Rockhampton, Australia, a town up the coast north of Brisbane. Bloody remote outpost near the Great Barrier Reef. No doubt you'll ask what I'm doing here, so I'll tell you. A government fellowship to one of your country's finest, which I took on the presumption that it would be a two-year vacation with a degree at the end. I was wrong, though. The bastards have put me to work," and he laughed. "Serious studies they expect. Plus no one told me how blessed cold it gets here. I've been freezing my balls off."

"It must be an adjustment then. A cold adjustment. You must get lonely."

"Not really. Well, I take that back. I do miss my family. But the crew here is a decent lot, and there's plenty to do. I must confess that I favor your view of the scholarly life much more than I do our friend's. You're much more realistic. The thought of living the rest of my life with a bunch of dead boring political science books is too grim for words. I'd be envious of your friend, too. I've set my sights on government work as well, once I get back home. Some civil service post in the State Department might fit me well."

"What are your prospects?" McIlweath hissed, and Mulrooney burst out laughing.

"Very good, I should think. The government's already picking up the bill for this little excursion. I'd think they'd want some return on their investment. I'm focusing on American foreign policy. The State Department back home might find my views useful when they have to deal with you Yanks down the road. That's what I'm counting on."

"Any problems adjusting to the States?"

"An unqualified no. It's all a matter of being resilient, and that's expected of us no matter where we go. I mean, if I'd gone off to Canberra I'd have been called upon to make as many adjustments in thought and action as I did in coming here. In fact, it's easier here. People see you're a foreigner and they have much lower expectations. They're ready to dismiss your transgressions, but if you're a known quantity they'll hold you accountable. I must say I've enjoyed that. I could go punch Joel in the gob if I wanted and explain that it's an Aussie custom to smack the host before you leave. People would just nod and say how quaint it all was.

"I suppose," he continued, "that that's a bit overstated, but you see my point. We all have to make a break sometime. Whether that break takes us across the street or across the sea is immaterial. Ultimately you're left on your own. That's how I look at it."

McIlweath nodded. Before he could reply, a freckled blonde, strikingly attractive, came up to join them. Her hair curled under her ears to the sides of her delicate neck whose slender length made her appear taller than she actually was. Her sweater and jeans fit tightly enough to show a firm, thin body with high breasts and narrow hips. Her hair hung casually over her forehead covering her eyebrows but stopping above her translucent, crystal blue eyes. Freckles lined her cheeks, chin and the blade of her nose. She radiated health, confidence and place, a sense that she belonged well wherever she found herself. Her mouth, small with reedlike lips, fixed itself in a smile.

"One thing, Tom, that's made the transition palatable is the gorgeous females you have here. This is one of them," and Mulrooney leaned down to kiss the girl on the cheek. She laughed and kissed him back. "Kathy, I've been making a new friend. This is Tom McIlweath. Tom, Kathy Keane, a lass after whom I've lusted wildly these several months."

"Ignore him, Tom," she said with a throaty laugh. "He'd have you believe he's quite the ladies' man."

"Well, I am, aren't I? My accent and polished good looks should entitle me to something with you birds, shouldn't it? I'm only asking for my fair share."

"Kieran, you're horrible. Are all Australians governed by their libidos? Anyway, I'm interested in talking to this mysterious stranger that I've never seen before. Be a dear and get us some more beer while we get acquainted." She shook her empty bottle at Mulrooney, who bowed from the waist, took it, then grabbed McIlweath's too before he disappeared into the kitchen.

"He's a sweetheart," said Kathy. McIlweath perceived that she had already had a fair amount to drink. She seemed completely relaxed. Or perhaps it was just a casually relaxed personality, the kind McIlweath saw too little of these days.

Almost instantly Mulrooney returned with their new beers, stayed with them a few minutes more, then moved on. "Some more folks here I want to check in with. Tom, give me a call sometime. We'll get together for a meal or a drink, hey? This place does get frightfully dull. I'd be glad for the new company. My number's in the directory. But then I'll see you in the library, I'm sure. Good luck," and McIlweath was left alone with Kathy.

The beer worked to put him at ease, and he felt none of the tongue-tied shyness that usually plagued him in conversations with attractive young women. His confidence rose like a thermometer in the direct sunlight of Kathy's relaxed demeanor. And, my God, she was purely beautiful.

They stood and talked at length, the flow of their conversation undulating between the serious and the silly. No one disturbed them, and McIlweath thought it peculiar that none of the people around them should try to break in on their discussion. They both finished their beers, then each got another, then another. McIlweath knew that he had crossed the line of intoxication and was moving progressively deeper into that rare territory. He felt terrific.

"So you're a competitive swimmer. I'm impressed." McIlweath had been regarding the gentle curves of Kathy's face. He was not certain how they had moved to this topic. "I swim, too. Three times a week. It's about the only exercise I get."

"I'm surprised I haven't seen you at the pool. I go there as often as I can, whenever I want to drop everything and feel good about myself again."

"Oh, now," she cooed, "do I detect a note of self-pity? What is it that makes you feel bad? About yourself, I mean."

"The fact that I'm here. The fact that I'm doing what I'm doing, which strikes me as hopelessly meaningless."

"Why?" Kathy became serious. "Didn't you choose all this for yourself?"

"Yes, but I chose it under different terms. As an undergraduate, things were more diverse. By contrast with my other studies, Classics excited me to the core. It still could, I suppose. My argument isn't with the discipline as much as how I have to approach it here. And the way of life. We're dead here, only we don't know it."

"You're lonely, Tom. Forgive my saying so, but there's something in you that seems so damn hollow. I hardly know you, so maybe I'm being presumptuous, but what you've said, what you've been saying all night, points me to loneliness. Hell, we're all lonely here, in one way or another. But, am I right?"

"Yes, I am lonely, and because I don't have enough self-confidence to assume responsibility for my current state, or so I've been told, I blame it on my environment. The fact is, I've met few people here I'd care to share my time with, and even fewer who are inclined to drag themselves away from their own studies to develop anything close to a friendship. I'm stranded, like a hermit."

"Joel's parties are the cure for that. He brings people together with no expectations other than to be yourself, to relax and to forget about any stresses of the moment. There are good people here, but it's sometimes hard to find them. Joel is something of a social guru. But, you have no one here in Boston you'd consider a friend?"

McIlweath drew his lips into a sardonic smile, then drank his beer. "Actually, the reason I'm here at all is a woman. I came to Boston to be close to her. She's at Harvard Med. The irony is that I rarely see her now, and when I do, I leave more unsatisfied than ever."

"You sound bitter."

"I don't know what I am." McIlweath with a start remembered the time. He glanced at his watch: 10:06.

"What's wrong? Do you have to leave?"

"I'm supposed to meet her for a late dinner. We were going to talk, although she might not know that. You know, this may sound bold, but I've had a richer conversation with you tonight than I've had with her in months."

Kathy smiled. "That *is* bold. I'm flattered."

"I mean it. She's so remote. All her life she's driven herself, step by step, to her goals. That's all I've been to her: another goal. A convenience to keep her company when she needs it and then only on her terms. There's precious little emotion there. She hides it well, and she's dismissed passion altogether. I'm a logical conclusion. A syllogism, nothing more."

"Why have you stayed with her?"

"Expectations. Besides, what else have I had?"

"Anything you would have wanted, I would guess. You seem to have a lot to offer."

"I've never thought so. I stayed with Anne because she was secure, even if cold. She did fulfill some of what I needed, too."

"Not enough, though. That's obvious. Anyway, you have to go meet her."

"No. I've given up enough of myself for her fancies. I'd rather stay here and drink some more."

"Are you sure? Insecurity can be a fierce thing, you know. And you already have a lot invested."

"But at minimal dividends. It's past time to reevaluate it all. I was going to do that tonight with her. But I can do it just as well without her, and it's far more pleasant."

"I feel fortunate that I've never been in a relationship like that. All my entanglements have been much simpler. I've never come close to being in love, and I'm thankful for it."

"Why thankful?"

"Too complicated. At this stage of my life nothing is settled. I want a career, I know that. I want to be an editor and I'll do anything I can to reach that particular goal. A man would be a distraction. There'll be plenty of time once I get where I'm going. But getting there is the thing. Do you know how many English grad students want to be Maxwell Perkins or Henry Luce?"

"Do I detect a hint of competitiveness?"

"I see what I want and I go after it. I'm willing to work my way up from the bottom, and I don't feel the need to steamroll anyone along the way. But I want the eventual prize."

"Does that apply to things other than your career?"

"It applies, my love, to everything," and she ran her arm around McIlweath's shoulder and kissed his ear. She was now drunk enough so that when she leaned toward him she tottered. Her hand fumbled for the collar of McIlweath's shirt, missed, then tried again. She held onto him there. McIlweath, aroused, slipped his arm around her waist. The flesh beneath the sweater was tight, firm, smoothly molded.

"Get me another beer," she purred. McIlweath unwrapped himself from her with some effort, for he, too, was drunk. He had eaten nothing; the beer had gone straight to his head. He wobbled into the kitchen, grabbed two full bottles and headed back to Kathy. The kitchen clock read 10:15. There would be hell to pay when next he saw Anne, but, really, how would that be any different from what was likely to occur tonight? Hell takes diverse forms, and breathes ice as well as fire.

Kathy Keane, he learned, had been born and raised in the Midwest—born in Missouri, raised in Springfield, Illinois. "We used to go to Lincoln's tomb to make out when we were in high school. There are so many hidden places there. Imagine, grasping a boy's penis in sight of the remains of The Great Emancipator."

She had grown up self-assured, intelligent, quick, witty and uncommonly attractive. Kathy had, in fact, made a name for herself amid the thousands of anonymous undergraduates at the University of Illinois. She captained the girls' tennis team, earned national debating honors and graduated magna. Professors came to know that if Kathy were in their class, the entire term would be a series of probing, pointed questions, complex constructions and animated disagreement. Kathy Keane was intimidated by neither age nor wisdom; she spoke her mind. Some professors actively sought her out for their courses. Many saw her name on their rosters at the beginning of a term and groaned. "She never lets you relax," complained one in a letter of recommendation she had chanced to glimpse. "That's a terrible burden for a man of tenure."

Upon graduation, she headed east because that was where the publishing jobs were. She would go to the best graduate school, make the proper contacts and get a degree that meant something. From there she was confident that those contacts would pay off with an offer of a nonprestigious job at a prestigious publishing house. Once her foot was in the door, she had no doubt that she could make the right people notice her considerable talents.

Joel's party this evening was not her first. "Grad school is unbelievably dull, isn't it? You become so grateful for even the slightest diversion, even if it's something you might not actually even want to do." She barely knew Joel and, like McIlweath, had no idea of his last name.

"Why have you spent your entire evening speaking with me?" asked McIlweath. "There are far more attractive men here who must be better conversationalists (his drunken mouth stumbled badly over this word) than me."

"Don't sell yourself short, my friend. You intrigue me. You looked a bit lost. Not forlorn or marooned, mind you, but somewhat bewildered. Especially when you were talking with that pompous idiot—what's his name? Olin? Who cares? I heard everything. God, he's awful, but grad school's loaded with that type. So stuck on themselves, capable only of justifying what they do through these silly rationalizations. That's really all they're capable of. Then when you were talking with Kieran you seemed like a decent person. You wanted to know him, so I thought I might try to know you. And, yes, there are more 'attractive' men here, but I don't like dealing with their cheap charms. I didn't feel like being asked to go to bed by someone shallow or smug."

"So I looked safe?" said McIlweath with a smile.

"You looked lonely. Besides, you're new. And you're a swimmer, and you read dead languages, and you're from California, which I've never seen, and you have a bitchy lover who keeps you for a pet. All that intrigues me."

"Of course, you didn't know any of this when you first came up to me."

"No, but if I weren't intrigued I would have left you and you'd have gone off to your bitch."

McIlweath saw the time on the far clock. It was a quarter to midnight. Anne by now would be seething. She probably would have called and grown angrier with each unanswered ring. 'It would never occur to her to be worried about me,' he thought. 'I could be lying in a hospital, but all she'll think about is her lack of a dinner and the insult of being stood up when I've always been as punctual as a full moon. Let her seethe.'

"I'll deal with her in due time. And please don't call her a bitch. She has some wonderful qualities."

"Which she keeps hidden and dusts off only when absolutely necessary. I know the type. You're much better off with me tonight."

"You two still at it?" boomed Kieran Mulrooney loudly as he came up behind them. "Jesus Christ, Tom, give some of us other horny blokes a chance, won't you? You can't show up a stranger and monopolize the most delicious girl in the place all night. It isn't proper." Kieran threw his arms around both of them and draped himself between them.

"I should think you two would be well enough acquainted by now. How about some affection, love?" He leaned his head toward Kathy who, with a giggle, kissed him quickly on the lips. "Oh now, what's this? We've done better than that."

"So we have," she responded, "but you're old news. I've found someone fresh tonight."

"Come on, Kath. I'm as fresh as there is. You know that."

"Okay, I've found someone untried. You've heard what we Americans say about variety."

Kieran flopped his head toward McIlweath and squinted at him with mock seriousness. "I don't know, Kath. He looks a bit undernourished. No meat on him at all."

"Lean and mean," said McIlweath with more effort than it should have required. "I'm tight, see? No fat." He patted his stomach with his free hand. His other arm he wrapped around Mulrooney's shoulders as a sincere rush of friendship swept through him. He liked this tall Australian very much. He wanted to know him through and through. He clutched Mulrooney's bony shoulder in a wave of affection, in respect for the distances he had come for reasons so personal, and of warm envy.

Mulrooney smiled at McIlweath's reaction. "You seem a reasonable soul, Tom McIlweath. We shall spend some time together, and it shall be good time, time well spent. But tonight," he disengaged himself, faced McIlweath and bowed deeply, on wobbly legs, "tonight I will leave you to your lass. Take good care of her for there is no one like her, even remotely like her, on this campus, in this cold city, and in this decaying country. Take care of her, I say," he waved a finger with affected gravity, "and I shall bid you good evening now. You may not have noticed, but I've had quite a lot to drink."

"Pining for the Outback, Kieran?" teased Kathy.

"After a fashion, my love. But that is not the reason I am now so drunk. I am now drunk simply because, like Mount Everest, it was there." With that, Kieran Mulrooney kissed Kathy Keane on the cheek, then turned and kissed McIlweath similarly.

"Be careful going home, Kieran," said a blushing McIlweath. "Do you want a ride?"

"He only lives two blocks away," said Kathy. "He'll be fine. Won't you, sweet?"

"Very fine. Good evening once again," and the thin figure stumbled up the stairs for his coat. Neither McIlweath nor Kathy noticed him come back down.

The crowd had thinned to a scattered few sitting, no longer standing, around the living room and four people near the liquor in the kitchen. "We're left with the long ball hitters," said Kathy. "This group won't break up until 3:00 or 4:00."

"I don't know if I can handle that," said McIlweath.

"Normally I'd hang with them, but I'm too drunk. Let's have one last beer before we go." McIlweath dutifully fetched two bottles from the kitchen. Kathy leaned against the doorframe, her sweater riding up above her belt, a languorous smile on her tilted head. She watched McIlweath's every move. Her blue eyes reflected green in the dim light and a lock of rebellious curls fell across her cheek, a wisp of blonde spray against her ruddy skin. As he turned back toward her, bottles in hand, and saw her there, Heloise in the doorway, McIlweath thought that she was the most beautiful woman he had ever seen.

"Your beer, miss," he barely whispered as he walked to where she leaned, the fairest of barriers.

"Thank you, M'lord. Let's finish these quickly and get out of here."

They threw off their beers in four or five swallows. By now the bitter, stinging flavor no longer affected McIlweath. He did not really like the taste of beer. He had been relieved when he realized that his drunkenness had carried him to the point where the beer was just a presence on his tongue and had no definable flavor. The beer went down now as easy as water.

What he and Kathy spoke of while they drank the final beer he did not know. He paid only enough attention to make replies that were not completely inappropriate or offensive. He tried to avoid non sequiturs. Glimpses of Kathy laughing and smiling told him that he must be fairly entertaining, or at least relevant, though he did not know exactly how he was doing it.

McIlweath knew that he faced the endgame. The moral demons that otherwise would be ripping apart the tender flesh of his conscience had been banished, for the moment. They would return, he knew, fiercely. But let them wait until tomorrow. Tonight, for one night of a forlornly frustrating life, he knew what he wanted to do.

Kathy shook her empty bottle in his direction. "We seem to have finished what we set out to do. I want to go."

McIlweath took Kathy's bottle and returned it to the counter with his own. He walked back to her, but before he could say a word Kathy locked her hands behind McIlweath's neck and kissed him hard on his astonished lips. They tasted like orchids. He responded, and felt himself grow tumescent. After several seconds he drew back; she smiled up at him. McIlweath could feel the firm pressure of her breasts against his chest, so he did not move. Kathy ran her hands down McIlweath's back and kissed him again. Her impish tongue played along the insides of McIlweath's mouth and along the corners of his lips. They stood in close embrace for uncounted minutes, oblivious to the others near them and unconcerned about how their show might be regarded.

Kathy at last paused and whispered, "Take me home, Tom. I want to leave now."

McIlweath's mind was too disoriented for him to respond

immediately. "Tom," she repeated, "take me home now."

"Oh . . . yeah. Of course, yeah. We should leave. Shall we pay our respects to the host?"

"You do it. I'll go get our coats. Which one is yours?"

"Blue jacket with a yellow lining." McIlweath sought out Joel, who was in a corner of the living room engaged in animated, drunken discussion with three other people, one of whom was a thin redhead whose hand had found its way to the inside of Joel's thigh.

"Joel," interrupted McIlweath, extending his hand. "I'm leaving. Thanks so much for asking me by."

"You're not leaving alone, I hope? That would defeat the purpose of a Joel Pleasance ('There it was, the last name. I'll remember that.') party."

"No. Kathy asked me to drive her home. We're leaving now."

Joel whistled deeply, as did the other man in the group. The girls just smiled. "Some pretty impressive company, friend. Well done." Joel shook McIlweath's hand warmly. "Really, you didn't meet everybody, and I think you should. You'll have to come back."

"I'd love to. Thanks, Joel. See you around?"

"Count on it. Be careful tonight, okay?"

"I'm well enough to drive."

"That's not what he meant," piped the other man, and they all laughed. McIlweath clapped Joel on the shoulder.

"Good night. I'll see you," and McIlweath left to friendly farewells. Kathy was waiting for him in the entryway with her coat already on. She helped McIlweath pull on his.

"Respects paid?"

"And respect won. Let's go." They walked out into the cold and down the street to McIlweath's car. The street was black and still.

"How did you get here? Do you have a car?"

Kathy hung onto McIlweath's arm. He tried to lean against her as they walked but he was afraid of losing his balance altogether and bowling her over.

"I walked," she said. "I only live a few blocks away. A lot of students live in this neighborhood. It's cheap and it's safe, at least as safe as Boston can be."

They reached McIlweath's car. He fit his key into the door on the passenger side after three futile attempts. When he entered on the driver's side, Kathy slid next to him, then grabbed his collar with both hands and pulled his face to hers. They resumed their position there, in the cold, sprawled across frozen leather seats. The windows steamed. Kathy reached for McIlweath's hand and guided it to her breasts where he plied the firm, sweet flesh while she ran her own hands the length of her companion's rigid, excited body. She filled his nostrils, his mouth, his ears—all senses focused themselves upon the young figure around him. He licked her, he breathed her scent, he heard her yip in small gasps of pleasure.

After some time of groping and fondling, Kathy slowed her pace and straightened up in the seat. "This is so juvenile," she panted, "and I haven't done anything in a car in years. There's a more comfortable place." She leaned over and whispered in McIlweath's ear, her lusty breath running through the cavity and down his spine. "Take me home."

He started the car and wiped the steam away enough to see. The street looked blurry. Kathy gave directions, and McIlweath drove slowly, concentrating on his drunkenness to make it ebb long enough so he could get them safely where they were going. He made several turns and had no idea where he was.

"It's right here. Turn in at this driveway." McIlweath navigated the car into the narrow lane between two dark houses. "The upper flat is mine."

"You live alone?"

"Yes. The landlords live downstairs but I have a separate entrance. Step lightly."

They walked as quietly as they could to the back of the old house on their right. Kathy unlocked the back door and led McIlweath up a stairway. Her flat was far more tastefully decorated than his own: bright colors, books neatly arranged, impressionist prints on the walls.

"Let me take your jacket." She hung it up with her own in a large closet off the main room. Then, with her blue eyes flaming, she grabbed her young man's wrist and led him to the bedroom. There she let him go and began to undress herself slowly, smiling teasingly at McIlweath's intense stare.

"You finish," she purred after pulling off her sweater and unbuttoning her blouse. McIlweath ran the blouse off her shoulders while Kathy kissed to tips of his nose and lips. With her own hands she unzipped the young man's slacks. When McIlweath removed her bra he gazed with wonder at Kathy's gentle breasts, the first he had ever truly seen. He ran his hands over them so lightly that he barely touched them at all. He fingered her nipples as if convincing himself of their reality. Within a few minutes, a long time given the simplicity of their task, they stood naked, their hands roaming into the nooks and crevices of each other's youthful body. For Tom McIlweath, respect flooded him and mixed with naive awe. He floated outside himself; he viewed what was happening from across the room, across the city. He would remember it better that way, detached in mind while his body reveled in its senses. Across the room, across the city. Across the city. Anne . . . Anne.

They climbed into bed. McIlweath's passion did not eliminate his inherent fears. The alcohol had strengthened him, but he believed it only fair, only right, to let his partner know the implications of what was at hand.

"Kathy," he whispered, "I think it best to let you know that I've never done this before. I'm what you would call 'inexperienced.'"

"So I should be gentle with you?" she giggled. Then at once she grew serious. Her eyes widened and she looked up at McIlweath with genuine surprise. "Oh my God . . . you're serious. You mean you've never made love to this girl you told me about? After all those years, you never once made love to her?"

"No. We've never slept together. I'm embarrassed to tell you that. I've never made love to her, or to anyone else."

She stoked his hair. "Through her choice, I presume."

"Through mutual consent."

"Meaning you were always afraid to press it. Am I right?"

"Yeah. Yes, you're right."

"Oh Tom. You look so sad," and she held him, asexually, as tightly as she could. "You poor sweet innocent," she whispered. "You good, good man. Make love to me, Tom, as hard and as long and as richly as you like. As you can. Pour yourself into me. I can make you whole again. I can make you what you deserve to be."

Tom McIlweath returned Kathy's caresses. He ran himself over her breasts and neck, over her stomach and the musky, mysterious, uncharted territory between her thighs. Each part of his own body came alive with intense, spasmodic pleasure. He thrust himself into her, time and again, reaching into his core to create the power and the grandeur of the redemptive act, thrusting deeply into Kathy Keane, thrusting deeply into the sweet, warm, cleansing darkness there and in losing his innocence, regaining it, this time permanently, this time to be clutched with the fury of life itself and never relinquished, upon penalty of death. The womb received him after so many years ago releasing him into savagery and frustration. A joy, a wordlessly throaty ecstasy, crept through him as his muscles tightened in a final explosion, and with it he expelled his youth, his temerity, and the quick, fast bonds that wrapped his tender conscience.

Their bodies parted. Without speaking they smiled at each other and shared a last kiss. Tom McIlweath dropped off at once into a deep, dreamless slumber, unbroken until the smell of coffee prepared by his new lover brought him back to consciousness the next morning.

CHAPTER XIX

*I shall die as my fathers died, and sleep as
they sleep; even so
For the glass of the years is brittle wherein
we gaze upon for a span.*

—Algernon Charles Swinburne, *Hymn to Proserpine*

The preceding day, several hundred miles to the south and well before Tom McIlweath's cleansing had begun or even been considered, Conor Finnegan pulled his car into a parking space marked 'Visitor.' He bounced out of his old machine and locked the door behind him. Despite the cool air that typified a Washington winter, although a temperate contrast to the wet, penetrating, slushy chill of his past four winters, Finnegan's blood ran warm. Tiny droplets of perspiration popped out on his forehead just below his hairline. His heart pumped grandly.

He crossed the parking lot and entered the low white building. At the reception desk he asked to see Mr. Carrecker. The lady behind the desk, a brittle, unsmiling, prickly creature, picked up a phone and dialed a single number. After speaking a few words the Finnegan could not hear, she asked, "Your name, sir?"

"Conor Finnegan."

"You have no appointment." This was a statement and not a question.

"No, ma'am. I was hoping he might be free for a few minutes."

"This is highly irregular."

"I know, ma'am." Finnegan tried to muster his most appealing and boyish demeanor. "My grandfather may be referred here in a matter of days. I'd like to speak to Mr. Carrecker before granddad comes. If he's not free, I can come back, but I was nearby on other business and I thought I'd take a chance."

The hedgehog relayed this to the voice on the other end, who paused and then squeaked something in response.

"Have a seat, Mr. Finnegan. It appears Mr. Carrecker will be right with you."

"Thank you. Thank you very much." Conor sat in the empty lobby. He would have expected someone else to be here, some casual visitor or possibly a vendor, but he was alone. He had seen other nursing homes where patients sat in the lobby to look out the front windows or to chat with whomever happened by. Some kept private vigils for the visits of family or friends. But not here. There was no point in that here. The poor souls here were bereft of hope in any form.

Finnegan had returned for a final look. Griffith Ross's admonition, that whatever he found here had to suggest some practical legislative step, had been difficult to swallow. Conditions in this facility had so outraged him that he felt obliged to the point of compulsion to do whatever he could to put Brandon Carrecker and the bandits who supported this enterprise out of business. He had been truly surprised when Ross had dismissed his initial report, and he could not believe that in the face of such abuses a United States senator could be so powerless. He attributed Ross's reluctance to a conservatism that had become more apparent the better Finnegan had gotten to know him. Ross was, above all else, a pragmatist. Why risk alienating people, and powerful people at that, if there were no assurances of anything to be gained? Finnegan thought that, at the very least, his report might spur the senator to urge a complete investigation by the VA of facilities receiving their patients for long-term care. But if Ross needed a more practical angle, Finnegan would try to find one.

After more than a little thought, some of it fueled by glasses of wine, Finnegan came to the idea that the processes of certifying these facilities might be intensified. If, as Ross contended, these homes must meet certain standards, yet at first glance those standards were not only broken but thoroughly shattered, then the certification processes must be too lax. It takes time for a healthcare facility to degenerate. Perhaps the VA could be legislated into more frequent inspections. In the meantime, until the practicality of that idea could be more fully evaluated, along with the sources for the budgeting the VA would need for increased inspections, Finnegan thought he might pass on a new, more detailed report of this hellhole to the VA's enforcement office. They might then be compelled to look more closely before throwing additional funds—in the form of infirm, helpless old men—in this direction. Whether he succeeded in conjuring a practical legislative approach or if he would have to content himself with a vindictive strike carried out through existing channels, Finnegan concluded that another visit to this septic backwater was in order. He had to refresh his memory, and reinvigorate his outrage.

In a few minutes a young girl came out from the hallway and motioned to Finnegan. "Mr. Carrecker will see you now, sir. Come with me."

Carrecker received him behind his wide desk. He shook Finnegan's hand weakly, with neither warmth nor strength. Again, Carrecker struck Finnegan as having no blood.

Carrecker sat back in his chair with Finnegan seated opposite. The older man laced his fingers in front of his chin. "How may I help you, Mr. Finnegan?"

"Well, sir, as you recall when we spoke earlier, my grandfather was about to be referred here. The poor man had some health setbacks, though, so he had to stay in the hospital longer than we had planned. He's due to be released again in a couple of days and he'll most likely be coming here. I thought, with your permission of course, that I'd like to look around again. Granddad is awfully nervous about coming here. If I told him I just visited again it would do a lot to calm him down."

"Hmmmmm," responded Carrecker. His face knitted in feral thought and when at last he spoke, he spoke slowly. "What is the exact nature of your grandfather's health problems, Mr. Finnegan? Why is he in the hospital and why will he be coming here?"

"Lupus. He's growing progressively weaker. It's eating away at him and he'll never get better, as you know with this type of thing. The doctors seem to have slowed his deterioration a bit. On some days, in fact, he says he feels strong and wants to go home. But then another spell hits and it's always worse than before. It breaks my heart to see him like that. I want him to be comfortable wherever he goes. So you see, I've come back as a means of assuring him that he'll be well cared for when he gets here. And to reassure myself, too, I suppose."

Carrecker paused again for several seconds, and looked away at a nearly blank wall. When he turned back to Finnegan, he spoke slowly and with great deliberation, measuring each word fully before letting it go. "Mr. Finnegan, why do you wish to harm my little business?"

"I beg your pardon?"

"I asked, sir, why you wish to harm my business."

"I don't understand your question. I mean you no harm."

"Whatever game you're playing must come to an end."

Finnegan's cheeks blushed hotly. A deep shade of red grew from his mouth to his forehead. He had always blushed on those rare occasions when he had been caught in a lie. It was involuntary, and he could not begin to control it. He was a lousy liar.

"I still don't understand you. What are you saying?"

"After our first meeting, where I injudiciously broke my personal policy of never giving impromptu tours, I became somewhat concerned that my hastiness to accommodate you might come back to haunt me. Consequently, I did some checking. There is no one named Finnegan on the faculty at Georgetown, neither regular faculty nor graduate assistant. There is, however, a Conor Finnegan employed by a United States senator. If this person is indeed you, then you have devised the flimsiest of gimmicks to get inside my facility.

"Even so," he continued, "I believe I have nothing to fear from you, despite your clumsy and juvenile efforts. You and your senator are of little consequence. Here we comply with the laws as they are written and enforced. If you seek to change the laws, we shall comply with whatever you come up with. And you have no enforcement power."

"But I might call down an enforcement body upon you. Have you considered that?"

"Briefly. But I am a man of many friends, some of them quite well placed. They would let me know well in advance of any melodramatic gesture. One does not prosper in this profession without learning some tricks of self-preservation.

"I hope," he continued, "that you have learned something from this little charade. And now I shall tell you that if ever I see you near my premises again I shall have you arrested for trespassing and harassment. And if ever the senator or another member of his staff chooses to pick up the torch you're now dropping, those charges will be applied to them. That would no doubt prove quite embarrassing to a man of his stature, don't you think? The press would love to hear all about it." Carrecker smiled menacingly through his paper-thin lips. Finnegan stared him in the face without response.

"And now, Mr. Finnegan, it's time we part. I shall have two of my orderlies show you out. Gentlemen," he called, and two large, unsmiling gorillas stepped into the room. They had evidently been just outside the door throughout all this.

"Show Mr. Finnegan to his car. Mr. Finnegan, good day to you. Remember my words. I mean them sincerely."

Finnegan rose, mortified, wanting this humiliation to end as quickly as possible. He walked out of the office in front of the orderlies, both of whom were taller and wider than he was. Each appeared quite capable of beating him to jelly. Where they had no doubt spent most of their time tying down weak, defenseless old men, they might actually enjoy a spin with a younger target who could be more of a challenge. Finnegan did not look at them, and he did not speak. He kept his eyes straight ahead. He wanted to do nothing to provoke them.

He reached the door, one of the orderlies reached around him to open it, and he was back out in the parking lot. The perspiration had returned to his forehead and run down his collar. The cold air dried it; he felt clammy and stale.

Finnegan drove back to Capitol Hill sullenly. His battle had been lost, and the way the loss was recorded offered neither glory nor honor. Losing, difficult to accept, difficult to reconcile, stung him deeply.

When he returned to his desk he found atop his mess a note from the senator. "See me when you get in." Finnegan's first reaction was that Carrecker had put in a call. He stared out the window to collect his thoughts.

'But no,' he reasoned. 'Unless Carrecker called immediately as I left, the senator has no idea of what went down. And why would Carrecker do that? He's already won his victory. He's too clever to keep this thing alive, in any form.'

Having reassured himself, Finnegan walked back to the senator's office. "Is he in, Joyce? He asked to see me." Months of working alongside this red-haired goddess had not reduced his appreciation of her elegant beauty, or quelled his simmering lust. The staff speculated on what services she might be providing their man over and above the call of duty. Everyone knew that the senator was not fanatical about his marriage. Finnegan, for his part, shared in the speculation and secretly envied his boss for his access to whatever sensual pleasures this gorgeous young woman might bestow.

"Yes, he is, Conor. Go right in."

The door to the private office was open. The senator sat behind his great desk reading legislative briefs. Finnegan was surprised to see him wearing reading glasses. He would never do so in public.

"Senator, you asked to see me?"

"Yes, Conor," he said, looking up and putting his papers to the side of his desk. "We have a project ahead of us that I'd like you to handle."

"Of course. What's up?"

"Partly due to your enthusiastic work with the elderly, Griffith thinks we can score major points with this constituency if we conduct a series of hearings on one of their central issues. He believes we should look into their housing conditions, where they live, what they pay, where they're coming up short, all of that. You've already put together some statistics on this, he tells me?"

"Yes, sir. According to HHS definitions, more than 30 percent of all people over seventy lived in substandard of dilapidated housing last year. The percentage is higher in certain areas, northeastern states in particular. And this group spends a disproportionate amount of their income on housing expenses. The absence of affordable housing combined with predatory rental and housing control practices have forced huge numbers onto the edges of real poverty."

"Right. We can build on that, I think. It's a humane issue that few people realize, and as long as we keep it noncontroversial, we should be well received. I want two days of hearings in mid-March. I've scheduled one of the hearing rooms in the Russell Building for the 19th and 20th, from 1 to 5 each day. Work around that schedule. You fill up the time for me. Find me some storytellers. I don't want witnesses who'll quote figures all day. Figures are dull, and no one would pay any attention anyway. Find some people who've lived it, who can bring a tear to your eye. We'll coordinate the hearings with opinion pieces on the topic in the major California dailies, so we need to make it compelling."

"Are we looking for legislative solutions? I could bring in some of the directors of senior agencies and associations. They're loaded with ideas."

"Perhaps. If anything obvious comes out of this, we'll follow it up later. Mostly I want pathos. Little old ladies who look like everyone's grandmother telling how they eat cat food twice a week because they can't afford to pay their rent, that sort of thing. Keep it varied, too. Different types of people, and make sure you throw in some minorities. Put together a tentative roster within two weeks and let's review it. We'll still have plenty of time to make changes then, if we have to, and to coordinate testimony. I'll want complete outlines of each witness's statements. You'll have to draw up relevant questions that correspond to their stories, that fill in the gaps and build out the impact. I don't want any surprises. And don't promise anybody anything."

"Would these hearings include institutional care facilities?"

"No, Conor, they would not. We're likely to offend some folks I'd rather not offend if we go down that path, and that's not what we're out to do. It's also complex as hell. I'm not even certain that would be an issue in any case. Institutionalized care is adequate, from what I can tell. We want something everyone can sympathize with. Stick to private citizens trying to get by on their own. Keep me posted on your progress."

"Senator, I'd like the chance to sit down with you after these hearings are done to evaluate what we do in response to them. If we can show some definite action, legislative or otherwise, stemming from what we've brought forward through those two days, then their impact on the voters will be multiplied. Also, we'd be extending any media coverage to include our own responses."

"We'll see what happens, Conor. Let's get them together first, then see how they go. It's too early to talk about what we'll do afterward."

"I know that, Senator, but I think we should be aware of their potential going in."

"I am aware of that. That's why we're doing them at all." The senator smiled. "I know you'll work hard in setting them up, Conor. Find me some people, and let's put on a good show."

"Thank you, Senator. I'll do everything I can."

"I have every faith. Check in with me in a few days to show me what you're doing."

Finnegan walked back down the hall to his own desk, jammed in a corner of the crowded suite where the middle-level staffers were corralled. The assignment, he knew, meant something special. The senator still had confidence in him. That was important, especially in light of that day's earlier fiasco. He might have a future in this profession after all, he mused, particularly if he could do a good job with these hearings. He spent the rest of the day drawing up an outline of whom he wanted, then speaking with his contacts in the field to feel them out about housing issues and asking them so submit their thoughts on the most pressing impact points. He needed to sort through the various ideas, devise an agenda and go back to them for their help in uncovering suitable messengers. Be systematic, he told himself, and involve a lot of people.

As the day wore on, Finnegan's Friday mood brightened further by Glynnis's impending arrival. While she spent most weekends with Conor, her visits never failed to fill the young man with anticipation. The little boy in him emerged at the thought of being with her. He could not possibly be casual about it, nor did he try. He swore to himself that he would never take his time with her for granted. She would be taking the train again, and she'd be with him in five hours, in four hours, in three hours. He counted the time, and the afternoon slowed to a crawl as Finnegan's anticipation quickened.

At 5:30 he went into the men's room down the hall, shaved with an electric razor he kept in his desk for such occasions as evening receptions or his lover's arrival, then splashed on a fresh coat of cologne. He relished the quick transition from professional to personal, so quick that the two overlapped. That was as it should be. He enjoyed making himself fresh at the end of the day, and he enjoyed projecting the simple comforts that lay ahead.

His renaissance complete, Finnegan walked out into the cold night. The lights of the federal buildings bit through the darkness. The angular green dome of the Library of Congress and the brilliant lines of the Capitol stood out sharply against the black sky. 'What future societies will view the ruins of these great structures,' he found himself thinking, 'and what will their thoughts be as they find these mossy stones? Will they have grace and power and dignity to match our own, or when these buildings fall, as they inevitably must, will those concepts fall with them? Are we destined to be philosophers or scavengers?' Finnegan reached his car, climbed in and drove the short distance down the hill to Union Station.

For a Friday evening, the great station was remarkably uncrowded. Most of those waiting for trains were young. The businessmen and government officials had already gone home. Students, poorly or casually dressed, carrying well-worn travel bags, their hair shaggy, shuffled through the high and echoing cavern. Finnegan looked at them with a certain envy: they were where he had been just a few months before, and that time had been glorious. He had passed that stage, and it had locked shut behind him. Finnegan was not commonly given to nostalgia, but he knew that as the years progressed he would come to regard the marvelous, expansive days of college with increasing fondness. As long as he could continue to infuse his current existence with wonder and novelty, he might be able to keep that nostalgia in check. He was certain, though, that it could not be eliminated, nor would he want it to be. It was all part of growing older.

Finnegan stood by the track where Glynnis's train would arrive. He still had a few minutes. He always liked to get to the station early. There he could gently stoke his anticipation through quiet time with no expectations, and nothing to do but watch others go by.

Glynnis's train steamed in on time, the massive iron torpedo crawling down the tracks with a gnash of metal and the clanking of its brakes, its cycloptic eye shining its path. It stopped with a perceptible groan, an old man whose bones protested both stopping and starting. The doors swung open; Glynnis stepped from one of them several yards down the platform.

She looked, as always, radiant. The softly molded features of her delicate face shone out from beneath her winter cap. Finnegan considered her most beautiful in winter. In contrast to the cold around them she exuded serenity and warmth. The brisk air instilled a gentle glow that rose from some deep well within her body. Finnegan relished those winter nights when the two of them stayed inside against the cold, nestling in a warm spot in defiance of the brutal assaults of the harshest seasons.

Glynnis spotted Conor and smiled softly. God, he loved her smile, its sly curve, its inference of wisdom and hint of mischief, its inherent quiet splendor. She walked to where he stood, put down her bag, and they embraced. On the way to the car Conor told Glynnis about the upcoming hearings while Glynnis informed her lover that nothing was new, that, indeed, she had plodded dully through the week.

The clear night air allowed the magnificent sights of the capital to sparkle almost translucently. They seemed artificial, fanciful creations that, if touched, would sprinkle apart like snow.

"I didn't tell you," said Conor, "but Dan's gone home for the weekend. We've got the place to ourselves."

"Oh, I was looking forward to seeing him. He's hardly around anymore when I'm here."

"He's a busy guy these days. It turns out he has to be a real student, or they'll kick his formerly lazy ass out of here. Besides, I'd think the obvious advantages of his absence might soothe your disappointment somewhat. I love being completely alone with you," and he smiled.

"It's too bad he picked this weekend to go home," Glynnis replied, slowly and with a bit of a halt.

"Why do you say that, Glyn? What's so special about this weekend? Aside from your being here, of course." He reached over and squeezed her gloved hand.

"Conor," Glynnis spoke deliberately, the words rehearsed several times over. "I want to go back tomorrow night. There's a train that leaves at 6:00, okay?"

"You're kidding. Why in God's name do you have to do that?"

"There are just some things I have to get done. There are some things I have to do."

"I've heard that before. Could you be more specific, please?" Annoyance was creeping into Finnegan's voice despite his best efforts to suppress it. But it was an acid etching through gentle tissue. This all made no sense to him. Glynnis's evasive response would only provoke him further.

"A lot of things. There's a project I want to finish, and I want to do some writing. Letters and such. I'm so out of touch with everybody."

"And that can't wait until Sunday night? Why do you feel compelled to slice our weekend in half? In less than half? This all seems pretty flimsy."

"Oh, Conor," Glynnis sighed. This was so difficult. Conor's trusting, boyish innocence, now offended, only made it more so. "I don't get time to myself during the week. Not enough. I suppose I just want some time to devote to myself alone, with no expectations and no one to attend to. To be honest, I was hoping to spend a quiet weekend doing simple things. I like being in the studio with no one around, and I like reading books I don't have time for during the week, and I like sitting at my desk writing letters with music in the background and the wind outside. There's just been too little time for that, Conor, and I'd like to devote at least one day to being uncluttered."

"At the expense of spending time together. There's been too little time for that as well, so there's something of a price to pay for this 'uncluttered' state you prize. Can't you carve some time for yourself during the week?"

"There are enough demands so that I can't. And even at the end of the day when I do get some time, I'm so tired that all I want to do is go to bed. I know I'm not being fair, Conor, but please try to understand. I had my heart set on a day completely alone."

"And I had my heart set on the two of us for the entire weekend. Jesus, Glyn, things can be tough enough down here without you pulling surprises on me. I spend my whole week thinking about you, about our time together. Lately that time has been too limited anyway, and now you want to slice off a weekend for some vague notion about having time to yourself, about being uncluttered, whatever the hell that means. I would have thought you'd prefer to be with me."

"Now who's being unfair?" said Glynnis lowly, but Conor kept on.

"Besides, what the hell do you do on those too-frequent weekends when we're not together at all? Doesn't that provide you with enough time alone? Or are you really alone?"

"Conor, you know I am. I would never deceive you like that."

"Perhaps you'd deceive me in other ways. Glynnis, you live alone. Every night you go back to an empty apartment and climb into an empty bed. Even if you're tired that should give you enough opportunity to clear your head. You needn't rob time from us."

"I'm sorry, Conor. I know I can't expect you to understand." Finnegan remained sullen and mostly silent during the rest of the drive. Glynnis, who had seen Conor in this humor only rarely but often enough to know its intimidating dimensions, did not want to venture further into a remote territory laden with hidden traps. She remained quiet, too.

How, really, could she expect Conor Finnegan to comprehend her mysterious moods? Glynnis knew her excuse sounded weak, but it was all she could think of. Lying was painful for her, and there was, after all, an element of truth in what she said. She did want a day to herself, to do various small things she had put off, to be for a while unhurried. But there was more to it than that, of course, and it was her real reason that she wanted to keep obscured, not that she would have been able to articulate it clearly in any sense.

In the shadow of Conor Finnegan, Glynnis felt herself to be manipulated. Her weekends with Conor had become a microcosm of the intellectual and emotional realms of their relationship. Glynnis came to him, placed herself in his security, and Conor filled their time as best he knew. In every way during their time together Glynnis became absorbed into Conor's world. She became part of his frame of reference. And worst of all, Conor expected it to be this way with an unspoken, assumed surety that sat poorly in Glynnis's heart. Glynnis, who had long been reluctant to cede the governance of her life to someone else, saw it happen piecemeal each time she came to Conor Finnegan. She had remained in Philadelphia despite Conor's pleas to come live with him in Washington. Now she feared her weekends with Conor were more subtle forays against her cherished independence. Conor had lost through a frontal assault; now he was trying to capture her through guerilla tactics that, with his style, his innocence, his intelligence and passion, he made so seductive. Yet the temper of her blood rose each time she perceived herself sacrificing another shred of her true self to Conor Finnegan. She loved him deeply, but she was not ready to anchor herself in his harbor.

Finnegan that night had planned to fix an elaborate dinner, complete with wine and after-dinner Grand Marnier. Without having to watch for the comings and goings of Dan Rosselli, they might then let youthful passion run its free course. But Glynnis's peculiar desire to go home early had cast a pall over Conor's romantic mood. He would have resented losing time with Glynnis had there been a good reason, but her rationale now was beyond him. Finnegan had always tended to get upset when things did not go according to his plans. When those plans centered on Glynnis, his reaction was more severe. He could not take the higher pathway of intensifying the joys of the time with Glynnis that circumstances had allotted. Instead, he fumed over what would be lost, and so the entire weekend, not just the half he would have to spend alone, became tainted.

And to deepen it all, Glynnis had rarely looked so beautiful as she did that evening. Her gentle face had caught the cold sufficiently to make her high cheeks glow softly pink, her glorious brown eyes sparkled with no bottom in the city light, and her forest of hair curled at the ends that fell over her shoulders and breasts. There was, as always, a graceful feminine elegance about her. It had all been accentuated tonight.

Glumly, Finnegan set about preparing their dinner. Glynnis sat on the couch in the other room sipping at a glass of wine and listening to music. The planned enchantment of their evening had evaded them. Tomorrow at this time she would be gone, and Finnegan would be without even Dan Rosselli's clever wit to keep him amused. During dinner, Finnegan found himself talking about Brandon Carrecker, the senator's indifference to genuine social issues, and how dull the winters were in Washington.

Afterward, their stomachs full and their heads lightened by food and wine, Glynnis stood at the kitchen sink rinsing off plates. Conor had retired to the living room, expecting Glynnis to follow.

"What are you doing in there?" he called.

"I'm just taking care of these dishes."

"Leave them until morning, Glyn. They'll keep. Better still, leave them until tomorrow night. It'll give me something to do."

"You know, Conor," she called back over the running water, "everything you attempt you end up doing quite well, including feeling sorry for yourself. I apologize for not being as predictable as you'd like."

"God knows I've never thought you predictable. If ever I had, these past few weeks would have shattered that notion completely." Finnegan rose from the couch and walked to the kitchen as he spoke. Glynnis was drying her hands. She had turned to face him as he entered the room.

"Oh, Conor, stop it. You've been pouting all night. I didn't expect to have to put up with such childishness."

"And I didn't expect to have to put up with our weekend being ripped apart. You make no sense sometimes, Glynnis, do you know that? I'm not even certain I buy your simplistic and rather hollow alibi."

"I don't give a damn whether you do or not. I'm leaving tomorrow night. You can either deal with that fact like a mature adult or you can go on being a spoiled little boy. Whatever you do won't change a thing, so you might as well come to terms with it so we can enjoy the time we do have."

"A spoiled little boy, is it? It seems to me I've been just the opposite. You set the terms of your comings and goings, Glynnis, and I'm expected meekly to go along with everything you propose. Forgive me for being hurt. If you see my reaction as childish, then you're more spoiled than I could ever be. Perhaps you've made too few sacrifices."

"And perhaps I've made too many. Maybe I'm afraid I'll cease to be Glynnis Mear altogether."

"How the hell can that happen with you tucked away a hundred miles up the road? You've preserved your identity quite well, it seems to me. Both logic and emotion dictate that we should be together, Glynnis. Not being so is the greatest sacrifice I can think of, for either of us. I don't think you're giving up anything more important than that." Finnegan's voice softened; his anger ebbed. "Sometimes I ache to have you with me, Glyn. It's almost a physical thing. I miss you, and this heavy throbbing crawls up my chest and into my throat. I see you with me, I smell you, I almost feel you as if your image is powerful enough to have weight. And knowing that I'll be going home to nothing just deepens the ache. You've made a cavity within me, Glynnis, and how do I fill that? When you're not with me a wind blows through, and it makes a vicious howl."

Glynnis came to him, closed her eyes and wrapped her arms around his neck. They stood in each other's embrace without speaking, simply feeling the warm and solid reality of their presence.

"Oh, Conor," she whispered, "I do love you. I love you so very much. And I'm sorry to hurt you. Please understand."

"It's not easy for me, Glyn, to be without you. Everything I say and do revolves around having you with me. Forgive my anger, my love. It means nothing against what I feel for you."

Glynnis kissed Conor on the lips, on both cheeks and on his nose. She smiled gently, her eyes softly widening. Conor plumbed them and found no bottom. She grasped his wrist and led him to the bedroom. There, in the pliant darkness, walled against the bitter winter, they made love with a ferocity they had never shared before. Conor threw himself against Glynnis like a hammer shattering concrete, and in response Glynnis discovered vaults of wild, primitive passion that had been scarcely glimpsed and never opened. She panted, she issued small screams, groped and heaved and rolled, her eyes locked shut in a heated trance. Conor ran himself the length of her body, turned her over, placed her on his lap and lost all illusion of control. He was an Aztec priest devouring the heart of his victim, Van Gogh slicing his ear. Their orgasms, when at last they came, left them both breathless and barely conscious. Glynnis's long hair wrapped around her neck. She lay facedown; it flowed along her back. Conor buried his face into its lilac-scented softness and, under his breath, said a prayer of thanksgiving.

"Are you certain you want to go back tomorrow?" he whispered.

"No, my love, I am not certain. I'm certain of so few things these days. But, yes, I'll go back tomorrow. Don't be angry with me, please."

"I'm not, Glyn. You worry me, though, sometimes. I never seem to know quite what it is you're thinking."

"Nor do I. Part of the charm of being a woman, this sublime confusion. Sometimes I grow fearful that you'll tire of putting up with me, and I'll lose you."

"No chance, my love. You will never lose me. I'm yours until death, and beyond."

"I don't know whether to be comforted or frightened."

"Take comfort. I'm as solid and as secure as the earth itself, and as faithful as the sweetest air you draw through your delicate lips:

> *Nay, but you, who do not love her,*
> *Is she not pure gold, my mistress?*
> *Holds earth aught above her?*
> *Aught like this tress, see, and this tress*
> *And this last fairest tress of all*
> *So fair, see, ere I let it fall? . . ."*

Finnegan ran his hand through Glynnis's hair as he recited. Glynnis looked up at him, thoroughly rapt.

"You charm me, young Conor. Whom have you quoted?"

"Robert Browning. A fair poet, although not Irish. The Irish can truly control a lyric. I wish I knew more poetry."

"That you might intoxicate me with your words and have your way with me?" she smiled. "There's no need, my handsome lover. You are poetry itself. Lyrical and fragile. It's not your words, but your soul that runs through my blood."

"And will be there forever, I promise you, if you will have me."

"Make love to me again, Irishman. Take me in your strong arms and fill me with your power. I want you tonight through every vein and pore."

"And will you want me with you always?"

"I love you, Conor. Tonight I love you with all my heart. There should be joy enough for both of us in that."

CHAPTER XX

O God! O God! That it were possible
To undo things done; to call back yesterday!
That Time could turn up his swift sandy glass,
To untell the days, and to redeem these hours.

—Thomas Heywood, *A Woman Killed with Kindness*

Tom McIlweath stumbled from the narrow bed still warm with the radiation of his own body, and of Kathy Keane's. Upon awakening he had had an instant of disorientation. The strange walls out of position, his body reclining in the wrong direction, the unfamiliar angle of the light had all formed a quick mystery that dissipated when, after a luxuriant stretching yawn, he recalled the wonder of the night before.

Surprisingly his head did not ache and his stomach did not churn, his usual effects of drinking too much beer. He pulled on his pants and sweater. As he walked out of the bedroom in the direction of the smell of brewing coffee, McIlweath took inventory of himself. All parts, he concluded, were in good working order.

Kathy stood by the stove about to pour scrambled eggs into a frying pan. She wore a floor-length robe that made her body monolithic, a pyramid of folds. McIlweath startled her as he approached from behind. She turned around quickly, spilling some of the whipped eggs onto the stove.

"You surprised me. I didn't hear you get up."

"I'm sorry."

She finished pouring the eggs, then kissed him lightly on the lips. "Don't be sorry. But I did want to fix you breakfast and bring it to you in bed. You were sleeping so soundly I thought I could pull it off." She dropped two slices of bread into a toaster.

"I slept better than I have in months. It must have been the company."

Kathy looked over her shoulder at him and smiled forth her genuine gratification. In the morning, her bit of makeup had worn off, and her tousled hair falling across her slender shoulders like thickets of hewn wheat rendered her absolutely gorgeous. McIlweath read compassion in her small and graceful movements. Her quietly radiant face hinted a satisfaction she would not have been able to hide despite any intent. Kathy Keane, of anyone McIlweath had ever met, seemed consummately in harmony with who she was, what she was doing, and the world in which she was doing it.

McIlweath poured coffee and sat at the kitchen table content for the moment to watch this unforeseen piece of great good fortune finish preparing their breakfast. She heaped the eggs onto two plates, buttered the toast when it sprang up from the slots, and poured two glasses of cranberry juice.

"Why are you smiling?" she asked as she brought the plates and glasses to the table.

"Was I?"

"You were. You look moonstruck."

"Just the simple pleasure of watching you move about the kitchen. That's enough to make any man smile."

"I don't believe you, but I'm flattered anyhow. At least you didn't tell me I look like a Vermeer painting." She sat down opposite him. "So you're not wracked by guilt this morning? You're not rolling in the throes of a brutally wounded conscience?"

"No," McIlweath smiled quietly. "No, none of that has set in yet. I doubt it will."

"I'm glad. You have nothing to be guilty about. I get the feeling that you've owed yourself a great deal for a long time and you're only now beginning to collect. Forgive me for saying so, but that lady of yours seems to be smothering all the life out of you. Perhaps if she deflates you totally you'll fit more comfortably into her pocket."

"Actually, I haven't given Anne much thought since last night, for obvious reasons. I suppose I'll have to deal with her soon, although I'd rather not try to guess how that will be. In any event, it won't be pleasant."

"You're evading my observation. I think that woman's very bad for you. She's consuming your better parts."

"You're certain of that after knowing me for, what, thirteen hours?"

"I know what I see. I told you last night that you looked lost. After you told me about this woman, how cold she is and how you're just another gear in her little machine, I could see why. I've seen your type before, Tom. You've been too insecure for your own good. You've given up far too much to this woman. And it's never enough for her. The more you feed her, the more she'll want to eat until there are only a few crumbs left."

"I don't want to talk about Anne. I'll be having my fill of her soon enough."

"You reached a turning point last night, my friend, whether you admit it to yourself or not. In your more conservative moods you'll no doubt try to deny it. I'm not talking about losing your virginity, although I can't imagine how you lasted so long, poor thing. In any case, that's no great matter. But I think that the very act of putting yourself in the position where it could have happened signified something important for you. Something lasting. Am I right?"

"Are you always so analytical with your lovers?" McIlweath was enjoying this. He was also impressed. Kathy had astutely interpreted what he had taken painful weeks (years?) to understand.

"No, but you fascinate me, Tom. You really do. I'm not sure I've ever met anyone so . . . well, so tolerant. You're incredibly patient. You must be. You've been patient with yourself to go so long without what you truly desire. You must've been more patient with this woman than she's ever deserved."

"One needs to be confident to be so patient."

"Or desperately lost. If one can't conceive of any alternatives, then all he can do is wait for matters to change of their own accord. He's then swept along by what he dares not attempt to control."

"Maybe, then, the best thing you've done for me is to replace that misdirection with a hint of self-assurance."

"Have I really done that?" she asked earnestly, leaning forward on the table. "Did I really have the power to do that?"

"Not alone. It's been coming for quite a while, I think. Since I got to Boston, and probably well before. But you've certainly helped the process, Kathy. If nothing else, you've catalyzed what was probably inevitable. For that I will be grateful to you the rest of my life."

"Provided only that you do something with what you've gained. Don't let this heroic talk the morning after come to nothing. Then you'd be worse off than ever you were before. You'd have seen the Promised Land without having the courage to cross into it."

"Can I see you again, or was this just a one-night rescue?"

"We're friends, Tom. You can see me any time you want. There's so much more about you I want to learn, and that will no doubt take some time, don't you think?"

"I hope it takes a great amount of time. Perhaps I should start to be more secretive."

"But you must promise me that you won't be too serious about this or come to regard me as more than I am. You mustn't expect more than what I can provide."

McIlweath looked her in the eye and said nothing. Kathy looked back through blue eyes of flame.

"It would be a huge mistake for you to want to substitute me for Anne. That's not what you need right now. If you lose her, she'll leave a gap and you'll want to fill it with whatever's handy. That's only natural. But you should let it fill itself while you get on with the other parts of your life. You've left them unattended for too long and you're growing bitter because of it."

"Let's take matters one step at a time, shall we?" responded McIlweath. "Let me get used to the exhilaration of your friendship first. I don't choose to look beyond that."

"And neither should I, I suppose. I shouldn't project like that, and I'm sorry for it, but I am concerned about you. And after so little time. You're a good and decent man, Tom McIlweath, and you've inspired my affection."

"Then I am a fortunate man as well."

* * *

The fortunate man drove directly to Anne Newbury's apartment later that morning. He had considered calling first, but he knew matters had to be dealt with, face to face. If nothing else, it was the honorable thing to do.

McIlweath walked up her stairs slowly with a reluctance he had presumed he had mastered but which reared itself again now that the confrontation was a few feet before him. His legs dragged from step to step with ponderous thumps as his boots landed heavily on each stair. He recalled similar thumping up the rickety steps of the house in New Brunswick. The sound brought it back, but those thumps usually manifested the excitement of coming home, of hopping up the narrow stairs two or three at a time. These thumps presaged a death march. The door loomed above him as some mythical time-portal to transport him back to an older persona. It remained to be seen whether the conclusions that evolved during his brief release would sustain him as he passed through to the other side. McIlweath had rarely felt so tested.

He knocked three times on the white door and waited. After several seconds, Anne's muffled voice seeped through the plasterboard. "Who is it?"

"It's Tom, Anne," and then silence. He presumed Anne was mulling over some new equation into which an unknown variable had been introduced, trying to find the proper formula to solve it.

"Anne, can I come in? We've got to talk." McIlweath heard the door unlatch. His own voice reverberated around the stark hallway walls into a ringing echo. It mingled now with the metallic sliding of the chain, a peculiar chorus. The door swung open brusquely.

Anne stood, one hand on the doorknob, the other perched combatively on her hip. She never slept late, even when she had the opportunity, so she was fully dressed. Most likely she had been dressed for hours. When some incident occurred that she could not control, something which she had not predicted, she often had trouble sleeping at all. It may have been this restless agitation that accentuated the angularity of her features; it may have been anger left to seethe. Her face locked in a deep scowl, her brow furrowed, her lips grimly set into a straight line. She gestured with one hand for him to enter, and McIlweath obediently accepted her ungracious command. His initial supposition from the night before had been correct: Anne had not been worried about him.

"Have you come to make amends?" Her voice spat forth like a flat, hardened dart seeking soft flesh. This would not be pleasant, another supposition verified.

"In a way." McIlweath's own voice, to his chagrin, had assumed its nervous, too-high pitch. He would not be well served by what he regarded as a shaky avian squawk. Convictions should resonate. Anne would seize upon his tone as an admission of guilt. Well then, so be it. The substance of what he had to say would far outweigh its form.

"I'm sorry," he continued, "for not showing last night. I really am sorry, Anne."

"I waited up until almost 1:00, damn you, thinking you might still be coming. You must have been held up, I thought, or maybe you just lost track of time. Where the hell were you?"

"I was at a party. Someone I knew had a party last night. He asked me to stop by, and since I wasn't meeting you until later, I did. I thought I would only stay for a bit."

"And you forgot about the time and you forgot about seeing me. Damn you, Tom."

"No, Anne, I didn't forget." They stood now, face to face, near the center of Anne's small living room. McIlweath denied himself all exits.

Let the battle begin, if it was to be so. "I didn't forget," he repeated. "I simply chose not to come."

"You what?" Anne had genuine difficulty with this. Her mouth dropped slightly ajar in wonder.

"I chose to stay at the party. I was having a good time, a better time than I have had in weeks. Probably a better time than at any other point since I came to this godforsaken place. There were challenging, intelligent people there. They talked to me, really talked in words that were worth saying, instead of the narrow, dull, banal garbage I've had to put up with for so long. I can't explain to you how fine it felt to be with such a diverse group."

"You were drunk, weren't you? You must have been."

"I'd had a few beers and maybe I was a little drunk, but that changes nothing. If anything, the alcohol made me relax enough to enjoy myself. You can't dismiss it all by saying I was drunk."

"Couldn't you have called to say you weren't coming instead of leaving me hanging like that? I swear, sometimes you are so inconsiderate."

"I could have called. I don't know why I didn't."

"You didn't want to disturb your good time." Anne turned to look out her window. She folded her arms across her chest. "What the hell was so special about this party that you couldn't break away?"

"Anne, what have I done with myself since I got here? I've made no friends, I speak to no one but you. All I do is study and wait for you to spare some of your attention for me. I've lived like a hermit in some remote cave, and you've been the only light, the only sound to filter in. That party last night took me out of my cave for a while. It brought me together with new people who were animated and bright and alive. I left my cave, Anne. I just didn't want to go back in, that's all. For a while I didn't even want to be reminded that it existed."

"You self-pitying bastard," Anne bit off the words beneath her breath. Her scowl darkened fiercely.

"You're right, Anne. I am self-pitying. That was why I went to the party in the first place. But at least I did something against it. I turned over my situation for a little while. And you resent it, don't you? It's not so much that I stood you up, although that's a handy pretense, and my fault entirely. It's that I did something purely for myself, without your knowledge or consent. We would have had this conversation even if I had met you for dinner last night."

"You're talking nonsense. God damn you, Tom," she was nearly shouting. "How dare you try to turn this back onto me. For once in your life take responsibility for your mistakes. You owe me at least that much."

"That, my love, is exactly what I'm doing." McIlweath spoke slowly, quietly, evenly, a contrast to Anne's fury. All this was too long overdue. "The greatest mistake I made was letting myself become cloistered away in this unholy place. You've dictated the terms of my life as completely as if I had surrendered to you on a battlefield. Unfortunately, I was never aware that we were fighting a war. I had always thought our destinies, if that's the proper word, were somewhat in harmony. I didn't realize that I had been steadily, dumbly and mindlessly forfeiting mine to yours. That was my greatest mistake, Anne. That's what I'm taking responsibility for.

"You see last night as more than rudeness," he continued. "You see it as an act of rebellion. By going to that party with a crowd you didn't know, I suddenly became less pliable. I might have formed new friendships or come to new conclusions uncensored by your peculiar insights. I might have become more my own man and less yours."

Anne faced him from the window. Her chest rose and fell with angry breaths drawn sharply. McIlweath had never seen her so full of rage. Fitting, he thought, that it should be that way. Anne's face twisted into a burning glare, her blue eyes almost electric with their razor-like fury. McIlweath judged that his words had hit a soft and tender target.

"You paranoid, self-absorbed fool," she hissed. "Do you believe I devised such elaborate schemes to keep you prisoner? Do you believe I would waste my time that way?"

"In a way, yes. This morning, as I got ready to come here it, occurred to me that you've never shown any tolerance for the things closest to me. You had absolutely no use for my college roommates, who were like brothers to me. In fact, you made it clear that you didn't like them in the least and you thought they were a poor influence on me. You wanted to spend as little time on my turf as possible. What were you afraid of, Anne?"

"Those three were unthinking, brutal, crude animals. You should have seen that for yourself if you had any self-respect."

"Those 'animals' are all doing exactly what they want to be doing with their lives. They're all making some sort of contribution to the world around them. And where am I?" McIlweath observed with a bitter smirk. "I'm the only one who's lost, it would seem. I'm the only one who's been unthinking. They've all gone the way of their own choosing. They defined what they wanted, and then they pursued it, with every ounce of their intelligence, creativity and passion. As I recall, at one point you told me quite plainly that you were better for me than they could ever be. Perhaps such well-defined personalities unnerve you, or was it that you thought they might set a dangerous example for me? Perhaps they'd pull me out of your orbit. And in the meantime, I've drifted along with my classics, not really sure what I wanted to do with it but purely incapable of making a decision and sticking to it, purely incapable of constructing my own course. So I relied on you, which is exactly what you urged me to do. No, Anne, you have it reversed. If I had any self-respect I'd consider myself unworthy of them."

"You can hardly blame me for that. I've tried to help you find some direction, but you've resisted every suggestion I ever made. You were content to float along, 'trying to find yourself,' or whatever they call it these days."

"If I've resisted your suggestions, then why the hell am I here? Good God, can't you see that you're the sole reason I came to Boston? Are you that blind, or is it part of your selective memory to forget all you've meant to me? Anne, you brought me here. That's how you've tried to help me find my direction. That's all it amounts to, wanting me near you as an amusement when you get bored or lonely."

He went on, his own rage starting to rear itself. "I have been your man, and not in the romantic sense. I have been your man because I did what you wanted me to, gone where you directed, colored my attitudes with your hue, thinned the roster of my friends to suit you, spent my time where you thought it best, dressed, talked and slept in your image of me. Anne, I have been your man totally. I've been your indentured servant. Last night I threw you off for a few hours. It was bound to happen, and you resent the hell out of me for it."

"I resent your coming here today and trying to imply that it was my fault."

"It was not your fault, Anne. I never said that. Letting you wait for me like that was wrong, and I'm sorry for it. But you've got to understand why it happened. I barely understand it myself, but the more I think about it the clearer it becomes. I'm trying to share that with you as gently as I can. I don't want to get angry or see you upset. That's not my purpose at all."

"Oh Tom, God damn you, you're talking nonsense. I don't understand any of it, and I don't want to. You were wrong, that's all there is to it. You were callous and rude and base and stupid. Don't you dare try to make me feel guilty for how I've helped you or what I've meant to you. That's cruel. That's the cruelest thing you've ever done." She was on the verge of tears now, her rage enhanced by the frustration of this unpredicted turn of the discussion. If anything, she would have expected a penitent McIlweath, a runaway puppy returned to be spanked with a rolled-up newspaper.

"Anne, whether you know it or not, whether or not you recognize it, you've controlled me since we first met. And I let you. Our whole relationship has been on your terms, me coming to you. Let me ask you something: did you try to call me last night when I was late?"

"No, I didn't."

"Why not?"

"You were supposed to be here by 10:30. I don't feel compelled to track you down when you're late. You weren't home anyway, so what good would it have done?"

"Do you recall that, as always, we agreed to get together at your convenience? I hadn't seen you for several days. I hadn't so much as spoken to you since early this week."

"What can I do about that? What do you expect, Tom, would you tell me that? I'm in medical school. I've worked my entire life to be here, and I'm going to do the best I can. That takes time. It's not like curling up with your dusty Latin books, you know. There's so much to learn and it's all crucial. Perhaps you don't understand that, having spent your life on frivolous things. What I learn is not open to interpretation, like some Homeric ode or a Roman fresco. And if that takes time away from you, that's too damn bad." She turned back again toward the window. The ticking of the clock on her bookshelf beat a haunting and hollow rhythm, the only sound in the room for several minutes.

McIlweath at length broke the silent tension in a voice so laden with regret that it rose scarcely above a whisper. "Anne, I think we need some time apart."

Anne's voice, too, had lost its rage, faded now into a concern for changes so obviously taking place. "It sounds to me as if we need some time together."

"No, I don't think so. Perhaps we've taken each other for granted. We've been too ready to assume that we're looking for the same things. I've been too accommodating, and you've been too presumptuous. We need some time apart to sort through what we want, and who we are. We need time to miss each other, if we will, and feel a need to be together rather than an obligation."

"How much time?"

"I don't know. Time enough to come to one conclusion or the other. Anne, we simply have too many expectations of each other. They started out as idealizations, and they were delightful once, but they've taken on a life of their own. Sometimes I think all we see are our expectations, and we've lost the reality behind them. We've lost ourselves. We fill a role for one another, that's all. We've drawn each other as we want. But the pressure to sustain that is just too great. It's worn us away."

"You make it sound so grim."

"You've never had to look at it. Perhaps for you it's not a problem. But it's been so difficult for me, Anne, and the odd part is that I never knew it. I had thought it normal, and I've been so afraid to lose you. You're all I had, or so I believed. Even now I'm afraid, more than you can know, but I know it's what we have to do if we're ever going to have any chance. We might find that we mean too much to each other to be apart. Like it was at the beginning."

"Or we might learn that the effort isn't worth the reward," said Anne bitterly. "But it's been no effort for me, Tom. I wouldn't do anything differently."

"I wouldn't have expected that I ever presented a challenge for you. You've never had to bend."

"Don't start again, please."

"No. You know what I think now, and I'm sorry it's been so hard."

"I still don't understand you, Tom. I *am* good for you, that I know. I really can't see what brought this on. What happened to you at that party last night to make you so God damned self-pitying and so hateful?"

"Nothing happened that shouldn't have been done long ago. Just that it was there, and I went, and I saw myself as such a contrast to everyone else. The party didn't start anything. It just confirmed what I had been feeling for a long time."

"Is that what your classics have taught you, the art of melodrama? There'll be no chorus coming through the door to chant a lament of your cruel fate. The gods won't take pity on you and turn your poor melancholy life around with a click of their fingers. I recall telling you once that you think too much. I was right then, and you've proven it to me beyond any doubt. You don't know how good you've got it."

"Only because I still have the freedom to change it. "

"You want some time apart," Anne said, the boldness at once returning to her tone. She spun around again to face him. "Okay, take as much time as you want. Think to your heart's content and let your veins burst with angst. Is that what you want, poor Tom? I'm willing to grant it."

"By your good graces."

"I'm willing to grant it," Anne repeated. "Come to whatever conclusions you wish. Sort out your feelings toward me. Separate the wheat from the chaff and the lambs from the goats. Consult Aeschylus and Socrates and Ovid. If, after all that, you don't arrive back to where you are now, then you are a hopeless fool."

"I suppose I should be envious of that typical Newburyian certainty. Don't any doubts ever creep in to shake that secure little world?"

"But know this," ignoring him, Anne continued. "For my part I'm not going to waste any time pondering either my faults or yours. I know what I want. I know what I'm doing with my life and I know the kind of person I am. And I won't change any of it. I have no time to indulge myself in any of this ridiculous posturing.

"So take your time, with my blessing," she went on. "But at the end of it, if you come to your senses and decide you want me as I am, you take the chance that I won't be waiting for you. My life will go on as it is in the meantime. It will close itself up when you leave it and there may not be room for you to reenter."

"What could be clearer than that?" said McIlweath, almost to himself. Anne's words had run him through. She had again become impenetrable. A strange, nostalgic sadness overran him.

"I'll call you in a couple of weeks," he said. "Perhaps we can talk then."

"You decide. Assuming you're capable of making a decision."

"I am sorry, Anne. I truly am."

"You have a great deal to be sorry about. You can't know what you're doing. You can't know what you've done."

"I know so little, of that I have no doubt."

Anne said nothing. She stood with her back against the window, her arms folded. McIlweath turned around and put his hand on the door. He opened his mouth slightly, but nothing he could say now would be right, not after this. Anne's hurt had translated back to rage. She had a unique talent to use her offenses as she needed them; McIlweath did not wish to add to that perverse arsenal.

He opened the door and walked down the stairs into the cold. He had not removed his jacket during his time upstairs, which in retrospect had not taken as long as he would have expected. The cold winter air crept into his pores and took away the heat of the argument. Anne's apartment had stifled him so that he might have suffocated without knowing it. He drew deep breaths as he walked to his car, and the fetid, hot vapors that weighted his lungs disappeared.

Later, when he was alone, his sterile apartment still lifeless but not as tomblike as he had seen it before, McIlweath sat in review of Anne. In the stark quiet loneliness of late afternoon, as the light faded and the shadows in his apartment deepened before the blackness swelled out of the far corners to envelop his rooms entirely, his analysis differed little from the thoughts he had drunkenly woven the night before. He had expected nostalgia, a sweet remembrance of the comforts they had shared, to stir his insecurities and make him remorseful. Yet, while he could indeed think softly of the fine times, the moments of elation, the silent communion of unspoken harmony and the subtle gelling of unfathomable emotion, he saw it all as belonging to a past existence, an earlier life that had been tragically extinguished and which his current incarnation could understand but not repeat.

For Tom McIlweath it was all a process of annealing himself against his emotion, and it was that process, rather than the loss of tenderness itself, which saddened him. Was this, then, an inevitable part of growing older? Must moving forward always exact such a cost, and once lost, could the raw joy of discovering a new posture, a new partner, ever be regained? So modestly, so imperceptibly had his embryonic love for Anne passed that he could now regard it only as illusory. Time alone would determine whether he had suffered permanent damage, although he doubted it. He was extricating himself just in time.

'Why,' asked McIlweath, more than once, 'why do I not feel the affection that so marked our early days together? When and how did I lose it?' He saw the core of their relationship played out through his sense of duty combined with a desperate fear of loneliness. But loneliness, he saw, came in different forms, as did suffocation, and paralysis, and catatonia. The time he had spent welded to Anne had been the loneliest period of his young life.

McIlweath sat at the window and rotated these thoughts over and over. He kept waiting for the sadness. He kept waiting for the remorse. He kept waiting for the lead to crawl down his throat and sink through him to his toes, dragging with it the light and the airy buoyancy of his youth and throwing him into a self-loathing depression. He kept waiting to miss Anne and to feel sorry for his immense stupidity. He kept waiting for a surge of pain to tell him that he truly cared about her and wanted to be with her for the way she had reinvigorated him, propped him up, fed him affection and restored a battered self-confidence. He kept waiting for some part of him to scream that his asserting himself meant he was denying her, couldn't he see that? He kept waiting to replay the gentle moments and to see what would be lacking going forward. He kept waiting to conclude that he loved her. He kept waiting.

All night he kept waiting, and all night the only sound that came to him was the muffled swishing of the traffic below. At 10:30, after a forgettable dinner and four hours of staring without comprehension at a television screen, he went to bed. There was still time to sort things out, and perhaps tomorrow, or the next day, it would be different.

* * *

"How did it go?" The voice on the other end of the telephone was unmistakably Kathy's, although she had not bothered to identify herself when McIlweath answered.

"Kathy?"

"Yeah. How did it go with Anne?"

"Wait . . . How did you get my number? I never gave it to you, did I?"

"I have my ways. Nobody's anonymous around here. So talk to me, McIlweath. Did you finally become a man yesterday in more ways than the obvious?"

"I didn't realize you had such a burning interest in all this. Or are you just being catty?"

"I've got a stake in you, my friend. You're the first male I ever deflowered. I want to see you make an honest man out of yourself. I also want to see you happy, which you're clearly not to any eye that bothers to look closely."

"Should these things be discussed over the phone? If you're evaluating whether or not I'm a new man, shouldn't you be looking me in the eye?"

"You're right. Fix me breakfast and tell me everything. Do you have enough food for two? And I mean things like eggs, toast, coffee and juice, not hot dogs and tortilla chips."

"I can make do. But you're coming for conversation, not food."

"I'll come for both. If the conversation is lousy, I can at least fill my stomach. Where do you live?"

McIlweath told her, then began fixing breakfast. His food was ordinary but he tried to overcome it through a dash of enthusiasm: he grated cheese for the eggs, brewed the coffee instead of boiling water for instant, and spread the toast carefully with a thin layer of margarine, then put his sole jar of jelly on the table. Surprised by Kathy's bright call, McIlweath went about tidying the apartment in the short time before her arrival. He straightened his desk, piled away the old newspapers in the closet, made his bed and arranged his clothes. Even so, the place still seemed dismal, austere and dark. Its heavy colors and tatty furnishings were somber, as was the neighborhood through which she would have to drive to get there. He wished he lived someplace else, someplace light, someplace that lifted him past the clinging muck of his daily routine as soon as he walked through the door. Where he lived now was part of that dank routine. It was too much Anne. He hoped that Kathy would not be too much put off by the sterility of this sorry place.

McIlweath heard footsteps on the stairs and opened the door before it could be knocked. Kathy Keane sprang upon him before he said a word. She leapt into his arms to cover his face with her warm mouth. McIlweath caught her foraging lips with his own and they stood there on the landing for several minutes until Kathy at last said, "Aren't you going to ask a lady in? It's cold out here."

"Sorry. I didn't want to break my rhythm."

She walked by him into the apartment pulling off her gloves and unzipping her jacket as she looked around. "I hope you don't pay much rent for this."

"It's rather simple, isn't it?"

"It's a tomb. How do you get any light in here?"

"You don't. It's the darkest place I've ever seen."

"I'd go mad here inside a week. Where's breakfast?"

"On the table, my lady, waiting to fall past your tender lips."

"Cut the bullshit, McIlweath, and feed me."

They sat down and began to consume what, to Tom McIlweath's unadorned lifestyle, constituted a plentiful meal. The food warmed him and returned a rashy glow to his cheeks. He recounted his discussion with Anne. All the while Kathy sat rapt, staring hard at McIlweath as he spoke, studying him, studying his reactions to what he related. She said nothing until he had finished with the particulars—the coming, the going, the words themselves, the anger and the hurt.

"What will you do now?" she asked.

"I'll wait to see how I feel in a few days. Eventually I'll call her, and we'll talk again. I'm not hopeful we can salvage anything."

"I wouldn't think you'd want to. The woman has no soul, Tom."

"Kathy, however you perceive her now, you have to realize that there's a thick cord of shared experiences that runs back years. That's not easy to sever. I'd still like to remain her friend if I could."

"You shouldn't. You should leave her completely. Any other way and you'll risk being sucked in again. Your moods will change. They'll flop back and forth like a loose gate in a windstorm. She can play on that if she wants, and the terms of any future surrender are likely to be fierce."

McIlweath shook his head sadly. He inspected the creases in the tablecloth. "You know," he said, "the most tragic aspect of all this is what I feel toward her."

"Which is?"

"Nothing. I can't explain it, Kathy. It's a numbness, as if I'd been beating the heel of my hand against a wall until I can't feel anything anymore."

"Or like being left in the cold too long. Emotional frostbite."

"Maybe. There's no anger, but there's no real affection either. And there should be. Oh God, there should be a deep well of emotion spilling over the top. But there's nothing. I throw a pebble in and it rings off the walls.

"I think of her," he continued, "and there's no regret. I mean, now, when there should be this huge sense of loss, there's just the idea that I surmounted a hurdle. I passed a test. When I think of what we've done together and what she's meant to me, I should be nostalgic at least, but whatever longing that's running through me is not for her. If anything, it's nostalgia for the condition of my life when we first met. I miss being excited by what I'm doing. I miss feeling as if my life is a mosaic and I all need to do is find the right pieces. And Lord knows I miss my friends, my old roommates. We carried confidence to the point of hubris, and it was all so very sweet. We would never get old, and we would never fail, and the four of us loved one another like brothers. Anne came into that, and lent a richness to it. She's a bridge for me now, back to that simple and promising time. Sometimes I get morose thinking that that phase of my life is ended. That's the form my nostalgia takes."

"She's been a symbol for you. No wonder you idealized her for so long."

"Even so, she lingered over my life like a threat. She never let me feel secure. Maybe I was to blame for that. But I catered to her constantly. Do you know I used to call her every time I went to the store to see if I could pick up something for her? It made me feel useful, and that in itself was a compensation for what she made me lack. Sometimes I'd call her at night before I went to bed, to hear her voice but also to have her with me so I could feed my fantasies. She was like a cat, so arrogant and so intent upon going her own way. I'd chase after her and try to please her, all the while hoping she'd consent to have me as company."

"And of course you never slept with her. That strikes me as so odd. So cold. I assume that wasn't your doing."

"No. Anne was never physical. For the longest time she'd pull away whenever I got close to her. Our physical relationship crept along like ice melting. For a while I'd strategize about how to get her to be more responsive. I'd think of what I could do to get her to want me to hold her. Once, when we were alone, I managed to spill some soda on the front of her blouse, then I insisted that I wipe it away before it stained, thinking that the presence of my hands near her breasts might arouse her. Pretty childish I know, but I wanted to cover every base. Nothing worked. After a few months I gave up trying. I thought that in due time she's come around, but she never did. I was always the aggressor. I came to think that even my advances violated her, even though nothing ever became of them. A transgression against her idealized state, they were, and I felt terribly guilty."

"I suppose you took a few cold showers, you poor thing. I can't imagine putting up with such frustration."

McIlweath went to the kitchen counter and returned with the coffee pot to refill their mugs. "It's ironic, too, that she would have been so cold. We swam together nearly every day. You've seen racing suits. They leave nothing to the imagination. You'd think that might help her develop an appreciation of her body, and mine too."

"Do you honestly think the two of you have any future in any form? Why this delay in leaving her? Talking to her in a few days doesn't seem to me as if it would serve any purpose."

"There's no future, Kathy. That was apparent yesterday when I left her apartment. The extra time is to eliminate all conceivable doubt."

"You have no doubt."

"She might understand things better if she takes the time to think about them. It might make it easier for her. That chance is slim, but I feel like I owe her at least that."

"Tom, I doubt she cares."

"As I said, I wouldn't mind remaining her friend."

"I can't see it. If you leave her now, you've probably earned a foe for life. She's not accustomed to seeing a part of her tidy little world rebel. She'll resent it forever."

"She was angry when I left, even though she feigned indifference."

"It may not have been a feint, my friend. Don't call her. If she cares to salvage anything, let her come to you."

"Then I've heard the last of her."

"In which case, as you told me yesterday morning, you are a most fortunate man. Now," she stood and walked around behind McIlweath's chair. She leaned over and ran her hands down his chest while she whispered in his ear, "Now that you've fed me . . ." Her blond hair fell against McIlweath's cheek. Her hands ran lower, into his lap and beyond. "I want you to answer the rest of my needs." Kathy's voice rode on the tongue which probed the curves of the young man's ear. McIlweath rose and, taking her hand, led her to his bedroom, too long in wait of this peculiar sacrament.

* * *

The train north clacked a rolling, uneven beat like the sound of a swordfight in an old adventure movie. Yet in the distinctive twists of context that cast differing connotations to identical items, no thoughts of adventure unleashed themselves. There was only despair and isolation against a monotonous jostling that annihilated all peace of mind. Across the deserted open space of Maryland and Delaware few lights provided any perspective. The train rumbled through a hollow darkness devoid of all dimension. Hollow night, hollow land, hollow time.

Glynnis Mear rode the train north from Washington, looked out her window and saw nothing. There was nothing to see. The interior lights reflected back and she saw her own image in the glass. Beyond it nothing emerged save a swampy blackness that reminded her of pulling a sheet over her head as a child when she lay awake at night. She breathed in bored sips, she wrestled about in her seat, and closed her eyes. She wanted the time to pass, the train to arrive, the cab to take her back to her small apartment. She wanted desperately to go to bed so that the limpid demise of this day could be put behind her forever.

A stubborn will had brought her here when she so clearly would have preferred the bed of Conor Finnegan. She regretted her current circumstances, but she did not regret the sentiments that created them. She and Conor had not fought again after their first flurry, although the young man made it obvious that Glynnis's resolve, which he hoped a night of impassioned lovemaking would shatter, displeased him no end. He had been quiet all day from the time that Glynnis averred that morning that she would be returning to Philadelphia on an evening train. Conor never addressed the point directly, but he radiated a pouting, sullen martyrdom that Glynnis was only too happy to leave. She could not stand that sort of childishness.

Conor expected so much, and although she did truly love him with a power she had never believed herself to possess, she could not sacrifice the parameters of her own character. She loved him, she adored him completely, yet some tremendous subconscious caveat held her back. She could not fathom exactly what it was, but its pull was incredibly strong, a tendril around her ankles that held fast and dragged her inch by inch, patiently waiting for her own strength to ebb, as surely it must should she be unable to loosen the firm grip. The thought scared her so greatly that she tended to dismiss it as exaggeration. There was so much to lose on either side. For now, she would go about preserving the depths of Glynnis Mear and trust her lover's constancy while she sorted out the right course.

That night, after unpacking and a long, hot bath, Glynnis went to bed early. She dreamed that she received a telegram from her sister saying that their mother wanted to see her, that it was important to get home as quickly as possible. In the dream, Glynnis arrived home that same day to find all three of her siblings dressed in black and walking through the house in rigid half-steps.

"She's dying," said Martha, said Bobby, said Peter. Just that, in lifeless, leaden voices, and nothing more. Glynnis felt no reaction to this, but went to the hospital alone. She had never before seen this building, though, and it was a massive, cavernous, sandstone structure. She could not tell what part of town she was in or how she had gotten there. The hospital had no name. When she went inside she found no one. The information desk sat empty, the gift shop had closed, neither doctor nor nurse nor orderly walked the hallway tunnels. Glynnis set about finding her dying mother. At the ends of the corridors shadowy figures moved in a great hurry, but they were too far away to be addressed and as she neared the places where they had been she saw no one.

Glynnis entered room after room, each empty. Discouraged, she began to cry. Her frustrations overwhelmed her; she sat on the floor to weep alone. Huge convulsive sobs swept over her so that she could scarcely breathe. In the midst of her sobbing, she heard her mother's voice. "Glynnis." She rose and walked into the room outside which she had been sitting.

Her mother lay flat on a narrow bed. Nothing else furnished the gaunt room. There were no chairs, no windows, no charts. The walls, too, were bare, painted a hideous shade of gray.

"Mother," said Glynnis in a whisper. "I heard you were not well."

"I am dying, Glynnis. Someday you will die, too."

"Father is dead. We shall be with him together then, won't we?"

"He is gone, but I do not pity him. I pity you."

"Why, Mother?"

"I pity you," she repeated. Nothing reflected in her eyes. They were two flat black rings, dimensionless buttons.

Glynnis noticed the tubes in her mother's arms. Four of them, two in each arm, ran to a huge plastic bottle to the side of her bed.

"What do they give you through these tubes, Mother?"

"Nothing, Glynnis. They give me nothing."

"Then why are they there?"

"To drain me. They are draining all the fluids out of me. When they are done, I shall be dead."

"Is it painful, Mother? Do you suffer?"

"No, Glynnis. It is the most pleasant sensation. I do feel quite wonderful. I do not fear my death, if it comes like this."

"I must leave you now, Mother. I must go home."

"With the others?"

"No. By myself."

The dying woman frowned. "You will not see me again, then. I shall be gone before you return."

Glynnis felt suddenly serene. She did not kiss her mother goodbye.

She only turned and walked to the door of the gray cubicle. "I must go. Goodbye, Mother."

"Goodbye, Glynnis. It's an easy thing to do after all, isn't it?"

"Yes, Mother. It is all so easy." But her mother had closed her eyes before Glynnis finished her words. Lying there, she began to shrink, her head growing smaller and sinking under the sheet pulled to where her neck had been.

Glynnis woke the next morning with the dream before her in vivid detail. She lay in bed trying to erase it, but could not. She took a long shower to steam away the uneasiness that had been seeded by the restless night at the end of a restless day. Glynnis walked off campus to a coffee shop that students frequented, hoping she might see someone she knew, but there were no familiar faces. Over breakfast she read the Sunday paper, all thoughts of shrinkage, death and dying blown for the moment off her shoulder at last, like the unwelcome specks of dust they were.

All afternoon Glynnis worked in the sculpture studio in the fine arts building. Normally an active, crowded place jammed with tools, materials and the mediocre talents that wielded them, the studio on Sundays was completely empty. She enjoyed the solitude. She tried to plan most of her sculpting for the late night when few people were apt to be around, or for the weekends. Glynnis did her best work when she was alone here. She could not see how anyone could be creative during the loud, hurried weekday hours.

She knew little of sculpting and her confidence lagged terribly. Consequently she worked slowly, meticulously studying each facet of whatever she was about, running her long fingers over its evolving shape and reestablishing her image of the outcome before making the next cut or gouging the next cavern. She worked mostly with clay. Stone, in all its solid permanency, intimidated her. She was reluctant to capture her mistakes in something so indelible. Clay allowed her to retreat, and she loved the slippery, spongy feel in her hands. She prodded, poked, pulled and smoothed with the greatest deliberation. In the quiet Sunday afternoon studio, she aspired to the ideal and unwound the tightly spun tension of her day with Conor Finnegan.

That was it, she admitted to herself. There was a tension now between them, new, subtle, yet so demanding. She realized that a part of her had to remain on guard whenever she was with him. She could never totally relax, or she might be taken away altogether.

'He expects so much. He expects me to listen to his stories and to share his frustrations. He expects me to smile at the proper time, to squeeze his hand when he needs reassurance. I'm to trust him as he sets our time together. I'm expected to be interested in what he reads and whom he knows. He expects our thoughts on every topic to be compatible. I'm expected to bring my mood into harmony with his: to be down when he's down, to be dreamily idealistic when he is so, to be loving and tender when he wants to hold me. And at night, I'm expected to give my body to him as he gives his to me. He expects to fill each corner of my mind and soul, to infuse me with new and Romantic perspectives, to eliminate the mundane, to elevate my very being through the magnificent, graceful power of his character.

'And I can do all these things. I love to do them for him, for can there be any doubt how thoroughly he reciprocates? But I have always done so by choice. I will not yield that option of choice, even though emotion's dictates are too overwhelming to be ignored. Conor doesn't understand this. He has come to expect what cannot, should never, be expected, but which can only given by choice.

"I do love him. His web is so kindly woven, so warm and gentle, so seductive. But it's still a web. He cannot absorb me; I will not let myself be drained away. There is far too much at stake.

'Poor Conor,' she continued her thought. 'I am not the obedient child; I have never been. I pray that I do not lose him through this confusion. And I pray most of all that I do not scar forever the tender flesh of his delicate, Romantic nature. He is too rare to be hardened like other men. But he cannot have me on the terms he sets.'

Shortly before the time when Glynnis would have left the studio to prepare her dinner, the door opened at the far end of the large room. She did not hear it, had not heard the footsteps in the hallway as they approached. Glynnis did not hear the intruder until he had walked nearly to where she stood smoothing the bad lines of her rudimentary creation, a dancer *en point*. She heard him at last, and turned with a startled drop of her scraper. When she saw who it was she relaxed at once and lifted a hand to her chest to quell her alarm.

"Oh, Michael," she said, smiling warmly now, "You startled me. I was beginning to think that you'd forgotten. Let me get cleaned up a bit, and we'll be off."

CHAPTER XXI

Life is a very sad piece of buffoonery.
because we have . . . the need to fool ourselves
continuously by the spontaneous creation
of a reality (one for each and never the same for
everyone) which, from time to time, reveals itself
to be vain and illusory.

—Luigi Pirandello, "Autobiographical Sketch" in *Le Lettere*

Conor Finnegan charged into the preparation of the hearings as a starving man devours a steak. The task nourished him; it made him strong. And as the hungry man turns over the bone to inspect closely all nooks of it in order to find the sweetest meat after wolfing down the obvious, so Conor studied all aspects of his topic to find scarcely known nuances to complement the more apparent facts that constituted what the senator had laid out as the core of these hearings.

He read everything he could grab on the housing conditions of the elderly. He sought out books—scholarly gerontological studies and less authoritative anecdotal compilations—and scoured periodicals of the last several years. He spent hours at the Library of Congress, sometimes staying throughout the day and checking in with the office for his messages. He would take with him the better studies and read them when he got home until his eyes and mind grew too weary to absorb anything more. He took voluminous notes on everything he read.

Armed with his newly won knowledge, Finnegan searched with the fervor of Diogenes to substantiate what he had learned. He knew the lobbyists, of course: well-dressed gentlemen and gentlewomen who represented the major federal groups, pensioners, health care associations and public membership advocacy groups such as the American Association of Retired Persons. Although they seemed pleased to learn of the senator's call for hearings, they remained skeptical that any practical good would come of it. Without exception, they suggested their association presidents as ideal witnesses.

Finnegan concluded that, while one or two well-fed and handsomely dressed association presidents might contribute something of value, he could not construct two days around just them. For one thing, the senator would be bored to tears. For another and more important reason, though, these people had, at best, limited empathy. They were no more than poorly reflective mirrors that gave a general outline of an image without defining its contours. Finnegan wanted these hearings without those blurry lines.

And so on most days he spent some time invading the neighborhoods. He spoke with the leaders of community organizations he had come to know and trust. They in turn pointed him to the saddest of the sad. Finnegan went to see them, the human faces that constituted the numbers he had learned, and touched the flesh that lived the reality of the studies he had read and the stories he had heard.

He found them as they were: inarticulate, frightened at first that a man in a suit should be coming to see them, gracious when they were convinced he meant no harm. Finnegan did his best to show that he was innocuous, that he was in fact on their side of things. He indulged their tendencies to ramble on about personal topics he could not understand, he smiled as much as he could, he kept his wide eyes fixed on theirs. He did everything he could to appear young, to appear eager and charming, to prove himself an ally. Most of those with whom he spoke abandoned their initial distrust simply for the unexpected joy of having another body in their homes. Most had not heard of Finnegan's boss, nor were they overly impressed that he represented a United States senator. They were gratified solely because he was company. He interrupted their all-too-finite procession of useless days.

Finnegan, somewhat timid at first in thrusting himself into the homes of feeble, fearful strangers, rapidly came to relish talking with them. They in turn regaled him with stories of their families, old pictures of places their younger days had taken them and opinions on the decline of modern society. Finnegan's understanding of the simple pleasure his companionship provided filled him with satisfaction. He vowed to keep in touch with many of them after the hearings concluded.

What he found, though, very nearly broke his heart. Everyone with whom he met, man and woman, black and white and Hispanic, lived in abject squalor that even the best efforts at dignifying could not hide. These are good, decent people, his brain screamed as he lay at night in his comfortably warm bed. They deserve to live humanely. They deserve to be free from worry, and spend their days in peace. My God, what have we done?

His explorations took him into the city's worst neighborhoods. He spoke to one old gentleman who claimed to be ninety-two and lived in a one-room apartment on the southeast side. Great gaping holes pocked each wall where the drywall had fallen completely away. In some spots the plumbing was visible. The old man had tried to cover them once with sheets, he explained, but he had come to need them for himself as his other linens deteriorated. The tenant fixed him some tea, which was served in his only uncracked cup, and they talked at length there, in that single desolate room. Finnegan sat in a tatty mildewed chair, and noticed that there were no windows to distract his view.

"Been here twenny-fi' years," said the old man, whose name was Moses, "and I ain't never once seed the man who owns it. He sen' his boy aroun' ever' month to collect the rent. I pay on time ever' month."

"Do you like it here?" asked Finnegan, and wished at once he could retract such a foolish question. "Do you feel safe?"

"Hell, I don't know. I'm used to it. Where the hell else am I s'pose to go? I'm old, and I'll end up dyin' here, boy. You can count on that."

"Do you have enough money to get by, Moses? With rent and groceries and all?"

The old man chuckled. "Nobody got enough, son. We can always use some more now, can't we? I get my pension and Social Security."

"What's the rent here?"

Moses told him. It was almost as much as what he and Dan Rosselli paid for their own much larger, much cleaner, well-maintained apartment in a fine neighborhood. "Do you know you're being overcharged, Moses? You can find a much better place for the same money."

"An' how I'm gonna get there? Who's gonna move me? What place is gonna take in an old man who's gonna drop dead on 'em some day? I can't live no place but here."

"Has your rent been raised lately?"

"Ever' year it goes up some. The man charges me more ever' year, maybe ten dollars a month, maybe a little bit more than that. His boy say he got to do it to make ends meet."

Finnegan saw the pattern again and again. Landlord raised rents regularly. There were no contracts, at least none that fixed rents beyond the short term. The old people, who like Moses had nowhere else to go, had to pay it. Most landlords would not hesitate to pitch them out if they became delinquent. And the waiting list for limited public housing alternatives usually ran longer than their life expectancies.

"What do you eat, Moses? It seems to me that if your rent keeps going up, eventually you're going to run out of money for food."

The old man chuckled again. "Ain't gonna be no need for food in a while. I eat a hot dog, and maybe some cereal. Corn flakes and such. I eat bread during the day, and I drink my tea. It's all the same when you get right down to it, ain't it?"

"Have you ever eaten pet food, Moses? Really now, tell me the truth."

The smile grew faintly sorrowful, a light burning dimmer. "Like I say, it's all the same. You get so ya don' notice no taste. You just look for whatever's gonna fill your belly and don't cost you too much."

"If your rent were lower you could eat better."

"So could you, boy."

When they finished their conversation, Finnegan made a point of returning the teacups to the kitchen area. As he put them into the sink he glanced upward at the pantry, which had no doors. Cans of dog food, cans of cat food, lined the bottom shelf. The first time he had seen this it startled him; now he had grown accustomed to it.

Finnegan found a lady a few blocks over. She seemed more fearful than the others he had met. Her name was Agnes, and in contrast to the surrounding neighborhood she was white. Despite Finnegan's assurances that he had been vetted and sent by her social worker whom he named and whose identification number he cited, she let him in only with the greatest reluctance. Her narrow, bony face displayed an underlying sentiment of terror.

Noting several pictures of young children scattered around the single-room flat that was in only slightly better repair than Moses's place, Finnegan kept the conversation on her family until she relaxed a bit. There were her grandchildren, she explained, who lived in California, Texas and Minnesota. She did not know them except through their pictures, but they were all lovely, weren't they? Her family had all moved away, so she related a synopsis of each of them and what they were doing. She alone had remained in Washington, and now it had come to this. They wrote her, and sometimes they sent her money, but there was nothing she could do about seeing them. This place was all she could afford. There was nothing leftover for either travel or entertaining out-of-town guests. She was living off Social Security and the money she got from selling her house, a large place in suburban Oxon Hill. That was several years ago. Trying to conserve her resources for what she had hoped would be a long retirement, she had taken this place in the city.

"But it's gotten much worse since I moved here," she said. "The neighborhood has gone downhill so quickly. And there's no way I can get anything repaired here. The landlord won't come around to fix anything without charging me for it, and I just can't afford to spend any money."

"Isn't he required by your lease to provide routine maintenance?"

"No. I checked it thoroughly, too, you know. He has the right to charge extra fees for fixing things. I didn't suspect that when I signed, and of course you never read the whole document when it's that long. It was only afterward, when the flooring beside the bathtub cracked and sank, that I looked for that clause, but then I was stuck. I suppose he believes he can let everything go until I die, then repair the whole place at once for the next tenant. It's cheaper that way, and he can market a freshly renovated apartment."

Finnegan looked upward at a series of weblike cracks splaying across the ceiling. One ran to the far wall and, a finger tracing in the sand, slid down the wall to the floor. Dusty shards of plaster lay in spots on the ragged carpet.

Agnes turned in her chair looking away from Finnegan. She ran a jagged clawlike hand along the side of her face and stared at something the younger man had no way of seeing. Finnegan noticed Agnes's eyes shone a stinging blue. They had not aged nearly as much as the remainder of her spare form. The stark setting made them incongruous, two blades of bright light in dim shadows. What was it that she kept alive, burning there where no one could see?

"You now, young man—I'm sorry, I've forgotten your name. And so soon."

"It's Conor, ma'am."

"Yes, of course. Conor. Such a lovely poetic name, I think. You hear that name so seldom these days. Conor, you are the first person quite so young to speak to me pleasantly in weeks. It seems like years. I'm very grateful."

"Don't you go out at all, Agnes? You must know some neighbors, and they certainly have children."

"You've seen the neighborhood. A frightful place, it truly is. Sometimes I fear we're condemned, all of us, because we're so eager to relapse into the worst forms of barbarism. There must be some flaw in our blood that makes us so easily brutal." Agnes's scratchy voice broken but she kept in, speaking slowly and searching her wall as she cradled her face in her hand.

"My neighbors have children, yes, and I do know them. About a year or two ago—God, even longer than that, I fear—five young men who live near here . . . well, I was walking down the street. It was afternoon, late, and they came out of nowhere, these five. They stood around me, in broad daylight with people everywhere, they were so sure of themselves. They were so sure no one would stand up to them. They had me in the middle and pushed me back and forth to one another, calling me such foul names. I was sport to them. Every time I thought I'd fall they catch me and throw me to someone else. They didn't want to break me because that would end their game. Finally they grew bored with me and pitched me to the sidewalk like an old rag. I feared I broke my hip, it hurt so much to move, but it was only a bruise. Two days later I still hadn't gone out again, and one of them came to my door and forced his way in. He slapped me twice and demanded money."

Agnes wept silent tears. They fell down her cheeks, the silky trails streaking softly downward from her blue eyes. "I gave him what I had, and then he said he'd be back for more every week. As long as I paid him each week, I'd be safe. If I didn't, he and his friends would come by and resume their game."

"Protection money," whispered Finnegan.

"Yes. I'm sure I'm not the only one they've targeted."

"So, for more than a year you've been paying these thugs every week. How much, Agnes?"

"Usually $50 each week. Whatever I have at hand. They have no set amount."

"That's $200 a month. You've not gone to the police, I take it."

"Of course not. They told me they'd hurt me terribly if I went to the authorities. I'm certain they would. And they'd know, too, as soon as an officer came to my door or snooped around any of them. Besides, I don't really know who they are. They're just neighborhood boys."

"Agnes, you've got to do something. Why don't you let me go to the police for you?"

"No," she said firmly, and then softer, "No. The police would have a hard time catching them."

"Perhaps you could arrange to have an officer nearby when they come to collect."

"I never know when they're coming. Even if they were to be caught, I'd have to face them again eventually. They'd be back on the streets soon enough to do their damage. No, young man. Let it be. There's nothing I can do." And then the woman gave herself over to her sadness, and silently flowed copious tears, the convulsive, dangling paeans to a once-proud existence, now reduced to its lowest denominator. Finnegan fought back his own tears. He stayed with her the remainder of the afternoon and when at last he left, his depression overwhelmed him. It seeped like melting snow into every crevice. *Reductio ad absurdum. Reductio ad nauseum.*

Finnegan continued his investigations. Everywhere he found the plights of Moses and Agnes duplicated with their individual nuances. He found the elderly living in fear, in hunger, in filth, in poverty so pervasive it stifled all hope, in the hollow emptiness of existence for its own sake, of existence without substance and with minimal form. The more articulate among them he evaluated as witnesses. Theirs were the stories to be told. And while most had no interest in trudging up to Capitol Hill to expose hardships of which they were horribly embarrassed, Finnegan found a few who still maintained a combative spirit. Those few who still had the power to assert their dignity with pride and conviction came forward as potential witnesses.

One, an elderly gentleman named Arthur who lived alone within a mile of Finnegan's office, said, "Hell, I can't wait to get up there. It's too much for me to take to be pissed away like this, the bastards, after all I've lived. I should be a national treasure, God damn it. I'm plenty mad, boy, and I'll tell the whole world why. You don't mind me using bad language, do you?"

"Say whatever you like, Arthur. The senator should see some anger. It would do him no end of good."

"Well, then, I'll be angry. I can't help but be angry for being pissed away like this. I live in a rat hole."

At home in the evenings, with Dan Rosselli still at campus, Finnegan listened to his music and pondered his conclusions. What, after all, had these poor people done to merit their situations? Merely grow old, an inescapable process. But growing old had made them weak, depriving them of any social or economic leverage in a fluid, dynamic society. They had become prey, rabbits in an open field under the gaze of circling falcons. Not enough money, not enough friends, no place to go, with nothing to trade, they cannot resist the falcons.

Finnegan's conversations brought home to him the realization that society ran by buy-and-sell, with precious little room for simple compassion. We are, all of us, mere products in a grand marketplace. How easily, how conveniently, how devoid of conscience as we devour our own.

In time, Finnegan sat down with the senator to review his progress in putting all this together. He had prepared a complete two-day schedule and had begun to fill in the slots with specific names. He had typed a paragraph summary of each witness—name, address, circumstances, likely testimony. For those slots still open, he indicated the type of individual he would be looking to fill them. He had saved for last the witnesses from social agencies and government bureaus because they would be the easiest to secure. For now, he wanted to show his boss the slate of private citizens he was lining up who could forcefully state a case of which the senator was only dimly aware.

The senator perused Finnegan's synopsis while the younger man sat silently in a chair opposite the great hardwood desk. He looked pensive as he read: his brow furrowed and he poked the paper with dartlike eyes. His mouth contracted into a small round nut.

"What will you have for media coverage?" he asked, turning to Finnegan in his swivel chair without taking his eyes from his reading.

"I'm arranging it with Peter. I'd like to get the majors, certainly."

"What did Peter say?"

"Definite coverage by all California majors—L.A., San Francisco and San Diego prints and electronics. Possible on the networks, at least for a blurb on the evening news, provided we come up with something worthwhile, but it's too early to be sure. The *Post* and the *Times* will be there."

"Good. I'll want summaries from each of these witnesses well in advance, and a complete line of questioning for each. I won't tolerate any surprises up there. And when you talk to them, try to drag out the most lurid side of things. That stuff piques interest. Now, how about the other witnesses?"

"I'll be getting them in line this week. They'll be no problem."

"You might want to trim back two or three of these old folks. See what their testimony will be first, but I think we've got too many street people. We don't want to be repetitive. If we turn the media off the first day, they'll never come back the second. Just take the best."

"Senator, these are the best. I'll have a hard time cutting them back."

"See what you can do. You've got no one from HHS slotted here. Why not?"

"I saw no need. You said you wanted stories rather than facts and figures. Besides, aren't they the eventual target of all this? That's where any legislation will most likely be aimed."

"I'd still like someone on the slate. Creates a balance and helps keep the administration from getting too pissed. They can always deflect criticism by saying that they were part of the process."

"I'll get somebody, Senator. An undersecretary, probably."

"Conor, strike these two slots for association representatives you've got on the second day. We'll hear from two on the first day. That should be plenty. They tend to be a bit too academic anyway."

Finnegan had not found them so. In fact, he had enjoyed his contact with the lobbyists and he knew that they expected to be heard. Cutting their time in half would ruffle some feathers. "I'm not certain that's a good idea, if only for political reasons. These people carry some pretty good clout, and their associations are huge."

"I don't want these hearings to be repetitive in any way, Conor. Edit out two lobbyists. We can't be saying the same things over and over. We'll cripple our coverage if we do." The senator flipped the schedules onto his desk. "Other than those suggestions it looks fine so far. Keep Peter on top of the media and talk to me again at the end of the week. I'd advise you to fill up that schedule as soon as you can. We may need to do some rearranging yet. Keep me posted, Conor."

Finnegan did not rise at the obvious dismissal. He had come to this briefing prepared to raise a point. In the face of what he had uncovered during his investigations, he thought it important to do so, even at some risk.

"Senator, one more thing. You'll notice that I've got three slots marked 'Open' and I explain in my notes that I'd fill them with appropriate witnesses from groups not represented elsewhere."

"I presume those will be witnesses from community groups. Possibly a social worker or two."

"That's not exactly what I was considering. Senator, I'd like to bring in some witnesses from nursing homes."

"Out of the question."

"But Senator, that's a big portion of the poorly housed we're discussing here. And conditions I've seen there are nearly as bad as the majority of private housing. Worse, if you consider what they're paying to be abused like that."

"It's too damn risky, Conor. You start raising testimony like that and you create the impression that the entire industry is corrupt. Everyone focuses on the renegades. They create so much of a stink that even the good ones start to smell foul. There's no need to chance offending an industry that's probably 95% clean."

"Assuming you're correct, should we sweep the 5 percent under the rug for the sake of keeping things tidy? There are some definite problems with our long-term care facilities, Senator. If we look at housing for the elderly without mentioning those problems, then we're not doing our job."

"Our job, my friend, is to get re-elected so we can all keep these comfortable positions for another six years. On the scales of relative electoral importance, the elderly are damn near too light to be counted. I don't want to risk offending anyone we needn't offend, especially for such a low payoff.

"If we produce these hearings correctly," the senator continued, "they'll have a broad appeal beyond the elderly themselves. Old folks don't vote, Conor, but their families do. There's a ripple effect. And people tend to vote on the basis of emotion rather than logic, that's very clear."

"So these hearings are to create an image rather than address a substantive issue?"

"The issue is part of it. But don't ignore the fact that we can't address the issue on any level unless we generate some broad-based sympathy for it, and that's emotional."

"But we can't be thorough, we can't be truly substantive, if we ignore this part of it."

"If anything, this aspect would belong in separate hearings on health and health care, not housing. If we got into that it could be a package in and of itself. And all it would accomplish would be to get people angry, or scared. Who wants to throw grandpa down a sewer hole?"

"Senator, I think it's important that we—"

"I don't give a God damn what you think, Conor. Forget your little cause. We'll all be happier if you do. Get on with what you're supposed to be doing. Don't think. Don't try to strategize. Just do your job."

"Yes, sir. I'm sorry if I was out of line."

The senator smiled. "You were, but apology accepted. Let's get back to work, shall we?"

Finnegan left the office without feeling chastened at all. 'At least the man knows I can come up with a few ideas if I have to,' he thought. Nor did he discount the possibility of working on this issue surreptitiously by placing one or two witnesses on the docket who could address it under the guise of another topic. He would have to think that one through, but he was fairly confident he could pull it off if he wanted to. If he did it cleverly enough, the senator might not even notice the subtle shift in focus.

The young man had minimal respect for his boss's intellectual capabilities anyway. He had considered himself to be sharper, more versatile and better able to formulate original concepts. Even though the senator's educational pedigree was outstanding, Finnegan saw scant evidence that it had done any practical good. Finnegan, although not purely contemptuous, rarely took the senator's pronouncements seriously. The man seemed to be a compilation of impressions rather than ideas, shaped by q-factors and public relations. Too, Finnegan had noticed that the senator had virtually no hard and fast convictions of his own. He followed the better arguments, those usually constructed around expediency, rather than any innate belief or principle. That in itself made him vulnerable.

Finnegan returned to his desk and looked through the revised agenda. On one point at least, the senator was correct: it was time to get to work.

* * *

The conflicting currents and eddies that swirled through Glynnis Mear intensified by the day. Where once she viewed her reconstructed existence with a quiet, placating serenity, there now churned a maelstrom without direction, a centrifugal turbulence that pushed one way, then another and left her farther away from her nexus than ever before. She swam through the waves of doubt, of remorse, of stubborn resolve to keep herself intact.

When first her uncertainties appeared at some indistinct point several months ago, she had expected them to be settled of their own accord. All the while she assumed that the result would be clear, that she would indeed cast her fate with Conor Finnegan as soon as she came to her senses enough to realize her prize. She blamed herself for her hesitancy, felt guilty about it, and tried to suppress it. She forced herself to be patient and lived in secretive dread that her lover would tire of the distances she imposed as she waited for enlightenment.

Yet the process she had envisioned had not come about. Her hesitancy deepened. Conor, as she had foreseen, was indeed becoming more impatient. Each time he spoke of some form of commitment, even the most tentative and reversible, she grew defensive. Her character, the distinctive essence of Glynnis Mear, came to be more rigidly protected than ever she had predicted it would need. Sacrifices to time and convenience became less frequent. Conor expected her very soul, but it became more difficult for her to lend him even a piece of it. Conor's expectations, unspoken and so innocently preserved, she came to resent.

Perhaps, she considered, the doubts had been there all along, overwhelmed at the start by the pungent intoxication of her young man's devotion. Conor was, without question, the most compassionate, diversely intelligent and Romantic man she had ever known. That he, with his unique perceptions and brimming heart, should have pursued her with such ardor and, in so doing, developed a rich affection for what he had regarded as her unadorned simplicity, touched her deeply. It also obscured the perilous state of her singularity. Now that his attachment to her was intractable, she realized the potential cost. Had she not always realized it, but kept her fears tamed because Conor himself was an uncertainty? He was secured now; she had license to think of herself.

Her time with Conor became increasingly strained as, each weekend, she insisted upon a Saturday return to the world of Glynnis Mear. Conor's assumptions had been overturned. Unclear of the specific reasons despite Glynnis's halting efforts to articulate them, he reacted petulantly. Glynnis remained stubborn, and they enjoyed themselves in each other's company less and less. The unspoken tension that pervaded even their most tender moments weighed them down like a steel net. Each was reluctant to address it. Their discussions resolved nothing and only led to a festering resentment, and quiet heartache. The tension grew now as a single-celled creature, pulling apart and doubling its strength as the soft, cushioning plasma in which it swam incubated it.

Conor's hearings served to distract him. He threw himself into them headlong, and spent his evenings mulling over his problems there instead of evaluating the challenging nature of his lover. In light of the pressures put upon him in constructing this project, he expected his time with Glynnis to be more precious than ever. It was a compensation, a counterbalance to the week's less-subtle struggles. The project agitated him; it stayed with him as a viscous, clinging substance that could not be washed off.

Such were their states when Conor picked up Glynnis, once again at Union Station on an early Friday evening. Finnegan recounted the week's progress and problems as they drove to his apartment. Glynnis saw him to be animated, consumed with what he was doing. He had, as always, come directly from the office, and he could disengage himself from it only slowly. Glynnis sat quietly, saying little as Conor told his tales.

When they arrived at the apartment, Dan Rosselli, dressed in a sport coat and slacks that fit poorly on his still-expanding girth, was pulling on his overcoat. Rosselli had some destination in mind, although Finnegan never kept track of his friend's coming and goings. On the weekends when he didn't go back home to the Jersey shore, Rosselli made himself scarce in accommodation of his roommate's romance. He would either dine with some friends or spend the evenings studying at some neutral site. Sometimes he would go to a movie alone. Always he was solicitous of Finnegan's unspoken requests for privacy. When he came back from his wanderings, with Conor and Glynnis already in bed, Rosselli made no noise. The next morning, when the young lovers finally rose, he would often be gone again. Rosselli, who genuinely liked Glynnis, would have preferred to spend some time with the two of them, but he respected Conor's privacy too much to intrude. For this added consideration in an already deep friendship, Finnegan loved Rosselli all the more.

"Hey, you two," said Rosselli as Conor and Glynnis opened the door. Glynnis greeted him warmly and kissed his cheek.

"Danny boy, what's up? Where you off to?"

"A friend and I are going out to dinner and a film. I'm not sure where we're going or what we intend to see, but it's something to do."

"Do you have to run right now?" asked Glynnis. "I don't get to see you enough. Stay and talk for a while."

"Yeah, come on, Dan. Join us for a drink. I've barely seen you all week myself. All I see of you lately is a trail of discarded clothing leading to your bedroom."

"And my coffee cup in the sink."

"Are you working hard, Dan? Of course you are," said Glynnis. "That's a silly question."

"Not for Dan it's not. You never saw this guy operate in college. Danny's the only college student I've ever known who could keep a full primetime television schedule. Each night he'd be flopped down in our old chair, watching some garbage, eating popcorn and dressed in his underwear."

"Those were surgical greens," replied Rosselli. "And as I recall, we watched together most nights."

"Only documentaries and PBS." Finnegan had taken Glynnis's bag into the bedroom and hung up their coats. "What do you say, roomie? Stay for an aperitif?"

"If you don't mind."

Glynnis squealed a girlish "Good," and then said, "Come sit down next to me. Conor can play bartender." Rosselli did so and Glynnis slid her arm around his shoulders. "I'm so glad you're staying."

"What would you guys like?" yelled Conor from the kitchen.

"White wine, hon," said Glynnis, and Rosselli asked for scotch.

"So, sweetie, how've you been?" asked Glynnis. "Really now."

"Busy, Glynnis. But you know Conor's right. I never worked this hard as an undergrad, yet I don't mind it in the least. It's not like work at all. Sometimes I think I could spend all my time at the med school—sleep there, eat there, everything. That's maturity, I suppose."

"Forgive me, Dan, but that sounds almost gruesome. And lonely. No women in your life?"

"Only my cadaver, but she doesn't put out. Good listener, though. A little like Anne Newbury."

Glynnis laughed. "You should have gotten to know my friend

Lynda. She'd have been perfect for your underworked hormones. You two share a mutual interest in anatomy."

Conor returned and distributed the drinks. The mention of Lynda's name froze him; he clutched, perceived the context, then sat down wordlessly.

"She was friendly then, huh? Where is she now? Somewhere near D.C., I hope."

"No such luck, tiger. She's in upstate New York wasting away with some corporate insurance firm. She's horribly misplaced. Lynda's not the corporate type, wouldn't you agree, Conor?"

Finnegan swallowed some scotch. "I suppose it's her stab at respectability. Something we all have to face at some point, unless we're incredibly fortunate. We're all doing it. We're all facing The Big Chill."

"Still," Glynnis resumed, "Lynda never leaned toward practicality. She always indulged herself, physically and otherwise. She liked to seize the moment, as she put it. The girl had little regard for long-term consequences, and she never questioned anything she did. At least not to me."

"That's rather dangerous, isn't it?" said Finnegan. "Particularly when she's not acting alone, and that's most of the time. Her impulses might satisfy her for the moment, but if they involve other people then they might well have consequences, even if they're not hers."

"How do you mean?" asked Glynnis.

"We just don't act in a vacuum, that's all. Where other people share our actions, they share the results, good or bad. Whether we act out of rebellion or lust or charity or revenge, or just a love of pleasure, everything we do reflects off someone else. Whether you see it or not, Lynda's impulsiveness is dangerous. You just can't know who you're going to hurt."

"A rather grim view, roommate," said Rosselli.

"Conor, you're always so careful. Sometimes you even border on being stuffy. I think you could use some of Lynda's impulsiveness. Everything isn't laden with some deep meaning."

"But Glynnis, everything is. And I hardly think I'm 'stuffy,' God damn it."

"Face it, Mick. I've known you like a brother for almost six years. You're too straight, and you're far too serious. Not everything is a life-and-death matter. I confess I'd prefer Lynda's approach. She sounds like she has more fun."

"I have fun enough, Dan. But I never want to lose sight of what I'm about. I can't see myself without a purpose that's right in front of me all the time. I can't imagine living my life with no set plan."

"Plans should be flexible, my love. And you can always put your purpose on hold for a time. It's important not to take yourself too seriously."

"I do believe I've heard that before," sighed Finnegan.

"It's true," insisted Glynnis. "I think you'd benefit no end from a little mindless hedonism. Your ethics are too confining. They restrain you, babe. They make you see everything you do as part of some great, grand process. It's not that way at all."

"But by definition, every act has to be part of a process. Nothing stands alone."

"Oh, Conor, not everything. You have to relax sometimes. You have to let yourself cool, if only to regain strength."

"No, Glyn. It's all related, everything we do. Our ethics define us completely. Every act, every thought, without exception. The more fundamental among us would refer to that as morality, but I tend to steer clear of that word. Call it whatever you think fits—ethics, morality, standards, conscience—but whatever it is, it defines us. There's no possible way to step around it. It's in everything we do."

"You leave no room for flexibility," said Rosselli.

"Hey, come on. My ethics allow flexibility. They allow me to relax that seriousness you make fun of, even though you think I never do. They permit me to follow the impulse of the moment. But what they don't allow me to do is throw away, even for a second, the basis of what I believe, and where I think I fit in all this. You absolutely have to keep your principles intact if they're to have any meaning at all. Not that you have to be mindful of working for world peace, say, or feeding starving children every time you go to a movie or spend a day at the beach. But your basic ideals you carry with you. In one form or another they're part of each action you take. They construct your very identity."

"So it's a matter of degree then," said Rosselli, "of how many layers you're willing to strip away from the core."

"You could look at it that way. Superficial actions are essentially meaningless. We complete them without a second thought. Going to the supermarket, for example. But if we're going to the store and we see a car hit a child, then try to speed away, we're faced with a serious test. Do we ignore it, or do we speed after the driver to get a license number, even at the risk of our own safety? How we respond is based on what we believe, on who we are. That stays with us always."

"Alas," said Rosselli, "I cannot. I have to be getting along."

"Oh Dan," cried Glynnis, grabbing his elbow, "you haven't even finished your drink!"

"No time, love. I have to meet my friend."

"Couldn't you call him and tell him you'll be late? Better yet, call him and cancel. Stay and have dinner with us." Glynnis's voice became a plaintive, silky whirr. Finnegan said nothing, miffed that his philosophical eloquence had been brushed aside.

"I couldn't, Glynnis. You two want to be alone."

"But I never see you, Dan. Stay with us. Please. Conor, you don't mind. There's plenty of food, isn't there? Tell him to stay."

"The lady wants you to stay, Danny boy. But of course it's up to you." Finnegan assumed Rosselli could read his tone.

Glynnis now had both hands wrapped around Rosselli's arm, and she looked up at him with pleading eyes. Finnegan caught the scent of lilacs. He knew his friend could smell it, too. Glynnis had made herself thoroughly appealing.

"Really, Glynnis," said Rosselli, his conviction now apparently fading. "I shouldn't intrude on you two."

"Nonsense. You live here, too. I think it's unfair for you to be turned out every time I come down. You're staying for dinner, Dan. I won't have it any other way. Are we agreed?"

Rosselli smiled sheepishly, caught between impulse and duty, their philosophical discussion come to life. "Well, if you two really don't mind. I can call Carl and tell him something came up."

Finnegan's house of cards caved in and became a random deck, disheveled, on the table.

"Oh Dan, I'm so glad," Glynnis bounced on the couch in her excitement.

'At what?' thought Finnegan. 'At Dan staying, or at yet another victory?'

"This will be wonderful. We can talk the whole night. Conor, get me another drink, won't you, love?"

Finnegan rose without a word and tried to engineer a pleasant expression. He took his time in the kitchen and, after rejoining Glynnis and Dan, said little. He continued that way throughout dinner. Resentment seethed through him like a fire. He had planned on steaks, wine and candlelight, now adaptable for three. Rosselli, increasingly aware of Finnegan's ill humor, avoided his friend's gaze as much as he could. Despite the veil of tension, Rosselli found himself entertained and enchanted by Glynnis, who spent most of her energy on her lover's friend.

After dinner they returned to the living room. Finnegan broke away to clear the dishes, then decided to wash them as well while Glynnis and Dan talked together. At an early hour, shortly after 11:00, Dan Rosselli stretched, yawned and, aware fully of Finnegan's resentment which lent an awkward air to the entire situation, went to bed. Conor and Glynnis bade him good night, alone at last several hours after Finnegan had anticipated.

He began immediately. "Why did you insist he stay?" he hissed between lips barely moving.

Glynnis's calm smile and tender gaze disappeared at once. She had found the evening delightful. She had, of course, sensed Conor's attitude, but she had not calculated the depth of his mood. It was one of the few times her normally impeccable instincts came up short. "What do you mean?" she asked through the ominous thunder of an approaching argument.

"Come off it, Glyn. You know damn well why I should be upset. Why the hell didn't you leave well enough alone? We could have had at least one evening to ourselves. Instead you chose to spend our normal pitiful allotment on my roommate."

"And it was time well spent, Conor. I enjoyed myself completely."

"Well, then, perhaps we should include Dan in all our plans. We can become a happy threesome, like Tom, Huck and Becky Thatcher. Shall we ask him to join us now, too? I could sleep at the foot of the bed and you two could chatter the night away."

"Conor, I hate you when you're like this. It's ugly. I consider Dan my friend, too. I rarely see him. Every time I come down he runs off somewhere because he's so certain we want to be alone. I feel guilty chasing him out of his own home. He's a friend, can't you understand that? I enjoy spending time with him. There's no rule between us that says every moment together has to be alone."

"It seems as if there are no rules between us at all anymore."

"Stop pitying yourself."

"It's true, Glynnis. We spend so little time together as it is. I want the time we do have to be just us. I swear I still don't understand how we got this way."

"I've told you time and time again, Conor. You just don't want to hear it. I know you resent the fact that I have a life of my own away from you. You expect me to focus my entire existence on what you want."

"I don't want to get into this again. But you know I love you and want you with me. I presume the feeling is mutual. You say it is, although I'm beginning to wonder. It makes sense to be together, not to pencil each other in as a one-day diversion."

"No, Conor, you want me to be a permanent diversion. You have a place for me, fit to your specifications, and you expect me to fill it. You want me to be one piece in your grand Romantic mosaic: the fawning damsel."

"You exaggerate, Glynnis. I've never given you cause to think that."

"The hell you haven't. It's in everything you do and say. It's one of those principles you argued were always with us, and that's always with you. You live by your ideals, Conor, and you've got an idealized view of me, too. You picture your entire life as an allegory. Everybody has a role, and up until now I've been just what I should be."

"So you're keeping me off-balance to make me more appreciative of you, is that it? I hate playing games like this."

"God, I could scream when you say things like that," and she turned away from him violently, only to turn back a second later. "Not everything revolves around your thoughts and feelings, you egocentric bastard. I'm not trying to make you more appreciative of me. I'm trying to figure out where I belong. And it's no game. I just don't feel like making myself into a stereotype just yet, and I won't be hitched to your orbit while you go about saving the world."

"Glynnis, you know damn well you'd never be just a satellite. Haven't I made it clear that you're at the center? You don't want to see that, it seems."

"Prove it, then. If I mean that much to you, if you truly want to be with me and if I'm the central purpose of your life, I want you to prove it."

"How can I do that beyond what I've already done?"

"Give up your job and move to Philadelphia. You can move in with me there, and we'll be together as you want."

"And surrender everything I'm building for myself here? That's crazy, Glynnis, not to mention unfair, and you know it. I have a career here that's just beginning to . . . "

"Then it's not too late to change things. You're not set yet."

"It's what I want to do with my life, damn it. I'm not going to drop it because you want to put me to some arbitrary test. I have more at stake here than you do where you are."

"Conor, you can't see what's at stake. You've proven nothing to me. You're only making matters more difficult."

"By not forfeiting my career!? Jesus Christ, Glynnis, it should be obvious that there's room in both our lives for any career we want and for each other at the same time."

"I'm not convinced, Conor. You expect me to fall into line with your other expectations. I won't do that, especially if I have to surrender what I've created for myself."

"And what the hell is that, Glynnis? You've created nothing yet. You're wasting your time up there."

"You arrogant bastard. You fucking arrogant bastard. You refuse to see anything except through your own narrow little prism. Any colors you don't recognize don't really exist, do they? I'm perfectly content doing what I'm doing. I'm as content as I've ever hoped to be."

"But what you're doing is so much more flexible than what I'm at. I have to be in Washington, there's no other place for it. There are graduate schools here, too, you know. You could come down and sacrifice nothing."

"You have no idea what I'd sacrifice. You can't see it, and no matter how hard I try to explain it, you don't want to understand. You always have an answer for everything. Christ, Conor, when did you become so demanding?"

"I've never changed, Glynnis. I can't say the same for you. You've grown more stubborn, if nothing else."

"And more rebellious. You can't deal with that. It's so unplanned, and it doesn't fit."

"You don't know what the hell you're talking about."

"I know only too well. Sharing our time with Dan didn't fit, either, so you're angry. He invaded what you had structured for yourself. You blame me because I asserted my friendship with him at the wrong time. Blame yourself, Conor. Blame yourself for being too inflexible. Sometimes you don't even let me breathe."

Conor sat quietly, then sighed with resignation. "Glynnis, we've too little time together to be spending it this way. Let's go to bed. For now we just have to be satisfied with not understanding each other the way we'd like. The way we should. We can't doubt our affection, though, can we?"

Glynnis rose from the couch without responding. She walked into Finnegan's bedroom and shut the door behind her. Finnegan followed, where he found Glynnis already undressing, not in the slow, languid movements of one preparing to receive her lover, but in the businesslike manner of a woman shivering on a cold winter night. She looked at Finnegan as he entered. Her eyes held his gaze flatly, her mouth sat without expression, a locked clamp frozen shut.

He approached her and tried to encircle her waist to draw her to him. The muscles in Glynnis's back did not yield. Her whole frame tensed against him and still her eyes showed no sign of softening.

"Let's not argue, Glynnis," Conor said. He had had enough of all of it.

"I agree. Let's not argue. It does no good." Her voice carried none of her usual lilt. She spoke as if reading a newspaper article on some bank merger or the visit of a foreign head of state. "I want to go to bed, and I want to sleep. I'm tired from all this."

Finnegan moved to kiss her to hasten this overly tardy thaw. She turned her head, and his lips found only the gentle grace of her cheek.

"No, Conor. We destroyed tonight altogether. We shattered it. I want to sleep."

Finnegan looked at her still hard face and saw she meant it. Anything he might do now would only seem desperate, which of course it would have been. He had been thoroughly robbed tonight. Not a shred of his expectations remained. The anger that had ebbed in resignation returned, stung into resurrection by the evaporation of the evening.

"God damn it to hell," he said with a bite, and spun away. He, too, began to undress with quick, short, asexual motions. Cold air pulsed against his naked chest and raised bumps on his arms like emery paper. He threw his shirt into the corner, then stomped into the bathroom. When he returned, Glynnis lay on her side under the covers. She faced the wall. Her long hair followed the contours of her shoulder and ribs. Finnegan climbed into bed beside her. Neither spoke. He accentuated his gestures, jostling the bed with the weight behind his sharp movements. He hoped to disturb her into some reaction. That was the only communication he allowed himself; words would be too destructive.

In a peculiarity of mood, a curious amalgam of anger, resentment, fear and remorse, Conor Finnegan abandoned a lost day that he knew prefaced only another of the same sort. There was no hope of redemption.

CHAPTER XXII

—Sophocles, *Antigone*

Divorced from Anne Newbury's unspoken intractable yoke, Tom McIlweath reinfused his existence with an enthusiasm his memory could scarcely recall. All predetermined constraints had been stripped away at once. The resulting freedom blew through him like a Chinook wind crossing the Canadian plains. It rose with a chilling persistence and swept forward with nothing to block its path, blowing in new air from a distant, unknown territory. The young man began to sculpt the contours of his maturity with a meticulous delicacy.

McIlweath resumed his studies with a fresh intensity. He rediscovered the stability of the ancient writers, their precocious grasp of mankind's most essential truths, the mystical lyricism of Greek and Latin. He read without heed of time, of place, of external demands. During the week his mornings dissolved under the fixed brown pages, his afternoon vanished through the musty texts. The critical papers he had postponed he now pursued with a dogged tenacity that showed itself in refined insights that excited him no end. The poems and sagas of a dead age sang to him again; he understood them with flashes of sophisticated brilliance, and expounded upon them in crisp scholarly prose.

For companionship he sought out Joel Pleasance and Kieran Mulrooney. They shared lunches and an occasional dinner. Joel's cavalier attitude and the Australian's simple quest to experience everything he could of a new society fascinated and pleased him. He knew, of course, that he could not hope to replicate the closeness he had shared with his undergraduate roommates, but the two young men answered an old need he had too long abandoned. He took tremendous comfort in knowing that, of all the swarming, faceless multitudes in this magnificent city, at least these two would welcome him warmly. They expected nothing of him but the promulgation of his wit and the presumption of his affections.

Kathy Keane, too, reinvigorated him. McIlweath placed no demands upon her time. She had been serendipitous, and he did not want to risk abusing her by prevailing upon her independence as he went about reestablishing his own. They got together each weekend, usually at Kathy's instigation. They explored the city as if it were an unclaimed province, and in so doing they explored each other. The two went to the theater when they could afford it, they walked through the Common and sought out the historical places, they browsed the shops on Newbury Street. McIlweath tried to see the early settlers lurking in the shadowy forms behind the buildings. He identified not with the blue-blooded Brahmins or the Italian or Irish workingmen, but with the distant images of the Puritans who had fled to this strange and untapped place to find something different, something they could create for themselves.

When they returned from their explorations they talked over coffee or wine, and nibbled on whatever food they could find. They talked almost ceaselessly. McIlweath told her in detail of the disjointed journey from coast to coast, of severing himself from the stark isolation of the empty years. Kathy spoke freely of the men she had known, her passionate love of the written word and her disdain for pretense. Implicit in everything she told him was her spirit of independence, of distinctive pride in the ferocious protection of her own inviolable identity. She took nothing for granted. Kathy's remarkable sureness bolstered McIlweath and reaffirmed his long-floundering confidence.

For those most fortunate, chaos resolves itself into enlightenment. McIlweath knew that the contentment he enjoyed now was only temporary. His life in Boston was artificial, no more than a stopover on the way to something else. That he had reconciled himself to it through the happy circumstances of the past several months did not change that fact. The personalities themselves were transient, the satisfactions they brought with them accentuated by the profound depression he had experienced before. He had broken out of that depression by sheer luck, and he knew it. He had created nothing for himself. That remained to be done, and so he recognized that his current state could not last. These people and the attitudes they fostered would move on. He vowed not to let himself be seduced once again by a flimsy and contrived sense of belonging.

Then, too, there was Anne Newbury. He had told her he would call her after a time, and she had feigned indifference. "I have no time to indulge in your Romanticism," she had said. "My life will go on as it is. There may not be room for you to re-enter." And, as the days passed and the turbulence she had engendered within him came to subside, McIlweath became more firmly convinced that he had no desire to re-enter her life, and certainly not as before.

Yet, paradoxically, a rumbling of affection had also returned during their separation. His puzzlement at the lack of warmth for her at the leavetaking had been replaced by the nostalgia he had first expected. Anne had shared a large portion of his recent life, the most significant portion to date, and the richest. She was part of his landscape, even as she receded into the background of it. Their relationship would necessarily have to be restructured if it were to continue in any form at all. He could no longer be pulled along as her shadow. McIlweath did not believe for a second that Anne would consent to a relationship on his terms rather than hers, but he nonetheless came to hope that something might be salvaged. His time with Kathy eradicated his insecurities; he no longer would tolerate Anne's distant, unyielding self-absorption. And he knew that it would be impossible to resurrect any romantic involvement, even if Anne should wish to do so, a fairly remote possibility in itself.

But he might treasure her friendship, one forged on an equal footing, one mutually supportive, altruistic and charitable, based on years of shared experience and the occasional good time. It would be a rare thing, a friendship such as that. He did not know if he were capable of it, and he doubted Anne would retain much in the way of friendly sentiments. There would be a thousand implications to overcome. The old emotional formulas would have to be redrawn, and their proprietary claims on one another would have to be shelved. It would be difficult, to be sure, but McIlweath was intrigued by the possibility. They had been through so much together, it would be a shame to lose it all.

He knew, in any event, that he would eventually have to see her again. The prospect cast a sinister shadow in the background; he drew the curtains to keep it away. McIlweath felt too revived to want to disturb his renascent spirit just yet. Anne would have to be addressed, of that he was certain. His rigid sense of honor made it unavoidable. But he was in no special hurry.

At the moment he set himself to the task of determining his next move. McIlweath knew enough that his present intoxication would not last. As pleasant as it was, if he did not use it to some positive, less transitory end, it would have been a waste of time. In fact, it could prove to be a burden if he were to lapse once again into a lingering melancholy. The present, he knew, always suffered by contrast. So in reality McIlweath acknowledged that he had not achieved anything of substance. That was still to be done. He had been given another chance, though. What he had now was a salve for a badly beaten ego and its derivative self-confidence. Comforting, yes, but the remainder of his task lay ahead of him.

* * *

Glynnis Mear reached for the glass of wine as it was offered. She had already had several and their effect worked through every part of her slender frame. Her back and arms unloosed themselves entirely. She marveled at how tight she had really been. For so long, endlessly it seemed now, she had been wound into a hard steel coil. It felt so good now to let the wine take over. It felt so good not to be tensed. Glass in hand, she eased herself back onto the sofa.

"I have a theory about your lover," Michael said as he resumed his place beside her. Glynnis had been speaking of Conor Finnegan, a subject she rarely broached in Michael's increasingly frequent presence. She had explained Conor's work in Washington, alluding only in the most general way to the pressure of his expectations, and then focusing that pressure more on him than on her.

Glynnis did not know why she had turned their talk to Conor. Perhaps it was the wine. He was always on her mind of late, as much as ever. Where previously those thoughts had been loving and filled with great longing, he now obsessed her as the most challenging dilemma she had yet to face in her young life, a challenge as great as her father's death, and just as sorrowful. She had thought it had to be the wine that made her mention Conor at all. She was relaxed; the subject usually inhibited by her companion broke free and ran assertively between them, a small puppy in a new house sniffing out all the corners. Glynnis had not spoken of her frustration and disillusion even though, as in almost all their conversations, she had done most of the talking.

"What," purred Glynnis, a vixen's smile spreading across her elegant face, "is your theory, Michael? Tell me. But this isn't at all like you, you know, forming ideas about people you've never met. And I've really told you so little."

"You've said enough for me to believe I might understand him. I've watched you, too. Sometimes I can read people quite well, when I have the motivation to do so. I can read him through you. It's like judging the angle of the sun by the way it refracts off the surface of a lake."

"You think you're so clever. What do you believe, then, about this man Conor Finnegan?"

"I believe he is living in the wrong age. Today we cannot tolerate him as he, although he does not know that quite yet. Unfortunately, sooner or later it will be made clear to him. His is a Romantic soul, Glynnis. There's no room for that now as he applies it to this complex, very un-Romantic age. He would have been much happier if he had been born two centuries earlier."

Glynnis narrowed her eyes in rapt attention. "Go on," she said.

"His problem, I think, is that he is trying to adapt that nineteenth-century Romantic idealism into modern forms. The two cannot be joined. We are not a Romantic society, not anymore if ever we were. Concepts of justice have become utilitarian, and the entire notion of perfectibility has been overshadowed completely by pragmatism. We seek only what works for us, and us alone. We've become too complex, too fragmented to worry about the cosmic questions with which your man concerns himself. When we divert our sight from the minutiae of making our lives comfortable, we're immediately overwhelmed. We're knocked back two or three steps, and we reel and stagger until we can collect ourselves again. We're too big now, too fast, and too determined, and the course of what we have set in motion has created a centrifugal force that no modern man can escape. Redirecting it is absolutely beyond our powers."

"You take a rather fatalistic view, especially for an artist."

"Like the society in which I was raised, my own idealism has been censored by a strong need to survive as well as I can. Notions of service and justice are well and good, but I fear your lover takes them far too seriously. And, no doubt, he takes himself too seriously as well. The impersonality of what we are now demands that our first service is necessarily to ourselves. Your man has lost sight of that simple truth. I daresay he puts too much weight on his own individuality: he believes he can meet whatever personal responsibilities he assumes while entertaining those inflated notions. I contend that he cannot. He can't assume the forms of this society while his temperament thrusts him so far outside it. There's a tension there that he will never be able to overcome."

"He's managed to be quite successful to this point," said Glynnis. She sat on every word. Michael's opinions, so rarely voiced, fascinated her in any case, carried to her ears by his sensual Spanish tongue. That he should attempt to analyze her lover's very nature was a strange, wondrous thing.

"Has he really been successful? His life until now has been a process of positioning. We're given so much latitude when we are young. We're allowed, then and only then, to be impractical, to be dreamers. And when we are, the common view is that we'll grow out of it, we'll grow up and become responsible, that dreams and ideals are for children. He has some natural talents, that's apparent. He would not be where he is now if that were not the case. You have told me that he's intelligent and strong and clever. And he's been given those talents in enough measure to set him apart from his peers. That's the root of his success, but it's also his curse."

He continued, "He's not done anything serious yet. He's gone to school, he's played his sports, he's made his friends and won his lover, and he's done exceedingly well at all of it. It's easy to build such high ideals, and such high expectations, when you're playing for such low stakes. But now the ante has been raised. In a practical society he has a practical role to fill. There's little room for frivolous notions. Society will accelerate its expectations of him—to hold a job, to perform the demands of that position, whatever it is, to obey its laws, to pay his bills, and so on—but those expectations are not his. He becomes a round peg in a square hole. He is now expected to survive, pure and simple, and there's no opportunity for anything beyond that. And if he is to survive well, then he has to play by the established rules. He cannot change them. The momentum is just too great."

"Must he seek change?" asked Glynnis. "Isn't it enough to live one's life according to principle, and make the best of what's at hand?"

"That's the best we can do, I fear. But, really, there's no interest in our principles. Our latitude disappears as we become more complex. The motivations behind what we do don't matter as long as we're meeting our responsibilities, and staying in line. If we fail in that relatively simple task, we're targeted. We're to be corrected. I believe your man sees things in reverse. Instead of acknowledging what society expects from him, he has his own expectations of the social order. He expects it to shape to his calling. There are harsh lessons he has yet to learn."

"When I first met him," said Glynnis sadly, "I told him that his heart was bound to be broken. There was something about him, Michael. A quality of trust. And expectation. He trusted the world to be a good place, and that all he had to do was point to the right things, and all would be well. As if he believed his marvelous good fortune would be endless, as if he really saw himself as somehow favored. Oh, Michael, he demands so much from everything he does. He demands purity. And because he believes so firmly in what he does, he expects nothing to stand in his way, or to question what he's about. It's just so hard to be near that naiveté, that constant certainty."

"He'll lose it in due course, Glynnis. You're right. He'll be terribly hurt. That will be the cost of his realization, although over time it will all be for the better. He's put himself in an impossible position. The great Romantics have condemned the social order, and in one way or another, estranged themselves from it. Byron, Whitman, Thoreau. Even Wordsworth, with his innocuous ramblings. Yet your man is deeply linked with it. He tries to draw satisfaction from it, he tries to play by its rules even as he seeks to alter its very focus. With the ideals you say he's embraced, he should be a renegade or a recluse. Maybe an artist. He should be living in a cabin in the Maritimes or a hut in the Pyrenees rather than an apartment in the heart of one of the world's most complex cities. He's a contradiction, Glynnis. He's lost sight of his own limitations. It's only inevitable that his contradictions will be resolved for him."

"And then," said Glynnis, "he'll have to reconstruct himself all over again."

"The cost of unrealistic principles in a rigidly pragmatic society. Most of us have more conservative expectations. We take whatever comes our way, and we're grateful for it. All our best efforts only push the walls back for a little more room."

"Poor Conor." She wished at that moment with all the power of her soul that she could go back to when they first met. She had been dazzled by him, stunned by his brilliant luminescence. Why, dear God, are we condemned to lose our innocence? Why can we not go forth forever in wide-eyed wonder at Your most precious gifts?

"We clutter ourselves so badly, don't we, Michael? It would be so much better if we could just know enough to take our pleasures where we find them and be content with that."

"It should be enough to create our own peace. All serenity, all order is internal. Our error comes in presuming order outside the self, where there is no order. And it's compounded when we expect to find our personal order, one we construct within ourselves, assumed by others. It is a dangerous illusion to believe that that order, which does not exist, is proper and correct. We can do so little for only a few. There is nothing beyond that but hubris."

"You make us sound so hopeless. And I'm sorry to say that I agree with you. But God, how I hate it. Think of how it robs us, Michael. How pitiful we are, and how utterly alone."

"Only if you fail to see that our limitations are quite natural, a function of the species. We need not be alone. We need only view our pleasures and our pains personally. There's no broad meaning to what we suffer and what we enjoy. Should we look for it, we only frustrate ourselves. There is no order, no meaning, no potential for anything beyond the immediate."

"Oh, Michael, you depress me. Sometimes I think I prefer Conor's naïveté."

"Which crushes you. No, Glynnis, I don't think you do. He may be charming, and I'm certain he is. He may be infectious, and charismatic, and inspiring, and all those vague qualities that compel us to come close. But he's a puppy, wide-eyed and panting, chasing his tail around and around, not knowing enough to see that he's really pursuing nothing at all besides a useless extension of himself. He's fortunate not to have been beaten or kicked by those passing by. He's fortunate no one's noticed him enough so far to care to hurt him."

"I wish you could meet him."

"I prefer to know him only through his lady. Do you mind speaking of Conor while you are away from him? If so, I apologize. I have perhaps said too much."

"It is rather unfair, but I confess I don't mind. He fascinates me. I've never met anyone even remotely like him."

"But he weighs you down. Forgive me, but that's so very apparent."

Glynnis sighed. "Yes. I can't keep pace with his . . . ideals. I almost said 'illusions.' They're one and the same, though, aren't they? Whatever we call them, they drag me along. I've lost perception of anything but through Conor. But we're traveling down two different pathways now, and it's ripping me apart. The sweet force of his personality is so strong that he seduces me over and over again. I go willingly when I'm with him. I let myself be taken."

"It's a law of nature that the deadliest poison smells the sweetest. Look to yourself first, Glynnis. That's all any of us can do. That's the only expectation we are required to answer."

"*Paradise Lost.*"

"What do you mean?"

"Cast out by the failings of our own soul, and never to be fully regained. We're a fated, sullied species, Michael."

"We are, sweet lady. But in the midst of despair we may yet find some beauty. You are here with me tonight, and we are alone. There is no Conor. There is no tomorrow. There is only Michael and Glynnis."

"You're a bit of a rogue to take advantage of a woman so perplexed," Glynnis teased. But her sadness sunk into her like a toxic vapor. It grew inside her. Her limbs thickened, her breathing deepened as a depressive miasma wafted in and around the small room. There was no avoiding it.

Glynnis knew what would follow. There was no avoiding that, either. From the first realization of Michael Halcón, it had been as inevitable as the seasons, as incontrovertible as the laws of gravity. She could not change it, neither by her strength of character nor by dint of her own expectations. She did not want to change it. No pleasure was involved; it was an act devoid of excitement. But it was necessary, that much she could see.

As the lights flickered off and the only illumination sifted through the windows from the outside streetlamps, Glynnis recalled the cold, shocking, fetid waters of the Raritan. She resurrected the tingle along her back and legs, the rush of cool air against her naked breasts. The rustling of her clothes as they dropped to the floor echoed the same sound, this time upon a softer ground.

* * *

The seed of despair sends forth deep roots; the cracked vessels pour out their waters and feed them. The waters seep through the indifferent dust, find the hungry tubers and are drawn up. It is as timeless as Man himself and as powerful as God. It grows strong, it grows strong, and ever it seeks the tender flesh. In the tendrils are carried the sharpest blades, the finest hooks; the flesh cannot resist, and it is torn asunder, carrion for the crows.

And in the vapid, desolate silence left behind, we can hear the eternal ringing of the exquisite agony that constitutes our humanity.

CHAPTER XXIII

Always do that, wild ducks do. Go plunging right to the bottom . . . as deep as they can get . . . hold on with their beaks to the weeds and stuff—and all the other mess you find down there. Then they never come up again.

—Henrik Ibsen, *The Wild Duck*

What now? What shall I do now? The question was as old as time, as immutable as the cruel snows of winter. In a finite world, old formulas cease to function, old certainties disappear. The currents that flooded through Tom McIlweath and swept him along in mysterious directions had lost their force, changed their bearings, and left him blinking into the sun on dry land, the tampy residue of surging swells clinging to his skin and hair like a mucus. He stood there where he landed, wondrous now at the absence of compulsion and resoundingly strong because he felt nothing pushing against him. He was amazed that he could no longer perceive any pressure.

It was the same sensation as when he stepped out of the pool after a particularly hard workout. The last few laps always seemed interminable, the water turning to molasses. He clawed and pulled and flailed, losing form and rhythm in a manic obsession to make his muscles respond, to finish it all now that he was so close. And when at last he touched the wall and let himself fall backward to float for a few seconds, gazing at the ceiling of the natatorium, the water regained its buoyancy. He would pull his aching body out of the pool and stand at its edge, his muscles throbbing. What a marvelous release he felt then, a serene elation that he had indeed come through the hostile water and conquered it. His spirit would fall into a counterbalance against the desperation of a few moments before. The absence of pressure, his muscles poised by rote to meet what would no longer be coming against him. He felt that now.

Yet McIlweath also knew it to be temporary. The currents would return, perhaps subtly at first, lapping at his ankles and running between his toes, but then stronger. He would welcome them because he believed at last that he was strong enough to ride them in the directions he chose, and not be swept along like seaweed. He could master them now, these currents. He could navigate the powerful ebbs and flows to position himself for whatever advantage they allowed. The horrible, smothering days in which he clawed for the breath of approval he had put behind him. They had been necessary, but now they were gone.

But the question haunted his peace: What shall I do now? Where shall I go? For Tom McIlweath acknowledged that he could not remain in Boston. His relationship with this place had been artificial, and there was less to validate it now. Had it not been for Anne Newbury, he would not be here. She colored the classrooms, the sweeping old college yard and the musty corners of the library. The fine dust of her image settled over his apartment. It rose from the harbor and floated over the narrow downtown streets; it perched atop Faneuil Hall and strolled along the Fens. He could not escape it, nor did he particularly wish to try. She had defined Boston for him, defined his life in this great city. In the absence of that definition it seemed be pointless to stay. This university, this city could be a glorious backdrop, but not for him.

Against the confusing ramble of his younger years McIlweath had sought a sanctuary. He has sought acceptance, stability, a sense of belonging. That was such a simple thing, wasn't it? To be in tune with those around him, to be in harmony. The idylls of his undergraduate years told him that it could be found, at least in glimpses. But where to find it now, and how to make it last? Where shall I go now? What shall I do?

Seeking a point of ballast, he thought of Conor. McIlweath imagined his friend now as he had always been: active, a participant rather than a reactant, casually accepting of his blessings and committed to putting them into motion. And always there was that air of excitement about him. He drew from what he did, it invigorated him and stifled the dark, brooding humors that must somewhere exist within him. McIlweath envied Finnegan now, just as he had since they first met. Of all the people he had ever known, Finnegan best embodied that esoteric harmony McIlweath wished to create for himself. That he had been won over by Finnegan's genuine affection had not decreased his envy. McIlweath, in watching his friend through the years, took comfort in knowing that what he so avidly sought was indeed attainable.

It was odd, thought McIlweath, how such opposites should be so strongly attracted. Their friendship had been an unexpected benefit of his undergraduate years. He recalled how he had blanched when he heard that Finnegan, of all people, would be going to the same college he had so carefully selected to be his refuge from an identity, a persona, that he wished to bury. It had been a non-identity, really, and he had feared that Finnegan would play to that, that he would carry it with him to distribute among the potential friends McIlweath so desperately needed at the time. He had feared that, after finally dropping the soiled and tattered cloak from his shoulders, Finnegan would pick it up and return it to him with the best of intentions but with the worst of results.

How foolish those fears had been. They had formed the closest friendship of McIlweath's life, a bond of shared emotions and shared reactions to a shared process. Finnegan's basic decency, his honest compassion and his great good nature had blasted apart McIlweath's apprehensions. In the panoramic love affair Finnegan had with the world at large, there was room for a struggling, shy young man lacking all self-confidence. McIlweath had found a degree of the acceptance he had sought in a place he had never thought to seek it. Finnegan's boundless optimism, his unwavering belief in his own quality, his appreciation of the gamut of human experience and his intense, joyous demeanor had won McIlweath over completely. Finnegan had been counselor, confessor, agitator, entertainer, provocateur. McIlweath assumed he had reciprocated in kind. They grew together naturally, and the singular result had been unlike anything else McIlweath had come across. Now, as he deliberated a next step, he wished that his friend were with him.

What shall I do now? McIlweath could not say; the point had been lost. He vowed not to repeat his mistake. This time his choice would be his alone, and made for legitimate reasons. He wrote letters endlessly and completed applications for scholarships and awards. He scoured scholarly journals and periodicals for notes of either professional opportunities or chances for further study in places better suited. He met with faculty to discuss government fellowships or research grants. At the root of it all he sought to maximize his options. Something would come along that would clearly be right. He could not say what it would be, but he would know it when it came. McIlweath thought of teaching, he thought of pursuing a doctorate, he thought of private employment, and he made corresponding applications in all directions. Something would come, of that he was certain.

What shall I do now? He would go away somewhere. He would leave this place for something new, something his own, something in tune with a nature he was just beginning to understand. He looked around himself and perceived only a brief respite in a general desolation. There was nothing for him here. Nothing at all.

* * *

Had Conor Finnegan had the time to reflect on his friendship with Tom McIlweath, he might well have come to the same conclusions about its evolution. Even though he still could spend time with Dan Rosselli, Finnegan missed the peculiar empathies that he shared with McIlweath and no one else, not even Glynnis. McIlweath had been the closest of the close. Rosselli, wrapped up in his studies and, to Finnegan's thinking, lacking the capacity for self-evaluation, did not have it in him to answer Finnegan's more introspective persona. The two shared good times; when they were forced to deal with the bad, they did so alone. As such, their friendship had become more superficial after their undergraduate years. Finnegan missed McIlweath in those randomly spare moments when he had the chance to feel his absence.

Those moments, though, came less frequently as the winter drew into spring. Finnegan, partly in frustration with Glynnis Mear's growing distances and increasingly mysterious humors, immersed himself in the preparation of the senator's hearings. They became for him both a catharsis and an animus. He saw in them a justification of the ethos that had led him to embrace this position from the start and, through periodic crumbs of gratification that had come his way, kept him energized.

His research had taught him that the problem to be addressed was more severe than he had anticipated. It compelled an answer. Through these hearings it would at least grab a bit of public awareness. That was the first step. From there, means of remediation might become more apparent. In any event, the best social and legislative minds would have had the chance to take notice and to formulate their own reactions. What eventually would come of this? Finnegan could not say, but he was convinced that, once begun, the process would necessarily lead to something positive, simply because it had to. There were too many good people of sincere intention involved for the issue to lie fallow. Finnegan sought to strike the right chords during these two days, to blend the vibrato of cold hard data with the trill of the emotional. He wanted those notes to share the pathos he had come to feel himself.

Finnegan worked hard, harder than he had ever worked before. He interviewed and reinterviewed his witnesses, he checked his research, he confirmed press contacts and media coverage, he retraced the logistics dozens of times, he read whatever he could find, took notes and evaluated new aspects of standard assumptions, he devised a thorough line of questioning so that the senator could draw out the best of each witness. Over and over he replayed in his mind how the two days would fit together, how one would progress into the other seamlessly. He made absolutely certain that no detail was overlooked, no point unmentioned, no argument underdeveloped. He had become obsessive.

The very concept of what he was doing thrilled him to the core. This was the practical application of the ideals he had nurtured, a manifestation of human compassion, evidence of the institutional response to human suffering, the central focus of how he intended to conduct the remainder of his professional life. He felt, not for the first time but certainly most deeply, the exhilaration of that rare juxtaposition of personal recognition, power and altruism. Finnegan was pushing along his part of the system with a clear-eyed, heady vision.

With the confidence of his own convictions, Finnegan became inflexible and argumentative. He saw the problem more precisely than anyone else, and only he knew how the hearings needed to be structured. He knew the issues, the language, the people. Suggestions from those less informed put him off. He told the witnesses what to stress and how to stress it. He demanded reports from HHS or NIH be produced on quick timelines and delivered as scheduled. He sidestepped the senator's press secretary more than once to discuss the type of coverage he wanted, and to tell the media what was coming and what they might want to feature. He badgered Griffith Ross to get more time out of the interns to help him with the legwork, the mundane running around to distribute testimony outlines or to fetch hard copies from the libraries.

At one point in pressing what he wanted from the other staffers, Finnegan snapped at Ross, "Damn it, Griffith, you're not giving me the support this project needs. Doesn't anybody around here give a damn about this?"

"Apparently not as much as you do, Conor. You're coming awfully close to making a fool of yourself. Peter tells me you've gone behind his back more than once to follow through with the media on your own. That's unprofessional, friend."

"I had to, Griff. Peter doesn't know what the hell this show is all about. He doesn't know what to feature."

"He knows what we tell him. He knows the view from the top, and that's all that matters. Most importantly, he knows enough not to go running off on his own."

"But he hasn't given this nearly enough attention. What's he done, a few phone calls? You know and I know that that's not enough. If you want to get the big boys out, you've got to tell them what to look for. You've got to badger the hell out of them. He hasn't done that, Griff."

"Finnegan, you keep this up and you're going to find your ass in a sling." Ross's voice rose in annoyance, and he pointed his finger directly at the younger man. "You've been stepping on a lot of toes lately, including mine. I don't much like the notion that you're going behind our communications man's back, one, and, two, that you're complaining about his performance. We do other things around here besides setting up these little extravaganzas. Let people do what they're paid to do. And if you've got a complaint or a suggestion, you come to me first. You don't go around doing other people's jobs."

"But, Griffith, that's not what I'm trying to . . . "

"I don't give a tinker's damn what you're trying to do or what you're thinking." The conversation was loud enough now to be overheard down the corridor. Staffers at other desks slowed what they were doing. Conversations ceased, time ceased. The angry words of Griffith Ross rang forth, incensed darts flung heatedly to penetrate the young man's insolence.

"You come here, fresh out of college, and you think you've got all the God damn answers. I'm sick of it, Conor. Everyone is. I've had it with your God damn self-importance. You're not the senator, even though you seem to lose sight of that little fact. Maybe someday you'll get the chance to run for office yourself, and maybe you'll win. But until that unlikely day, you don't make policy. You don't decide what's important. You're at the bottom of the food chain and that's where you'll stay unless you start to play a team game. I've got no stomach for prima donnas. Am I clear, friend?"

Ross's eyes glimmered hotly as he finished. His square jaw set pugnaciously, and a slight red flowed up his cheeks to points just in front of his ears. Finnegan blushed deeply, his face lost behind a crimson veil. The prickly sting of humiliation shot through his limbs and paralyzed them. He knew everyone was watching, that everyone had heard.

"Yes, sir," he replied quietly. "You're quite clear."

"Now get to work," barked Ross. "And watch yourself." Finnegan rose slowly, wordlessly, and went back down the corridor to his desk, head down, eyes down. He dropped to his seat and buried himself in a report which he could not read. He saw words but they did not register. No one spoke to him the rest of the day, fearing the taint of guilt by association.

The next day Finnegan continued his work, slightly daunted but still convinced of the essential rectitude of what he was doing. This work *was* critical, there could be no doubt. And if Ross's pragmatism trivialized it, so be it. In the end Finnegan would prove himself. The issue was such that even a coldhearted practicality could not stifle it. Finnegan resolved, though, to be more careful about staying in line. Ross's anger had been real, and he was not a man to be crossed. Finnegan was not accustomed to being upbraided, although he believed in his heart that what he had done had constituted no sin at all.

The hearings were scheduled for March 19th and 20th. The week before, Finnegan had worked himself into a nervous snit in putting together their finishing touches. Glynnis had not come down at all that weekend, but Finnegan barely heard her excuse. He was consumed by what lay immediately ahead. There would be time later for Glynnis. He could not have done her justice anyway. He would have been too distracted, and too irritable.

As the dates approached, Finnegan met with the senator almost daily to review each witness, to prepare specific lines of inquiry, or to confirm messaging. The senator occasionally suggested some changes in content, forcing Finnegan to go back to his witnesses and recast the points they were set to make. Finnegan had scheduled what he thought was a compelling slate, amalgamating the logistical with the emotional— government officials citing statistics, representatives of national and local association presenting overviews, social workers constructing theories, and the victims themselves repeating their tales of trauma, loss and degradation. Each would add something new. The senator seemed relatively pleased with this lineup as he came to know it.

Wednesday, March 12th dawned cloudy and cold, a last vestige of winter, a final affront to sensibilities impatient to lose the soggy, frigid malaise of the barren months. Finnegan had not slept well the night before. He had not slept well for several nights.

His father would have teased him about a guilty conscience, but that was not the reason. He kept waking during the early morning hours, his mind racing across the details of the days looming ahead and sorting them out as they arose. Finnegan's obsession plagued him ceaselessly. In time he started to look it. His face showed his fatigue, eyelids slightly heavy and hanging a bit lower over languid eyes, cheeks drawn, tiny weblike lines curving around his mouth. His social habits, too, had suffered. On most days he ate lunch at his desk alone, or grabbed a quick hamburger from the dining room. Sometimes he would eat the plastic food from the fast-food outlets as he drove around the city to see his people. He spoke rarely to his colleagues, even his friends among them, not because he felt alienated but because he didn't want to spare the time. He phoned Glynnis twice a week and unburdened himself to her for half an hour at a time, but that was the only indulgence he allowed his coiled spirit. He looked forward to spending a weekend with her, although that would have to wait until the task at hand was put away, presumably with overwhelming success. He was counting on it.

Finnegan arrived at the office early, shortly before 7:00. He liked to be among the first ones in. Those early moments when the cluttered suite was unusually empty soothed him. All this was his for now, and he relished the claiming of it. Possession was nine-tenths, he mused. It was calm then, before his colleagues filed in, before the lobby jammed with tourists looking for Senate passes or maps of the city, before the pressure really started and the suite became lost in a swirl of ringing phones, rushing bodies and the ceaseless clack-clack-clack of keyboards. Finnegan arrived, hung up his coat and set the coffee brewing. He sat at his desk, and in the quiet reviewed the *Washington Post*.

As he read the thick newspaper, Finnegan realized how horribly tired he really was. The walls sagged in on him and he did not have the strength to push them back. From an unseen corner an old radiator hissed wetly. Finnegan lost himself in the sound of it as it entered his ears and seized him. All he heard was the singular hiss. He floated with it across the room, entranced, oblivious to any intrusive sight or smell. For several minutes he did not move, saw nothing, felt nothing. He rose with the steam to the top of the suite and tucked himself into a corner where he hovered hypnotically.

Steve Krall broke the trance as he walked into the room. "Morning, Conor. Coffee brewed yet?" Finnegan looked at him for a second or two as if he were an anachronism, the court jester or a Greek bard. His thoughts refocused then, and he was away. But God, how tired he felt.

Finnegan spent that morning reviewing the proposed remarks of an assistant undersecretary at HHS regarding the previous year's public housing starts and median rents. Finnegan resented that he had been unable to get someone higher than a midlevel minion from a government body inextricably linked to the problem. Obviously, HHS did not share Finnegan's enthusiasm concerning these hearings. Finnegan had had to overcome a number of bureaucratic roadblocks even to procure this lowly soul. The department no doubt feared appearing callous or indifferent, thought Finnegan, but that's what they were. This witness was a straw dog whose testimony would be skewered by those sad faces who saw no benefit from these statistics, whose humble circumstances could never be remedied by sterile numbers reflecting the sterile construction of sterile buildings whose interiors they would never see.

Around 11:00 Finnegan was buzzed by the senator's secretary and told that the man would like to see him. He gathered his folders on the hearings and headed down. Another briefing, he thought, and was glad of it. He enjoyed holding the senator's ear. Joyce motioned him in, and he closed the door behind him.

"Good morning, Conor. Have a seat."

"Good morning, sir," he replied as he took his place in one of the thick leather chairs across from the senator's desk.

Usually they conferred at the table across the room. There they could spread out their papers and work side by side. This morning, though, the senator remained behind his desk. "I take it things are continuing to move along smoothly," he said.

"Yes, sir. I think both days are completely in order now. Is there anything in particular you want to review?"

"No, Conor. In fact I called you in to let you know that we have a problem, and I'm sorry for it. I've been asked to address the State Association of Manufacturers in San Francisco on the 20th. I've agreed to do it. You've done a commendable job on this project, Conor, and I'm grateful, but unfortunately, our hearings are cancelled."

Finnegan heard thunder in his brain. It drowned out the words that had to coalesce into some type of response. Great ringing peals clapped up from the base of his skull and pulsated the length of his body. He sat dumbfounded until the ringing subdued enough to permit him to arrange his thoughts.

"I'm sorry, Conor," continued the senator. "I know you've worked terribly hard, but, frankly, this is more important to me. To be honest, I'm not sure I liked the direction these hearings were starting to take. I think they may have become too sensational, too emotional. It's best we cancel them for now and take some time to reconsider exactly what we want to do with them, and what we want them to do for us."

Finnegan heard the senator's words, and knew what they meant. He heard in them all the base, dispassionate pragmatism he had come to loathe. He saw the pathetic underside of the human condition, and those who lived on its margins, cavalierly dismissed because it lacked utility. He saw thousands of people abandoned, once again, because they lacked the leverage to redirect an inert system. He saw the smug image of Brandon Carrecker. He saw the anguish of Agnes and Moses and dozens of others like them.

And ultimately, Conor Finnegan saw an illusion—pounded, bruised, twisted, stabbed and battered but somehow kept alive—now suddenly shattered into dust. In one gesture he had been rocked to the core, his Romantic ideals all at once invalidated. He had been cast to the sidelines. He had never in his life felt so cheated.

As the thunder died, rage swelled up to take its place. His fatigue robbed him of discretion. A frothy anger bubbled outward and could scarcely be contained. Finnegan tried, to be sure, fighting with himself to maintain composure in the face of such bitterness. But the Irish temper whose beneficence could be so sweet reared up in a black fury that could not be stemmed.

"And so that's it," he said at last, in something of a hiss. "A few words and the problem is swept away."

"I'm afraid so," the senator replied sternly, aware of the young man's humor.

"But of course how could I have expected anything different, given the way the scales tip. But God damn it, Senator, you can't do this."

"It's already done, Conor. There will be no hearings."

"So you can suck up to some more of your moneyed friends? You're turning your back on a problem that involves real people in real situations, can't you see that? Is every issue weighed solely in terms of votes? You're supposed to serve the great unwashed, too, or don't you remember? Because they lack influence doesn't mean you can ignore them. That's immoral, for Christ's sake."

"*Immoral?*" The senator shot forward in his chair, and his voice rose to meet Finnegan's. As he spoke he jabbed a finger in Conor's face. "Let me tell you something, pal. The only morality I care to recognize is whatever it takes to get re-elected. If you can't handle that, then get the hell out. I don't need some smartass kid lecturing me on morality. People only expect me to be moral with them and theirs. After that they don't care what I do for the other guy. You'll be carved up in this profession if you don't come to understand that simple fact. All your high-minded morality does is piss people off. People don't want to hear it."

"And you don't want to waste your time on an issue that provides only a marginal political return," countered Finnegan, still hot, "when you can pander to that sentiment and collect some campaign contributions. If that's your brand of morality, then what the hell's the point of even holding office? There's no point."

"The point is that if we're not re-elected we can't do anything for anybody. We can't . . ."

"*But we're doing nothing now!* If you do nothing with your office, then you *shouldn't* be re-elected. Those people you're going to address in San Francisco don't need you. They want to trot you out like a show dog and make you do tricks for them. At the end they throw you a bone and scratch you behind your ears. But while they jerk you around to feel important and you lick their hands to feel loved, there's an issue you're ignoring that calls for your attention. You can do something about this. Maybe not everything that needs to be done, but something. And by pretending it doesn't exist because the people it affects don't vote in great numbers or can't pitch huge sums into the campaign chest, you're dismissing your responsibility. What are you here for, then?"

"To stay here. My singular responsibility is to myself. I'm answerable to no one's illusions, Conor, least of all yours. I'm not responsible for your sensitivities, and I won't let you or anyone like you dictate my job. What the hell do you know about political reality, anyway? You come in here with your esoteric notions of 'morality' and 'responsibility' and you try to tell me what's right and what's wrong. What good is it all? What purpose does it serve when power if the final determinant? Is that your question? The answer is, power for its own sake. There's enough latitude in that to justify any morality. Face it, my friend: each morality is different, and so they're all invalid. Nothing works but in the most general sense, and I'm senator for all the people. There's no room for dogma, so take your preaching elsewhere. I've no time for your pious handwringing. Your hearings are dead."

Finnegan's entire body flushed in rage, and his eyes flamed. Everything had evaporated in a matter of minutes. "So this is my lesson in practical politics. Money talks, and the consequences be damned."

"Disappointment is part of the game. And get this through your head: you can't change anything here. You can't change war, or disease, or poverty, or death. All you can do is dab around at the edges. But the system won't bend, and the evils within that system won't disappear despite your best efforts. It's all self-perpetuating. It's built up so much inertia over two centuries that no soul, or group of souls, could kick it into a positive motion, or could budge it more than a few inches.

"But enter Conor Finnegan," the senator continued, "bright-eyed and brimming with principle, unlike the rest of us. You want to restructure politics and revamp an entire care system. You might even want to revamp the economy. While you're at it you might take a stab at world peace. Do you honestly believe that two days of hearings would alter the circumstances of even one life, would improve the lot of a solitary individual after our entire social and economic systems have dealt them out? That can't be changed. We can't all of a sudden create a new pigeonhole for these folks. The system won't permit it because there's no room. If there were, they wouldn't be on the outside. You'd have to tear it all down and start again from the bottom. All of it— industry, agriculture, education, the government itself—because what you're really talking about are questions of equal distribution.

"So what can a single senator do, let alone a junior staffer? Your hearings would have had no effect if God Himself had come down to testify. The odds are insurmountable. It's all a game, Conor. A game of image and commercialism and marketing. The sooner you accept that, the happier you'll be. Shelve your principles. The world doesn't want to hear about them."

"And nothing we do has any bearing?"

"Oh, we can do some transitory good, don't get me wrong. We might help some individuals cut through red tape or convince the administration to throw a few dollars where we want them, but that's the most we can expect. I'd be grateful from here on if you could remember that and climb down from your mountain. You're paid to do research, write speeches and shake a few hands on my behalf. You're not paid to do any thinking. You're not capable of it. Do you understand me?"

"You've made yourself quite clear, Senator. I understand you more now than I ever did before." Finnegan's blood was livid.

"Good. Now get the hell out of my office."

Finnegan forced his legs to move him through his rage. He spun out of the wide office and back down the corridor to his desk. A red-hot prickly fire burned around the edges of his vision; he saw nothing but a few feet in front of him. His heart pounded against his ribs, constricting his breath, and cold perspiration flowed down his sides.

At his desk Finnegan flung his folders angrily down on top of the clutter. Several loose papers blew to the floor. He sat down and buried his hot, hot face in his hands.

This, then, was the reality. All his efforts had been nothing more than self-indulgence. They had no meaning, and never could. His sharply defined idealism had been bludgeoned, and he felt absolutely foolish. All along he had been a curiosity, an anomaly, Tom Thumb trying to play serious drama.

Finnegan sat that way for several minutes until his humiliated rage subsided enough to allow him to move. He wiped his hands across his face trying to draw out the moist heat that rose there. Glancing at his watch he saw that it was not yet noon. Outside, the thickened gray sky shrouded the streets, making the day appear later than it was. Finnegan rose, put on his coat and walked out of the office. He did not return that day. Instead he went back to his empty apartment and collapsed on his bed, given up at last to the exhaustion he had felt all along.

* * *

As Conor Finnegan had his conclusions thrust upon him, Tom McIlweath reached his through quiet paces. He had time enough at last to sort things through. He was calmer now than he had been in recent memory, and he reveled in it. For the first time he believed his options to be limitless. He knew, too, that he would most likely never have the luxury of such freedom again. Whatever came next would change all that. A single decision would close the door forever on countless others. That was the way of things.

And so the fusillade of applications and inquiries he had discharged over the past weeks came back around, some hitting him broadly to capture his interest, most missing altogether. McIlweath had no timetable. His peculiar confidence that, finally left to his own manipulations he would find an appropriate alternative, never left him. More particularly, McIlweath believed that whatever direction he chose for himself would lend him peace. He would find the acceptance he had sought. He knew that he would be able to create it for himself under better, purer circumstances, and that those circumstances need not be perfect. No longer was he in quest of the Holy Grail; no longer was he Faustus, no longer Rachel nor the driven Jason. He could take his time.

In early April McIlweath received notice that he had won an obscure fellowship for which he had been recommended by one of his senior professors. He had, in fact, forgotten that he had ever applied for it, the endless reams of forms having long since blurred into indistinguishable memories. But the fellowship had come, and it was a good one. A very good one, and completely unlike the others. This one opened strange and romantic doors; it spoke in a lyrical brae. McIlweath let its impact sink in, then he reviewed its possibilities.

One night, a week or so after receiving his notification, a sleepless McIlweath rose after midnight, and poured himself a glass of wine. He took it to his desk, positioned now by the window that looked out on the dead street. There in the dark he sat quietly, watching nothing, observing the lack of light and sound and movement as if they were animate conditions, positive beings with personalities all their own. In the other room Kathy Keane still slept on her half of the bed they shared with increasing frequency. McIlweath had moved out of it slowly, measuring each step so that he would not disturb her.

A lack of light, and sound, and movement. A void. That's what it all was, wasn't it? What, then, could his expectations be? The base commercialism, the selfishness, the petty, meaningless, transitory gratifications, the mediocrity—that's what he could expect. Look at this street now, and consider the sleeping forms that haunt it by day. Do I seek to become like them? Shall I define myself by any other standard?

The huge, indomitable energy of this place, of this old city. Of this old country. How dare I defy it? It overpowers me; I am caught in an avalanche and rolled, blindly suffocating, down a sharp hill. All my life I have been suffocating. I am fortunate at least because I know that it is happening. But most, feeble against the accumulated force of sheer mass, are ignorant of it. What power do we have to stand against the immense, omnipotent sweep of that which seeks to conform us? What power at all? Is that the root of my discontent, this fetid rot that has eaten away at me for as long as I can remember?

A car drove down the narrow street. Its headlights made two yellow lines that blended together ahead of its hood. They appeared from McIlweath's right, parted the darkness as a knife through a loaf of black bread, then went on. The engine made a hollow clanking rumble before it grew fainter and disappeared in pursuit of some unknown direction.

'I have sought to be in harmony with my surroundings. I have sought to be regarded solely on the basis of my character—its talents, its shortcomings, its peculiar values, its emotional parameters. I have sought to avoid judgment beyond what I have brought upon myself. And I have sought, above all, a way to indulge my mind and fulfill my emotions apart from all imposed distinctions, and to do so in a manner purely consistent with the character through which I will be regarded.

'And I have failed.

'Perhaps I have been making false assumptions all along. Perhaps I have assumed that what's around me cares enough to identify my failures. Perhaps I have assumed that it would care enough to take note of my successes, the things for which I have been so hopeful. Perhaps I have assumed that, in crafting a singular identity, I might effect some infinitesimal alteration of an order that has defied me for so long. Am I really any different than Conor Finnegan?

'But the order is a great avalanche, and we are caught in it, Conor and I. We cannot stop it, or slow it, or cause it to move off its path for even the slightest bit. If we stand up to it, we shall be crushed and it will roll over us, gaining speed, gaining momentum as our bones crack and snap, rolling noisily until it hits some indefinable bottom with a cataclysmic thud.

'Conor, with your bold, Romantic, quixotic visions, have we not been after the same things all these years? In my introverted longings, in your idealistic clamoring, have we not both sought to divert this great avalanche away from us? We are both anomalies, Conor. We are both perversions that cannot hope to be tolerated. There shall be no final victories, not here. In due course we shall be beaten down by what's brought against us, by what we can neither prevent nor master, until we grow tired and bitter and full of despair. We shall be swept away then, when our resolve is broken, and we shall become exactly like all the others. We are brothers, Conor Finnegan, doomed by our flawed spirits to struggle against what cannot be overcome in a thousand lifetimes.

'There shall be no peace for me here. What I know of this place does not allow it. It may be that there shall be no peace for me anywhere. If so, then what do I have to lose?'

Another car came and went. Across the way, a few buildings down, a light flicked on above one of the small family-run stores. It stayed on for a minute or two, then went off.

'I shall not find what I am after if I remain. Perhaps it cannot be found anywhere. But the farther afield I go, the greater my chances will be.'

Kathy stepped out of the bedroom, a white robe wrapped around her slender frame lending an ethereal air to her natural beauty. "Tom?" she whispered. McIlweath turned in his chair and saw her there, her angular face peering through space the darkness did not allow her to perceive.

"Kathy," he replied. "I didn't want to wake you. I'm sorry."

"What are you doing here? Couldn't you sleep?"

"No. Through no fault of yours. I've been a little agitated, I guess."

She came up behind him and put her hands on his shoulders. He nestled his head between her breasts. So firm to hold me there, he thought, like a pair of hands.

"I haven't noticed, Tom. Do you want to tell me what it is?"

"Not now. It's nothing, really. Pondering my own future, that's all."

She wrapped her arms around the front of his chest and bent down to hug him, her head next to his as he leaned back against her. She felt the rasp of his unshaven face, then kissed his cheek. "That sounds serious."

"No, Kath. Not serious at all. Merely something we can't avoid. It hits us all from time to time, doesn't it?"

"But we don't have to deal with it at so late an hour. Come back to bed, Tom. It's much warmer. And tell me what you're thinking when we get there."

McIlweath rose and they embraced. He clasped her waist to lead her to the bedroom. Beneath the covers they huddled. McIlweath's chilled body rubbed against Kathy's warmth. She flinched at first as he pressed to her, then she moved her body back and forth against his to warm it.

"What was on your mind, Tom, that took you out of our bed?"

"It's late, Kathy, and it was nothing new."

"You're going to leave here, aren't you?"

"Yes."

"I'm glad for you. It must be awfully difficult, even so. You don't belong here. But you must know that when the time comes I'm going to miss you terribly."

"Let's not talk, Kathy. It would do no good." His embrace deepened, and Kathy moaned softly, not from lust, but from the pure joy of holding him. She felt at once the depth of his character, the hidden well of passion that quietly guided everything he did. She ran her hands along the scars that she knew must be there.

"I will miss you, Tom McIlweath," she whispered.

"You saved me, Kathy. I never want to forget you. But I'll be here tomorrow, and the day after, and for weeks to come. Let's not talk about leaving until we have to. Let's just hold each other."

And they did, as night closed back in around them to engulf their most fragile comforts.

* * *

An ephemeral glint caught in the eye burns its way onto the soft tissue behind it and stays there after the brightness has passed, hanging weightless, tied to the sightlines so that it turns with the eye, raising and lowering itself as the head moves, always there, just beyond touch, just beyond grasp, just beyond comprehension and wisdom. We are the tail of a comet, fleetingly brief in our dusty accident, luminous in part, mostly obscured, our energy artificial, an illusion or a hoax as it dissipates into the horrible void, and all that follows is a deathly, unearthly silence so deep that it hypnotizes the mind and befuddles the soul.

So joy passes through the great darkness, and so confusion, and so comfort. All pass, and only the darkness remains, so vast and indomitable—the ultimate chaos against which all knowledge struggles. So pass melancholy and resolution; so passes a quiet brilliance. All, all pass, yet the darkness remains in its immense, constrictive suffocation. In the end it is only this, and we cannot avoid its conclusion, the grimy epitaph that stands behind us as we lie motionless: we are ephemeral, and only darkness prevails.

It prevails against our most glorious intentions; it prevails against youth which ages, strength which weakens, love which fades, vitality which wanes, pleasure which grows tawdry, beauty which grows banal. It prevails against flesh and the spirit. It prevails against the lyrical, lusty laughter which rises in our throats, and there chokes it. It has always been there; it will always be so, and there is no hope for redemption but to deny that it will ultimately claim us, although in our most terrified, secretive thoughts we know better.

Still, we must deny the horrible, and it is that denial alone which keeps us functional and clear. We throw ourselves against the blackness, screaming defiance until we are strangled by our own phlegm, almost believing that the eternal destiny of Mankind will escape us, that somehow, through the splendid power of our splendid souls we shall not be sucked into the abyss, that we shall somehow stand true and honored and finally content, spared by Providence and our own valor from the endless horrors our subtle brutality has imposed upon us. But, in the end, after all fury is spent and all joys are exhausted, we must come back to what has never left us since we first crawled out of the primordial muck. And grief, which shall not die, laughs at us and our puny efforts, smiles at our hubris, then claims us against our will, against our expectations. There to die in the echo of our protests which are not heard, and finally, mockingly, the realization which we cannot escape is burned into our delicate sight—We are ephemeral; only darkness prevails, the great darkness against which the tail of the comet flashes.

CHAPTER XXIV

Because no battle is ever won he said. They are not even fought. The field only reveals to man his own folly and despair, and victory is an illusion of philosophers and fools.

—William Faulkner, *The Sound and the Fury*

Tom McIlweath walked sullenly up the familiar, narrow flight of stairs. For a brief second an image of the great Aztec temples had passed through him as he stood at the bottom. The final act, at last, and welcome. He had drawn a deep breath and placed his foot on the bottom step. The rest could be no more difficult than that. Compared with what had brought him here, it would scarcely be noticeable at all.

At the top of the steps he rapped lightly with his knuckles. In an instant he heard footsteps within, then the door opened thinly to permit the face behind it to look out. Satisfied that the threat that stood outside was not immediate, Anne Newbury pulled the door open all the way. She stood at the side of it, unsmiling, grimly serious, her features crafted in slate.

'No,' thought McIlweath. 'This will not be easy. But she can't touch me now. There is nothing she has of mine to ruin.'

"Hello, Anne," he said softly. Despite his best effort at composure his voice had once again risen in pitch. How could one sound confident and sure when his voice piped like a choirboy's? Such was McIlweath's curse, or one of them.

"Come in, Tom. Let me take your jacket." The voice that had once seemed so comfortably melodic when he heard it every day now sounded coarse and grainy. McIlweath could find no warmth in those few words, no compassion, no empathy. In all likelihood they had never been there except to an ear expecting to hear them. They had been echoing constructions of a desperately yearning imagination.

McIlweath gave Anne his jacket and stood in the center of the room. She told him to take a seat somewhere. Clinical, and to the point; an operation to remove a diseased or crippled part. He sat on the couch, and Anne sat across the room in an armchair.

"I'm sorry I didn't call you sooner, Anne. I know I said only a few days when we spoke last. How've you been?"

"As I've always been, Tom. There's been no change in me. How have you managed? Have you found your poor little lost soul yet? I assume that's why you called me."

"I called because I thought we should see each other, to set things in order. Or at least to be clear about it all. We left things in such a bad state. And I think I've finally found the strength to face you honestly."

"To see what we can salvage? How gallant."

"Not gallant. But after all we've shared I thought I at least owed you . . . an explanation, if nothing else."

"Perhaps an apology might be more in order. That is, if you want to salvage anything at all. Or is this just another one of your exercises in angst?"

"An apology would imply that I had done something wrong, and that you had been wounded by it. The first part isn't true. I've done nothing wrong, Anne, except to myself, and for that I'm solely accountable. As for the second part, I doubt if I've ever had the power to wound you in any way. I wonder if any man can."

"If you've come to insult me again, then please leave right now. I've no time to deal with your peevishness."

McIlweath turned to look out the window as he drew his thoughts. He saw nothing but an amorphous pattern of lights that ended abruptly at a black void that must be the park a few blocks away. The clock on the windowsill read 10:17. This part of the city had ground to a halt hours ago. What was left outside the window was only the winding down, the binding of the rag-ends that hung useless and limp. Wednesday night in mid-May, the beaten stump of a brutal year. The wind blew, hard enough to push vagrant papers and buds against the glass in a scattered rapping that seemed bored except when the gusts knocked the debris with such force as to evoke images of anger or desolation. It had rained that day; it would rain again tomorrow. On such a night there was no place else to be.

McIlweath had not planned to call on Anne tonight, although he knew eventually he must see her again. The sentiment had captured him as the afternoon plodded on its gray, leaden weariness. The weight of the entire year since he had come to Boston pressed down on him then. His alienation had been characterized in a somber campus, empty hallways and wet, blowing papers. He had spoken to no one that day, like few such days in recent weeks. There had been only the rain, cold on his face and hair, and there had been the wind swishing along what was unattached. It had not been a day to look forward to the impending next step. Rather, it had been a day for retrospection, sober and depressing, a day in which husbands and wives sat glumly on opposite sides of the dinner table to sip their coffee without speaking, before going silently and dispassionately to bed. The dampness in the air soaked through the skin, soaked through the bones and seeped into the heart. The wind made echoing, empty noises.

"No, Anne, I haven't come to insult you." McIlweath had all of a sudden become extremely weary. It took a concerted effort to force the words out of his lungs. "I just thought we should talk. To settle accounts, I suppose."

"And what accounts are those? What conclusions have you reached? After all this time you must certainly have something profound to tell me. Perhaps you've identified more of my faults, or determined other ways in which I've made your life miserable."

"I take full responsibility for the condition of my life, Anne."

"You're damn right, you do. I swear, Tom, I've gotten so tired of your self-pity. It's all been so childish, ever since I've known you. You've wasted so much time. And in the end you've always resented me for what you think I've made you do. Well, I've made you do nothing. You're where you are of your own accord. Whatever you've had to put up with has been the result of your own little schema, or lack of it."

"I know that, Anne. For the first time in a long while, I can admit that. Perhaps for the first time ever."

"All I've tried to do is give you some direction. It's always been up to you whether to accept it or not. But, God, you're so damn stubborn. I suppose that comes from timidity. You've been petrified to make a decision and so you've drifted along without aim, or rudder, or locomotion. You've ridden the currents, and you cry when you bang into the rocks."

"I've never been as driven as you, that much is true. I'm afraid I've been too conscious of my insecurities. I've let them sway me more than I should have. And you, Anne, have been my greatest insecurity. I've never told you that, but it should be obvious. You don't need me to tell you. You've played off that since we met. I've been your servant, and your pet, and your amusement, simply because I dreaded losing you. I've been everything but your lover.

"It's not that I've been lacking direction, Anne," he continued. "It's that I've ceded responsibility for my direction to you. I've run along after you for fear of being left alone, a puppy left behind when its owner runs to the store. That's been a horrible weakness, and I've paid for it dearly. I have no time to pay for it further."

"Oh, Tom, you God damn fool. I'm the best thing that's ever happened to you, but you're so lost in this sophomoric nonsense to realize it."

"God, you're so certain of yourself. You have no doubts. Anne, you have no answers for me. You're blessed if you have them for yourself, no matter how certain you are. But you have nothing for me.

"You say that I've been drifting and that I have yet to devote myself to anything lasting. But that's not entirely true. I've devoted myself to you, and so I've trailed you like a shadow. Yet you've always remained untouchable. You've dangled yourself just out of my grasp, and always I've kept trying to clutch you. I thought I needed that as much as I needed a roof over my head or clothes on my back. You've been a magnet; I've always pointed to you, true north, and that's been as much direction as I've allowed myself to see.

"It's been a hopeless situation," he continued, "but it's taken me years to recognize it. You wanted me in your orbit, but you were always going where you were going whether I came along or not. Yet when I accede to you and accept your terms, you call me weak."

"Perhaps," said Anne, "you accepted my 'terms,' as you call it, for the wrong reasons. You followed me out of insecurity rather than conviction."

"But you've always had enough conviction for all concerned," McIlweath replied. "My God, Anne, how can you be so certain of yourself? How can you be so certain of what's out there and where it all fits?"

"And how can you not be?" she shot back. "Christ, Tom, every move you make shouldn't be subject to some ponderous deliberation. You agonize over issues that should be taken for granted. You play Hamlet, or Byron, but you're not afforded that luxury. It's the simplest thing in the world to know what you want for yourself: you define it, then you go get it. But the more you question and second-guess and inspect and evaluate, the more likely you are of becoming so confused that you become paralyzed with fear. That's what happened to you. Act on what you know, not on what you don't. Act on what you want."

"What we want is determined by what we know. I have no definitive answers, Anne. I don't know enough to have them. But I'm becoming increasingly aware of the potential to acquire what's needed. And I don't think it can be done here. That's really what I've come to tell you."

"What are you going to do, Tom?"

"I've been offered a fellowship, Anne. I'm going abroad for a while."

"Where?"

"Ireland. University College, in County Cork. You've never heard of it."

"My God, Tom. I'd have never thought you capable of it." Anne spoke in a hushed voice, the sting of her words gone now. She had been caught short, and thoroughly surprised.

"Until recently, neither had I. You speak of acting upon what we know rather than what we don't. I understand that, for whatever reason or series of reasons, I'm not destined to be happy here. I know I can't feel comfortable within the expectations that have been set for me. Even if I found that I wanted to get a degree, or do post-grad research, or teach, I'll resist because I'll feel manipulated. Or else I'll go do it and feel absolutely miserable.

"Anne, we're all born to an order, and that order defines our possibilities. All my life I've felt alienated, never quite a part of what's going on around me. I don't know why that's been the case, but whatever the reason, it's been a part of me for too long. I've wanted to be accepted and respected above all else. I've wanted people to recognize the strengths and weaknesses of my character, its anodes and cathodes, and respond to them alone, away from any preconceptions. That's why I came east. That's why I was originally attracted to you. I've always held out an anticipation of that acceptance. I've thought that I've seen it in other people, so naturally it had to be in store for me.

"But as we grow older we complicate ourselves. That's obvious, isn't it? And we become more answerable to others' expectations. *More* responsive to what other people think, or expect, or demand, rather than less. You've conceived your own standards for me, and I've tried to honor them. That's what brought me here, and I've been abjectly miserable for months. Sometimes I think I'm getting away as a reaction to you, but it's really broader than that.

"I'm seeking something simpler, Anne. Something less cluttered. I want to know that I'm doing what I'm doing purely because that's my preference and not because I feel I have no other alternative."

He went on, "We see each other as types, and we so seldom look behind the façades. I want to study Classics, so professors look at me one way, students regard me another, and society in general places a price-tag on the end result. There's no Tom McIlweath in any of that. And so I've felt alienated here, and I want to get away from it. Perhaps it's no different elsewhere, but at least I have the capacity to wrench myself away from what I have here and build my own circumstances. If I don't take advantage of that now, then the chances grow increasingly remote that I ever will. The entanglements will just be too great. Do you understand that? No matter if you don't. I know that this is right for the moment. I'm only thankful I have the courage to follow it through."

"I see nothing courageous in anything you've said," replied Anne. "You're running again, that's all. Just a little farther afield this time. I imagine you'll sour on this in due course as well, then move on to something else. I do confess that Ireland impresses me. I applaud your resourcefulness, really. I had no idea you were ever interested in going abroad, so you've shown me something there. But actually, it's the same old story, isn't it, Tom? I've grown tired of it, and of you, too, I'm afraid. It's too much energy to bring myself along and drag you at the same time. I'm glad you're going."

"I wouldn't have expected you to grasp much of this, Anne. I'm sorry, but even now you fall back on your smugness. It's beyond you to acknowledge doubt. Where does that leave you? You're bound to be successful, I'm sure of that, but at what cost? You have no sense of wonderment. And without that, success is hollow. I'm sure of that, too. It'll be like punching a few buttons on a computer to find an answer instead of sweating through a thousand calculations and miscalculations until your mind is squeezed dry, but knowing that when you find it it'll be truly yours and there's positively no chance that it'll be wrong."

"At least I'm certain I'll find it by pushing those buttons. I've been certain all my life."

"I know. And that, I fear, is your curse."

"It's for you that I'm sorry, Tom. You won't let yourself be happy. I've done all that's in me for you. You've resisted me. You've resisted yourself. You're a brilliant, sensitive soul, but you're really no more than a child, self-pitying and indulgent. You'll never be more than that.

"So run then," she continued. "Run as far and as wide as you please. I have no desire to try to stop you. I'm not capable of it. And if you thought what you told me tonight would earn my respect, or make me wail and cry to get you to stay, you've deluded yourself. You're throwing away ambition and comfort and the satisfaction of striving, but I suppose you couldn't comprehend that no matter how clear it is. You're throwing away more than most people will ever attain. But as I said, you exhaust me. I can't take your grand, Romantic indecisions anymore. I can't take your breast-beating and hand-wringing and constant second-guessing. It's become as boring as it is tiring. Leave me if you must, or don't. It really doesn't matter anymore. There's no remorse, there's no nostalgia or gloom. There's only exhaustion, nothing more."

"Then there's no point in continuing," said McIlweath, the words a low exhalation barely audible. He, too, had been exhausted. But now his Protean exertions neared their end. It would shortly be all over.

"No, Tom. There's no point. Just go."

He rose with effort, the strain of this peculiar dismemberment having sapped his better parts. McIlweath felt as if this conversation had lasted several hours. In truth, it had been very short. It was neither bang nor whimper, and now that the end had come he felt vaguely cheated. It seemed as if there should be more points to be won, more flesh to be exacted. He had hoped there might be passion, the clashing and wrenching of joined souls. He had not expected fatigue, nor the overwhelming weariness that soaked his limbs, his lungs, his heart, his very spirit with a camphored numbness. The final salvo had been fired long ago, only he had been too deaf to hear it.

"I'm sorry, Anne. Perhaps more so than I've ever been in my life. Please try to understand what I've done, and what I'm doing."

"Be assured, Tom, that my life will not change without you. You've always been welcome to be a part of it."

"But always on your terms. I can't do that anymore, Anne. I was a fool to do it at all."

"You are a fool. Perhaps in time I'll come to worry about you. But not yet. I've nothing left to give you."

"I'd like to write you after I get settled. To let you know where I am."

"Do as you wish. I suppose I should wish you luck, although I'm not certain what luck would bring you."

"Merely some understanding, and some harmony. That's the best I can do." McIlweath opened the door. For some reason, a sentimental exaggeration of nostalgia, he paused to look around at the small apartment. "Goodbye, Anne."

She stared at him, unsmiling as when he had come, her eyes set in blue stone. Tom McIlweath turned and walked down the hollow flight of steps. They parted as they had come together, and the bitter, sterile gulf washed in behind them.

* * *

For Conor Finnegan, the grand and glorious fabric of his life had begun to unravel. Once started it could not be stopped. It was as if he had snagged a sweater on the corner of a table and pulled at the loose string that ran out of his garment, leaving it so misshapen that he would wonder how he had ever been attracted to it at all.

After the hearings were cancelled, Finnegan found himself consigned to a series of tasks and responsibilities he considered essentially meaningless. Griffith Ross had told him to "put the elderly to rest for a while. We won't be doing anything on that front for several months." Finnegan once again had protested and, once again, he had been sternly rebuffed. He briefly considered pursuing the issue on his own and completing the studies on nutritional problems and cost overruns in federal medical programs he had begun weeks before, but he knew that Capitol Hill had no room for freelancers, and that any such effort would jeopardize what little credibility he still had with the powers that be. Ross ignored him for the most part, and when they did speak, the older man did little to hide his contempt. Their conversations became terse. Finnegan reacted in kind and kept his distance. His indifference for Ross turned rapidly to dislike.

With his pet issue taken from him, Finnegan was left to pursue what he considered to be mundane research on antiseptic topics. He wrote position papers that were filed and ignored. He was assigned to develop arguments on amendments to maritime laws, interstate freight rates imposed by railroads, the budget for the Immigration and Naturalization Service and other issues equally boring to him. He wrote a bland speech for the senator to deliver before the California-Hawaii Elks Association. On two or three occasions he conducted tours of the office for groups of high school students. Some afternoons he was assigned to answering the phones and recording constituent comments, complaints and rants, the Siberia of staff responsibilities.

Finnegan worked fewer hours. When 5:00 came he was usually gone, the voracious appetite for doing what he did having disappeared. There was nothing to which that appetite could be directed, nothing meaty to bite. As the spring wore on, he came to the office increasingly late and left increasingly early. No one seemed to care. He wanted to get back to his apartment while it was still light so that he could make some use of the day.

The sour humor that clung to him intensified by contrast to the fortunes of his colleague Steve Krall, whose star had risen as Finnegan's had sputtered. Finnegan had grown closer to Krall than to anyone else on staff. During his first summer in Washington, when Krall had arranged for him to occupy his aunt's elegant townhouse, the two often spent evenings together after work sitting in the living room or on the narrow porch, drinking beer against the heat and swapping impressions of their co-workers, the nature of what they were doing, and the pervasive thrill of being young and free in such a city. When Finnegan came to Washington permanently, their friendship did not deepen, but neither did it wane. They remained close, eating lunch together when they could and occasionally going out for a night on the town. Finnegan considered Steve Krall something of a kindred spirit formed from a similar mold.

Krall was only four years older than Finnegan, still a very young man even by Washington standards. His background was parallel: an honor student at a fine university, a star athlete who had given up his sport for broader pursuits, an idealist who had come a great distance to be at the heart of a place where he might have an impact. Krall was a superb conversationalist who exuded a sincerity of conviction, a genuine appreciation of his fellow man. It was that appreciation which led him to take the wide-eyed Finnegan under his wing and show him what he should look for in a city that could be vastly confusing. Finnegan, too, was attracted to Krall's quiet expectation that ultimately he could affect in some small way the evolution of a pluralistic society with its share of injustices and heartbreaks. While Krall's Romantic tendencies were not nearly so rampant as Finnegan's, they were apparent to all who knew him.

What modified that idealism was a pragmatic instinct at which Finnegan marveled. Krall, it seemed, knew what would work in any situation. His grasp of political sensitivities was such that he knew where and how hard to push, what direction to turn his arguments, and when to step away completely. Krall worked extensively in issues affecting low-income traditional minorities. He had been instrumental in developing a series of bills aimed at regulating fair employment practices in both the private and public sectors. Finnegan had been impressed with Krall's thorough, meticulous substantiation of the conditions that kept people unemployed and locked in poverty. He had documented enforcement costs, administrative operations and logistical details to the smallest digit. The senator had been delighted with the effort but doubtful of the reception such legislation would receive, given the senate's current composition. It was Krall who suggested scuttling three of the bills, deferring two to the next session after the mid-term elections, and introducing only the remaining two immediately, but only if sufficient co-sponsors could be enlisted.

Among those bills scuttled was the one of which Krall had been proudest, a reorganizational bill that would have affected Department of Defense standards of promotion. When Finnegan asked him why he had been willing to drop it, Krall went into a detailed analysis of how the bill would have been brutalized in committee, who would have proposed which amendments, and where it all would have come to rest. It was simply not the time for it, he said.

"But by sacrificing that bill I convinced the senator that the others, because they were less extreme, had a chance, and that if we introduced the safest of the bunch with other co-sponsors we'd at least have something to build on in future sessions. He was all for it. You can make any point you want through comparison."

"You're leaving the teeth out of your package, though," Finnegan had countered. "You're really not doing anything with this bill. Wouldn't it have been better to introduce the entire series? Even if it were blown apart this session, you'd have planted the seed for next year. And you'd know who stood where and who you'd have to work on."

"We know that already. Why force a confrontation if it isn't necessary? And if the series had died in committee, anything we reintroduced would already have the stench of failure and could be ignored. The senator doesn't believe in Pyrrhic victories. He's against all bloodshed, especially his own. You should know that by now. We'll build on the proposal gradually, by steps. It might take longer, but in the end it'll be more complete than if we charge ahead full bore. You lose respect that way."

Finnegan had not been convinced. If you have an issue to pursue, then you pursue it, directly and simply, without constructing some elaborate strategy to get it done. Even though he was impressed with Krall's comprehensive understanding of the waters through which he had to navigate, Finnegan believed that any final product would be too compromised, that it would be flaccid and weak. 'Half of the problems we anticipate in this business never materialize anyway,' he thought. 'More than half.'

And so it was with consternation that Conor Finnegan saw Steve Krall, whom he considered an equal, benefit from both a title and a salary upgrade while Finnegan spent his afternoons yapping with angry constituents. Krall was moved out of the noisy, boisterous central suite where eight of them were jammed together in heat and squalor, into a semi-private office shared with only one other and located two doors down the corridor from the senator himself. In spite of himself, Finnegan seethed with resentment. It did not matter that Steve Krall was older, had been on staff longer, and had performed with professional impeccability. Finnegan felt slighted and his bitterness grew. Conor Finnegan hated to be off the front lines, and he resented those who were there instead of him. He had been too accustomed to his successes. For a while, until he could reconcile his reactions with the logic that dictated their immaturity, he thought it best to keep his distance from his erstwhile peer. He might say something he really didn't mean.

As his professional responsibilities became more menial and his quixotic aspirations more tarnished, Finnegan found little consolation in his private life. He still did not understand why Glynnis was distancing herself. It had been a gradual process, but there could be no mistaking it. Finnegan spent most of his free time trying to analyze this sadly peculiar momentum. There must be something he could do. But if he did not comprehend the source of the disease, how could he effect a cure?

Glynnis came to Washington most weekends, but she stayed only a day. She became more adamant about returning on Saturday afternoon. Finnegan's frustrations grew, and they argued frequently. Trivial matters could set either of them off.

One weekend he bought theater tickets for Friday night. When he picked her up at Union Station, he showed her the tickets as they walked to the car.

"The Arena Stage, Glyn, and an August Wilson play. It's gotten great reviews, and it's sold out, but one of the interns had tickets she couldn't use, so here we are."

"Tonight? Jesus, Conor, couldn't you have let me know?"

"How was I going to do that, Glynnis? I wasn't even certain I'd get the tickets until just before I came to get you."

Glynnis dropped Conor's hand and turned her head away. When she turned back, she snapped, "Did you ever think that sitting in a dark theater for three hours after a long week might not be the way I want to spend my time? And so we go there straight from here, with no chance to freshen up or even stop for a drink? Great. Just great."

Finnegan had been stunned, but disappointment fell back into familiar patterns of resentment. He made no attempt to soothe her. "Fine. Then we'll forget the theater. No doubt for a very nice, relaxing evening at home, just like always. I'll tell my friend that the play was outstanding, that we wished it would never have ended. How's that?"

"I see your martyrdom reflex is especially sensitive tonight. Conor, I don't want to have to consider anything deep tonight. I don't want art, or literature, or poetry. I don't want to have to think. About anything."

"Okay, then we can sit silently on opposite ends of the room. No thought required."

"You know, you can really be a bastard sometimes," and they both fumed away the entire night.

The simplest things could bruise them. They sniped and jabbed, making remarks in the course of ordinary conversation that were meant to keep the other defensive or, if their moods were particularly foul, to elicit hurt. Even their quiet times became strained. The wild passions that swept over them subsided in a black mist of aborted expectations and muted resentments.

Conor viewed his time with Glynnis through a singular lens: Why is she not here with me? For Glynnis, her resolve not to be consumed became indomitable. Their two characters were intractable—neither budged. His frustration smoldered constantly, and on those occasions when it flared, it was met with Glynnis's cold assertions. She withdrew from him into deeper and deeper recesses, and Finnegan in turn grew more frustrated. The question ate at him always, an acid dripping slowly, continually and unstoppably. It ate away until the structure that supported the two of them together began to weaken with each movement. Cracks appeared where there had been no cracks before, and they split wider without remediation. And always Glynnis remained there, so desirable, the very marrow of his contentment, but always just out of reach. His grasping fingertips brushed her, and she backed away, stung by the touch.

* * *

On a morning in early June Conor Finnegan plodded through a Department of the Interior report on some unimportant aspect of a topic in which he had absolutely no interest. The monotonous insignificance of his current assignments were accentuated by the softly warm and dry luster of early summer, before July's stifling humidity descended to choke off all needless motion and the enthusiasm that generated it. On such a morning the city exuded a crystalline vibrancy, so pungent that one could not help but breathe it in. The great marble monuments and museums reflected white, the rivers, creeks and pools sparkled in a rich, pure blue, the austere government buildings sharply etched in chiaroscuro line and shadow seemed almost majestic. In the intoxication of vernal clarity the city's mood brightened. Noises of the street—the abrasive honks of car horns, the resonant belches of the buses, the sullen shuffling of the sidewalk traffic, even the plaintive wail of the occasional siren—all seemed less harsh, their brutal contours relaxed by the reaffirmation of lost innocence. People had ceased to shiver and they had not yet begun to perspire, and so there was an uncommon equilibrium, a delicate balance. A morning so rare, then, and so deftly sweet.

Finnegan felt none of it. Had his circumstances been less demeaning, he might have shared the city's buoyancy as he had before. As it was, though, a burgeoning cynicism cut short any sense of rebirth. 'Nothing lasts,' he told himself. 'Nothing survives. And everything we see as wondrous, gentle and complete moves away from us, faster and faster. It's inevitable, yet we do not see it. We can only sense it, and when we do, we tell ourselves that our senses lie.'

Near noon Griffith Ross walked out of his office and down the corridor to Finnegan's desk. Even on such a day, Ross wore his customary scowl that usually deepened when he spoke to Finnegan. For a brief while Finnegan had chafed under Ross's obvious disregard, but now it did not bother him nearly as much. Their contempt was mutual. Finnegan knew the source to be irremediable. It was a clash of two fundamental philosophies, two ways of looking at the world. They had collided on enough occasions to put them permanently at odds. Finnegan was thoroughly convinced that Ross had torpedoed his hearings. Ross was the final arbiter of everything that went on in that office. Because Finnegan could neither change him nor function outside Ross's purview, he forced himself to be quiescent. Since the cancellation of the hearings and his reassignment to every task that no one else wanted to do, Finnegan had given Ross a wide berth. They spoke only when necessary.

Ross stopped at Finnegan's desk and gestured down the corridor. "The boss wants to see you, Conor."

Finnegan put down his report, a mind-numbing review of public sanitation facilities from which he was pleased to be released, although he did not know what was afoot. The senator spoke to him rarely these days, too, and then usually just to review or confirm a point of fact that might have surfaced in a position paper or press release. Finnegan's heart quickened just a bit. The thought leapt into his head that another reassignment might be at hand, something to get him back into what was meaningful. He would have to be cautious this time, he knew that. But he was anxious to wrap his arms again around something that mattered. 'I've spent my time in purgatory,' he thought. 'I've done my penance.' The prospect caused a glimmer of anticipation to run through him.

"What's this about, Griffith, do you know? Should I bring anything?"

"You don't need anything." Customarily terse, thought Finnegan. The bastard. Not a pleasant word to be found. The two men walked down the corridor at Ross's brisk pace without saying anything at all.

Ross walked into the senator's office with him and took one of the chairs adjacent to the large desk, behind which the senator sat with his fingers arched together at the tips. The young man, wary now, sat in a chair directly opposite the senator's desk. Joyce shut the door behind them. Finnegan sensed himself at the point of an uneasy triangle, exposed and vulnerable. His anticipation made a kaleidoscopic change to apprehension, opposite shades of the same color.

"Conor," the senator began, "I'll get right to the point. Last week I spoke with the majority counsel to the Joint Committee on the Library. He has an opening for a research assistant. You're going to fill it."

As Finnegan's mind frantically assembled the implication of these few words, the contours of the room melted into a jellied mass, in the midst of which swam the firmly set expressions of the two older men, one marked by something close to boredom, the other scowling deeply but with a hint of a smile cornering his lips.

The kick struck Finnegan between the eyes. His brain exploded in confused, stunning pain. He sat motionless as the blood drained from his face. His eyes, widened at the impact, could only stare at the senator's face, languid now for all this, and moving feature by feature in the slowest animation.

"You have talent, Conor," the senator continued. "There's no doubting that. You've got a quick mind, you're organized and you write quite well. You're also a bulldog. Once you get hold of something, no force on earth can tear it away from you. That can be an asset if you use it selectively.

"But you've got a great deal yet to learn, my friend. A great, great deal. We can't afford the luxury of teaching you while you go about stirring things up. We fight enough battles just trying to accomplish what we want for ourselves. It's too exhausting to have to fight internal ones as well. We have to act as one body which, for better or worse, I lead. At first you surprised me with your boldness, and I was impressed. That bulldog in you, a very striking quality. But you have to know when to let go, Conor. I'm sorry, but I won't have a renegade on this team, no matter how well intentioned."

"You've never really fit in, Conor." Griffith Ross spoke for the first time. His voice penetrated Finnegan's ears with a shredding, threshing rasp, and Finnegan felt violated by it. "And you never really kept to what you were expected to do. You're paid to do research and to write a few speeches when we tell you. You're paid to remain quiet until we ask for your insights. This may shock you, but I've never given a tinker's damn about your convictions. I've never cared for what you thought our policies should be or how you wanted to pursue things. That's not your place, but it's obvious that you're not comfortable with being a follower. All along, you were a piece of something more complex than you chose to understand. You were a part of the machine, not the steam behind it. But you never seemed to accept that."

Finnegan shook his head from side to side. What burned within him he could not identify, but he knew it to be hot, as torrid as anything that ever flamed inside him. When one mixes the most potent liquors, each strong in its own right, he creates something toxic. If he should manage to choke it down, it renders him senseless. It rips apart the delicate tissue there, it robs him of self-control and hurls him randomly in whatever direction offers the least resistance. Conor Finnegan could not sort through the passions that pulsed through his bloodstream, a concoction of his strongest, most intoxicating substances—rage, humiliation, frustration, futility, impotence, guilt. But as they swirled together within him they created a sublime fury surpassing reason itself. As one drinking that odd mixture of intoxicants, his subconscious screamed a desperate warning that his indulgence would make him miserable when it finally came to rest. It was ignored, this warning, overwhelmed by the massing torrent that unleashed itself.

"We want you to start there Monday. Take the rest of the week to tie up what's outstanding, and coordinate your work with Steve so that we can reassign it," Ross went on in his grating, authoritative snarl. "And try to stay in line over there. I doubt there's much potential for damage in such a remote outpost, but you never know, what with your ideals and all."

The senator began to tell Finnegan where the committee office was and who his superior would be, but Finnegan heard none of it. His eyes riveted on the smug face of Ross, now thoroughly enjoying all this, relishing Finnegan's banishment.

Finnegan's torrent at last broke free.

"Ross, you God damn son of a bitch," he bit off the words with a perverse pleasure, enunciating each syllable. His voice began as a hiss, then rose as he went on, more and more of his fury escaping, greater chunks of the damming wall washed away.

"Now listen, Finnegan . . . "

"No, damn you, I'll listen to you no more. So you've won. Congratulations, although I never realized we were at war. You've reconfirmed your absolute control over our man here, and all of us who work for him. You must feel wonderful, you heartless bastard. But take a good look at what you've won. And take a good look at why you're squeezing me out. You can't stand a conscience, can you?

"What the hell is anyone to you except a vote? Neither one of you bastards has the slightest notion of responsibility, or, God forbid, service. You don't know the meaning of those words." Finnegan stood up now, his voice rising to something close to a shout. Both Ross and the senator rose, too. Ross took a step forward, and the senator walked out from behind his desk, his previous expression of casual boredom replaced now by a look of uncertainty. Ross maintained his scowl.

"You sit up here in your comfortable offices," Finnegan continued in a rush, "and push papers around and shake people's hands, and tell yourselves how important you are. You're surrounded by a bunch of bleating sheep. 'Yes, Senator.' 'Of course, Senator.' 'Thank you for your time, Senator.' But it's all a ruse. We put forth an image of public respectability, and we talk about the right things without ever intending to do anything other than protect what we already have. We protect ourselves, and to hell with anyone else. So I'm a threat to you because I don't buy that illusion. I believe that if the idea's there, then we have to make at least some small effort to put some meaning behind it.

"You talk about idealism like it's some kind of disease. But I'm not an idealist at all. I'm more of a realist than either of you *because I see what's out there*. I see the squalid, rotten things that you take such care to insulate yourselves from. And I see what we have the power to do about raising those issues. But you deny that power. It's *your* ideals that preclude it. You two, with your precious role of the devoted public servant, are far more idealistic than I could ever be. And your idealism is perverse. It's grotesque. You serve no one but yourselves.

"You sit there and tell me that that's the way it has to be, that's the way the game is played. I say that's bullshit. You can be as forceful as you want to be. You can raise the uncomfortable things, and try to do something about them. And yeah, there are risks involved, but that's why you're here. There are supposed to be risks. But instead, you circle the wagons and assume a bunker mentality. You stay where you think it's safe, where no one can get at you to see how shallow, incompetent and callous you really are. For all you accomplish in that real world you boast of knowing so thoroughly, you may as well be cardboard cutouts. There's no dimension to either one of you.

"So exile me to some damn meaningless committee. You're right, Ross, you fat bastard, I don't fit in. Too principled, you might say. So you perform a minor operation to remove the only pang of conscience either of you has to face.

"But let me tell you this. You can continue to weave your little illusion all you want. There's no one to stop you. There never was. But at some point you're going to have to be answerable to people who won't be taken in by a winning smile and a firm handshake. You're going to have to justify yourselves to those same people you've ignored. And when that happens I pray to God they have the good sense to flush you two bastards away like the garbage you are."

Finnegan whirled around and with his forearm swept clear a table near the door. Framed photographs, glassware and a small lamp scattered over the carpeted floor. Something broke: a tinkling of glass upon glass crinkled above the muffled crashings.

In an instant, Griffith Ross sprang forward and pinned Finnegan against the wall. His left hand wrapped Finnegan's shoulder and his right arm pressed against the young man's throat hard enough for the suggestion of strangulation. Finnegan's chest rose and fell with his furious breathing. His face flushed bright red.

"You little son of a bitch," hissed Ross. "I feel like breaking that thin little backbone of yours right here. I feel like crushing your skull between my fingers." Tiny droplets of spittle rained on Finnegan's face. The tip of Ross's nose brushed against Finnegan's, and his lips curled back in a repulsive hate-filled sneer. Finnegan was so close that he could see the tiny red lines in Ross's eyes, and the pores of his face.

"You don't know enough to back down, do you? You don't know when you're beaten. You want to be humiliated, too, is that it?" Ross clamped down hard on Finnegan's collarbone. Pain shot down his spine. "If you so much as open your mouth to cough I'm going to smack your face into a bloody mess, you understand me? Then I'll have your ass arrested for threatening assault on a United States senator. You'll have about six months in a federal prison to ponder those wonderful ideals of yours. Is that what you want?"

Finnegan swallowed hard through a constricted windpipe. His rage had spent itself in the blind act of sweeping the table. He had had no control, although he did not completely regret that, even now. But his rationality had reasserted itself. His senses were fully alert to any subtle gesture, any tensing of any muscle that Ross could interpret as hostile. He knew he had to be cautious. His margin of error had been erased by his own violence, and Ross clearly meant his threat.

"I don't want to see your face ever again, Finnegan. If I so much as see you walking down the hallway to the dining room, I'm liable to punch you out on the spot. I've already had so much more of you than I ever thought I could stomach. You're the biggest fool I've ever met, and you're going to be ground into dust before you know it. I wish to Christ I had the pleasure of finishing off that process myself. Now get the hell out of here, you whining son of a bitch."

Ross took his arm from Finnegan's neck and opened the door. His other arm dropped to Finnegan's chest. With a quick and powerful shove, he thrust Finnegan backward out of the office with such force that the younger man lost his balance and fell on his side, his head narrowly missing the corner of Joyce's desk. Two or three faces stopped their work and stared down the corridor at Finnegan's demise. Joyce stared with naked surprise at the body that had been flung toward her. Ross stood in the doorway with an oily smile creasing his lips. He looked at Joyce, then back down at Finnegan.

"Conor's balance isn't too good these days," he said evenly. "Get up, Conor. And try to be more careful where you fall. You're liable to damage the furniture."

Finnegan rose slowly with Ross watching every move. He drew himself up and paused to fix his eyes intently upon the older man's scowling face. Finnegan took a deep breath. He became aware of the perspiration that lined his forehead and was cascading down his sides. His fall had dislodged his shirt from where it had been tucked into his pants. He felt completely defenseless as he stood there. What might there be left to consider? What might there be left to do?

Finnegan turned and walked back down the corridor to a desk it would take hours to empty. Behind him, the door to the senator's office had shut. The mundane sounds of work that had been suspended for a few seconds resumed, but the buzzing in Finnegan's brain, the relentless angry swarming of a million hornets, would not let him hear it.

For the remainder of the day not one of his colleagues spoke to him. He had become a pariah, and no one dared guilt by association. They were not certain of the crime, but they knew it must have been heinous. They wanted no part of the perpetrator. Finnegan made some outside phone calls to his contacts to inform them that he would be moving on and he would no longer be able to offer any assistance. He sent a brief memo to Steve Krall letting him know that he had free rein to reassign as he saw fit any of the responsibilities Finnegan was leaving behind, confirmed the access to his email accounts, and outlined what was in his files. At the end of the day Finnegan dropped his office key on the receptionist's desk, pushed his way between two tourists inspecting their senate gallery passes, and walked wordlessly into the austere, colorless hallway.

As he headed down the echoing corridor, nausea swept over him as rapidly as a breath of wind extinguishes a candle. The very building seemed to mock him, the great massiveness of it. The resonance of its reverberating voices, the clacks and clangs of footsteps, dollies and delivery carts, the familiar and nameless faces he had seen every day for the past year. All of it massed around him, a rancid, acrid odor that seared his nostrils and twisted his stomach into a Gordian knot. His head swam in dips and eddies. He became desperate: he had to get out of this haunted and haunting building. He had to get out. He had to get away from the dull sights and monotonous sounds and the common feel of the hard floor beneath his shoes. It had all become invalidated. *He* had been invalidated. This place was spitting him out like a watermelon seed.

Each corridor curled into another, each looking the same. Finnegan's familiarity with the pattern ebbed by degrees, then vanished. The mindless anarchy of panic crept into his veins. His heart raced. 'Which way? What shall I do now? Where shall I go?'

His breathing grew raspy and frantic. He tried a high wooden door that he thought was a stairway, but it was locked. He turned a corner and the corridor ended in a blank gray wall. Footsteps echoed around him. A beautiful long-haired blonde, Glynnis in a wig, walked past him. She raised her eyes and smiled. When Finnegan turned to watch her walk away she was gone, and no one was near.

Finnegan's desperation doubled back on itself. He had to get out. Which way? He had been invalidated. What shall I do now? He saw himself leaping out a window and making a high, sweeping arc over the city, his pant leg ripped by the headdress of the Indian on the Capitol Dome, and landing with a great splash in the Potomac where no one noticed and the waters closed back over his sinking head and the river went on as if nothing had ever disturbed it. He saw it in an instant, then it vanished, as everything did, leaving only the horrible darkness. He had been totally invalidated.

At the end of the corridor, a sign glowed 'Exit' above a doorway. Finnegan spotted it through the spinning, blurring vacuum. He broke into a run. This way, and the prospect of at least a temporary certainty. Sweat blinded him, and then the eruption, the heavy thrusting and pumping within him reaching its climax. As he approached the red sign, he saw another door to his right and knew he must use it, use it at once. The thunder in his ears had become a pounding shout, a deep, resonating basso cry that flushed away resistance.

Finnegan dashed through the men's room door on his right and raced to the sink just fast enough for it to catch his vomit. His hands gripped his sides. The pure white porcelain cooled him and he let the heaving gasps reach their peak, then subside. A silvery viscous thread hung from his mouth. He watched it there, languidly spanning to the brownish mess he had made. He did not want to sever it. After several minutes his panting blew it away. Finnegan turned on the tap and washed the fetid detritus down the drain. He swished the water to each corner of the sink to make sure he got it all, then cupped his hands to capture a good amount. Bending his head near the porcelain, he splashed his face to cool it. To wash away the last traces. No one had come in while he was there.

After a time he straightened himself and waited for the strength to flow back into his knees. Even then he still sagged at the joints. His body could barely carry itself, but at least his breathing had returned to normal. His sweating had ceased. Finnegan wiped his forehead with a paper towel, opened the door and found his way out to the street where the sun blinded him, a hot fist thrust into his face. He reeled, leaned against the building which was hard and grainy. While the tag-end of a Washington day walked by, he regurgitated the last few bits in his stomach onto the cracked pavement at his feet.

CHAPTER XXV

He who learns must suffer. And even in our sleep, pain, which cannot forget, falls drop by drop upon the heart, until, in our own despair, against our will, comes wisdom through the awful grace of God.

—Aeschylus, *Agamemnon*

Tom McIlweath sent most of his belongings ahead. He had taken several days to clean out his apartment and box up the relevant materials he wanted with him in Ireland, mostly books and personal effects such as letters, swimming awards and clippings from the student newspapers. What he did not want he either discarded or sold. His limited wardrobe he packed into three suitcases that he would take with him when he went.

When he went. While the concept had intrigued him and had reinvigorated again his spirit, the reality loomed, if not menacingly, then at least as something worthy of the highest respect. His Romantic detachment had been shelved in favor of the logistical details to be addressed.

His parents had come to visit him before he left. He had been gratified by the gesture but he found that they had very little to say. John McIlweath, who had traveled a similar path years earlier, behaved sullenly while his wife lapsed into a weepy sentimentality. Their admonitions, cautions and encouragements sat poorly with their son, who saw in his parents for the first time a subtle pressure of expectation. Although bystanders now, they retained ideals for their son that this most radical of acts obscured. Not that they opposed it. Rather, they did not quite know what to make of it, especially because its eventual value was not clear. They were merely visiting their son because they had not seen him for too long, and the next meeting was uncertain. Such were the limits of their interpretation of the young man's exile.

The McIlweaths had stayed a week. Tom showed them as much of Boston as he knew, and the rest of the time they spent in the apartment or going out for meals, talking or not talking depending upon their moods. Mrs. McIlweath fussed with Tom's clothes a great deal, repaired some things and helped him sort through his books. John McIlweath took no part in his son's preparations. He watched a fair amount of television and kept to himself. Not once did father and son speak alone at any length. The younger man waited, anticipating either a benediction or a curse. Nothing came, and at the end of the week Tom bade them a relieved goodbye. His mother wept and his father offered only a handshake. They climbed onboard their plane and flew west as their son stood below to watch the gleaming white cylinder as it shrank to an imperceptible sliver. His lack of sadness puzzled him. He felt guilty; he might never see them again.

It was early August, the thick part of the year. McIlweath's apartment had been emptied of all but the furniture that came with it. He sat at the kitchen table and watched a late afternoon sun spill in the window and paint his floor in butterscotch. Kathy Keane sat opposite him. She had helped him load his car, although there was not much to do since he was taking so little. They were finishing glasses of iced tea.

"It's so hollow here," said Kathy. "When you speak it echoes."

"This place has always been hollow. I'm glad to leave it."

"But you can't be sure you're going to anything better. You might end up in a huge stone room with a high ceiling and bats flying over your head. Drafts might come in through the cracks. They have those things in Ireland, you know," she said with a soft smile.

"The cold winds off the south coast."

"And a ghost. You'll most likely have a ghost. Or several, perhaps. I hear every corner of Ireland has its own ghost. How old is this college of yours?"

"Mid-nineteenth century. A Johnny-come-lately as European colleges go. Built as a sop to wealthy Brits stuck among the savages."

"Nonetheless, it's probably thoroughly haunted. Why is it that old countries hang onto their ghosts so much more fiercely than we do?"

"They've had more time to cultivate them. And they're no doubt proud of them. Ghosts give up their world reluctantly. So if you have them running about, then there's probably something around that's difficult to leave. Something unfinished they want to be a part of. I'm sure there'll be ghosts in my rooms, but not all of them may be native."

"Meaning?"

"I'll be bringing one or two with me," McIlweath replied with a thin smile. "Maybe more."

"I assume I'm one of them. Tell me without being maudlin."

"Yes. You're one of them."

"Good. I'd hate to think I could be so easily forgotten. I confess you'll be lingering with me for a good while, too." She paused, then turned serious. "Yours is a marvelous spirit, Tom. You deserved to be saved."

"If indeed that's what's happening. Sometimes I think about what might have occurred between us under different circumstances. If I had met you ten years from now when you'd be truly ready for me. I think we might have saved each other then, and allowed ourselves some genuine happiness in the process."

"Put away those thoughts, Tom. There's better for you than me, that I know. We'd kill each other before we knew it and spend the rest of our days like zombies. You know that as well as I do. You've already gone past me and there's no room for regrets. I've been your catapult, and now you're airborne. I'm awfully proud of myself for that."

Beads of condensation ran down their two glasses. McIlweath ran a fingernail across the moisture on his tumbler, drawing an abstract design. Before he could make any sense of it, more drops flowed over it and washed it away.

"I'm not afraid of what comes next," he said. "I'm not apprehensive about going someplace foreign. It's foreign here, but we tend to fool ourselves into thinking that we fit where we are because of the accident of where we're born. Temperament transcends heritage, though. It's all been foreign, to me. It's been foreign for years."

"So it doesn't really matter where you go?"

"No, I don't suppose it does. As long as I'm the final judge of everything that follows. I'm fortunate to be able to see that now."

"The loneliness doesn't scare you?"

"Kathy, until you surfaced I'd been lonely almost every day of my life. Any loneliness there will be of my own choosing. You've dismantled my insecurities, Kathy. There's a dimension of choice that overrides anything else. I've learned that. I don't know what I'll have there, and in one sense it doesn't matter. But for the first time in my life, *in my life,* I'll be working with raw material. I'm desperate to do that. Loneliness is only one factor, and it's a minor one at that. There's something greater at play. And if nothing else, this indulges my spirit of adventure."

"It's wondrous, this potential we have," said Kathy wistfully. "It's one of our greatest tragedies: that so few of us ever try to capture it. You and I are among the fortunate ones, I dare say. I include myself, Tom. I think that's probably why I was attracted to you from the start. You pricked something in my subconscious. I've just never felt compelled to go so far afield."

They were both silent. Random street sounds wafted up through the window, the sounds of Boston at sunset on a hot summer day— the press of traffic, the grating hoarseness of short tempers, the dull thudding shuffle of tired legs. The ancient city had been that way for generations; it would be that way for countless more. Ethnic or social character made no difference. Immutable Boston. Immutable Man.

"You're going south tomorrow, right?" asked Kathy after some time. "To Washington to see your friend."

"Yes. I have to see him before I go."

"You've told me about him. The heroic one."

"He's been on my mind a great deal lately. I haven't seen him in more than a year. We'd been as close as brothers."

"Will you stay with him long?"

"A day or two. Long enough to re-establish ourselves before we separate again. It hurts, Kathy, being apart from him. For years, he was my rudder. We spent our best years together, and I always took my lead from him. He gave me his best without ever knowing it. I've got to see him again."

"Well then, I can't blame you," she sighed. "Come on. We have one last night together. Let's begin it now." She rose and took his hand. McIlweath took a final look around the stark apartment. When he left it he felt as if he were stepping out of a tomb, Lazarus saved by an unseen power to embrace his own Magdalen.

* * *

The drive south the next day was gloomy. The night had brought in a heavy layer of clouds that pressed down on the landscape in colorless sobriety. It did not rain. McIlweath wished very hard that it would, and be done with, but the clouds did not unlock. They hung low and solid, sealing in the heat, making it palpable and smothering the entire seaboard. Perhaps it was only fitting, he thought. Forged in ice, freed in fire. His spirit hung motionless, as heavy as the clouds.

McIlweath had left in the early morning. With his body screaming its reluctance, he had disentangled himself from Kathy for what he knew might be the last time. The finality of it depressed him, and as he ate a vapid breakfast he spoke only a little. Kathy, too, had nothing to say, so they completed their brief morning tasks in an air of eerie silence. Their courses were set; too many words might weaken a determination so wrenchingly established, or, more likely, invite regret. They did not want to tempt themselves with pointless words. Sweet comforts they had shared would be resurrected later.

When the actual moment of leavetaking came about, it was necessarily swift. Kathy in her robe walked McIlweath to his car. There, on the empty street, they embraced. To the young man's astonishment tears spilled from Kathy's eyes. Then she was gone—forever, or long enough to seem so.

The long, tedious drive deepened his depression. New England's scenery which had once seemed so charming became monotonous in the gray light. McIlweath noticed chips in the pavement on the Turnpike, and near Chicopee a construction project narrowed the road to one lane. He was annoyed at the delay. When he reached Springfield he left the Turnpike to head south into Connecticut on I-81, which had neither tolls nor construction. He perceived an oily, sooty smell from the nearby factories, and it disgusted him. He drove on in a sullen, trancelike state and paid heed only to the road in front of him.

McIlweath skirted New York's urban web and passed through the flatlands of northern New Jersey. He recalled the first time he had come to the city as a freshman at Rutgers. The city held such unbelievable romantic magic then. He had seen New York as a microcosm of the human condition—all aspects of his real or potential experience, for better or worse, were contained there. It was the doorway to an inner universe, the perch from which the most comprehensive views of humanity had issued. Whitman and Wolfe, O'Neill, Fitzgerald, Crane, Lardner, Langston Hughes—they had all known it to be so, and that was why they came. He had come, too. God, it had been so glorious.

But then they had all gotten hopelessly drunk, and Conor vomited in the restaurant lobby, and on the walk back to the car they had run into some hookers. He had stayed away from the city after that. The power there, reverberating through the air itself, had been too much for him. It had sullied all of them, he and his friends, dragging them away from anything Romantic or grand. That night had alarmed Tom McIlweath, even though his friends always alluded to it thereafter with good humor. As they recounted stories of that night in the months and years to come, its significance diminished for them. But McIlweath feared what had taken hold of them then.

Now, as he drove past the huge towers and belching factories on a gutted roadway, the city and its surrounding fiefdoms repulsed him. He saw nothing romantic here anymore. There was only a grotesque ugliness to which most were immune. But today he saw it as the souls of the people living there turned inside out, cast in steel and stone.

Near New Brunswick, McIlweath was tempted to turn off the highway and drive through campus one last time. He toyed with the idea, then dismissed it. There was nothing to be gained. He did not want to sentimentalize his attachment to the place. Besides, there was no one there he cared to see. The ghosts would remain healthy and vibrant without him.

From there McIlweath lapsed back into a dank boredom. South Jersey, the neck of Delaware, Maryland's rolling rhythms, the distances between them all—it meant nothing. It was all indistinguishable, subtle shades of ink all run together on one sheet of paper. He stopped once to eat and twice for gas. For most of the day, he drove without thought or reaction.

As he neared Washington, clouds thickened again, enough to block the light of the setting sun, building a premature darkness. His blood began to pump, and his senses sharpened. Here at last he was reaching the end of this purgative journey. Conor Finnegan was only a few miles away. The day's heat lifted somewhat and a cool breeze blew through the open window. McIlweath's fatigue lifted, too, and his boredom with it.

The wooded hills south of Baltimore gave way to residential areas, the highway widened. By the time McIlweath turned on to the Beltway, lights in the houses, offices and stores had begun to come on. He looked forward to catching glimpses of the great monuments in the dark. Finnegan had told him that it was all beautiful after nightfall. Living there, his friend had said, he had begun to take it all for granted, but it still could take his breath away sometimes. It could be truly inspiring if one were given to such things. When McIlweath caught sight of the Capitol Dome, illuminated by spotlights that tinted its pristine whiteness with a gentle gold, he felt the rush of awe that Finnegan had hinted.

Perhaps it was not just the Dome itself, but the fact that Finnegan was a part of it. His friend had always seemed tailored for this city. He had been completely adaptable to its power and glamor. What McIlweath admired in Conor, this city amplified: the elegance, the command, the sense of control, the restrained enthusiasm channeled to positive action, and, in the end, the compilation of those traits into a single strong, attractive, irresistible entity. If hubris crept into it, that was to be expected and forgiven. It must be incredibly difficult to remain subdued when such obvious blessings had been bestowed.

McIlweath knew that, of all the people he was leaving behind, he would miss Conor Finnegan most fiercely. He had missed him terribly during the year they had already been apart. McIlweath could not have counted the nights he ached for the steady reassurances and insights of his friend. Had Finnegan been present then, perhaps McIlweath would not be doing this. Conor had been the constant embodiment of those distinctive qualities McIlweath sought for himself. With Finnegan, there had never been a question of acceptance or belonging. His exuberant self-confidence was infectious; it had stabilized McIlweath all the time they had been together. Finnegan lived his life with an unflagging passion for the infinity of his possibilities. In reflection, during the time they were apart, McIlweath realized that Finnegan confirmed the potential of youth itself, and that, at least in his own mind, Conor Finnegan lived in harmony with his own capabilities.

Where did that harmony come from? McIlweath did not know, but at least he could devise a theory. It existed because Finnegan assumed it did. He had spent his young life with the pretext that what he was and what he did reflected the best that the fates could possibly offer. Finnegan's life echoed an unarticulated collective longing for purification. Man was still pulling himself out of the muck, and if Finnegan was to be a part of that, then so be it. He assumed that what he claimed for himself and what he perceived as natural attributes merely fit in with that evolutionary pattern. Nothing had occurred to dissuade him, so, for Conor Finnegan, that simple assertion still held. All those assets he had amassed for himself were part of a greater process in which his life was destined to play a role. How could one not be in harmony with that?

McIlweath had no problem finding the right street. He pulled into the tiny lot behind a high brick apartment building and saw Finnegan's car. At seeing that familiar object his excitement leaped. He had reentered his friend's sphere, and here was proof. He noted, too, that Dan Rosselli's car was nowhere to be seen. All along, McIlweath had subjugated the notion of seeing Rosselli to the greater purpose of seeing Finnegan. Rosselli was an added benefit that he too often overlooked. The three of them back together for a night or two . . . it would be like stepping through a time portal, the brothers reunited again in a different context, strong again by being together, and able to put aside their singular struggles and frustrations and loneliness.

He hopped out of the car and headed for the door to Finnegan's end of the complex. McIlweath rang the bell below a piece of tape that said 'Finnegan/Rosselli', and a harsh buzz signaled that the door was now unlocked. He opened it and faced two stairways. Apartment D. He took the one on the right and by the time he was halfway up it, the door at the top swung inward and Conor stood beaming before him. McIlweath ran up the last few stairs.

Finnegan reached out his hand, and McIlweath reciprocated, but even the firmest of handshakes could not contain their affection, or could bridge the gaps of loneliness. They embraced there on the landing in a great bear hug, pounding each other's back and feeling the heft and strength of one another's shoulders. In retrospect, months later, McIlweath came to recognize that what he grasped there was more than just his friend. In the gesture he embraced the breathless final moments of his own receding youth. A long time would pass before he could sort through the emotion of that moment.

"Come on in, Mac. Give me your bag. Jesus, it's great to see you. Let me put this down and get you something to drink. God, you must be beat."

McIlweath obediently followed Finnegan into the apartment which, in its casual clutter, was exactly what he would have expected. What he had not expected was the change in his friend. At first glance, McIlweath could see a subtle alteration in both physical appearance and aura. After so much time together over the past several years, the two shared an instinct to read each other thoroughly and implicitly. McIlweath saw now a vague resignation that would have been imperceptible to anyone else. Where a stranger might see a proper, ambitious young man—warm, enthusiastic, intelligent and complete— McIlweath saw someone subdued. The face lacked a little of its usual vibrancy. Finnegan's eyes did not dart about as they usually did, eager to sight everything he could and not miss a glimmer of what was around him. Instead, they seemed tired, and, despite the tenor of his greeting, so did his voice. The lilt that made nearly every sentence he spoke a kind of song was not there. One of the few constants in his life had been Conor Finnegan, but some inner alarm told McIlweath that this constant had shifted.

"Nice place, Conor. Of course, now that you're a rising young professional I'd have expected nothing less. Where's Dan?"

"The school. He'll be coming home any time. Mac, you wouldn't believe the change in him. He's become responsible."

"Our lost friend Dan?"

"Has become a man. He's thoroughly in love with what he's doing. I think he's finally built himself some respectability. In fact, I rarely see him. Between med school and this new woman he's found, he's never home."

"You told me about this woman. Has our boy at last grown up?"

Finnegan was in the kitchen opening two beers. He raised his voice to answer. "He says he has. Apparently he's been, shall we say, consummated. She's rounded him out. Her name's Julie. She's a Georgetown undergrad, which means she comes from richer blood than ours. School of Foreign Service."

"I assume she's gorgeous."

"Like a lingerie model. Thin, fresh, and with an hint of innocence. Brown hair, blue eyes and dimples. Dan says he might actually be tempted to get serious."

"The worse for him. Sounds like that's the last thing he needs now."

"You *have* gotten rid of Anne, haven't you?" said Finnegan, returning to the living room and handing McIlweath a full glass. "That's quite a turnaround from the Tom McIlweath we used to know. The one who clung to a woman's security, despite all costs."

"A phase I've outgrown, Conor. Sad but necessary. Anne was the keystone of it."

"And without her you're back on the road to self-assurance. You've got your balls back. She weighed you down, Mac. You know that now, don't you?"

"Yes. You and Dan and Lanny saw it so clearly. To your credit, you guys were always decent about it. I saw it myself, but I never let on. I was too afraid."

"That's behind you now, thank Christ. There are other things to talk about. After a year and a half we shouldn't introduce a conversation with the subject of Anne Newbury. Or Glynnis Mear, if you're thinking about asking. Those are serious topics we can work up to."

"How is Glynnis? You haven't written me much about her recently."

"Ask me again around midnight after we've had enough to drink to make me honest. As I said, a serious topic. For the record, she's fine."

"I hope I haven't touched a nerve."

"You couldn't help it. It's dangling there exposed. Let's move on to some harmless small talk, such as where in hell in Ireland you're going. Start with that, and when we deal with why you're doing it, we can get into Glynnis."

McIlweath told him and stayed clear of anything deliberative. Finnegan's implication was obvious to him. This was what McIlweath had wanted, and he felt quietly relieved that his friend would not prove evasive. McIlweath needed a final accounting, an inspection and evaluation of his own course. That was why he had come. Conor, he presumed, would reciprocate. The result would be one of those exhausting sweeping discussions that left both of them drained yet intuitively and permanently wiser. Finnegan, of course, was correct. They would have to work up to it. But beforehand they would enjoy one another again in less stressful rhythms, the simple company of a parallel soul.

After they had been talking for half an hour, heavy thumping clomped up the stairs. "That could only be Dan," said McIlweath.

"Some things never change."

A key in the lock, the door swinging open and the glowing form of Dan Rosselli. His smile was incandescent, a huge Cheshire-cat grin that radiated pure joy.

As McIlweath had perceived an alteration in Finnegan, so he perceived a similar yet opposite transformation in Dan Rosselli for whom the pendulum had swung the other way. McIlweath had never seen Rosselli so alive. That was obvious to even the untrained eye. The conflict between expectations and reality that had eaten away at McIlweath in Boston, and that now seemed to be affecting Finnegan, was nowhere to be found in Dan Rosselli. Dan had always relied somewhat on what McIlweath had identified as an Etruscan fatalism. More than any of them, Rosselli had been content to go with the flow, dipping his oar into the water only now and then to direct a general course. Perhaps, then, his expectations had been limited. If so, then the satisfactions that he had found in his current state had exploded into his mind, and into his heart.

"Mac!" shouted Rosselli, and the two men came together in the middle of the room to embrace. Rosselli threw an arm around McIlweath's shoulders and hugged him to his side. "You old son of a bitch, how've you been?"

"Great, Dan. You look super. You've lost weight."

"I've been eating Conor's cooking. That would take weight off an Ethiopian refugee. Speaking of which, do we have dinner plans or are we just going to drink all night?"

"I want to take you two out somewhere," said Finnegan. "To celebrate our reunion, brief as it is. There's a Spanish restaurant on Connecticut that I like."

"When did you become so generous?" asked McIlweath.

"Don't question it, Mac," replied Rosselli. "Conor's making a pretty good dollar. He can afford it."

"Right. The largesse of our rich Uncle Sam. Actually, it's because I'm the only one of us who has a respectable job. I have to spend my money somewhere, so it may as well be on food and drink with my lost brothers."

"There were times this past year when I would have given five years off my life for a night like this," said McIlweath.

"You were pretty alone up there, weren't you?" asked Finnegan, suddenly serious. "I wouldn't have expected that."

"Yeah, I was alone, Conor. And I certainly didn't anticipate that. Even with Anne, I was completely alone. Until the end, that is. I got some relief toward the end. That's why I was able to leave, I think."

"You cleared your accounts?"

"I couldn't leave under the circumstances that existed for most of the year. I wouldn't have been able. But that's too complex to go into now. I'd rather eat. Let's go," and the three of them filed back down the stairs and out the door, their voices commingling in excitement, their very souls once again overlapping as they had done for so many years.

The restaurant was a short drive over the Wilson Bridge, then up 18th to Connecticut. Thankfully short, to McIlweath's thinking, for he had suddenly become extremely hungry, as hungry as he could remember. It came on in an explosion, and a burning flare ate away at his stomach and crawled up his ribs. His depression had been shattered, and with it his body's subdued response. All day he had merely been going through the motions. Relieved now, his system erupted back to its normal state and required compensation. McIlweath wanted to eat anything he could reach.

They ordered from the menu and started in on the imported beer that came first. McIlweath devoured handfuls of the thin tortillas placed in front of them. Because his stomach was empty (or hollow, as he might have considered it) the beer took immediate effect. A warm glow rose up from his core and radiated down each limb, sapping away whatever tension lingered. He thought briefly of the Prodigal Son.

The evening for all three of them turned into a reclamation. Qualities of their youth had slipped from them without notice or recognition. Now, in the complexities they each had assumed, they realized that what they had lost could only be regained with each other. There was no other way. The simple physical comforts they enjoyed that night, the food and the drink, revived them and confirmed what they had once been. The meal was a sacrifice, a Eucharist laid out on the altar of a common passion. What would ensue for the remainder of their lives would only reshape the possibilities they all had shared at a distant point. And so, on this haunted evening, infested with the silent ghosts of past lives, they commemorated that quickly fading point, that diminishing dot on a broad horizon, that would never disappear entirely but was destined to become so remote that its contours would become amorphous, shifting and therefore mythical.

They stayed at the restaurant several hours, eating a huge meal and drinking the thick, dark European beer they preferred. Through it all, McIlweath and Finnegan kept clear of the weighty topics that, by their earlier implications, would be the meat of the discussion to come. Rosselli, though, ignored all bounds. He carried the conversation, his obvious excitement with the course of his own life providing the constant theme. Rosselli relished the evening; he relished the presence of his friends. He had fallen hopelessly in love with the conditions of his existence, conditions he had not imagined as they had developed, and so the harmonious sweetness of his life was deepened by its serendipity.

At one point, McIlweath remarked, "Dan, I can't believe how happy you are. Not that you were unhappy before, but now you seem to be so much more complete."

"And I can't believe how well everything has fallen into place," Rosselli beamed in reply. "It's like I've been singled out. You know, I used to be envious of you two."

"And now you're not?" said Finnegan playfully. "Have Tom and I made such a mess of things?"

"Not at all. But in college you guys held all the cards and I didn't think I had anything to match them. I mean, here's Conor Finnegan, America's Golden Boy, honor student, outgoing, personable, good athlete, with a gorgeous woman on his arm, and there's Tom McIlweath, intelligent, albeit a bit insecure, captain of the swim team, honorable mention All American, squiring around a woman of his own, even if it was only Anne. And what was I then? A struggling pre-med, looking for a good time. I was never certain anything would come of me. I was always afraid my ambitions were out of reach. I was never quite sure that I was good enough for med school, that I was smart enough or had enough discipline to put myself through it, even if I could get accepted."

"You hid that pretty well," said Finnegan. "You always struck me as confident to the point of being smug."

"A smokescreen. You two had the discipline. You had the intelligence and you had the guts. By contrast, I was scared. I was afraid I'd end up as some frustrated mechanic working in a garage on the Jersey shore, married to an Italian girl growing fatter by the day."

"Instead," said McIlweath, "you'll be a well-known surgeon with a huge manor in the suburbs and a summer house in North Carolina, married to an oversexed blonde who gave up a career as a fashion model to be your wife, driving a Ferrari or a Lamborghini, and with at least two mistresses on the side."

"And," continued Finnegan, "you'll publish articles in the best medical journals, join a country club and retain a small army of stockbrokers to manage your investments. However, at the height of your glory, one of your delicious mistresses will slap you with a paternity suit. There'll be a scandal, your wife will divorce you and the country club will rescind your membership. You'll be so distracted that in surgery to repair someone's hernia you'll inadvertently cut off his penis, thereby destroying your reputation and sending your malpractice insurance into default. To meet your alimony expenses, which will be huge, you'll have to sell your

Lamborghini and take a job in that same Jersey shore garage."

"What you're saying," laughed Rosselli, "is that the pendulum can swing both ways. And that we're fated to whatever we get."

"It does swing both ways, Dan. Viciously."

"Well, if that's the case, then all I can do is enjoy what I have for the moment. But I don't expect my allotment to be meager. I'm not going to worry about protecting my flanks. I'm charging straight ahead until I get the things I want."

"So," said McIlweath, "part of your current bliss is based on the conviction that you're on the way to the type of lifestyle you want for yourself."

"Absolutely, although I do enjoy what I'm doing for its own sake. There are satisfactions I never recognized before. It's satisfying to have a positive impact on someone else's life. But in the end we have to secure ourselves before we can think about securing others. That's what I intend to do." The exchange with Rosselli was the closest they would come to serious conversation this night. Finnegan and McIlweath each recounted in noncommittal terms the course of their past several months. Mostly they reminisced about the common years of their embryonic emergence, the secure years of anticipation.

"Take this, all of you, and eat it. This is my body, which will be given up for you. Do this in memory of me."

* * *

They drove back to the apartment several hours after they had left it. Rosselli suggested stopping for a drink, and Finnegan took them to a bar he knew in Georgetown, not one of the loud, cramped, raucous student bars, but a quiet place in one of the better hotels. It had no entertainment, so few people went there on weekends. Finnegan liked it because it seemed so sane. Perhaps, after all, he was aging beyond his years.

Shortly after 1:00 they got back to the apartment. As soon as they shut the door behind them, Rosselli yawned, setting off a chain reaction. "I've had enough for one night," he said. "Mac, where are you sleeping tonight?"

"Conor says the couch."

"Good idea. We need someone as a first line of defense against the cockroaches. I'm going to bed."

"You want a nightcap, Mac?" asked Finnegan.

"Yeah. I'll stay up for a while."

"See you guys in the morning. You're not thinking of getting up too early, are you, Mac?"

"No way. I'm beat."

"Good. I'll see you guys around noon, then. Good having you here, Mac. Conor's gotten boring. You're a welcome change of pace."

"But I'm boring, too."

"I know, but I'm not used to you yet. Good night, you guys."

Finnegan returned from the kitchen with two snifters. He handed one to McIlweath, who held it up to the light.

"Grand Marnier," said Finnegan. "You'll like it."

"You can afford the good stuff now, I see."

"An acquired taste. One of the few I've managed."

"A reflection of your new and rising prominence?"

Finnegan snorted. "A reflection only of some latent pretensions. There's a Rossellian strain that runs through me too, I think."

"There's nothing wrong with that. In moderation, of course."

"Now, when have you ever known me to be moderate?" asked Finnegan. The night all at once seemed emptier, and Finnegan's mood shifted to something flatter. McIlweath tried to read it, but it had too many layers. A blend of depression, frustration, and. . .what? Loneliness? Was that echoing in those few words, too? Something new was in there as well, and completely unexpected: cynicism. It was a potent mixture, and more than a little unnerving.

"Well, I've never thought of you as extreme," said McIlweath.

"I've never considered myself that way either. Until recently. I've had some evidence that I might push the borders a bit. In retrospect, I may have always been extreme. It's just that my perspectives had never been put to the test." He raised his glass in a quick toast. "To Ireland, Tom, and the grand things that go with it." They clinked glasses, then sipped the heady liqueur. Its fumes raced up McIlweath's nostrils and pierced his brain right behind his eyes. The thick orange flavor hung on his palate, and his full stomach received the syrup warmly. Little darts of heat ran to his far corners.

"I don't know if there will be grand things there, Conor. I don't really know what's going to be there. It'll be a sorting out, that's all. A purgation."

"Because of Anne?"

"Indirectly. There's no need to purge what never really penetrated in the first place, is there? Anne's a symbol, Conor. She epitomizes my subjugation. She played upon every insecurity I ever had. She tucked me into her bag like one of those medical instruments she carries with her now, only I'm not as sophisticated. I'm leaving Anne, that's true, but I'm leaving more than that. I'm leaving myself.

"My life's been random for a long time," he continued. "It's been predicated on the expectations of other people, so it's never had the legs to find a direction of its own. That's my fault exclusively. I've let myself be too answerable to people who have no permanent stake. Anne's been the most obvious example, but she's not the only one by any means. I've been moved too much by impression, Conor, so I've lost my bearings. Ireland's a means of claiming control again."

"That seems like a fairly drastic step."

"It has to be. I want to get as far away as I can. I have to strip away any and all temptations that might lure me back. That's the only way for me. I want to find some place that's purer than anything I've ever experienced. You know, I think I can finally understand the mentality of the ancient Essenes. There's something to be said for going into the desert for a few years and eating nothing but locusts. This is my desert."

"It sounds as if you're trying to punish yourself."

"No. Not punishment, just—realignment. Conor, there are some real attractions to what I'm doing. Ireland's not the end of the world. From what I can gather, this whole situation is likely to be rather quaint. I suppose all I'm looking for is some time, and maybe a little space that's all my own.

"And I'll tell you something else," he went on. "If I'm going to do this right, I have to get away from every influence to which I've become accustomed. Do you realize that each time you so much as walk down a city street, that you're subjected to a thousand different assumptions? I imagine that because we're the Great Melting Pot we've become fanatical about absorption, about conformity. We've built systems, and everyone's supposed to have a place somewhere, and be happy with who they are and where they land. There's little room for exploration, or for growth. We tolerate deviation very poorly."

"You're right, of course," said Finnegan. "But can we ever escape that? There are assumptions no matter where we go or what we do. We're always answerable to the thoughts or impressions or perspectives that other people craft for us."

"I'll hold judgment on that. Look, I'm not implying that I'm about to devote myself to some radical scheme, and I'm not saying I've become misanthropic. All I want is a clean slate and some time to figure out what I want to draw on it. I can't do that here."

"You're running the risk of never coming back."

"There are worse fates. Yes, that's a risk. But what would I be giving up? And if I find that the substance of what I am and what I want lie outside what's come before, then why should I come back? I'm not bound by any overdeveloped sense of national identity. All I want to do is curl up with my books for a while, Conor, and not worry about where I'm going. Some course will become apparent. If not, I've lost nothing in the meantime. There's nothing mystical in that."

"What comes afterward?"

"Who the hell knows? I'm twenty-four years old and I don't have a God damn clue what I want my life to be. That makes me an anomaly. You see, I've broken the program already. It's that sense of obligation that I have to get away from. I don't know what comes afterward. Something more logical than what's come before is all. I'll let the specifics make themselves known as they come along."

Finnegan thought a while, then said slowly, "And here Dan and I thought you were leaving because of Anne—the heartbroken lover running away from his grief. You impress the hell out of me, Tom, and after all these years we've spent together, I wish I knew you better."

McIlweath stared down at the snifter in his right hand. He sought an articulation of the indefinable sentiments Finnegan's words evoked. Not finding it, not coming anywhere near it, he said nothing for several minutes. The room's only sounds were the muffled ticking of a clock across the way and Dan Rosselli's stertorous breathing from the bedroom.

As with sympathy, as with passion, as with life itself, the frozen moment faded before memory could respond, leaving, years later, only an echo. Silence, and the conclusion behind it, weighed down upon them almost palpably until they could no longer stand the burden, even knowing that it would leave its imprint crushed into them so that in the private moments to come they could dig a finger into it and drag their hands over its ridges.

Finnegan sighed, rose from his chair and went into the kitchen for the bottle of Grand Marnier. He returned and put it on the coffee table. "This has the makings of a long night," he said. "We'll keep this handy."

"No, Conor, it needn't be long. Not on my account. I've said all I have the power to say."

"I remember in high school, Mac. You were one of the most nondescript people I'd ever known. Sometimes you were barely visible. And I think of those idiots who ignored you just because they couldn't define you. You could condemn the whole lot of them now if you wanted. You're stronger than they could ever hope to be."

"I'm acting from necessity, as I see it. Nothing more. Don't romanticize it."

"It's a Romantic notion. That whole concept of self-determination, and all the wasted years. I can see now how wasted they were on both sides. For you and for me. The difference is that you've got the strength to pull yourself out of it."

"Strength is an ambiguous quality, Conor. It comes in different forms. We do what compels us to survive. We can go about developing some grand meaning to what we do, but what's the point? We put it onto order and slap labels on it. Very clinical, very scientific. I'm somewhere above 'survival' and somewhat below 'profound.' What you call strength might only be evolution."

"Perhaps then I've evolved poorly. Instead of becoming an intelligent, enlightened human being, I've become a subspecies."

"What do you mean?"

"Nothing, really," sighed Finnegan. "I suppose I just feel a little inadequate right now. I feel like some type of vapor, just taking the shape of whatever space I'm released into. After a while you don't even know it's there."

"You look tired, Conor. More than I've ever seen you. I noticed it as soon as I saw you. You're worn down to a thread."

Finnegan said nothing. He turned his head to look away from his friend. To focus, he let his eyes rest on a crack in the far wall, a thin line like a pencil mark against the faded white. He stared at the crack and studied the way the wall had been disturbed—a slight fissure now but destined to widen should no repair be made. The bumpy texture of the white paint stopped abruptly where the plaster had split. Were he a microbe, Finnegan could stand at the edge of the rift and stare into a bottomless abyss.

For Tom McIlweath, seeing Conor Finnegan dispirited—weak, timid, uncertain, his remarkably resilient confidence nowhere in evidence—was tantamount to a great natural cataclysm, like an earthquake or a flood. Something immensely powerful had been upset, as if the physical laws had been commuted, as if he had dropped a stone and it had flown up into the sky, as if he had gone to sleep one night and woken up the day before. As a friend, as a brother, McIlweath was rent himself. He felt the bleeding of Finnegan's spirit in his own.

"How's Glynnis, Conor?" McIlweath asked gently.

Finnegan continued staring at the crack. "I don't know, Mac. I really don't. I see her so seldom now. These past few months—I don't know, she's fading from me. She's a snow sculpture in the sun, melting from under my eyes so gradually that I can't see it. I only know that she's less than she used to be."

"What's happening, do you know?"

"No. I don't have a firm grasp of it at all. I'm not prepared for it, Mac, and I react to it so poorly. She has some fear, some phobia." Finnegan stopped, then turned his eyes quickly to his friend. "You might have some empathy with that."

"It seems as if she's afraid to let herself go," replied McIlweath, then smiled softly. "You can be pretty intoxicating, you know. You've drawn her in all this time, into your orbit. She might think she's caught there."

"You can empathize with that, can't you? Christ, you might even take her side."

"Is this a battle?"

"It's a war of attrition. The first person to wear down the other can claim victory."

"Then what have you won? Only resentment. And resignation."

Finnegan took a deep breath. "I know. There's no middle ground. If the battle's engaged at all, then it's already lost. The damage is too great. The battle itself is the defeat."

"You've lost her then, if you believe that."

"I've lost her, Tom. I'm losing her now and it'll all be done in a little while. Yes, I know that."

"You love her, of course. And she loves you? Still, I mean, through what's happening?"

"She says she does. That's not the motivation for any of this, the absence of love. It's more complex than that. As I said, I'm not very good at this. I have a hard time understanding it. She wants security. She wants affection, but she can't bring herself to offer her own security as collateral. She's afraid that if she gives herself to me she'll cease to be Glynnis Mear.

"But," he continued, "she can't see that that's going to happen one way or another, and there's absolutely nothing she can do about it. She's already ceased to be Glynnis Mear. She's clinging to an illusion while the reality changes of its own accord."

"That happens to all of us," said McIlweath. "We all grow along and leave behind what we used to be. But it's easy to see ourselves as what we were, or at least as what we considered ourselves to be. All that changes, though."

"Exactly," replied Finnegan. "We're one part reality and nine parts illusion. Are we that same people we were five years ago, or ten? No, and we should be glad of it. I think that as we age, as we assume these complexities we can't avoid, we become desperate for some type of guarantee, some evidence that the core is still in place and that it's essentially the same as it's always been, even though the outer trappings have been completely redone. Glynnis is afraid that if she gives over the trappings of her life, then her core goes with it. And with that core goes the security she craves. She's not consoled by the new type of security that's complementary to both of us. There's a line in a song by Richard Thompson—"You might be lord of half the world, you'll not own me as well." I hear that in her distance. At least, that's what I've been able to make of all this."

"I hope you can salvage this, Conor. I've never seen two people so thoroughly in love as you two. You and Glynnis—well, you were so clearly in step. To have anything happen to that would be a real tragedy."

Finnegan stared again at the crack. "You know what I can't get out of my mind, Tom? If she leaves me, I won't ever experience anything like her again. Do you know how depressing that is? What I've felt for her, and with her, will be dead forever. There'll be no way to bring it back."

"There are other women, Conor."

"Yeah, but they're not Glynnis. She's been more than a lover. She's an affirmation, Tom. She affirms that Conor Finnegan might be a little special. She's part of youth, and strength, and innocence, and promise. When she goes, if she must, all that goes, too. I die a bit. We both do. I suppose that's the natural course of things, but being natural or inevitable doesn't make it any less depressing."

"Perhaps," said McIlweath, "that affirmation has been false all along. Perhaps, in the end, you're no different than any of the rest of us, and you're destined to the same heartbreak and disenchantment we all have to face."

"Conor Everyman, shaped by the forces around him and helpless to resist," Finnegan said with a slow shake of his head. "That's hard to consider. The road has been pretty open until now, without a whole lot of bumps. Maybe that's made me weak. And now I feel like I'm at the mouths of the wolves."

"It's something to consider, Conor. Blessings, or talents, or strengths, or whatever you want to call them, do no good unless they take us down some hard pathways. Otherwise, they're nothing more than amusements, or self-gratifications. It's what we do with them that's important."

"I don't function as well as I thought I did, Mac. As bad as it is to lose Glynnis, it's far worse to see it coming, step by step, and know that the process is irretrievable. It's death by cancer."

"What will you do, Conor?"

"Try to resurrect myself a bit. Perhaps in another form that's harder. Someone not given to idealization. Not so wide-eyed and eager, or trusting. More deliberative and infinitely more careful. I'll have no underbelly left to expose."

"I think I prefer the illusion of Conor Finnegan to the one that you just described." McIlweath paused to sip his Grand Marnier. "You'll stay in Washington, I assume? This is what you want to do with your life?"

"Government, you mean?" Finnegan looked back at McIlweath, shifted in his chair and sipped his liqueur. "It's all I know at this point. Do you remember my rather smug assumption that the course of my life would take care of itself? That if I did the right things for the right reasons, the right things would happen?"

McIlweath nodded. "Not too much unlike what I just laid out about my own plans. Or lack of plans."

"I always thought that the right opportunities would make themselves known, and that all I had to do was be ready to see them. Just be alert enough to recognize what was out there, then let my natural abilities get it done for me. When that assumption proves false, though, you're helpless. You have to go back to Square One and reevaluate.

"In answer to your question, though," he continued, "yes, I'll stay in Washington for the time being. Probably for the foreseeable future. It's all I can do. It's all I'm prepared for. But it has no meaning anymore, if ever it actually did. I've been exiled by the powers that be. I'm fortunate to have a job at all."

"You wrote me that you left the senator. You never went into much detail. As I recall, you made it sound like a step up, although I couldn't see it. I mean, the committee you're with seems a bit obscure."

"As obscure as they come, Tom. The Siberia of Capitol Hill. I did inflate the importance of it, didn't I? I apologize. In truth, it's a trivial position with a powerless group on the far outskirts of government. I see no reason why it even exists."

"You had a falling out?"

"Call it a philosophical disagreement. My naïveté again. The senator and his top aide schooled me in practical politics and how the system really works. I didn't fit in, so they lanced me like a boil."

"I guessed as much, despite your letter."

"I suppose the circumstances were apparent, regardless of my smokescreen. They were kind enough to keep me employed on the Hill, but they made certain I'd be in a place where my ideals wouldn't get in the way. As you said, it's what we do with our gifts that's important. It's how we function that matters. So, I'm allowed to retain my illusions. I'm allowed to retain the glamor of working in government, walking through the corridors of power, even though the substance has been taken away from me. I'm not to be trusted with any of that, at least not until I prove myself more respectful of the ways of the world."

"Why do you stay with it, then? You sound bitter as hell. There are other things you could do."

"I *am* bitter, Tom, but I'm also much weaker than I thought. There's an element of comfort in what I do. It's not terribly taxing, the demands are reasonable, the pay is fairly good. Right now it's all I know. Sometimes I think about leaving it. I've thought about trying to land a teaching job in a prep school, teaching history and coaching basketball, maybe. I think I'd enjoy that. I've thought about law school, too, but the prospect of three or four years of intense study makes me tired. I couldn't take it. Finding a job in the private sector holds no appeal. It would be no different than what I'm doing now, just as pointless and narrow, so why should I leave for that? In a very real sense, Tom, I've lost my ambition. I've lost my hunger. I hope to Christ it's only temporary, but I can't tell."

"So you'll just float along, doing what you're doing and hating it until something else comes by? I'm surprised, Conor."

"And disappointed?"

"Yes. And disappointed."

Finnegan smiled, more to himself. "You know, Tom, up until now all the influences in my life have been gentle, positive and affirming. There's never been a need to stand up to them. Now that the need's arisen, I find I'm too weak to do it. It's too exhausting, and in the end we gain nothing from it anyway. So I'll play along, like everyone else does: I've become the type of person I always used to feel superior to."

"Not everyone plays along, Conor. There are exceptions. There have to be."

"I know. And I envy them. I envy you. You're better than I am, Tom. You're stronger. You've always been stronger, but I never saw it."

"I never saw it either, but it's been sweet to learn it. That strength was dearly won. It'll come to you, too. I'm sure of it. You've got too much going for you to stay this way for long."

"You overestimate me, Tom. Maybe you're still reacting to image, or maybe it's important for you to believe that. We'll see. Nonetheless, thank you for your confidence."

"I have to be confident in you. What you call an image has meant a great deal to me. In some ways, it's sustained me. That's a big part of what I'm doing now. A quiet inspiration, call it."

"My grandfather came from Ireland. When he was a young man. Nineteen, I think he was."

"Your dad's father, right?"

"Yeah. There was nothing for him there, or so he said. He was a farmer's son, at a dead end. He wanted something different, so he made the jump. I haven't seen him in, Jesus, ten years."

"He's still alive then."

Finnegan smiled. "After a fashion. Age has robbed him blind. But he's a wonderful old man and still pretty sharp." Finnegan drained off the last of the Grand Marnier and noted that McIlweath's snifter was also empty. "I hope I haven't depressed you, Mac. This is the new Conor Finnegan. The chastened version. Another drink?"

"No," replied McIlweath. "In fact, I think I'm going to call it a day. I'm exhausted, with the drive and all."

"When do you leave?"

"Two days, if I can stay that long."

"You're welcome to stay longer. As long as you want."

"No. My flight's arranged. I shipped most of what I'll need on ahead."

"What will you do with your car?"

"Find a dealer to take it off my hands for whatever the hell he'll give me for it. There's a lot of history in that machine."

"Another bond broken."

McIlweath just shrugged. "It has to be. I have the couch?"

Finnegan went to the hall closet and pulled out a pillow with some blankets. "I hope you'll be comfortable. If not, we can work something out for tomorrow night."

"No way. This is your place."

"Nonsense. It belongs to all of us. It's one of the last possessions we have in common." Finnegan tossed the bedding on the couch. "Good night, Tom. I've said it earlier, but I'm thankful you're here."

"I couldn't have left without seeing you, Conor. You're like a brother. I've told you that, haven't I?"

"It's good to hear. And the feeling's mutual." They shook hands, then embraced. Finnegan cuffed McIlweath on the back of his head. He turned then and opened the bedroom door. "See you tomorrow, Mac. Don't get up too early, okay?"

Finnegan and McIlweath spent their two days together running around the city. Rosselli occasionally joined them. In contrast to Finnegan's pensive brooding, Rosselli was continually ebullient, a small child on Christmas morning. He introduced McIlweath to his Julie, who was, as described, amazingly beautiful and prompted McIlweath to wonder how his roommate had attracted a goddess. Two relatively carefree days seemed to break Finnegan's depression. McIlweath saw it, and felt relieved, but Finnegan for his part had merely suspended matters for a bit. He knew nothing had been resolved.

On the morning McIlweath was to leave, Rosselli bade an affectionate goodbye before bounding out of the apartment on his way to the med school. His friend's visit had been yet another unanticipated pleasure in a life now teeming with them. Finnegan drove McIlweath out to Dulles. Neither said much on the drive.

McIlweath checked his bags while Finnegan sat adjacent the check-in counter. When McIlweath was done and had his boarding pass and baggage tags, Finnegan rose, and once again they embraced. Deep within him, in some uncharitable hollow space near the flickering ebb of his spirit, Finnegan felt a compulsion to cry. He resisted it, and his nerves aborted the sentiment. Later he would reflect on what was now being abandoned, and regret that he was not able to take closer note of it.

McIlweath went through security and his thin form disappeared down an escalator to the gates. Finnegan watched his back until it turned a corner, and was gone. He knew it would be years before they saw each other again, if ever. This was a divergence, so graphic as to be convulsive, one of the rare instances in a life when a point of departure lacks all subtlety and so cannot be ignored. Things would be different now, from this point. It had all been so swift, these rites of passage. They each were left to face alone the consequences they authored.

CHAPTER XXVI

When Conor Finnegan returned to his apartment that evening, having gone directly to work from the airport, a single letter sat in his mailbox. He saw the Philadelphia postmark; a dart of electricity shot through his tired frame, at once snapping his senses. He became aware, and his fatigue vanished. Aside from an occasional brief note when they could not get together for two or three weeks, or a frivolous card now and then, Glynnis never wrote him. They had always been too close for letters.

But this indeed had some length to it. Finnegan held it gingerly on his fingertips and felt its weight. To the kitchen, then, and to the scotch, which he poured liberally over a handful of ice cubes. He sat at the table there and sipped slowly, waiting for the strong brown liquor to take effect, to calm a heart beating too fast and a mind with all the wrong focus.

After some time he felt the quiet, gentle numbness claim his limbs. His breathing eased and he resigned himself to whatever might be in Glynnis's words. He rose and went to the kitchen drawer, took out a knife and slit the envelope. He pulled out the pages within, brought them to the living room and began to read as he burrowed himself into the couch there:

> *Dear Conor —*
>
> *This evening I spent in the studio trying to sketch an outline of a sculpture project, but I accomplished nothing. I can't keep my mind off you long enough to put two thoughts together, or to concentrate on anything at all. That's been a common condition lately. I thought that writing a letter might purge me enough to go on with the matters at hand.*
>
> *Conor, I love you. You must have no doubt of that. For the past few days I've been recalling all the stupid, unnecessary things I've said to you that might call that simple fact into question. I'm sorry for them all, and I'm sorry for the distance that we've come to keep.*
>
> *I don't know why I feel the way I do, why I'm so reluctant to give my whole being to you. All my reasoning seems so pale in the light of day. My fears are a sign of my own immaturity, and I pray that I'll be able to put them aside in due course.*
>
> *I miss you terribly on those weekends when we're apart. I know I would be happier seeing you, and on those rare logical moments, I know that I need you on more than just the weekends, that I need you every day. And I wish, oh God how I wish, I could answer the force that tells me not to. Yet when at last I do see you, when I want to rush to you at first glance and take you in my arms, I'm unable. And I know that I become defensive as soon as you start to question me. It could be a gesture, or the way you hold your body, or even the way you pick up my bag for me that lets me know how much you disapprove, how much you're hurt by all of this. You assail my defenses, and rightly so. This must confuse you no end.*
>
> *I can't know what offenses I'll commit when we're together again (They are offenses, aren't they?), but let me offer my apologies for them now. What I say is not based in malice or distance, but confusion. You confuse me horribly.*
>
> *You're a gentle and charming contradiction, salvation and condemnation in one.*
>
> *But I do love you. I can't possibly say that enough. Whatever lies ahead for us, tragedy or redemption, you must*

always believe that. My beautiful Irishman, I remember telling you when we first met that your heart was bound to be broken. I said it flippantly, although I saw in your uncluttered innocence a countenance too wide-eyed to survive as it was. There is something in you that cries for protection.

Perhaps we are both destined for a hasty and sad judgment. Perhaps as I struggle to avoid being dragged down by you I shall ultimately drag you down with me. Perhaps we shall both spend the rest of our years regretting the death of a precious spirit that once made us fresh.

I say now, without knowing whether I truly mean it, Wait for me, my lover. Please be patient. And if this feeling I express in these pages proves to be fickle or transitory, a last flickering glimmer of a cooling blaze, then know that it once existed as the fiercest fire that burns the human heart, and that you once lived within my soul in a place no one else can ever touch.

I shall cherish you always.
Glynnis

Finnegan folded the pages and sat motionless for an indefinable time. It would take him a while to put this into some type of order. He sighed, went to the kitchen and poured himself another glass of scotch. Yes, this would take some time.

He stayed with the scotch all night, a warm and customarily sticky summer night in Washington. He turned off the air conditioning, and breathed in the heat. Finnegan wanted to feel the night like a blanket, or a shroud. His glands opened and perspiration poured out of him, welding his back to the chair and causing his hair to fall across his forehead in disheveled wet ropes. Finnegan sat in his chair, played his music, drank his scotch. Periodically he picked up the letter from the corner table to feel its weight again. Ballast, it was.

What had he just read? A capitulation? No, not that. With her preframed apologies, it may in fact be just the opposite, a license to kill. Her passionate avowals of a deep and lasting love gave him some comfort. In recent months those had become rare, and he knew that it was easier to commit such sentiments to paper than to speak them to flesh and blood, no matter how close.

But why had she written it now? If, as it seemed to be on the surface, Glynnis's letter was a guilt-laden expression both of her love and her deep regret that it had come to this, what had prompted her to write it? Glynnis had always been rather stubborn, he considered. She admitted her defensiveness, and Finnegan knew it to be so. Each time he danced around the fringes of anything that sniffed of commitment, Glynnis crouched in a self-protective coil, ready to strike. Had her guilt over all this gotten the better of her? If so, why now? The prospect of guilt made Finnegan uneasy. There could be no guilt without transgression.

He considered all this in foggy terms, and the night drew on. Finnegan clinked the ice cubes against the glass, and warmth swelled up within him until it met the heat seeping in from the outside. The night grew hotter; his skin grew clammy. There could be no resolution. Not of this letter, not of Glynnis, not of the eminently flawed scheme of living that had placed him here tonight. It wasn't working. It wasn't working at all, and the black-hooded specter crept into the room, looked down at the slouching figure and smirked.

'You belong to me,' it whispered hoarsely. 'You've belonged to me from the start,' and Finnegan stared back, saw nothing and drank his scotch. 'Your precious blood has bought you a poor return. It could not buy you more. You spill it, and it soaks the ground. There is no other way. Look hard at my contours, study my form, and know this: You shall not die, although some days you will wish it. You shall not die, although only sand pumps through your brittle veins. You are the same as all the others, the ones whom you do not know, whom you have never comprehended.'

Finnegan stared back at what was not there. He stared hard until his eyes no longer focused and a thin, reedlike ringing jabbed at his brain. Before he could recognize it, the night caved in on him. His mind went black in the exhausted confusion of a long distance runner who cannot find the final turn.

* * *

He woke hours later. Blinking his eyes to bring them alive, he rose unsteadily and squinted at the clock in the kitchen. 11:47. Finnegan felt woozy; the day, the night, had sucked him dry. He entered now on the perverse underside of excitement, of engagement, of presence. He was scraps of shredded paper on the street after a night-long celebration, a glass quarter-filled with stale liquor.

Glynnis must still be up. Finnegan's cloudy brain told him to call. To hear her voice, that's all. To thank her for the letter. Perhaps even to say something in return. That was how the healing should begin, right? Someone makes a move, someone else responds. She could come down this weekend. She could do that.

Finnegan flipped on a light to see the phone, and a burning seared his eyes. He clenched them shut as they watered against the brilliance. Glynnis. Yes, it would be grand to hear the silky lilt of her gentle New England voice. Her voice had always transposed him to peaceful places, had always calmed him. He loved her voice, no matter the words that it carried. He did not quite know what he would say, but he knew that when he heard her voice the words would come. Finnegan opened his eyes gingerly and blinked hard until they could work in the light. His entire body felt slushy, his muscles turned to spring snow. He picked up the phone and dialed.

On the other end, the clicking of long distance, then the familiar tone of Glynnis's phone, the purring backside of the ringing. Twice, three times . . . She must be there . . . four . . . She usually answer by now . . . five, six . . . Come on, come on . . . seven . . . ten . . . twelve . . . Finnegan let it ring several minutes. She had not activated her voicemail, so there was nothing but the rings. Because of the scotch, because of the letter, because of Tom McIlweath, Finnegan desperately wanted to speak with her, to hear her. But she did not answer. On a Monday night, nearly midnight, she did not answer.

With the paranoid fear of an insecure lover, Finnegan traced through the possible explanations. Perhaps she was at the studio, or with a friend. Perhaps she had gone out for a late bite to eat. Perhaps she merely wanted to go to bed early and turned off her phone. Through the sheer force of his will, Finnegan calmed himself. He demanded no conclusions be drawn, not yet. He could try later, but no, he was too tired. And too drunk. He should just go to bed. This day had been enough. Tomorrow night he'd reach her. There was no point in getting worked up any tighter than he already was.

But the evening following was no different. Finnegan called at 6:00, at 7:30, at 8:00, and then at fifteen-minute intervals until midnight. The dry crackling brush had been ignited; his fears flamed up and consumed the kindling. Unless the cooling waters, the Healing Waters of Glynnis, splashed upon him soon, this fire might burn out of all control.

By Wednesday night, when again he got no answer, Finnegan had no idea what to think. There was no way of knowing now what to expect, what his reception would ultimately be on the other end. Something had happened, and he cared not to speculate on its details. Given the recent drift of their affair, Finnegan naturally presumed that whatever it was had to be negative. The flimsy rationales he had drunkenly constructed two nights earlier carried no weight. This was no doubt another chapter in an increasingly sour novella.

For most of their time he could have rebuilt her entire day from morning to night and specify whom she saw, where she was, what she talked about. But he realized now that, with the continental drift of the last several weeks, he no longer knew the particulars of Glynnis's life. Those incidentals lent dimension, and without them the entire landscape became foggier. She was vaporizing before his sight. Over the past few months she might be practicing Satanism for all he knew.

* * *

On Thursday, a rainy, stormy, glum day, Rosselli was already home when Finnegan plodded and dripped through the door. This was a rarity. Most nights Rosselli studied late, then stayed at Julie's place to repeat that pleasant pattern the next day. But tonight, as Rosselli explained it, he thought a change in routine might keep him fresh. Besides, Julie had midterms looming and needed to put aside the distractions of her lover for a week or so.

Rosselli had dinner prepared by the time Finnegan got home, soggy with rain and perspiration. Rain did not abate the heat, and the day had been smothering. Glynnis had occupied most of Finnegan's thoughts that day. His work, mindlessly simple, had not suffered.

Over dinner, a vapid Rossellian creation of a pasty cut of meat with some spongy green vegetables, they carried on something of a conversation. Finnegan was grateful for the contact. In his new position he had made no friends. Everybody on the committee staff tended to go a separate path. There were no common lunches, no Friday happy hours. Finnegan had begun to sense the initial stabs of a desperate professional isolation he had not experienced before.

Rosselli had assaulted his food with a primitive brutality, shoveling forkfuls into his mouth before he had completed dispensing with their predecessors. He finished his plate well before Finnegan, then got up to fill it again.

"Jesus, Dan, slow down. This crap's not that good."

"I can't help it. I'm starving. I took a swim this afternoon after my anatomy lecture."

"I'm surprised you gave yourself time. How far did you go?"

"Two thousand. I'm in horrible condition, but it felt great. I used to do five thousand without breaking a sweat. The only laps I've done lately are around my cadaver."

"We get old, Dan. Be grateful some kid isn't pulling out your liver and holding it up to the light."

"You haven't been too physical of late either, have you, Conor? I don't recall you playing ball for a while."

"I haven't played ball, or run, or anything. I think I've lost my fire."

"You've got the time."

"Now I do. But I don't have the energy anymore. I have very little in reserve at the end of the day. But I'm not working hard at all. I'm not doing anything, but I've got nothing left."

"Motivation," said Rosselli, tucking away a small mound of mashed potatoes. "You've lost your motivation. Find it, or you'll end up looking like me. Lovable and cuddly, but rather round."

"That may be the answer, Dan. Fat people are supposed to be jolly."

"All a myth. I've always been big but I've never really been happy until lately. Didn't one of your poets write something about that?"

"Several of them did. 'Only where love and need are one, And work is play for mortal stakes, Is the deed ever really done.' That's Frost. You seem to have found your love."

"In more than one form. Speaking of which, Glynnis is coming down this weekend, isn't she?"

"She said she would. But it's hard to tell these days what she means and what she doesn't. I've been trying to call her."

"No luck?"

"No answer. She's out every time I try. Frankly, I don't know what the hell's going on anymore."

"Hang in there, roommate. You two are about as ideally suited as any couple I've ever seen."

"But what do you see? Christ, any two people can put on a reasonable show every now and then. I thought so, too. I thought we were God damned perfect. But it's all superficialities. Time has a tendency to break those down into their component parts."

"Don't give me that, Conor. If you were only drawn to superficialities, then you'd be a hopeless motherfucking idiot, and I know you're not. I don't handle self-pity real well, especially from someone like you. There are better places for my sympathies."

"Thanks, roomie. Just what I wanted to hear."

"I mean it, damn it. Maybe Glynnis is going through a phase, or maybe she's changing her perspective altogether, or maybe she's just tired of all the pressure of a relationship. You know her better than I do. People don't stay the same. That's a fact, and thank God for it. I hope you two can work it out. I really do. And if you can't, then I'm sorry, but, hell, it's not the end of creation. There aren't any guarantees. Everybody loses a lover before he's through."

"Glynnis is more than that. She's more than a lover. She's . . . hell, I don't know. But it goes beyond the here and now."

"Wonderful. Does she radiate a white glow, too? Jesus, come

back to Planet Earth, Conor. That's always been one of your greatest strengths. I can see where Glynnis might feel some pressure. I'd hate to be thought of as someone's ideal."

"She's part of something broader, Dan, and I can't explain it. If I tried we'd probably end up in an argument, and you're the first friendly voice I've heard in three days."

"You're stuck with a pretty grim group at the office, huh?"

"Humorless bastards. They're all a few years older than me. They come in every morning, sit behind their desks all day—Jesus, most of them don't even go out for lunch. There's never any sense of activity, never any sense of urgency. Even though the work is essentially trivial, we can still infuse it with some vestiges of life, can't we? At the end of the day, off they go back to whatever little holes they come out of. I'm still trying to figure out cause and effect, whether dull work makes dull people or whether dull people are drawn to dull work. Either way, they're sad. There's no spark to any of them at all. Sometimes I wonder why they want to keep doing what they're doing, if it makes them so lifeless. But I'm a part of them now. A colleague."

"A process of absorption, Conor. Be careful."

"I know. These people are all taking the path of least resistance and it's killing them. There's no joy in what they do. I hate being around them. They're barnacles hooked to a ship's bottom, just hanging on for the ride."

They finished their meals. Rosselli cleared the dishes and put them in the sink. "I'll clean up, Conor. Go call Glynnis."

He did. But again she did not answer. Finnegan let the phone ring twenty times, then hung up with a curse. Tonight he knew would be no different except that Dan Rosselli would be around to observe his frustration. His humiliation.

That evening Rosselli stayed in the living room and read. Finnegan tried to concentrate enough to do some reading, too. He had read very little lately, his nights customarily a depressive stupor that exercised itself either through his music or the television.

A week earlier he had started *The Brothers Karamazov*. Upon leaving school Finnegan had come to recognize how pitifully underread he really was. He had spent four years exposed to the greatest literature, philosophy and history, yet had absorbed little of it. Often he had failed to complete his reading assignments at all. Early in his career he discovered how to extract relevant ideas from a written work without having to pore over its entirety. He knew enough to give his professors what they wanted, he learned to interpret them well, and to understand how they viewed the major points of their offerings. He found he could prepare himself to get his grades with minimal effort. Only he knew himself how tainted his Phi Beta Kappa key really was.

Now, out on his own, Finnegan perceived his shortcomings. He had spent too much time playing basketball, joking with his friends, or reading fluff. The allusions he came upon constantly in his research, in newspapers, in conversation with his better-read acquaintances or colleagues left him dry, and he saw his intelligence as narrow, lacking sufficient depth to be as flexible as he would like it. Consequently, he had committed himself to reading the classics he had spurned in college. When he had worked for the senator he had spent most nights during the week reviewing his work, planning for the coming day or following up on his research. Now that he no longer felt compelled to take his work home with him, his evenings were free for his own pursuits. His goal was to complete something worthwhile every three days. In this fashion, before things grew as dark as they were, he had run through a fair number of books he should already have read. He had knocked off most of Hardy and Fitzgerald. He had consumed all he could find of Steinbeck, that resigned, faithful cynic, T.S. Eliot, *il miglior fabbro*, Hemingway and the twisting mists of Faulkner. It had been a good start.

Of late, though, his concentration waned. Finnegan found it increasingly difficult to home in on a piece of literature, after dragging himself through days that numbed him and drove his expectations into dust. The immediate task at hand became the restoration of those peculiar Finneganian tenets in light of the unforeseen circumstances that had dismantled them. Although he had no doubt his readings could help him in the process, Finnegan saw his mind wander elsewhere. The intellectual pursuits in which he had taken such pride showed themselves to be luxuries afforded a more contented soul.

Finnegan picked up his Dostoyevsky and read, but he knew that little was sinking in. Across the room Rosselli seemed completely absorbed in one of the medical texts that Finnegan, in glancing through, had found impenetrable. Was there really any practical knowledge in all that? Does every ache and malfunction really have a name, and can they all be compressed into neat categories?

He read for almost two hours and covered only a few pages. He had reached the section wherein Alyosha recounts the life and thoughts of the saintly Father Zossima. Most of it struck him as the stunted philosophical angst of a neurotic Russia, a paranoid rationalization of inflexible thought. Yet Dostoyevsky's agonizing struggle to comprehend his people and his times, despite its technical defects, had fascinated Finnegan enough to accept the challenge implicit in opening the book. He wished he could appreciate it better.

Finnegan read Alyosha's manuscript on Father Zossima, and tried to make sense of the dying mystic's exhortation:

> *My friends, pray to God for gladness. Be as glad as children, as the birds of heaven. And let not the sin of men confound you in your doings. Fear not that it will wear away your work and hinder its being accomplished. Do not say: "Sin is mighty, wickedness is mighty, evil environment is mighty, and we are lonely and helpless. Evil environment is wearing us away and hindering our good work from being done." Fly from that dejection! There is only one means of salvation. Make yourself responsible for all men's sins. As soon as you sincerely make yourself responsible for everything and for all men, you will see at once that you have found salvation.*

Tension agitated him. He could not sit for long, yet moving between rooms in the small apartment did not satisfy him. He thought of taking a nighttime run, but the steady rain discouraged him and he felt weak. Finnegan had not run for days, for weeks. His body was growing a bit puffy. Dostoyevsky's wisdom rang hollow. He could think of nothing to do to break the edge. Only Glynnis, and the unfolding demise.

Near midnight he called again. He had no expectation now of hearing her voice. He called only to hear the ring, to affirm that indeed there was another end to this line even if no one was there to pick up. The phone gave back its familiar buzzes—eight, nine, ten, eleven of them. Finnegan waited. After a while, he put the phone down and went to bed, unaware that as he undressed, Glynnis Mear was just then sitting up in another bed with a start.

The room there was dark, its foreign geography casting odd shapes against walls that she could not decipher. Her chest rose and fell with a quick, desperate breathing set off by her nightmare. She did not remember what it was, only that she had been totally helpless. She had been the object of some irrepressible force that she could not escape, and whatever it was had taken away her capacity to move, to flee, to breathe. Her sudden waking had wiped the details clean. Only the panic remained for a few brief seconds until consciousness beat it back through its affirmation of darkness, quiet and peace.

Glynnis reoriented herself. The shapes, the smells were so odd, the angle of the veiled light so different. She blinked her eyes until things came into focus. She shook her head with a jitter to clear it, and felt her hair swish against her naked shoulders. She took a deep breath, then another. As she inhaled, her breasts pressed outward against the thin sheet, her only cover on so warm a night.

The broad muscular back on her right reassured her. He had not woken; there was no need to disturb him now. Glynnis sank back down on her pillow and rolled to her side against him. She threw her arm over his shoulders. The heat of his splendid body radiated through her and caused her flesh to cloy to his. The strong musky scent of him flared her nostrils. Glynnis took the nape of his neck in her mouth, feeling the short strands along his hairline. She ran her tongue and lips across the sensitive tissue there. She tasted the salt of his dried perspiration and let it linger in the front of her mouth. Gently, so as not to rouse him, she dropped her hand from his shoulders to his flat stomach. With the tips of her fingers she nestled the fine silky hair that grew from the center of his belly down to his loins. She sighed, and pushed herself closer against him.

'Please God,' she whispered to herself. 'Let there be no more nightmares.'

* * *

Conor Finnegan knew there would be no Glynnis on the Friday evening train. Still, he went to Union Station anyway. It was a futile gesture, but it bound him to those earlier and happier evenings when he would press himself through the crowd there to find her stepping off the hissing train. Perhaps she would be there, and they could instantly dismiss their complications in the sheer joy and surprise of their unity. Perhaps, by going to meet her there, Finnegan could transport himself across the past few months and, in so doing, find evidence of the crime yet to be discovered.

The rain had stopped that morning leaving the city neither cleaner nor cooler. Waves of sultry heat rose from street and sidewalk. The cavernous station held it all, a giant stone oven. The soggy heat made people cross. Women pulled their children along with harsh jerks and harsher admonitions. Men scowled, perspiration soaking their foreheads. Areas under people's arms and small of their backs were marked with dark gray rings of moisture. Even the ticket sellers and porters, locked into their stifling black uniforms, sneered with a general annoyance. The crowd as a mass moved slowly, an amoebic gelatinous fluid that shifted without direction, merely occupying the space it was allotted. No one spoke unless he had to, and then only in muted voices. It was too hot to be alive.

Finnegan moved carefully through the crowd to the platform for the Philadelphia train. He did not want to disturb anyone. Tempers were too short. He had already seen an argument in the grand atrium between two men who had been standing too close. One, a tattered old black man drenched in sweat, had clearly been the aggressor, but the other, a young white man perhaps twenty who might well have been a student, had not backed down, and the argument had nearly come to blows. Finnegan didn't know the issue. Chances were, it was trivial. People wanted to bark, to bite, to sink their teeth into the unbearable heat.

Down the track the cycloptic train made its turn into the station. The eye grew bigger, the sibilant hissing more demonic. Metal clanked on metal, there was some thumping, then a whirling screech of brake as the train slowed. Few people got out. The train had been nearly empty. Too hot to travel; too hot to go anywhere at all. Finnegan walked briskly from one end of the platform to the other, checking each open door to see who emerged. He looked behind him and saw the people heading up the stairs to the lobby, to the Metro, to their cars or to the taxis. The platform cleared and he stood there alone except for two porters who surveyed the area with obvious disinterest. The train continued to hiss malevolently. Finnegan stood for a few minutes. The emptiness seemed so anomalous; he had so much space all to himself. He could stay here, against the congestion, against the heated press of a snarly mass, and breathe the noxious fumes of his solitude.

One of the porters came up to him as he stood there, looking at nothing. "Can I help you, son?" There was nothing polite about him. His face frowned out his displeasure—with the heat, with his job, with this fatuous young white face in front of him. The porter was a burly man, taller than Finnegan, with a thick mustache above unsmiling lips. His eyes threw forth an unsubtle challenge.

"No," replied Finnegan, glancing up at those angry eyes then immediately looking away. "No. I just expected to meet someone who didn't show."

"Well, move on then, son. You can't stay down here."

Finnegan nodded, then walked back to the stairs. Why, he asked himself, had he even bothered to come? Hadn't he had enough of futile gestures and naïve symbolism? He gave himself back to the crowd, as latently hostile as before, and back to the overwhelming heat.

CHAPTER XXVII

*Welcome, O life! I go to encounter for the millionth time the
reality of experience and to forge in the smithy of my soul
the uncreated conscience of my race.*

*Old father, old artificer, stand me now and ever in good
stead.*

—James Joyce, *A Portrait of the Artist as a Young Man*

There was no heat in Ireland, or very little of it. The days adhered to each other through damp gray and rain, delineated only by the cool dank nights that evoked shivers even under the warmest of blankets. The moist air was almost palpable. One inhaled it and felt his lungs thicken with the physicality of something foreign, leaving a flat taste on the palate.

Ireland's south coast was sparse. The small college where Tom McIlweath had come to cleanse himself was easily the most notable feature in the immediate vicinity. The townspeople treated it fondly as their own peculiarity, a shard of meteor landed in their midst that, because of its accidental location, set them off from surrounding neighborhoods and gave them reason to boast a bit. Whether college or space-rock made no difference. Neither could have the slightest effect upon the daily lives of the natives. But the students were generally well-mannered, the masters spent their earnings in the area, and the college added a distinction that few could really comprehend. Theirs had been a part of the island given to famines and rebellions. A college was an aberration in the quiet patterns of their existence, one complete with its own traditions and legends. Most were glad they had it.

A wind seemed constantly to blow off the Celtic Sea from the direction of St. George's Channel. It brought with it a pungent odor that Tom McIlweath had never smelled before. He could identify its parts—salt, fish, tar, rotting wood—but the components blended indelicately. It was not unpleasant, but the odor had soaked irremediably into the flesh of the natives so that, even on calm days, the smell was everywhere. One could not escape it. The shops, the bakeries, the grocers, the pubs and the people who ran them all carried it. They did not notice it themselves. Having grown up with it and grown into it, they had become inured, yet it was as much a part of them now as their noses or their ears. To outsiders, though, the odor was a badge, a clear indication of the wearer's place of origin.

Given the sameness of that town and its environs, McIlweath could, after a few weeks, note the smell, look at the individual who gave it off, and piece together his or her entire background. There was no mystery to it: the options in this damp part of a damp world were extremely limited. McIlweath made a game of it. The men were often fishers or farmers. Their garb would give them away, the farmers carrying overtones of dirt, mud and peat, rough-hewn hands and sometimes with a number of rips or tears in their clothing. The fishermen were usually cleaner but more heavily dressed, wearing extra layers as if the chilling waters of the gray-green sea had washed through them with such force that their bodies could never be warm again. A scattered few worked in the handful of small mills or manufacturers. The merchants, shopkeepers, and tavern owners were better dressed than the other groups, although they remained casual. A smattering of bankers and businessmen were clean-shaven, and their hair was combed, moderate in all their pursuits, constituting what amounted to a social elite, although no one seemed to place much stock in place or status. As far as McIlweath could tell, these groups constituted County Cork.

Their backgrounds would be uniform, but this did not limit McIlweath's fascination with them. In fact, it heightened his desire to know the timeworn currents that had locked this part of Ireland into place.

The fishermen had always been fishermen. They had been born into it, the sons of fishermen. Boats would remain in the same family for generations. They were clanky, rickety things, barely able, it seemed, to chug their prows through the unpredictable sea. And the Celtic Sea was indeed unpredictable. Storms whipped up suddenly with terrific fury, sending ten- or twelve-foot waves pounding the shores and blowing a mist well inland behind vicious gales. The effect was truly frightening—one could not help but feel completely dwarfed, completely impotent, completely unimportant. Yet casualties among the fishermen were quite rare. The collective memory of their forebears gave them a sixth sense. When the boats came in early, a storm would surely follow, no matter how incongruous the current weather would make it seem. Despite the acquired knowledge of hundreds of years, these fishermen were hopelessly poor. They had always been so, and would always be so.

The farmers, too, were a struggling lot. McIlweath saw farmers and fishers as opposite sides of the same coin. Their fields differed, as did the crops they reaped, but their condemnation was the same. If anything, the farmers had a tougher go of it. There would always be fish, regardless of the market. But Ireland's coquettish climate made the farmers' livelihood more precarious. Witness 1846 and 1847. Moreover, traditional family farmlands were often divided, and many were purchased outright by conglomerates. The emigration of farm boys to the city or to other countries further weakened it all. Farm plots were often small, the damp, saline soil adaptable to only a handful of low-yielding crops: grains, beets and the ubiquitous potato. A farmer might only see the scantest of profits even in his best years. During hard times, or when the economy itself fell victim to international pressures that dictated recession, it would be all he could do to survive with body and spirit intact.

The merchants had the best of it, although by no means could they be considered secure. They had higher incomes, but they also had higher expenses, and more risk. This was no middle class. Some stores and homes had been mortgaged many times over. And many were themselves the sons of merchants, the same fate they would hand down to their own sons.

Nothing ever changed here. Nothing ever changed at all. Only the first names.

The women as a whole were largely nondescript. McIlweath saw them as an extension of a cultural conservatism, dictated by the Church, that impelled modest standards, adherence to moderation and an emphasis on the hearth. He noted few professionals—lawyers, doctors, or even shop keepers. It was as if he had stepped back a full century. Nearly all had grown up in the same area and taken husbands from the same pool of young men who were their neighbors. They had their friends, they gathered to chat and to gossip, they came together socially when they could, but their best energies were expended in the maintenance of their households, however they were defined. That was the way it had always been, and no one expected much more than that. A woman might feel proud if she had a loyal, sober husband, well-mannered children, food on the table and a regular seat at Mass. Many apparently considered anything beyond that to smack of pretension. Conceptions of a broader, more fluid society were well hidden. The college, along with its more progressive notions, kept to itself.

The town, the region, perhaps all of Ireland itself, seemed impervious to time, impervious to change. The struggles of existence were the same as they had always been. The roles were identical. McIlweath might well have been stepping into the eighteenth century. Only the manner of dress and the appearances of modern devices made this any different. The people in their nature had not changed since the days of Pearse, of Cromwell, of Brian Boru. Borderlines remained drawn in the same places as during the time of Parnell or Wolfe Tone. And always the pungent odor blew in from the sea, the everlasting sign of their everlasting fate.

The people around him allowed themselves no variances; they could imagine none. A man's fate came to him through his bloodlines. It would be passed on intact, and that was that. Existence, the daily pattern of struggle and reconciliation, of victory and defeat, of gain and loss and all the panoply of glorious emotion, had absolutely no meaning beyond the souls themselves that preserved it.

Rare was the individual who ventured afield from this enforced order, who left to find a new place, a new purpose, a new self. The remainder had been robbed of any context. They were merely and solely part of a greater process that not even the smartest or most intuitive among them could understand. They took what little the land or sea or town afforded them, chewed it up mechanically and fed it back. It was not theirs. Nothing was theirs, not aspiration or definition or imagination. The boldest personality, the quickest wit, the strongest grip counted for nothing because nothing they ever did counted for itself. Theirs was a subdued existence, absent of design, of mystery, of potential, and so it was a dead existence. They may as well have been rabbits in a warren.

The realization brought McIlweath to the brink of physical illness as he sat in his rooms one Sunday afternoon and regarded what he had come to conclude. He lay down on his bed and waited for the nausea to leave him.

For reasons he could not fathom, Conor Finnegan kept running through his thoughts. His friend haunted him now as thoroughly as any disquieted spirit in this ancient land fixed to the site of its doom.

A new ghost had risen in Ireland, hardly a rare event. The youngest Finnegan had joined the wandering specters of his wretched ancestors.

For his part, McIlweath had no fixed world view, no *Weltanschauung*, to complicate the task at hand. He needed to identify the fundamental fibers and currents of his own life before he could begin to consider where he fit in the broader scheme of things. He had been driven by a near manic compulsion to rid himself of all expectations.

By contrast, Finnegan had never been one to study what he assumed was already in place. With his own affairs in such good order, it had been easy for Finnegan to be outgoing, enthusiastic, charming, and ultimately wedded to ideals rather than processes. Better, thought McIlweath, if Finnegan had used his immense gifts—the active and agile intelligence, the congenial wit, the boyish good looks, the ruddy athleticism—to make certain first of his own destiny. To know himself before seeking to know others. Now, unprepared, he moved through a practical world that had no stomach for fanciful inventions. He had become another rabbit in the warren.

The rock that had jammed in McIlweath's insides gave no sign of dislodging. It rolled over several times causing the walls of his stomach to lurch and spasm. McIlweath had taken rooms in one of the smaller residences, a ponderous stone building erected in the 1890s, drafty and dank but not unpleasant. His rooms, a bedroom where he now lay and a sitting room where he kept most of his books, were comfortable enough, if a bit unadorned.

The spirit of the place served as its principal decoration. This was Ireland, boggy and sorrowful, and this was a modest seat of learning in the Land of the Saints. His bedroom window opened to a wide courtyard. Usually there was some sound rising up—the swish of the traditional academic gowns worn by the masters and required of all who entered the dining hall to take their meals, perhaps casual voices, or maybe the shouts and calls of a game of football. Today, though, there was nothing, a dead stillness on a barren, pensive afternoon. It had been too much. McIlweath's head began to ache in echo of his stomach, and a weariness claimed his limbs. He closed his eyes and let sleep take its hold.

He awoke two hours later to a gentle knocking on his door. He rose unsteadily, the disorientation of new surroundings causing him to hesitate, and shuffled through to the outer room. To his relief, his nausea had disappeared and his head felt clear, the dull throb that had risen up beaten back by his nap. At the door stood the broad, amiable face of Gowan Phelan, a fellow graduate who had taken a great liking to the unassuming Yank. McIlweath had reciprocated, taking pleasure in

Phelan's open and obvious goodwill. McIlweath had found a number of friends here in a very short time.

The Irish students were drawn to Tom McIlweath's quietly sincere demeanor, the peculiarity of his American identity aside. Most of the Americans they had met on campus had been more boisterous. The Yanks came bounding through with an overflow of self-assurance, willing not so much to learn as to teach. They set a fast pace, darting here and there, trying to piece together a comfortable, unpressured situation, and many grew resentful when they looked back to notice that the natives were not following. The Irish set their own pace, unhurried and deliberate. What attracted them to McIlweath was that he honored what was in place, and sought to absorb it rather than amend it. McIlweath let it be known early on that he was a visitor, not a proprietor. He was there to sit among them. They swapped stories and impressions most night in someone's rooms, getting to know each other with a delicate mutual respect for the others' experience. No, this Yank was quite different from most of the others who had wandered through over the years.

Had there been any doubters about McIlweath's adaptability, they were dispelled one Saturday afternoon in late September. McIlweath had joined a group of his mates as they loped away from campus to the playing fields behind the spired chapel. He was out for a run, saw his acquaintances heading out, and ran with them out of the courtyard. He had not noticed that one of them was toting a rugby ball. When they got to the fields they began to choose sides for the match, and McIlweath stood aside watching them. Gowan Phelan was among them.

"Rugby, Gowan?"

"Right, Tom. You've never played, I'll bargain. Most Yanks don't know anything about it."

"Do you mind if I give it a try?"

Phelan was genuinely surprised. The Americans he had known had treated the sport with disdain. If they had not played it in the States, then certainly it was a silly and unimportant pastime. A good number refused to play because they were afraid that under the game's liberal rules they might be targeted for a special pounding. But here was a Yank eager to join in.

"You know the rules?"

"As I see it, there aren't a whole lot. Pass the ball backwards and get it over the line."

"That's about it. But it does get choppy out there. Think you can handle it?"

"Don't know. There's something to be said for trial by fire, though."

"Come on then. You're a winger."

Those who played and the few who watched saw the young American throw himself at their game with a reckless enthusiasm. He did not shy away from tackles, even when the burliest of his opponents hurtled across the field at him. He dove at their churning knees and leapt on their backs to wrestle them down. McIlweath was the slightest player, a slender reed in comparison to those bigger men who had played this game most of their lives, but his speed served him well. He ran the ball fearlessly, absorbing the blows of his tacklers with a cavalier resiliency.

McIlweath did not play well. He made numerous mistakes, running when he should have kicked, and conversely. He was worthless in the scrums because he was unsure of just what he was trying to do. But he played hard, as hard as he could. Each time he was knocked down he bounced up quickly, relishing the grit of the Irish soil on his knees, elbows and back, rejoicing in the taste of his own sweat. He applauded his teammates and clapped the backs of his opponents. At the end of the game, McIlweath made a special point to congratulate them all, smiling broadly. He thought his team had lost, but he was not certain. It didn't matter, of course. What he had done, what his purpose had been, was to claim another small variable. This was Ireland, and this was rugby, and the two went together, and here he was with something he had never done before.

Yes, this Yank was not like the others. Both his teammates and his opponents took him under their wing from that point on, pleased in fact to know this considerate, pensive, adventurous newcomer.

Now Gowan Phelan was at his door. "'Evening, Tom," he said. "I hope I haven't disturbed you too much. I thought you might like some dinner in town for a change of habit."

"Jesus," said McIlweath. "Is it that late? I was taking a nap."

"It's nearly six. I'm sorry. I must have roused you. Poor timing once again."

"No, not at all. Dinner would be great. Come on in while I revive myself. There's some port next to the smaller bookcase. Help yourself."

"You're a hospitable man, McIlweath. Shall I pour you a glass?"

"Of course. I'll be right out," he called from his bedroom. He changed his slacks and put on a sweater. He also splashed himself with cologne, an act of defiance against the pervasive sea-scent. No one wore cologne here.

He stopped, then, to look out onto the courtyard. In the glimmering final throes of yet another woolen day it appeared harshly somber, its thick green carpet drained of color so that it appeared a putrescent, loamy gray. The spired buildings around it, created in a pretentious neo-Gothic that seemed completely anomalous in so simple a setting, faded to mere outlines.

McIlweath moved from his bureau to the window so that he could take it all in. Not that there was anything to see. What he wanted to absorb was the flood of satisfaction this common scene engendered.

His life here was as uncluttered as ever he could have imagined it. All elements had been reduced to their simplest denominator. McIlweath had resurrected the joy he had found years before in his studies. The mysteries spoke to him again, their melodic words and strange symbols titillating his imagination. Antiquity had been recreated. There in his study, the dim light of evening eking through his window in a lyrical, battered land, McIlweath constructed for himself a vicarious identity with the long-dead classical writers and statesmen. He shared in their profound excursions by having embarked on his own. The symmetry of it inspired him. Their very names, once flat echoes it pained him to hear or read, now undulated poetically, magically before him: Livy, Ovid, Themistocles, Virgil, Aristophanes, Aeschylus, Catullus. This place, in its stolid testament to the durability of man's creations, had brought them alive to him once more, and he reveled in the rediscovery.

Rediscovery. That was the key to it all, wasn't it? He could not tell whether the reclamation of his spirit would be permanent. In fact, he tended to doubt it. Something ahead would likely derail him again so that the agonizing process of recalibration would have to be repeated. At least he knew what would be necessary now.

McIlweath gazed across the yard. The falling night and its attendant misty reflection transformed the solid building into nebulous shapes, jagged in their massive points and sweeping vertical lines. Illusion, all of it. He knew enough to see it as such, to see through it to where the cold, hard weightiness stood rooted in the soil.

But he knew enough not to be afraid of even the most deceptive illusion.

McIlweath realized that not one person in this yard or its surrounding buildings, not one, had denied him, even subtly. He walked among them as an equal, as if he, too, were part of the damp, gritty Irish loam. Perhaps it was the accumulated wisdom of an old land that permitted him to take his place here without expectation, without demand. Whatever he generated, for good or ill, would be its own determinant. If he proved fallow, so be it. He alone would have to address the consequences. But if he showed himself to be a rich and creative contributor to the ancient fabric of this place, if he should show a ready curiosity and peculiar wit, illustrate disparate avenues of a developed mind, sport a strong set of shoulders and a rapid gait, if he, in short, proved himself—as he must—a unique, capable creature of some dimension, he would be welcomed without affectation. That much had become obvious. The remainder now rested solely within his own temperament, within his own spirit. One could not ask for more than that.

The courtyard this evening, like life here generally, was simple, unadorned and quiet, broad enough for each observer to impart whatever interpretation he chose. He found the view comforting. The evening chill came so quickly, all at once, as to be visible between the spires. McIlweath pulled on his heaviest sweater, but even then he knew that it would not be enough. He would need a jacket as well. And wine. He would need several glasses of wine.

For quite some time he had wrestled with the ageless questions each young person of some promise and awareness had to pose: 'Where shall I go now? What shall I do? Where will it all come together, and be right?' McIlweath had let those questions torment him. They had wrenched him into contrived poses in the expectation that, should he stay in his contortions long enough, he would grow into them and assume the forms they demanded. He had condemned himself as weak, and let others do likewise.

And now, on a cool Irish evening, he looked out at the site of his evolution's latest chapter, enraptured, content, yet cognizant that the questions would not go away. 'Where shall I go now? What shall I do?' Because, of course, this satisfaction could not be permanent, nor could his stay within these walls be prolonged.

But none of that mattered.

Tom McIlweath recognized that his mistake had been in presuming that the questions demanded answers. They did not. What mattered was the asking. It was the questions themselves, that was all. Should he ever fail to pose them, should he ever reach the point where the coming mystery would be once and forever resolved, should he ever come to believe that his course was obvious and irresistible, that all creation pointed him in a single irreversible direction, he will have perished.

'Where shall I go now? What shall I do?' That would be the point— to keep the questions alive forever, so that he should be alive with them.

McIlweath turned from the window and went back to the outer room. Phelan was already halfway through his glass. With a gesture of his hand he indicated McIlweath's glass on a corner table. McIlweath crossed to it, and without a word raised it to his lips. Phelan smiled and said something which McIlweath did not hear above the interior sound of his swallowing. The heavy taste of the wine clung to the roof of his mouth, and a warm shaft trickled down his throat to an empty stomach.

"Take this, all of you, and drink it. This is the cup of my blood, the blood of the new and everlasting covenant."

CHAPTER XXVIII

*The world breaks everyone and afterward many are strong
at the broken places. But those that will not break it kills.
It kills the very good and the very gentle and the very brave
impartially. If you are none of these you can be sure it will
kill you too but there will be no special hurry.*

—Ernest Hemingway, *A Farewell to Arms*

Conor Finnegan did not know what part of his disrupted spirit compelled him to undertake such a melancholy journey. Was it some longing, unarticulated, in his bloodlines, or possibly a last measure to derive a logistical understanding of what had deserted him and why? It was an act of desperation, founded in frustration and fed by the constant memory of dissipated expectations. He had run short of options, so he had to head for the heartland. Go for the heart.

And so he pushed his car westward through a chilled and rainy autumn. It took two days. The rain, which never ceased, not for a second, plastered the fading greenery against the rolling cornucopia of Pennsylvania and drenched the flat checkered farmlands of Ohio and Indiana, darkening what already lacked color or dimension. The highways Finnegan followed took him through small anonymous towns, horribly depressing in their unchangeable stolidity. He could not relate to what he saw: the old drafty houses with chipped drab paint, the family stores, the decrepit, dusty diners with their broken signs. The people here echoed their timeless desolation, although they would not have seen it as such. They had lived in these towns all their lives. It was all they knew, and they found it to be sturdy and secure. A form of modern-day Calvinism this was: here they would live, and here die, generation after generation with little variance. Those who left were mavericks, or worse. Many eventually came back.

The towns with their peculiar names slid by indistinguishably, and still it rained. The monotony of the scenery, the monotony of the people within it, made Finnegan feel old. All time had been abandoned, the standards of movement had been displaced. He was beyond the pull of gravity. He was weightless and a pawn of relativity, so he did not age, but the thrust needed to break away had drained him thoroughly. He might have been eighty years old, groggy and feeble, for all the resistance he had left in him.

Finnegan had left in mid-morning, having first called to make certain that he would be welcome. Until he picked up the received and heard the crackly voice on the other end he was unsure he would truly bring himself to make the trip. It all seemed so nebulous, so inexact. But his promise, to the brittle man with whom he spoke, to arrive within two days forced the issue. He would have to go now, and there was nothing he could do about it.

The first day he drove as far as he could stand. Night fell early then; the darkness heightened his fatigue. More than once he lapsed into a mild trance, hypnotized by the wet sameness of the vacant landscape so that it all blurred together, his eyeballs spasmodically losing their focus. Finnegan lost track of the hours as they piled on top of one another. At one point, late in the day, he glanced at his watch and found it to be two hours later than he had thought. He stopped for the night in a shabby motel near the highway in a town whose name he had never heard. Somewhere in southwestern Ohio, it was, probably near Dayton. Everything was near Dayton in southwestern Ohio. Finnegan peeled himself off the seat that had adhered through the humidity to his shirt and jeans. He took a room, showered, and collapsed lifelessly onto a hard bed where he slept soundly, despite an air conditioner he could not shut off and did not need.

The next day Finnegan crossed Indiana and headed up the spine of Illinois. Only near the northern end did his boredom begin to lift. Here lay the city. Finnegan could smell it, a brawny reclining animal from which the scent of the hunt emanated. The hot loins, the panting tongue, the smothering musk of a thick, impenetrable pelt. Finnegan would have known he was close even if his eyes had been closed and his hands bound. He could have recognized the pulsing of latent energy, the limitless potential for brutality and gratification that radiated in his direction. Buildings clustered, the sounds grew harsher, the odors more fetid. In the distance, because there were no breaks in the flatness to obscure his view, Finnegan saw the great glass and steel pillars rise. Alive now, his pulse revived, Finnegan drove into the maw.

There exists in every major city a singular rhythm, an imperceptible pace all its own. Shaped by a multitude of factors—commerce, arts, attitude, style—it is as distinctive as a set of fingerprints, and just as unalterable. Hidden in the deafening roar of its daily life it silently instills an order and a context, a thread so thin as to be invisible, yet unbreakably binding the random beads into a solid chain. Finnegan's invigoration at once again being in a city, at being delivered from the bleak and barren rural graveyards through which he had had to run, was only temporary, and he knew it. Soon, once that muted rhythm worked itself into his psyche so that it became identifiable and thus the norm, soon his exhilaration would lapse back into a subtle, constant, unyielding depression. He would be reminded of the task at hand, the somber quest for an unlikely salvation. Everything else would fade into unobtrusive background noise.

Finnegan crept through the late afternoon traffic aware only of the general direction in which he was to head. He had an address and a map. Putting the two together, he followed streets that he presumed led to the proper way. His journey progressed block by block, subject to the mercy of traffic lights and the endless mass of cars around him.

The striking steel towers of downtown gave way in small doses to humbler designs. The buildings became squatter, less ornate, obviously older and more worn. Apartments mixed with the offices, then dominated. Narrow row houses—brown, gray, sooty—replaced the modern apartments. The streets closed together, the buildings crammed in, and on the sidewalks the polished, well-groomed professionals had vanished in favor of rougher types. The young people here had a hard look about them, coarse and bitter, already deporting themselves with a dayworn resentment that negated their youth. They were black, white and brown, moving about in separate groups. The older people, too, looked coarse, but they maintained a cautious and almost cowering demeanor. Age had taught them their vulnerability, and they respected it. All about was a pall, a resignation to the forces that beat against them, both young and old, forever brutalizing, forever critical, forever deadening.

Finnegan found the street he sought and checked the numbers through the wet gloom. The lighting was poor so he had to peer through the dimness while driving as slowly as he dared. In due course he found his number. The building to which it belonged was a crumbling brownstone, the worst of the block. It had no external adornments. Its bleak façade consisted solely of windows and uneven brick above a narrow wooden doorway. The neighborhood itself appeared foreboding, a hint of casual evil wafting in the soggy air. Up and down the street were similar brownstones in somewhat better repair. At the corner was a grocery store with iron bars over its front windows. Finnegan had seen this type of neighborhood too many times before, and he remembered the stories of those he had come to know living in these places.

To his relieved surprise, next to the building was a small driveway. He noted that only a few of the old structures had room for such a luxury. They were jammed together as closely as books on a shelf. Finnegan turned his car into the driveway, stopped the engine and stepped out onto broken asphalt. He stretched and took a deep breath of fusty city air. Finnegan moved up the rickety, slanting steps and rang the middle of three doorbells. A sharp buzz unlocked the door. He entered and was met immediately by an overpowering stench of mildew. His nostrils flared as he climbed the dark, dank staircase before him.

On the second landing a door opened. Stepping forth was an ancient, jagged figure, brittle to the touch. His hair had long since become a shock of gray. It fell haphazardly around his razor-thin head. Deep lines creased his face in all directions. Between the creases, a pair of fiery brown eyes burned outward. Yes, it was those eyes. Despite age and poverty, these eyes were still very much alive. His eyes reflected an intensity that Finnegan rarely saw in people six decades younger. The old man's body sagged only slightly. He carried little fat on him and his limbs no doubt had as much strength in them as could be allotted to someone of his years. Finnegan knew him to be nearly ninety although he did not know his exact age. The old man himself had never told him.

The elder figure stepped cautiously, in the slow and measured movements of an aged body, and regarded the young man coming toward him up the stairs. The corners of his mouth broke into a wide smile. Finnegan saw it, saw the old man, and smiled back, bounding up the final steps two and three at a time.

"Conor!" the old man cried.

"Grandpa," and the two embraced in a hug that lasted several seconds. Conor's grandfather would not let him go. The younger Finnegan reveled in the elder's strength, the sureness of his clinch.

"Holy Mother of God," said the old man at last, releasing Conor and stepping back to look at him in full. "You've grown up well, boy. Of course I wouldn't have expected any different now, would I? But you look to be the best of us."

"Good food and clean living, Grandpa."

"Ah, the devil. You're a Finnegan, that's all. But you seem to have outdone all the others I used to know. You're a prize, Conor. Come in."

Finnegan walked into his grandfather's flat. The worn and faded look, the cheap furniture, the decrepit appliances soiled permanently with grit and soot—all of it had been predictable. Finnegan had been in so many such places, and they never failed to depress him. The tail end of mortality was always so present in them. Here was no different. His grandfather would shortly be dead. He could not help but be near the end of his complex journey. His grandfather had to know it and, if he were at all like the dozens of people Conor had met in similar situations, he might even welcome it. Yet the buoyant vivacity Conor had remembered in his grandfather still shone forth. It remained there, in those remarkable eyes, still hungry to absorb whatever they located, and in his lyrical voice which gave no evidence of faltering. If his grandfather truly recognized his imminent passing, then he would at least save his pride by not bowing to it. Let it come, if it must, but he would keep those precious parts of his mind, body and soul alive in the face of a closing darkness.

"You look well, Grandpa. You look strong."

"As strong as an old man's health allows. I have no complaints. The occasional pain in one extremity or another, but that's about as far as it goes. Have a seat and I'll make some coffee. Or would you prefer something a bit more spirited?"

"More spirited? You're still at it, aren't you?"

"An old man has scarce few pleasures left him, Conor. Don't try to deny me one of the best."

"Well, then, let's have a drop or two. It's been a long drive."

"Just the thing," said the elder Finnegan and ambled slowly into the kitchen. Conor followed him. His grandfather opened a pantry door. "Here, let me," said Conor, and reached by him to pull down two tumblers. "Where are the spirits?"

"Next cupboard. Whiskey is all I've got. That's all that appeals to me these days."

"Fair enough." Conor found the lone bottle and poured an amount into each tumbler. At the refrigerator, a dilapidated thing with chipped enamel and a broken handle, he fetched an ice tray and dropped three cubes into each glass.

The old man took his glass and raised it toward his grandson. "God's blessing on you, Conor. To your health, to your joy, and to the everlasting glory of your spirit."

"And to yours, Grandpa."

"What little there's left of it, aye."

The liquor burned the back of Conor's mouth and seared its way down his throat. He had been thirsty, although this whiskey was not the answer. He would have preferred something soft. But the prospect of sharing a drink with the grand old man, this ancient, hoary font of legend and inestimable respect, meant far more than slaking his thirst. This was their first drink together, and most likely among their last. They had so little time.

The two returned to the living room and sat, Conor on the couch, his grandfather in an easy chair adjacent. In the corner a yellow canary twittered impulsively.

"It's good to see you looking so well, Grandpa."

"Yes, and a trifle surprising too, I'll wager. At my age each day's a blessing. An unanticipated gift of sorts."

"I don't believe that," responded Conor with a smile. "You make it sound as if you're just sitting back and letting life go by. That's never been your style."

"No, you're right. But I do get lonely here, Conor. Loneliness so deep it's like a wound. Unfortunately there's not much I can do about that. Petey keeps me company," he inclined his head toward the bird, "and there's the television. Those are the only animated voices I care to hear. This isn't the safest of neighborhoods any more, you know. The lady upstairs, she's about sixty. She goes to the store for me when I don't want to go out. She looks in one me from time to time. Mrs. McCarthy, her name is. She tells me she keeps a gun on her nightstand," he chuckled. "Can you imagine?"

"I thought I might buy you dinner tonight if you're up to it."

"No," he snapped. "I don't want to be bothered. I haven't seen the inside of a restaurant in at least twenty years."

"Well then, I'll go out and bring something back. Sandwiches maybe."

"If you want. Conor, let me put one thing to you right away. You needn't be solicitous of me. In fact, I'd prefer you knock it off altogether. I've never been comfortable with anyone thinking they have to do things for me."

"But Grandpa, you don't—"

"I don't want to hear it," he interrupted sternly but with good nature. "Treat me like your grandfather, not some old, feeble hermit. We'll get on fine if you do. If not, you'll most likely make me feel old and grouchy. Now, how long do you want to stay?"

"How long do you want me?"

"No one's going to kick you out."

"In that case, maybe two days or so. Let's play it by ear. See when you get tired of me."

"How's your dad?" asked the old man. "You know, that bastard's forgotten how to write. I hear from him every six weeks or so when he calls, but you'd think he'd pick up a pen and jot out a letter every now and then. How is the boy?"

"Dad never was much for writing. When I was in college Mom would write all the letters. I got maybe two from Dad in four years. But he's doing well as far as I can gather. He'll be retiring in a year, maybe less. That's hard for me to believe. I can't picture him not working."

"Ah, then there'll be two nonproductive Finnegans on this earth. It'll be up to you to pull enough weight for the lot of us."

Conor smiled. "He sends his love, Grandpa. When I told him I was coming to see you, he made me promise to say that."

"Of course," replied the elder. "It's always easier to work through a third person. I do appreciate the sentiment but tell him I'd appreciate it more if he delivered it in the flesh."

"How long's it been? Over a year, right?"

"Damn near four. He and your mother visited one June, if you recall. They came through after your graduation. But they've not been back since then."

"You know how many times Dad's asked you to move out there with them. I'm sure that offer still stands."

"It can stand until Doomsday. I'll never leave here. I've grown into this place by the roots. If you rip me away I'll die. I'll die anyway, but it stands to be more pleasant if I remain. I've no interest in cluttering your father's life through a misplaced gesture of good will. I've been here almost seventy years, for God's sake."

"That's a long time."

"You're damn right. And I had nothing when I got here. Nothing. Just my clothes in an old suitcase and a few dollars. But that was enough to get me by until I could build a stake. I slept at the mission for three weeks before my first paycheck came and I could get a place of my own. That was on Irving Park, and it wasn't too bad except it had no furniture. Here I thought everything came complete and when I unlocked the door it was totally empty. I slept on the floor in my clothes for about four months. I bought some things then, and everything was fine."

"Why Chicago, Grandpa? Why not Boston or New York?"

"Boston scared hell out of me. I'd never seen anything so damn big and crowded and dirty. There were Irishmen there, but they were different. They were bitter and hard, and they'd been whipped. Kicked by people who just wanted to hear the sound of flesh thumping. I stayed two weeks and I hated it. I'd lived on a farm all my life until then. I missed the open space. I missed being able to walk by the sea or walk for miles down a path without running into another living soul. But in Boston it was all elbow to elbow. There was cursing and sweat all around, and always those same whipped expressions.

"One day," he continued, "I was sharing a glass with a fellow in some pub and I was feeling particularly miserable, regretting the day I'd ever decided to come this way and figuring I'd made the biggest mistake since Judas. This fellow started telling me about the Midwest, the Great Plains. Farmland, he said, for as far as the eye could see. He'd never been there, mind you, but he desperately wanted to go. He was certain it was glorious there.

"So I got to thinking. There were no breaks for me in Boston, that was obvious, and I felt if I stayed long enough I'd end up either starving to death or becoming a thief. I had enough money to get me to Chicago. I'd never heard of the place, but that was the city he mentioned. I figured it was probably some little village compared to Boston. Something like Waterford, or maybe Cork at the worst. I thought I'd come here and head for the farmlands, hire myself out until I got enough money for my own spot of land."

The old man chuckled softly. "Instead I found something three times as huge as Boston and twice as dirty. On the train ride I sat by the window and watched all this green land go by. Miles upon miles of farms and small towns. I thought I was as close to paradise as a man could be. But then the train stopped here and I had to get out. Only now I didn't have any money left. There was no place else to go."

"And you've been here ever since."

"And I'll die here. And you know, Conor, I couldn't be happier about it."

They spent the night talking. Conor's grandfather told story after story, and Conor sat, enraptured. The old man had lived a demanding life, but his sense of purpose, and above all his sense of self, had never diminished, and it led him onward. He told Conor of making his own liquor because it was cheaper and better than what he could buy. He did so without guilt, but with a righteous indignation that a man should be forced to such trouble to secure his pleasures. He recounted fights, mostly verbal but some physical, with those who sought to cheat him because they equated his accent with an innate stupidity. He relived his courting of his beloved Molly, who had, he said, saved him from his baser passions and lent a sweet stability to his existence. She had justified him and given him his ultimate purpose: to make her equally happy. Their lives had fused into a joyous amalgam of her gentility and his commitment. They tempered each other with their best parts. When Molly died he had been lost, helpless for months, just sitting alone in a now-empty flat. But his old dignity rose again to restore him. His grief would not claim another life. He vowed to himself to go on with his narrowing routine, but he also vowed never to leave this place where he and Molly had shared the best of their lives.

The next day the stories continued, and the day after that. The weather improved enough, the rain ceasing and air warming smartly, so that Conor coaxed his grandfather into taking slow, ambling walks. The old man's limited endurance kept them short, although they were long enough for the elder to point out scenes of his own past, and that of his son. The corner store, now secured behind bars, had once caught young Edward Finnegan stealing a candy bar, a crime for which the boy had been grounded for two weeks. Here was the corner they turned to get to Wrigley Field, and there lived a delicate little blonde girl for whom Conor's father had carried a torch. Conor reveled in the memories, whose telling brought a wistful lilt to his grandfather's voice.

Toward evening they sat in the flat and drank a single glass of whiskey. That apparently had become his grandfather's ritual, a prelude to dinner, an exercise in making it more palatable. Conor would be leaving the next day. Over them both hung a somber pallor based on their common realization that this would most likely be their last time together in this earthly vale. Even the grandest of old men must pass, and young men age to take their place.

They sat there then, in the gloaming of a cool night, the last shred of daylight permeating the tattered room through dusty white curtains. The television droned out the news, but neither wanted to hear it. Long silences passed between them, not awkwardly—as if one or both believed that conversation was essential to fill a dead time, but respectfully, each weighing the presence of the other's life on his own. It was an evening for balances, a night for final reckonings.

Conor saw in these quiet moments why he had come here, why he had sought the company of his aged grandfather. He hoped for an osmosis, a transfer of strength and perspective. By breathing the same air as the one whose boldly confident yet charming character had been the stuff of legends throughout his childhood, Conor hoped for a transformation. He might discover an insight he had overlooked, a nuance he had discarded, the Conor Finnegan that had died. He might find it though his grandfather's words, but then again, it might be in one of the cautious movements of his old body or in the arrangement of his furnishings. It might lie in the couch cushions like a lost coin. It had to be there, this mysterious power, this life-giving ingestion. His own grandfather, the drying flesh of his own flesh, the thinning blood of his own blood, had to have it for him, whatever it was. This would be his last chance, his final opportunity. Conor Finnegan, a supplicant to the Oracle at Delphi.

In the silent night, after a long break with no speaking, no street noise, no sound at all, the old man sipped his whiskey with an audible slurp and asked, "Where do you go from here, Conor? Back home?"

Conor smiled with a sadness borne of whiskey upon the indomitable press of time. "Home. That can be a rather ambiguous concept, don't you think? Yeah," he sighed. "I'll be going back to Washington."

"But with none of the joy that should belong to you. Only you know why. I couldn't begin to understand it even if you should explain. It's a personal matter, whatever it is that's sucking you dry like this. But it's obvious that there's something. I know the feeling, Conor. Believe me when I tell you that. That's why I'm here, dying in this grimy old flat, and that's probably why you're here with me now, isn't it?"

Conor sighed again, this time very deeply. He took a long draught of his whiskey. He waited for the flame to rise up within him, burning outward from the vault of his stomach, but it did not come. When he spoke, the words were released with the measured pace of resignation.

"I have a friend," Conor began slowly. "My age, essentially my background. In most respects just like me. In fact, we went to school together, both high school and college. To look at him you wouldn't think much was there. Tall and scrawny, not terribly attractive but not unattractive either. Just something of an Everyman at first glance, and if you talk to him he really doesn't belie that. He's quiet. Most of the time he goes out of his way to avoid making any kind of fuss. To be honest, I never paid him much attention. It wasn't until we went away to college together that I really got to know him. I got the chance to reach behind that unassuming exterior.

"And Grandpa, this shy person that we all pretty much ignored, or even felt sorry for, this cipher that we never saw even when we were staring right at him, turned out to be wiser than any of us. Tom is his name, and I love him like a brother. I haven't seen him in three years.

"Tom was going along like the rest of us, trying to make some sense out of the hand he'd been dealt. Only he didn't like it much. In fact he hated it. He hated what he was doing and who he was doing it with, and even why he was doing it at all. For quite a while he didn't think there was anything he could do about it. Like the rest of us, he'd been pulled along by circumstances that others were dictating. He'd been trying to do the right and proper thing, trying to meet everybody's expectations but his own. Tom had no expectations. He hadn't allowed himself any. So he felt trapped in a situation he'd let other people create for him, and he was miserable for it. Absolutely wretched.

"But," continued Conor, "Tom was too smart, too strong to let it eat him alive. He broke away, Grandpa. Just when he was feeling as helpless as he had ever felt before in his life, he broke away. He threw everything aside, wiped the slate clean and started over again on his own terms. And God, I love him for it."

"What did he do?" asked the grandfather.

Conor smiled. "He went to Ireland. The south coast, in fact. Cork."

And the old man smiled in return. "Ah, Lord," he said. "I think I'd like this lad."

"You would. Immensely. He's more your grandson than I am. He went over for a year and found he loved it there. He's been there ever since. I get letters from him occasionally. He's teaching at the college there while he finishes his doctorate. I suspect he'll be married soon, to an Irish girl he makes reference to with increasing fondness. He's writing now in terms of permanence and he's happier than I've ever known he could be. I don't think he'll ever come back to this country. And why should he, really? He's got everything he ever sought, and he did it totally on his own, in his own manner. In the process he found what was inside him that no one else ever recognized or valued. He defined Tom McIlweath."

"Your friend is indeed a rare man," said the grandfather, "and a courageous one. He's authored his own course of things, his own contentments. There's precious few among us who can say the same. I daresay you're not one of them."

"And I'm terribly envious," replied Conor. "But there's nothing I can do. Unlike my unassuming friend, I fear I lack the strength to turn everything over."

"Conor," said the old man, quietly and with deliberation, untapping now one of his last remaining reservoirs of conviction. "Long before you were born I was dying. I had years left to me, but they wouldn't have mattered. They would have choked me with their barren dust, choked me into a grave I would have welcomed. My life there made no sense to me, it had no point. What would I have been but what my father was, and his father before him, and on before that? What possible difference would it have made if I had come into this world or not? Man isn't meant to live like that, just occupying space. It was no one's fault, but that was how it had all built up. The easiest thing in the world, though, would have been to stay, running one step ahead of poverty and two steps ahead of starvation in what everyone else thought to be the natural order of things.

"We're like a magnet, Conor, dragged through the sand. We pick up little bits of filings, tiny shards of metal, without feeling them on us. But in time they weigh us down. Their heaviness accumulates until we no longer believe we can move at all. But Conor, we have to. Your friend had the strength to shake them away. It can shatter your heart and cause the flesh of your soul to bleed with a thousand wounds, but it's the only alternative we have."

Liam Finnegan was not a gentle man, but neither was he brutish. He regarded his grandson, read the haunting echoes of death in his eyes, and prayed he was mistaken. Yet the premonition that followed him that evening remained with him the rest of his days, and the morbid fear that the sins of the father had been visited upon his heirs never left him until they lowered his casket into the silent earth.

Conor, the grandson of Liam, finished his whiskey, kissed his grandfather on his ancient head, and went to bed for a night of unsettled, tormented slumber, the kind of night to which he had lately grown accustomed. He rose the next morning with nothing changed.

It would take more time than that.

ACKNOWLEDGEMENTS

This novel came to life after a long and intense gestation, with a number of midwives. When I began the writing of it, I had little idea what I was doing. But I knew I needed to do it, that I needed to try making sense of the maddening and unfathomable processes that make us who we are. Along the way I had more help, counsel, support and encouragement than any writer could ever want.

Pat Conroy showed me early on how the written word can dance in lyrical gyrations that create music and carry truths like fresh winds. I did not know him well, but I'm proud to say that I knew him, and that he encouraged the early stages of what became this book. Pat made me brave enough to do this. His passing robbed us all of the most passionate and generous of writers. I've drawn from the brilliance of many other writers whom I have no illusion of approaching – Niall Williams, Colm Toibin, Owen Thomas, Fergal Keane, Amor Towles and countless others whose work elevates language and thought to the highest planes. I am deeply grateful to all of them for their craftsmanship and inspiration. But Pat Conroy has always been my brightest beacon.

My great good friends Tom Cierzan and Kevin Johnson were the first to read the manuscript. Their honest reactions helped move the book along and give it focus. Gerry and Marlys Evans, my second parents, took the time to read the rough draft, as did Ruth Shiltas. David Welch read the final draft with amazing care and attention to detail. His insights lent a critical perspective in shaping the final product. And Caroline Jam Miller, whose sensitivity, humor and kindness nurture everyone who knows her, encouraged me through the final stages. She remains one of the most insightful people I have ever known.

Bill Evans and I, who grew up together playing baseball and following the Dodgers, discovered a couple of years ago that we were both writing books. He's an amazing storyteller. Bill has been an essential partner as we've navigated together the confusing and intimidating waters of creating words for others to read.

John Koehler had the courage to publish this novel despite its length and the pretentions of its author. His care for and nurturing of writers should be the standard for every publisher. I'm immensely grateful for his faith and encouragement.

Joe Coccaro and Elizabeth Marshall McClure buffed and polished a manuscript heavy on words and sometimes lacking precision. They've sharpened the finished product in ways I never could.

But none of this would have mattered were it not for Lynn and Michael. Lynn's beauty, intuition, and strength have sustained me for more than two decades, from the day she rescued someone desperately lost and confused, and showed him that there might actually be someone worth treasuring. She saved my life, then together we raised a son, who has infused that life with immeasurable joy, purpose and pride.

This book, and whatever worth it might hold, is for them.